BETWEEN WRATH & MERCY

JESS WISECUP

Copyright © 2022 by Jess Wisecup.

All rights reserved. Printed in the United States of America. No part of this book may be used or reproduced in any manner whatsoever without written permission except in the case of brief quotations embodied in critical articles or reviews.

This book is a work of fiction. Names, characters, businesses, organizations, places, events and incidents either are the product of the author's imagination or are used fictitiously. Any resemblance to actual persons, living or dead, events, or locales is entirely coincidental.

For information contact:
jesswisecupbooks@gmail.com

Cover design by AMDesignstudios
Internal Art by Eternal Geekery

First Edition: February 2022

For all the mothers who still dream to be part of the fairytale.
And for me.

Also by Jess Wisecup

The Divine Between Series
Between Wrath and Mercy
Between Despair and Hope – Late Summer 2022
Between Book 3 – To Be Determined
Between Book 4 – To Be Determined

Author's note
The Divine Between series should only be read by mature readers (18+) and contains scenes that may make some readers uncomfortable. For a full list, please visit my website. I do promise a happily ever after for our heroine, but guard your heart along the way. It will be hard-earned.

PRONUNCIATION GUIDE

NAMES:
EMMELINE HIGHCLERE – EM-MUH-LEEN High-clear
Lucia Highclere – Lou-see-uh High-clear
Elora Calvert – El-or-uh Cal-vair
Rainier Vestana – Rain-ier (like "tier") Vest-ah-nuh
Lavenia Vestana – Luh-vin-ee-uh Vest-ah-nuh
Soren Vestana – Sore-in Vest-ah-nuh
Shivani Vestana – Shiv-on-ee Vest-ah-nuh
Dewalt Holata – Duh-walt Hole-ate-uh
Mairin – My-reen
Thyra – Tier-uh
Cyran – Sigh-run
Ciarden – Kier (like "tier")-den
Aonara – Eye-uh-nar-uh
Rhia – Ree-uh
Hanwen – Han-when

Places:
Vesta – Vest-uh
Mira – Meer-uh
Ardian – Are-dee-un
Ravemont – Rav (like "ravioli")-mont
Olistos – Ol-is-toes
Cinturon Pass – Cent-er-on Pass
Astana – Ah-stahn-uh
Lamera – Luh-meer-uh
Nara's Cove – Nar-uh 's Cove
Folterra – Fol (like "fold")-tair-uh

Mindengar – Min-din-gar
Evenmoor – Ev-un-moor
Nythyr – Nith-ier (like "tier")
Kieża – key-ay-ż (like the "g" in mirage)-uh
Creatures:
Onaán – Oh-nah (like the "a" in "cat")-on
Tírrúil – Tier-rue-il

THE THREE KINGDOMS

AEWY SEA

GLENHARBOR

ERILIMAN FOREST

AESIRO BRIDGE

DARKHOLD

FOLTERRA

SEAT OF THE MYRIAD SUPREME

LAMERA

EVENMOOR

VARMEER

THE CASCADE

MINDENGAR

NYTHYR

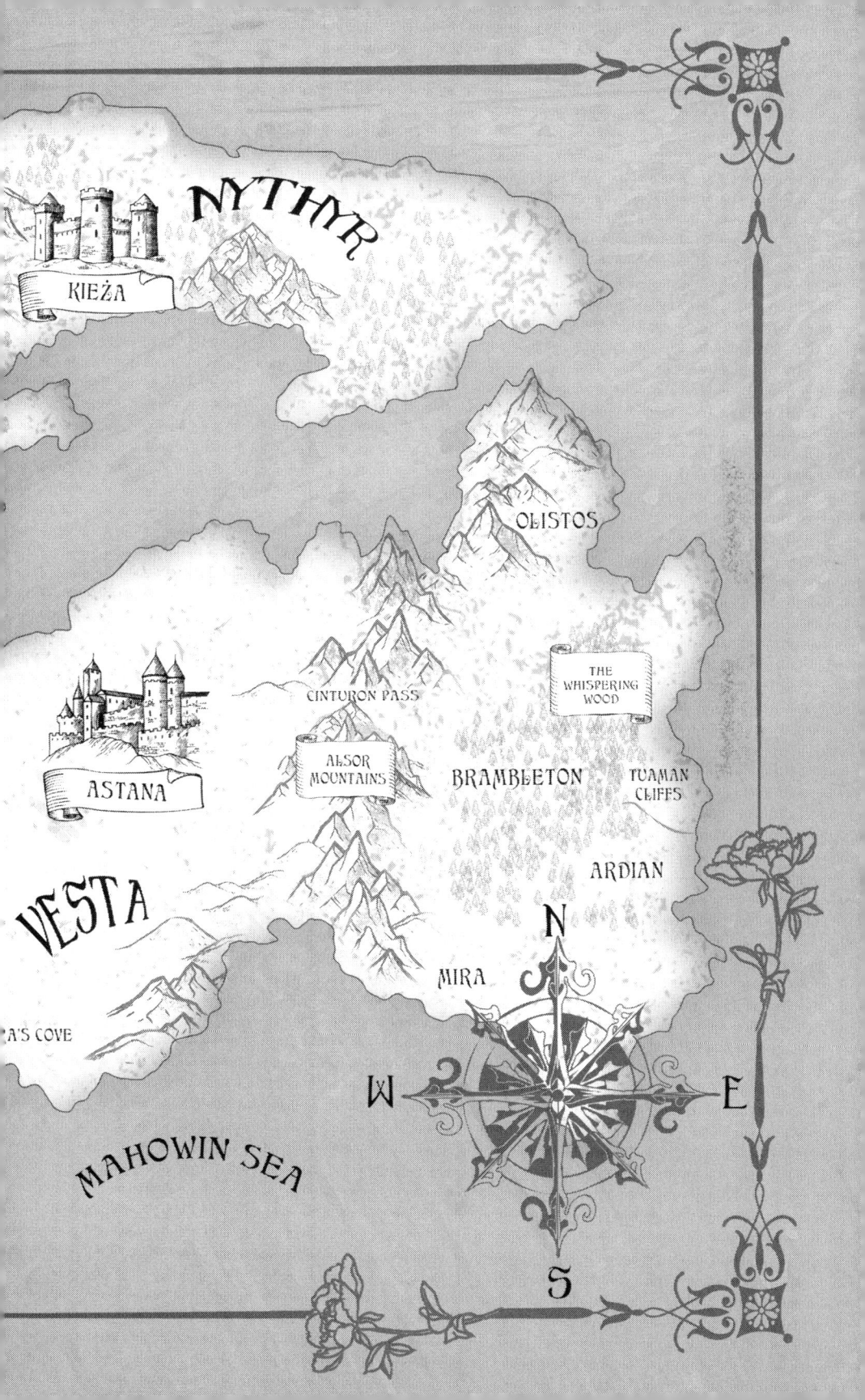

KIEŻA

OLISTOS

THE WHISPERING WOOD

ASTANA

CINTURON PASS

ALSOR MOUNTAINS

BRAMBLETON

TUAMAN CLIFFS

ARDIAN

VESTA

MIRA

A'S COVE

MAHOWIN SEA

N
W   E
S

PROLOGUE

It was a good thing Lucia was the Beloved; if anyone could change the world by sheer force of will, it was her.

"It's not fair. I want you with me at court." A scowl formed on my sister's face. We had been over this topic many times before.

"You know I can't. Father won't let me."

"When I'm Crown Princess, I'll make Rainier offer you a position in our guard. Then Papa won't expect you to stay at Ravemont and marry Faxon."

I grinned.

"I'm not good enough for that! Besides, you don't need me." I put my hand up to my chin in mock thought. "Although I really don't want to marry him, so maybe a quick death from a would-be assassin would be preferable."

We both laughed and threw ourselves back into the grass, her white hair mingling with my golden brown. My twin looked over at me, eyes soft.

"Of course, I need you, Emma. I've never been without you." Tears limned her eyes, threatening to spill down to the ground and water the wildflowers we laid in.

"You're going to have hundreds of years to get used to it," I teased, but in my heart I was serious. I'd be dead and gone just a blink into her reign. I heard her take in a shaky breath. "We'll find you a conduit to perform the ritual with. We'll send out missives first thing tomorrow." Her voice was a bit frantic, as if she had forgotten how many times we had been over this.

"Lucia, there's no point. There aren't enough left. I doubt they'd want me, anyway. My divinity is pathetic."

"Don't say that. Besides, it isn't true." Lucia's tone of admonition took over the frantic energy with ease, ever the eldest sister, even if only by a few minutes.

"Which part isn't true? That no one would want me or that my divinity is pathetic?" Lucia ignored my sarcasm.

"Both, you idiot. But I know one conduit who wants you."

"Gods, Luce. Don't start."

"When he talks to me, he pretends he's talking to you."

"It's all just games. None of it is real."

"I'd call it all off for you, Emma. Just say the word."

And she meant it. Or at least she'd try to call it all off. Between the Myriad and King Soren, she didn't stand a chance.

Later, in the quiet of my room, I'd think about what Lucia had said—her offer. I had told her none of it was real, but it felt real. Alone in my room, in the stillness of night, my divinity was transcendent. A white-hot tether in my mind, listening to the sound of his far-off heartbeats, mourning the loss of something I never had.

CHAPTER 1

16 Years Later

Everyone in my home had a death wish, and as time went on, I was becoming more and more likely to oblige them. I'd spent the last two weeks mentally preparing myself to let my teenage daughter leave on a trip with her father. They had both been working on me since his last trip to Mira—Elora begging any chance she could, and Faxon giving me an expectant look, allowing her to pester me. He had brought her a book and a beautiful necklace with a single ammolite stone embraced by a teardrop setting. She had squealed, claiming it looked like a dragon scale, and thanked her father profusely. And then Faxon, the traitor, told her she could go with him the next time he went to Mira and pick out matching earrings. My eyes had nearly bulged out of my head when I turned to look at him.

"What?" He had shrugged. "Come on, Emma, it'll be fine. She's fifteen, not five."

I could have killed him.

"Mama, *please, please, please*. I promise I'll be careful. Please, Mama!"

We'd only ever gone as a family to Mira, and the last time was a few years ago. As Elora grew older and her divinity began to manifest more clearly, it had been too dangerous to risk going to any of the major cities. We'd even begun to avoid Brambleton. Though the town was small and not well-off, there were plenty of people who might notice her abilities. And it might have proven problematic if they thought they could get some sort of recompense for the knowledge. I didn't want to risk it. She just didn't have enough control of her abilities yet. The last thing we needed was anyone to see her white hair and her fingers spark. They'd jump to the obvious conclusion. Her eyes were wide and hopeful as she stared at me, reminding me of a much younger version of her.

"I'll think about it," I had said, accompanying the statement with a glare toward Faxon. He raised a brow at me and smirked like he'd won a battle against me.

It was typical of him to cast me as the bad guy. He'd been doing it the entirety of our marriage about everything, let alone Elora. It was somehow my fault that our daughter had been born the Beloved. It was my fault she had the shock of hair, pure as freshly fallen snow, and her eyes glowed white when she cried. It was my fault we had to leave and hide her from the Myriad. It was my fault he wasn't currently busy running Ravemont.

When our parents realized Lucia's divinity was extraordinarily strong for a child, they reached out to the Myriad temple in Ardian, proud and eager for her potential to be Aonara's favored. The day my sister was formally identified was our eighth birthday. Mother had put her in a white dress to match her hair while I was given grey to blend in. I was not allowed in the temple with them, so I stayed outside with Father, keeping my eye on the doors, waiting for my sister to come back out. I could have sworn I heard her screaming, but when I told Father, he denied hearing it.

It's fine, Emmeline.

Shortly after, the doors burst open. My mother was holding Lucia's hand, a triumphant look on her face. They had a Myriad Master on either side of them, escorting them down the steps. When I looked at Lucia, I wondered why I was the only one to notice the crumpled exhaustion written across her features. She averted her eyes from me, and it marked the beginning of a change in our relationship. We both were on different paths from that point forward, and I would always miss the time before that warm summer day.

The next day, the Myriad had distributed an official proclamation formally identifying Lucia as the Beloved. The one person prophesied to bring peace to the Three Kingdoms, the Myriad believed the Beloved to be someone blessed by Aonara, the Goddess of Light. I never found out what they did to confirm my sister was goddess blessed. She would never speak of it. Considering she was dead, leaving the prophecy unfulfilled, they had been wrong.

When Elora was born, I vowed I would never let her go through that. I would never let her be officially declared, especially considering it caused Lucia's death, and they hadn't even been correct about her. I wouldn't let Elora be used as a pawn for political alliances or face the same dangers my sister had faced and ultimately succumbed to. So, when we had to leave Ravemont Estate and go into hiding, that was obviously my fault too, according to Faxon. Regardless of my feelings toward Faxon and his eagerness to portray me as the problem, I did feel empathy for Elora. She'd never had a normal childhood. The minute she was born, looking so much like her aunt from birth onwards, I knew she'd be hunted, and it was our responsibility to protect her. Sometimes that meant tough decisions. But because I felt bad for her, I chose to think about it rather than just say no outright.

Every night since that conversation, either Elora or Faxon would ask me if she could go to Mira. It was over a three-day ride to the port city, and they wanted to spend a few days in town, so, finally, they cornered me, forcing me to make a decision.

"Why don't I come along, too?"

"You need to meet with Lord Kennon the same day we need to leave. I can't leave any later for Mira, or I won't be there for the shipment." I rolled my eyes. He'd placed an order months ago for a specific type of grain from Nythyr, and part of the purchase contract included Faxon paying in labor to help unload the ship.

"What is Elora supposed to do while you're busy with the shipment?" He couldn't expect her to just sit at the docks all day.

"The ship will be in before dawn. She can stay in the room and read until I'm done." He glanced at me with annoyance, his dark brow furrowing while he rubbed his hand over his thin lips and mustache. The man had never been handsome, and age had not done him any favors. His hair was thinning noticeably on top, yet he insisted on trying to adjust what little he had left to cover the bald spot. I didn't understand it. He wasn't fooling anyone. I'd offered to shave it all off, to help him own his appearance, but he'd screamed at me until he grew hoarse, and I never mentioned it again.

Looking over at Elora, I raised a brow.

"You know, you can read at home." It was a half-hearted attempt to get her to change her mind. I knew she would much prefer to be reading at the inn in Mira.

"Mamaaaa . . . " She was much too old to be whining at me. They'd be leaving in two days if I allowed her to go. I needed to decide now if she were to have time to prepare.

"Fine. You can go. But you must keep your divinity in check. No showing anyone any fun tricks. And you have to dip your hair in brun root." It went against every instinct I had, but the look on her face told me I made the right decision.

"Mama, thank you so much!" Her book flew out of her hands as she jumped into my arms. I pulled her in close, running my fingers through her long, curly hair. I gripped her upper arms and pushed her back to look at her, taking in her white mane and how it contrasted with her tanned skin, darker than my own. Reading outdoors was her favorite pastime, and it showed in her freckles and warm glow. She was radiant.

"Promise to be careful." She'd always listened to me and taken every precaution I'd asked of her, but all the same, I felt the need to reiterate.

"I promise." She nodded, a serious expression on her face, looking much older than fifteen.

That night, when I slept, I dreamt about Lucia and Elora. The three of us sat in a field making daisy chains. My sister was alive and whole again, forever seventeen, not much older than my daughter sitting beside her. The two were almost indiscernible from each other except for Elora's curls—my daughter took after us. She didn't look at all like her father, and I felt secretly triumphant. It was rare, Lucia visiting in my dreams. My subconscious fought to stay there with her. Just one more moment with my sister holding her hand and laughing with her was all I wanted.

The next morning was brisk, a sharp breeze cutting into me despite the sun. There were brown and red leaves all over the ground, blowing in the wind. The crisp grip of autumn had officially descended. As Bree trampled up the back alley to the entrance behind Mairin's infirmary, I pulled my cloak tighter and my hood down and forward to shade my face. The town couldn't afford the services of a conduit, the cost of utilizing someone's divinity too high, and Mairin did the best she could. After revealing my abilities to her, she'd call for me on occasion under the promise of anonymity, and this morning was one of those times. I wanted to help when I could, but it was too risky for anyone in Brambleton to know there was a benevolent conduit living just outside its borders, unwilling to accept payment for something that should be shared freely. And so, I moved in shadows, and those who benefited from it paid in secrets instead of coin.

The leaves softened the clatter of Bree's hooves on the cobblestones, but Mairin still heard me arrive. Flinging her back door open, she yelled for me to hurry. Jumping down, I grabbed the extra rags from my pack and ran inside.

It was a small cabin made entirely of wood. Going through the back door, I crossed into a small, cramped kitchen before coming into the front room, which doubled as her living room and examination room. Mairin slept upstairs, an area only accessible through a small ladder that hung on the wall of the main room. The dark green curtains were shut, blocking the light, but a thin breeze behind them told me she had cracked the window for air. As I rounded the corner into the front of the cabin, a piercing wail met my ears. Mairin shoved the baby in my arms to check her while she attended to the mother. The infant was small but had strong breathing sounds. I held her still, focusing my abilities. I closed my eyes and reached out, flinging my divinity toward the fragile child in my arms, and listened for the tiny heartbeat, a small tug connecting us. The baby sounded fine. But when I'd reached out to the babe, I'd been overwhelmed by a louder stampeding rhythm. Looking at the mother, I realized why Mairin had called me. I swaddled the baby and laid her on a pile of blankets in the corner of the room.

"Toxemia?" I asked the healer. The mother's eyes were closed as she lay on the bed, her extremities swollen. Though the room was comfortable, on just this side of cold, the woman had sweat beaded across her brow, and her features were ashen, her dark hair soaked. Mairin met my eyes and nodded.

"Gertie, can you tell me where you are?" Mairin's voice was smooth and calming, an amazing juxtaposition from the fear I saw on her face. Gertie did not answer.

I lowered myself to my knees on the other side of the woman. I placed my hands on her neck, trying to slow her racing heart. This was a bit outside of my experience. I was used to healing wounds or broken bones. It was unusual for Mairin to call me to her during a birth. My healing abilities had gone untested against something like this. Regardless, I felt my hands heat up as I placed them on the woman. Normally, I would picture wounds knitting together or bones snapping back into place, but this time I imagined cool waters and winding streams—hoping to bring her heart rate back to normal. I passed my hands down her arms and across her chest. Down her legs and back up, doing the best I could, not quite confident in what I was doing.

"As long as she doesn't seize, I think she'll make it. Keep going," Mairin whispered to me. After smoothing sweat-streaked hair from Gertie's forehead and placing a cool cloth on it, she pulled her own hair back with a cord. The long orange-red curls were bursting at the leather, and I thought it was a true miracle it didn't break. Her freckled skin was ruddy with exertion. I wondered how long Gertie had been in labor, Mairin desperate to reach me, knowing full well toxemia was often fatal. The messenger, Mr. Gunderson, my neighbor on the eastern edge of my property, didn't seem too fussed to pass along Mairin's request until he'd already talked to me for twenty minutes about his plans for his crops. The minute I realized, I hurried, knowing the healer only called for me when she truly needed me.

After nearly an hour of attempting to heal Gertie, she seemed like she was resting comfortably. The swelling in her hands and feet had gone down, and her heart rate had slowed—still accelerated, but a vast improvement. Mairin went to the babe, swaddled and asleep.

"I'm going to let Gertie rest before I bring her the wee one, but I think she'll make it. Thank you, Emmeline. You're a miracle worker."

I glanced at Gertie when Mairin said my name, glad for a few reasons she was peacefully sleeping, before turning my attention back to the healer. She swayed her hips, rocking with the baby. Mairin was a young widow and had no children of her own, but clearly adored every child who crossed her threshold. She offered services to even the poorest townsfolk, accepting nothing but the scraps from their table which pride forced them to shove into her hands. She was the closest thing I'd had to a friend the whole time I lived here, even if she'd only met Elora once. When Mairin had first arrived in town a decade ago, I barely saw her. Her husband wasn't known for his kindness or his social graces, and he seemed to hide her away. When he died, she began seeing patients as a way to make ends meet, and she was great at it. When I went to her, offering up whatever assistance I could give, she was wary, but eventually, we developed a trust and camaraderie.

"I'm glad it worked. I was truly just guessing."

"No, you weren't. Your divinity knows better than you do." She smiled a half-smile at me, always encouraging.

"Faxon is taking Elora with him to Mira tomorrow."

"And Mama Bear is allowing it?" she chided. She never understood why I didn't let Elora come into town with me.

"Under duress." I forced a smile. "I'd better get going; I have to help her pack. Let me know how Gertie does."

"I will. Let me know how *you* do."

I rolled my eyes at her and went out the back door.

On my way home, I stopped and gathered some brun root in a small grove of oak trees near the house. After bringing it inside, I set it on the hutch within the kitchen, bumping a drawer shut with my hip as I did it. The squeak of the wood on wood and the stick of the drawer told me I needed to rub wax where the wood met. I glanced around the room—the whole thing needed updating. The hutch held my nicer dinnerware Nana had sent me from Ravemont, and I kept the piece of furniture in good condition, but everything else had fallen into disrepair. The shelving holding my copper pots and pans was bowed in the middle, the white paint was peeling from the paneled wall in places, and the hearth had some loose bricks which drove me crazy. It functioned though, and that was what mattered.

When Elora came into the room, she took one sniff and eyed the brun root I'd brought and groaned.

"Do I have to? It stinks so bad." She had a point, but I wasn't about to agree with her.

"Do you want to go tomorrow or not?" I retorted. I watched eyes the color of my own roll so far back in her head that I was genuinely concerned they might get stuck. I watched her for a moment as she stood on the other side of the table from me. She'd grown so tall; she was nearly as tall as me. Since Faxon wasn't much taller, I figured she was done growing or close to it.

"Fine, but I'm going to complain the whole time."

"I expect nothing less." I stuck my tongue out at her. She stared at the brun root for a few moments, arms crossed, before she peered up at me and heaved a sigh.

"Thank you, Mama, for letting me go. I know you hate the idea."

"I just worry, Elora. You know why."

Because you are so like her.

Because she is gone, and you are not.

Because being favored by the gods is not any sort of blessing.

"I won't go near the temple, Mama. I promise. I'll stay in the room and read when Papa is busy. This is good practice." My heart ached. Conduits generally came into their full divinity between the ages of eighteen and twenty-two, girls sooner than boys, and she had every intention to go explore Vesta when it happened. And I had no true desire to lock her up in a tower or put her to sleep for a hundred years, no matter how much I might want to. She needed a chance to live and grow. I wanted that for her. I wanted her to live—for my sister who never got the chance, for myself who had only lived for the two of them, and most of all for her. She'd be able to protect herself once her divinity reached maturity; she wouldn't need me anymore.

"Absolutely do not go near the temple. If you see any novices on the street, turn around and go a different way. You promised me, so you better keep your promise." I realized my voice was stern. I hated being strict with her, but it was purely to keep her safe.

"I will. Do you want me to pick up anything for you while we're there? I want to go to that bookstore and pick out something new. Papa has horrible taste." She giggled, gesturing toward the small stack of books that sat between the two armchairs by the window. He brought her a book back anytime he went, but sometimes I wondered if he just walked in and bought the first thing he saw.

"No, honey. I don't need anything. Thank you." She walked past me toward the hall, and I gently tugged on her braid as she went. She smiled and flounced up the stairs.

I'd been in bed for over an hour when Faxon stumbled up the stairs. He didn't bother skipping the creaking board at the top step. It had squeaked as long as I could remember, and since it was right outside Elora's bedroom, I'd made it a habit to step over it early on, trying not to wake her. The habit stuck. I'd gone up early, not feeling well after using my abilities on Gertie. The toll from using my divinity would often leave me fatigued, and in some circumstances, I'd end up with terrible headaches. I'd had worse, but the light ache behind my eyes was enough to send me crawling into bed. I listened to the man in the hall bump into the wall, sounding like he caught his hip on the corner closet. Faxon drank most nights, rarely in excess, though tonight seemed to be an exception. I wondered why since he had such an early start in the morning. As I heard him, my body tensed, and I considered trying to slip into the bathroom before he came in and wait him out until I heard his snores on the other side of the door. But when I noticed his steps dragged more than usual, I figured he'd fall asleep the minute he laid down, so I stayed put.

He crawled into the bed next to me, reeking of alcohol. Ever since his delusions of grandeur were interrupted by the exceedingly real threat of having the Beloved for a daughter, he'd sunk further into the cup. When he married me, he and my father both had dreams Faxon would run the estate one day. Before Lucia had died, we'd both told Father I would be perfectly capable of running Ravemont with or without Faxon. Lucia argued with Father more boisterously than I ever had. She'd even tried to guilt him, arguing that without any of us performing the bonding ritual, she'd outlive us all. Our parents would both die sooner rather than later, and I'd age and wrinkle while she sat on the throne for hundreds of years, leaving her alone with no one but Prince Rainier at her side. She wanted me in the capital with her, in Astana, looking for a conduit to perform the ritual with so I could be by her side always.

But then she died first. Our parents had tossed me off to Faxon within the week. I didn't particularly care anymore that he was mortal and I'd never perform the ritual. I didn't want to live too long anyway, not without Lucia.

I was lying on my side, facing away from Faxon, when his body slammed into the bed, and I felt his warmth as he sidled closer to me. I froze. The drunker he was, the more likely he was to pursue intimacy with me, and that was not something I cared to argue. Again. I tucked my hands between my thighs and squeezed.

"Don't worry, I won't badger you tonight, though I should," he slurred, hot breath into my ear.

"And why should you?" I snapped back at him.

"Because you're my wife."

"And that gives you the right to use me as you please?"

"Careful, hen. I said I wasn't badgering," he hiccupped.

My marriage with Faxon was a loveless one. He wanted Ravemont, and he'd gone through me to get it. Fifteen years my senior, and lacking any especially attractive qualities, he'd never interested me. Though living in isolation to protect Elora wasn't what I'd wanted, I couldn't help feeling mollified he didn't get his way. I allowed him my body in those early months. A large part of me was disgusted he'd been able to look at me then, given the state I was in, and find any bit of arousal. But he did. And when Elora had been born, I'd decided I would not allow him to father any more children with me. Since her birth was extremely difficult on me, and Elora was my priority, I didn't want to risk another child. To have another to worry about. Knowing full well he'd never consistently take the precautionary tonic, I decided I would no longer allow him to touch me. In the beginning, he was irate, screaming at me and throwing things whenever I denied him, but he never forcibly took what I wasn't willing to give. I wasn't sure if it was one of the last shreds of honor the man had or if it was a well-founded fear of what I would do to him if he attempted.

For what it was worth, it was only when he was drunk that he pushed the boundaries. When Mairin took on her role as healer, I convinced her to tell Faxon what he needed to hear. I wasn't sure what she said, perhaps that another pregnancy would kill me, or something like it. Whatever she insinuated worked, and he left me alone, for the most part, barely bothering to guilt trip me anymore. When he was drunk enough I felt fear, I'd lock myself in the bathroom or sleep with Elora. As time went on, it began to happen less and less, making me wonder if he had a woman in town. I didn't care if he'd found other outlets for his release. It kept him off me.

He moved over to his side of the bed, and snoring followed shortly after. I rolled onto my back and looked over at him. He wasn't the worst of men, necessarily. I knew countless other women who had husbands who intentionally hurt them every time they drank, significantly worse than the fingerprints Faxon left on my arms. And he never did it sober or in front of Elora. That wasn't the case for a lot of the women in town. He was decent to Elora, and he helped protect her. He taught her to fish and helped support her passions. He was a good father, but he'd never be more than that in my eyes. To me, he simply existed. Another body occupying space in my home. I'd been served to him on a platter with Ravemont Estate, and he'd eagerly taken my father up on the prospect. I'd had no choice in the matter, especially after Lucia's death.

Don't marry him, Em.

I wondered how things might have been different if I had listened to him then—when he might have been able to help me. I fell asleep, remembering green eyes flecked with gold.

CHAPTER 2

The next morning, I struggled to roll out of bed when Faxon lightly pushed on my shoulder as he got up to relieve himself. I'd gotten little sleep; vipers made of shadows and the sounds of endless screaming plagued my subconscious. I woke up in a hot sweat a few times, gasping for breath. Faxon rarely woke during my nightmares, and last night was no different, for which I was thankful. My nightmares had grown rare in recent years, only making an appearance when I felt particularly stressed. On the rare occasion I'd wake him, he'd just grumble and go back to sleep.

When he came out of the bathroom, he was already dressed and ready for the day. Reaching for the glass of water by my bed, I nodded to him, and he gave me a small smile as he walked out the bedroom door. Though I felt no love for him, in recent years we'd fallen into a sort of friendship. I didn't mind his company when he was sober. He could be quite funny, and he loved Elora. As much of a pain in the ass he was for me, Faxon had never been anything less than a dutiful father to her. I gulped down some water and laid back, pressing my hand to my eyes. After saying goodbye to Elora and Faxon, I'd need to head straight to the meeting with Lord Kennon.

Groaning internally, I forced myself to sit back up and reach for my hairbrush on the nightstand. As I pulled it forcefully through my tangles, I reminded myself, not for the first time, that I should braid it before going to bed. In sleep, the long, golden-brown hair turned into a rat's nest. Looking at my brush, full of errant strands, I was cursing my forgetfulness. I went to the bathroom, filling my hands with water from the ewer, and ran my fingers through my waves, smoothing the unruly frizz which plagued me regularly. Looking in the mirror while braiding my hair, I noticed one side of my face was a bright, rosy pink from laying on it, explaining the heat I felt radiating from my cheek. I leaned forward toward the mirror, noticing the crease between my brows, and began to rub at it in a misguided attempt to smooth it. Mother had always told me if I didn't stop scowling, it would become permanent. It pained me to know she was right. Walking back into the cramped bedroom, skirting past the wardrobe which sat at the foot of the bed, I slouched my nightgown off into a puddle on the floor. After my dream of Lucia the night before, I wondered if she and I would still look similar. We'd always been the same exact height and build, though that last year, I'd started to gain more muscle. We'd never been slim, but I wondered if comfortable palace life would have made her more plump. Would she have any children now? Would we have complained about the changes our bodies went through together? Would she have slathered lotion all over our growing bellies? The line of thought pained me.

Throwing open my wardrobe, I dressed for cold weather. I'd be traveling, so the dark brown breeches would keep me warm, and I chose a long-sleeved, button-down shirt. I debated skipping the bodice but knew I'd be better served to wear it and skip the lecture, considering this one didn't have boning and was rather comfortable. He'd only just stopped harassing me about wearing pants instead of a dress. After finishing the ensemble with socks and boots, I headed towards the stairs, prepared to wake Elora on my way, but her door was open and the room empty. She must have risen before the sun.

"Mama! We're about to leave, hurry up!" She shouted up the stairs in her singsong voice she always used when she was in a wonderful mood. I could practically hear her vibrating with excitement as I made my way down the steps.

"You may want to tone it down, little miss. Your father isn't used to your morning exuberance, especially before his coffee." Elora was sitting in an armchair, completely dressed and beaming. Either she or Faxon had set a kettle to boil in the kitchen and pulled out the cheesecloth and coffee grounds. Watching her, I smiled. Even though I was nervous, seeing Elora this happy made my heart soar. Theo, our neighbor who helped us from time to time, had asked to go as well, and Faxon had agreed after endless needling from Elora. Theo was a couple of years older than her, and I'd known him since before he reached my hip. He'd always cared for her like one of his siblings, and I felt a little less nervous knowing he'd be there too.

"Mama, Theo says I look stupid with this big, heavy, winter cloak. Do we have anything lighter?" Elora was looking out the window at the boy in question and picking at her hood—dark grey with a lining of rabbit fur on the inside.

"Elora Mae, I packed an extra cloak in your bag, but have you even looked outside? It has done nothing but rain, and it's cold. If you want to freeze because you can't handle Theo's teasing, be my guest." Raising a single eyebrow, I stared at Elora, waiting for the challenge. She whipped her head over her shoulder and glowered at me. I chuckled, knowing every bit of her attitude came from me.

"Alright, you two." Faxon walked back inside and interrupted the staring match. He reached for the coffee I'd poured for him, eyeing the two of us with caution, before he drank it all down fast. He belched and rubbed at his belly, and I swallowed my distaste over his poor manners. "Elora, it's time to go. Tell your Mama goodbye."

Elora jumped up from the armchair, the hood of her cloak already on and ready. Running over to me, she slammed into my arms for a quick hug, and I gave her a peck on the forehead.

"Please be safe, sweet love of mine. Listen to your father." I could feel the excitement racing through her veins as she kissed me on the cheek and started for the door, her frantic heartbeat pushing against my senses.

"Love you too, Mama, I will!" And she was out of the house before she finished speaking.

"Someone is excited," I muttered, a smile still on my lips. I knew this meant the world to Elora, and I was glad for it. She deserved to do things normal children did. She didn't even know about the prophecy, let alone that she was the Beloved. I'd never told her. She knew we lived in hiding because she had the same rare abilities that caused her aunt's murder, but nothing more. I had never told her the Myriad would consider her to be Aonara's favored, blessed with abilities only the Goddess of Light could bestow. I never saw it as a blessing, but rather a curse.

We were so far away from the major cities she had never even seen a member of the Myriad, only having walked past the temple in Mira. It was easy to keep the secret from her, the true magnitude of what it meant. Faxon and I had argued about it on more than one occasion. He had no intentions of ever telling her she was the Beloved, but I knew we needed to eventually. She had a right to know about the prophecy. Watching her sprint out the door, I made up my mind. I'd tell her when they got home, Faxon be damned.

"Try not to worry. I'll keep her safe." As he passed me to get his hat off the coat rack, Faxon put his hand on the small of my back and leaned in, kissing me on the cheek. "Goodbye, my love." When he turned to walk out the door, all I could do was stare. He rarely showed affection, probably because I never returned it. I watched him pull on his cloak and leave the house, glancing over his shoulder at me with a strange look on his face. I couldn't quite put my finger on it, but the interaction left me feeling uncomfortable.

I pulled on my cloak, a deep, rich blue—almost black—with pale yellow flowers I'd embroidered on the hood. Following my family outside, I stood on the porch and waved. Faxon led the way with Theo and Elora behind, giggling with each other. I couldn't stop myself and smiled wide. It was comforting to see my daughter do normal things like flirt with the neighbor boy when so much of her life hadn't been what I'd wanted for her. Her hood fell back, and I saw she had done what I asked and darkened her hair. It was still lighter than mine, but the brun root had darkened it enough to look natural. It would suffice, as long as she kept her hood up. I called out to remind her, and she waved an annoyed hand at me and pulled it back up.

"Love you to the moon!" I shouted, attempting to annoy her further. She turned, shooting a glare at me before smiling over her shoulder as their horses disappeared around a bend in the path.

I walked out to the stable to ready Bree for the trip to meet with Lord Kennon. While Faxon and Elora were going directly south, I'd go southeast to the meadow where we met every month. It was a long ride but an easy one. As I walked into the stable, I heard Bree softly nicker at me from her stall.

"Hush girl, I'll be there in a minute." Muttering, I pulled out my quiver and bow from the empty stall at the end of the stable. The yew bow was a gift from Faxon a few years ago, and I cared for it tenderly. Once Elora was a bit older, I had started leaving her with Faxon, and I would lose myself in the woods hunting. My father was as generous as he could be with his stipend, however, supplementing it with any meat I could find helped us live more comfortably. I glanced at the short sword leaning against the back corner and grimaced. That was not how you cared for a weapon. It had been a few weeks since I'd last sparred with Theo. He'd grown busy preparing for winter: adding compost to their garden, clearing all the brush from the trees he and Faxon had trimmed over the summer, and making all of the necessary repairs around their property. I knew he was occupied, and for good reason, but it meant I hadn't sparred with anyone in a long while. I supposed I should have pushed Elora to learn, but it was next to impossible to pry her books out of her hands, let alone get her to do any chores around the house. She would much rather read or practice using her abilities. It was another thing she had in common with Lucia—neither cared about weapons in the slightest. Sometimes I wondered if I was only as keen as I was in order to feel useful, to have a skill uniquely my own.

Why would I ever need to arm myself? I have you and Rainier to protect me.

The memory was a slap, and it was one that came to haunt me regularly. Oh, how wrong she was. I could hear the trill of her voice, much higher than mine. She'd been teasing at the time, as she had been more powerful than me, but it turned out to be a crueler joke than she could have imagined. I tried to ignore the pang in my heart. They were more rare as time had passed, but certain things could trigger a memory when I least expected it—I'd be in tears if I thought of them for too long. I shook my head to focus and walked over to the stall housing my headstrong, stubborn, and temperamental mare. Bree let out a great sigh to let me know she was glad for my attention.

"Good morning, Bree." I rubbed my hand along her muzzle. She was a beautiful bay horse with a red body and black mane and tail, and she gave the false impression of approachability. Giving her a quick brush, I began to prepare her for the ride.

"Did you see Theo this morning? Of course, Faxon didn't tell him to get you ready too, huh," I cooed at Bree. Maybe if I kept talking to her, one day she'd answer. Leading Bree outside, I realized I was running late. I ran back into the house to get my bag and attached my dagger to my thigh. I always left armed for these meetings. I'd be coming back with enough money to entice thieves, even if I'd never once run into one.

Pulling out the old pocket watch he'd gifted me as a child, I confirmed that Lord Kennon Highclere was late. It was two hours past noon, and Bree and I had made up for our late start, and still beat him to our meeting point. The meadow where we met sat near the banks of a stream leading all the way east to the Tuaman Cliffs. The rolling field of grass and wildflowers had been a destination of peace for me and my sister. It was only a two hours' ride from Ravemont, so when Lucia began to feel the stresses of what it meant to be betrothed to the Crown Prince of Vesta on top of being the Beloved, we would often ride out here. We also took the prince and princess with us quite a few times when they came to stay at Crown Cottage, one of the royal residences on this side of the Alsor Mountains. There were days we'd all ride out in the morning and sleep in the grass, warm from the sun and the Nythyrian wine in our blood. That last summer we spent a lot of time outside, either in the meadow or the olive grove. During a particularly stressful time when the Myriad Masters came to see a show of Lucia's talents, she disappeared with Princess Lavenia and Rainier's best friend Dewalt, leaving the prince and I to make excuses. She'd been sheepish and apologetic when they returned. Lucia had slipped the guard who was assigned to accompany her that day, and he was beaten for it. She was so angry that she convinced our father and the Crown to let Prince Rainier and Dewalt be her personal guard. They were just as well trained, and both were more powerful than any of the guards, Rainier especially. After that day, we spent even more time in the meadow, the five of us, and it turned into our own personal haven. The meadow was one of the only places near Crown Cottage and Ravemont that didn't bring back cruel memories for me.

I left an apple for the trip back, but the rest of my food did not stand a chance. I hadn't eaten anything since the coffee that morning, and I chuckled to myself, imagining my grumbling stomach would alert predators on the path. When I finished, and there was still no sign of Lord Kennon, I began to worry as I pressed my healing hands against Bree's joints, keeping her comfortable. The man was getting older, and though his path to the meadow from Ravemont was much easier than mine, he was mortal and aging, more fragile than he'd like to let anyone believe. I started to ready Bree, about to continue the ride to the estate, when I saw him on the horizon. Instead of meeting him halfway, I waited. He'd be insulted if he thought I doubted his abilities.

"Emmeline." Lord Kennon uttered my name as a particularly disappointing fact. He looked the same as I'd seen him last month. His stomach and shoulders had grown rounder with age, and his beard and hair were going white. His skin was a bit more sallow and pale than the last I'd seen him. Considering the ride, I was impressed by his perfect tidiness. Ever the lord, he wouldn't tolerate a single hair out of place or garment looking unkempt.

"Father." I attempted to match his contempt and immediately regretted it. I loved him so much. But the tragedies he faced—we faced—had made him a shell of who he used to be. When Lucia died, all three of us were husks. Mother passed not long after. She was a healer like me, and I didn't have nearly enough time to learn everything I could from her. Although she was a conduit without a bonded lifespan, like I was now, she was still considered rather young when she died. I believed it to be from a broken heart. She'd always favored Lucia, and somehow, she managed to take it harder than Father and I. She'd been quick to pawn me off on Faxon and usher me into a different wing of the estate after the wedding. I think seeing my face, Lucia's face, was too much for her. It was too much for me too. It was quite a long time before I stopped avoiding mirrors. After Elora was born, I thought Mother was relieved. She orchestrated the move to Brambleton, set up the stipend, and ensured Father, and only Father, would deliver it to me this way. It hurt a bit, knowing she'd rather not see me. I knew just seeing my face brought untold agony to her. But I understood. I understood it better than anyone. I didn't see my mother again before her death, and I missed the burial. Since Father hadn't sent a messenger when she passed, I found out here in the meadow after it was all said and done. Part of me would never forgive him.

"Where is Elora?" He glanced around in confusion, drawing me out of my thoughts.

"She went to Mira with Faxon."

"What a shame; I wanted to see her." He gave a sad smile. Would he have been a better grandfather than he was a father if he'd ever been given the chance?

"I'll bring her next time. She sends her love. Faxon says thank you, as usual." The lies came easier every month.

"It's nothing. Here." My father leaned down and passed me a small satchel. "The same as usual," he added.

"Thank you, Father." I rubbed the back of my neck, feeling my face flush. I hated this. All I wanted was to have a normal relationship with the man, but this was all I ever got from him. His formality only increased as the years passed.

"Sorry I cannot stay longer; I must be off. The servants are in a frenzy. The Crown has business in Ardian and has requested to stay at the estate rather than ride straight from Crown Cottage. They will likely arrive midday tomorrow." My father seemed rather annoyed by the whole prospect. Since Lucia's death, his resentment for the monarchy only grew. He suspected King Soren knew of the threat the Folterrans posed and simply allowed her to die. I couldn't understand that line of thinking. Lucia's powers bound to the prince's would have made the future king and queen the most powerful rulers Vesta had ever seen. Why wouldn't King Soren want that?

"What business does King Soren have in Ardian this far into autumn?"

"Ha! The old mongrel probably doesn't know how to ride a horse anymore, let alone find Ardian on a map. It's the Crown Prince. As for what business he might have in Ardian, I am not one to question the motivations of royalty. However, I am told it has to do with the temple."

I froze. Crown Prince Rainier would be at Ravemont tomorrow night.

You are poison.

The last words he'd said to me after Lucia's burial rang through my ears. He'd been down on one knee, holding his side after I'd just stabbed him. I had spent the better part of the last sixteen years hating him, just as he hated me. He was the reason I still had nightmares from that night.

"Send him my regrets for my lack of attendance. Tell him I hope he understands."

CHAPTER 3

I BEGAN THE RIDE home, lost in thought with an aching feeling in my chest. I had tried, unsuccessfully, not to think of Prince Rainier during all the years I'd been in hiding. After Lucia died, it was common knowledge Queen Shivani had searched for a replacement to perform the bonding ritual with the prince. As if Lucia had merely been a pawn. As if anything about her were replaceable. The queen presented eligible conduits, hailing from all over Nythyr and Vesta, hoping to find someone suitable for Rainier, but as far as I knew, they hadn't decided on one. If I could have felt anything back then, it would have been disgust—for more than one reason. At the time, I wondered if the queen counted down the days after my sister died, waiting for the appropriate opportunity to find Rainier a conduit to replace her. Did the queen feel inconvenienced by how long she had to wait to avoid appearing callous? Did Rainier grieve for her? For what we'd done?

I would always mourn my twin, though any official mourning period had long passed. Even sixteen years later, any time I thought about her, I felt this pinch in my nose, and I'd need to remember to breathe. My sister and I had always been two sides of the same coin, and ever since she'd been taken from me, everything had been off balance. I didn't think the wound would ever heal completely. Like an ache in my knee during the cold months, the hole left by my sister would stay inflamed forever. For so long after Lucia passed, I didn't eat, didn't sleep—I merely existed. I floated through the halls of Ravemont Estate like I was the one who'd died. Less than a week after the attack, I was married to Faxon. It was my eighteenth birthday—our eighteenth birthday. I didn't remember much of it, moving through the day in a fog. Faxon and I had retired to the west wing of the house, a mirror of the east wing where Lucia and I had grown, and I let him do what was expected of us—if only because I didn't have the energy to fight anything. I hadn't even known I was pregnant with Elora until I felt her flutter kick in my stomach months after the wedding, my body out of sorts.

When I finally felt her, I'd found a reason to survive. I began to eat for Elora, not myself. When she was born small, I blamed myself for those early months of malnutrition, but she thrived. I poured myself into her. I gave her every part of me, and, in doing so, I saved myself. When she wrapped her tiny hand around my finger, it was an anchor, bringing me back to the ground. Every smile from her was a gift, a reminder of what I stood to lose. Looking back, I realized, without her, I would've drifted away completely.

My thoughts moved to Elora in the present, off on an adventure with her father and Theo. The boy and his parents were who I heard most of the court gossip from. They'd told me of Vesta's push to claim Varmeer, the island which lay between Folterra and Vesta. South of the Alsor mountains and west of the port city of Mira, the island would prove to be a weakness if inhabited by Folterran forces. When King Dryul's armies began gathering on Varmeer, King Soren sent his son to bring the Folterrans to their knees. And by the sounds of it, he did. That had to have been a decade ago now. They'd even pushed into Folterra itself and built a fort on the peninsula jutting out of its southeastern side. Theo's father, John, long since dead, had painted a bloody picture when he talked about what the Vestian armies had done. Prince Rainier had brought hell down upon their armies. When I'd heard, I'd hoped the prince had shown the same cruelty to the Folterrans as they had to my family.

The last day I saw the prince, he told me he would bring me King Dryul's head. He'd told me those who were responsible for my sister's death would pay with their life. I had pulled my hair off my neck and bared it to him in response. We were the ones who took down the wards that night. We were the ones who deserved to pay. My sister, my best friend, my confidante—was dead. Because of us. I would never forgive myself, and I would never forgive him.

It was late, nearing dinner time, when I heard a scream from what sounded like a small child. Pushing my heels into Bree, I urged her toward the source of the noise. Coming around a bend in the path, I found two children and one angry pony. An older boy, maybe around ten, knelt next to a smaller child, a little girl with hair the color of sunshine. Bree nickered and came to a halt some distance away from the small, stamping horse.

"Can I help? What happened?" I climbed down from Bree, noticing the tears streaming down the girl's face. If I had to guess, the pony either bit her or threw her. Her older brother was wearing a mask of bravery, but his heartbeat told another story. I pulled back; I hadn't meant to listen, but it was just second nature sometimes.

"Poppy threw her off, ma'am. I think...I don't know, her arm don't look good. Mama is gonna kill us. She said Junie wasn't allowed up, but she wouldn't stop crying, so I let her. And now look. Junie, this is all your fault!" At this, Junie began to wail.

"Alright." I shot a warning look to the boy. He wasn't helping the situation. "Hold on honey, let me have a look."

I kneeled next to Junie, and her cries tapered off as her lower lip continued to quiver. Booboos and bandages were long past with Elora, and I missed this age. I rolled up her sleeve and saw the contortion of her wrist. I was amazed she wasn't screaming.

"Junie, you are a brave little girl. Do you mind if I try to fix you up?" She nodded. "This might hurt a little bit. I want you to use your other hand to grab onto your brother. Hold on tight and squeeze as hard as you can."

Children's bones were difficult; they were so bendable it was hard to know when I'd fixed them. Sometimes it was an injury I'd have to revisit afterward, just to make sure it healed properly. I delicately placed my hands on the little arm before me. Heat radiating from my palms, I guided the bones back in place. Junie gasped, and I saw her brother's face twist with pain. His sister was not only brave but strong—her grip on his hand like a vise. There was a pop, and Junie cried out. I held her arm a while afterward, the heat warming her skin, until her sobs subsided, and I pulled my hands from her.

"There we go. Now let's get you—"

"Are you a conduit?" A small furrow of suspicion appeared on the boy's brow as he spoke.

"Yes, I am. Although, this is about all I'm good for." I gave a smile, trying to assure him. Conduits were rare, more common among the gentry, and tended to live on large estates or in cities and have enough wealth to not bother mingling with mortals, let alone poor ones. I'd kept my divinity to myself for a reason. I didn't want to draw suspicion toward our family or Elora. I took in the sight of the children: their clothes a bit too tight and ragged and their teeth showing some signs of malnourishment, and despite my desire to remain unnoticed, I decided I wasn't done with them.

Junie leaned over and gave me a one-armed hug, surprising me. "Thank you," she whispered.

"No worries, little one. Let's get this wrapped up, and I'll help get you two home." I turned toward the boy. "Go reach into my bag and grab the apple out of it. Let's see if it will settle that one down." I glared over at the pony. Devilish thing.

As the boy gave the mean thing an apple, I ripped a strip off the bottom of my cloak and helped wrap Junie's arm into a sling. I should have already replaced this cloak anyway; holes had started to show in the fabric. I had set the bone and attempted to reduce the swelling, but she would still need plenty of rest. This wasn't the first time I'd wished my divinity was stronger. The image of Lucia lying crumpled on the ground came to me, and I shuddered, pushing it away.

"How far off the road is your home? I'd like to explain to your mother how to care for her arm." I looked toward the boy, who reddened immediately.

"It's fine, ma'am, just tell me how to do it. I'll take care of her." He started kicking at the ground beneath his feet.

"Now listen, I have to tell your Mama. She's going to know something happened, best to face it head-on. Also, I'd appreciate it if you'd stop calling me ma'am. Miss Emma will suffice." Nothing made me feel more like my mother than someone calling me ma'am. The boy sighed.

"Just about a quarter-mile west, ma—Miss Emma." He grinned.

The boy, whose name I learned was Thomas, had predicted his mother wouldn't react well, but she was full of nothing but gratitude. She insisted I stay for dinner, and, after smelling the simmering stew, I was disinclined to say no. I made myself a tiny portion, knowing the moment I stepped over the threshold, they must have been struggling. This knowledge sat alongside the fact she'd be deeply offended if I declined to eat. I rarely visited with people who weren't in my immediate family. As good as the stew was, the chaos and excitement which radiated off the two children, happy for a guest to join them, were what truly warmed my soul. My house would be empty and quiet when I arrived home, the first time I'd witness it as such. As Elora had gotten older, she'd gotten quieter, but her presence was still vibrant. I wasn't looking forward to the empty house for the next few days.

"Thank you. The stew was delicious and the conversation a delight. Would I be able to come back in four- or five-days' time to check in on Junie's arm? I just want to make sure it's healing properly." The little girl was asleep in her mother's lap, limbs askew and mouth open, and the woman, Lillian, nodded.

"Thank you so much, Emma."

I waved as I let myself out, hoping to make it home within the hour. I made a mental note to talk to Mairin about a salve for the dry, rough skin that climbed up Lillian's arms from her hands to her elbows. I tucked it away in my mind with thoughts of Theo's little brother, a boy a bit taller than Thomas, and how I'd inquire about hand-me-downs his mother might be willing to spare.

For the remainder of the ride, my thoughts were drawn to Elora and how much she'd grown. I missed pulling a tiny, little girl into my lap, kissing away tears as I made her whole again. I'd been feeling sentimental a lot lately, as Elora wanted more independence. She was growing into a smart and sufficient young woman, and soon she'd leave, onto a life belonging only to her. I worried she would never be completely safe, but she was already pushing back against me so much. Her divinity was on par with Lucia at that age, and she was stronger than me. I couldn't keep her sheltered away forever, or she'd grow to hate me. I'd have to let her go. I wondered what I'd do then. Perhaps we'd return to Ravemont—Faxon would like that.

After a deafeningly quiet first evening by myself, I was relieved when someone rapped on the door the second night. Sweeping the curtain aside, I saw a mass of fiery red hair and smiled wide.

"Mairin! What a surprise!" I realized then perhaps she was only there to summon me for help, but her answering grin told me her visit was for pleasure, not business. She came in, her arms loaded with a heavy basket.

"I've brought sustenance." She waggled her eyebrows as she pulled out a bottle of wine and passed it to me. "A newer Olistos, but hopefully, it still does the trick." Olistos was the northernmost city in Vesta, known for its wine. Olistos wine was good, but any true wine authority knew the best wines came from Nythyr, the kingdom to the north of Vesta. Either way, I was grateful for both her and the wine. I smiled. It was nice to have a friend.

"What else is in your goodie bag?" I reached into the hutch, carefully pulling out two wine glasses and placing them on the counter.

"A little bit of this, a little bit of that," she retorted as she pulled cheese after cheese out of the basket, followed by meats and fruits.

"You didn't have to do all of this! If I knew you were coming—"

"I don't do things for my friends because I have to. I figured you might be lonely."

"You figured right," I supplied as I pulled the bottle of wine closer to me, taking the bottle opener to it. After I got the cork out, I poured us both a glass and sat down at the table.

"So, how many nervous breakdowns have you had?" Mairin followed suit, sitting in the chair across from me, a smile playing on her lips.

"None, thank you very much." I returned the smile, even though she was intentionally annoying me.

We spent the rest of the evening at the table chatting. After finishing the Olistos, I went into the pantry and dragged out my last bottle of Nythyrian. Mairin nearly clapped with glee. I looked across at my friend, my first real friend in a long time, and smiled. I was grateful for her—for helping me pass the time. After a while, our conversations grew more serious.

"She's a conduit too, isn't she?"

I nodded.

"But not like you?" It was a question I could tell she already knew the answer to. If Elora had been like me, it wouldn't have been as much of a necessity to keep her cut off from the world.

"No, she's not like me. She's like my sister."

Mairin nodded slowly at this. She didn't know who my sister was. She knew she was dead, but she didn't know she was the Beloved. I found myself wanting to tell her, to confide in someone.

"What are you going to do when she fully comes into her divinity?"

"I'm going to do the best I can." My chuckle came out more nervous than I'd intended. Mairin tilted her head and arched an expectant brow. "When she comes into her full divinity, she shouldn't need me anymore." My smile was sad. I didn't want her to need my protection, but protector was a role I took on gladly.

"A girl always needs her mother." Mairin reached across and squeezed my hand.

"In a way."

"That still doesn't tell me what you are going to do."

The truth was, I'd barely begun to think about it.

CHAPTER 4

FIVE DAYS AFTER ELORA and Faxon left, I took a ride southeast to check on Junie and her arm. With me, I brought a few shirts and pants for Thomas, though the knees were in dire need of darning, and a skein of green and pink floral-patterned fabric I'd found stashed away in a closet. I'd intended to use it in the spring for something, but thought Lillian could use it to fashion Junie some more clothing. When I handed Lillian the small container of salve, she flushed bright red and rolled her sleeves down over the flaking skin. I assured her I'd brought it only to help, knowing it had to bother her, and told her Mairin in town could always get her more if she needed it. The flush left her face, but I still wondered if maybe I'd overstepped. But she reacted so positively to the rest of the items I brought that I thought if I did hurt her feelings, she'd forgive me sooner rather than later. Junie's arm was healing well, and I headed home with a full belly, Lillian insisting on feeding me for my efforts. I didn't want to risk the potential of offending her further, so I ate graciously. It was midday as I approached the creek near home. Just on the other side of it, the babbling water between us and the house, Bree tensed.

"Come on, almost there." Coaxing the stubborn beast, I pushed her forward. Bree refused to take one more step. Climbing down, I walked in front of her, thinking maybe she'd seen a stick she thought was a snake or something else on the path. I didn't see anything that would stop her from proceeding. But then I heard something. I froze, my hand resting on my dagger the second I heard a voice.

"How much longer are we supposed to wait? I wanna go back to that tavern. You saw how that maid was eyeing me, Charlie?"

I tiptoed back to Bree, quiet as I could, and slipped off my cloak. My bow and quiver were strapped to my pack, and I quickly retrieved them. The voice I'd heard speaking belonged to a tall, lanky man who stood in the clearing in front of my house. The sun was bright, so I was able to get a clear view of him as he turned.

and I noticed a dark red port-wine stain taking up a good portion of his face. I wasn't sure who he was, but he was clearly waiting for me. I certainly didn't want to be found unarmed. He made his way up the steps on my front porch, kneeling on the bench in front of the window as he peered inside.

A laugh barked somewhere to my left, and I heard someone relieving themselves in the trees, though I couldn't see anyone. "She was just wondering if you could afford her!" My uninvited guest pulled himself away from my window, making his way down my porch steps.

"Hey, fuck you, Charlie. But you're right, aye, why pay the maid in Brambleton when we can just wait a little longer here?"

That statement was what sealed his fate. These men had plans for me, and they were not of the friendly sort. Maybe I should have waited for Charlie to approach as well, so I knew where both of them were, but the threat I'd just heard terrified me, causing me to act without thinking. I grabbed an arrow, notched it, pulled back, and released. He turned to the side, and my arrow went straight past his ear.

Shit.

"AY!" He dropped down, crouched, looking into the trees for the source of the arrow. I frantically reached for a second one.

When I shot this one, it didn't miss. It hit him in the chest, and he fell to the ground without a sound. I knew Charlie would come looking for me soon, so I pulled another arrow out, my bow ready. I slowly walked up the path, scanning the clearing for the other man.

To my left, I heard a twig snap, and I whipped my head around. I didn't have more than a second to react before Charlie rushed me. I'd stupidly expected him to go to the clearing to check on his friend after hearing his cry, and I'd spent so much time controlling my divinity, only using it when I called upon it, that I hadn't been listening for his heart. He must have realized what was happening and crept through the trees. He smacked the bow from my hand and grabbed me by the neck, pushing me to the ground. I was pinned, arms folded under me. I needed to get a hand free. I would not let this man kill me or do whatever else he planned. Hot, sour breath washed over me as he pushed my shoulder down to the ground, torquing it painfully. I cried out in pain, the pressure of his body on mine hurt, and I couldn't move. His face was sallow, with dark circles under his eyes, lank hair hanging down into his face—into my face. He weighed more than me and was holding me down by the throat, and I could hardly breathe.

"Got you, bitch," he spat at me. "Dom had that coming. Too bad he'll miss out on the show." He sneered down at me, shifting his weight and pressing his arm down across my chest as he began to pull at his breeches with his free hand. The second he let go of my throat, I started pulling in gasping breaths, not as deep as I needed since he was still pushing down on me.

My vision began to suffer from the lack of air, and I felt my panic rising. I tried to pull my knees up to knock off his balance, kick him, knee him, anything. His legs were over mine, and I was thoroughly pinned. But he did pull back just enough so I was able to free my left arm. I reached for his face, dragging my nails down the side of it, ripping through flesh.

A flash of light and pain burst through my skull at the temple. He'd reared back and punched me in the head, hard.

I laid still for a second, blind. He sat back a bit, grappling with the buttons on his breeches. As he struggled, he lifted some of his weight off my chest, and I rallied, bringing my other arm out from under me. I was free to reach for my dagger, strapped to my thigh. I strained, stretching for it, pulling my leg back toward me. My fingertips barely brushed the hilt, just out of reach. I began to panic. This man was going to rape me and kill me when he was finished.

My brain was racing for some way out, my breaths gasping, as I reached for his face again, but he'd sat back out of reach trying to pull my pants down, not bothering with the buttons. Without him pushing me down, I was able to start trying to wiggle away from him, kicking and pulling at the ground behind me. And then I felt the tip of one of my arrows. My quiver had spilled out when he threw me to the ground. This particular arrow was broken, the head and shaft only about the length of my hand.

I palmed the arrow just as he successfully pulled my pants down past my hips, exposing me to the cool autumn air. I felt my flesh crawl as he surveyed the length of my body, eyes landing on my face. He grinned as he reached for himself. I couldn't hesitate.

Drawing my arm up, arrow in my fist, I slammed it into his throat as hard as I could. He had a look of shock as he watched his blood pour onto my chest, and then he collapsed.

Grunting, I pushed the man off me as best I could while covered in his blood. It was hot and sticky, and I'd never felt more disgusting. I jumped up, pulling up my undergarments and breeches as I did. Hearing Bree nicker from behind, I strode over to her, absentmindedly patting her muzzle as I caught my breath. I stood there, looking at the body on the ground. The body of a person who had just tried to rape me. A part of me wanted to run to the stable and bring a hatchet back to chop off the appendage he'd been trying to use. I shuddered at the thought of what I'd just narrowly avoided and turned, burying my head into Bree's neck.

Who were these men, and what did they want from me? Did someone know I'd be alone, and Faxon would be gone? Finally, I pulled myself out of my thoughts and moved, leading Bree toward the stream. Picking my way across the stream, I spotted two horses tied at the front of the stable. With Bree safely settled inside, happy with the fresh oats I'd given her, I went to search the other horses, but found nothing of import. I got them settled in the stable, unsure of what to do with them. Moving back into the clearing, I kicked at the man from the porch—Dom, as his friend had called him—his body spread on the ground before me. He was dressed in all black, his young face marked with acne. That youth and clear inexperience explained why he died so quickly; he hadn't even tried to take cover after I shot my first arrow. I searched him, finding nothing, and did the same to Charlie's body. Nothing.

Walking past him, I went to the stream, doing the best I could to clean the blood off me. I untied and took off my bodice, thankfully free of blood save for one single drop, and then took my shirt off, fully submerging it in the water. I wasn't sure I'd ever get all the blood out, but at least I could use it for rags.

I walked back to the house, throwing the shirt on the porch railing. I was exhausted physically and wasn't up to laundering it. I didn't pay attention to anything else as I trudged up the stairs, my mind racing. How long had they been waiting? Who were they? Did they know about the stipend? Charlie hadn't seemed to care about money when he was on top of me.

I went into the bedroom, tugging off the rest of my clothing before finding myself in front of the mirror. I'd gotten most of the blood off at the stream, but there was still some on my face, some of it my own. I poured water out of the ewer into the basin and grabbed a washcloth. I touched the wound, wincing, before I started to scrub, erasing his existence from my body. What if I hadn't gotten him off me? What if he'd—I stopped myself. He didn't. I hadn't been able to stop him from exposing me, and I felt violated. Moving down, I scrubbed my body with the cloth, not satisfied until every part of my skin he'd touched was pink and smarting, but it still wasn't enough. I slid down to the ground with a sob.

After I calmed down a bit, I realized I'd have to tell someone about what happened. Should I go to Mira? Did these men see Faxon and Elora on the road? Maybe one of them had mentioned something about me being alone, not realizing someone could do something terrible with the information. I didn't know what to do.

I had left the bodies where they fell, but I guessed the best course of action would be to go to Brambleton and let someone from the guard know what happened. But that meant drawing attention to my home. And to me and what was almost done to me. I crawled into my bed, still naked, and let my thoughts run wild. My body was exhausted. Even though my mind was racing, I couldn't stop my eyelids from closing, pushing me to unconsciousness.

I couldn't have slept for long because it was still light outside when I heard it. A groan. Someone was in pain nearby. Jumping out of bed, I fumbled around for my robe, pulling it closed around me and tying it tight. There was another sound, and it was louder this time. It sounded like someone was right under the bedroom window. Opening it and throwing my head out to look down, all I could see was a black lump on the ground, but it was moving. I raced down the stairs, grabbed my dagger from the table where I'd left it, and slammed out the door. Rounding the corner behind the house, the black lump on the ground turned into what was clearly a person. They had a cloak on their head. I pulled it off and jumped back, immediately regretting my decision. He'd clearly been beaten. A mass of purple, swollen skin and likely broken cheekbones explained the moaning. The man groaned again and blinked at the light of the sun behind me.

They took her. On the road."

I gaped at him.

"Theo?" His voice was the only thing familiar which registered. He closed his eyes and nodded. "What are you talking about? Who took who?" The panic started to rise. I knew what he was trying to tell me.

"Elora. They took Elora."

After placing my hands on Theo's face for a little while, the swelling had gone down a bit, and I was able to get him comfortable enough to begin talking. His dark blonde hair was slicked back with blood, and I was so glad he was alright. While I healed him, I told him about the men. Their deaths seemed to bring him relief.

He said they had stopped for lunch, almost a full day from Mira when they'd been taken. A dozen men galloped up to them, coming north up the Mirastos Path. They'd thrown Elora onto a horse, and the man who seemed to be in charge climbed up behind her. Faxon had run to Elora while Theo attacked the men.

"I tried to stop them. I—I did everything I could. They hit me, and I… I fell."

"It's alright, Theo." He was crying.

"When I woke up, they…they told me to bring them here. I didn't want to. I didn't want them to hurt you, Emma."

"They didn't. It's alright, I'm fine."

"They said they'd find Mama. I... I'm sorry."

"Theo, stop apologizing. Did they say anything? Anything about where they were taking them? Do you know how many days it's been? Did they take Faxon, too?"

I sank back on the ground next to Theo.

"I didn't see what happened to Faxon, but I think they took him, too. Before I—I heard him yelling at the men, and he had his sword out, but I don't know what happened next. I don't know how many days. They said something about a ship. The younger one, he said he'd never been on one, and he was sore to be missing out."

Did that mean they were taking them to a ship? Where were they going? Who were they? Folterrans? It had to be. How could they have known about Elora? Father was always careful with the information he shared. He rarely visited anyone or had visitors. None of the servants knew where we lived, but it wouldn't have been exactly difficult to find where we were. All they'd have had to do would be follow him to our meeting spot, then follow me home. But we trusted them.

"Emma, who would take her? Why would they be putting her on a ship?" I shook my head, hoping it was enough to stop his questions. I didn't have the energy, and he probably wouldn't believe me, anyway.

"Is there anything else you can remember about these men? Did they have an accent? Were they conduits?" I pleaded. Maybe these were Vestian renegades who had no idea what they had in their possession. Theo shook his head. The poor boy. He'd been through a lot, and I was not exactly being delicate with him.

"The...the man in charge said something I didn't understand. He said 'the best part is the Bloody Prince has no idea she even exists.'"

I stilled. They knew. They knew what she was. I'd heard that phrase in recent years. The Bloody Prince was what the Folterrans called Crown Prince Rainier.

I sprang into action. Bringing Theo inside, I set him up in the armchair and started a fire in the hearth. Sprinting up the stairs and flinging my robe off in the hallway, I gathered clothes and dressed in a hurry. I dragged a brush through my hair, not bothering to take the time to wet and braid it. Catching a glimpse in the mirror, I reminded myself of the images of Rhia, the Goddess of Fertility. She was always depicted with her long black hair floating out around her face, caught on an invisible breeze.

Grabbing the spare clothes where I'd tossed them on my bed, I put them in a pack and ran out of my room, thundering down the stairs. I grabbed my boots by the front door and carried them to the other chair near Theo.

"Stay. Rest. Eat. Please look after the horses. Take care of your mama and your brother."

"Emma, I want to come with you. Please."

"Theo, you'll only slow me down. Please, just do what I ask and get better. Thank you for coming back to me. I'm sorry for what happened." I finished lacing my boots and stood.

"I came back 'cause I'm a coward. I should've let them kill me."

"Well, then I really would have been mad." I tried to smile at him. I reached down and ruffled his hair. If he hadn't had a growth spurt recently, he'd still have the chubby cheeks of adolescence. But he was becoming a man. He had tried to protect Elora, and I was grateful for him.

"You are not a coward. Oh, and please get this to Mairin." I found a scrap of paper and wrote a hurried note, asking her to help Theo handle everything and explaining what had happened. I grabbed a few more supplies from the kitchen and headed out to the stables.

Panic was threatening to bubble up in my chest. Ever since Theo told me Elora was taken, I'd been in a daze. I gathered my clothes and took care of the last few things around the house in a state of shock, successfully keeping the terror at bay. I climbed my mare, and we took off. It drizzled off and on the entire ride. Any other time, I'd have been freezing, but terror and anger warmed me. As the forest whipped past me, I did my best to fight off intrusive thoughts. If they wanted her dead like they had Lucia, she already would be. They wouldn't have taken her. She was still alive. She had to be. A part of me felt like I'd know if she weren't. The world would stop spinning, the trees and grass would turn to ash, and life would have shifted. I wouldn't allow myself to think of any possibility where my daughter was not alive.

I couldn't stop thinking about what Theo had told me. They were pleased the Bloody Prince—*Rain*—didn't know she existed. Did they plan to use her as a weapon against him? From what I knew, the prince had been busy at the fort on Folterran lands or busy on Varmeer. I'd thought after his initial brutalization of the land and their army, relations with the Folterrans had been tense but peaceful. I did wonder why Rainier took the defense of the island as his personal mission and wouldn't assign it to one of the Vestian generals. It kept him away from Vesta most of the time, a fact which surely didn't please Queen Shivani.

Why would they be happy the prince didn't know she existed? How did the existence of the Beloved affect Rainier? Did they think he would have used her as a weapon against them? That didn't make any sense. He'd planned to wed Lucia, not use her as a weapon. Unless they viewed the bonding ritual as such, as an act of aggression. Although, the more I thought about it, giving Prince Rainier the same powers as Lucia in addition to his own would make a devastating enemy.

The forest on either side of me began to fall away and cleared into the meadow. It was dark outside, my pocket watch telling me Father would be drinking his nightcap, when I finally let Bree fall to a walk. The horse would need to rest. As Ravemont Estate came into view on the horizon, lit up on the inside, I wondered if I had made a mistake. Elora was likely already in Mira, based on the fact Theo had come almost all the way back to Brambleton after she was taken. If we left right then, not stopping to sleep or rest, using my divinity to heal her as we rode, I could likely make it to Mira by this same time the next night, but what would I do by myself? I had no authority, and I certainly couldn't take on the abductors by myself. I knew I needed a larger presence and assistance from the Crown. I also knew exactly where a large force of the Crown would be located, and I made the choice which would be more likely to bring Elora back to me. If the prince would even help me. I pushed the thought from my mind. I'd make him help me. He owed me.

As I eased closer to Ravemont, my breath caught. I took in the limestone facade, a beautiful tan color, and saw it hadn't changed at all. In fact, it looked like it had been recently painted, though it was hard to tell in the dark, the crescent moon doing little to illuminate the grounds. The climbing hydrangeas were no longer blooming during this season but had spread to take up more space on the front of the estate, spreading from one end to the other. The east and west wing both jutted forward from the front entry, a fountain in the middle. In the center of the water fixture sat a little girl blowing on a dandelion, but instead of air coming out of her mouth, it was water. Small hedges surrounded the fountain, creating paths that meandered around it. I'd played tag in those hedge paths with Lucia more times than I could count, running through them until eventually we were tall enough to jump over them. The game wasn't as fun once we were grown.

The servants were closing all the windows, and I could see white gauzy curtains inside blowing with the breeze. The giant oak tree Lucia and I used to swing from was still present in front of the east wing. Our rooms had been on that side of the estate. We'd watched out our windows to see the squirrels and birds call the oak tree their home.

I wished Elora were here for this. My return to Ravemont was supposed to be triumphant. In my head, I had imagined coming home with her, finally able to live without the fear of tragedy. I wasn't sure how my imagination had hoped to accomplish this feat, but that didn't stop me from hoping and wishing. I felt the threat of tears at my lashes, and I focused my attention on stopping it from happening. If I started, I would never stop. I would be useless to Elora.

I directed Bree straight to the front entry. There would be a servant there who I could ask to take her to the stables. I navigated us past the fountain and stopped right in front of the steps leading to the place and people I used to call home. Dismounting my mare, I took a deep breath in. Nothing was going to stop me, and yet all I felt was nerves as I stood in the footprint of the immense building in which I'd grown up.

As I started going up the stairs, the door creaked open before me. I looked up, only able to see the silhouette of a person in front of the well-lit entry.

"Mistress Emmeline?" Mr. Carson had been the butler since I was a baby, and I was shocked he still held the job. I took a few steps up so the light behind him wasn't blinding me, and I could make out his aged face. He regarded me in confusion, with the hint of a smile on his lips. I gestured out the door to Bree behind me.

"Can you see to my horse? Please make sure they're extra sweet to her."

I pushed past him, watching the competing questions he wanted to ask lose steam as he glanced between me and my mare, his facial expression one of exasperation. I marched inside, not caring that I was dripping all over the entryway tile, as I headed toward the back of the estate where my father entertained, hoping they were all still awake. I yelped as I ran square into a squat woman, soft and warm, and nearly knocked her over.

Nana tottered, and I grabbed her elbow. She gaped at me like she'd seen a ghost, not the child she'd been a nurse, confidante, and teacher to.

"Mistress Emmeline! You're bleed—"

I gently moved past her. I'd have time to speak to her later. As I crossed the dark oak floors, which ran from east to west, I scanned my surroundings, hoping not to run face-first into any of the servants who were surely bustling throughout the house due to the Crown's visit. But when I took in the person standing to my left, my steps faltered.

"Emma?"

Lavenia looked exactly the same. Slim and wiry, she still had the same long black hair, currently plaited into tight braids falling down her back, and that same golden-brown skin, a shade darker than her brother's. Her eyes were a deep brown, so dark they were almost black. So different from Rainier's eyes. She didn't look much older than the last time I'd seen her. Had she performed the ritual? The princess I once knew always had a grin and a joke waiting, but the woman looking back at me had her mouth slightly open, standing frozen, almost as if she was stuck to the spot she stood. She stared at me in confusion and what seemed like something else. Anguish, perhaps. I dipped my head but didn't have the words, the sense of urgency flowing through me. I turned back to the doors of the audience room and made my way the final few steps, feeling Lavenia turn to follow behind me. I gained momentum and slammed the doors open. A hush fell over the room as I locked eyes with my father. He was seated on a small sofa, surrounded by people I didn't know or hadn't seen in years.

"They have her, Papa." His head tilted in confusion.

"Who?" I wondered if it was shock making him struggle or something worse. He should have known who I meant.

"Elora. The Folterrans have Elora."

Everyone in the room turned to stare at me, and no one uttered a single sound. Father's lips started to move, but he was unable to follow through with any words. I scanned the room, noticing it was mostly untouched since the time I'd lived there—the dark grey-green wainscotting and cream walls above it, stamped with a tiny floral pattern, looked exactly the same. Even the cream-colored rug which sat in the middle of the room was unchanged, and I couldn't help but notice the dark spot where Lucia had once spilled a glass of juice. My eyes found Dewalt, the prince's second. He stared at me in shock and something verging on horror. He appeared the same as I remembered, as if he'd barely aged a day. I couldn't see a single wrinkle on his face. His long, jet hair was tied behind him, without a hint of grey. Had he performed the ritual too? After a long moment, he broke the trance within the room.

"Emma? Is that... Where have you—" he stammered as he rose to his feet, and I saw his fist clench and unclench a few times.

"Darling, what do you mean Elora has been—" My father tried to rise from his seat beside Dewalt, clearly confused.

"Where is he?" My voice was more of a demand than it should have been, considering what I was asking. It came out much louder than intended as well. The room was large, causing my breaking voice to boom. The light blue curtains which hung over the floor-to-ceiling windows did little to help muffle the sound.

The room was too silent, the stress too vast, and I started to tap my foot. I was coming undone.

"He'll be back." Thankfully, Dewalt knew what I meant and didn't scold me for my delivery. His eyes watched me with caution as he looked at me from across the room, something about it unsettling. He'd filled out. He was still tall and lean, taller than Rainier ever was, but he had muscle to go with it now and a fair amount of it. His laugh lines were still there, and I realized that was what unsettled me—the absence of his smile. I'd rarely seen him without one.

"What's going on, Emmeline?" My father was sitting on the edge of his seat, giving up on jumping to his feet, but his face was a mask of concern. He was seated on the button-tufted sofa before the fire, the wooden frame still bearing the scratch marks from the winter Lucia and I had snuck one of the stable-cats inside. With Dewalt seated on one side and a younger woman I didn't recognize on the other, my father looked older than I'd ever seen him. By the familiar way the woman had her hand placed on my father's shoulder, I assumed there were things Father had kept from me during our monthly meetings.

I took in the room once more to determine what information I could share. One of the older servants, Miss Suzy, was in the back of the room with her hand over her mouth. She knew of Elora and what it meant for her to be taken. I checked behind me to see Lavenia and Nana had followed me into the room. I started to wonder if I made the wrong choice, that I'd wasted time by coming here and not going straight to Mira. I started to lose control of my emotions and felt the fear rise in my throat. As if sensing what was coming, Lavenia grabbed me by the hand, which I just noticed had begun to shake.

"Emma...Emmeline. Let's sit you down." She gently pulled me toward a wing-backed chair across from the sofa on which my father still sat. I was grateful she took control of the situation. My father clearly wasn't in any state to handle it, and I barely was myself. Lavenia sat down on the matching ottoman situated at my feet and watched me, never letting go of my hand. Kindness and concern were all I saw in her charcoal eyes. I didn't see a hint of resentment from the woman I'd once called friend. I took a deep breath and began to explain.

"My daughter. Elora. She—" I hesitated. Everyone in the room, save for possibly the woman sitting next to my father, knew Lucia was the supposed Beloved all those years ago. What some of them didn't know was that Elora even existed, let alone we suspected she was the Beloved. Those in the prince's court didn't know the true reason why I hid away. I leveled my gaze upon the woman sitting next to my father.

"Would you please give us a word in private?" I asked in as even and measured of a tone as possible. The woman glanced between me and my father before nodding. As she rose, Father stopped her.

"Emmeline, she can stay. Gemma knows everything." I stared at my father. He had chosen to reveal the truth about my daughter to a woman I'd never met? Now was not the time for me to deal with it. I narrowed my eyes at them both before I pushed my frustration down. I needed to focus my energy on getting through to arguably the two most powerful people nearby, after the prince, wherever he was.

"Elora is my daughter. She's like Lucia." I watched Lavenia, dreading the recognition in her eyes. Lucia had been hunted for what she was. Understanding and sadness looked back at me as my old friend's gaze met mine. "They were attacked on the Mirastos Path, a day's ride north of Mira. Elora and my husband were taken. Two men came back to the house to... I don't know, kill me, I guess."

"That was their last mistake, I presume?" Lavenia looked so much like her brother as her mouth twitched. I didn't reply as I watched her eyes flit up to the side of my head where I'd been hit. I realized with a start that because of the rain and the fact that it was still bleeding when I left, I probably had blood all over my face. I ignored it.

"I found our farmhand nearly beaten to death afterward. The men had brought him back, used him to find our house. He told me what happened, and he thinks they are taking them to a ship. I came straight here. I knew Rain... Prince Rainier was supposed to be here, and I thought, well, I didn't know what to do and—" I felt the tears welling up and was grateful for Lavenia's interruption.

"He will help. *We* will help. Of course, Emmeline." Lavenia glanced over to Dewalt for what I assumed to be approval. He wasn't looking at her, though; he was looking behind me, toward the doors to the hall. I felt my skin prick as I sensed his presence behind me. The servants in the back of the room dropped to their knees, and I remembered myself. Sliding down to my knees and turning toward him, keeping my head down, I gave myself time to catch my breath and calm down.

"Lady Emmeline, stand up. You've never once knelt before me—why start now?"

CHAPTER 5

He must have been in Ardian today.

The thought came to me as I eyed the light brown mud coating his black boots. In all my imaginings of what would happen when I arrived at Ravemont, I never got to the part where I'd actually see him and have to speak to him. I swallowed audibly. I needed to get up and face him. I didn't know what I'd do if he said no, but I knew I had to ask for Elora. A small part of me felt I'd deserve it if he said no. Even if I did deserve it, I wouldn't let him. I couldn't. I'd been so hateful to him, but the events of that night still haunted my dreams. *He* still haunted my dreams. He owed me.

I stood and raised my eyes to the prince. Despite the grand room we were in, his presence was formidable, seeming to take up more space than he truly did. He'd always towered over me, but the last time I'd seen him, he was all arms and legs. Now, the broad shoulders of a warrior tapered into a trim waist and long, thick legs. He pulled off his cloak, revealing a thin, black shirt, and I couldn't avoid seeing the taut muscles in his back press through the fabric as he turned away from me. I brushed away the strands of hair in my face, suddenly aware I'd never braided it back that morning. I probably looked like a wet dog. A bloody, wet dog. As he turned back toward me, I lifted my gaze to his face, studying all the ways it had changed. His jawline was less rounded, more square than it used to be, and covered in stubble. His golden-brown skin was less smooth, dappled in scars that told a story I found myself desperately wanting to hear. He'd cut his hair shorter, no longer the mass of curls I was used to. Although I could see the crinkles at the corners of his eyes and laugh lines around his mouth, it was hard to believe the man in front of me laughed much at all. I was shocked at how imposing he appeared now. Gone was the slim young man I remembered, and in his place was someone who I could only describe as powerful. I counted my heartbeats as I tried to balance my fear and attraction in my mind. Fear of what he could do and fear he wouldn't help me raced through me as strongly as my pulse thundered in my ears.

Goddess, help me.

When I saw his eyes, I realized he had been doing the same thing to me. His gaze was roaming over me, and I started to feel myself flush. I was sure I looked so different from the last time he saw me. When I left Brambleton to come here, my mind had skipped past this reunion and what it would entail. When his eyes finally met mine, deep green like the olive grove we'd once run in, I realized I'd been holding my breath. I held his stare as I inhaled deeply. He did not smile, and I could see his jaw was clenched, his temple throbbing. He did not move. I felt the heat rise to my face, remembering the last words he'd said to me.

You are a cruel fool, Emmeline.

I heard Dewalt mutter something to Lavenia, both of them standing behind me. The woman stifled a laugh, and I wondered what could possibly be funny in this moment. Rainier turned to look at the two of them, standing off to the side next to Nana.

"Leave us," he ordered in a low, quiet voice. I went rigid at the sound. His voice was deeper than I remembered. This was the voice of a man who commanded armies and destroyed Folterran forces. Lavenia and Dewalt skittered out of the room like two chastised children, and out of the corner of my eye, I noticed Gemma leading Father out, the servants ahead of them. The prince walked across the room to the ottoman his sister had perched on and took a seat, looking up at me expectantly. When I sat down across from him, he passed me a handkerchief, watching me with an expression I couldn't quite place.

"Clean yourself up. Coming here covered in blood was unnecessary but an effective tactic, nonetheless. I will help you get your daughter back."

I stared. I wasn't sure how long he'd been standing behind me, but he must have heard my explanation. I'd been bracing myself, waiting for all the cruel things I had imagined him saying to me over the years. All the questions, all the accusations. I'd been ready for it. I'd even been ready for his refusal. I was not ready for how quickly he acquiesced. Nor was I ready for the tone he took with me—the cold detachment in his words. His eyes were narrowed on me in what I could only interpret as suspicion. Did he think I'd shown up covered in blood on purpose? I felt my blood heat.

"It is no tactic, *Your Highness*. I came here directly after I was attacked. I must admit I left my jewels and satin at home."

His eyebrows lowered as he glared at me, watching me wipe the rain and blood from my face. I immediately regretted the level of disrespect I'd just shown him, considering he was my best shot at finding Elora. The fact he thought my disheveled state might have been some sort of act offended me more than he likely thought it would. He took a deep breath before he spoke, looking down at his hands dangling between his legs, opting not to reply to my last statement.

"I assume, since you have been . . . away," he said, body tensing, "she is likely to be the Beloved." He looked up, waiting for me to nod. "Which means the Beloved is in the hands of our enemies. Even if we did not share a *history* . . ." He paused after forcing the word out and cleared his throat. "Even if we did not share a history, I would be obligated to assist in retrieving her. Who knows she is the Beloved? Many here?"

"A few of the servants here, yes."

"And her father is with her?" His eyes narrowed. "Faxon?" I nodded once more. I noticed his jaw clench again. My eyes were drawn to the pale line cutting vertically through his left eyebrow. No hair grew on it. The scar seemed old, but was one he had gained in the time since I'd seen him last.

"Is there anyone else you've trusted with this information?" Something in his voice made me pause before I answered. He was clearly bothered by something.

"No. No one else." The quick tilt of his chin was his only response.

"We will rest and leave for Mira before dawn. You, Lavenia, Dewalt, and I will go ahead, and my men will—"

"That's too late!" My heart grew frantic. "We need to get on the road now!" I felt a shiver roll up my spine, and it wasn't entirely due to my soaking wet clothes. Even if we left now, we might still not make it before she was gone. I knew it was possible, even likely. Hell, they had already been in Mira for days before Theo got back and was able to warn me. But riding to Mira would take at least two days we didn't have to spare. As it was, it was unlikely we would get there in time—she'd be gone, on her way to Folterra. Once she was on a ship, the journey to retrieve her would be drastically different. I felt the panic rising in my chest, heartbeat rocketing. I stared down at my hands as they began to shake. A large, calloused hand closed over them, that old familiar tingle of heat rocketing across my skin.

"Em, we will rift there." His tone was soft, as if he was talking to a child. I took a deep breath. Of course. Prince Rainier's divinity manifested as organic manipulation. Hanwen's blessing upon the crown prince had been bountiful. He could reform earth, harness rivers, and possibly more useful than the rest, create windows into other locations. *That* was how he had planned for us to travel in the morning. It was how we'd traveled after we took down the wards that night. I hadn't thought about it in years—repressed it so much I'd almost forgotten it even happened. I tried to control the shudder rippling through me at the memory. He noticed and abruptly pulled his hand from mine and stood, not looking at me.

"Get some rest. We will leave before dawn." He stood and walked toward the hall, likely to call Dewalt back in. I rose from my chair and followed after him, hoping to find Nana, needing to find out if I could sleep in my old room. I traced the line of Rainier's shoulders and neck with my eyes, the tension in them likely mirroring my own. He stopped walking, nearly forcing me to run into him, my arms up between us. He turned to me and grasped my hands in one of his. The intensity of his stare made me want to avert my eyes, but I kept them opened and fixed on his own.

"Over my dead body will another Beloved's death be on my conscience, Emmeline. Nor your own." He released my hands as I tugged them back, the intensity and contact too much to bear. I didn't want to think about the possibility of her death. Part of me wondered if he was truly worried about my conscience, finally understanding the guilt I'd felt all these years. He stood there, staring down at me as if expecting me to reply. His expression held the same tenderness it always had, and the sight of it closed a fist around my heart and squeezed. His hand reached up to my temple, his fingertips gently brushing against my hair before they slid down to my neck, and I froze. The touch was light as he traced the marks on my skin from the attack.

"Did you kill the men who did this to you?" His voice was low and quiet, not quite soft, but less harsh than before.

"Yes." I swallowed. I had no choice.

"You did them a kindness they did not deserve."

He pulled his hand away from my neck and spun, heading out the door. I waited until the faint heat from his touch had dissipated, until my breathing calmed, before I followed.

When I couldn't find Nana, I headed towards my old room, hoping it wasn't closed off. White flowers slip-printed atop a golden-yellow wallpaper adorned the halls—new—and I hated it. The bright yellow almost felt garish, especially paired with the white wainscotting below it. This estate didn't know that kind of happiness, not anymore. I had gone to my old rooms, the one I'd grown up in, not bothering to go toward the west wing of the estate to find the suite I had once shared with Faxon and a newborn Elora. I wanted the familiarity I once knew. I looked around, taking in the four walls that had been my sanctuary in my formative years. It hadn't changed at all. Even Lavenia being perched at the end of my bed was not too far out of place due to how often she visited us. She was sitting there, eating grapes and crackers off a platter likely intended for me. This was a common occurrence when we were younger, and surprisingly, it brought me comfort. I slid the tray farther into the center of the bed and sat down on the other side of it.

"I assume we are leaving in the morning?" Lavenia raised a questioning eyebrow.

"Yes, before dawn. You, me, Dewalt, and . . . the prince." I hesitated, not sure what to call him.

Lavenia snorted. "The prince? I don't see you calling me princess," she hedged. I rolled my eyes. I did not feel like unpacking this situation ever, let alone now. I didn't know what to call Rainier and using his royal title felt safest.

"Lavenia, I appreciate the levity, but my daughter has been taken by the Folterrans." My tone was dry, although a part of me did value Lavenia trying to distract me. I needed it so I wouldn't fall into hysterics.

"I'm sorry. It's just so weird seeing you, of all people, being so formal with him." She eyed me a certain way I chose to ignore. Her gaze softened. "What's she like?"

The question surprised me. I had no idea how badly I'd wanted to talk about her.

"She's like Lucia. Strong like her. Remember when Lucia's eyes would glow when she was mad? Elora's do too. She looks just like her because of the white hair. She loves to read; fantasy is her favorite. Sarcastic—"

"Wonder where she gets that from." Lavenia smirked, and I glared. It was strange, returning to this normalcy of friendship with her so quickly. Lavenia had been closer with Lucia, but she was still dear to me.

"Sarcastic and curious. She's everything I could ever ask for." I took a deep breath as Lavenia reached over and squeezed my hand.

Suddenly cold, I realized I was still soaking wet from the ride. I'd forgotten my pack with Bree and wasn't sure if any of my clothes here would still fit. I didn't want to go down to the stable, so I started digging through the wardrobe, a thought occurring to me as I searched.

"Lavenia?" My old friend glanced over, mouth full of grapes. "What were you laughing at downstairs? What did Dewalt say?" My eyes narrowed as I saw the look on Lavenia's face. As if she'd been caught red-handed. She hastily shoved another grape in her mouth. I sighed. "Gods, Lavenia. What is it?"

"Dewalt was just being Dewalt." I was surprised she was able to get the sentence out, considering she probably had about seven grapes in her mouth.

"That doesn't sound good," I chuckled.

"It never is with him." Lavenia continued to evade my question, chewing more thoroughly than I thought was necessary.

"Well?"

She sighed, swallowing the remainder of what was in her mouth. "He said he wasn't sure if you and Rainier were going to fight or fuck."

"What?" I whipped my head back to stare at her, eyes wide.

"Well, you both just stood there staring! It looked like you were either going to rip each other's throats out or clothes off. You can claim to hate him all you want, Emmeline. Doesn't make it true. We all saw it." She raised a challenging eyebrow in my direction.

I turned back to the wardrobe, heat on my face. I hadn't seen the prince in sixteen years. And our *history*, as he had put it, meant I couldn't be curious how time had changed him? I found an old nightgown, a light blue paisley print, and slipped behind the dressing divider to shimmy out of my wet clothes. I pulled the old thing over my head and grunted as I struggled to pull it over my hips. It would have to do for the night.

I went back to my bed and climbed in, leaving Lavenia on her side, staring at me. I could sense she wanted to talk about...well, everything. I was not ready for that.

"We all thought you were in Nythyr all these years. You weren't I take it? Was that you or Lord Kennon's doing?"

I knew Father would have made excuses for my whereabouts, but I'd never known what he told everyone. "His. I didn't have anything to do with what he told people."

"Were you here this entire time? In Vesta?"

"Yes, near Brambleton."

"Just you and Faxon? And Elora?"

"Yes. When she was born crying with glowing eyes, well, we all knew we had to hide. We left Ravemont soon after."

Lavenia nodded solemnly. She seemed to understand. I truly hadn't cared whether I stayed at the estate or left. Faxon had wanted to stay, of course, but I didn't care. I was still a ghost then. Haunting the halls of the estate, mourning the loss of a part of me. But I knew I had to leave for Elora.

"Do you love Faxon?"

I smiled sadly. How could I love a man I was forced into a marriage with days after I buried my sister? How could I love a man I ran from? That had allowed his father to get away with what he did to me? How could I love a man who resented our life and the way we were forced to live it because of our daughter? I loved the fact he didn't ask me about Lucia, whether it was for my benefit or for his. I loved how he read to Elora when she was small. I loved his love for her. But I didn't choose him. I hadn't chosen anyone, save for Elora. And he'd given me her. I realized then that none of my fears about the abduction had been reserved for Faxon, and I felt a tinge of guilt.

"In a way." Lavenia tilted her head, waiting for me to continue. "He gave me Elora when the night was darkest. I'll always love him for it."

Lavenia nodded, watching me thoughtfully. I laid back and found myself starting to think about how scared Elora must be, and then, more horrifyingly, about how loudmouthed my daughter could be sometimes. I was grateful Faxon was there with her. As long as Faxon was still alive, he'd do everything he could to protect her. Gods, I hoped he was still alive.

At some point, Lavenia curled up in the bed next to me, a scarf wrapped protectively around her braids, and she quickly fell asleep. It was comforting, and I was able to drift off.

Warm arms wrapped tightly around me.
A hand traced the curve of my jaw, lips gently chasing the same path.
Lips on mine. Fumbling hands.
A gasp. A groan. "We can't do this."
Pain jolting through my arm, over and over.
"They're here."
Fear.
Sweat and tears and blood filling my nostrils.
A scream.
"Lucia! No!"
Hands on my back. Shouting. Falling.
Darkness and water. So much water.

"Emma. Emmeline, wake up. It's alright." Lavenia placed a soothing hand on my clammy forehead. It was pitch black in the room, too early to be awake yet. I rolled over to face Lavenia, even though I couldn't see her, wiping a mix of tears and snot from my face the best I could. My throat felt raw; I must have been screaming.

"I'm sorry," I whispered.

"Don't be. I was there too. I know." She reached out and grabbed my hand and pulled it to her chest. I was touched by the fact she remembered my ability, knowing it might soothe me. I focused on her heartbeat. Hearing her breathing and heart slowing, I was pulled into a trance, slowly falling back asleep. One thought wouldn't leave my mind as I finally drifted off. I *wasn't* there. Not when I could've done anything for Lucia. Rainier had rifted me away.

CHAPTER 6

I WOKE UP AT the sound of Nana's quiet knock and stretched. It was funny, recognizing exactly who knocked and the purpose of it all these years later. I heard her footsteps head down the hall, choosing not to linger after waking me. The bed here was so much nicer than my bed at home. The sheets were softer, and I couldn't feel any feathers poking through the mattress. Looking around my old room, the faintest light coming in through sheer curtains, it was as if I'd been transported back in time. The walls were still a light blue, and I wondered if Lucia's room was also unchanged. She'd picked a deep red for her walls, joking about the blood of her enemies when Mother asked why. She'd been so different from me in so many ways. Lucia was confident in her abilities and found her destiny an honor, even if it was a burden. I would have hated the responsibility. Even the expectations of me as the Beloved's sister sometimes proved to be too much.

Lavenia was still in bed with me, snoring softly. I decided not to wake her until I was finished getting ready, giving her more time to sleep. Since I never fetched my pack, I sighed, knowing I'd have to put my still damp clothes back on. Based on the way my nightgown sat on my hips, I wouldn't find breeches here that would fit me. If I even had any breeches here to begin with, a garment I rarely wore until I lived on my own, away from the expectations of being a lord's daughter. When I undressed and my hand brushed against my face, it felt oily and a bit gritty. I had pushed Bree yesterday and never cleaned up from the road. Searching desperately for a brush to pull through my mass of hair, I guessed there was likely one in the bathroom I'd shared with Lucia. I pulled my dirty shirt over my head, not bothering with the bodice yet. There was a small amount of blood on the collar I cringed over, but I had to wear something. Turning the knob as quietly as possible so as not to disturb Lavenia, I went into the bathroom.

Catching sight of myself in the mirror, it was then I realized how insane I must have looked rushing in after the ride from Brambleton. With wet hair a mess, blood on my face, and eyes ablaze, I must have looked mad. I pulled open a drawer, found a brush, and began to tame the wild mane of hair. Peering into the same mirror I'd used growing up, too short to see it for the longest time, I simultaneously felt at home and lost—a ghost misplaced in time.

Knowing rifting wasn't always the smoothest form of travel, I chose to braid my hair, starting above one eyebrow and crossing to the opposite ear, pulling the strands away from my face as I went. I smiled as I remembered the first time Rainier had rifted with me. We had wanted to go further east along the stream toward Tuaman Cliffs, where it grew wider. We stepped through, and, not understanding the angle we were positioned, the prince stumbled backward down a slope, landing hard in the water. My sides had hurt from laughing so hard. His accuracy was dependent on how distracted he was. One time, after a particularly dreary meeting with the king and a Myriad Master, he'd rifted us ten feet above the meadow and barely managed to bring the earth up to us to soften our landing. To his credit, neither of us were watching where we walked, too busy kissing one another to pay attention. And of course, the last time we rifted came to mind, but I pushed it out of my head.

I finished the braid and turned on the water, splashing my face as quickly as possible. One of the things I hadn't realized I'd missed was having hot, running water. The servants kept the water boiler filled and stoked during the day, and I was grateful they'd already attended to it. It was something only the gentry and royalty generally had, so I'd had to get used to using an ewer and filling up washbasins. I found a washcloth and bar of soap smelling of lilacs and violets, and it brought back a rush of memories that blended in my mind. The smell of a thousand different mornings spent with my sister and our friends. I inhaled the scent desperately. Nana hadn't sent any for me in a long time. I never buttoned the top half of my shirt, so I took the washcloth to my skin, attempting to rid myself of the grime from the day before. With the water running and my eyes closed, appreciating the hot water, I didn't even hear the door open.

"Shit!"

Startled, I looked up, eyes wide. Rainier stood in the doorway, staring at me through the mirror with his mouth open.

"Get out!"

I pulled my shirt together as fast as I could. He couldn't possibly have seen much, but it still felt like an invasion. It was more of my skin than anyone had seen in a long time. Where skin was considered, I couldn't help but notice Rainier was shirtless—pale scars I didn't recognize splashed across his tawny skin. Driven by the sight of my scrambling, it must have dawned on him that he couldn't continue to stand there frozen in shock and horror. As he whirled to the door, I noticed one long scar across his muscular back, the puckered slash starting on his shoulder and moving diagonally across toward his opposite hip. He slammed the door to Lucia's room behind him. I hadn't known anyone had been given Lucia's quarters, let alone him. I kicked myself for not thinking I'd be sharing the bathroom. I finished washing up and pulled out a new washcloth and set it on the counter for him before tentatively knocking on the adjoining door.

"I'm finished in here. I—sorry." I couldn't get out of the bathroom fast enough, slamming the door shut behind me accidentally. I came face to face with Lavenia, still rubbing sleep from her eyes.

"What's going on? Why are you slamming doors?" She gave a sleepy smile as she brushed past me, headed toward the door I'd just hurriedly slammed shut.

"Wait! Rainier is in there!" I rushed out, not wanting the incidental bathroom run-ins to continue. Lavenia stared at me in confusion, and something akin to amusement fluttered across her face.

"You...were in the bathroom together?" She raised one eyebrow slowly as she studied me. Understanding what she was insinuating, I scrambled to defend myself.

"No! I mean, yes. I was there first, and I didn't lock the door. I didn't realize. Anyway, I just finished, so he's probably in there now. Give him a minute."

Lavenia, thankfully, didn't say anything else and avoided looking me in the eye after. She padded over to a bag against the wall and started digging through clothing. I hadn't noticed it there the night before, and it hit me. This was the room she had been staying in, and I barged in on her last night; she hadn't even mentioned it or asked me to leave.

"Why didn't you tell me this was your room? I'd have found somewhere else to sleep." No wonder Rainier was in the other room, sharing the suite with his sister. She shrugged.

"I knew you wouldn't want to be alone. I planned to come to you wherever you ended up." My heart ached, and I felt a small tinge of pain in my nose. She had always been so kind.

"Thank you." I meant it.

I heaved a sigh, found my boots, and slipped them on. I was going to have to get over this. I'd been friends with Rainier for years before everything went to hell. I needed to figure out how to interact with him as an adult. We were so far removed from our past it was practically a different life, and he was my best shot at finding Elora. It didn't matter what had been said or left unsaid between us. It didn't matter that he was helping me out of obligation or guilt because of Lucia's death. All that mattered was finding Elora.

***

An hour later, Lavenia and I were waiting in the entryway as Rainier discussed our plans with the royal guard. While we were searching in Mira, they'd cut west across the Whispering Wood, headed toward the capital. I wondered why none of the guard were coming with us. Did Rainier expect us to be able to free her ourselves, or did he think Elora wasn't even in Mira anymore? I shuddered at the thought, no matter how likely it was. If Elora was already in Folterra, her rescue would become much more complicated. Taking a Vestian-born Beloved into their territory was an act of aggression, and King Soren would have input in how to handle it. My mouth went dry. I wasn't sure what King Soren would want, but the idea of war had never phased the old man. I didn't want to think about what that could mean for the people of Vesta, but what I did know was my daughter would become a bargaining chip. I would not let that happen. I would figure out a way to get her back myself, even if it meant going to the Folterran capital myself. Though the appeal of sneaking into Darkhold was nonexistent, I would do whatever was needed to get my daughter back.

Dewalt sauntered over to us. He'd been Rainier's best friend as long as I'd known them and had been arrogant the entire time. I'd hoped age would have matured him, but from what Lavenia told me last night, I knew that wasn't the case in the slightest. His hair was loose and hung down in a shiny, soft wave, nearly as long as mine. The last time I'd seen him, it barely hit his shoulders. It suited him.

"Heard about your little bathroom run-in this morning." He smirked. His grin was wiped off his face a fraction of a second later, after Lavenia landed an elbow straight into his gut. I chose not to dignify his insinuation with a response, but I felt my face turning red. I was a married woman, let alone the fact that my daughter was missing. As if I could possibly entertain such inane ideas. The sheer fact that Dewalt or Lavenia could have thought any of this struck a nerve. Had I not made my feelings and intentions clear enough all those years ago? Whatever we'd had, which wasn't much it turned out, had been obliterated when Lucia died.

"Are we ready?" The prince, thankfully, had missed Dewalt's comment. I nodded. I'd already grabbed my bag from the stable where I ensured Bree would be cared for and forced breakfast down my throat at Nana's insistence. The prince looked to Dewalt and Lavenia, both equally serious now. Lavenia's mouth was closed tightly in a straight line. She was all business. She seemed to have taken on a certain sadness ever since I spoke of Elora the night before. I wondered if my depiction of Elora, so like her old friend, had affected her more than she let on.

Rainier nodded. He rubbed his hands together as if to warm them up and then pushed them straight out in front of him. There, in the entryway of my father's house, was an opening into a forest, dappled with light. Dewalt stepped through first, then Lavenia. I took a deep breath, pushing the nerves down into the pit of my stomach, and walked into the rift, Rainier following closely behind. Once he stepped through, the rift closed.

I scanned our surroundings, confused. We were standing on a path in the middle of the woods. The trees above us had bent over it, creating a tunnel of orange and red leaves. I'd never seen anything like it. I knew when the light grew stronger in the afternoon, it would look like fire. It was loud in the way only a forest can be; birdsong and a distant stream burbled nearby, while two squirrels chased each other through the foliage. It wasn't the type of loud that indicated we were anywhere near a port city. Wherever we were wasn't Mira.

"You missed."

"No, I didn't." Rainier's voice was flat, maybe a bit annoyed. There was a bench on the path behind him, and he walked over to it and sat, pulling a small canteen of water out of his pack. I blinked at him for a second. We were clearly not in Mira, but allegedly he hadn't missed. When he continued to sit and not explain, I glanced at Lavenia, and she chuckled.

"Mira is too far for him to rift us there in one go; he has to rest." He hadn't ever tried to rift us far in the past, but I didn't ever realize he had a limit. Since conduits didn't have endless access to divinity, it all made sense. There was a give and take. Like my headaches.

He glared at his sister, who just laughed again.

"I don't have to; I prefer to. I'm more accurate when I have time to rest in between." His glance darted over to me when he mentioned accuracy. I tried to keep my face empty of thought or reaction, and instead, I focused on the small statues next to the bench. There were four, waist-high, and they depicted each of the gods. Along with coins, they held water and a bit of debris in their cupped hands. A divine statuary. A place for prayer.

"Where are we? Near Ardian?" I tried to think of locations between Ravemont and Mira.

"Just outside it," he confirmed, taking another swig of water. I nodded. Rainier had to focus on different locations and picture them to open up the rift to step through. He once described it as folding something in half, forming a wrinkle in reality. He'd been here before, and likely recently since he remembered it well enough to rift to it.

It was beautiful here, so it wasn't surprising. Looking to the east, the path quickly turned, but to the west, the tunnel of leaves stretched as far as I could see. The bench and statues seemed out of place in the middle of the path, but maybe it was intentional. Secluded and beautiful, it would be a nice place for reflection.

I knelt in front of the statues. Hanwen and Ciarden, the gods of wrath and dark, were on the right, their heads tilted downwards and their faces grim. They were indistinguishable from each other in the form of these stone statues, but in the colorful Myriad texts, they couldn't be more different. Hanwen was always depicted with bronzed muscles and golden hair, while Ciarden had skin of ivory and hair of the blackest night. To the left were Rhia and Aonara, the goddesses of fertility and light. Their heads were tilted upwards, and their faces were radiant. These two, like their counterparts, could not be more different: Aonara with pale skin and white hair, and Rhia with dark, umber skin and long, black curls. Yet, they appeared the same when etched out in limestone.

I'd never been religious or prayed to any of them, even though Lucia had been Aonara's favored. I believed she prayed to Aonara, but we never discussed it. A niggling feeling in the back of my head told me maybe Lucia would be alive, or Elora wouldn't have been taken if I'd just humbled myself to pray. I felt my breath hitch in my throat. I reached into my pocket, hoping to find a coin or something of value to place in the outstretched goddess's palms, but I had nothing. I sank back on my heels with a sigh. I supposed if they were truly real, they'd understand if I didn't have anything to offer other than the intense helplessness and sadness I felt.

"Here." A warm hand was on my shoulder. I hadn't even heard him get up, but Rainier held out a coin and pressed it into my palm. I willed myself not to burst into tears when I made eye contact, seeing the look of sorrow and compassion flooding his features. He nodded and made his way back to the bench, giving me privacy.

I placed the coin into Aonara's outstretched palms and bowed my head.
Please.

No other thoughts came into my head as much as I tried. I tried to think of a compelling argument to convince a god to intercede on my behalf. But all I could do was beg. On my knees, I pleaded, and I felt tears start to roll down my face. I didn't care.

I wondered, not for the first time, if Lucia could hear me. If she truly was Aonara's favored, it stood to reason praying to Aonara might reach her. I hadn't visited her grave since the burial, hadn't tried to talk to her all these years. I couldn't. She died because of me. She could have done so much more with her life than I ever did with mine. But Elora was my chance to make it up to her. My chance to show Lucia I'd still done something good.

I opened my eyes and realized the sun had risen, the light breaking through branches to illuminate the statues in front of me. We needed to go. I would not weep for my daughter; I would find her. Wiping my face and sniffling, I stood up and turned toward the others. Dewalt and Lavenia had walked down the path a bit, but when they saw I was standing, they headed back toward us. Rainier was still on the bench, watching me as if I might break in half. I felt hot anger rise in me. I didn't want his pity or compassion; they'd only slow me down and cause another breakdown I didn't have the time for.

"Did you get enough beauty rest? Can we go now?"

Dewalt barked out a laugh, and I was surprised to see Rainier smile as he stood.

"You tell me." He smirked, and I felt my temper flare.

After we stepped through the rift, finally in Mira, I couldn't help myself.

"You've gotten much better at this." Looking over my shoulder at him, I saw his mouth form into a straight line. I'd struck a nerve.

"I've had some time to practice." He stared at me pointedly. Not sure if he was commenting about the time that had passed or about the last time he'd rifted me, I chose not to ask for clarification or speak further. He grimaced and rubbed at his temple, and I wondered if he'd pushed himself too far with his divinity. Pondering for a moment, I realized our second rift would have been a much farther distance.

Dewalt cleared his throat, and all three of us turned to him. We were in an alley in the middle of the city, or so I thought. I didn't hear the ships or the market dock, which would have been serving up breakfast for the hungry fishermen. Nor was it quiet enough to be near the temple in the northern part of the city. The alley where we stood was distinctly cleaner than I'd have expected, though Dewalt carefully led us farther away from the main road past a questionable pile of debris with an unpleasant smell. He took on an air of seriousness I didn't remember him being capable of.

"Let's separate and meet back here in one hour. Ask questions, but don't give any details. Ask about a girl with white hair, a group of men. Don't get more specific. See what we find."

"It's darker right now. Normally it is white. I—I made her change it that morning with brun root. It's more blonde than white right now." The memory of the sun glinting off Elora's hair made my breath catch and my chest tighten. Dewalt nodded grimly.

"Blonde hair. If you get a lead, return here, and we will go together. Do not go any further by yourself. I don't want any of this getting out of hand." Lavenia shot him a glare before she took over.

"I'd say it's already pretty out of hand, but alright. I'll go through the shops on the northern side of the market toward the temple. Rainier, do you want to check the docks? Dewalt, you take the marketplace. That leaves the weapons vendors for you, Emmeline." I was surprised Lavenia and Dewalt took charge while Rainier maintained his silence. It was unlike him to not take the lead. Though he did have an air of leadership when he eyed each of us in turn, his gaze settling on me. His eyes, today a deep green not unlike the forests north of Ardian in spring, met mine as he spoke.

"No risks." I held his gaze defiantly, tilting my chin up. "Emmeline." His eyes narrowed on mine, and he tilted his head down. His voice betrayed him. He knew me better. I'd risk everything and more to get my daughter back. I didn't know why he bothered to say it.

"Come on," I said, leading our way out of the alley.

"Emmeline, I'm serious. You came to me for a reason. Maybe I flattered myself by assuming you needed me more than just my ability to rift. Maybe you know just how dangerous this will be. Don't be reckless." He stood in the alley, arms crossed, staring down at me. I swallowed and nodded, and they finally filed out behind me.

I'd been to Mira a few times before. The last time we went as a family, Elora was around ten years old. Every time Faxon traveled to Mira for supplies he couldn't get in Brambleton, he made sure to pick up a book for her, but the memory of her grin when we stepped into the building full of books warmed my heart. Part of me wanted to go explore the book shop, knowing if Elora had been able, she would have made a line straight to it. She'd been enchanted by the floor-to-ceiling shelves and the comfortable furniture spread throughout the corners of the shop. Since Lavenia was the one headed in that direction, I was grateful for the conversation I'd had with her about Elora, about how my daughter liked to read. I headed toward the main road with the others, Dewalt and Lavenia turning right, leaving Rainier and I to turn left. If I remembered correctly, it would be about a ten-minute walk before Rainier would branch off. I hoped he'd maintain the silence. I didn't know how to talk to him, and I wasn't sure I wanted to remember.

He wore black breeches and boots and a light tan cotton shirt covered by a deep green cloak. The sun hadn't had a chance to warm up the dark bricks underneath our feet, so it felt cool and crisp even on the main road directly in the dawn's path. There was no sign of his crown, of course, something he only wore for formal occasions. I'd only seen him wear it twice. The first time was his arrival at Crown Cottage, when King Soren and Queen Shivani announced his betrothal to Lucia. He'd been sixteen years old, the crown threatening to slide off his head at any moment. It seemed like a lifetime ago. The second time was the last time I saw him.

He walked so he was positioned between me and the street—ever the gentleman, even though the roads weren't busy yet, only one lone horse and its rider in sight. The whitewashed buildings we walked past were private residences, easily distinguished by the state of disrepair of the roofs. They were row houses, all connected down the length of the street. One window was thrown open, and I could hear humming, a soft lullaby sound, perhaps a mother comforting a baby.

A young woman came out to dump a pail of water. She froze when she saw Rainier, and it wasn't because he was recognizable as the prince. I watched her lick her bottom lip slowly, her hand coming up to rest on her chest, which was blooming a light pink color across her pale skin. I felt my eyes narrow on her, and she glanced at me for just a moment before running back inside. I was no obstacle, yet I struggled to push my satisfaction away at the fact she thought I might be. I started to wonder again why he hadn't found someone else to perform the bonding ritual with. Surely King Soren would be worried his son hadn't bonded to another conduit. I knew there would have been interest. We passed an older lady walking in the opposite direction, pushing a cart full of apples. She gave a curt nod but gave no indication she recognized the Crown Prince of Vesta was walking toward her. Sensing my confusion after two different people failed to recognize him, Rainier took a breath and spoke quietly.

"I haven't made my presence known in Mira in over ten years. They forget me."

"At least you don't have people falling over themselves to speak to you."

His brows furrowed, but he said nothing.

"I'm sorry about—"

"My apologies for this morning," he spat the words out, like he needed to say it and be done with it.

"It's nothing. I should have locked the door."

"Yes, you should have." I threw a glare in his direction, but if he saw it, he didn't react to it, his face impassive.

We continued walking in silence and came to a split in the road. Rainier would need to go right toward the docks, and I would go left to the metalworkers. He contemplated me for a moment as if he was debating what to say. He settled on a gruff "good luck" and veered to the right, suddenly picking up his pace.

I went into the first shop on the corner. Noticing a display of bows in the window, I suddenly remembered I'd only brought my small dagger with me to Mira. My bow was likely in the stables of Ravemont with Bree. The shopkeeper was an elderly man, round in the spine, with more hairs coming out of his nose than there were left on his head. He didn't have any information which might concern Elora, but he was kind and pressed a mint into my hand as I left.

I visited shop after shop for the better part of the hour before I started walking back toward the alley, feeling defeated. My thoughts ran wild. I knew high tide was within the next few hours. It was probable Elora and her abductors were already gone, but there was a chance they'd be headed out today. If the others hadn't found anything, would we start searching the ships scheduled to leave? The panic started to bubble. What if Elora was already halfway to Folterra? Hopefully, she had her pack and cloak; she'd need the warm clothes for the trip. She'd never been on a ship before; would she get seasick? Would anyone comfort her? My heart started racing, and I took a deep breath. I couldn't spiral here. We had no leads yet, and I needed to control myself. I was passing the old man's shop, the mint aftertaste in my mouth still present, when I spotted something that made my stomach drop. One of our horses.

"Allegro!" I sprinted toward the dapple-grey horse, shouting his name, trying to get the attention of the woman riding him. Allegro was Faxon's horse.

"Ma'am, excuse me!" I shouted up at the woman. She was around the same age as me, holding a bundle in her arms. A sharp cry told me it was a baby. The woman took me in, made a gesture, and pulled the rein, pointing Allegro away.

"This is my husband's horse, and he's missing. Where did you get it?"

The woman would not respond, and rage started burning through me. I grabbed her by the ankle. I'd pull the lady off the horse, baby and all, if I had to.

"Emmeline, stop." A commanding voice rumbled much closer to me than anticipated. Rainier placed a surprisingly warm hand on my shoulder, pulling me back. I shrugged it off.

"She can't understand you."

I whirled to face him. "What do you mean?"

Rainier looked up at the woman, and he began to speak another language. She smiled before nodding and rearranging the baby against her chest, and from what I could tell, exchanged pleasantries with him. I looked back and forth between the two of them, dumbstruck. He put his hand on the small of my back, and I did my best to ignore the heat that flew through me at his touch. When he turned to me, his eyes were twinkling with amusement, a soft smile on his face that broke my heart. A smile so familiar and yet foreign. A stranger in the body of someone I'd once known almost better than myself. His hand slid to my waist before he tugged me closer to him, and every nerve in my body was focused on where we touched. I didn't know what he was saying to the woman, but she watched me, her eyes softer. She glanced between the two of us, a strange expression on her face as she started speaking again. Rainier said something, and she started speaking slower, drawing out the words. This went on for a few moments longer, Rainier sometimes squinting with concentration, as if he was trying to formulate the correct sentences. Eventually, he lightly tapped Allegro on the rump, and the woman and her baby rode off.

I stared at him, open-mouthed. He gently removed his hand from my waist and stepped away from me, putting an appropriate distance between us. I was surprisingly disappointed he moved, but I chose not to think too much on it.

"I saw you accost her." The right side of his lip twitched. "She tried to tell you. Did you not see the armband she wore? She's from Skos." It made sense—the kingdom across the Eastern Sea didn't use the common tongue.

"How did you—"

"I'm not too good at it, but a few of my soldiers are from Skos, so I learned a bit." He shrugged. "She told me she bought the horse from a man at the inn on the north side of town. Come."

I didn't argue as he turned and led the way. In fact, I intended to spend the rest of the walk in silence, feeling stupid. I felt like a fool for not knowing the woman couldn't understand me. She'd worn an armband, and I was blind to it, my judgment clouded by fear. It was embarrassing. It also surprised me that the prince bothered to learn the language of a handful of his soldiers. We walked in silence for a little while before I couldn't stand it any longer.

"What else did you say to her?" I was thinking about the looks on both of their faces when his hand slid around my waist. "Did you tell her I was sorry? I—I didn't know. I feel terrible. I was about to—" I stopped myself. Despite my outburst, I didn't want to tell Rainier I was about to pull the poor woman off the horse.

"You were about to what? Drag her and the babe to the ground? I saw that hand on her ankle." He turned his head toward me; this time, the right side of his mouth definitely tugged up. The way the sun hit his face made his green eyes shimmer, and I felt a flop in my stomach despite myself. "Why do you think I stopped you? And yes, I apologized on your behalf. I also told her you'd be feeling guilty about it for the rest of the day. At least that's what I hope I said." He stared off into the distance as if he wasn't sure.

"Thank you," I quietly spoke. I rubbed my forehead, attempting to smooth the space between my eyebrows. I needed to pull myself together; there was no time for hysterics. I was glad Rainier was there to stop me. His presence was equally comforting and disarming, something I would think about later.

"Here." His voice was gruff as I turned to watch him pull something out of the front pocket of his shirt. He pressed it into my hand, and when I realized what it was, I stopped walking to examine it. The conch shell sat perfectly in my palm. The outside was faded to a whitish blue, but the inside was a bright, striated sapphire. Turning it over in my hands, I rubbed my fingers over the bumpy ridges on top where the shell swirled in upon itself. I looked up at him to see he stopped a few paces in front of me, turning back to peer over his shoulder. His face was illuminated as if the sun shone only for him. The light played off the sharp angle of his jaw, and I struggled to breathe.

"Why?"

"A vendor was selling them," he supplied, averting his eyes. "Do you not collect them anymore?"

I was shocked he even remembered.

"I haven't been to the beach in a very long time."

He tilted his head, a response waiting on his tongue before he turned away and cleared his throat. "Come on, Dewalt is going to be annoyed with us if we're late."

I slipped the shell in my pocket, holding it while my thumb memorized the dips and whorls across it. I took a few quick steps to catch up to him, and we continued back to the alley in silence, a bit more comfortable than before.

Lavenia and Dewalt hadn't been able to find any leads on Elora. Rainier shared that he knew of one ship scheduled to leave in the hour, but he'd already searched it. The captain graciously allowed him on board when he learned he was speaking to the Crown Prince of Vesta. After sharing the information from the woman who bought Allegro, Rainier turned to Lavenia.

"You went inside the inn, correct?"

"Yes, but there wasn't anyone downstairs other than the keeper. He wasn't exactly forthcoming."

"And you didn't force him to be more forthcoming?" Dewalt had a grin on his face as he interjected.

"I was told not to let anything get out of hand." She glared at him.

"D, I want you waiting at the docks. If you see anything, send an impulse." I hoped Rainier meant to be the only recipient of the impulse and not all three of us. Dewalt had the ability to send jolts of energy to people he had some sort of association with. The impulse felt shockingly like slamming your elbow on a table. Hard. It didn't leave any permanent damage, but it did give you full-body tingles for a short while. That was what brought us back to the cottage the night Lucia died. He'd sent two to each of us, and we knew it was something bad. Rainier opened a rift immediately, and we had walked back into chaos.

"Lavenia, I want you to ask around about a man selling horses. The woman we spoke to said it was someone at the inn last night, and we don't have much more to go on. Emmeline, I want you to stay with me. I want to talk to the innkeeper and see if he will let us do a sweep of rooms. Everyone understand?" We all nodded.

Dewalt left to go toward the docks while the three of us turned to the northern part of the city. The route Rainier and I had gone earlier was a steep decline. This route was the opposite and a longer walk. My thighs began to burn. I didn't need to imagine Rainier was in much better shape than me, and I imagined Lavenia was as well if she accompanied him on his missions. After about twenty minutes of walking at this angle, I felt a bead of sweat at my temple. I wiped it away, hoping no one would notice. I was still keeping pace with Rainier and Lavenia, though they were ahead, but I swore Rainier slowed a bit. My eyes narrowed, watching his footsteps. Every one of his strides was at least two of mine. Had he always been so tall? He'd put his cloak in his pack since it had warmed up, revealing the muscled swells of his back through his shirt. I tried not to ogle. He was so different and so similar, all at the same time.

The sight of Mira's Myriad temple distracted me. A tall, whitewashed brick building with intricate stained-glass windows stood in the midst of the square, out of place against the filthy buildings nearby. Outside, one of the Myriad novices was dressed in a white cloak. Though their hood was up, they also wore the white covering over their face, a symbol of humility so early on in their training. They weren't there to be seen or to be heard, just to serve. The Myriad were incredibly unsettling. The vast majority had taken a vow of silence and communicated through official proclamation, though some of the Masters and the Supreme chose to speak. I hadn't interacted with any of the Myriad since Lucia's burial. I shuddered, picking up the pace to get past the novice, and averted my eyes.

As we finally approached the inn, Lavinia spotted a few people gathered around benches outside. There was a tavern just next door to the inn, and people seemed to be coming and going rather frequently. She nodded to us as she turned off to engage with the people who lounged about. Rainier took a step up onto the front porch of the inn and pulled the door open, hanging back so I could walk through. I stepped inside and immediately tensed. The room was small and dark. I wondered if all the rooms were as tiny and dank as the front room. The innkeeper came out from behind a curtain leading into what I assumed was a back office.

"Hello, I'm here to ask you a few questions about some of your recent patrons." I wasn't sure how I'd managed to be so polite. Based on the look Rainier was giving me, it surprised him too. I bristled and ignored him. The man turned his head a bit to the side, directing his ear toward me, and pushed his glasses farther up his nose.

"And what kind of questions would those be, lady?" The man's voice was gravelly, as if he'd spent his entire lifetime smoking a pipe. I didn't like the tone either when he referred to me as "lady." It sounded sarcastic.

"We are looking for a girl. Blonde hair, about this height . . . " I gestured for the innkeeper. "She may have been with a man. He would've been a bit taller than me, black hair and a mustache?" I cringed a bit as I described Faxon in front of Rainier. I didn't know why I cared what he thought, but I did.

"No, never had anyone check in here like that." I began to reply, but then I heard it. His heartbeat was hammering in his chest. Other than patients with Mairin, or my family at home, I tried not to use this ability. It felt invasive, intrusive. With my family, it was second nature. But now, as we were questioning this old man, I realized I'd been listening for it, to see if he was lying. I turned to Rainier, who had been watching me, waiting. He hadn't forgotten my abilities at all. I shook my head once. Rainier's eyes narrowed in recognition as he turned to the man.

"I'd like to check and make sure if that's alright with you?" Rainier put his elbow down on the counter in front of him and leaned down so he was eye to eye with the man. "You wouldn't refuse the Crown Prince, would you?"

The old man backed up a step and raised his hands in surprise. He took a moment to study Rainier's face before he gathered himself together.

"Your Highness, yes, of course. Follow me." He raised part of the counter, and we followed him through the curtain.

CHAPTER 7

THE MAN AT THE desk escorted us back into an office and storage area. It was extremely cluttered and small. Thin streaks of light slipped between the boards of the back wall, illuminating dust particles in the air. Using his cane to push things out of the way, the man stumbled to a desk toward the back and opened a case full of keys which hung on the wall behind it. He pulled out a few and shoved them into my hand.

"These are all the rooms that have been checked out within the last few days. Feel free to check them, but please make sure you knock. None of them have come to return their key yet, so they may be inside. I pay my debts with discretion, so please do not pester my guests more than you need to." He looked down and leaned against the desk.

Rainier stepped forward and examined the keys. It appeared that only three rooms had been checked out.

"When were these rooms reserved?" He didn't waste a glance on the old man as he asked.

"Two were reserved two days ago and one today...Your Highness." The man's heart still beat rapidly. I wasn't sure if it was because he was lying or perhaps he was just nervous that the Crown Prince of Vesta was in his dingy back office, questioning his business. Either way, I believed we were on the right track. Something seemed off. It was likely he knew nothing, but a man who was prized for his discretion must have reasons for not wanting to know what his customers did. Rainier clearly felt the same as he strode out of the room, through the counter, and approached the narrow stairs directly next to it, while I followed close behind. The inn consisted of three levels, with only the top two floors containing sleeping quarters. We had rooms to search on each one.

We knocked on the first door and heard voices on the other side of it.

"Just a minute!" The pleasant, singsong voice was a striking contrast to the dank surroundings. I glanced at Rainier, but he was staring straight ahead at the door.

The stubble on his face was so much fuller now, unlike the sparse fuzz he used to sport. A young woman answered the door, a blanket wrapped tightly around her. Her lips were red and slightly swollen, her hair mussed. Rainier raised an eyebrow and glanced over at me.

"Uh, excuse me. We are looking for a young girl, fifteen, blonde hair. Have you seen her?"

"No. We ain't seen nobody since we got here this morning. I ain't paid to leave the room. I'm paid to stay in it." The crooked smile she gave and the wink which followed was more information than I needed. I felt my face turn red as I turned away from the door, moving onto the next room.

"Thank you for your help." Rainier spoke, and the door shut a second later. I glanced over my shoulder at Rainier, wondering what he thought of the woman. But his mouth was set in a straight line; he seemed unaffected by the interaction. We continued down to the next room and knocked. After a moment of waiting for an answer, I reached out, listening for heartbeats within.

"Nothing," I mumbled to Rainier, fitting the key into the door. I pushed it open and saw the room seemed untouched. I took a step in, Rainier filling up the doorway behind me. My first instinct had me checking behind the door. I knew there was no one there, but still. Looking around the room, I felt uneasy. Walking over to the nightstand, I pulled open an empty drawer.

"You've never seen a libertine before, have you?" Rainier mirrored my actions on the other side of the bed.

"A libertine?" I'd never even heard the term, so how would I know if I'd seen one?

"The woman back there. They accept payment for . . ." He trailed off as he pushed the nightstand shut, observing me with an arched brow and a carefully curated straight face.

"Oh, no. I haven't. I mean, I knew there were women who—"

"And men."

"*People* who did that. I've just never met one before. She seemed happy?"

"Mira is small enough; she might have established clients who treat her well. I think it depends on a variety of factors."

"Like what?" I truly wanted to know. I'd always thought to do work like that would be degrading, something one would only do if they had no choice. I didn't want to know why Rainier seemed to know about libertines, but I was curious.

"Well, some libertines choose the lifestyle. They're not all forced into it. If she has kind customers who pay her well, it makes sense she'd be happy." He shrugged while I made a thoughtful sound.

"You learn something new every day." I gave him a faint smile as I dropped down to look behind the nightstand.

He nodded, not a trace of a smile due to my naivety, and continued searching the room, pulling the curtains back to check behind and under them.

"I take it you've been staying out of the cities?" He seemed to genuinely be asking, but I couldn't help feeling guilty. Like I'd been keeping secrets from him. Which, I guess I had been.

"We've come here a few times, but mostly we don't go anywhere bigger than Brambleton."

"Is that where you've been? Brambleton?"

"Just outside it." I was surprised Lavenia hadn't told him any of this, but I supposed she hadn't had a chance.

"We were told you were in Nythyr. Lord Kennon mentioned it in a letter once." I took a chance and glanced at him then, and his face was a slate, not a single muscle out of place.

"I suppose he must have made up something. I've never even been to Nythyr." He chuckled, but I saw something flash in his eyes which didn't match the lighthearted smile he gave.

"Here I was, imagining you cavorting across Nythyr this whole time, drinking all the wine and dancing at all the festivals."

I gave a small smile. "I still drank the wine, just had to settle for the import."

"A shame." I heard a smile in his voice.

Rainier stood back up; he'd been on his knees searching under the bed. "Whoever stayed in this room didn't leave anything. It doesn't even seem like they slept on the bed." His lips had gone into a flat line, the muscle in his jaw taut.

Stepping over to the closet, I pulled it open. There was a broken chair inside, leaned up against the wall, and a high shelf which appeared empty. Rainier walked over behind me.

"Hang on, there's something up here." He reached over me onto the top shelf of the closet, slightly pushing into me with his chest, and I stumbled further into the closet. I reached my hands forward into the small space and caught myself. A sharp pain and twisting in my stomach shot upwards. I needed to get out. Before I could stop myself, I elbowed my way out, digging straight into his stomach. He let out a burst of breath and a grunt as I shoved past him, taking deep, panicked breaths. I'd felt trapped, and my instincts got the upper hand, forcing me out of the small space. I took a few steps into the room, trying to regain control of my breath. Deep breath in, hold, exhale. I hadn't intended to elbow the Crown Prince of Vesta directly in the stomach. I stared at him as he straightened back up.

He turned to glare at me, lightly pressing one hand on his stomach where my elbow had struck. He didn't say a word as he handed over what he'd pulled down from the top shelf. It was a text from the Myriad, one of the small books they handed out to people during the religious celebrations. I flipped through it, noticing the usual depictions of the gods and goddesses. I stopped at Aonara, the goddess of light. When Lucia was declared Aonara's favored, we should have known then what would happen to her. Playthings of the gods were expendable. I finished flipping through the book and set it down. I turned to Rainier, ready to apologize, but he walked past me, as if he couldn't wait to be away from me.

"Let's check the next room," he grunted, pushing the door open and going back into the hallway.

We walked toward the landing, the prince leading the way up the stairs. He had to duck once we reached the third floor, the ceiling lower and halls narrower. He stopped a few steps into the hallway and paused, turning slightly to let me pass. I had the key to get into the room. It took all my concentration to slip past without touching him. I felt bad for the elbow to the stomach and was afraid to get close. I paused at the door, reaching out with my senses to hear a heartbeat. I didn't hear any from the room we were going to, but I did hear a faint and frenzied one from the room at the top of the stairs.

"Wait," I told Rainier as my gaze turned to the occupied room. It hadn't been checked out in the last few days, so this must have been a long-term occupant. The closer I got, the louder I could hear the heartbeat. There seemed to be only one, and it was quieter than I was used to. Rainier followed close behind, but made sure to keep a bit of distance between us. I lightly tapped on the door.

"Hello? Is someone in there? Can you help me?" I tried to be delicate. Whoever this person was, they were either terrified or ready to attack. I had a feeling it was a child. My suspicion was confirmed when the door creaked open, and there were two large, brown eyes looking up at me from just above my waist. The child, a boy if I had to guess, just stared at me. He caught a glimpse of the giant of a man behind me, and his eyes widened, his heart racing even faster than before. I knelt to address him at his level.

"Hey there, my friend and I are looking for my daughter. She's a few years older than you. She's got blonde hair right now, but it might have turned white." The boy opened his mouth in awe. "She looks a lot like me. Do you remember seeing her anywhere?"

The boy peered back and forth between Rainier and me. I reached out gently and took his hand.

"I know he looks big and scary, but he won't hurt you, I promise. If you could help me, I'd be so grateful. I love her very much, and I could really use your help finding her. Have you seen a girl like that?" The boy gulped and nodded.

"You've seen her?" I asked quickly, making sure I understood. He nodded again. "Where? Where did you see her?" I glanced over my shoulder to see Rainier watching me with an openly sad expression. I glanced back at the child as he pointed to the room we had yet to check. When the boy gestured, Rainier quickly walked back to the empty room.

"Did you see her today?" The little boy shook his head no. My heart dropped.

"Yesterday?" He shook his head again.

"The day before?" The little boy nodded.

Shit.

I knew she wasn't in there; I'd already listened at the door.

"Did you see anyone else with her?" The boy nodded again. I wondered if he could speak or if he was too scared of us. "How many people were with her?"

He held up a few fingers and shrugged. When I described Faxon, asking if he'd seen my husband, the boy nodded again. Relief flooded my veins. Her father was with her. I knew he would do his best to keep her safe and unharmed. A surge of worry and a bit of guilt went through me then, hoping he'd stay safe. I hadn't thought about his well-being more than a passing second since I found out she'd been taken. Faxon wasn't stupid though, and I had a renewed sense of hope; he'd find a way to get them away.

"Thank you so much for your help." The little boy nodded and shut the door.

I made my way down the hall where Rainier waited. I reached for the key, and he put his hand on my arm. I stopped and looked up at him, tethered by the hand he lightly wrapped around my wrist.

"Emmeline, I know you didn't hear a heartbeat on the other side of this door, or we'd have knocked on it first. The boy saw her two days ago. Let me go first and prepare yourself for the worst, just in case."

I swallowed, realizing in horror what he was suggesting. He thought she could be dead. The idea hadn't crossed my mind. If the boy saw Elora two days ago, and I heard no heartbeat, it would mean Elora was already gone on a ship to Folterra. I was prepared for that outcome. In fact, it was the probable one. It made no sense for them to smuggle her away and kill her; they could've just done that on the road—why take her to Mira? Mindful of his concern, I took a deep breath, nodded, and turned the key.

The room appeared just as the other one had, undisturbed. After Rainier's warning, I breathed a sigh of relief. I didn't think they'd have killed her and left her here after the hassle they went through to get her. Rainier stepped in first, and we started the same routine as before, though I avoided the closet this time. There was no sign of Elora here, and we were at a dead end once again.

"Big and scary, huh?" Rainier tugged the curtain in the room back as I searched a small desk up against the wall.

"You've seen your reflection, right?" He chuckled as he searched the nightstand.

"And how do you think the kid saw you? Short and sweet?" He teased. "Though it *was* nice to see you without a scowl."

"Shut up." He was getting comfortable with me, and I didn't think I could risk that, didn't think I could afford it. All he did was give me his crooked smile—the one that had always melted me—before he bent down and checked under the bed.

"Hang on."

My heart stopped.

"What is it?"

He stood up, holding something in his hand, a thin chain hanging down.

"Give it to me." I snatched it from him. Elora's ammolite necklace.

I sat down at the foot of the bed and held my head in both hands. I started to tremble and felt like I couldn't get enough air. I was panting, trying to breathe deep. But I couldn't—I couldn't expand my lungs enough. My chest tightened, and I was able to take small gasping breaths, just enough to keep from passing out. I was doing everything I could to keep it together, but now what? How did her necklace break? It looked like someone had ripped it off her, the clasp gone. She wasn't here. She was halfway to Folterra by now already. What if—

"Giving up again, Em? Get up." I could hear Rainier's smirk in his voice and the command in his tone.

I raised my head from my hands and stared. I took a slow deep breath, effectively quelling the panic as something like rage started to simmer.

"Are you joking?" I nearly spat the words at him.

"You're used to giving up, aren't you? Not used to fighting for something."

"You have no idea what you're talking about." The sheer audacity.

"I think I do, Emmeline. It was easier to give up than face what happened. Did you know I came back to Ravemont after you left with Faxon?"

I didn't know. He'd tried to see me once while I was still there, heavily pregnant with Elora, but I wouldn't see him. Couldn't see him. I didn't know he came back a second time. The expression on my face must have given me away because he nodded slowly, his eyes narrowing.

"Oh yes, even though you tried to kill me. I came back to explain some things to you that you weren't ready to hear. But you were gone."

"First of all, I didn't try to *kill* you, it was first blood. Gods, you're dramatic." I did not hold back my sneer as I stood to face him. "Second of all, I never asked—"

"You're right, you didn't try to kill me. You just ran. You ran from the thing you needed most." His voice was deep and cold, and my stomach clenched. I reached out and felt the steady heartbeat, if a little fast, thundering below his skin. He looked down his nose, still towering over me even though I was standing. "It seems like maybe you've learned that, though. Maybe you've realized some things are worth fighting for." I saw red and started in on him.

"The thing I needed most? The thing I needed most was my sister, and she's dead, thanks to us. If you meant you?" I let out a dark laugh, watching his nostrils flare. "'We can't do this,' remember? What choice did you leave me?" I shook my head and looked down. I was mad, certainly, but I couldn't help feeling a small sting over the rejection I'd experienced all those years ago. "Gods, I hate you. I've never stopped hating you." I glared up at him, my eyes narrowed and chin jutted out, and I watched his jaw clench as fire whipped up in his eyes.

"I bet that poison tastes like honey on your tongue." His gaze pointedly moved down to my lips as he took a step closer to me, and gods damn me if my eyes didn't move to his mouth in turn. If I breathed too deeply, my chest would have pushed against him. He leaned his face down so his lips were a breath away from mine. I stood my ground, refusing to be the one to give in to this strange battle of wills. "You seem angry, Emmeline." I felt his words on my lips as a shudder rippled down my spine. Hoping I controlled my physical reaction, I stepped back before I lost my mind.

His win.

"That's because I *am* angry, Rainier."

"Good, you're much more useful when you're angry." He shot me a grin then, and realization slowly dawned on me.

"You did that on purpose?" Indignation clear in my voice, I crossed my arms so I wouldn't slap him as I glared. All he did in return was shrug.

"Can't have you breaking yet. Best to rile you up instead." Amusement flickered in his eyes, and his nonchalant tone made the anger he roused in me simmer like a pot over a flame. I stepped back toward him, close enough to touch, and took a breath, pushing myself into him. I knew he felt the same energy I did, and if he wanted to play with fire, then fine. We would play.

"I've always known there were things worth fighting for, Rainier." My voice dripped with that honeyed poison. "Did it ever occur to you that maybe I didn't want to fight for someone who wouldn't fight for me?"

His mouth snapped shut, and his jaw tensed, but Rainier didn't say a word. His expression had shifted into what I assumed was a mirror of my own face. I could almost feel heat radiating off him. He finally took a step back, rubbing his hand over his mouth and chin in frustration.

My win.

I stood there for a moment, staring at him as he averted his eyes. I took a few steps toward the closet, the last place we needed to search before I could leave the room, the movement helping me achieve some necessary space between us. I was not ready to have conversations about that day, about Lucia, about anything with him. I doubted I ever would be. I was also embarrassed I'd told him just how much his words had affected me, given I still clearly remembered after all these years. I took a sharp breath; this would not do. This animosity couldn't continue if he was going to help me. He didn't have to be here. I needed to maintain the delicate balance of friendship with him. After this was all said and done, I could go back to hating him from far away. But until I had Elora back, I needed him. I needed his cooperation and advice. His presence wasn't all bad, and he'd even helped me stay calm today. Once with Allegro and just now with the necklace. I took a deep breath before I spoke.

"There are other ways to make me angry, you know." I said it while facing the closet, but my tone was softer. I was offering an olive branch. I didn't think he was being truly malicious, only attempting to pull me out of the spiral he was about to witness. He didn't reply while I searched, and, after I turned from the empty closet, I found him silently leaning near the door. Our eyes met for just a moment before he pushed off the wall, walking toward me slowly.

I couldn't help it as I flinched when he roughly cupped his hand to my face, and he paused, guilt and anger mixing in his gaze, when he noticed my reaction.

"Should we talk about how you let those bastards hurt you instead?" At this, he tilted my head to study the bruises on my neck, which were hopefully fading, his eyes finally landing on the cut at my temple. "I'm disappointed, Em. I thought I taught you better than that."

What happened when the man tackled me played out in my mind. The tackle and the struggle. The man on top of me, pushing me into the ground. My pants getting pulled down, the cold autumn air on my body juxtaposed with the warm blood pouring out of his neck, all over my face and chest. I shuddered, trying to shake the thought. I was fine, they were dead. Some emotion, anger if I had to guess, crossed Rainier's features, and I almost swore he saw my every thought. His body tensed even while I felt his hand on my chin relax.

"Did they fucking touch you?" I knew he wasn't talking about the bruises.

"No." I looked down, not wanting to be caught in the intensity of those eyes, the gold flecking his irises resembling embers from a flame. "I killed them before…" I let my voice trail off as he tilted my chin gently to look up at him, his eyebrows raised and together, true concern washing across his face.

"But they tried?" His voice changed. Still quiet and precise, but gentle at the same time. He was less intense, his features softening with the shift in his demeanor. I nodded, and he let out a sharp exhale. He closed his eyes and inhaled deeply, and I sensed he was trying to calm himself.

I was surprised when he folded me into his arms, pulling me tight against him. He had his hand pressed against the back of my head, pulling it into his chest. I couldn't help inhaling his scent. He smelled of petrichor, earth and ozone, fresh and familiar. It was comforting and heartrending at the same time. How many times had I dreamed of him holding me like this? I allowed myself a moment of weakness, a moment to think. I knew Rainier had been trying to distract me from a meltdown before, but in his arms felt like a good place to be when I expressed the fear I'd been repressing.

"What if they—do you think they've hurt Elora?" I hadn't voiced what had been in the back of my head since I found out she was gone. Those men were trying to hurt me, and I wasn't even who they wanted. He pulled me tighter to him, his thumb grazing my scalp where his hand rested on my head.

"I don't know, but I doubt it. Someone has likely paid a high price for her. They'll want her in one piece." I felt my lower lip quiver, and I hoped he was right. His chin hovered just above my head, and his fingertips danced over my temple where my skin had split. "This will never happen again. Ever." I watched his arm as his fingertips traced across the bruises, noticing a small circular scar on the inside of his wrist. I stopped breathing as I pulled away and gazed up at him, something in his eyes I couldn't quite place. "You and your daughter are under my protection from this point forward. You should have been this whole time."

He gently traced his fingers down my neck to the hair that crossed over my shoulder, and he tucked it back, keeping eye contact with me the entire time. My heart was pounding in my chest as he touched me. I took a small breath, not sure what to say. Would he keep us under his protection when we eventually went back to Ravemont? I watched as Rainier's eyes dipped to my lips, and I locked my eyes shut, wishing I hadn't seen. There was no point in denying the attraction was still there. But it had always been more than just attraction for me. It was why

I knew this was dangerous. Everything about being around him was dangerous for my heart, but what choice did I have? I had to choose between two types of destruction, and, even then, I might still get both. Destroyed by my daughter being lost to me forever or ruined by the man who had done nothing but set my life aflame. There was no question in the matter, no price too high to get her back. I'd steel my heart against everything and work through it. Work through the guilt of being with him and being around him, being alive with him while my sister rested in a grave I'd never visited. I was drawn from my thoughts when we heard shouting and the sound of someone running up the stairs. I grabbed my dagger as Rainier's hand left my neck to rest on the hilt of his sword. I closed my eyes and reached out. The little frantic heartbeat across the hall was drowned out by two others moving up the stairs.

"Two," I spoke softly, opening my eyes to find his peering into mine. He nodded and turned, walking to a position which put him between me and the door.

It slammed inward a moment later.

CHAPTER 8

Dewalt marched into the room as Lavenia skidded to a halt in the hallway.

"Are you two about to kill each other?" Lavenia gaped at us from behind Dewalt, confusion and surprisingly authentic concern crossing her face.

"No! We thought—" I started to explain as I put my dagger away.

"Don't stop on our account," chuckled Dewalt. His dark brown eyes crinkled at the corners.

"What are you doing here, Dewalt? Why didn't you send an impulse?" Rainier cut in sharply. He clearly was not in the mood for his friend's line of teasing.

"Yeah, why did you bust the door open?" He scared the hell out of me.

"A ship left yesterday with Elora on it." His face was grim, brows knotted. My stomach dropped.

You knew this was probably what happened. It's not much worse than we already thought. We will get her back. It will be alright. Inhale. Exhale. Steel your heart.

"How do you know?" I demanded, desperate for more information.

"I paid a libertine." He shrugged. "She wouldn't leave me alone while I was waiting." He kicked up a grin then, and the ghost of a swaggering teenage Dewalt appeared before me. "So, I paid her to leave, but not before asking if she'd seen a girl."

"She definitely saw Elora?" How many girls could be getting smuggled out of Mira? It was likely if there was a girl there, it was my daughter, but I still asked the question.

"No. *She* didn't. Her client from this morning did, though. Said he paid her generously, and she asked him why. I guess he's a deckhand for a different ship, but he helped smuggle them out on another ship his captain owns. It left this time yesterday."

"Where is he?" Rainier demanded with a ferocity that gave me pause. I watched him, arms crossed and jaw clenched. He looked like a statue of Hanwen, wrath personified.

Dewalt grinned. "The cellar. That's why the innkeeper was shouting. He wasn't thrilled with the idea."

"Wasn't thrilled, my ass. He smacked you over the head with his cane." Lavenia rested a gentle hand on Dewalt's shoulder, and the look of concern she gave him as she inspected the welt over his eye disarmed me. I blinked. Shocked I didn't realize it before now, I gawped at the two of them. They had performed the ritual. That explained a lot. The fact neither of them appeared much older than their early twenties was something that tinged me with a bit of jealousy when I'd first seen them, but now I understood.

"Anything else we need to know before we question the deckhand?"

It was Lavenia's turn to look grim. "I found out who sold the woman your horse." She turned to me. "It was Faxon."

I stayed silent on our way down the stairs. I knew after finding her necklace the odds weren't good for us, yet I was still devastated. But I withheld my tears, my agony, and pushed it down into a deep pit in my stomach. I'd have time to cry about it later. Instead of thinking about the increasing helplessness of our situation, I tried to organize my thoughts about Faxon. It didn't make any sense to me. Why would Faxon sell our horses? Were they making him sell them before they forced him onto the ship? It was the only thing that made sense. Lavenia had asked around about a man selling a horse and found he'd sold both two nights ago. One of the men Lavenia spoke to even knew his name, and his description matched.

They'd been at the inn, and Faxon sold the horses. A man helped arrange passage for a girl. Had Faxon gotten away from the captors and sold the horses for passage in order to try to free her? I was bewildered by all the different scenarios running through my head, and I stayed silent while I thought.

All four of us and the old man crammed into the dingy back office, the innkeeper resigned to the fact the Crown Prince would be using his cellar for an interrogation. Dewalt moved a heavy barrel of unknown liquid, some type of alcohol perhaps, off the top of the cellar door. Lavenia lifted the door and pulled it open. All I could see were stone walls and wooden stairs leading down into the dark. Carrying a lantern, Dewalt led the way down ,with Lavenia close behind. Rainier followed, but paused on the top step before turning back to me, face drawn.

"You don't have to watch this, if you don't want to." His face was grim, his full lips pressed into a thin, tight line. I took his warning to mean he'd torture the man if he needed to.

I shook my head and stepped forward. I needed to see it. I needed to hear everything. He started down the stairs, reaching back with his hand for my own, and I let him lead me down into the dark. His calloused hand engulfed mine, and he squeezed it tightly before he let go.

Dewalt had put a satchel over the man's head, and his hands were tied with a rope behind his back. Dewalt kicked him as he walked past, with a casualness that told me this wasn't the first time he'd interrogated someone. I wondered exactly what his role was during his time with Rainier—when they were working against the Folterran army. Had he been tasked with torturing people for information? It was a bit difficult for me to reconcile my friend, the rascal with an easy smile, with someone who could be capable of anything resembling torture. He pulled the deckhand up to his knees by his shirt and yanked the satchel off his face. The man, whose greasy face seemed to match his greasy hair, turned and spat at Dewalt's feet. He looked at each of us in turn before his gaze settled on the prince. I watched with some small amount of satisfaction as fear took over his frame.

Rainier's presence was intimidating in general, yet in this small cellar he evoked the gods. He had to tilt his head down to even stand in the tallest point of the cellar. The room was barely larger than the size of my bathroom at home. While boxes were stacked against the stone wall behind the steps, the rest of the walls were made of earth. The cellar had been dug straight into the ground and felt cool and damp because of it. I took steadying breaths, in through my nose and out through my mouth. The size of the small room and the musty scent of water, earth, and stone were bringing up a memory I wished didn't haunt me. Part of me wanted to walk back and sit on the steps behind Rainier, but then I'd have to see the man's face and that seemed worse.

The deckhand was on the ground in the middle of the dirt floor, and Rainier stood directly in front of him at the base of the stairs. The man's body was strung tight as he glared up at his prince, face screwed up in a bitter grimace. Lavenia stood at the back of the cellar where the ceiling was lower while Dewalt crouched off to the side of the man on the ground. He faced Rainier, and I was surprised to notice the muscles across his back press against his shirt. He'd always been lean and tall—taller than Rainier even—but he had filled out quite a bit since I'd been around them last. Not as drastically as Rainier, but still enough that I was taken aback. I decided to stand next to Lavenia, out of the way. I knew it would be a test of my fortitude, but I wanted to be here, needed to be here. I focused on the stone wall and the stairs in front of me. Being underground was not something I anticipated or something I was sure I could even handle, but this man had information about my daughter. I didn't want to wait to find out. As long as I focused on the task at hand, I could keep my head clear.

I will get out. I can get out.

"What did I do?" The man had a high nasal voice, but his response sounded feral. I reached out, listening to his heartbeat, finding it slightly accelerated. Not surprising, considering he'd been bound in a cellar and was currently being questioned by the Crown Prince.

"Did you arrange passage for a girl on a ship that left harbor yesterday? Blonde, about this tall?" Rainier's voice was commanding as he repeated my earlier description of Elora.

"No, I don't know what you're talking about." The deckhand's heart rocketed, as if it would beat right out of his chest.

"Lie." I interjected, surprising myself. I sounded calmer than I felt. Rainier met my gaze, his eyes flashing with surprise and something else. His mouth spread into a wicked grin.

"The lady has called you a liar. Do you refute her?" Rainier's voice dripped with venom. He was baiting the man.

"I ain't a liar!" The deckhand yelled over his shoulder at me. Rainier knelt, closer to eye level with the man. I didn't need to listen to his heart to retort this time, a growing frustration within my body propelling me. He knew where this was going to lead. Why wasn't he talking?

"Lie."

Rainier's eyes shot up to mine, laughter in them. His lips spread in an almost seductive smile. He was enjoying this, and I didn't know how to feel about it. He kept his eyes on me for another second before his gaze slid back over to his captive. Rainier's hand slid up, cupping the man's cheek in what could have been mistaken for an intimate gesture in any other circumstance, but in truth, it was anything but. The deckhand attempted to pull away, but I watched as Rainier's fingertips pulled his face back where he wanted it.

"Last chance for honesty. Did you arrange passage for a young girl?" I stared at the prince's mouth, the smile still present along with a malicious glint in his eyes. He *wanted* the man to lie again.

"I didn't do anything." The deckhand was either stupid or brave—potentially both. When I didn't say anything, Rainier peered up at me through impossibly thick lashes.

"Well, darling?"

My reply was instant and steady, though I couldn't help my surprise at the intimate intonation of his voice.

"Lie."

Rainier clapped his hand against the man's face, almost gently, before standing. I watched his fingertips twitch as I felt a rumble below us. The earthy scent of mildew permeated the air more than it already had been. I took a step to the side as I realized what was happening. The earth beneath the man started to shift away and his body fell deeper into the ground. Dirt stopping halfway up his chest, he sank, his hands still tied behind his back. I grabbed onto Lavenia, bracing myself. A trickle of water started running down the wall behind the stairs. I wasn't sure if Rainier disrupted something when he opened up the ground or not.

"What the—" the man cried out.

"You seem like a forgetful man. Hopefully this will remind you." This time Rainier spoke with the low growl matching someone who could make the earth below us swallow someone whole. I tensed. It wasn't often Rainier used the other aspects of his divinity, and his other abilities had a certain reckless wild which made me nervous.

"I didn't do anything!" The man was desperate, flailing his upper body around. He looked like a fish flopping around on a dock. Rainier caused the earth to shift even further before he spoke, his voice deathly quiet.

"Where?" A demand.

"Folterra!" the man yelped, realizing how truly desperate his situation was.

"Which port?" Rainier spoke precisely. Terrifyingly.

"I—uh..."

"The next time you fail at answering a question the first time I ask it, you will not like the consequences. Which port?" His tone was casual, but the fire in his eyes as he looked at the man was anything but.

"Mindengar."

"How many did you arrange passage for?"

"I...I don't remember."

Rainier stood up and kicked the man straight in the mouth.

I stared at the prince, eyes wide. I'd never seen him be cruel, but I'd also never seen him interrogate someone. He rolled his neck, stretching, before he turned back to the man. I saw him clench his fists, the frustration radiating off him, and I felt guilty. I was the reason he was having to do this. I watched the water spilling down the wall behind Rainier, the sound distracting me from his fists. The trickle grew louder in my ears, and I felt myself going to a place of panic. I took a deep breath, inhaling. My heart had started to race. Getting lost in the sound of the water made it hard for me to focus. I began counting in my head, trying to calm myself down. I needed to stay down here, listen to what the man had to say.

The deckhand spat blood and teeth onto the ground before him and turned his head up to Rainier. I could hear the sneer in his voice as he spoke.

"Eleven men and the girl."

"Was the girl hurt?" I froze when Rainier asked the question. I wasn't sure I wanted to hear the answer.

"No." The man's head tilted. "No, she wasn't hurt. Her father was with her. He was the one who arranged the passage."

His heartbeat was normal. A little accelerated, not unusual for someone who'd just been kicked in the mouth, but not racing like before. I could feel the color draining from my face. Rainier glanced at me, his brows furrowed.

"Were the rest of the group Folterrans?"

"I think so, the accents—"

"Was the girl struggling? Her father?"

"They ended up putting ropes on the hellcat. She bit someone's ear off when they were boarding."

Shit.

Rainier raised his eyebrows, a ghost of a smile on his lips before he gave me a pointed look which said *like mother, like daughter.*

"And her father? Was he bound?"

"No."

Rainier asked another question, but I didn't listen for the answer. Faxon had purchased passage and wasn't bound. There were only so many things it could mean. The water trickling down the wall was all I could hear. I couldn't breathe. Suddenly, it felt like the walls around me were closing in. The smell of mold overpowered me, and I needed to get out. The edges of my vision blackened, and I ran toward the stairs. Rainier watched me as I pushed past him, frustration burning in his eyes. For me or Faxon, I wasn't sure. I made it to the top of the stairs, bursting through the door straight into the sunlight. Hands on my knees, I began to retch.

CHAPTER 9

After I'd lost my breakfast in the street, Lavenia suggested I take a short nap while Dewalt and Rainier dealt with the man in the cellar. I didn't know what dealing with him entailed, but I wasn't exactly curious to find out. I sat down on one of the benches outside, head between my knees, waiting for Lavenia to get us a room. I didn't think I had much left in me, but it didn't stop the bile from rising.

Elora had been bound—from biting off someone's ear no less. As much as it pained me to know she probably made things worse for herself, a small part of me still swelled with pride. She was fighting back. But what was Faxon doing? Why wasn't he bound? Why had he paid for their passage? It didn't make sense, and nothing was adding up. A heavy feeling settled into the pit of my stomach, and I didn't think it would budge until I saw them both again.

There was something there, something I didn't want to think about—the deep insecurity I felt about Faxon's loyalty. The fact I was sitting there questioning his actions and not trusting him completely told me more than it should have. The idea shouldn't have crossed my mind, yet something was just not right. I started reviewing every interaction I'd had with Faxon recently which might have struck me as odd when I heard Lavenia approach.

The princess walked to my bench and held out her hand to lead me inside. We went up to the top floor, across the hallway from where I'd seen the small child, next to the room where we found Elora's necklace. I reached into my pocket and palmed it, rubbing my thumb over the ammolite. Lavenia walked across to the small window, set off-center in the wood-paneled wall, and the thick green curtains, moth-eaten in some places, served their purpose when she pulled them shut, dimming the room. The furnishings were superior to the other rooms we searched; an armchair and a small table holding glasses and a sturdy clay pitcher sat near the window while a mirrored dresser stood by the door. I sat down on the bed, filled with feathers like my own in Brambleton rather than the soft cotton

I had appreciated the night before at Ravemont, and slid off my shoes. Lavenia fetched a glass from the table, filled it with water, and brought it over to me.

"I'm going to go downstairs, see if I can help the boys. Rest. I'll come wake you when we know more."

I nodded and gulped down the water. While the little sleep I got the night before had been comfortable, it hadn't been restful, and I'd barely been eating. I'd need my strength; Elora was on her way to Folterra. I kicked off my pants and threw them on the ground. I heard a dull thud when they hit the floor, and I reached for them, digging through the pockets. Finding the conch shell, I said a silent prayer of thanks that I hadn't accidentally broken it. I rubbed my thumb over the bumps and whorls and felt myself calm a bit. I was surprised Rainier remembered my collection, even more so that he added to it. I couldn't help but think about how he was managing to calm me when he wasn't even here. I placed the conch on the nightstand, crawled into the bed, and sank into my thoughts once again, a bit calmer than just a few moments ago, but still terrified, nonetheless.

After being responsible for Lucia's death, I thought perhaps I brought this upon myself. Wouldn't that be justice? If my own husband was partially responsible for my daughter's—*our* daughter's—abduction? But for him to do something to Elora still made no sense to me. He loved her. He'd always loved her and cared for her. It was the one thing about him I never doubted or resented, the one thing I had complete faith in. So, why was I now uncertain of even that?

"NO!" The shout died on my lips as I was enveloped by blackness.

I landed on my knees, hands thrown forward, and I winced as pain shot through my abdomen. I couldn't see a thing. The ground beneath me felt damp and cool. I spread my arms wide, hoping for a wall or something to grab onto. I could hear a faint trickle of water, and the realization hit me like a slap. Tuaman Cliffs. I was inside the complex system of tunnels and caves we had spent the last week exploring, somewhere behind the cavern where Rain and I had explored each other only hours before.

I slowly stood, arms outstretched, and finally made contact with a wall. Why did he send me here? I felt a tickle on my face and reached up to wipe at it, barely touching the sliver of open skin at my hairline.

Lucia.

Though I was disoriented from my fall and inability to see, I quickly began to panic. We'd been running, the soldiers overtaking us. I had been bleeding into my eye, struggling to see as we fought our way through. She was sending bolts of white light into chests as we ran while I kicked knees and slashed across hands and necks, disarming more than injuring anyone. She had given me a shove and yelled at me.

"Keep going!" She had marched forward as she shouted, moving away from me. I stumbled and threw my arms out, reaching for her. I wasn't going to leave her. She turned a moment before I grabbed her, and she shoved me so hard, I fell backwards. I watched as a bright light erupted out of her, and my vision went white as I lay there on the ground. Blinking, I realized the bodies of those who had been chasing after us were on the ground, unmoving. I gasped, knowing she had emptied her well of divinity with that blast of power. Black tendrils of smoke began to envelop her, vipers undulating within the clouds. Lucia let out an earth-shattering scream and fell to the ground. I clambered to my feet, running towards her, but then Rainier was behind me, grabbing me around the waist from behind and dragging me, legs flailing, before he tossed me in a rift.

He closed it.

I was alone.

I started screaming. Lucia was hurt, and I could help her. She needed me. I had to find my way out of the cave system and back to them, back to her. But I had no idea where I was. The cavern was right at the opening of the cliffs. It had been beautiful, and we had no reason to explore back further into the caves, so I had no idea where I was. I started shivering from the cold at first before it shifted into something more, and my lips turned up into a rueful smile. The blanket Rainier and I had been laying on was probably where we left it, along with the lantern and bottle of wine we'd polished off. It struck me then—the wards. We'd lowered the wards.

It was our fault.

Divine hell, it was all our fault.

I stopped moving, my heart in my throat. I had to fix this. I needed to get back.

I held my hand against my side, fabric wet with my blood, as I made my way through the caves. I walked for hours, sometimes having to crawl, as I made my way through the dark. I had been following a promising path, only for it to end in rock-fall, making the way through impossible. I let out a scream of rage and slid down onto the ground. Rain didn't follow me, and the rift closed. I was well and truly lost, helpless. I focused my energy, reaching out for a heartbeat. Hoping against hope that Rain was nearby, searching for me.

Silence surrounded me, enveloped me, suffocated me. I leaned back against the cave wall and closed my eyes, the cool rock behind me soothing the ache in my head. I didn't know how long I sat there before I felt the water lapping over my feet.
  High tide.
  I jumped to my feet, running and crawling back towards where I started.
  I was stuck. I was going to die in these caves.

I woke up drenched in sweat. Being in the cellar earlier had pushed my mind to a place it rarely went, somewhere it hadn't gone in years. Rainier had rifted me into the cave system by accident, intending to send me to the cavern we'd discovered days before. But he'd been frantic, panicked, and he missed his mark. I ran a hand over my face. I did not want to start thinking about this again. Those were some of the worst hours of my life, second only to the hours following.
  The room was surprisingly full of light, and I assumed it was late afternoon. I rolled over, confused, sure that Lavenia had closed the curtains.
  "Feeling any better?" Dewalt was sitting in the worn velvet armchair in front of the window with his feet propped up on the table, resting dangerously close to the pitcher. When my eyes found his dark ones, he was staring at me, seated with his hands crossed on his stomach and an uncharacteristically soft look on his face.
  I sat up, pulling my blanket higher.
  "A bit. Where's Lavenia?" My tone was harsher than I meant for it to be.
  "She's with Rainier. We got some more information out of Ratshit downstairs, and they're going to follow up. I was instructed to stay with you."
  Ratshit. The nickname was a good one. "A note would have been fine; I didn't need you watching me like some kind of creep." When we were kids, Dewalt was like an older brother to me, and my favorite part about that had been pestering him. He was always extremely confident—too confident—and he could be rather annoying, so it was important to knock him down a peg whenever possible. It was easy to go back into the same dynamic.
  "Hey, I was reading!" He gestured to the Myriad text under his propped feet. "You snore, by the way." I snorted. A small smile was evident on Dewalt's face, but there was worry in his eyes. Considering what I was dreaming about, I doubted I'd been relaxed enough to snore.
  "What did you find out?"

Dewalt's smile faltered. "I'll let them explain when they get back." I narrowed my eyes at him. "It should be soon," he added, almost apologetically. It felt invasive, but I reached out and noticed his heart was beating faster than usual.

"I hear your heart racing, asshole. Just tell me. She's my daughter; I deserve to know." I snapped at him, and his eyes shot to mine. He contemplated it for a moment, his face unreadable. He could look intimidating when he wanted to, with his strong brow and high cheekbones working with his expressions to make him seem unapproachable. His face was a handsome one, and his long straight nose gave him the appearance of nobility.

"We don't think Faxon was being held prisoner. The rat mentioned he'd met him before." He watched me, pity in his eyes—dark brown to go along with his onyx hair. I stared at him for a moment, willing him to tell me more, and his bronze skin darkened at his cheeks.

"What do you mean?" I demanded. My stomach writhed. I knew something was wrong. Faxon kissed me that morning when he left. That was when I should have known he had no intention of coming back. My skin crawled where he'd placed his lips to my cheek.

Dewalt heaved a sigh and brought both of his feet down onto the ground in front of him. He leaned forward, head down, and put his hand on the back of his neck. He truly didn't want to tell me.

"Debt. He owes debts all over the city. Rainier and Lavenia are looking into them now."

What? How could he have debts? Everything was paid for by my father. He went into Mira every couple of months, but it was to visit shops we didn't have in Brambleton. What kind of debts? I started spiraling a bit, a list of questions about to tumble off my tongue. I couldn't breathe properly. Steeling myself, I eyed Dewalt, knowing he'd see fire.

"Get out." I ordered. He gaped up at me, dumbstruck and unmoving. "I just want to put my damn pants back on. Get out for a minute."

He sat there for another second before he realized what I'd said. He made for the door just as there was a light rapping on it. He glanced over at me, as if seeking permission to open the door I had just told him to leave through, and I groaned in frustration. He opened it and stopped Lavenia from entering the room as he pushed out.

"Evidently, Emma doesn't like to wear pants when she sleeps." Dewalt couldn't have been more annoying if he tried. I heard Rainier's low rumble of a laugh in the hallway, and I felt myself flush.

"Just give me a minute." I muttered as Dewalt stepped out and closed the door behind him.

I ripped out of the bed and caught a glimpse of myself in the mirror above the dresser. My hair was halfway out of the braid I'd worn earlier, so I finished the job and ran my fingers through it as my thoughts went to Faxon. That *asshole*. That absolute piece of shit. We were at home, relying on the stipend from my father, making minimal trips to stay hidden, *sacrifices* to stay hidden. And he was traveling to Mira, racking up debt gambling, no doubt. Did he say the wrong thing to someone? Did they find out about Elora? I was simmering. With fear, with anger. I reached down onto the floor and pulled on the breeches I'd left in a pile, doing the buttons with rage-shaking hands. I stalked to the door, a picture of wrath.

"*Your Highnesses*," I gritted out between my teeth as I showed them into the room. I abruptly realized Dewalt may have some sort of title since he was Lavenia's bonded partner, but I didn't care enough to find out at the moment.

"There she is." Lavenia gave me a lopsided smile that didn't reach her eyes as she walked in.

"Be careful, Ven, she assaulted me. Don't push her," Dewalt warned, a small smile on his face as he entered the room.

"Assaulted you?" What was he talking about?

"You heart-checked me!"

"Oh, that. Not sorry." It wasn't as if I had hurt him by doing it.

Rainier had taken a seat in the armchair, one elbow on an armrest. His chin rested in his hand, and his eyes were simmering with an emotion I couldn't quite place. I was embarrassed. He'd warned me not to marry Faxon, as if I had much of a choice. But here we were, years and years later, and he was seeing just how right he was. My pride was hurt. Rainier had rejected me, and then I'd married someone who gave me nothing but Elora. And now, whatever Faxon had done had taken her from me.

Dewalt stood next to him, leaning against the wall. I was sure he told them in the hallway that I knew some of what they had to tell me. Lavenia perched on the end of the bed and watched me as I paced back and forth between the window and the door. She looked tired. I wondered if she'd used her ability to compel anyone while they were out. She didn't like to do it for a few reasons, the exhaustion one of them. She once told me that it felt gross, forcing people to do and say things against their will.

"Well? Out with it." I barked at no one in particular. Lavenia cleared her throat.

"Faxon has been gambling. A lot." I'd already figured as much. He must have been weaseling away some of the money from my father and bringing it here to waste. "He owed debts to—well, almost everyone." I nodded, still pacing.

"Including libertines." Dewalt felt the need to add insult to injury today, apparently. It wasn't helping. I threw up my middle finger in his direction without sparing him a glance, and I heard Rainier stifle a snort.

"Yes, including libertines." Lavenia's tone was sad. I didn't give a single rat's ass who owned his debts. I didn't care about his patronage of libertines. It's not as if I had ever been amenable to his advances, and I wasn't stupid. I'd already suspected he'd found his release somewhere else. I just figured it would be some girl from Brambleton. Someone *free*. Lavenia watched me sadly, pity in her eyes, and I felt my face flush.

"I get it, not surprising. You're not going to find me weeping about it." It was embarrassing, but not astonishing. Having to reveal it to the three of them hurt more than any sort of claim against his fidelity. I couldn't help but notice Rainier adjusting uncomfortably in his chair. I exhaled, just wanting to know more. "Did someone take her to force him to pay?"

"That's just it." Her face was grim. "It appears he paid off most of them last night."

"What? How?" I didn't know the numbers, but I knew we didn't have money lying around to pay off debts to every creditor in Mira.

"No one knew. He still owes money to a few of them." Of course he did.

"Where did he get all the money?" No one in the room answered, and my stomach hollowed out, dread filling me.

"He told the remaining creditors he'd send the rest of the money—that he had investments in Folterra." There was sympathy in her midnight eyes.

My mouth went dry. What kind of investments?

"Why didn't he just run from the creditors and take all this money from his—whatever this business in Folterra is? Why pay everyone off?" I felt chills race through me. Had he made some sort of deal involving Elora? I immediately rejected the idea. He would never. No matter what he'd done, the debts he'd accumulated, he would never risk Elora—would he? What kind of person would?

"You." Rainier had his hands clasped between his legs as I whirled to face him.

"What do you mean, me?" His gaze met mine, his green eyes burning and eyebrows raised, as if he were the one asking the question. He sat there for a moment before he spoke.

"What you suggested may have been his original plan, but when he rode in with the Folterrans, he ran into a few people who planned to make good on his debts.

He paid off everyone he could and made assurances to everyone he didn't. He's been a regular for years, Emmeline. They knew where he lived, where *you* lived. He paid to protect you. And to protect his own neck as well, of course, but you were still part of it."

I stared at him a beat too long before I laughed.

"Fat lot of good that did." I gestured to my face from the previous day. "Aside from the fact it doesn't make any sense, where did the money come from? How could he pay everyone off?" I rubbed the spot between my eyebrows, sick nausea creeping up my throat.

"Emmeline." Something in his voice made me nervous, sick.

I knew. I knew all along; I just needed someone to put the words to it. It was all I could do to stay upright.

He heaved a deep breath as he watched me. "He sold her."

That feeling in the pit of my stomach exploded. I let my gaze sweep across the three of them, waiting for someone to explain that what he'd just said was wrong.

"From what we've gleaned, he sold her for a large sum. When his creditors got word, many threatened to kill him where he stood and burn your home to the ground with you in it if he didn't pay up. They knew he had the money, so he paid them all to save his own neck. And yours."

"Why?" I didn't know exactly what I was asking, but my voice was quiet. Rainier only shook his head with his eyebrows raised and hands outstretched. He didn't know either.

"The money, that's our only guess." Lavenia supplied, choosing to answer why he'd sold Elora. Why he bothered to save me when he took Elora from me was left unanswered.

"There has to be more to it. She's our *daughter*."

No one spoke. My shallow breaths were the only sound in the room. In a daze, I walked back over to the bed and sat down, staring at the floor in silence. The sun was setting, and I watched as a ray of light moved across the floor. I vaguely felt Lavenia move, the weight of her body leaving the mattress, but I didn't bother to see where she had gone.

How could he? He sold his own daughter to the same people we'd spent the last fifteen years hiding her from. I felt my hands ball into fists. Anguish rising, I threw my head back and screamed, louder and more guttural than any sound I'd ever made.

To their credit, no one stopped me from yelling or attempted to comfort me while my screams of rage turned into heaving gasps for air and eventually melted into quiet sobs. Dewalt and Lavenia left the room, probably in search of dinner. My back against the headboard, I leaned forward, bringing my head down onto my knees. I couldn't comprehend the information I'd just been given. Faxon had sold his own daughter to our enemy to pay off gambling debts and to keep his creditors from killing me. How did he not see he was killing me himself?

I felt the mattress shift next to me, and I glanced over. Rainier had taken his shoes off and climbed up next to me, leaning against the headboard. He looked absurd in the small bed, his body taking up more than half of it. I watched him situate himself, crossing his arms over his chest and one ankle over the other. He glanced over, finding me staring at him, and he seemed so startled, I snorted. He watched me, eyes wide, as a small smile formed on his face. I couldn't help it as I started laughing. And once I started, I could not stop.

He looked at me incredulously. "What?"

"You!" I cackled. "This!" I gestured to him on the bed. What had my life turned into? I never thought I'd see him again, let alone see him here next to me, looking like a giant in a child's bed. I never thought he'd be the one to tell me my husband sold my daughter. The events of the last day were mind-boggling, and it clearly had gone to my head. He stared at me, expressionless, and his face sent me even further into my fit.

"This is all ridiculous!" I was howling with laughter. The corner of Rainier's lip tugged upward, but his face flooded with confusion and worry.

"I've spent her whole life protecting her, and her own father sold her!" I was losing my mind. "And now you," I snorted. "You! Of all people, *you* helped me find all of this out." I threw myself backwards, my laughter slowly turning to quiet tears. "What am I going to do?" I felt my face crumple. I should have known. I should have seen something wasn't right. "I'm such an idiot."

I started slamming my fist into my thigh, over and over again, wanting it to hurt, wanting the pain of my body to match the pain of my heart.

Rainier reached out and grabbed my wrist between punches, and I whipped my head toward him. His face was calm, but his eyes tracked my features. He was studying me again as he had on our way to Mira, like I was about to break in half. I hated it. He lowered my wrist as he intertwined his fingers with mine. I caught my breath as I looked down, focusing on his thumb gently rubbing the back of my hand. I could feel the calluses on his hand, but his touch was delicate. I sat there for a few minutes, just watching his thumb circle while my tears slowed.

"I should've guessed you'd be the first person I'd have to stop from hurting you." I could hear the smile when he said it, but his voice was quiet and soothing, almost as if he was afraid to talk too loudly. I gave a choked laugh and drew my free hand to my face, wiping away the tears. I felt his eyes on me, and I focused on my small hand resting in his large one. The difference between the two was drastic, and it made me smile. It was almost comical. I felt the heat of Rainier's arm next to mine, and I couldn't stop myself as I put my head on his shoulder. His arm was warm underneath my cheek. I wanted to just sink into him, letting myself only think of the heat, the smell of him. Our hands stayed clasped between us, and I tried to relax. I could feel my divinity slipping out of control and heard his steady heart. I counted the beats and basked in him while I focused on my breathing. I needed to calm down and get myself together. What just happened couldn't happen again—it wouldn't save her. After a while, he reached over with his other hand and pulled my chin up to look at him.

"We are going to find her. And then I'm going to kill your husband." The voice belonged to the Bloody Prince, but his soft expression belonged to Rainier. It belonged to Rain. *My* Rain.

"Alright." I didn't have any doubts he meant it.

Dewalt and Lavenia walked back into the room a while later and exchanged a weighted glance. I sat up and pulled my hand from Rainier's. I had no idea how long I'd been sitting there with my head on his shoulder. It was dangerously easy to fall back into friendship with him. Could I even call it that? It was strange, coming back to this world, to this life. In some ways, it felt like no time had passed at all. Lavenia was still kind and Dewalt was still annoying. I had loved all of them. But when Lucia died, she took part of me with her. I wondered if I'd ever be able to forgive and forget. Did I even deserve to? Did any of us deserve it? Sometimes I wondered if the part she'd taken was my ability to love. Or maybe the ability to love *them*. At least with Elora, it was intrinsic. I loved her because she was mine.

"Everything alright?" Dewalt drawled.

Rainier chuckled. "Emmeline was just having a laughing fit because I told her I was going to kill her husband." It wasn't exactly true, but not far enough from the truth to refute.

Lavenia snorted. "If she doesn't do it herself first, Hanwen help her."

I cringed, remembering how I had told Lavenia I loved Faxon in a way. The thought tasted like sulfur, slimy and disgusting. He was a traitor. He betrayed me, and he betrayed our daughter. There was no punishment I could think of to fit his crime. I wondered if I had tried to love Faxon, maybe he wouldn't have done what he did. But there was no point even thinking about it. We were in this situation because of every decision the two of us had made over the years. The choices he made all those years ago made it impossible for me to love him. And the choices he made now were unforgivable. Maybe I would find myself praying to the God of Wrath after all.

"You could do it together—it's a unique bonding experience." Dewalt deadpanned over his shoulder, placing a tray on the table. Something about the way he said it made it seem like he spoke from experience, that he'd shared a kill with someone before. The tray he carried was filled with an assortment of meats and fruits, as well as a pot of what smelled like chowder. As he began to divide out the food in plates and bowls, I inspected the room and wondered where we could all sit and eat and not make a mess. I ended up cross-legged on the floor with my back against the foot of the bed, and Lavenia plopped down on the floor next to me—you'd never know she was a princess. Rainier sat across from me, back to the closet door, legs outstretched. As Dewalt started bringing over our dinner, I suddenly grew curious about his and Lavenia's relationship. I needed a distraction, and their love life was a welcome one.

"So, when did you two perform the ritual? You were most definitely not in love when I saw you last."

"I was wondering if you noticed." Lavenia's smile was almost shy. "It'll be ten years ago in the spring. And no, we were not *in* love then or now. He's my best friend and has been for a long time. We know each other's minds and love each other. It's enough for the ritual. You know how rare conduits are." Lavenia shrugged.

Though conduits themselves were rare, it was rarer still for anyone who performed the bonding ritual to not be in love with their partner. Conduits not only shared divinity, but they shared their lives after they performed the ritual—forever connected emotionally, physically, and spiritually with the person they chose. Because the Myriad gave bonded conduits access to the font, the life-giving gift from the gods, the lives of conduits were long, spanning hundreds of years. It wasn't unheard of for royalty to perform the rite to form alliances or to gain power, such as what was supposed to happen with Rainier and Lucia, but as a second-born child, I'd always expected Lavenia to choose someone for love. Though I supposed she was right, conduits were a dying breed.

Dewalt brought his meal over and sat on my other side, across from Lavenia. "We love each other like we always have. She is my best friend, and I am hers. I would do anything for her, just like I'd do anything for Rainier."

"The only reason he didn't pick me is because Lavenia asked him first." Rainier chuckled.

"If I'd have known you were interested . . ." Dewalt's eyebrow arched, a lascivious smile on his face.

"Firstly, I have no interest in doing the Body aspect of the ritual with you. Secondly, your abilities are too weak to help a future king." Rainier smirked at Dewalt, who in turn gasped in mock offense.

I was sure Rainier was joking about Dewalt's abilities being too weak, but I wondered if it was why he had never completed the ritual himself. I couldn't help but feel a small pang, knowing how pathetic my own divinity was compared to theirs. Healers weren't uncommon at all, as far as conduits went, and I wasn't even close to being one of the best. And, though my ability to listen to hearts was rare—I'd never met another with my gift—it wasn't exactly useful. Had Queen Shivani not been able to find someone for him with adequate abilities? Lucia had been more than suitable, but was there no one else for him? I didn't know what came over me, but I decided to ask him.

"Why haven't you performed the ritual, Rainier?" I took a bite of a strawberry as I watched him, oddly nervous for his answer.

"That's an awfully intrusive question, isn't it, Highclere?" One of his eyebrows was raised, and the smirk he'd been wearing only a moment ago was gone. I glowered at him, knowing he only used my family name to irk me. I tried my best to be nonchalant and shrugged.

"You don't have to talk about it, *Vestana*. I'm just curious. I figured there would be courtiers lining up to bond with Crown Prince Rainier." I saw a hint of a smile when I used his own family name, but Lavenia cut in before he could speak.

"Oh, don't flatter him." She groaned, and I saw Rainier's eyes flash something close to relief. I decided to let the topic drop; I'd get it out of him later.

"Anyway, the conduit pool is rather low, and, at the time, nobody was doing anything for me." Lavenia laughed as she continued. "Dewalt was a choice made in desperation." Rainier started chuckling, and I was relieved to hear the sound of it.

"Excuse me!" Dewalt's words didn't match his face, full of laughter, as he looked at Lavenia.

"But you do what the ritual demands?" After the Mind ceremony, they would have had to be together physically for the Body, and they'd be connected from then on, continuing to renew that bond regularly. It was part of the ritual where the mind, body, and soul of the conduits would meld and combine to make them both stronger. I couldn't imagine doing that with a friend, no matter how close we were.

"We do. We are not monogamous though, if that's what you're truly asking." Dewalt grinned.

"Don't tease her. Dewalt and I, well, not so much Dewalt, but I pursue relationships outside of the bond. If either of us were to find another conduit to perform the ritual with, we'd revisit our arrangement." Lavenia smiled at Dewalt, who glared at her after her comment about his relationship status.

"But so far, it hasn't been an issue." Dewalt finished for her.

"So, what did the Myriad make you both do for your tasks?" I'd never seen any part of the ritual performed. Rainier and Lucia were to be the first one I'd ever seen. I wasn't completely ignorant, though. Each partner was given a task from the Myriad to complete, to prove their worthiness to the other before they'd be allowed to proceed with the ritual. Sometimes it was a quest, sometimes it was settling an old grudge, and sometimes it was something as simple as bringing a smile to your partner's face with a unique gift. I had no idea how the Myriad Masters decided this and honestly thought it might have been purely political. For matches they didn't want to occur, they'd assign impossible tasks, forcing the conduits in question to give up.

"They made me meditate," Dewalt said derisively. I snorted.

"I'm sure it was no small task. For how long?"

"Until I had a vision. Which, given that I had smoked draíbea before I left, it wasn't long before I was hallucinating." Rainier started laughing hard enough he had to wipe a tear from his eye.

"Tell her what you told them." Rainier grinned at me, raising an eyebrow and nodding. I knew whatever he said, it was going to be good.

Dewalt grinned. "I told them I saw my dead mother, telling me I'd made a good choice in Lavenia." Lavenia rolled her eyes as I joined Rainier in his laughter. Dewalt's mother had famously hated the royal family, disowning him when he chose to join the royal guard. During the time I knew him, she'd sent a yearly letter, asking him if he had come to his senses yet.

"Well, there's no way that's what you actually hallucinated." I was grinning at him, but the moment I saw Dewalt's features close off, I felt my smile fade.

"It's nothing worth mentioning." He stared down at his hands.

"He saw his own death." Lavenia's voice was sharp, cutting through the quiet with a bluntness which surprised me. Dewalt was still looking at his hands, but I saw his slow blink before he focused on me.

"I had a feeling the Myriad wouldn't appreciate that vision." An artificial smile rested on his face, and I saw the pain in his eyes. I wouldn't ask, but he must have seen something bleak.

"I had to bring him an heirloom from my family. A weapon to give him to protect me with because I'm a helpless woman." Lavenia's voice was bright as she interrupted, annoyance and amusement mixing to drown out the unpleasantness. "So, I skipped down into the crypt and grabbed one of our grandfather's swords." She shrugged, and I chuckled at the thought of her grave robbing her own grandfather.

"How was the ceremony?" I jumped on the change of subject, wanting to relieve Dewalt of the grim look in his eyes.

"LONG!" "BORING!" It worked, as they both shouted at the same exact time and laughed.

"Mind and Body was the night before. Then Soul the next morning after the Myriad confirmed our divinity."

"Confirmed it?" I didn't know what she was talking about, and Dewalt began to explain.

"Well, the Mind ceremony is what we did in front of everyone, the part where we made all those obnoxious promises." Dewalt laughed when Lavenia glared at him before she continued.

"Then the Body ceremony was later that night. A Myriad novice waited for us to demonstrate our shared abilities. Dewalt had to wake the novice up—they'd fallen asleep in an alcove in the hall. Thank the gods they can't talk. It would make it so much worse." Lavenia was cringing telling the story.

"They just waited there all night?" I was shocked and mildly disgusted. Dewalt chuckled before he answered.

"You're not supposed to leave the room until you've—well, until your divinity is fully shared and you can demonstrate it. Lavenia was lucky mine was *so weak* we had no problem." Dewalt shot a glare at Rainier, who grinned.

"Anyway, the novice escorts you to the temple the next morning. Drank from the font, all that nonsense." I was curious about what "all that nonsense" was. I'd never met a conduit who had done the ritual, other than the king and queen, and didn't think it was prudent to ask questions.

"Lucia used to joke that the font had to be full of the finest Nythyrian wine since the Myriad is so stingy with it." Dewalt's voice softened as he spoke. Rainier shot him a look, maybe of warning, but Dewalt continued. "She used to say it was why the Myriad didn't talk, because they couldn't string together words since they were drunk all the time." He smiled at me, albeit sadly.

I felt a pang in my chest. Faxon never spoke of Lucia. Elora only did in passing; it was hard for her to think of a dead aunt she'd never met. But hearing our friends speak of her? It hurt, but in a freeing sort of way, like pulling out a splinter. She had been an important part of all of our lives—the most important part of mine. And she'd been ripped away so abruptly.

"Well, was she right?" A sad smile formed on my lips.

"No, it tasted like shit." Dewalt laughed, the smile lighting up his face.

"I miss her." Lavenia's voice was quiet, barely more than a whisper. Rainier nodded in agreement.

"We missed you too." Dewalt reached out and lightly smacked my leg. And I felt lighter.

CHAPTER 10

We ate the rest of our meal in companionable silence. I wondered if they would come with me to Darkhold or if I would be on my own. Rainier had said he'd help me find Elora and then kill Faxon, but there was no way he'd actually be able to. The Crown Prince of Vesta couldn't drop what he was doing for me and my daughter. It was probably something he said in the heat of the moment when I was clearly on the verge of breaking. I knew it was something I'd have to deal with alone.

A rather loud part of me didn't want to do it alone. I'd been doing everything alone for years, and that hadn't gotten me anywhere, and this was possibly the most important thing I'd ever done. I planned to get some rest and arrange passage in the morning. I hoped Rainier would be able to help me with payment. He could ask my father for it. I assumed he'd be heading back to Ardian to finish whatever business he had with the Myriad there, and he could ask him then. I felt bad for assuming my father would cover it, but promptly decided not to care. Maybe Lavenia or Dewalt would accompany me. I wouldn't ask them, but I wasn't sure I could do this myself. Could I be trusted to make the decisions necessary to get her back?

"I plan to book passage to Mindengar in the morning. Thank you for everything you three have done for me."

"What?" Dewalt dropped his fork onto his plate with a clatter.

"I don't expect, nor will I ask any of you to come with me," I clarified.

"No." Rainier's voice was low, his eyes narrowed on me.

"No, what?" I retorted. His plate and bowl were on the ground next to him. One leg resting on top of the other, he still leaned against the closet door behind him, his arms crossed. He didn't look anything like a prince, leaning there so casually, but his tone and demeanor left no doubt.

"You're not going to Mindengar by yourself. Shit, Em, you're not going to Mindengar at all." His eyes flashed as he stared me down, recognizing my posture as combative. He still knew me well.

"She's my daughter, Rainier. I'd like to see you stop me." My chin lifted as I stared at him in defiance. As if sensing Rainier and I would enter yet another battle of wills, Lavenia gently put her hand on my arm.

"Emmeline, once they get her to Darkhold, she will be so heavily guarded, none of us would stand a chance at getting to her."

"What's your plan, Emma? Even if you can find her, how will you both get out? Alive, I might add." Dewalt's voice was kind, if patronizing.

"So, you would have me do nothing?" I didn't care if they were right. Rainier leaned forward, emerald eyes meeting mine, a glint of ferocity sparking in them.

"Of course not, Em. I expect you to wage war."

Rainier planned to petition his father, the King of Vesta, for forces and permission to negotiate. Rainier had a small contingency of his own, but not enough to take on the Folterran armies at the capital. He and Dewalt both explained that the abductors would not linger in Mindengar for long, but would take Elora straight to Darkhold, straight to the King of Bones, King Dryul. I shuddered at the thought. What could he possibly have in mind for my daughter? I hated that my only comfort was the fact she wasn't already dead.

Since the guard was already on the way west through the Whispering Wood, Rainier wanted to meet up with them on the Mirastos Path, a few days north. Dewalt had sent word by messenger crow that the plans had been updated while he and Lavenia went to get us dinner. They must have made the plans before I even knew what Faxon had done. For some reason, it meant quite a bit to me, although I guessed it might have been more for the sake of the Beloved than it was for me and my daughter. Either way, I was grateful. We would take the Mirastos straight north, past Brambleton to the Cinturon Pass. It was the only way through the Alsor Mountain range, to the west of which sat Astana, Vesta's capital. Rainier couldn't rift us that far in one swoop, and it had been so long since he'd been on the Mirastos he didn't trust his ability to pinpoint locations for rifting to break up the trip.

Once in Astana, Rainier would appeal to King Soren. I had little confidence he'd be able to convince his father. Rainier's presence demanded respect, and he'd grown into a strategic and revered leader. His father, on the other hand, didn't have a reputation for being amenable. The man I remembered was cold and calculating, seeming to view Lucia's death as no more than an inconvenience.

A vivid memory of Rainier fighting with his father came to mind. It was a memory I'd forgotten in the years since, but talking about the king had brought it to the forefront of my memory. In the hours after Rainier returned with me from the caves and the hours before Lucia's burial at Ravemont, I'd seen Rainier and his father arguing. They were walking the grounds while I sat inside my room, staring out the window, enveloped in the shroud of grief which would be my companion for a long time to come. I'd watched in a daze, not truly paying attention, until I saw flames at the tips of King Soren's fingers. His hands were at his sides, a picture of calm, while his son was the opposite, all flailing arms and what appeared to be harsh words. When Queen Shivani met them in the garden, I was relieved and closed my curtains.

"What if your father says no?" I asked, wary of his ideas. My daughter's life was counting on his cooperation.

"He won't." Rainier's eyes were a forest at night and held the same danger. "If he says no, I have enough pull. I'll get us the soldiers we need." Those eyes looked into mine, full of sincerity. "I promise, Em, I'm with you on this. Until the end."

Dewalt and Rainier began to talk strategy, referring to different groups within the Vestian armies and where they would be best suited for a siege on Darkhold. How was it less than a week ago I was telling my daughter goodbye and to be safe, and now I was with the Crown Prince of Vesta, planning to go to war for her? I was feeling particularly useless. I had nothing to add to their strategies. I was so far outside my depth that just trying to listen to them was making my head ache. Not that any of the day's events had been any easier to follow.

Elora was on her way to Folterra. *My* Elora—the baby I nursed at my breast, the toddler I'd taught letters to, the little girl who loved to read, and the teenager who was just starting to understand her responsibilities. The desperation I felt made my stomach hurt and bile rise in my throat. But underneath the sick taste, coating my throat and clawing through my insides, was anger. Bitter anger. I started to think of Faxon and his gambling. How could I have no idea what he was doing? I would have called him a wolf in sheep's clothing, but Faxon was no wolf. He had always been terribly average. He had acted meek and mild, relying on his father to instill fear in me, but I'd never once doubted his love for Elora, even if he did the bare minimum as a father.

I started retracing my memories, searching for the moment things might have fallen apart. He'd always resented moving to Brambleton. After Lucia's death,

Faxon's offer for my hand was the only one that still stood, and my father didn't hesitate. Ravemont was thought to be cursed after what happened, so he was eager to hand me off before Faxon could change his mind. My husband was willing to risk a curse, but he didn't expect to get shuffled off to the middle of nowhere with a small stipend to sustain us. But was any of it more than a nuisance when it came to keeping our daughter safe? I did everything right. I left my life at Ravemont behind. I left behind the chance of any sort of reconciliation with my friends, regardless of whether I wanted it at the time or not. It was something I had thought about a lot over the years. I poured myself into protecting her and running our household, only for him to waste all my efforts over debts he caused. I could feel it then, a knot growing in my stomach. A hard and sharp knot telling me if I ever saw him again, he'd be dead in one way or another. But I wanted to be the one to do it. I pictured watching the light flicker out of his eyes and did not feel anything but fury over what he'd done.

If I'm Aonara's favored, you're Hanwen's. No one would ever cross you if they knew the wrath you'd bring upon them.

Lucia's voice flowed through my head, like the ripples thrown off by a tossed pebble hitting water.

"You know, Lucia always hated Faxon." I blurted it out loud. Dewalt and Rainier looked confused for a moment, as if what I said had anything to do with strategy. I'd spoken of Lucia earlier, and it was like a dam had broken. I wanted to talk about her with people who loved her. I'd been deprived of it for so long.

Lavenia snorted.

"Who didn't?" I glanced at her, surprised. No one but Lucia had ever voiced how they felt about him. Not even Rainier, other than that last day when he told me not to marry him. But my father had already accepted the offer by then. Dewalt's head turned slightly to his best friend, an expression on his face I couldn't quite read.

"I barely knew him. I only met him once, that last summer at the cottage." Dewalt didn't take his eyes off Rainier as he spoke. I didn't know why he seemed worried about Rainier; it wasn't as if he'd wanted me either. He'd said as much before we felt the impulses in our arms, only moments after he'd slid himself inside me, pulling us from the cavern before we had time to finish anything, let alone our conversation. My parents were bound to give me to the highest bidder as soon as possible, and, as luck would have it, Faxon was the only bidder.

"I didn't know him either." The laugh I gave was cold. "He was persistent with Father, and he was the only one still interested after—after Lucia died. I never understood her hatred for him, though."

"The others withdrew their offers?"

"You knew there weren't many to start with. Father accepted the morning of the burial, the same morning the other offers were rescinded. He was the only one who wanted me." My laugh was bitter. Faxon's dreams of being the lord of an estate such as Ravemont were not fazed by a potential curse. I glanced up to Dewalt and saw him snap his jaw shut, eyes wide at Rainier, who let out a long breath, as if he'd been holding it.

"You know gods damn well that's not true." Rainier finally looked at me then, eyes violent, and I wished he hadn't.

"Do I? Only one offer sat on my father's desk that morning, Rainier." I tried to match the anger in his eyes, but all I felt was sadness. And I was sure he saw it. He never took back his words, never said anything to make me think otherwise. I'd begged him on the cliff side, but he didn't give me another option, hadn't wanted to. He'd told me the same thing in the cavern the night before. We couldn't. But none of it mattered. Lucia was dead, and I didn't care what happened to me. I didn't care if my parents wanted to get rid of me. "I didn't have a choice." My voice was almost a whisper, my eyes only on Rainier, the others forgotten.

He watched me for a moment, contemplative.

"Maybe none of us thought we had choices back then. But we were wrong. We did. We had choices, and we still do." The violent flicker in his eyes had gone out, replaced by sadness which matched mine.

Still do.

"Lucia knew you deserved more, Emmeline, needed more. And she knew Faxon couldn't give it to you. It's a shame she turned out so right." Rainier shook his head and sat up straight, graciously ending the conversation.

I sat still for a few minutes. He was right though; Lucia had always wanted more for me. She knew I didn't want Faxon. Even if I had never confirmed to her I'd wanted Rainier, it was plain enough I would never desire the man I ended up marrying. She even thought I could be appointed to her royal guard, which, looking back, was almost laughable. She was a dreamer. And I hadn't accomplished a single thing she'd dreamt for me. Except maybe to have a family, but even that was flawed thanks to my traitorous husband. I hung my head, sensing the heat of Rainier's gaze on me, feeling a rise of flushed skin up my neck.

"He thought he'd be Lord of Ravemont by now. Is that why he'd betray us?" My voice was small. I was grasping for some way this wasn't my fault. I hadn't seen what he was doing. I hadn't loved him the way someone should love their husband. I'd been a fool to trust him.

"Does it matter why he did it? Does it change anything?"

I shook my head no. Either way he would bleed.

My eyes popped open, and I was disoriented for a moment. I was in bed. I must have fallen asleep on the floor listening to Dewalt and Rainier strategize. Lavenia was asleep next to me, and I had a vague memory of Rainier rousing me and helping me get into bed, pulling the blankets over me. The door creaked shut, and I realized it must have been what woke me. The tall figure in the doorway turned, bolting the door, and when a streak of moonlight from the window hit Rainier's face, I relaxed.

He unbuckled the scabbard he was wearing and gently placed it on the floor. I watched him, taking in the man he'd turned into. It was strange to see him so much older. It was something akin to reading your favorite childhood book as an adult. There was a comfort in the familiarity, and yet a different appreciation for things gone unnoticed before. He walked past the foot of the bed to the chair by the window, moving with a feline grace. He'd been trained in all manner of skills, including stealth, and his movements were proof he retained the mastery. Turned slightly away from me, he unbuttoned his shirt, and a sliver of moonlight moved across his back. He sat down in the chair and removed his boots. I realized he had been keeping watch, likely where Dewalt was now. Having only traveled with the prince once, to participate in the Summer Solstice event in Ardian, it was easy for me to forget what it was like—always prepared against a potential threat. He leaned back in the chair, hands behind his head and limbs outstretched, bare heels propped on the ground. My eyes followed the long line of his legs. Though he had breeches on, I could tell he was more muscular than the man I remembered. My eyes traced up the strip of bare stomach and chest, muscles taut in his stretch. He was so different but so much the same. I wondered if he thought about me that way. Did he notice all the ways I'd changed? My gaze lifted to his face and found him looking back at me. Instinctively, I shut my eyes tight.

"You awake, Em?" He spoke quietly, almost seductive.

"I just woke up and thought you might want a blanket," I lied.

"No, I'm warm enough. A pillow would be nice, though." I could hear the smile in his voice. Grabbing one of the pillows I'd been sleeping on, I tossed it at his face. I regretted it within the same instant as I heard a thump on the ground and realized I'd knocked the conch shell off my nightstand.

"Hey now, don't start something you can't finish." I smiled despite myself as I climbed out of bed.

"Sorry about the pants." I stopped and looked down, not sure what he meant when I saw my pants on and intact. "I know wearing them to bed isn't your preference, but I thought you'd be more mad if I removed them." He shot me a wolfish grin.

I huffed a laugh. "You were right." I lowered myself to the floor as I bent over.

"What are you doing?" I heard the amusement in his voice.

"Trying to find the shell I just knocked off the nightstand."

"Do you want me to open the curtain more?"

"Sure." I was on my hands and knees reaching underneath the bed, tracing my fingertips over the floor. I knew the light of the moon wouldn't be much, but it would be better than nothing. When the curtain opened, silver light spilling over the floor, I lowered myself down to search under the bed instead of just reaching blindly. I froze when I heard a small grunt behind me.

I sat up, still on my knees, and turned to look over my shoulder. Rainier was still seated in his chair, but his eyes were on me. I couldn't read his expression in the dim moonlight, so I cocked my head to the side in question. He didn't reply. "It's rude to stare." I bent back down, continuing in my search. I was oddly attached to the shell Rainier had bought for me, and I wanted to put it safely in my pack.

"Oh, that's rich. You're allowed to look at me all you want, but I'm not allowed to look at you?" His quiet words sent my heart racing.

I slowly sat up and eyed him over my shoulder. Surely, I misunderstood what he meant. My eyes met his, moonlight illuminating the side of his face, and I saw something in them I hadn't seen from anyone in a long time, let alone him. I watched his gaze trace hungrily down my body, stalling over my backside. I felt my pulse quicken, and I couldn't help myself as I reached out, listening to his fast heartbeat. A part of me felt triumphant, knowing I was having an effect on him, as he was on me.

So, I did it again.

Bending back over, I resumed my search, only half looking for the shell at this point. I didn't know why I did it, maybe to torture him like he'd been torturing me, or perhaps because it felt good to know he still found me appealing after all these years. I heard a long, slow exhale of breath behind me and knew I'd accomplished something. But why did I want to? Spreading my arm wide under the bed, my fingertips brushed up against something cool and smooth.

"Yes!" I whispered in satisfaction as I found the shell and sat up. I heard a disappointed noise come from Rainier as I stood up and took it over to my pack in the corner. I turned to the window Rainier sat in front of, reaching past him to pull the curtains closed. He was relaxed back in the chair, his legs outstretched and hands clasped across his stomach, the strip of skin from his open shirt visible in the moonlight. I didn't bother stopping my eyes from their sweep down his body as he watched me, able to tell exactly what I was doing.

"You just look so different. It's strange, almost like you're a completely different person. Your muscles have muscles now." I felt embarrassed at the admission, but at the same time proud of myself for being honest. "I'll try to stop, since it bothers you."

He let out a huff of laughter. As I turned back to the bed, he lightly grabbed my wrist.

"I never said it bothered me. You look quite different, too." I watched him as his eyes searched mine, the moonlight hitting my arm where his hand held my wrist. "You're somehow more beautiful now." I felt my breath hitch at his words, and I averted my gaze, lightly tugging my wrist out of his hand before I returned to the bed.

"Goodnight, Rainier." I laid back onto my single pillow, significantly less comfortable than two.

"Goodnight, Emmeline." I heard stirring and peeked up to see him completely remove his shirt. Even when his eyes caught mine, I didn't look away.

I'd pushed my back against the wall of the cave, and water was coming up past my knees. Shaking from cold or fear, I wasn't sure, I began to wonder if I should just give in to the water. It wouldn't be too difficult to just sit down and lay in it. I wondered if I'd freeze to death first or drown. Would I be able to stop myself from treading water or would my reflexes fight my death? Would anyone find my body before I was nothing but bones?

I realized then, almost reluctantly, that Rain would find me long before my body decayed, but too late to do anything about it. He'd search every cave until he found my bloated corpse. I hoped he wouldn't blame himself, although this was entirely his fault. It wasn't his job to keep me safe. In fact, it was his job to keep Lucia safe. I couldn't think about her right now. She'd collapsed, and Rain had haphazardly tossed me through a rift. He would have rushed to her side and helped her escape the cloud of...vipers. My healing abilities were no match for large injuries, but surely, I could be of some use, at least until a true healer could get to us. But I was of no use in this cave and would be of no use in general soon.

For some reason, I was completely calm as the water slowly rose halfway up my thigh. I was wearing my favorite dress. I couldn't see it in the dark, but I could feel the bottom of it floating around me. It was blue-grey linen which matched my eyes. It was simple, but it accented the curves of my body in a way I appreciated. Lucia had a matching dress in crimson. Mother loved when we wore them at the same time. "Fire and ice, my darlings." Which of course I hated, but Lucia loved. My mother had always been closer to my sister than she was to me. Lucia loved the political intrigue which accompanied being betrothed to the Crown Prince. She loved to dress in the exquisite gowns and charm everyone. It wasn't the dresses I hated though. It was the fact I would never shine as bright as her, something everyone accepted and didn't question. Except Rain.

As if prompted by my thoughts of him, I felt a dull hurt between my legs. Even though he'd been more gentle than I could ever imagine, and it only lasted a moment before we had to stop, the ache remained. At least the cold water did something to numb the pain, though it did nothing to soften what he'd said. Gods, it was pathetic that I was on the edge of drowning, and yet embarrassment was going to be one of my final emotions. I really was stupid enough to think he was going to tell me he loved me, and then he'd done the opposite. What a fool I'd been. One good thing about letting myself die meant I'd never have to talk about it.

The water had come to rest at my shoulders, and my feet were numb. I realized my body might not be able to fight, whether I wanted to or not. I began to jump up and down in the water in an attempt to warm myself. Images of fires and Lucia's warm light flickered behind my eyes. Coals in the kitchen when the servants baked. Oh, warm stew in my stomach. A warm hand on my stomach, warm lips on my bare shoulder. A warm body pressed into mine. Blood rushing through my veins, my heart pounding. His heart pounding.

Wait.

I splashed myself in the face with water. I'd lost my mind, and I was freezing. I wasn't hearing anything. That didn't stop me from reaching out again.

There it was. A faint heartbeat, and it was sprinting.

"I'm here! I'm here!"

I doubted they could hear me. It might be someone above me, observing the ocean as waves pounded into the cliffs, unaware of my demise in the ground below them. But it wouldn't explain why it was racing. It had to have been him.

The heartbeat was getting louder.

"Rainier! I'm here!" I was sobbing and screaming, terrified he wouldn't get to me in time. It was rising too fast, and I had to start treading water, the cave ceiling swiftly approaching. At the rate it was filling, I thought I only had moments.

Our heartbeats echoed, the only sound I could hear over my gasping breaths.

I heard the sound of a rift opening, and it was him. Rainier was here, soaking wet, barely tall enough to stand. But he was here, and he'd found me. He must have rifted into cave after cave, searching for me. He pulled me to him, pressing me against his chest as I let out a sob.

"I've got you, Em. I've got you."

CHAPTER 11

The next morning, I woke up frustrated. I hadn't dreamt about the caves in years, yet the memory had taken over my subconscious. Questioning the man in the cellar was apparently a bad idea. Being around Rainier probably didn't help, either. I was angry that I kept revisiting old wounds in my sleep. So, when my eyes finally opened and everyone else was already awake, Dewalt and Rainier staring at me, I popped up onto my elbow and lost my temper.

"What? Why are you two staring at me?"

"We were trying to decide who would have the displeasure of waking you up." Rainier gave me his crooked smile, but it still didn't quell my annoyance.

"And you both decided to stare at me until I woke up?" I glared.

"Well, we were going to draw lots, but you just looked so peaceful." Dewalt was sitting in the chair Rainier had slept in, picking at his nails. His raven hair was braided down his back, and I watched as his tongue darted out in concentration.

"We aren't leaving until midday, to time our meeting up with the guard. We're used to being on the road. You aren't. We thought you should get as much rest as possible." Lavenia's voice grew softer as she spoke only to me. "You've tossed and turned a lot; I know you're not sleeping well."

My chest felt tight at the realization she'd been paying that much attention to how I was doing. "Well, thank you." I inhaled, pulling my emotions together as I sat up and beheld the two men in the room. "I could do without the scowling, though."

"I'm not scowling." Dewalt harrumphed. "But if you want me to be honest, I was looking because I'm still in shock you're even here." It almost felt like he was expecting an apology.

Lavenia averted her eyes from me, glancing at her brother. He was leaning against the wall across from the bed, one arm crossing his body and the other arm up, a fist resting against his mouth. The sleeves of his white shirt were rolled up—the fabric crisp against his brown skin, showing the curvature of his muscles.

No one had any business looking so handsome quite so early in the morning. Dewalt might not have been, but Rainier was definitely scowling, his crooked smile replaced by a clenched jaw. His eyes were a mossy green color today, and they softened as they met mine. As I held his gaze, I noticed his jaw relax and the tension release. I never would have imagined myself here either. With people who had been family to me, with a man I thought I loved all those years ago. It wasn't easy for me either. My heart ached, and I felt my face fall. Rainier didn't break the contact, continuing to watch the warring emotions crossing my face. Maybe I did owe them an apology. Dewalt and Lavenia hadn't done anything wrong, it was me. I blinked, breaking my trance, and I turned to Dewalt.

"I know it's probably strange for you. It's strange for me too. This is all under terrible circumstances, but—" I paused, taking a breath. The three of them had dropped everything for me the moment I asked. I wondered what would have happened if I hadn't pushed so hard and so far away from them all those years ago. If I had been able to forgive myself and Rainier, if I was there to comfort my friends and let them comfort me, things could have been different. I wondered if Rainier and I would have been friends, successfully moved past what happened between us. "But I'm glad I'm here. I—I have a lot of regrets." Dewalt stopped picking at his nails to glance up. He wasn't smiling, but his frown had lessened. I took it as a good sign.

"Thank you for helping me." I looked around at the three of them. Dewalt and Lavenia both nodded, but Rainier didn't indicate he had heard me at all, an inscrutable expression on his face. I wondered if he had regrets too. His expression made me wonder if he knew most of mine involved him. Did he find it as hard to be around me as I found it to be around him? I met his gaze and held it. I wasn't certain about any of this. There was too much between us—time and pain—to even begin to delve into. I decided it was best not to entertain any of it.

"While Lavenia and I make necessary arrangements, you'll be training with Dewalt." Rainier suddenly pushed off the wall, walking to the door. "Unless you've been practicing?" He tilted his head, a smile tugging on one side of his mouth. He probably already knew the answer. I glared at him, but I was actually grateful. The scuffle with the men at home had been too close for my liking. I was still good with my bow, but my hand-to-hand combat and sword fighting were lacking. I'd only had Theo to spar with, and it wasn't exactly challenging to train with him since I'd been the one to teach him what he knew. Not to mention he had quite a few responsibilities, so it had been a while since I'd been able to train with him at all.

Lavenia and I had trained together when we were younger. My father had been reluctant to allow it until Lucia intervened, arguing with exuberance for her protection, and even then, he barely approved. Dewalt and Rainier would take time to teach Lavenia and me outside of our other lessons, Lucia shouting encouragement from under the shade of a tree. I fondly remembered the first time I ever disarmed Rainier. He'd gotten cocky since he had a much longer reach than me. He had attempted an overhanded swing when I was just too far away, and I'd pushed forward at the last second, smacking his sword to the ground. He'd tackled me afterwards, playfully angry he'd been bested. We'd all been in the meadow that day, drinking in the sun and laughter.

"Don't worry about him. He's gotten lazy with his sword the more he relies on his divinity." Lavenia grinned. I was curious to see what she meant. He'd gotten better at rifting, by far. But I wondered what it was he could do that made him less reliant on his sword. I'd seen a bit of it in the cellar, but it wasn't far off from his capabilities as I'd known them. That reminded me.

"What happened to the deckhand? After the cellar?" I questioned.

"He found himself without a head." Rainier had the audacity to shrug as he said it. I stared.

"You *killed* him?" I was shocked. The man was a criminal, but that didn't mean he deserved death. A vision of Rainier kicking the bound man in the jaw entered my mind, a savagery I'd never seen from him before.

"War has a price, Emmeline. You know that better than anyone. I cannot afford to be weak. The man was a traitor, whether he knew Elora was the Beloved or not."

I wondered what else he'd done so as not to appear weak. What exactly had earned him the title of the Bloody Prince to the Folterrans? Beheading a traitor was a start.

"You sound like your father." I knew I was crossing a line, but I didn't care. King Soren was vicious and ruled with an iron fist. Rainier had always detested his father's methods, and it bothered me to know he'd do something so much like him. Today wasn't going to be a good one. I hadn't even gotten out of bed yet, and I was comparing Rainier to a man he'd sworn to never turn into. His next words chilled me.

"I know."

Dewalt and I went down the large hill to a small beach near the docks. The ground was more rocky than it was sandy, but it would do. The port city was built atop the sprawling ruins of a temple created to praise one of the old gods. Within the less populated areas of the city, it was easy to see some of the still-standing ruins upon which Mira had been built. Large slabs of rock, polished by the sea, made up most of the shoreline. We found a flat area, which was no small feat, and cleared out some of the bigger rocks still in our way. Dewalt must have truly lost all faith in me because he told me not to bring a sword, and he only wanted to work on physical conditioning. I knew I was going to be sore after.

Starting out with stretching, Dewalt was still uncharacteristically quiet.

"What is it?" I sighed, one arm across my chest, stretching as far as I could reach.

"Nothing, Emmeline." If he wanted to be quiet and weird with me, fine. Everything had happened so fast, and it only made sense he might struggle with it. I knew I was struggling.

After stretching, he made me do squats followed by a jump into the air. Over and over again. When I was finally done with the repetitions he desired, I was sweating. I wiped my brow with the back of my hand and reached for the canteen I'd brought down from the room. It was Rainier's, but since I didn't have one, he let me borrow it, handing it over to me without a sound before Dewalt and I left the room. After taking a few swigs from it, I was still panting.

"You wanted to start with swords, and here you are, huffing over squat-jumps." His normal joking tone was missing, and his demeanor was aggressive with arms crossed over his body and a glare pointed in my direction.

"Well, I haven't been getting into many sword fights in Brambleton. Apologies." I could tell Dewalt was on the verge of something, and I didn't want to be on the receiving end, so I attempted to remain lighthearted.

"No, you've just been hiding in Brambleton like a coward." I froze, the canteen halfway to my mouth, before I lowered it again.

"I was protecting Elora, I had to." He struck a nerve. I did feel like a coward almost every day. Scared to live, scared to do anything. Cold fear dominated my decisions and every interaction I ever had.

"And we're seeing firsthand what it got you." I physically jolted backwards at his words. I didn't think I'd ever seen Dewalt this angry at all, let alone with me. Even after I'd come back, he'd been easygoing and playful, never indicating he might feel so strongly about this situation. It didn't feel good.

"I've never known you to be cruel." I was willing to let the three of them say things to me I knew I probably deserved—within reason—but he crossed a line. He dragged a hand down his face, clearly frustrated.

"You're right, I shouldn't have said that, but . . ." He trailed off, like he had thought better of what he wanted to say. With his mouth a thin straight line and his brows furrowed, he seemed older. His anger transformed him into one of the Bloody Prince's most trusted advisers and captains. I was surprised I hadn't seen him as such until now, when his anger was directed toward me. I tried to hide my expression, the hurt probably clearly visible on my face, and he let out a long sigh. "I just need to say some things to you and then move past it. I don't like this—" He gestured in the air between us. "And I want to go back to annoying the shit out of each other, but I have to get some things off my chest."

I didn't say anything, just watched him and waited. He was standing, arms still crossed, tapping a foot irritably. Finally, I nodded, submitting to his demand to speak. I hoped it would be quick because I wanted to move past it as well. I wanted to move past everything. I wanted to stop having nightmares, I wanted to find my daughter, I wanted to figure out my place in this new world.

"You weren't the only one who lost Lucia."

My eyebrows shot up. "I'm her twin."

"Shut up and let me talk." I nodded, feeling properly reprimanded. I had agreed to let him speak, and I was interrupting. "Losing Lucia was the worst thing that's ever fucking happened to me. But then we lost you too. *He* lost you too. And you've just been in Brambleton, having babies, and doing what? Nothing?"

"Baby. Singular. And I've been protecting her, Dewalt."

"Protecting her from who, us? Where is she now, Emma?"

"I'm not going to deal—" I spun away from him, ready to head back to the inn, when he grabbed my wrist. Lightly enough it didn't hurt, but hard enough I'd have to pull free from him. I knew better than anyone how terribly I'd failed at protecting my daughter, and his reminder rubbed raw what little control of my emotions I had left.

"You destroyed him that day, at the burial. Do you even know who healed him, Emma? After you stabbed him?" His eyes were hateful daggers, regarding me in disgust. He acted as if I'd caught Rainier unawares, stabbing him out of hate. I didn't know who healed him after though. I'd left, rushing back to Ravemont from the family crypt. I didn't remember much from that day. I remembered talking to Rainier at the cliff side near the crypts, and he'd blocked my exit when I wanted to leave. To run. The memory forced itself upon me clearly, as if the autumn wind whipping around us was only the beginning of a summer storm from long ago.

He grabbed me, pulling me toward the cliffs. It began to rain, a cool summer drizzle driving the temperature down. I remembered feeling the slick stone underneath my shoes, willing myself to slip, to fall, to hurt. To feel. I remembered the black dress I wore that day—Lucia would have hated it. It was itchy, and too many layers of the thick linen in the summer heat were making me sweat. Running from Rainier added to it. He'd cornered me before the burial too, talking to me about who was responsible. I'd escaped him after insisting it was us who deserved to pay for her death.

"Don't marry him, Em."

"What do you expect from me, Rain? I have no choice."

"I can talk to my father to stop it."

"Why? Lucia is dead because of us, and you've made your feelings clear enough. What else do I have? Faxon will take care of Rav—"

"And what will you do, Em? You want to be mistress of Ravemont, popping out heirs for Faxon? Planning little parties and deciding what color flowers the garden will be each spring?" His tone had turned hateful, and I was grateful for it. Anger was easier for me to handle than anything else.

"You know that's not what I want."

"Then why are you doing it?"

"Give me a reason not to!"

"Because it isn't what you want!"

"Then what do I want, Rainier? Who do I want?"

His shoulders sagged as his gaze met mine. His throat was working, but nothing came out. His eyes begged me not to ask him; we already knew the answer.

"Exactly. Give me a reason not to or let me go."

"I—I can't, Em. It's not—we can't. It's not up for discussion."

I remembered the anger and the hurt and the shame. His words echoed what he'd said in the cave before we were called away. We can't. And yet here he was, asking me to defy my father, my parents. The two people who just buried one daughter due to actions from the other. I had no interest in marrying Faxon, but I had even less interest in hurting them further for no reason. I had begged him. I'd begged him for a reason, and he wouldn't give it. Noting the sword across his back and the other strapped to his hip, I challenged him to first blood. When the words registered, the look on his face was one I hoped to forget.

"First blood, and you'll let me go. Completely. I don't want to see you again."

In the moments that followed, I realized part of him gave up the second I made my request. When I hit him in the ribs, drawing blood, I turned to leave. It was then when he'd said those things to me, kneeling on the ground with his hand on his side.

"You are a cruel fool, Emmeline. Your words are poison. You are poison."

I stepped closer to him, only having to bend slightly to reach him, and kissed him softly on the cheek.

"Goodbye, Rain."

And then I ran.

"Who healed him?" My voice was quiet and weak in the aftermath of that visceral recollection. I hadn't thought about him then, even if I spent many moments over the years wondering about what happened after I left.

"Your mother, Emma." She'd never told me. "But what's worse is you didn't even have the decency to see him when he came to Ravemont. We didn't even know you left until, what, a year after? We heard rumors you left Vesta. We searched for you. We've *been* searching for you.

"But I thought he was finally over it and moving on. For the good of the kingdom, but also for the good of himself. And now you're back, and I am happy. We all are. You have no idea how hard it was at the beginning without you both. You destroyed him when you left, and, while I hope he forgives you for shutting him out, I'm finding it difficult."

I wondered how recently they'd been looking for me. Surely, he only meant at the beginning, right after I left. When Rainier had gone to Ravemont, and the welcome wasn't *she won't see you* and became *she isn't here*. I didn't understand why he would still care after I was gone. He'd made everything perfectly clear to me. It wasn't up for discussion, so why was he having to move on? I did him a favor by removing myself from his life. But what if it hadn't been? What would my life have been like if I didn't cut them off and run away? Would Elora be safe right now, protected by the Crown? Maybe Rainier and his father could have prevented my marriage. I wouldn't have Elora, but who knew where my life might have gone. I swallowed, pushing the feeling of regret down as deep as I could. Dewalt noted the movement, and he took a breath.

"I swear to the gods, if you destroy him again, Emma…If we get your daughter back and you disappear again, Hanwen help me I will not be held responsible for what I do. Do not make him lose you twice. You have no idea what his life has been like since that day, none."

Something in his eyes surprised me. I'd never seen Dewalt so earnest. As if the thought of watching his friend go through something like that was too much to bear. I wondered for a second how Rainier reacted back then to make Dewalt this protective. He was watching me expectantly, wanting assurances I wasn't sure I could give. I didn't know where things would fall once I got Elora back. I knew we couldn't go back to Brambleton, just the two of us. The secret was out, and I clearly needed more capable protectors, at least for a few more years. Could I just fall back into this life with them? And Rainier—I stopped myself. I'd think about it once Elora was back.

I stared down at my feet. I wasn't sure when all my fear and sadness and anger from all those years ago started turning into nothing but regret, but it was making me come to uncomfortable realizations.

"I'm sorry." I knew they probably thought what I did was selfish. And maybe I should have seen Rainier when he came to Ravemont. But each time I saw his face, all I could think about was the look my sister gave me when she saw us run through the rift, disheveled and red-faced. I'd betrayed her on her last day, and we were the cause of the attack. She probably died hating me, and I hated myself for it. And seeing Rainier back then brought it all back up for me. I was angry with him for convincing me with his crooked smile and a stolen kiss to bring down the wards so we could sneak to the cavern. I was angry with him for throwing me in those caves. And I was angry he didn't love me—not in the way I did him. I didn't have the benefit of time then, to work everything out. My sister died, I was married, I was pregnant, then I was a mother—all within a year. I was a mother with a child who was destined for the same fate as my sister, and I'd barely had time to process any of the rest of it by then.

I'd had plenty of time now, though, to prepare myself to see his beautiful face without feeling the guilt try to suffocate me. Now, it stoked regret more than anything else. Regret that I'd let my guilt and anger turn us into strangers.

"Just promise me you won't disappear again, Emma."

"I promise. I promise I won't disappear." It was a promise I hoped I wouldn't have to break. For their sake and my own.

After another hour of exercising on the beach, we headed back to the inn to meet up with Rainier and Lavenia. I was glad Dewalt got the things off his chest he needed to, and he kept his word and went straight back to annoying me.

"I saw the dagger, but do you have anything else on you?" My hand traced the hilt of the blade strapped to my thigh, worn and perfectly suited for my hand.

"None here. My bow is with Bree."

"Helpful. I, too, like to leave my weapons somewhere else, rendering them useless." I shot a glare at him.

"I don't see you carrying all your weapons! All you've got is your sword." He lifted a regal brow at me and stopped, bending down to lift up his pant leg. An ankle sheath was hidden below it. He grinned up at me.

"I have my bandolier in the room." I hadn't seen the bandolier, but it didn't surprise me. Dewalt had always loved throwing knives.

"Point taken. I'll have my bow when I have my horse. I'm still good at that, at least." He smiled then, and I was hopeful things would be better between the two of us.

On our walk back, Dewalt began to update me on the king and queen. I'd heard rumors of King Soren's ailing health, but Dewalt explained just how bad it had gotten in recent years, the king's temper significantly worse because of it.

"He was always an asshole, you probably remember. Cruel."

I remembered. Always paranoid and quick to extinguish any perceived threats, I'd thought King Soren wasn't much better than the Folterran king. My heart sank. As much as I didn't like the fact Rainier executed the man from the cellar, to compare him to his father was low. Even for me.

"But now," he gave a low whistle, "he's even worse. I think it's part of why Rainier has been so involved with the Cascade. To stay away."

"The Cascade?"

"The fort in Folterra?" He watched my expression and one of surprise crossed his face. "I'm shocked you haven't heard of it. It's Rainier's project. Even though the two kings haven't come to any sort of agreement, we've been laying the groundwork for a treaty."

"And King Soren approves of this?"

Dewalt huffed a dark laugh. I looked up the hill. We were only halfway up, and my thighs were already burning.

"Of course not. He knows the fort is there but doesn't know Rainier has been quietly working with the locals. The Folterrans there are pretty bad off. Honestly, having the fort nearby seems to be helping them. The soldiers spend money in their markets. And I've personally trained the men and women who are stationed there. Rainier thinks it's good planning for the future, once his father is gone."

"And the King of Bones? He doesn't have a problem with the fort being there?" I surprised myself when I mentioned my sister's murderer and daughter's captor so nonchalantly. I felt my blood start to simmer in a mix of fear and anger.

"From my understanding, the minute we set foot there, he wrote off the peninsula. The soil isn't particularly fertile, the people are mostly women and children, the men being forced into his armies. I'm sure if we pushed farther into the kingdom, it would be a problem, but so far he's done little to deter us."

I nodded. I was surprised about Rainier's willingness to work with Folterra. These were the people responsible for Lucia's death. Though I supposed the villagers were innocent—they didn't kill my sister. I was more guilty than they were. I was having a hard time reconciling the Rainier who craved peace with the one who killed the man from the cellar and promised me someone's head. Not even counting the Rain I'd always known who sat somewhere in between. It was difficult to wrap my mind around. We turned the corner and saw Lavenia and Rainier outside in front of the inn, saddling the horses.

"It drives Queen Shivani crazy. She wants him at the palace."

"Then why isn't he in Astana?"

"We were staying at Crown Cottage after our last visit to the Cascade."

I shuddered. Why would he want to stay there? I couldn't think of the place without thinking of that night.

"Trust me, I struggle with it too." Dewalt's voice was soft as he noticed my shudder. "But the alternative is Astana with the queen. She's worried. King Soren is over 900 years old, and she doubts Rainier's seriousness about the Crown when he hasn't performed the ritual."

"Why hasn't he? I'm sure the queen has found him a suitable conduit."

"Yes, and a few of them would bring some sort of benefit or alliance to Vesta, and yet he refuses to perform it." He glanced over at me, a soft expression on his face as I saw Lavenia approach us from the corner of my eye.

"You two ready? We could only find three horses with this short notice. So, I guess you two get to pick who is sharing with me until we meet up with the guard." She flashed a grin.

"Not it." Dewalt and I replied simultaneously.

We'd been on the road for about an hour, Lavenia firmly planted in front of Dewalt, when I reached into my pocket and realized Elora's necklace was missing. Trying to keep calm, I thought about the last time I'd held it. I couldn't remember touching it once today, and I wondered if it fell out of my pocket onto the floor and got left behind at the inn. I'd been distracted with the confrontation with Dewalt and the exercising, keeping my mind from the idle thoughts which terrified me and made my blood run cold. Those thoughts were what had been bringing the necklace into my hand, turning it into a worry stone of sorts. And now that I was on the road with nothing but thoughts, I noticed its absence.

Rainier and Lavenia had packed our bags while Dewalt and I trained. I was about to hop down and start digging through them, to get my shell out and trace its edges to calm me, but instead took a breath and counted to ten. I could do this like a sane person. I pictured myself bursting into hysterics on the side of the road over the missing necklace, and I wanted to tamp down that energy. Instead, I turned myself back toward Dewalt and Lavenia, riding behind me.

"Ven, did you see Elora's necklace this morning when you packed up? I can't find it." The automatic use of her old nickname surprised me, but if it showed on my face Lavenia made no notice.

Her brows met, and she shook her head no.

"Did you ask Rainier yet?" I grimaced before turning forward on my mare.

Rainier was quite a bit ahead of us on the path. He had surged forward shortly after we got on the road, and I had the sense he wanted to be alone. He hadn't said more than formalities since I compared him to his father. A knot formed in my stomach. I needed to apologize; it was unfair of me to say what I did. After talking to Dewalt, it was clear I didn't know much about Rainier anymore, what he'd been doing under his father's nose. I pressed my heels into my mare, pushing her until we caught up with him. His back was unusually straight, and he wasn't wearing his cloak, the sun beating down on us warm enough. He was holding his head in such a way he wasn't Rainier to me, but the Crown Prince, something I'd quickly shaken off in only two days. As if he sensed me staring at the back of his neck, he reached up and rubbed it, almost wearily. I pushed my heels in again and forced my mare next to him.

"Hello." I blurted out, cringing a bit. He turned his head slightly and gave me a smile which didn't reach his eyes. I would never get used to seeing his eyes again—the different shades of green had been in my dreams and nightmares alike. They looked more gold than green as we made our way through the forest full of fall leaves, their oranges and reds reflecting into his irises.

"Hello, Emmeline." He nodded to me, a picture of civility.

"Dewalt told me about the Cascade." I felt like I needed to make up for what I'd said to him earlier, when I'd compared him to his father. His cold demeanor caught me off guard and apologizing to him became my top priority. I'd ask him about the necklace after I fixed things.

"Did he, now? And what do you think?"

"I can't say I understood it at first." I let out a breath, watching him for a reaction before I continued.

"And now? I wouldn't think you'd be very pleased with the idea of working with the Folterrans." He was guarded, as if he was waiting for me to strike at him, and I felt that tinge of regret again.

"Dewalt explained. It's a good idea." I surprised myself with the admission, but it was true. The Three Kingdoms had been looking for an easy way out with the Beloved, not willing to work on their actions themselves to fix the problems. "I've always thought you'd make a great king one day."

He grunted, as if he didn't believe me. "That's not what you seemed to think this morning." The arched eyebrow didn't hide his annoyance.

"I'm sorry for what I said. I probably shouldn't make a habit of saying horrible things to someone trying to help me."

He huffed a laugh. "Too late, don't you think?"

I deserved that.

"I'm sorry, Rainier. I mean it." Whatever his reasons were for killing the man, it fell shy of King Soren's cruelty by a long shot. But, at the same time, what had Rainier turned into in recent years? He'd clearly earned a reputation.

"He put your daughter into the hands of our enemies. He put the kingdom at risk. He may have been the catalyst for a war, Emmeline. I do not regret it. There were other reasons I had as well." He gave me a dark look. "Elora wasn't the first unwilling girl he helped smuggle onto a boat." His mouth was a straight line. I let the realization settle in my bones as I felt my whole body break out in goosebumps.

"Shit. Well, I guess it's good you killed him." Though this specific instance appeared justified, I decided to continue anyway. "But as far as catalysts go, that was Faxon, not the deckhand. I am as well. I hid her from the Crown and the Myriad, so she had no protection, and then Faxon sold her. Am I not a traitor to the Crown?" I didn't know why I was pushing him, as if I wanted him to have a reason to find me guilty.

"Faxon is a catalyst, and I already told you he would die for it. Unless that is no longer what you want?" He stared straight ahead, shutting me out. I paused, wondering if what he was asking me meant more than the simple answer. I bided my time.

"I would think I do not have much sway in the matter." I mirrored him, keeping my face a solid slate, shutting him out as he had done me. He let out a long, low breath.

"You have always had more sway with me than you should have, Emmeline." His voice was a low rumble, and in it, I felt a deep sense of regret and longing and maybe something else. I could feel his eyes on me, but I willed myself to keep looking straight ahead, to not let him see his words affected me. If not for my traitorous skin flushing, I'd have thought I succeeded.

"I still want his death. But should I not also want my own?" I thought what I was doing in hiding Elora was the best thing for her. To grow up away from the influences of the Myriad or the Crown. But now I was second guessing every decision I ever made with her. Maybe the Crown would have been more successful in her protection than I was. And Faxon would have been living the life he wanted, making his betrayal less likely. I heard Rainier inhale deeply beside me.

"Did you believe what you were doing was protecting her?"

"Of course, it was to protect her. I've been terrified her entire life, I still am." I rattled it all out in one breath. Saying it was claiming it, and I didn't want to claim the fear right now. To deal with it.

"Then I'm willing to take intention into consideration Em, at least with you. Always with you." He heaved a sigh like it had been weighing him down, while a small smile played on his lips. "You did your best." Maybe one day I'd believe him.

"Thank you. I appreciate you helping me. I—I was afraid you might not.".

He stared at me, stricken for a moment. Then his mouth went tight, the small smile gone. "I am not the monster you seem to think I am." I felt an ache in my chest.

"That's not—" I decided not to get into this conversation with him, not now anyway. I should have apologized and got straight to the point. "The reason I came up here actually was to ask you if you'd seen Elora's necklace? It was in my pocket last night, but I wonder if it fell out onto the floor at some point."

"Shit, sorry. Here." He reached into his cloak and pulled out the jewelry in question. Face still closed off, he passed it over to me. I took it into my hands and rubbed my thumb over the ammolite stone, the dragon scale. Running the tiny chain between my fingers, I noticed something.

"You fixed it?" When he pulled it out from under the bed, the tiny clasp had been missing.

"I found it this morning after you and Dewalt left. I had someone fix it while I got supplies and Lavenia found the horses." He shrugged as if the gesture meant nothing, as if it was expected for him to do all the things he'd done for me the past few days and still find the time to fix a necklace, inconsequential as it was. I was happy to see some of the tension ease from his face when I looked over at him.

"That was kind of you, Rain. Thank you." He watched me as I pulled my hair back and put the tiny necklace on. If I wore it, I'd be less likely to lose it.

"Don't thank me. Just keep calling me that." He turned forward, and I noticed him swallow. I hadn't even realized I called him Rain until he mentioned it. I'd been actively avoiding it, wondering about the implication of using the name I used to call him. The name I used *before*. The name I used for him before he broke my heart and everything went wrong. I decided to hell with my careful approach and hesitations—I'd give myself over to the comfortable familiarity, even if it hurt me in the end.

"I think I can do that, Rain." And the smile I gave him was the first genuine one I'd given since Elora was taken.

CHAPTER 12

The Mirastos Path was well-traveled and properly maintained, large enough to fit two wagons across. The dirt road was so frequented that it was flattened, any rogue pebbles sunk deep within the earth, making easy travel for all those who took it. The woods to the westernmost side were thinner, more sparse, leaving a clear glimpse of the Alsors which awaited our crossing farther north. The Whispering Wood to the east was darker, more dense, and spoke of quiet danger. The normal sounds of the forest were almost muted to our right as we traveled north, as if the air was thicker. I wasn't frightened as I remembered all the stories told about this forest, but I was less relaxed here than I had been in the osage tunnel, the warmth of the sun through those red and orange leaves lighting up like fire. I wished that was the path we were taking. Rainier's guard would be cutting west from Ardian through the Whispering Wood, possibly taking the same tunnel of trees I'd prayed in. We timed it just right so we wouldn't get too far ahead and would likely run into them the following night.

Rainier kept quiet in the front of our group, leading us deeper into the woods. I followed in equal silence, with Dewalt and Lavenia riding behind. After I thanked him for the necklace, I fell back, wanting to give both of us space to think about what we'd said. I didn't think he was a monster. A monster wouldn't do what he was doing now. A monster wouldn't drop everything to help me find Elora. He wouldn't take me with him to petition the king for an army. I realized if he was only helping because Elora was the Beloved, he might have chosen not to bring me with them. The fact I was in attendance meant he was doing this for me too.

Even during the months after Lucia's death, I didn't think he was a monster. I thought we made stupid decisions together which caused her death. I thought he robbed me of a chance to say goodbye to her and almost killed me doing it. I didn't like to admit to myself he also broke my heart that night, but I never thought he was a monster. And I wondered why he got that impression from me.

Because I treated him like one.

Because I flinched when he approached me.
Because I told him I didn't think he'd help me.

None of it was because of him. I didn't know why I flinched. Maybe I expected him to grab me and yell at me like he did at Lucia's burial. Or maybe I was accustomed to not being touched, and I was afraid if he crossed the distance between us, I wouldn't be able to maintain it any longer. But when he held my hand on the bed and promised to kill Faxon, something changed, and I wasn't so sure of myself anymore.

I told him I didn't think he'd help me, not because he wouldn't want to, but because I'd been so terrible to him, I wasn't sure I deserved it. I stabbed him at my sister's burial and let those words be the last things said between us. He'd come to Ravemont once after that, right after I felt those first kicks with Elora. It hurt to turn him away, especially because with Lucia gone, I had no one to talk to. And I was terrified for so many reasons. Could he have helped comfort me? Would he have wanted to, after finding me pregnant with Faxon's baby? I'd never know because ultimately, I chose not to see him. He could have forced his way in as the Crown Prince without repercussion, but he never did, calmly accepting my refusal. I wondered if things would have changed if he had. But if Dewalt spoke true, they'd searched for me. I couldn't understand why. Rainier had made his feelings abundantly clear when I begged him to give me a reason.

I hadn't been able to look at myself in the mirror for over a year; Lucia's face was all I saw. And every time I thought of her face, it took me back to that night, and I relived it. The look of shock when she saw Rain and I return together that night. I'd never told her my true feelings about him, never indicated it was more than flirtation. He was going to be her bonded conduit, her husband. That night haunted me frequently, and I relived the events once more in my self-inflicted solitude.

Once Rain rifted us back to his bedroom at Crown Cottage, we found his door ripped wide open as if Dewalt had come to find him. It had only been minutes since we felt the impulses, but he was nowhere to be found. Rain had grabbed his sword from his room in one hand and interlaced his fingers with mine in the other as we crept down the hallway. Dewalt's room had been empty, but as we rounded the corner, we heard the chaos. Then Lucia was sprinting to us, my sword in her hand.

After asking where we were, she had thrust my weapon at me as she studied me, lingering on the hastily adjusted neckline of my favorite dress, my disheveled hair, my flushed features, suspicion crossing her face before she eyed Rain, realization dawning. She had scowled at me, so severely I started to rush to explain, to tell her she was right all along about my feelings for him. She cut me off with a jerk of her hand, uttering words which would haunt me so many years later.

"The Folterrans are here."

Rain's voice had been calm and steady when he asked where Dewalt and Lavenia were, despite the fear I saw in his eyes. And when I saw that fear confirmed by Lucia's rapidly increasing horror, my divinity had gone uncontrollable, and I heard his heart nearly beat out of his chest. Dewalt was out front with the rest of the guard, but Lavenia had gone into the gardens to look at the night-blooming starflowers, their first buds only appearing that night.

With a curse on his lips, Rainier had taken off running, rushing down the servant staircase to reach the back gardens. I hesitated for only a second, letting my sister's eyes weigh heavily against my skin before I followed. I could hear the clash of swords and shouts of soldiers from the other side of the estate as I rushed out the large, glass doors Rain had left wide open. I spotted Lavenia a moment before he did, her light blue dress still visible despite her attempt at hiding within the garden. I had begun to run toward them when I heard Lucia gasp behind me.

Three rifts had opened around us, and soldiers poured out.

We had fought for our lives. Lucia and I became separated from Rainier and Lavenia, encircled by soldiers who kept pushing us back, moving us away from the estate. Even as I shoved my sword through a Folterran neck, my eyes kept darting over to Rain to ensure he was alright. He didn't have time to rift, entirely engaged in combat, Lavenia using his dagger when she could. My attention had been drawn to the man in front of me, and I cried out as his weapon found purchase in my side. Lucia had been able to rid me of the man before he could do worse, but my eyes met Rain's for just a moment as I clamped my free hand to my stomach. Rain had roared as he began to mow soldiers down left and right in an attempt to reach me. I tore my eyes from him as I engaged with yet another soldier, but I lost track of him as Lucia and I had been herded into the open.

Fighting back-to-back, she had sent out bursts of light, more like lightning than anything else, knocking enemies to the ground. Dewalt and Rainier had trained me well; I held off enemies to her back, incapacitating or killing when I could, but I was quickly overwhelmed. A soldier grabbed me by the neck and threw me into a tree where I slammed my face. I had felt my forehead split and my knees give out before I dropped my sword. Then a bright light broke across my vision, and Lucia grabbed me under the arm, pulling me up. And we ran and ran until we got overwhelmed again. All I had was my dagger, but we had managed for a while—until we didn't. Until Lucia stopped and pushed me. Until Rainier caught up with us. Until she died, and I never got a chance to explain. She died thinking I'd betrayed her, and she would have been right. And I blamed him because it was easier to blame Rainier than it was to blame myself.

We had lunch before we left Mira, so when we stopped for dinner, we stopped for the night. Rainier and his horse left the path, veering through the trees to our right, into that smothering, impenetrable wood. He cut in quite a ways, crossing over a stream, until he found a small clearing, the diminishing sunlight barely cutting through the thinning canopy above. By then, my ears had adjusted to the strange heaviness, the sounds of the forest normal again, if a little quieter than usual. The foliage itself was thicker on this side of the path, filtering the lingering daylight almost completely. I was nervous about camping on this side, but Rainier insisted, arguing that we'd be better sheltered and protected amongst the dense trees. He dropped to the ground in a fluid motion before walking a quick perimeter of the site.

I thought all four of us felt introspective on the ride, lost in our own thoughts. No one spoke, even Lavenia and Dewalt maintaining a quiet, comfortable solitude. I decided if I was going to continue to be here with my old friends, I couldn't keep revisiting past wounds. I needed to get it all out and be done with it so I could focus solely on Elora. I was going to have to face all of it head on. I would start tonight.

Dewalt and Rainier began setting up our tents using wooden stakes, ropes, and a bit of leather. There were two, each big enough for two people, and they erected them next to one another. The three of them offered me my own tent so I'd have a full night's sleep, not having to worry about being woken when someone had watch. I protested, but the other three wouldn't hear it. Lavenia pulled a wool blanket from one of her packs and threw it down on the ground in her tent before divvying up the rest of the bedding. I began gathering kindling for a fire, my hands already freezing. In my rush to get to Ravemont, I hadn't brought warm enough clothing.

After the tents were set up, Dewalt started working on the fire while Rainier began to pull out hard tack, breads and cheeses, and apples for our meal. He had packed light, knowing we'd hit Brambleton before we took the Cinturon Pass to the west. As I bit into the apple, I remembered Junie and her grumpy pony and wondered how her arm was doing. She'd been mostly healed when I saw her last.

Shit.

I'd been attacked on my way home from seeing her. The bodies. Theo and Mairin. Had Theo reported the bodies to the guard in Brambleton? Was he alright? I was sure between my healing and what Mairin would do for him; he'd be fine. We'd be in Brambleton in three nights, and I could go home and check in before we headed west. I needed to. But did I want the others to come with me? The thought of bringing my old friends to my home didn't sit well in my gut, almost like crossing a boundary. As though by allowing them to see that part of my life, I was opening a door to them, inviting them in. I was accepting this as my new normal, and I wasn't sure I wanted that. Well, they didn't need to come with me, but I needed to tell them my intentions.

Face all of it. Head on.

We'd been sitting around the fire in easy silence, Lavenia sharing a log with me and Dewalt resting across the fire from us. I'd watched, fascinated, as Rainier pulled dirt up into a rudimentary chair. He offered to make me one, but I was comfortable on my log.

His abilities had always intrigued me. Although conduits had access to their full divinity upon maturity, some of the more difficult or consuming abilities took years to hone. Though he came into his full divinity one winter away from Crown Cottage, the Rainier I knew wouldn't have been able to craft a chair straight out of dirt. Instead, he'd have created an entire hill and have to slowly carve with his ability to get to the desired outcome. Once, when we'd been eating lunch in the meadow, he'd attempted to fill a pitcher with water from the nearby creek using his divinity. Instead, he sent a wave at us, and we both got soaked, laughing because we couldn't scramble away fast enough. We'd dried off in the sun afterward, the day unusually warm for the season, and we fell asleep with my head on his chest. He gave me my first kiss when we woke—soft, warm, and breathtaking. He'd said I smelled like sunshine and spring. He took me to the willow tree after, and we kissed beneath it for hours, drunk on affection. It was the first time our lips explored the other, something we began to do often and in secret after that day. Until Lucia died. Drawing myself out of the memory, I broke the silence around the fire.

"I need to go home. It's just east of Brambleton."

"Why?" Dewalt's expression was one of confusion, not contradiction. I wasn't sure if I imagined Rainier's back straighten in my periphery.

"Well, I want to check on our neighbor, the one they beat. And my—my friend, Mairin, likely has some questions. Not to mention the bodies. I need to take care of things. I can branch off and go home and then meet back with you as soon as I'm done." I definitely noticed Rainier relax with my reply.

Lavenia snorted. "Divine hell, I forgot about their bodies. You just left them?" Honestly, I had almost forgotten as well, the last few days a blur.

"The minute I realized what happened, I packed up and left for Ravemont. I hope Theo dealt with it. I owe the boy." I grimaced. If he hadn't dealt with it, I'd have to when we got there, and I didn't anticipate it being a pleasant experience.

"If he hasn't, it's a good thing I'm here to do it for you." Rainier sent a crooked smile toward me, but I was confused. I didn't intend to bring him with me. Plus, I wasn't going to ask him to bury week-old bodies. He looked at me and chuckled. The ground at my feet began to shake, tiny pebbles vibrating on the dirt.

"Oh." I huffed a laugh. "Thank the *gods*, just imagining the smell was nauseating. You'd make quick work of it." I was surprised at the ease in which I joked about dead bodies. Before Lucia and I were overrun that night, I had killed a decent number of soldiers. I didn't know how many. It must be easier to not care about killing someone when they deserve it.

"Tell us about Mairin." Lavenia's voice was quiet and curious, as if she'd seen me crack the door open and wanted to know if I'd let her in. I debated for a moment. Everything in my mind was telling me to keep it closed, not to let them in. But if Rainier was coming with me to help bury bodies, they'd see my home, my life. Her questioning was friendly, and I followed that pull from my heart, the one telling me to open up, to rely on them, to share with them.

"She's the healer in Brambleton. They can't afford a conduit. I help her sometimes, secretly of course. She actually kept me company one night after Faxon and Elora left. She got me drunk and asked about my future." I chuckled. "She's funny and kind. Honestly, she's my only friend." I stared at my feet, embarrassed.

Dewalt was sitting across the fire from me. He looked like something out of a children's story about a warrior of old. His arms were crossed, and the corded muscles were particularly visible in the firelight. The tunic he wore had no sleeves, and his bicep had a tattoo on it, something he didn't have all those years ago. It was a pattern of lines circling his arm in varying thicknesses. I'd have to ask him what it meant. The look on his face told me now was not the time. The fire flickered in his eyes. His long, black hair was hanging down either side of his face, and he seemed drawn in by the red and orange licks of flame before him. He didn't look up as he spoke.

"Did you ever see us in your future?"

I paused. I'd barely thought about the future, but no. I didn't ever see them in it.

"Actually, when she asked me what I planned to do after Elora reached her full divinity, I had no idea. I guessed I'd go to Ravemont with Faxon." I blew air out between my lips then, a sound which showed my disdain for the idea. "But no, I didn't predict any of this."

"Would you have ever come back if you didn't need our help?" All the warmth in Dewalt's voice was missing.

I studied my hands in my lap. I didn't know what to say.

"It's alright." Lavenia reached over and patted my hand. She had always been so kind—to everyone. Even if they didn't deserve the kindness.

"You should come with us—after. You should stay." Rainier's voice was quiet. He was watching me, eyes lit up by the fire and something I didn't want to put a name to. His words caught me off guard, and I chose not to think about them too much.

"Where, Crown Cottage? No, thank you." I shuddered.

"There, the capital, the Cascade—you'd be welcome at all of them." I glanced at Lavenia, who nodded in agreement. Rainier's gaze had stayed on me. He'd been around me for barely more than two days, and he was already offering me to accompany his court. I couldn't let myself think about what that might mean. If it meant anything at all.

"I don't think I could ever go to Crown Cottage again." I exhaled a thin breath.

"I thought that too, Emma. But I was wrong, and I'm glad for it." Lavenia's voice dipped low and quiet. "They took so much, but I wouldn't—*won't*—let them take the good things. The olive grove, the weeping willow, the meadow, I won't let them have it."

No one had ever told me what happened after Rainier sent me through the rift that night. When he brought me back, Lucia's body had already been retrieved. The same healer who came to see if there was anything to be done for my sister tended to my side where the dagger had pierced my skin. She worked as I stared at the sheet-covered body on the chaise next to me. I would wonder for years why it hadn't been my mother to tend my wounds. I didn't see anyone else until the burial the next day. I had no idea what happened in her final moments, how the others had survived. I felt like this was a decent enough time to ask them, to find out what I'd wondered for all these years.

"What—" I cleared my throat. "What happened that night after you rifted me?" My eyes found Rainier. He'd been the one to remove me, so he could be the one to explain it. He hadn't tried back then, and I hadn't asked. I hadn't wanted to know. The fire danced in his eyes, but I could feel the weight of the sadness behind them. In my periphery, I saw Dewalt lean forward, elbows to knees, across the fire from me, and I felt Lavenia stiffen.

"Please. I need to know. I—No one ever told me." I swallowed, trying to keep my voice from wavering. Dewalt surprised me by being the first to speak.

"When Lucia used her light to take down the soldiers surrounding you both, I was across the field, still weaving against the soldiers near me." In addition to the impulse Dewalt could send, if he was able to touch someone, he could create visions in their head, weave a sort of illusion. He could make them think their friend was the enemy, make them run in fear from a threat. The only downfall was the necessary physical contact. He was always the one to train me since he was used to fighting in close quarters. "When I saw the flare, I started running to her." I heard his voice break, still emotional about it all these years later.

Rainier spoke next, eyeing his friend cautiously.

"I was running to catch up with you both. I was behind you when she shoved you. I saw you hit the ground, opened the rift, and tossed you through it." He had the decency to cringe when he said it. "You saw her fall. When she did, she never got up."

"Was she awake?" I had heard the scream before she fell. Saw the vipers forming around her, twining up her body.

"I got to her first. She wasn't breathing." Lavenia inhaled deeply. "When he called his shadows back, they…they came pouring out of her body. She opened her eyes for a second, but she never spoke. I—I stayed with her." Lavenia's voice was quiet, strained. I refused to look at her, knowing I'd see tears in her eyes. I couldn't do that yet. Instead, I reached my hand out to her, and she held it.

"He was on the outcropping you both were running toward—King Dryul. Not one of his minions or his son or anyone else, it was *him*. It was why the soldiers were chasing you, pushing you both toward him. I was exhausted, but I tried to pull the trees to him, to hit him or kill him, I don't know. It was useless. But he called his shadows back and vanished, right as I sent the trees flying at him. He just . . . did what he came to do and then left." Rainier drew a breath. "I ran to Lucia to see if I could do anything, but—"

"But she was gone, Emma." Lavenia squeezed my hand.

"And Dewalt . . . " He glanced at his best friend then, pausing a second before continuing. Rainier's eyes were full of devastation as he watched the man. "Dewalt was screaming for you, to see if you could do anything, but I'd already rifted you." Rainier had one elbow down on his knee, and his head was in his hand.

"So, I rifted to the cavern then, but you weren't there." I hadn't realized he'd started looking for me so soon after he'd put me there. The cave system must have been huge, since he didn't find me for hours, and I didn't hear his heartbeat until right before he found me.

"While he looked for you, I found survivors. Dewalt—" Lavenia glanced at her bonded partner, the man she'd chosen to spend her life with, and sorrow flooded her features. "Dewalt stayed with her. I sent for our parents first. I don't know if I did it right. I didn't know what to do." She had only been fifteen or so when it happened, and with Lucia dead, her brother searching for me, the small guard stationed there decimated, she had to make some tough decisions.

"I'm sure you did everything the right way, Ven. Thank you." My voice came out quieter than expected. Calmer. This was their trauma too, and I was asking them to relive it for me, for my closure. And they were willing to do it to help me.

Rainier was watching me carefully. I wasn't sure if he was afraid I was going to break down or not, but I felt his gaze on me as I glanced at Dewalt across the fire, his expression still cold and lifeless. I didn't have words to thank them for what they were telling me, for helping me find closure. Maybe I would one day.

"When your parents got there, you weren't back yet. None of us knew where you were. I didn't know Rainier had rifted you, just that he left. For those few hours we weren't sure if we lost you too. Or even Rainier." Lavenia let out a sigh. "We just waited."

I didn't know that. I pictured my mother, thrown across Lucia, and my father pacing. Waiting, wondering if I was dead too. I thought about the hell they'd have felt if that were the case, if both of their children were dead in one fell swoop. I imagined their lives wouldn't be much different than the ones they lived anyway with me alive. I did die that day, just not in the same way Lucia did. I died, and I was reborn a timid, cowardly creature who ran and hid.

Rainier sighed, head down, running a hand over his scalp. "I didn't know what I did—where I sent you. I'd been shooting for the cavern. I knew you'd probably start trying to run back to us, so I went to search the beach, but saw no footprints in the sand. Then I went into the back of the cave, trying to find you, but I reached a dead end, and you weren't there, so I started exploring. I was searching for hours. And the longer it took, the more panicked I became. You know how it worked back then, any sort of stress and my aim was off. And I couldn't pinpoint where I was going at all, I was just bumbling along trying to find you. I walked and ran a lot of the paths between rifting. One of the times I rifted into a flooded cave. I tried to send the water down, push it out. But it was too much, and I was too weak—from the battle, from rifting, from all of it. I barely had enough strength to rift back out so I could breathe. I had to rest for a while after, in a cave where the water was only up to my thighs. But then I finally heard you." Rainier lifted his head, his eyes immediately finding my own. They were shimmering, and I wondered if I'd asked for too much in having him tell me this story.

"I heard you, Rain. I heard your heart, so I started screaming. I'm surprised you heard me."

"No, that's the thing Em. I—I didn't hear you screaming. I know this sounds crazy, and I know it's impossible, but I've re-lived it for years—awake *and* in my dreams. I could hear your heartbeat. I followed it to find you."

"That's impossible," I whispered.

"I know it is. But I found you, didn't I?"

I nodded. He did. And now, I'd found him.

CHAPTER 13

I WAS SORE. My thighs ached, and the base of my spine was killing me. I'd been on horseback more the last few days than I had been the last few months, and I was paying for it now. The others discussed who would stand watch first, and I offered to take a shift as well, so everyone could get a little more sleep. My offer was met with a resounding no.

"No offense, Emma. You're out of practice. I want to see you with a sword before I trust you to guard us with one." Dewalt smirked. I rolled my eyes, not about to admit I hadn't touched my sword in two months. Nonetheless, I was prepared to argue the point.

"You're the one who wouldn't let me use a sword back in Mira. Spar with me when we get to Brambleton, I'm not that rusty." My pride was wounded. I'd been better than Lavenia and almost as good as Dewalt and Rainier. Granted, I hadn't spent the last half of my life in skirmishes as the three of them had. I hadn't had to defend myself either, but I thought I was more than capable of standing watch over my friends.

My friends.

"I'll spar with you. I deserve a rematch." A hint of a smile played on Rainier's lips as he peered up at me from under lowered brows. I was shocked he even brought it up, and it showed, based on his expanding grin. The crooked smile he'd always had was disarming, but when he gave me his full smile, it felt like the sun coming out from behind a cloud, shining only for me. He had always laughed easily, his personality engaging and welcoming, and it had always been one of my favorite parts about him. He chuckled. "I held back then, but this time?" He shook his head. "Not so easy."

His admission confirmed what I suspected all those years ago—he had held back, but why? Because he knew he couldn't give me what I wanted? Because he knew I needed the distance from him? Because once I requested it, he knew there was no going back? I was surprised he was able to joke about the last time our swords had crossed, let alone offer to spar with me. But if he was willing to joke about it, I'd follow his lead. "From what Lavenia said earlier about how lazy you've gotten, are you sure you want to?" Rainier's eyes lit up, accepting the challenge.

"To surrender this time, not first blood." He had always been better at tiring out his opponent. First blood meant dancing around one another until you could get the hit in. To surrender was a different beast. Even if he had been trying all those years ago, it was still probable I would have made first contact. He was more patient. He could take the hits and then wait for who he was facing to drag and slow. I could be patient to an extent, waiting for the right opening, but once I made the first mark, it was a struggle to pace myself. It was a weakness of mine he was more than familiar with.

"No divinity?" I asked. Maybe he'd grown as much out of practice as I had.

"Of course not, it wouldn't be fair." His eyes glinted with delight. "Although, if you'd patch me up when you're through with me, I'd be much obliged." I rolled my eyes.

"As if you think I'll even get a hit in. Terms?" I knew better than to answer a challenge from Rainier without discussing terms. He chuckled and examined the ground as he thought.

"You win, you get what you want. You get to stand watch. If I win, you come to court with us after we find Elora. Try it out for a year." His gaze met mine, smile no longer reaching his eyes. He seemed nervous. Though they'd broken off for their own conversation a while ago, Dewalt and Lavenia turned to pay attention once more, her brows raised and his lips firmly tipped up in a smirk.

Go to court. For a year.

"Well, that doesn't seem very fair. First of all, does the time before we get Elora back count toward the year? Secondly, all I get is to stand watch?" I crossed my arms. "No way."

"Sure, your time can start now. As for your prize, is there anything else you'd want instead?" His expression was sincere. What did I want? What was commensurate with spending a year at court? I didn't need anything. After all of this was done, we'd go back to Ravemont as long as Father would have us, and Elora and I would want for nothing. I couldn't think of anything I wanted other than the obvious. For Elora to be here. For Faxon to not have betrayed us. For Lucia to be alive. But Rainier couldn't change the past, and he was doing his best to help me get my daughter back. I contemplated for only a moment when a small voice in the back of my head whispered.

Revenge.

"If I win, you'll let me be the one to give the killing blow to the King of Bones if it ever comes to that." I heard Lavenia's sharp intake of breath. Rainier's face hardened, the grin gone.

"We don't even know how to kill him, Em." He rubbed a hand up the back of his neck in what I thought was exasperation.

"I imagine he bleeds like the rest of us; I just have to get close enough." His eyes were hard as flint as he took me in. "You have to let me try. He killed my sister and took my daughter."

"Two years at court." His eyes were on mine, glowing in the light of the fire. I stood, staring into the flames as I contemplated.

"Fine."

I walked over to him, grasping his hand in mine, attempting to ignore the warmth spreading within me at his touch. We shook on it, his eyes still on mine.

"Then it's a deal."

Rainier took the first watch. Dewalt wasn't ready to sleep, mentioning he needed to talk to the prince about something important, something private. Leaving the two of them at the fire, I crawled into my tent. Rainier and Lavenia had acquired bedrolls for everyone, and I'd already tossed my pack in after the tent was set up. I pulled my sweaty shirt off and swapped it for a fresh one, and I was grateful I'd be able to take a bath when we stopped at the house, feeling disgusting after only a few days.

"Emma? Come keep me company." Lavenia called from her tent. "I'm cold, and Dewalt won't come to bed."

"Give me a minute." I smiled, pulling my hair out of its braid and rubbing my scalp where my hair had caused tension. When I was done, I crawled out of the tent, noticing Dewalt and Rainier leaned in close to each other. It appeared as if they were arguing. Dewalt turned and caught my eye, nodding at me. Feeling like I'd been caught doing something wrong, I scurried into the tent with Lavenia.

She pulled her blanket up, and I crawled in next to her, ready for the warmth. I had accidentally left my cloak, and I was already freezing from the few steps over to her tent. Lavenia instantly started chattering about anything and everything—soldiers from the guard who I'd known and what they were doing now, members of the older families from the western side of Vesta who had ruled her stories every spring when they came back to Ravemont. It made my heart happy to know so many of the soldiers had married and created families, most of them still members of Rainier's guard. But I couldn't stop myself from asking about the families of those I knew had died the same day as my sister—I hadn't forgotten them. Eventually, she started to tell me about some of her friends at court, and I gladly listened. I was sore and tired and needed to rest, but her stories were keeping me distracted, allowing me to relax without being sucked into my own thoughts and worries.

"Raj is Rainier's other captain, along with Dewalt. He's in charge of the Cascade when we aren't there. He was a transfer from our father's guard a long time ago, so he's a bit older, but he's good. I think Rainier trusts him more than Dewalt sometimes."

"Are there any other captains?"

"In Rainier's forces? Just one, Brenna. You'll meet her in Astana. She's the most beautiful woman you will ever see," she laughed, "and the meanest."

"And you know this from experience?" I teased, smiling at her in the dark.

"Oh yes, lots of experience." The tone of her voice told me all I needed to know.

"Is she among the relationships you pursue?" Lavenia chuckled before growing serious.

"She couldn't wrap her head around the bond, it was part of why we didn't work out."

"I kind of understand that though, especially for a mortal." The bond between two conduits was something even I was intimidated by. It would be difficult to be in love with a person who was bound in mind, body, and soul to someone else.

"I did too. It was why I offered to stop being with Dewalt, let his divinity fade out of my blood, let the bond break. He agreed to it, but it wasn't enough." She spat the last words out, angry with her former lover.

"You must have loved her quite a bit to offer to do that." Dewalt's powers were tremendously helpful in battle, and to give them up after ten years of use was a big sacrifice to make. Not to mention that, should the bond break, they would no longer be allowed to drink from the font. I wasn't sure if they'd start aging normally again or how it worked, but since only bonded conduits were allowed entrance, Lavenia and Dewalt would no longer be allowed access. Brenna must have been incredibly special to Lavenia for her to offer all that.

"I did. The bitch." Her voice quieted, the insult backed by sadness rather than anger.

"I hope you sent her an impulse after things ended." I tried to cheer my friend up, and it worked, based on the cackle I received in return. Her laughter lightened the mood, and she changed the subject, beginning to explain all about the Cascade, down to details I didn't truly care to hear. But I smiled. One day he would be king, in charge of the entire Vestian army, but it was still strange to hear about it now, even if I always knew it would happen eventually. The wind howled outside the tent. It was made of thick leather, keeping our heat trapped inside, with flaps at the front that could be tied together. We didn't bother since Dewalt would eventually want in, and I'd have to go back to my tent. It kept the heat in relatively well anyway, without being tied. With the blankets, bedrolls, and body heat, we were relatively cozy. I almost dreaded going back to my own empty tent.

"It's strange to be going to the capital. I've never been west of the Alsors, let alone to Astana."

"It will be strange for all of us. The three of us haven't been there in over a year. We bounce between the Cascade, Crown Cottage, and Nythyr mostly. Although, I suppose Nythyr will be off the table now, since you're back."

"He doesn't have to stop what he's doing in Nythyr because of me. I plan to win our match anyway. I'll be out of the way as soon as Elora is back and the King of Bones dead."

Lavenia rolled over, almost aggressively.

"Goddess, help me. Dewalt told me to expect little when I talked to you, but this defies expectation. We went to Nythyr *because* of you." Her upper lip curled in disgust. It was so unsettling on her normally kind face I blanched.

"Because of me?" I didn't understand.

"That's where we thought you went, remember? When you wouldn't see him, he decided to give you space. He went to do Father's bidding for two years. I think he figured you'd be willing to talk to him when he came back, and he needed to get his head right anyway. You wouldn't care to know I'm sure, but he was in a bad place after everything happened." Her brows furrowed, glaring at me. "But then we found out you went to Nythyr. It renewed something in him, and we went for the first time soon after. Every time we go, he talks to all of his contacts in the major cities, makes new ones. We spent a lot of time in Kieża, figuring the capital would have been a good place to start searching. We spent almost an entire year there the first time, and we've been going once a year ever since, searching for you. We just got back a couple of months ago. He goes on the anniversary." Her face softened a bit by the end.

Dewalt had said Rainier searched for me, but I didn't realize the extent of it. I laid there in shock, feeling the heavy weight of guilt in my stomach settle into a curled-up ball of cold nerves.

Here I was, imagining you cavorting across Nythyr this whole time, drinking all the wine and dancing at all the festivals.

I wondered if he went to the festivals and looked for me.

"You know," Lavenia cut through the silence, "You didn't have to strike a bargain with him. If you had just asked him, he'd have done everything to give you what you want." I doubted it, but I didn't tell Lavenia as much. "It'll be nice to see you at court though." She elbowed me in the ribs.

"Knock, knock." Dewalt peeked his head into the tent. "May I have my bed back, Lady Emmeline?" He mocked a bow, and I snorted as I made to get out of the tent.

When I stood up, I saw Rainier still sitting at the fire, hunched over with an elbow on his knee and chin in his hand. He was staring into the fire with a look on his face that told me whatever conversation he had with Dewalt wasn't a pleasant one. When I took a step, he turned, and his eyes found mine, expression soft.

"Hey." His voice was quiet, and he tilted his head toward the log next to him, beckoning me to come sit. I walked quickly across, glad to be next to the fire, and sat down next to him.

"That conversation seemed intense," I offered. I didn't expect him to talk to me about it, but I wanted him to know I was there if he wanted to. It struck me how natural it was to *want* to be there for him.

"You could say that." He let out a low chuckle before his eyes moved back to the flame before us. "Dewalt likes to remind me of things I'd rather forget."

"What else is a second for? It's why I don't have one." I gave him a small smile, and the side of his mouth quirked up, though he never broke his gaze with the fire.

"I'd wager, Em, you don't have a second because you don't need one. Unless you've been raising an army in Brambleton?" I laughed at the thought.

"Maybe you're right. Or maybe I don't need a second to remind me of the things I cannot forget." I knew it was a dark thing to say. I wished I could forget so many things—it would've made everything so much easier. I cleared my throat, deciding to change the subject.

"Thank you for talking to me about that night. I've always wondered, and my nightmares filled in the gaps. Honestly, the truth is a lot easier to handle than what my subconscious made up." I didn't know why I offered the information to him, but it was true. It sounded like she'd gone more peacefully than I'd ever imagined.

"I still have nightmares, too. Rare anymore, though."

"Mine were rare too, until the last few days." The stress had made them almost a nightly occurrence.

"You had one last night, didn't you?"

"How did you know?" He let out a huff, almost a chuckle.

"You were talking. You kept saying 'you found me.'" There was no judgment in his tone, only a hint of concern. "I almost woke you, but you quieted soon after, so I let you sleep."

"I'm sorry I disturbed you. I hadn't dreamed about the caves in years. The cellar must have done a number on me." I let out a shaky laugh.

"You didn't bother me; I wasn't sleeping yet. I've been in my head a lot since you got here." He stared into the fire, not looking at me. I didn't know what to say. "So, the panic in the cellar?"

"I—it was the water. And being underground." Although I'd never hesitated to blame him before, I wasn't sure it fit anymore. After all the admissions and the emotion in his voice, I didn't want to make him feel guilty when he acted on impulse trying to protect me.

"When I bumped into you in the closet and you elbowed me, I figured it wasn't just out of spite. There had to have been more to it." With his gaze still on the fire, it almost seemed like he was talking to himself more than he was talking to me.

"Sorry. It wasn't intentional."

"I know. I'm sorry you have to deal with all of that because of what I did." Peering over at me, his eyes were still burning even though he'd torn them away from the fire.

"It's because of the caves, not because of you." I'd never made the distinction before. The separation. We sat there in silence for a while, both of us lost in thought.

"You should sleep. Another long day tomorrow." He nodded toward the tent, far enough from the fire that I shuddered at the thought of walking over to it. He chuckled.

"Here, take it." He pulled his cloak off and held it out to me. "I don't need it with the fire." I hesitated a moment before I took it and wrapped it around me, inhaling his clean, earthy scent deeply before I caught myself, hoping he hadn't noticed.

"Thank you." He nodded as I ran off to the tent as quickly as I could. I climbed into it and kept his cloak on me while I rolled up in the bedroll. The fresh petrichor scent on his cloak was tinged with a bit of smoke, but it was purely Rainier. I allowed myself to breathe deep. I got so distracted with my conversation about nightmares at the fire, I hadn't had a chance to think about what Lavenia had said. He'd gone to Nythyr once a year this entire time? For me? I wondered what he would have done if he had found me. Tried to get me to come back to Ravemont? To court? I wondered if he would have been able to convince me.

Would he have been willing to help me protect my daughter and still keep her secret from the Myriad? I hoped the news of Elora disrupting the Crown Prince's plans hadn't been shared publicly. I didn't want anyone to know until the last possible moment. And I certainly wouldn't let the masters do any tests on her when we got her back. I made a mental note to talk to Rainier about it. I knew I was borrowing trouble, since we hadn't even rescued her yet, but a tiny part of me was more afraid of what they'd do and expect of her than I was of the Folterrans. They hadn't killed her, just taken her. I didn't know what their plans were, but I couldn't hold back the feeling that she still wouldn't be safe, even after we got her back. I fell asleep worrying about the punishment Elora likely received for biting someone's ear off.

Elora was sitting cross-legged next to me, weaving a daisy chain while she spoke about the book she'd been reading. She let out a heavy sigh and gave me a dreamy smile, dropping her hands to her lap.

"I can't wait for someone to kiss me like that."

"Not for a while, baby." I put my hand on her soft cheek. Her skin was glowing, contrasting with her white hair and her mint dress. She looked like a siren from one of her stories. Radiant.

She grabbed my hand tight.

"Mama, the Folterrans are here." Her voice was not her own, my sister speaking through my daughter in warning, her voice crueler than I remembered.

I wrenched her up from the ground, and we ran.

Elora was ahead of me, throwing blasts of light in our path, leading the way. I had a sword in my hand, and I used it with fervor. Cutting down the torso of one soldier before beheading another, whipping around to slice the throat of the next. Faceless bodies falling in a heap.

We were running, and I felt the ground empty out below me, dirt falling out from beneath my feet as I ran. I sank down, down, down into a narrow hole, pulling me deeper until my head was the only thing above ground. I didn't know when it happened, but my hands were bound behind me, my sword gone.

I was stuck, but she kept running.

When I saw the shadows surround her, the vipers merging and dancing around her ankles, I began to scream. She stopped running and turned to face me, her voice her own again, loud in my ear despite the distance.

"I'm alright, Mama, I've never been afraid of the dark."

Then she fell.

CHAPTER 14

A BLAST OF COLD air hit me, and I gasped, a scream stopping in my throat. When I realized it was just another nightmare, sobs of relief tore through my body. Elora wasn't safe by any means, but what I'd seen wasn't real.

"Em, you're alright. Hey, it's me." There was a warm hand on my ankle. I tried to respond, but the best I could get out was a small moan as the sobs still tore through me. The hand left my skin, and I heard soft voices coming from the other tent. A short second later, I felt the cold air again when the flaps of my tent opened, and Rainier crawled in, smelling of smoke.

"I'm sorry." My voice came out as a moan I almost didn't recognize.

"Don't apologize. It was Lavenia's turn to stand watch anyway. You just woke her up a little early." He sat on the other side of the tent, cross-legged with his head ducked down, too tall to sit up all the way. I practiced my breathing, in through my nose and out through my mouth. Slowly.

"You don't have to stay, I'm sorry. I know sitting like that isn't comfortable." I sat up, rubbing my hands over my eyes and pulling my hair off my neck. I'd grown sweaty, and my hair was sticking. The light was dim in the tent, but given our proximity to the fire, I was able to see Rainier's eyes on me.

"I'm comfortable enough. Do you want to talk about it?"

"I—Not yet." I was afraid if I told him about the nightmare, I'd start crying again, and I'd only just stopped.

"Would you like me to talk about something else? A distraction, perhaps?" He twisted his body, stretching his legs out and leaning back on his elbows.

"That sounds nice." I laid back down, turning onto my side and looking up at him.

"Hmm, what would you like me to talk about? Family or friends? Past or future?" His tone was playful, and I was happy to participate, to push the nightmare out of my mind. I tilted my head back and closed my eyes, debating on what to ask him and finally settling on something I'd been wondering about.

"Family, but present. I've heard it's been a while since you've seen your mother?" I was curious. I'd always looked up to Queen Shivani. She was centuries younger than the king, a third wife for a man who had no heirs. She came from Olistos, and little was known about her before she became queen other than her status as the last siphon, able to take from the divinity of those she touched and use their own abilities against them. I had been eager to know her when Lucia had been set to become her daughter-in-law.

Rainier let out a sigh clearly annoyed.

"Dewalt doesn't shut up, does he? She doesn't think I'm serious about being king."

"And are you?" I countered, already knowing the truth. I just wanted to hear him explain. He shot an annoyed look at me, and I smiled.

"Of course, I am. My entire life I have been serious about it, you know that. I have wanted so much more for Vesta than my father has been willing to give." He eased further back onto the ground, hands under his head.

"So, why does she doubt it?" Rainier had always dreamt of change for Vesta, righting his father's wrongs.

"Because I refuse to be used as a political pawn and make the alliances her and my father want." He snapped.

"They want you to wed." It seemed as if this was the answer to my questions about his performing the ritual. It wasn't because the queen hadn't been able to find a conduit worthy of him, but because he didn't want to be used.

"Yes. They wanted me to bring power to Vesta and intimidate Nythyr and Folterra with your sister. Political scheming, and we know how that turned out. I promised myself I wouldn't . . ." His voice was dark and biting as he trailed off and shook his head, clearing his thoughts. "Since your sister died, I told myself I would only ever bond and wed for love. Nothing less."

I supposed he hadn't found love. I didn't know how to feel about that.

"So, you avoid them?" I felt a small tinge of jealousy. If I had the option to leave and tell my parents no, I wouldn't be married to Faxon. But then I wouldn't have Elora, either.

"She claims I'm avoiding my duty." He gave a dark laugh. "My duty is what has kept me from doing many things I've wanted all these years. But, considering the way my father has supposedly been ailing, maybe she's right. If he dies and I have not drunk from the font, the crown will go to Lavenia."

I didn't know that. It had been centuries of King Soren's rule, so the ascension process was foreign to me. "And what would be the problem then?" Lavenia was strong and smart and a gifted conduit.

"The problem would be that she does not want it and has not prepared as vigorously as I have. It's my duty to the Crown and to Lavenia to ensure it does not pass to her. Besides, do you think Vesta could survive with Dewalt as king?" I laughed as he sighed, rolling on his side to face me. It brought me back to all the times we would lay in the meadow, talking about our dreams and fears. By the beginning of that last summer, those talks would often end in soft kisses and whispers of a future which would never exist. I found myself smiling at him, and I was rewarded with the crooked one I still loved. "Enough talk about the insufferable monarchy, it's your turn."

"Past or future? Friend or family?" I replied, echoing his words from before.

"Tell me about her. Your daughter." He propped his head up on one arm, still laying on his side.

"I don't know where to start." I fingered her necklace. "Her name is Elora Mae…Calvert." I hesitated with her last name. I had hated not being able to give her mine. While Faxon had let me keep my own surname, a boon after my punishment, he had not allowed me to give it to Elora.

"I always thought Faxon had a more dignified family name than he deserved." He chuckled. "Beautiful name, though. Wasn't that Lucia's middle name?" I was surprised he remembered.

"Yes, Lucia Mae. And she takes after her aunt not just in name. She looks just like her." I thought of the happier dream from weeks ago, the one which had the three of us weaving daisy chains. "She has the same white hair, but it's curly—one of the only things she inherited from Faxon. Eyes like mine. She's just as tall as me." I was smiling thinking about her as Rainier snorted.

"That isn't much of an accomplishment, Highclere." I kicked him in the shin, and he laughed.

"She loves to read. She's a dreamer. It's been hard all these years, keeping her locked away. I know she wants adventure, excitement. A knight in shining armor. Even though I told her the majority of knights are older and uglier in real life than in the stories." He chuckled.

"She sounds lovely. How old is she? When I first saw you, I had assumed she was a small child for some reason, but I doubt a small child would be capable of biting someone's ear off." There was definitely some amusement in his voice at the thought.

"She's fifteen." I sighed, worried for Elora. "I'm still trying to process that. I wouldn't think she had it in her." Only because I failed at training her.

"She's yours, Em, of course she has it in her." He made it sound like a compliment.

"I hope they're not punishing her for it." My thoughts turned dark. "In my nightmare, the shadows got her, the vipers. And I couldn't do anything." I took a breath, trying to control my voice.

"It wasn't real." His voice was soft.

"I know. And they'd have killed her by now if that's what they wanted." Hoping for Folterra to have a plan for my daughter disgusted me, but the alternative was worse.

"Does the boy who warned you know about her divinity?"

"He knows she's a conduit, but I don't think she's ever shown him." Unless she broke my rules, which I doubted.

"Did she use her abilities that day?"

"Actually, no, Theo never mentioned it. Why wouldn't she?" I rolled onto my back, staring at the leather above me.

"Obsidian, probably. They use chains inlaid with it." The volcanic glass was the only known thing to subdue divinity. "They knew what they were getting into with her." He sounded angry, remembering Faxon was the one responsible for their information.

"I didn't tell—Elora doesn't know about the prophecy. I was going to tell her after this trip, but I never got a chance." I squeaked the words out, ashamed. I had done so little to prepare her like I should have.

"When we get her back, you can tell her." Rainier's choice of the word 'when' instead of 'if' meant a great deal more to me than he likely knew.

"Something tells me she will already know by then." I stifled a yawn. Sleep was calling me, but I didn't want Rainier to leave. "I hope she'll forgive me." I should have told her sooner. She should have known all along.

"You'd be surprised how easy you are to forgive, Emmeline." He rolled over onto his back, his leg against mine, the heat reassuring. I knew for a while he'd forgiven me, at least for some things, or else he wouldn't be here. But hearing it was nice, all the same.

"I don't think she will agree with you." I laughed. "Will—" My smile disappeared, sobering over what I needed to discuss with him. "I don't want the Myriad to do to her what they did to Lucia. But I'm sure they'll have to know, after all of this?" I rolled over to take him in as he nodded slowly, a guarded expression on his face.

"We will figure it out, Em. If you don't want her tested, if she doesn't want to be tested, she won't be."

"Is that even up to you?"

"It is now."

"What do you mean?"

"I mean, it's important to you, and I will not let something happen that you don't want to happen."

"But your father—" He cut me off, shaking his head, a bemused half-smile present on his face.

"I don't think you understand. Things have changed in the last sixteen years. My father is not nearly as in control as he once was. I have more sway and respect than he ever did. I don't have to petition him for soldiers; we will have them either way. I am doing it this way to maintain that sway and respect."

I nodded slowly. The information made me feel better, knowing he'd pull through for me no matter what. I wanted to know more though. How had he gained this influence? And then I looked at him, truly looked at him. I already knew the answer. He gained his influence by being the Rainier I'd always known. Patient, kind, poised. Just and fair, only quick to anger in certain circumstances. He'd earned the influence.

"I'm in a very different position than I was sixteen years ago." His gaze was intense as he watched me. I nodded and rolled onto my back, getting pulled into thinking through all the decisions I'd made which led me here. Maybe I should have trusted him sooner or at least seen him to find out how much more sway he had, to see if he could have offered his protection sooner, his promise to keep the Myriad away. Rainier was still on his side, watching me when I let out a yawn, and he sat up. "Before I go back to my tent, I want you to know I've thought about that moment pretty regularly over the years. When I rifted you. I was scared, and it was stupid. I'm sorry." He was staring down at his hands, his voice quiet but steady.

"I forgive you." I'd been slowly coming to the conclusion that I forgave him, at least for that, with time on my side to realize he acted out of fear. But hearing the story of what happened from the three of them today made something shift into place. It had been the unknown of her death which haunted me. I was so angry for so long because I thought he'd pulled me away when my sister needed me most, when I could have done something. But I was no match for King Dryul, and my healing abilities would only have prolonged her suffering—if they'd have done anything at all. He may have taken my chance to say goodbye when he rifted me, but was it so unforgivable when he thought he was protecting me from a fate like hers? My forgiveness wouldn't change the nightmares I still had or anything else that happened that night, but it was something I could give him in exchange for the hope he'd given me.

Even in the dim lighting, I could tell he was surprised. I did my best to shrug from where I was laying, trying to take the intensity out of the way he watched me. "You'd be surprised how easy you are to forgive, Rain. Especially when given so long to think about it." He huffed a laugh as he moved to leave the tent. When the cold breeze blew in, it solidified what I'd been thinking a moment before. "You don't have to swap tents—if you want to stay in here, you can." I burrowed lower into his cloak and my bedroll, oddly embarrassed. I hadn't meant anything by it, other than just wanting his company and his warmth.

He glanced over his shoulder at me, still on his knees about to climb out of the tent, an appraising look on his face.

"I'll be right back."

I closed my eyes, ignoring the way my heart started pattering, as I rolled over to face the empty part of the tent. I heard him murmur something to Lavenia and walk the few steps over to the other tent. There was silence, followed by a quiet interaction between Dewalt and Rainier I couldn't make out. Rainier seemed agitated.

Before I had a chance to wonder about what they'd said, he was climbing back into the tent with a bedroll tucked under his arm. Sitting back on his heels, he spread it in the empty space next to me. He sat down on it, and I watched as he took his boots off and placed them next to the opening of the tent, his muscles visible under the back of his shirt as he bent over. I closed my eyes and burrowed farther into my own bedroll while he struggled into his, an awkward enough task in a small tent that I didn't think he required an audience.

When he seemed settled and comfortable, I opened my eyes. He was propped up on one elbow, watching me, as a smile slowly spread across his face.

"You look like a caterpillar." I glanced down and started laughing. My eyes and nose were the only thing visible at the top of the bedroll, the rest of my body bundled tightly inside it. The sweat which had accumulated on my body during my nightmare had dried, and I was cold now.

"A rather cold caterpillar." I burrowed farther into the bundle for emphasis.

"So *that* was why you asked me to stay." There was a shimmer of amusement in his eyes.

"I didn't ask you to stay, I offered." It would seem I had to argue with him about everything.

"Semantics, Em." He laid down on his back and patted his chest. "Come here." I hesitated. It felt dangerous or inappropriate, even though he was someone I cared for deeply in my past. *Especially* for those reasons. I was freezing though and heavily considered it. I was startled when I heard his heart, not realizing I'd been reaching out. It was a little faster than it should have been just lying in the tent, and I realized he was as nervous as I was.

"Have you heard my heartbeat again? Since the caves?" I stayed in place, wanting to see his face while he answered.

"Not the past few days, no." He lowered his voice and turned his head from the tent above him to face me. I noticed the stubble on his face had grown a bit in the days I'd been with him. It gave him a rough, intimidating look. "The last time I heard it was the burial." When I stabbed him.

"Did you ever hear anyone else's then? Lavenia or Dewalt?" I wondered if somehow, I'd projected some of my abilities onto him. I didn't even know if it was possible.

"No. I only ever heard you." His lips parted as he looked at me, and I found myself wanting to bring mine to his and feel if they were as soft as I remembered. Even in this low light, I was sure he could tell where my eyes were fixated, and I stopped myself. Now was not the time, if ever. Everything between us felt like an impassable canyon, and I wasn't sure if we'd ever be able to get over it, capable of coexisting without being laced with hurt—from both sides. Not to mention he was soon to be king. It was unrealistic to even think about. But we could be friends again, that was easy. Truly, he'd been my first real friend other than Lucia, and I wasn't sure family counted. Friendship had always been our strength; it wasn't until we added more to it that things turned sour.

"Well, I'm lucky I guess, that you're some sort of freak." He laughed at the deflection but stilled as I scooted over and put my head on his chest. After a moment, he exhaled, lowering his arm to wrap around me. I closed my eyes, breathing him in. This was the Rain I'd missed all along. He was so warm, and I was so tired, I fell asleep quickly, feeling his hand gently playing with my hair.

"It's dawn, wake up." Dewalt's voice called from outside the tent. He sounded mildly aggravated, but that wasn't far off from his normal morning personality. I kept my eyes closed, refusing to move. I was extremely warm and cozy, and I knew the minute I moved, cold air would find a way into my cocoon and stressful thoughts a way into my mind. Rainier and I had rolled to face each other in our sleep, both of his arms around me with my head tucked under his chin. I was surprised he didn't have his arm tucked in his bedroll with him given how cold it was. I inhaled deeply, content to never move again, enveloped in his smell, his calming and cleansing scent after a storm. Rainier tugged me closer, the gesture painfully intimate. I felt something catch in my throat before he stretched his arm upward and his whole body followed, everything going taut. I took the opportunity to stretch as well and pull away from him, my heart needing the distance. The pull of him was too great.

"Good morning, Emmeline." He reached down and brushed a strand of hair off my face. I stilled at the motion, and he noticed, pulling his hand away. With that one small gesture, it made me realize I had let things go too far. I shouldn't have crossed this line; it was something I should have left alone. I thought it wouldn't mean anything other than two friends sharing warmth on the road but waking up in his arms felt distinctly like more than I'd bargained for. I didn't want to walk down this path again which led to nothing but heartbreak and destruction for us both, full of mistakes and regret. I also felt a clear sense of disgust with myself, for even thinking about things between Rainier and me when my daughter was in the hands of the enemy. I knew we needed to rest the horses and sleep for the night, and I was on my way to do everything I could for her, but there was shame roiling in my gut. How could I possibly think of anything other than her in a time like this?

"Morning." I rolled onto my back, stretching. I sat up, blanket still wrapped around me, and pulled my fingers through my hair, brushing it out and braiding it into a coronet on top of my head, pointedly not making eye contact or conversation with Rainier. To his credit, he did the same. He put on his boots before passing me mine, then climbed out of the tent without a word. He could probably tell something had shifted with me, and I hoped I hadn't hurt his feelings.

I dressed in fresh clothes, and my thoughts turned to what Lavenia and Dewalt had said to me yesterday. Dewalt had been so angry with me, accusing me of destroying Rainier, when *he* had been the one to destroy me. He and I pulled down the wards when he decided to take me to the cavern. He had been the one to tell me we couldn't be together. Twice. I couldn't let myself care that he searched Nythyr for me over the years. I couldn't let this go further than it already did. Even if we could get past all of it, there was no possible future for us in any way. I'd get Elora back and then go to Ravemont. I was sure Rainier would at least help provide a guard to protect her, and then he would go on to rule Vesta, hopefully enacting the change he desired. I'd inherit Ravemont, Elora would live her life, and that would be it. Maybe I'd keep in touch with my friends, maybe I wouldn't. But I couldn't let myself get close like this again.

CHAPTER 15

By the time I left my tent, Dewalt and Rainier had already packed up the other and Lavenia was packing our supplies. Everyone was working quietly, and I ignored the way my stomach twisted when I caught Rainier's gaze.

"Go fill up the canteens, Emma." Dewalt's voice felt more like an order than a request, and I remembered the mumbled exchange between the two men the night before. I hoped Rainier staying with me didn't start some sort of issue between the two of them. I grabbed the canteens and went walking to the creek, a little farther north than the campsite. I stayed alongside the water, going farther than I needed to, wanting to put some distance between myself and the man who was currently haunting my thoughts. I stopped when I came to a point in the stream where it opened into a serene pond. It was beautiful, and that strange quiet, the smothering silence, didn't touch me here. It was almost as if I was in another forest altogether. I'd never explored the Whispering Wood before, having been trained to fear it as a child, but we were close enough to the Mirastos I figured it was safe enough.

I crouched down on the bank and put our canteens in the water. It was so clear I could see the tiny multi-colored rocks at the bottom of the stream, their opalescence glinting in the sunlight. When I dipped my hand in, tiny fish scattered across the bottom of the stream bed. After I filled the canteens, I sat back for a moment, taking in the serenity of the area. I was reminded of the small pond near our home in Brambleton where I'd taught Elora to swim. There was a willow there, and she used to hide in its leaves to frighten me. Those brief moments of terror, not knowing where she was, listening for a splash or cough or anything to find her, were awful, and she got punished accordingly whenever she did it to me. Now, that same fear was leaching into me, and I was experiencing it at all times. The only respite was being around the others, distracting myself from the intrusive terror threatening the borders of my mind. Most moments not spent keeping myself busy had me thinking about Elora and what might be happening to her. Even though we were going to Astana to use the best resources I could find, I still felt like a failure. I knew weeping and wallowing wouldn't get her back, but I felt like I could be doing more. I knew being distracted by Rainier was just another way of coping, but I needed to be more careful.

I startled when I felt a warm hand on my shoulder. The man in question had snuck up on me, almost as if I summoned him.

"Gods, warn me next time!" My heart was in my mouth. He gave me an apologetic smile and pulled me to my feet, holding my hands after I stood, and rubbing his calloused thumbs across the backs of them. I stilled for a moment, glancing down at my hands in his. His eyes were on me when I lifted my head, the early morning light playing in them, giving him a mischievous look. Rainier's mouth curved up, and I couldn't help but stare at his lips. I didn't move when he put his hand up to my cheek, gently caressing my jaw with those rough fingertips. I'd just told myself this had no future; I couldn't let this continue. But here he was, and I wasn't sure about anything.

"I—Rain, this won't ever—" He put a finger on my lips, quieting me. As much as I hated myself for it, as much as the shame roiled in my stomach—when he leaned down to kiss me, I did not stop him. A distraction and nothing more. That was what I told myself, what I had to tell myself.

His kiss was feral as he nipped at my lips, a hand going to my waist. The soft and warm kisses I'd remembered were no more, and in their place was this frustrated and wild passion which surprised me. He pushed me backwards against a tree and pulled one of my legs up around his waist, grinding into me. I gasped, taken by surprise until I felt his hardness pressed against my softness, and I couldn't help it as a moan slipped past my lips. He took a firm grasp on me, tilting my head, as he lowered his mouth to my neck. His teeth grazed against my skin, and I felt it pebble. This was so unbelievably stupid and irresponsible, and yet I couldn't—wouldn't—put a stop to it.

Wrapping my arms around his neck, I gave in, completely embracing what my body wanted, what *I* wanted. His hard edges pressed perfectly against my soft curves, every part of him melding precisely against me. If it was only a distraction from my worry and fears, fine, I'd take that diversion gladly. I tilted my head away from him, giving him better access to kiss my neck. There was a warmth traveling down my body, pooling low. Why did he wait until now? Why didn't he unleash this fire last night when we truly could have done something about it? Would I have?

He started tracing his hand down the leg I had around his waist, reaching down to grab my ass as he pulled me toward him, and he snaked his other hand up my shirt, palming one of my breasts before he squeezed, almost painfully. It brought me to my senses. I started to think about what this might do to me mentally, and I had second thoughts.

"We can't do this. Not here, not ever." I started to push him away. We needed to get back on the road, get to Astana, get to *Elora*. I wanted him badly, but I couldn't let myself think like this, get lost in this. He pushed back into me again, pulling my lower lip between his teeth before he went back to kissing my neck. And gods help me, I got lost in the sensation.

"Emmeline, I want you to grab your dagger." My eyes were shut, letting Rainier drag his lips across the sensitive spot where my shoulder met my neck, the skin pebbling. The voice was familiar, but it made no sense, and it took me a moment to fully understand. I opened my eyes, looking towards the path I'd taken, and blinked.

Rainier and Dewalt stood on the path, watching me with grim horror.

My eyes widened in shock while I felt a sharp pain in my neck.

"It's an onaán." Rainier's voice was low. He was carefully circling around me, assessing and searching for a way to get to me.

"Can you reach your dagger? You'll have to get its heart." Dewalt had an arrow notched, waiting, but the onaán was too close to me for him to get a clear shot. I reached down for the weapon strapped to my thigh. I knew I needed to do something soon. Its hand on my breast had turned into a claw, and I nearly cried out as it started digging into me. I knew it was draining me. I was already feeling lightheaded in the moments since it latched onto my neck. Blade in hand, I pushed the creature back from me a little bit, and it pulled the claw out of my shirt, grabbing onto my neck, holding me still as it latched on even harder, pushing back into me. I let out a small yelp and looked desperately at Dewalt in my line of vision. I tried not to look at the onaán, its body starting to change. It still looked like Rainier, but its skin had turned mottled—bark-like and a dark greenish brown.

"I can't—" My voice faltered, and I noticed spots in my vision. I started pushing against the monster again, desperate and flailing. I was going to die.

"Stop, Em! It's going to tear your throat." There was real terror in Rainier's voice. "Just stay with me."

The ground below us gave out, and I screamed as I fell, the monstrosity landing on top of me, and a searing pain in my neck. A second or an hour later, I wasn't sure, a splash of warm and wet splattered down over me. I peered up through blurry vision and saw Rainier holding the onaán's head, no longer attached to its body. The next thing I knew, Rainier was lifting me, gently and with ease, cradling me to his chest. I heard, more than felt, the ground below us move as Rainier held me, maintaining pressure on my neck. I vaguely knew I was bleeding, excessively based on my suffering vision. I closed my eyes, relaxing into the weightlessness.

"You can't sleep right now, Highclere. Open your eyes. Look at me, Em!" Rainier hovered over my face, the emerald-green eyes flooded with concern and fear. "Go get Ven's kit, now!" Rainier's yell would have been deafening if I wasn't on the verge of unconsciousness. Leaning into his warmth, I realized Rainier had seen me kiss the onaán, and I thought maybe the embarrassment of it would keep me from passing out. It didn't.

I woke up to a canteen being held against my mouth.

"Em, drink." I pulled it to my lips. It was a struggle, considering everything was bouncing, and it took me a moment to realize I was on horseback. I drank deeply, soothing my dry throat. Rainier's arm was around my waist, helping keep me balanced on top of the horse.

"How long was I out?" I sat up a little straighter, stopping myself from leaning back into his arms.

"A few hours. Lavenia patched you up and said to let you rest. We knew you'd kill us if we waited on you, so we packed up and left."

I couldn't believe I'd been knocked out for a few hours. I surmised that the onaán must have taken a lot of blood, considering how weak I still felt, but at least I wasn't dead. I glanced down, sure I'd still be covered in blood, but I saw I had on a fresh shirt with my cloak wrapped around my shoulders. A surge of embarrassment flowed through me. Not only had I been caught kissing a creature I thought was Rainier, someone had changed me out of my blood-drenched clothes, and they had to get me up on the horse. Mortifying. Thankfully, my stomach started growling loudly enough to drown out any of my thoughts.

"Let me grab you something to eat." After fumbling around in one of the saddlebags, he pulled out an apple and passed it to me. I bit into the piece of fruit ravenously, throwing the core when I finished.

"Thank you," I paused, "for saving me. Sorry for the trouble."

"I was surprised to see the onaán so close to the Mirastos. I'm glad we got there in time." I felt his arm tighten around me, pulling me closer to his body. Whether it was intentional or not, I didn't think about it and just relaxed into his hold.

"I should have been more careful." I should have known Rainier wouldn't throw me into a tree and forcefully kiss me, especially not after our limited exchange when we woke up. After everything we'd been through, all the things we'd said in hurt and anger, all the time that had passed? How stupid was I?

"How could you have known? Onaán are surprisingly convincing." His voice didn't hold an ounce of amusement, and for that I was grateful. I knew the stories of many different creatures supposedly wandering the Whispering Wood, but I thought most were legends. I didn't realize they were real, and I'd never heard of an onaán before. I wouldn't make such a mistake again.

"How do they work? How did it know to mimic you?" Why did it appear to me as Rainier? Why did it try to kiss me?

"That's only the second one I've seen in all my travels, but they tend to appear as someone you'd trust. Their goal is to get close and drain you, so they'll appear however they think they can do it, using your own thoughts against you." I almost snorted, entertained by the idea of Rainier being the person I trusted the most right now, although the longer I thought about it, the more I realized just how right the creature was. I heard a sound to my left as Lavenia approached.

"Ah, you're awake! How are you feeling?" She gave me a smile that didn't reach her eyes, clearly worried. She seemed tired, and I noticed she'd thrown her braids on top of her head into an elegant bun. I wondered if it was to keep it clear of the copious amounts of my blood she had to deal with.

"Tired. I know I just woke up, but I could easily go back to sleep, even on top of a horse." With Lavenia next to us, I thought perhaps I should pull away from Rainier, but I was nestled in his arms rather comfortably. Still, I didn't want to give her and Dewalt more fodder for their insinuations.

"Here, eat this." She reached over, handing me a hunk of bread. When I lifted my arm to take it from her, she noticed Rainier's arm around my waist and let her gaze hover there for a moment. I ignored it. It was just an arm, after all, and I'd been unconscious only minutes ago.

"Chew on this if you have any pain. It's a shame you can't heal yourself. What's the point of your divinity if it can't even help you?" She teased. She handed me a small pouch full of leaves. I sniffed them, and tucked them away, put off by the scent. My neck wasn't hurting quite that bad.

"If only. Mairin will check on me when we get to Brambleton." I reached up and felt the bandage on my neck. "Pretty nasty, huh?"

"You're lucky Rainier killed it when he did, before it could just rip your throat out. I'm still shocked it wasn't bleeding more." Lavenia grimaced, and Rainier made a low sound in his throat before he spoke.

"I thought you were dead, there was that much blood. Too much. But by the time I got you to Lavenia, it had slowed, and I could tell you were breathing."

"You're lucky." She eased off, falling back behind us. I laid back in Rainier's arms in silence for a while, already about to doze off again. Eventually, I felt him stiffen behind me.

"Did you mean what you told the onaán?" I racked my brain, trying to remember what I'd said to it when I thought I was talking to Rainier. I couldn't remember much of anything that was done in the moments before I passed out, let alone what was said. Everything from the encounter was so jumbled. I was glad in the moment, sure that whatever I'd said wasn't something I would've wanted him to hear.

"I don't remember. Everything is such a blur." I wondered if he saw it grab my ass. Considering he heard me speak to it, I thought the odds were good.

"Never mind, it doesn't matter." His body relaxed slightly, his arm loosening around my waist. "I do have to ask; how did it manage to seduce you? Onaán can't speak, not without giving up their ruse. Am I so alluring, Emmeline?" I felt my face flush in embarrassment, and the mischief in his voice did something to me I wanted to ignore.

"Maybe that in itself was the allure. He looked like you but didn't speak." I didn't want to admit every part of me had wanted him in the moment, even if I fought it. He barked out a laugh, and I felt his body shake behind me. I pushed farther into him, his presence warm and comforting. He leaned down a bit, putting his mouth right next to my ear.

"Well, Highclere, the next time you want me to be quiet and kiss you, just tell me. I'll even bite your neck if you want."

A flash of heat tore through me, and I willed myself not to react, choosing not to reply to him. I was sure he heard my sharp exhalation of breath before I gained control of my reaction, but he didn't say anything, thankfully. The confidence of his statement made me start to wonder. He was handsome and the Crown Prince, so I was sure he could have and would have been with other women since the last time I saw him, but part of me bristled with annoyance. I'd only been with Faxon, and it was years ago, and not out of any real desire. I couldn't even think of the last time I wanted to be around a man, let alone have one kiss me. And yet, I'd wanted that from him just hours ago. It had to be an omen: the one time I'd felt anything close to desire in all these years, and I'd nearly died because of it. Feeling a tinge of possessive jealousy made me decide to chew on one of the leaves Lavenia gave me and try to sleep. If I didn't, I was worried about what stupid things I might say.

When I gagged at the taste—a mixture of cherry, mint, and lavender—Rainier chuckled, and the sound melted down my spine.

"They don't taste great, but they definitely work. Are you comfortable? I suspect you'll sleep for a while." I nodded as I scooted farther into his hold, head tilted back. As I drifted off, I swore I felt him kiss the top of my head.

It was close to dusk when I woke, and it was significantly louder, voices surrounding me. I sat up in a start, eyes wide, hand going to my dagger. Rainier's arm squeezed around me.

"Easy, killer." A low chuckle vibrated against my back. I looked around, forgetting my wound and wincing, and I realized we were surrounded by his guard. My neck began to throb—more sore now than it was before.

"They ran into a little trouble in the Whispering Wood. A tírrúil attack—a lone female." Contrary to the onaán, I knew tírrúil existed. They were a certain type of wolf, especially large and especially deadly.

"Was anyone hurt?"

"She took down one of the pack horses, and one of my younger men broke his arm. They set it in the field, and Lavenia took a look at it, he'll be alright."

"Why didn't you wake me? Help me down. Let me see him." I pulled his arm off me.

"Em, stop, you're too weak. You can check on him when we make camp, we're stopping soon."

I didn't like being told my limitations. "I'm fine. I'm not going to let someone suffer longer than they need to. I'm awake now, let me fix him." When he didn't lift his arm from me and showed no signs of listening to me, I decided a different approach might be necessary. "Please, Rain. They're all here because of me." I felt him still before he exhaled quickly.

"Fine." Rainier let out a sharp whistle and pulled us to the side of the group, turning his horse toward the end of it. "Dickey, where are you?" Rainier called out, trying to find the injured soldier.

"Here, Your Highness." A voice from the back of the group called out, hidden behind the pack animals and wagon. I was shocked when everyone else surpassed him, and the boy was revealed. He couldn't have been much older than Elora. His bright red hair and freckles across his face reminded me of Mairin. Why did Rainier have someone so young in his guard?

"Hop down, Dickey. Lady Emmeline wants to inspect the break." Rainier's arm was still around me, and I pulled it off, making to get down. "Would you be patient?" He huffed at me, annoyed. He jumped down, lithe as always, before grabbing me by the waist and putting me down on the ground in front of him like it was nothing. I felt dizzy and grabbed his arm for support. "See, this is why I wanted to wait. You need to rest."

"The longer I wait, the longer Dickey, here, is in needless pain. Besides, I can just go right back to sleep when I'm done." Dickey smiled at me when I mentioned his name, but I noticed the wince when he got off his horse and his arm jolted from the movement.

"Sit down at least, so he doesn't have to catch you when you pass out." I heard Dewalt's drawl before I saw him, ambling toward us on his own horse, no doubt wanting to see what we were doing. I knew he was joking, but it wasn't the worst idea he'd ever had. I threw my middle finger up at him as I delicately sat down. Rainier laughed, and I was happy, hoping to get rid of his annoyance. I motioned for Dickey to sit down across from me.

"Take the sling off him, Rain." Dickey gaped at me in shock and something verging on horror. "What? Does it hurt that bad?" Rainier did as I asked, gently lowering the boy's arm so the broken limb rested in his lap.

"No, I just—You were so informal." The boy hissed the last part of it, peering at Rainier as he walked back to stand next to me.

"Our friendship goes far back, Dickey. Don't worry, he won't have my head over it."

"Don't be so sure," the prince retorted.

I couldn't contain my grin as I examined Dickey's arm. There was definitely a break, close to the elbow, but considering it was a tírrúil attack, I was shocked he didn't have any abrasions. "What happened?" The boy's cheeks reddened.

"The horse I was on spooked. We both fell, and the horse landed on top."

"And you weren't attacked? You were easy pickings."

"It was occupied with the packhorse." I remembered with a start how they intended to bring Bree to me. I hadn't been looking for her when we waited for the guard to pass, but I didn't remember seeing her.

"Rainier, where's my horse?" I felt my voice rising in pitch as I began to worry. I tried to keep myself occupied and began to work on Dickey, pushing his arm into the most conducive position for healing.

"I'll find her." Rainier jumped back onto his horse and rode off, leaving Dewalt to help me if I needed it. I rubbed my hands together and placed them on Dickey's arm, feeling the heat pouring into his wound. It took more concentration than it normally did, only because I was tired. I could feel the bones mending, and, by the grimace on Dickey's face, he could too.

"I need water." I glanced up to Dewalt, wincing as my neck reminded me of my own recent attack.

"Water? Why?" He was confused, clearly thinking I wanted the water for the healing process.

"Because I'm thirsty?" I watched the corners of Dickey's mouth turn up as Dewalt turned away with a huff, ruffling through one of the packs.

"Lady Emmeline, you're going to get me in trouble."

"Is that so, Dickey?"

"Well, if you keep talking to them like that, I'm going to start laughing, and it won't be pretty for me."

"Don't worry Dickey, if you laugh at them and get in trouble, just blame me." He smiled through his pain, and then his face turned serious.

"Are you Lord Highclere's daughter?"

"Yes, I am. One of them, anyway."

"Ah, yes. Martyr Lucia. I'm sorry for your loss." I felt my skin pebble, shivers racing down my spine. Martyr Lucia threw me. I kept so isolated after she died, I didn't even realize the Myriad formally recognized her as a martyr. It was something my father clearly failed to mention.

"Thank you, Dickey. It was a long time ago."

"I know your daughter was taken by the Folterrans too. Does that mean she's the Beloved?"

"Prince Rainier has been rather helpful in my pursuit of her. She's not much younger than you." I didn't mention the prophecy, and thankfully Dickey either didn't notice or decided not to pursue it. He could tell in my tone I was asking him a question.

"My father used to be a member of the guard before he died. It was just the two of us, so when he passed, I decided to join. All I'm in charge of is the horses." He gave me a shy smile.

I took Dickey's arm in my hands, bending it and twisting it. "How's that feel?" The grin I received told me the answer. "Alright, Dewalt. Put the sling on him again."

"You fixed him, why does he need the sling?" Dewalt questioned me as he walked back from his pack but worked to put the sling back on Dickey anyway.

"It was a bad break; I don't want him to use it for the rest of the day." I turned to Dickey. "Take it easy tonight, don't use it. I don't want you on any watches either, I want you to rest. Who makes your watch schedule?"

"I'll take care of it right now." Dewalt passed me a canteen before spinning on a heel and promptly mounting his horse. I sat there with the canteen, gulping the water back with only Dickey and his horse as company.

"My lady, would you like something to eat? I have some cheese in one of these." The boy got up, rummaging through the packs.

"Dickey, say no more. I would love some, thank you." He brought me a hunk of cheese, and I ate it ravenously. I'd slept most of the day, and I was starving. I couldn't wait for us to stop for the night and eat dinner. I was nearly finished eating when I saw Rainier riding back, appearing disheveled. My heart dropped, and my face fell. Bree, my beautiful, stubborn mare, had been the packhorse to die in the attack.

"She's not dead." Relief flooded through my veins as Rainier casually dismounted. I was grateful for his directness, knowing where my thoughts had likely gone. "But she is not here. She is at Ravemont." My confusion must have been evident on my face.

"Mr. Carson had a farrier called. He found infection under a shoe. They're treating her, and they expect a full recovery." I was disappointed, but glad she was checked out before she'd made the journey.

"Did anyone bring my things?"

"Yes, they did, I already grabbed them." He turned to Dickey, "She fix you up, boy?" Dickey nodded, face stuffed full of food.

"Dewalt is taking him off watch tonight, he needs to rest. He should be back to normal tomorrow."

"Good. We need to get going. I wanted to be further north before nightfall." He held out his hand and pulled me up. My knees buckled, the cheese and water not being nearly enough to help me regain the energy I'd lost between nearly bleeding out and healing Dickey. I managed to stay standing, but Rainier studied me in concern.

"Your Highness, her neck." I heard Dickey and realized I must be bleeding again. Rainier put a hand on my waist and turned me toward him.

"Gods dammit, Em." He heaved a sigh and picked me up, gently positioning me on top of the horse. He hopped up behind me, as graceful as a cat, and berated me the entire way back to Lavenia who took one look at me and groaned, angling her horse off to the side of the throng. Rainier repeated the process of plucking me off the horse, and I was too weak to object. His hands held steady on my waist, and I was grateful as I swayed on my feet.

"You know, if you'd just have waited until we made camp, it would have been easier to take care of Dickey *and* yourself." Lavenia's voice was laced with annoyance.

"When have I ever been easy?" I did feel bad for making trouble, but I'd never feel bad about healing someone when they needed it. Rainier barked a laugh.

"Take her bandage off, Rainier." Lavenia began digging through her pack as Rainier gently pulled at the wrapping on my neck, and I found something on the ground rather interesting as his fingers brushed my skin.

"The bruises on your face are almost gone." I'd completely forgotten about the punch to my temple. After peeling off the bandage, he lightly traced the marks on my jaw. "One injury almost gone, and then you get another. That's familiar." He quietly chuckled, and I felt my lips tug upwards. I had always been rather accident prone.

"Move." Lavenia shoved her hip into her brother, pushing him away from me. She took a wet cloth and pushed it against the wound. I hissed as it burned, my skin feeling like it was bubbling. "Quit whining, it will kill any infection. I think you probably needed a couple stitches, but I didn't want to do it out here in the field. You need to take it easy until it's healed more or I'm going to have to stitch you and risk infection."

"Yes, ma'am." I made eye contact with Rainier as I said it, and he pushed his hand to his mouth in a fist so Lavenia wouldn't see his smile. "Sorry, ma'am." Lavenia leveled a glare at me that would have sent half of these soldiers running, tail between their legs.

"You're older than me. And you definitely look like it." Lavenia lifted a brow as I snorted, and Rainier let out a loud peal of laughter. "I mean it, Rainier, I don't want to do stitches until we make camp." She gave me a sly smile, glad I laughed at her insult.

"Yes, ma'am." Rainier retorted and dodged as Lavenia reached out to smack him.

He darted to me, staying out of his sister's reach, and placed me on his horse as if I weighed nothing. I settled in, and Rainier was behind me a moment later, tenderly wrapping an arm around my waist and pulling me against his chest.

"You should sleep. You're much more docile when unconscious." He chuckled, his breath warm on my ear. I took in his intoxicating smell and obeyed.

CHAPTER 16

THE LAST LEG OF travel that day passed by much like the rest, with me asleep. When the horse finally slowed to a stop, I opened my eyes, disturbed by the silence around me. I reached down and grabbed Rainier's arm.

"Where are we?" My panic was eased by the fact I knew Rainier was still with me. I carefully looked forward, trying not to disturb my neck too much. A large, grassy area stretched before us, full of wildflowers. Everything was a shade of blue underneath the tiniest sliver of the moon, but I knew in the light we'd be surrounded in color, a beautiful sight in the midst of the forest. Crickets played their melodies, and the air was still. I imagined there were all manner of critters who frolicked here during the day and called this place home. It was beautiful even in the dark. Almost more beautiful in the dark, for the imagination I used to picture it during the day.

"I wasn't quite ready to put you down, and I wanted to let them set up camp before I woke you, so I took us exploring and stumbled upon this." His voice was quiet, reflecting our surroundings.

"It's like the meadow." I sighed. Though the meadow from our childhood had no trees as far as the eye could see, it had the same calm as this place.

"I knew you'd say that." He paused as he lowered his head down, speaking quietly, a whisper in my ear. "I thought you were going to die today. I'm glad you didn't." Something stirred within me, and I tried to ignore it.

"Me too." I smiled; It was a silly thing to say.

"You just came back to me, and we've barely had a chance to talk. You can't die yet." I froze. I wasn't sure how I felt about what he'd said. I hadn't come back to *him*, I'd come to him for help. I wasn't sure if I should make the distinction out loud to him, so I chose not to. Part of me wasn't sure I wanted to make the distinction. Were the two options much different? I'd found him either way.

"I'll try not to." My stomach growled loudly, as if to make it clear I might die if I didn't eat soon. Rainier huffed a laugh as he turned us around, I assumed to make way back to camp.

"You mentioned you work with a healer in Brambleton. Is there anything else you've been doing?"

"Yes, I've been working with Mairin for a long time. Hmm, what else? I maintain our garden." I could practically hear Rainier's eyebrow raise behind me. "I know, you have no idea how long it took me to successfully grow something." He had seen the mess of a garden my mother had forced on Lucia and me. She'd pushed flowers and shrubbery on us, trying to find us a hobby befitting a lady, but what had resulted was an abomination of weeds and dead plants the servants had to take over. Green beans and tomatoes, potatoes and strawberries—those were easier for me. "I've taught Elora all her lessons over the years. And lately I've tried to help her train." Though my divinity barely registered compared to hers, I did the best I could to help teach her.

"That's it?" Rainier sounded surprised, and it twisted something in my gut.

"Yes, that's it." The question bothered me. "I know it doesn't compare to the life of a crown prince." I began hearing the sounds of camp and could see a fire I wanted to hold my hands over.

"Weren't you bored?" The way he asked it didn't come across as rude, more confused than anything. "What about Faxon? What did he do?" The tone he reserved for Faxon was more openly hostile.

"Faxon did different things over the years. Most recently, he wanted to start harvesting grains." My stomach clenched, remembering the "special order" he'd made which had all been a ruse to get our daughter to Mira. I felt my anger rise, rage boiling up my throat. I didn't have any qualms with killing the man I'd shared the last sixteen years of my life with, and I was only partially bothered that I didn't care. "It hasn't been the most exciting life, but it's been safe." Until now. Until I failed because I put trust in someone I thought would never betray me. Betray us.

"I bet you're a wonderful mother." Wonderful mother, save for the fact I let my daughter get taken. I took a shuddering breath, wanting to argue with him, but chose to stay silent instead. "Elora withstanding, do you ever feel like you made a mistake?" His mouth was beside my ear again, and the shiver that went down my spine mingled with the rage brewing from my thoughts of Faxon and spun, like fibers on a wheel, to turn into an angry, dark thread. I didn't think before I tugged on it.

"I accept the decisions I've made. Do you?" I bit back at him, my voice flaring in frustration I wouldn't have known surprised him if he hadn't jolted away from me. My eyes stayed on the fire growing larger at our approach, feeling my own fire rising in me.

"Emmeline—" He stopped himself, stiffening as I pulled his arm off me. We were breaking through into the camp, and I didn't want to be on this horse with him a second longer.

"I meant every word I said to the onaán, Rainier." Remembering our earlier conversation, I'd finally been able to pull what I'd said to the creature from the banks of my memory. "We will never. Asking if I think I made a mistake suggests you offered me an alternative. I begged you, Rain." I shook my head, wincing at the pain in my neck. "The only mistake I made was you. Breaking the wards with you, betraying my sister in her final moments with you, all of it. I will regret *that* until the day I die, but not the decisions I made after. *You* didn't choose *me*. It sounds an awful lot like you're the one who feels they made a mistake, not me."

You are poison.

"Let me down. Now." I'd had my eyes on the fire the entire time I spat my venom at Rainier. He'd walked us straight into camp, not stopping for me to finish yelling at him from a position of solitude. Our friends were at the fire watching us, Dewalt's mouth in a thin straight line and Lavenia wearing a look of concern. There was no way they hadn't heard what I'd said. She made eye contact with me before her eyes roved to my neck. Rainier pulled his arm away from me, finishing the job I'd started. I clumsily slid down off the horse, the victory being that I managed not to fall.

"Take me to my tent." My voice was hoarse as I ordered Lavenia, and I was grateful she didn't remind me she was a princess and could have my head for such disrespect. We walked between Dewalt and Rainier, the two men maintaining eye contact. I wondered, not for the first time, if they had some secret connection, able to talk to one another without actually exchanging words. I considered the impending argument with Dewalt, but I decided I didn't care.

The tent Lavenia brought me into was huge. There was a small brazier in the center of it with a hole in the top of the tent to vent the smoke out. I could stand in the tent as well, not having to crouch inside. A small table with a chair was set up along the back wall. For what purpose, I could not know. There was a pile of furs and pillows to the left of the desk and a pallet to the right. I'd barely been awake the entire day, and my anger was coursing through my veins so fiercely I didn't think I'd be sleeping anytime soon. I heard the tent flaps close behind me as Lavenia entered, carrying a small pot of water.

"I need to deal with your neck. Take your bandage off." I knew she'd have loyalty to her brother, but I had hoped she wouldn't be cold. Nonetheless, I did what she asked and gently pulled the bandage off as she placed the pot on top of the tray on the brazier. I took my boots off and laid down on the pallet, my head toward the bottom so she'd have full access to my neck. I knew I needed to brace myself; it was going to hurt. Lavenia grabbed the desk chair and set it near me, placing all the items on top, including the pot of hot water.

"So, do you want to tell me what that was all about?" She dipped a cloth into the water and carefully began cleaning my neck. It hurt and felt good at the same time.

"What if I say no?" I nearly hissed the words out as she hit a particularly sensitive spot. It felt like my skin was sloughing off.

"You're not going to say no." The words were a challenge, one I knew I'd lose.

"It's nothing. He keeps bringing up the past, like it's my fault for the way things turned out." I winced as she pulled the cloth away, thin pieces of my skin clinging to the fabric.

"It's not nearly as bad as it seemed earlier. I probably won't need to stitch it." I grunted as I felt the familiar bubbling on my skin when she poured something on it, killing any chance of infection. "What do you mean about the past?"

Like I had some sort of choice. Like I could have done anything differently.

"Lavenia, he told me we couldn't be together while he was still inside me." I felt her stiffen at the description, but I didn't falter. "And maybe time has changed his thoughts on the matter, but it doesn't change the fact I made decisions based on what he said—with what he *repeated* when I begged him later. I will not make apologies for how I chose to repair myself after he br—The decisions I've made and the life I've lived are my own, and I will not apologize for a second of it." My heart had cracked when he said what he did. The crack had spread when I saw Lucia's face. And it shattered when she died.

"I didn't know he said that. I've always thought you were just so broken it caused you to make some questionable decisions afterwards." Her voice was quiet as she applied a salve to my wound. It smelled of mint and felt amazing on my torn skin.

"Of course, he didn't tell you that part." I snapped. "Did he tell you the part where Lucia looked at me like—like I betrayed her by being with Rainier? It has haunted me ever since." Even though I bit the words out, I could feel the tears welling up and couldn't stop them from crashing down onto my face. I'd had years to accept what I'd done, that some of Lucia's last moments included discovering my omission, my deception. I'd convinced myself a few times if she'd only had time she would have understood, forgiven me. Forgiven us. But an overwhelming part of me still felt nothing but disgust whenever I thought about it. Which, given my company, was more frequent than I ever had before.

"I'll get you some food." Lavenia packed up her supplies and left the tent, giving me privacy.

I repositioned on the pallet so I was laying with my feet toward the fire. I let the tears welling up crash over me, just to get them out. Of course, I had wanted a different life for myself, but if Rainier thought I'd dreamed of a life with him, he was mistaken as well. I'd barely let myself dream of a day with him before everything happened, let alone a life. Even if he hadn't said what he did, even if I'd somehow stopped my marriage to Faxon when I ran, where would that have left us? He'd never have been allowed to court me, let alone marry me. Even if I had made a different decision, I doubted my life would have turned out much differently. Forced to marry Faxon a year later rather than immediately didn't seem like much of a different life to me at all.

I was lying on my back, staring at the leather above me, when Lavenia returned with food. The light of the brazier and the small lamp on the table showed what appeared to be veins from whatever poor creature ended up as this section of tent, and oddly, I felt a bit bad for it. Lavenia also had my pack with her and a bottle of wine tucked under her arm.

"It's stew. Don't ask me what meat it is, I don't think either of us want to know." She sat down on the end of the pallet by my feet and put the bowl on the chair. I sat up and gladly took it. I was ravenous. I didn't care what the meat in it was, just that it was thick and hearty, full of potatoes and carrots. Delicious. As I ate, Lavenia wrapped the bottle of wine in a fur and started banging it on the ground. I watched her with amusement, wondering what she was thinking and then finally the cork popped out.

"Neat trick." I smiled as I dredged the bottom of my bowl for the last mouthful of stew.

"Comes in handy." Her grin widened before she took a swig and then passed the bottle to me. I took a deep drink and felt the warmth spread in my stomach.

It probably wasn't wise to drink too much wine after copious blood loss, but I didn't care.

"Rainier is sending his spies into Darkhold." She offered the information casually but tracked my reaction. I wasn't sure why she cared.

"I didn't know he had spies."

"He has a few everywhere but keeps his most trusted on a short leash. They're shifters."

That interested me; I'd never met a shifter before. "I think they might be offended by your choice of wording." She snorted before taking another swig of wine.

"They don't shift into dogs, they wouldn't mind. Right after I brought you in here, he went to meet with them. They leave at dawn." The look on my face must have told her what I was thinking. "Yes, I will wake you for it." She smiled.

"He has two?" They were rare enough, like most conduits, that I'd never seen one, let alone two.

"They're twins. You'll like them. They have the spy personality mastered. Very quiet, very mysterious." She laughed as she passed the bottle of wine back to me. I felt my heart lurch to think of another set of twins. A complete set. The smile left my face as I began to imagine, not for the hundredth time, what life would be like if Lucia were still alive. She would be a princess. Hell, she might have had children with Rainier by now. The thought actually made me feel a bit nauseated, not heartsick like I would have imagined. Oddly enough, I wondered for the first time, if they'd have gone through with the bonding ritual, would I have ever crossed Rainier's mind?

"We'll get her." Lavenia mistook my melancholy expression for thoughts of Elora, and I felt guilty it wasn't her I was sad about at that moment. "The twins have been instructed to extricate her if they can do so safely. When we get to Astana, we will figure something out. Negotiations or concessions, violence if necessary. We will get her." Her voice was full of confidence I didn't have.

"I hope so. I'm starting to feel rather worthless. All I've successfully done is have a panic attack and puke everywhere and then get attacked by an onaán. You three have been busy dealing with more messes I've made than anything else."

"Dewalt said the onaán looked like Rainier." She studied me, clearly wanting an explanation.

"I thought it was him. I let my guard down."

"Let it stick its tongue down your throat is what I heard."

I groaned. "To be fair, it's not like I had much choice. It pushed me into a tree."

"Uh huh."

"You're killing me." I was exasperated and embarrassed. Mortified, even.

"You spent the night together, I figured it would have been out of your system." She shoved the wine bottle back into my hand, and I gladly took a deep pull from it.

"Don't act like you weren't listening for something while you were on watch. You know as well as I do that nothing happened." Lavenia threw her head back laughing, and I glared, but the corner of my mouth tugged up all the same.

"How'd you know I was listening?"

"Because I'd have done the same thing." I grinned, taking another swig of wine before I passed the bottle back to her.

"You know, our mother can grant you a divorce." I started and let my wide eyes meet hers. That wasn't even on my mind.

"Since Faxon will no longer be alive after I see him next, I'm not sure if it's wholly necessary." She laughed but the smile didn't reach her eyes.

"Well, maybe not. But you'd be free to remarry after."

"Lavenia."

"What? You'll be at court for the next two years anyway. I know what he said before was atrocious, but..."

"You need to stop. Even after I get Elora back, you and I both know it would never happen. My divinity is a fraction of Lucia's, of the other conduits who the queen has selected for him. I have a *child*. No matter what anyone wants, if he even did want that, it would never happen. Not to mention my choice in the matter. *I do not want him*. I may have forgiven him for a fraction of the things that happened, but I will never forget them. Even if I did want him, I could never. Lucia's memory is more important, and since we are responsible for her death—"

"You still think—" I silenced her with a look.

"I swear to the gods if everyone doesn't stop talking to me about this, I will lose my mind. I have bigger worries to think about than someone I thought I loved over a decade ago." I passed the wine bottle to her after taking a long swig of it. I meant it. I was so sick of everything turning into a conversation about my relationship with Rainier that if it weren't for the access to an army and spies I didn't have, I would've already made a go at Folterra on my own.

"I'm sorry, you're right." Lavenia's hands were up, the bottle of wine between her crossed legs. "I've only ever heard Rainier's side of things, what he's been through since you left, and even then, it's not like he liked to talk about it. I'm just glad you're back. I won't say anything again." I scowled at her. "I promise."

"Good. Also, what makes you think I won't win our duel? Two years of court, ha." I shook my head. "I think I need to sleep now; I'm feeling pretty exhausted.

Thank you for the food and for bringing my bag." I knew my friend meant well, but the line of conversation had tired me. And I was sweating in the heat of the tent. Nothing could make a bad mood worse than being sweaty during it. Lavenia picked up the bottle of wine and put the chair back under the desk before she left.

I stripped off my dirty clothes; my clean shirt from before had blood on it from my neck, and my pants had green stains on them that smelled absolutely foul. I assumed it was onaán blood, and I was grateful I hadn't smelled it before this moment. I examined my breast where the foul creature had clawed into it. Surprisingly, the scratch marks were almost gone, but small, purple bruises remained where it had squeezed with fingertips I'd imagined doing other things—softer and more pleasing things. I shook my head and blew out a breath. I needed to get my head straight. I went and grabbed the pot of water Lavenia had brought in to help clean my neck and found the cleanest part of the shirt I'd just taken off. Dipping it into the pot of water, I used it to bathe as well as I could, especially around my collarbones, where there was some dried blood. I stripped off my undergarments but kept my socks on, not risking taking them off, and stood close to the brazier. Even though I'd been sweating moments before, I was cold with no clothes on. I turned to my bag and grabbed a fresh shirt and put it on, not bothering to button it yet. The fire was warm on my back, and I enjoyed it as I pulled my braid down. I heard the tent flap open, and assumed it was Lavenia again. I glanced over my shoulder, surprisingly careful of my neck despite the circumstance, and saw Rainier standing there. He was just too tall for the tent, his figure imposing in the low firelight from the brazier.

His sleeves were rolled up and he had a faint sheen to his skin, like he'd just been doing something strenuous. I saw the muscle in his arm twitch as he clenched a fist. Turning my head forward again, I started working on my shirt, but I could still feel the heat of his gaze roam over me. I tried to maintain my composure, not allowing him to see how he affected me, but I couldn't help but struggle with the buttons as my hands shook.

"You're hurt."

"My neck is fine. Get out." His footsteps came closer to me, doing nothing like leaving as I'd just ordered. I finished buttoning my shirt, but knew it was entirely too short to be standing here like this with Rainier's eyes on me. I froze as rough fingertips lightly grazed the back of my upper thigh, and I winced. I *was* hurt. I hadn't even realized.

"Let me help you clean it." He spotted the pot Lavenia left and put it back over the brazier to heat it up.

"Fine, if you turn around so I can put underwear on." He froze and spun on a heel, walking straight out of the tent. I snorted at the speed with which he fled. I must have done a good job pulling my shirt down if he didn't realize I wore nothing under it. After I pulled fresh undergarments on, I examined the back of my leg the best I could manage. There were two scratches up the back of my thigh, both red and inflamed. Since it was the leg I'd hooked around the onaán, I figured it must have grabbed me through my pants as we fell. Thankfully, the scratches didn't seem too deep, just irritated. When I heard his throat clear at the opening to the tent a few moments later, I couldn't help but chuckle.

"If you did that the last time you tried to come in here, you wouldn't have gotten an eyeful." He didn't say anything as he walked in, but I watched his eyes roll over me, and I felt my cheeks pink. I turned to the fire, breaking the contact, as he went to the desk and dumped an armful of supplies across it. I held my hands over the flames as he organized the items on the desk, attempting to calm my racing pulse. My efforts were in vain as he approached, crouching to examine the wounds. My stomach clenched, and I internally cursed the man as he traced gentle fingers across my skin.

"It doesn't seem deep, but I want to clean it. Onaán are nasty." I shuddered, not wanting to be reminded I'd been desperately kissing one.

I sat down on my pallet, keeping the bad leg tucked up, knee against my chest. Now that I knew it existed, it hurt when I touched it. Pain had a funny way of doing that sometimes. I pulled a blanket over me, hoping to maintain some sense of modesty.

"She said to just keep it in your pack." Rainier grinned as he pulled out the salve from the pile of items on the desk. I matched the smile despite myself.

"She has a point." I laughed, a burp coming up at the same time. "Sorry, your sister plied me with wine." He knelt next to me, the pot of water on the ground in front of him.

"Sounds like her." He was eye level with me, and I wasn't sure if it was the wine or the blood loss, but I found it hard to breathe when those green eyes, mossy in the low light, met mine. Despite my anger with him, there was no denying the man was beautiful. The scar through his eyebrow gave him a bit of an intimidating look, the asymmetry drawing attention to how expressive his face was. The slightly crooked nose, a bit upturned at the tip, led my eyes down to his lips. The true crime of the onaán was not getting the exact softness right. At least not how I remembered them. The urge to verify my suspicions with my mouth nearly overtook me before I traced the rest of his face with my gaze. The stubble on his jawline accentuated the sharp angle of it; it hadn't been so defined when I'd last seen him. Time had been kind to him.

"You're going to need to lay on your stomach." He broke our silent stare before he looked pointedly away, letting me situate myself. I wasn't sure how to do that while keeping myself covered as completely as possible. I pivoted on my hip and laid down, keeping the blanket over me. Once I got comfortable, I tugged my shirt down to cover my underwear, knowing he'd likely see them anyway when he pulled the blanket down. I made a mental note that I could have insisted on Lavenia coming to help me, an acceptable request, but for whatever reason I didn't.

I'd think about it later.

I pulled my arms underneath a pillow, resting my head on it and nodded at Rainier when he looked at me for permission. I stopped breathing as he began to pull the blanket down my leg. I'd just been yelling at Lavenia about him, but here I was getting butterflies in my stomach from the man. Pathetic.

I do not want him. I do not want him.

He pulled the blanket back just enough to show the scratch, and I felt my neck and face flush as he tugged my shirt down. Clearly, I had not been as successful in covering myself this time. The scratches were longer than I thought. He took the cloth and gently cleaned from the top of my leg, dangerously close to the swell of my backside, almost all the way down to the back of my knee. It didn't hurt nearly as bad as my neck, but I was still glad to be treating it. I was surprised I hadn't noticed it in the saddle, though I supposed the pain from the scratches must have melded with the soreness of being on a horse so much the past few days.

He opened the tin of salve and used one finger to gently apply it to the length of the scratches. He was careful to not touch anything other than the wounds.

"I don't think it's worth bandaging since it's not bleeding." He pulled the blanket back on top of me, resting his hand on my back afterwards. "Dewalt set up the tents for us and made an assumption. They're sharing tonight, but you'll be with Lavenia tomorrow." He stood and walked over to the other side of the small desk to the pile of blankets and pillows, and I realized there was a second pallet underneath them. I felt stupid for not realizing I'd be sharing this tent. It was too huge to only be mine.

"I'm sorry, I didn't know. I can sleep somewhere else." I could find another tent; I didn't want to intrude, and I doubted he wanted to be around me. He let out a long-suffering sigh, annoyed.

"Do you want to sleep somewhere else?" He sounded tired. Which it was very likely he was, considering he didn't sleep the entire trip today as I had.

"I—Not particularly." I was rather comfortable where I was.

"Then it's fine. Goodnight, Emmeline." He turned back to his pallet and started to unbutton his shirt. I'd have to move and turn my head the other way to avoid watching him, and, even though I told myself it was because of my neck injury, I knew in the back of my head that wasn't why I stayed still. Once his shirt was off, I saw the latticework of marks across his back. The light skin of the scars contrasted against the rich golden-brown underneath, and I found myself once again wanting to know the history of each injury. How he got each one and what he did to the person who gave them to him. I cleared my throat.

"Goodnight." He turned, giving me a glimpse of the side of his body, and I did everything I could to maintain eye contact. "Thank you for cleaning my leg." He nodded, then put a lid on the brazier and blew out the lamp before climbing into his pallet.

Plunged into darkness and silence, I let myself think, decidedly not about the man who lay mere meters away from me. Instead, I thought about Elora and her life. I wondered if we could have kept her hidden at Ravemont without the Myriad ever finding out or if we could have kept them away. I wondered what would have happened if I didn't cut Rainier off and married Faxon anyway. If he still would've been a part of my life while I cared for Faxon's baby. I wasn't sure what I wanted the answer to be, not that it mattered. None of the past mattered anymore. What mattered was finding Elora, destroying Faxon, and hopefully killing the King of Bones. After, I'd let the gods decide. I couldn't let myself think of the future like that, with the most important part of that future being forcefully separated from me. I laid there for a while, tossing and turning despite my neck, listening to Rainier's breathing grow deep and consistent.

Finally, almost in desperation, I reached out and listened to his heart. It was slow and steady, and I felt myself counting the beats, remembering the nights I'd counted his heartbeats all those years ago.

CHAPTER 17

I WOKE SHORTLY BEFORE dawn. I turned my head a bit and didn't feel any pain from my neck. It was strange; I'd gone from bleeding out and Lavenia thinking I needed stitches, to barely any pain within a day. The bubbling solution she'd used, however awful it felt, must have worked wonders. Rainier was still asleep, his back turned toward me and the blanket around his waist. I took a moment to appreciate the smooth swells of muscle in his shoulders before I turned to my bag on the floor, putting on a fresh pair of breeches. I was soon to run out of clothing, but I wasn't about to put the pants with onaán blood all over them back on. The scratches on my leg didn't hurt at all, thanks to the salve still sitting on the desk. I tucked my shirt in and was starting to braid my hair when Rainier stirred on his pallet.

"We are going to have to get you some new clothes in Astana." His voice was low, still groggy with sleep.

"Oh? Why is that?" I kept braiding my hair.

"The styles from the capital are much more comfortable." He rolled onto his back, an arm behind his head. I tried not to look at him. It felt too intimate to see him shirtless for some reason, even if I'd seen his bare torso countless times before. It felt different now.

"These are comfortable enough."

"Do you have anything appropriate for court?" I closed my eyes, bringing up a mental inventory of my clothing. No, I had nothing that would work. My nicest dress was plain cotton, dyed blue—nothing like what the frivolities of court required. None of the nice clothes in the attic would fit me anymore, either. I supposed I could pull one down and try to take it out at the seams, but I wasn't sure it would be enough at my hips.

"I have one dress that might work, but you're right. I'll need to get something so your mother will even let me in to see the king."

"Bring the dress. It will work until Lavenia's dressmaker can make you a few gowns."

I nodded and finished my braid while I started calculating in my mind just how much it might cost. "I don't have any money. I have a small purse in Brambleton I was going to grab, but not enough for something fine enough for court. I can ask my—"

"Should I be offended that you think I cannot buy you a few gowns?" I gave him a sheepish smile as he watched me with a fondness in his eyes that made me look away.

"I can't accept that, Rain." I walked over to the desk and gathered the supplies from Lavenia and shoved them all into my pack.

"You can, and you will." The way he said it told me arguing would be futile, so I chose silence instead. I carefully peeled the bandage off my neck and bent over the pallet of the infuriating man who didn't know how to take no for an answer.

"How does it look?" He pulled his arm out from under his head and reached his fingertips to the wound, his eyes widening.

"It's gone. I mean, it's red, but..." My hand shot up to my neck, knocking his finger out of the way, feeling for the skin that surely should still be sliced, and only found smooth flesh. Sore, but smooth.

"What? How?" I had no idea how it had healed so fast. Rainier sat up at my alarm, the blanket falling away from his chest.

"Your divinity?"

"It has to be, right?"

"Have you ever been injured like this before?"

"Not like this, no. Cuts and scrapes but nothing like this."

"And did those heal like normal?"

"I guess. I never paid much attention to them. I mean, the bruises on my neck healed normally, right?"

"Maybe it doesn't work for small ailments?" There was no way to know. I stayed crouched beside him, trying to think of any injuries I'd sustained since I came into maturity.

"Elora," I whispered. "When Elora was born, I nearly died." I closed my eyes, remembering the blood. "I *should* have died. The midwife was shocked I didn't." I'd lost too much blood and had been going in and out of consciousness, hallucinating, a whole ordeal. I woke a day or two later and was finally able to hold my baby, but according to the midwife, it had been touch and go for a while. Rainier studied me, something in his eyes I couldn't read. "My divinity. Did it—"

"You saved yourself. Emmeline, that's amazing." He lifted his hand as if he wanted to touch my neck, but I stood up before he could. I started pacing by the fire. How could I not have realized I could heal myself? This was quite the revelation for me. I didn't know what to do with the information, but I knew I didn't want to stand idle. The lingering frustrations from my infuriating conversations the day before in addition to the newest rush of adrenaline had left me with energy I needed to spend. I grabbed my pack and left the tent without another word. There was a soldier sitting by the main fire outside, warming his hands.

"Can you tell me where Dickey is?"

"The kid?" The man seemed surprised I'd be asking about him.

"Yes, I need to check on his arm."

"Ah, the boy is probably getting the pack horses ready." He pointed me in the right direction.

"Thank you!" I called back over my shoulder, already on the move. The man at the fire was right. Dickey and another soldier, also young, were packing up.

"Lady Emmeline!" The boy perked up at the sight of me.

"Good morning, Dickey, let's see that arm." He finished what he was doing and turned to me, rolling up his sleeve.

"Good as new!" He grinned. The redness had faded, and as I turned his arm this way and that, he didn't react in pain at all.

"Good, I need a favor."

"What can I do for you?"

"Do you have a training sword? Two, preferably." The other boy looked at Dickey, and they both flushed.

"How did you know we'd have training swords?" He was embarrassed.

"Just a hunch. Could I borrow them for a little while, please?"

"I'll get them." The other boy skittered off into the group of soldiers who were waking and breaking down tents.

"Thank you. Maybe I can help train you both." It would give me something to do, to help feel useful. "As long as Dewalt approves."

"I—No offense, Lady Emmeline, but I don't think—"

"Don't think I could teach you much? I'm going to let you in on a secret." The boy seemed mortified. "I am very good. I know I looked like I was about to drop yesterday, but, well, that wasn't a fair fight."

The other boy ran back up then with two wooden swords in his arms.

"Thank you, boys." I practically skipped off to find Dewalt.

When Dewalt and I walked back from the meadow to join the camp, I had a faint sheen of sweat on my body, but I was proud. Rainier was standing at the fire and turned back to look at me with a single raised brow when he saw me carrying the training swords.

"You ready to leave?" I was a bit breathless when I asked him, worn out from the sparring I'd forced upon Dewalt. During training, I'd decided to pretend the conversation with Rainier hadn't happened. He was here helping me, and I couldn't let our past control how we interacted now. Besides, if I thought about it too long, I'd get angry again and blame both of us for various indiscretions in my head. I decided to skip all of that and do my best to forget it, for my own sanity.

My friend had been pleasantly surprised by my efforts, although I expected he was taking it easy on me in the beginning. Practicing with wooden swords wasn't my favorite thing, but since Dewalt hadn't been eager to put a real sword in my hand at all, I figured this was the next best thing.

Where Dewalt had only been a bit better than me all those years ago, now he was an excellent swordsman. He anticipated every move of mine and met me with more force than I'd have imagined. It made sense, as he'd been participating in combat like this for years. He had long held onto the tradition of the old gods and kept his hair long because of it. When I had known him, it had rested just above his shoulders, but now it hung well past his waist, proving his prowess, and it showed in his swordsmanship.

At one point, I thought I might get the upper hand when I hit him in the shoulder and he stumbled, but he quickly recovered and kicked my foot out from under me. When he helped me up, he gave me quite a compliment, and I hadn't stopped grinning since.

"Almost ready. I had Dickey rearrange some things on the horses so you can have your own." I wasn't sure how he managed it considering one packhorse had been killed in the tírrúil attack. I was grateful for some space between us; it would make it easier for me to distance myself from our conversation the night before.

"Dewalt said you'll have your hands full with me." I nodded to the training swords in my hand.

His voice was deadpan when he retorted. "I didn't need Dewalt to tell me that." I didn't think he was only talking about sword fighting.

"Here ya go, Lady Emmeline. This is Clyde." Dickey joined us with an older buckskin horse and a smile. "I think I have all your things but let me know if you need anything." He practically ran back to where the pack horses were.

"Thank you, Dickey!" I called out to him and got a wave in response.

"He's a good kid. He's going to love you forever for fixing his arm and being so nice to him." Rainier smiled as he watched Dickey run off.

"Are people not nice to him here?" I crossed my arms. I was about to find out who was mean and have it out with them.

"That's not what I meant. A lot of the soldiers just don't have time for the young ones, but you made time."

"He was injured." I shrugged.

"You missed it this morning." Lavenia came walking up to me with a hand on her hip. I stared at her blankly, not sure what she was talking about. "The shifters."

"Oh no," I groaned. "I completely forgot."

"I'm sure you'll see them again one way or another." Lavenia smiled as she walked off to her horse. In truth, part of me hadn't wanted to see them. The twins. It was almost a punch to the gut to think about. I turned to my horse and saw my bow and quiver were there, sent from Ravemont while Bree was kept behind. I added my pack I had with me and strapped the training swords to the horse as well. I approached Clyde and held out a hand, and the good-natured old horse pushed his snout into it.

"Well met, friend." I smiled and petted him for a moment before clambering on the saddle, in a lighter mood than I had been. I'd worked out some energy, discovered new aspects of my divinity, and felt more hopeful than I had in days.

CHAPTER 18

I SPENT THE DAY in my thoughts. I couldn't believe I was finding out things about my own divinity this far into my life. I was extremely grateful for it, as I would have been dead without it, but I was still processing the shock of it. Was I stronger than I thought, and I just hadn't practiced enough to know? Maybe I could have helped Lucia. I'd just wrapped my head around the fact that there was nothing I could have done, but now I began to second guess. But I tried to banish the thoughts, remembering that I hadn't even come into my full divinity when she died. Still, it gnawed at me. I began to wonder about the limitations of my abilities. Obviously, my divinity couldn't heal me if I had my head chopped off, but would it work if I was stabbed in the heart? Would the onaán have killed me if not for my divinity? Curious, I pulled out my dagger, and sliced my palm open.

"Hanwen's asshole, what are you doing?" Dewalt rode up alongside me, confusion and surprise warring on his face. I snorted as I closed my hand, doing my best to focus my divinity on the sliced skin. "Did you cut yourself on purpose?" Dewalt was practically shouting, distracting me from my task.

"I'm testing something, calm down." I felt his eyes on me, but he stayed quiet as I opened my hand, the skin healed. "Huh. It worked."

"Sure, but now your hand is all bloody, and it's going to get all over your bread."

I glanced over at him, not realizing he'd brought me food. I spotted a large roll, bigger than my fist, and I reached out with my clean hand to take it. It smelled delicious, like the honey bread Nana used to make.

"Ravemont. They sent quite a few provisions." Dewalt could tell by the look on my face as I devoured the bread that I wondered where it had come from.

"Thank you. Sorry we missed breakfast." He shrugged.

"It was worth it. I have to say, I was surprised you were still so good. I didn't imagine you were keeping up with your skills all this time. Did you teach your daughter any of it?"

"A bit. She hated it, just like Lucia." The sad smile spreading on his face told me he remembered. "She didn't want to bother."

"Lucia always said it was pointless, no matter how many times I begged her to practice with me." She'd always laugh and flirt with him to get out of it every time he asked her. "It doesn't matter if she was right. She could overpower any of us, even Rainier."

"She was impossible." I laughed. My sister had definitely been stubborn.

"We can practice again in the morning if you'd like."

"That would be nice."

"Oh, and you can bunk with Lavenia tonight. I'll share with Rainier." Even though he stared straight ahead, I could tell he was curious but thought better of asking. I wasn't going to give him any satisfaction.

"Thank you, I appreciate it." He nodded and then fell back, leaving me in peace.

The rest of the ride passed with no problems. Dinner was stew once again, and since I was less hungry when it came time to eat it, I did put more thought into what kind of meat it was. I didn't think it was as bad as Lavenia assumed, just rabbit, and I was used to eating that to supplement everything my father provided. Opting to take the next morning off, I spent a small amount of time sparring with Dewalt. Dickey and his friend, a stocky boy with honey-colored hair who I'd learned was named Sam, came to watch. Both boys taunted their captain until Dewalt let out a warning growl that sent them running to do some unnamed task. I had to stop for a moment because I couldn't stop giggling. Dewalt's smile was grumpy at first, but he soon joined me in my laughter. Later, Lavenia and I shared a tent, and I went to sleep feeling fulfilled and tired enough I didn't have time to devolve into terrifying thoughts of Elora or confusing thoughts about Rainier.

Hours later, I woke up to the thundering of heartbeats around me. None were racing or unanticipated, but it was strange and startling to hear over fifty hearts at once. It wasn't often that I heard hearts by accident, generally only occurring when I was tired or stressed. In slumber, I must have let my guard down. I struggled to stifle the sound, wanting to return to my dreamless sleep, but it was like a storm in my head. Lavenia was snoring softly, and I heard coughing nearby from one of the soldiers. Between the cacophony in my mind and the sounds around me, it wasn't likely I'd fall back asleep anytime soon, so it only made sense that my bladder would add to my annoyance. With a quiet groan, I slipped out of my pallet and pulled on my breeches, boots, and cloak before I made my way out of the tent.

One of the things Rainier did both times we made camp was dig holes downwind for everyone to utilize. It wasn't something I looked forward to having to use, and I was eager for my own private toilet I'd have access to the next night. I passed a few sentries and nodded to them on my way, quietly slipping past tent after tent of sleeping soldiers. When I'd finished what I came to do and was buttoning up my breeches, I heard a howl. Every hair stood on end when it split into two octaves, the call of the tírrúil. And it was close. When other voices joined in on the baying, I raced back to camp. The sentries had heard the sounds and were busy rousing soldiers and ushering them south, the direction the horrifying noises came from. I went straight to my horse, hitched with Lavenia's behind our tent, and climbed atop with my bow in hand. I led him to the large fire in the center of the encampment. Tírrúil were afraid of fire.

"Why am I not surprised you're one of the first ones out here?" Rainier's voice was low and chiding as he approached. Disheveled from sleep, it was unfair how handsome he looked.

"I wasn't sleeping."

"Really? I figured you'd be tired."

"Exhausted. It was the heartbeats. Normally I can tune them out, but," I shrugged, "I had to pee."

Rainier chuckled. "Fair enough."

A scout came running to the fire, panting with breath. "Donya saw eight or nine, Your Highness, all coming from the south." I wondered if the lone tírrúil had somehow led her pack to us. Rainier had said she ran off before they could kill her.

"Shit." Rainier's facial expression mimicked the unease in his voice. Eight or nine tírrúil could easily cripple the guard.

He put two fingers into his mouth and let out a series of whistles which clearly meant something to everyone around us.

"You should go back into your tent." He didn't even turn his head when he said it, but when I glared at him in response, he finally locked eyes with me. "Or not, that's fine." I watched his cheeks darken as he peered up at me, but his facial expression was still wary.

"I'll stay here with Clyde next to the fire. Don't worry."

Everyone around us was in motion. The horses were corralled near the large central fire, no small feat considering all of them were on edge. I suspected my own steed had some hearing loss because he only became tense when he could tell the horses around us were unnerved. I saw Lavenia with a group of soldiers to my right, and Dewalt with a group in front of me—the southern group. The way they moved was seamless, a sense of purpose and camaraderie taking over that had been earned over the years. It was fascinating to watch, and I couldn't help but feel almost reverent.

Rainier walked over to speak with a soldier to our left. She was tall, with olive-toned skin and long, blonde hair, the sides swept back in small intricate braids meeting in a ponytail at the crown of her head. She was easily just as tall as him and looked every bit a warrior. She seemed to push back against something he was saying, and I saw her grip on her ax tighten. Something about the way she talked to him gave me pause, and I made a mental note to seek her out, wanting to know more about her. Dickey and Sam and a few of the younger soldiers were behind me, running around trying to keep the horses from bolting. The thundering of noise in my head had reached a level not unlike boulders crashing to the ground, and it was causing my own heart to race. Under all of it, I heard, no, *felt*, a low rumbling and turned toward Rainier to see his hands fisted and his eyes closed.

"A trench around us. If one falls in, the roots will take care of them." He answered the question I hadn't asked yet as he walked back toward me. Dewalt let out a low whistle, and we both snapped our attention to him. It was too dark for me to see the trench, but I could see eyes glinting in the distance. Three sets of eyes in the dark, slowly circling the camp from the southern edge. I watched as the trees on either side of the path slammed down, somehow narrowly missing every set of those luminous eyes.

"If I knock any more trees down, they'll just serve as a bridge." He sounded resigned as he watched the beasts approach, picking their way over the trees or around them. One of the sets of eyes blinked slowly and then raced to the edge of the trench. The animal that went flying over the gap was enormous. Easily three times as big as the average wolf, it was a mass of black matted fur, and teeth as long as my hand. When it jumped, I saw one of Dewalt's archers let an arrow fly, and, while I knew one arrow wouldn't kill it, we all heard its screams as it fell into the trench below.

"That's not going to work a second time. We aren't near a stream or else I'd just set this whole area on fire and put it out when they were dead." He walked back over to his men to my left, pulling his sword from its sheath. He glanced at me over his shoulder and nodded before he barked out orders to the guard surrounding him. This was my first time seeing him as a commander, and I was shocked at how well fitted he was to the role. His presence demanded respect from his guard, and those around him seemed eager to fight beside their prince.

As if encouraged by the howling of the fallen tírrúil, the rest of the horde moved at the same time. Growling and screaming surrounded me as they jumped over the trenches from every direction. From what I could tell, at least one more fell into a trench on the side where Lavenia was posted. She and I were separated by the fire, but I made sure to watch her the best I could. I was keeping a mental tally of the fallen devils. I erred on the side of caution and assumed there were nine in total. With two in the trenches, that left seven.

As I scanned for Lavenia, I saw she was closer to the fire, surrounded by a few soldiers. The rest of the guard on her side were hacking away at two creatures in their midst. I watched helplessly as one man fell underneath a dark brown mass of fur. I realized what Lavenia was doing when a large grey blur slammed into the dark brown tírrúil and they rolled, a pile of matted fur and gnashing teeth. She was compelling one of them to attack its own. I was surprised; I didn't know her divinity could work on something inhuman. I couldn't imagine having to infiltrate the mind of a beast. While the two masses of teeth and fur fought, the dark brown one kept lashing out at the soldiers in the vicinity, and they surged forwards to help the compelled tírrúil, working with it to attack its own brother. I wondered if Lavenia would loosen the compulsion before the soldiers had to take down the grey one. I knew part of her consciousness shifted into whomever she was compelling. She'd be cognizant of the pain if she maintained the connection until its death.

A flash of light caught my attention from the south, firelight reflecting onto a sword. Dewalt's soldiers had already taken one tírrúil down while a second one, much bigger than the others I'd seen, danced out of the way. That left three unaccounted for.

A scream from my left pulled my gaze in the direction of Rainier and his soldiers. One of the monsters had the blonde warrior's arm in its maw. I notched an arrow in my bow and was about to fire it off when Rainier and a few others overpowered the creature. I would've hit one of them with my arrow had I released it. I let out a long breath when I saw the blonde woman stand back up. She clutched her arm up to her chest but was still wielding her ax from her other hand. I realized then I'd have my excuse to meet her if she'd let me heal her. A gleam in the woods across the trench caught my eye. The predator, much smaller than the rest of the pack, was watching the soldiers, growling and pacing. If I counted this juvenile, there was still one beast left.

Clyde jolted forwards, and I looked down to see the horses around me pushing south, away from the fire. That's when I saw them. There were two tírrúil prowling quietly through the tents toward the fire, toward the horses. One broke away, moving behind tents and out of my sight. They had to have circled around the encampment and jumped the trench from the north. I grimly noted Donya's count was off at the same time I saw a shock of ginger hair.

"DICKEY!" I saw the boy and his friend on the other side of the fire, attending to a horse trying to pull them through it. Dickey gaped up at me right as the monster lunged. I couldn't get a good angle from where I was seated on Clyde, so I pulled my legs out and stood. I hoped that with all the horses pushed so closely together, Clyde wouldn't be able to move much, and so far, he didn't seem to care I was standing on his back. I couldn't see Dickey or Sam from where I was, but I could see the beast, another black one, attacking them. I pulled my arrow back and released it, launching it through the flames of the fire. The creature stumbled, telling me my aim was true. I finally saw Dickey's head, and it seemed like he was dragging Sam with him. I set off three more arrows, all hitting the creature, the last arrow landing true, right in the eye, and it fell. As much as I wanted to run for the boys, I searched for the other predator that had been prowling with the one I killed. I'd lost track of it, and the soldiers wouldn't expect to be attacked from the interior of camp.

I scanned Lavenia's group. They were killing the one she had compelled, and she was sitting on the ground, head in her hands. Based on the limited fight it was putting in, Lavenia was wholly focused on maintaining the mental link she had with it. She wouldn't risk any soldiers getting hurt. Dewalt and his soldiers were still dancing around the biggest one, but it was surrounded and wounded. It wouldn't be long. Clyde was getting pushed a bit, and I was struggling to maintain my balance.

Finally, I turned back to Rainier. The smaller juvenile that had been on the other side of the trench had finally found its courage and decided to join the fray, so his soldiers were focused there, not paying attention to the tírrúil coming up behind them.

"RAINIER!" My voice was hoarse from my scream to Dickey, and I thought maybe he hadn't heard me. I turned and dipped my arrow in the fire before I shot it off, right as Rainier's eyes found mine, wide in shock. My arrow hit it in the shoulder, and its soulless black eyes turned to look at me before letting out an earth-shattering howl which sent the horses around me moving. Clyde, bless him, planted himself. Maybe it was the knowledge his rider was standing atop him, maybe it was fear, I couldn't know. But no matter how strong and stubborn he was, he wasn't a match for the frightened horses that surged forwards when the tírrúil I'd shot came flying over them, mouth open and teeth bared. As even Clyde went hurtling away, I fell backwards toward the fire, down to the ground right on the edge of it and threw my arms over my head. The horses, gratefully, stayed away from the fire, and, although I felt like I was melting and it was hard to breathe, I counted my blessings. I pulled my arms down as two horses came screeching to a halt, screaming because of the monster that prowled in front of them, growling at me. This one had an intelligence to it I wouldn't have expected. The eyes that met mine weren't bloodthirsty but calculating.

I knew keeping the fire at my back might be an advantage, depending on how afraid it was. I also knew if it decided to be brave, I'd get thrown backwards into the flames. I grabbed my dagger from its sheath, knowing it wouldn't do much, but it was still better than nothing. My gaze was drawn to Rainier, who argued with the tall warrior beside him, her injured arm still tucked up into her chest. His soldiers had all gathered around him, the juvenile dead behind them. I readjusted my grip on my dagger as the tírrúil prowled slowly toward me. I needed Rain to make a decision, but it was clear he didn't want to attack the walking nightmare in front of me and have it knock me into the fire. Though I couldn't make out the words, I could hear him shouting at the female soldier, and he seemed angrier than I'd ever seen him, a vein in his neck bulging. I breathed a sigh of relief as he startled, a dumbfounded look on his face, and he opened a rift in front of him. My relief faded as nothing appeared next to me. He closed it and rubbed a hand over his face and tried again. Again, no rift.

He couldn't do it.

I was out of time as the beast in front of me lowered its head—fangs bared, and its hackles up—ready to attack me at any moment. I didn't want whatever happened to be on his shoulders, no matter the outcome, so I took it out of his hands. "I'm going to run this way," I shouted, pointing to my left, toward the edges of the camp. Rainier's arms were at his sides as he stared at me, helpless. His rifting had failed him again, but I could get out of this situation at least. "Once I'm over—" I didn't have a chance to finish as the predator's ears flicked, and I started running, not hesitating a moment longer.

Too slow.

The impact of the beast wasn't as bad as the burn I got down my back from sliding backwards over the rocks and dirt. My dagger flew out of my hands the minute it hit me. I had one arm around my own neck, trying to protect it from the snapping teeth, drool flinging all over me. I screamed as its teeth latched into my arm, the pressure almost unbearable. I swore I could feel teeth on bone. It pulled my arm away from my neck as the mouth clamped down, and I sobbed as I kicked at its stomach, trying to find any leverage to push it off me. My mind went to strange places as I began to picture my imminent death. I wondered if Rainier would still rescue Elora for me but instantly knew he would do anything to save her, especially if I was dead. I hoped he would tell her how hard I'd tried. To get his help, to get to her, to save her. Would he kill Faxon and make her an orphan? Would he take care of her? Drool from the gaping maw of the tírrúil flicked into my eye, bringing me back to the pain.

Fire would have been preferable.

I didn't know if it was instinct or something else that had me reaching for the animal with my other hand. Bringing it up, I started pushing through the matted fur on its neck.

Slow. Calm. Slow. Slow down. Relax.

I shoved my free hand through the mats, trying to reach some sort of bare skin. If compulsion worked on animals, maybe my abilities would work too. I started picturing calm and cool waters like I'd done with Gertie.

Slow. Slow. Slow. Sleep. Rest. Heavy.

It was working. The tírrúil started to sway on its feet, and I felt its jaw loosen around my arm. A blow from its side knocked it over onto me, and the force of the fall had my arm twisted in its mouth, but I was able to wrench it free. A guttural scream got past my lips as I pulled. The blow hadn't been a killing blow, the creature still alive but sleeping. I tried to get up, but the weight of its limbs kept me on the ground, so I tried to scoot backwards under its legs, but I wasn't strong enough. Someone, the female warrior, reached over me and pulled a leg up so I could push out a bit farther. She let go of the leg and put a hand under one of my arms and hoisted me up.

"You are rather stupid." Her accent was thick as she grinned at me. I wondered if she was one of the soldiers from Skos. "And brave."

"It's not dead, just asleep." She stared at me in confusion and then focused her attention on the beast on the ground.

I scanned the vicinity for Rainier and saw him running toward me, panting and eyes wide. Relief flooded through his features as his eyes met mine. I pulled my bad arm up into my chest, wincing as I did it. I didn't think it was broken, but the punctures from the bite were definitely bleeding. I'd never tried to use my abilities in any particular direction, but I stilled, closing my eyes, and imagined the low golden light of my divinity encircling my wounds, not sure if it would do anything. I only did it for a matter of seconds before I stopped, knowing I couldn't waste any more time.

"Dickey! Where's Dickey?"

I started running to where I'd last seen the boys. They were nowhere in sight, but I saw blood on the ground where a body had been dragged. Following the trail around the fire, I came to Lavenia hunched over Sam while Dickey sat next to him, his friend's hand in his own and his face ashen. The honeyed locks of Sam's hair were darker, tainted by too much blood.

"Move!" I ripped the boy's shirt open and put my hands on his chest, ignoring the pain in my injured arm. I reached out and listened for a heartbeat, but I found nothing.

"He's gone, Emma." Lavenia put her hand on my back, and I shrugged it off.

I didn't dare look at his face, not yet. I needed to get some of this skin sewn together to slow the bleeding, to get his heart going again. I slid my hands through the blood to find the source of his injury and focused my healing there, where his neck and shoulder met. I envisioned the wound knitting from the inside out. The blood circulating and his heart beating.

"Pump his chest." My voice was hoarse as I barked out the order.

Someone did as I asked while I continued running my hands over him, searching for any other wounds. The worst of them was healed, but he hadn't woken up, his heart still refusing to beat on its own. I hadn't realized how different a living heart sounded from the one being forced to beat below my hands. There was no spark, and I could tell. I stayed there for a long time, waiting, hoping for a tiny glimmer of life in him. He couldn't have been more than seventeen or eighteen years old. A child.

Finally, the hands pumping his chest slowed and stopped.

"Em, he's gone." I looked up, startled. I didn't realize it was Rainier who had come to help. I collapsed backwards to the ground, my arms on my knees as I brushed sweat out of my eyes. "Bring me the rest of the wounded." My throat hurt, and I felt like I was choking.

"We can take care of them; we've had to do this before."

"Bring me the rest of the wounded." My eyes met his as I enunciated each word, trying to wrestle the emotion out of my voice. Out of all the patients I'd lost with Mairin, none of them were this young, this full of life. I'd heard his playful banter with Dewalt, his shy embarrassment when he fetched me the training swords, the way he and Dickey acted like brothers, reminding me of Dewalt and Rainier. And his young life was snuffed in an instant. Maybe if I'd gone straight to him and let Rainier and his soldiers deal with the beast that ultimately attacked me, maybe Sam would still be alive.

Rainier's eyes cooled as he stared into mine. He was frustrated, but I didn't care. After a moment where I met his gaze, he finally put his fingers into his mouth and let out a coded whistle. I searched our surroundings for Dickey, wanting to say something to the boy, some words of comfort, but I didn't see him anywhere.

"Do you need this?" Dewalt came walking up and dumped my pack next to me. Lavenia's pack was there as well from when she tried to heal Sam.

"Yes. Alcohol?" Dewalt nodded and headed off. I turned to Rainier who was still seated at my side, watching me hesitantly.

"Help me rip my sleeve." I offered my arm to him, and he followed the tears in the fabric from those long, vicious teeth and carefully ripped, trying not to jostle me. I heard his sharp intake of breath, and I glanced down at my arm. It looked like shredded meat.

"Divine hell." Dewalt let out a low whistle as he came back with a few bottles of alcohol in his hands. There were four deep gouges that went across the top of my forearm, and I could see the muscle underneath, knowing if I looked hard enough, I would see bone. One of the gouges was bleeding significantly worse than the others, and I wondered if the teeth nicked an artery. If it had, the divinity I'd pushed toward my arm was saving me from bleeding out. Dewalt set the bottles down, and I handed one of them back up to him with my good arm. I turned to Rainier, grabbing his hand with my bad one and braced myself against his shoulder.

"Pour it on my arm." I directed Dewalt, who gaped at me. "Oh, don't be a baby, just do it. Hurry up, so I can make it stop bleeding."

Rainier held out the bad arm with one hand and used his other to bring me toward him. He held the back of my head against his shoulder as Dewalt poured, and the liquid fire raced across the open wound. He held my hand in his, no matter how desperately I tried to pull back, no matter how loudly I screamed. I was groaning and panting, feeling sweat break out across my brow. After Dewalt was done, I sat there for a few moments while catching my breath. Rainier didn't speak, holding me close as his fingers tangled in my hair.

"Fuck." I panted, pulling away from him. "Let's see if this works." I attempted to smile at Rainier, but I was sure it came out as a grimace. In the light of the fire, his eyes were bright, and they held worry and what I thought might be admiration in them. The way my heart began to soar at his silent praise was quickly tempered by the pain in my arm and the disappointment in myself, in my inability to save Sam.

I put my good hand on top of the wounds and closed my eyes. First, I focused on the blood. Slowing it, clotting it. Then, I focused on the gouges as a whole, only trying to speed the healing process a little bit so I could focus on the other injured soldiers. I imagined the deepest part of my injury and pictured mending the blood vessels and knitting together the muscle. It wasn't the same as when I healed other people, but I could tell it was working. It burned, and the taste of metal filled my mouth. When I opened my eyes both Dewalt and Rainier were staring at me, waiting for me to speak.

My voice came out softer than I anticipated. "I'm alright."

Both men spoke at once.

"Are you sure, Em?"

"Don't you think you should rest?"

I offered a humorless laugh, appreciative of their worry. "I'm fine. Will you please find Dickey? Tell him I'm—I don't want him to be alone right now." I would tell him I was sorry myself. Rainier studied me for a second, his eyes full of sorrow, before he nodded and grasped Dewalt's outstretched hand to help him up.

"Send someone for me if you need me."

I nodded, and they went to attend to the chaos surrounding us.

Examining my arm, I saw the gouges were much shallower, and the bleeding had stopped. It was still tender, but I didn't want to waste what divinity I had when there could be soldiers much worse off than me. I finished tying a bandage on my arm as the first injured soldier stumbled over to me.

CHAPTER 19

I tended to seventeen different soldiers with varying degrees of injury. Among the worst was an older man with a pretty disastrous neck wound and another younger man who had been gutted. Because so many were wounded, I had to ration what I could do for everyone. The man with the neck injury had lost so much blood by the time someone dragged him to me, I dropped my other patient to focus on him. Thankfully, the young woman with a mild scalp abrasion was more than understanding. Knitting the man's wound from the inside out had proved difficult, and he still had a large gash on his neck by the time I was done with him. I disinfected it a second time and bandaged it, sending him off with another soldier. Not long after I finished with the understanding woman's scalp, a man with his innards spilling out was brought to me. That was particularly harrowing. I had to have someone hold him down as I shoved my alcohol-drenched hands into his stomach and traced his intestines for damage before I closed the wound. I was afraid he still might not make it. If infection set in, there would be nothing I could do. The rest of the injuries were minor—most were similar to my own.

The last soldier was the blonde warrior who called me stupid.

"Little dyrr." She smiled at my confusion as she sat down across from me. "Deer. You ran like frightened deer to momma." I flushed in embarrassment and a bit of frustration. I may have acted like a frightened deer, but I killed one of the beasts and rendered another one helpless. I could have done worse. At the look on my face, she chuckled.

"But then you rocked tírrúil to sleep like a baby." She grinned. "Good job." I smiled back.

"Thyra." She reached out a hand, and I gave her mine, small in comparison. Everything about this woman, from her actual size to her personality, seemed large.

"Emma."

We sat in silence as I disinfected her wound. She didn't even flinch as I poured the alcohol over it and sat quietly as I held my hands over her. It took a lot longer than I'd have liked, my divinity exhausted and my head throbbing. I glanced up and the light of the sinking moon had a haze over it, the brightness making me wince. Between the headache and light sensitivity, I knew I was headed for a terrible day of recovery from overusing my divinity, probably my worst day yet. Over her shoulder, I saw Rainier leading Dickey into a tent, his hand on the boy's back. I hoped he was alright; I hadn't had a chance to check him over. My attention turned back to Thyra when she made a small sound, low in her throat.

"Peas in pod, those two. Not fair." I murmured in agreement. It wasn't fair, not at all. And it was my fault. My fault they were even here, my fault I didn't run straight to him, my fault I couldn't heal him. I cleared my throat, needing to change the subject.

"You're from Skos?" I wasn't sure, but based on her coloring and accent, it seemed to be a safe bet. She nodded.

"Yes, but it has been a long time since I've been home." She gave me a sad smile.

"What brought you here? To Ra—To Prince Rainier?" I felt like I needed to be formal with her about Rainier, that she deeply respected him, and to address him the way I normally did might offend her. She shrugged when I asked.

"He is a good man, and I owe him my service." Her eyes shuttered, and I chose not to pry. When her wounds were no more than deep surface cuts, I bandaged her, and she helped me pack up my supplies. When I turned to head to my tent, she stopped me.

"Thank you, little deer. I see now why he changed plans." She patted me on the shoulder before she headed the opposite direction. I wondered briefly at what she said, but I was too tired to think much on it.

By the time I got to the tent, dawn was breaking, and it was a struggle to keep pushing my feet in the right direction. I was exhausted, and it felt like there was an icepick in my brain, digging in. Rainier had sent an order, what seemed like hours ago, for everyone to rest and plan to leave at midday. I was about to duck into my tent when someone grabbed my pack from my arm. I turned around, too weary to be annoyed.

"You're with me." Rainier stood there with my supplies under his arm as he reached for Lavenia's pack. I handed it to him, grateful to not be carrying anything; it was enough work just to stay upright. I was too tired to question it, so I just followed him to the next tent over. He went through first, holding the flap open for me as I ducked in.

"Lavenia gave too much today. Dewalt is helping share the load." I didn't know what that meant, but I was too drained to ask. My eyes were on the ground as I kicked off my boots and moved toward the pallet. I swayed, and even though I wasn't going to fall, I was grateful for Rainier's steadying hand under my elbow. "Em, are you alright?" Though he'd had just as little sleep as I did, he wasn't nearly as exhausted. Perhaps it was the exhilaration of battle or the fact I'd used my divinity to the point of pain, but he barely seemed affected.

"Just exhausted." It was an effort to speak. "And the headache is pretty bad." He kept his hand under my arm as I lowered myself down to the pallet.

"You gave too much, too." His lips turned down into a frown.

"I didn't give enough." I bit out as I stared down at my bloody hands, thinking of the boy who died beneath them.

Rainier's eyes were drawn down as well, and, as I peered up at him through forming tears, I could see the understanding flash across his face.

"I know, Em. I know." His voice was soft as he busied himself with something at the brazier before tearing into my pack, searching for fresh clothing, I assumed. I slithered out of the disgusting pants I'd worn, forgoing modesty. I was covered in blood, in pain, and didn't quite care. He'd seen me without pants anyway, thanks to my idiocy with the onaán.

"Everything in there is dirty." I didn't want to bother with changing into fresh clothes, I just wanted to sleep. I nearly collapsed backwards onto the pallet, but I was grateful I had some sense of control when I leaned forward instead, putting my head in my hands. I could have passed out right there, but I needed to get the blood off me. Sam's blood, the blood from one man's neck and another man's intestines. Thinking about it made me nauseated.

"I can see that. Smell it, really." He made a face as he shoved the clothes back into the pack. I could feel the corner of my mouth lift as I watched him. He gave me a small smile, infinitely charming, and walked over to his pack in the corner of the tent. He pulled out a cloth and a long-sleeved button-down shirt that looked entirely too fine to be packed with his traveling gear. I lifted a brow as he turned to me with it.

"I had plans in Ardian when you interrupted them." He shrugged as he placed the shirt over the back of the chair sitting at the tiny desk. He turned to the brazier, and I saw what he'd been fiddling with before—a pot of water. Taking it off the heat, he brought the pot over and knelt before dipping the cloth into the water. When he pulled one of my hands into his and gently started scrubbing at the blood, I nearly started crying at the tenderness. I was so used to handling everything myself, the act of someone caring for me felt intimate beyond comparison.

"Dickey said you killed the tírrúil that was attacking them." He kept looking down at my hands, getting the blood out of the creases in my palms and around my fingernails. I watched the small line between his eyebrows and the downward slant of his nose.

"Not fast enough." Not before it killed Sam. Pain tore through my head, and I started breathing in through my nose and out through my mouth. I imagined the arrows going through the beast that had just ended a boy's life and remembered my bow. I'd been holding it when I almost fell into the fire. I sighed, knowing it was likely in pieces.

"No. I suppose not." He glanced up to me through his lashes, and I had to catch my breath. There was a fire in his eyes as he watched me, something fierce and prideful. "But then you warned me of the other one and killed it too."

"I put it to sleep."

"Same thing." He shrugged. "I'm sorry I couldn't rift to you. I—That's the first time that's happened since—since that day." His eyes lingered on my arm, and I knew he was feeling responsible for my injury. I wondered why his rifting always seemed to act out for him when I stood to lose the most from its failure. I faintly entertained the idea that maybe that was exactly the problem—my involvement made him unable to use his divinity properly. I dismissed it as fast as it came.

"I'm here, aren't I?" I gave him a faint smile, and he looked back down at my hands, now clean, giving them a quick squeeze. The throbbing in my temple intensified, and I winced.

"Here, use the cloth to clean the blood and...drool?"

I inspected myself before I nodded in confirmation; I did indeed have tírrúil saliva all over me from when it tried to eat me. He tossed his shirt to me, retrieving it from where it rested on his chair. It was a deep, emerald green I knew would match his eyes in better lighting. The fabric was soft as silk but without the sheen. Before he even finished turning around, I was already unbuttoning my filthy shirt. It was disgusting and ripped half to hell down the sleeve. Based on the breeze at my back, I assumed it was shredded from when I slid across the ground. I got the shirt off, and then lightning flashed behind my eyes, and I bent over, catching my head in my hand, smothering my cry. I couldn't see, a thousand tiny stars clouding my vision, and I let out a sob from the pain. Rainier was crouched next to me in an instant, and I struggled, lifting my other arm to cover myself.

"Come on," he whispered as he gently tugged me to him, adjusting me as he laid me down on the pallet. I curled into myself, turning my back to him as he pulled a blanket over me, the pain behind my eyes feeling like a thousand needles. After lying there for a few moments, the tiny stars faded, but the pain remained. I kept my eyes shut. I wondered if Lavenia's head ached as badly as mine did and hoped Dewalt was taking care of her too. As if sensing what I was thinking, Rainier spoke quietly, his voice a low rumble.

"One of the good things about the bond is sharing the cost. As long as Dewalt is touching her, he can take some of this away. The pain." He had taken the cloth and dipped it in the warm water, starting to clean my back. I tensed a bit, feeling the rash from being pushed across the dirt and rocks. He was gentle, and I could tell he was tracing the worst of the scrapes, making sure to get them clean. The pain in my eyes hadn't lessened, but it had stopped getting worse, so I focused on the strokes of the cloth, soft and warm.

"Their divinity is increased by being bonded, and when the after-effects can be shared, they can push themselves further. They can borrow from each other too if they need it. Lavenia pushed too far today by staying inside the tírrúil's mind while it was slaughtered." He gently lifted my braid away as he washed the back of my neck, down my shoulder and injured arm, staying away from the bandage.

"Do you want me to take your braid out?" Not able to form words, I gave a soft grunt of assent, and deft fingers began to gently pull my hair free from the tight plait. The release of tension at my roots felt painfully delightful. It was short-lived, as my head gave a tense throb behind my eyes. I let out a whimper, unable to stifle it, and he stilled his movements. After a moment he continued, and when finished, he gently massaged my scalp for a few blessed seconds. He pulled away, but not before softly tracing his fingertips over a spot on my neck.

"You spread yourself too thin, Em." I heard him wring out the washcloth and dip it back into the water right before he brought it up to my neck, to the same area he'd touched just moments before.

"I had to, Rain." My voice was quiet and trembling. I was in so much pain.

"I know." He kissed my shoulder after he said it, and I didn't mind, the implication felt less romantic than it did appreciative. He reached over me with the washcloth, cleaning my neck and collarbones. I closed my eyes and tried to breathe through the pounding in my head as I rolled back toward him, lying flat on the pallet. I wanted the blood and grit and saliva off me more than I cared about my modesty.

The only indication he cared was a slight hitch in his breath I could have imagined. I kept my eyes closed and used both hands to massage my temples, continuing to focus on breathing through the pain while Rainier carried on washing me. Once I rolled over, he was able to get a better angle on my chest and clean the rest of the saliva off my neck. Slow inhale and slow exhale as the cloth moved lower, over the swell of one breast then the other before dipping to the valley between. There was nothing lascivious about the way the cloth touched my body, only quick and thorough swipes to clean me off. By the time he finished, my head was still aching, but I was able to sit up as he helped me into his shirt. The buttons were on the opposite side of what I was used to, so I struggled a bit, and he leaned in to help me, his rough knuckles gently grazing my soft skin. When he was done, he traced his thumb over my lips as his hand cupped my cheek, and I looked at him, too worn out to put my thanks into words, hoping he'd see the gratitude written on my face. His eyes softened even further before pulling me to him, and he brushed a light kiss across my brow, soft and gentle.

"I've been wrong this whole time." He whispered it against my brow, and I kept still.

"About what?"

"The blue. I'd imagined the Mahowin Sea all along."

I started to pull away, confused, but he circled me in his strong arms and pulled me close.

"Your eyes. The Mahowin Sea doesn't do them justice."

I felt my heart begin to race, and I swallowed, overwhelmed by the conflicting emotions flooding me, my breaths coming too fast.

"Sleep, dear heart." He whispered and laid me back down. He pulled a blanket on top of me, and, despite what he'd just said, the exhaustion overpowered me. I was asleep before I could hear him settle down across the tent.

I woke to the sounds of the camp packing up outside. We were still a half day's ride from home, and I was eager to crawl into a real bed, feathers poking up out of it and all. My head was still a dull ache, but I managed to keep my eyes open without any sharp stabs of pain; I hadn't moved the entire time I slept. I could tell the day was well underway by how stifling the tent had become. With the brazier going and the sun warming us from above, it was no surprise I had a thin layer of sweat covering me. I threw the blanket off my body, wanting to get some air before I remembered I didn't have pants on. I rolled over quickly, noticing the lack of pain on my back, and saw, thankfully, that Rainier was not in the tent. I relaxed a bit and sat up, pulling my mass of hair out of my eyes. I stood and flipped my hair over, using my fingers to massage my scalp, and a small moan escaped my lips. When I flipped back up, Rainier was standing just inside the tent.

"Sorry, I was coming to wake you." I watched his eyes trace my face then slowly move down to the hem of his shirt. It ended halfway down my thigh, shielding me better than the shirt I'd worn the day he bandaged my leg. How had that only been two days ago? I crossed my arms, feeling oddly self-conscious, like he hadn't seen me half naked just hours ago. I saw his jaw tense as he pointedly turned his body away from me, and I spun, grabbing my dirty ripped breeches off the ground behind me. I stumbled into them, teetering on this too-fragile edge of . . . *something* he and I shared in the early morning light. Rainier cleared his throat before he spoke, still giving me privacy by facing away.

"We lost a few horses this morning. When they ran, a few went into the trench and broke their legs. The soldiers had to put them down."

"Why didn't you tell me? I could have done something." I hoped Clyde was not among the fallen horses. He'd earned a place in my heart by staying calm when I needed him to.

"What could you have done? You were spent by the time you finished with the soldiers." He whirled to face me, his expression a challenge, jaw tight and brows lowered. He was right. I had nothing left, *still* had nothing left. The normal light thrum of my divinity was gone, reduced to the barest hint.

"Clyde?" I sounded pitiful, but for some reason the safety of that one horse felt like it could break me.

"That's what I came to talk to you about. Would you mind sharing him with me today? The old beast was on the other side of the trench." That crooked smile lit up his face, a twinkle of amusement in his eyes.

"He jumped it?" I was incredulous.

"Sure did. I fixed the trench before bringing him back; I didn't want to tempt fate twice." He laughed and walked over to me, his boots crunching the ground below him. "So, you'll share?" He was close enough I needed to look up to speak to him, but my eyes couldn't get past his lips. Based on the way the corners of his mouth lifted, he noticed my struggle.

"Yes, we can share." I almost whispered it and stepped back, focusing on pulling up my shirt to check my arm.

"That color suits you." Rainier took a step forward, closing the distance I'd just made, and started rolling up my sleeve in a much more practical manner than I had. When the shirt was rolled up, I peeled the bandage back and found nothing more than scrapes already scabbed over—I'd healed quite a bit in my sleep. Rainier moved to grab our packs, and I began to braid my hair again, wincing a bit thanks to the headache I still had, however mild it had become.

"You should leave it loose."

"What?"

"Your hair."

I laughed, surprised he had an opinion on my hair. "You'll change your mind when it's whipping into your face the rest of the day."

"I won't. Leave it down." Something about the way he said it made me pause.

"Fine, let's see how long you last before you beg me to braid it." Based on the breeze that ruffled the tent, I didn't think he'd last long. His answering grin told me he'd bear with it, just for the satisfaction of winning.

Within the hour, the camp had been packed up, and after giving Clyde some extra special pats and an apple, I was seated on the horse, waiting for Rainier to finish speaking to Dewalt and Thyra. I wondered if I could convince him to leave me Clyde in exchange for one of the horses I'd gained in my stable in the last week. It would be a good trade for him. I stared ahead at the horizon, wondering how much longer it would be until I had my child back in my arms. I'd known she was missing for five days now, and it had been almost two weeks since I saw her last. It felt like a lifetime. I tried not to think about how much longer we had to go. The trip from Brambleton to Astana would easily take a week. Going through the mountains was treacherous, especially this close to the winter months. And then once we arrived, Rainier would have to convince King Soren to make a move on Darkhold or, at least, render control of more of his army to Rainier. If they chose to negotiate instead, it could be months before I saw my daughter again. I took a deep breath, and it caught in my throat. My headache was still there, and I was feeling queasy on top of the exhaustion still clinging to my bones. I'd barely rested after the attack, but the urge to move was taking over. I needed to leave, move toward the destination that got me back to Elora.

I watched Rainier, still deep in conversation with Thyra and Dewalt, likely discussing where we'd make camp once we reached Brambleton. He had asked if I had enough land for the soldiers, and I'd told him I did, but my home was out of the way, and I wouldn't want them to have to backtrack. He didn't mind, insisting to accompany me to deal with whatever fallout was left at my home. The guard would make camp in a field on the other side of the stream that ran through the southern portion of my property, and tomorrow would be spent going into Brambleton to replenish supplies and give the horses a day of rest. I stared at the back of his head, willing him to turn and look at me. I wanted to leave. Finally, after a few long moments, the three of them dispersed, and Rainier met my gaze. He didn't stumble, but I could tell he was taken aback to find me staring. He didn't give me any sort of smile as he approached and climbed up behind me. Letting out one of his whistles, he urged Clyde to walk.

"What have I done now?" There was worry in his voice as if I was angry with him rather than just eager to leave.

"I don't know, Rain. What *have* you done?" I chided, and it coaxed a laugh out of him. I felt his body shake as he put one arm around me, grasping the reins, and placed his other hand on my hip. I was conscious this time, so the threat of falling off the horse was not there. I let him keep his hand on me anyway, not minding the contact.

"You were staring at me like I was in trouble. I'm quite familiar with the look, you know." I could hear the sly smile in his voice.

"No, I was just eager to leave." I paused, debating to tell him where my mind had gone before deciding to share. "I—When I'm still for too long, my mind wanders."

He made a small sound low in his throat, understanding what I meant. "Do you want to talk about it?"

"I don't think I can." I'd start to spiral and wouldn't be able to stop.

"I'm here if that changes." He squeezed my hip, and every ounce of my attention went to where his hand was on me.

"Thank you." I put my hand on his knee and squeezed back.

CHAPTER 20

To his credit, Rainier did not once complain about my hair blowing into his face. Though, to be fair, I eventually put my hood up and leaned back into him for a nap, keeping my hair out of his face for him. I was still exhausted although my headache had finally eased enough to be manageable. I woke up when we finally came to the crossroads of Brambleton, the noises of the town louder than I ever remembered. There were countless people gathered on the streets when they realized the Crown Prince was in their midst, the guard ruining any hopes of anonymity. We turned east toward my home, and as we drew alongside the inhabitants of the town, I pulled my hood down lower and attempted to hide from view. I wasn't sure if it was out of habit to lie low or something else, but Rainier noticed.

"How many of them know you're the one who helps their healer?" His breath was warm on my ear, and he had to feel my shudder at his proximity.

"The ones who know have never acted like they do. Mairin is pretty strict about respecting my wishes."

"Will we meet this Mairin?"

"I expect you will. Oh, gods." I hadn't considered the full extent of the conversations I was about to have with not only Mairin but probably Theo and his mother as well. They deserved to know everything, but I was not eager for the repercussions. "She is going to be mad."

"Why is that?"

"Well, I left her two dead bodies and only a note to explain it." I laughed. "She didn't know why I was in hiding, so I'm going to have to tell her the whole story." I dreaded it.

"You never told your only friend?" I was more stunned he remembered she was my only friend than I was annoyed at his judgmental tone.

"Well, I—no. No, I did not." When I thought about it now, I felt guilty, but I had never considered risking our safety by telling anyone. I thought maybe Rainier was judging me for my choice, but what he said next surprised me.

"That must have been lonely." He sounded sad. I didn't want him to feel sorry for me; everything I had done, I had done by choice. I could have tried to confide in a friend. I could have—and probably should have—told Elora she was the Beloved. There were many decisions I'd made over the years which, in the end, were lonely ones, but they were all mine. I chose not to say anything and instead laced my fingers through the hand he held on my hip, feeling the slightest squeeze in response.

When we finally reached the clearing in front of my house, the soldiers had already turned south to make camp in the field, leaving Dewalt, Lavenia, Rainier, and I alone in the clearing.

"Well, at least one of the bodies is gone." I gave a nervous laugh as Rainier steered us to the stables.

"Is there room for these two in here?" Dewalt hopped down from the horse he and Lavenia were on, leading it to the stable when he saw me nod.

A wave of emotions came crashing down on me, and I felt overwhelmed. My daughter wouldn't be there when I walked in the house; her musical laughter and voice wouldn't welcome me home. It would be silent and dark—a physical reminder of her absence. Another part of me was unsettled by having my three childhood friends here, something my mind was struggling to comprehend. Watching Lavenia dismount and lean against the pell in the yard while Dewalt walked the horse into the stable—*my* stable—created some cognitive dissonance within me. I knew it was happening, but it was so outside the realm of possibility even two weeks ago that I was struggling to keep up. Because of all these conflicting emotions, I felt a pulse of laughter rising in me, and I did my best to stifle it. Rainier jumped down from Clyde and helped me before he followed Dewalt into the stable.

I looked over at my porch, noticing my blood-stained shirt I'd left on the railing was gone. Someone had taken it in, or it had blown away. I walked down toward the path to the stream and confirmed the other body was also gone. I wondered how Theo handled it. I had started for the porch when I heard a yell coming from the stable. Lavenia and I exchanged a glance as we both jogged over.

Rainier came walking out, laughing so hard I saw a tear glimmering on his lashes. Though the sun was low and almost setting, the way it hit him sent a flood of warmth through me. Gods, he was handsome. Dewalt followed behind him, cradling his hand, and I saw a gleam of red.

"She bit me!" Dewalt moaned, and it took all I had to keep myself from joining in with Rainier's laughter. Bree had every right to be grumpy; I'd abandoned her for almost a week, and then two strange men came into her space. But . . . that wasn't right?

"Wait, how is Bree here? I thought she was at Ravemont." No sooner had the words crossed my lips, I heard my front door open, and I spun around. Rainier's hand was on his sword, the other two taking a fighting stance before we realized who it was, and my jaw fell open.

"Nana?" I called, not believing my eyes. Why was she here?

Lavenia and Rainier were busy starting a fire while I was inside with Dewalt and Nana. We all desperately wanted and needed a hot bath, so Rainier volunteered to use his abilities to make it easier on everyone. I had checked on Bree before I made my way inside with my injured friend, and he was all the more grumpy because of it, claiming I liked the horse better than him. I wasn't sure if he was wrong, though.

"You're lucky Bree didn't take your finger off." He had made the mistake of approaching her without me, but I hadn't exactly warned him. I hadn't even expected her to be here. Nana was busy behind me at the hearth, readying dinner for the five of us while I disinfected Dewalt's hand, already swollen and red.

"I should have expected a creature of yours to bite first and ask questions later." He was scowling until Nana snorted from behind me, causing a tentative grin to break out across his face. I glowered at her but was glad she made him smile. The old woman looked as if she could be his grandmother. They both had red undertones beneath their brown skin, similar eye shape, and high cheekbones. But where Dewalt was tall and dignified with a strong, straight nose, she was squat with a round, tomato nose. Her hair might have been black like his at some point, but it had only ever been dark grey as long as I had known her.

Once satisfied with the disinfection, I placed my hand on his. I decided to risk healing him fully, hoping we would be relatively safe for the next day, and my divinity would continue to recover. When I finished, he rubbed his hand and complained of the itch.

"Better an itch than losing your hand," I retorted. I waited for Nana to scold me for my rudeness, but when I turned to rid myself of the bloodied cloth I'd been using, I realized she'd slipped out, quiet as a mouse. Rainier walked in then with a hand up and his finger hitched, like he was dragging something behind him. I tilted my head in confusion.

"Where's the tub?" Realization dawned on me as I saw what lingered behind him in the air. A long, thick stream of water leading back to the pot above the fire followed him. I scrambled away from the table, pulling Dewalt with me into the study. In the back of the room, next to Faxon's desk, there was a storage closet which housed the enormous copper tub we used to bathe. It was something I bought for myself one year after squirreling away excess funds from my father. I needed help pulling it out, and Dewalt gladly reached in to help me, setting it upright in the middle of the floor. The moment we placed it down, Rainier came into the room, and with a flick of his wrist, the undulating mass of water slowly poured into the tub, filling it. I was distinctly jealous. I never filled the pot at the fire more than a third because I couldn't carry it in to dump into the tub. It usually took me a few trips, depending on how much I spilled, the work required for a bath generally necessitating one. Rainier walked back out to the porch, and I watched as water flew out of the well and replenished the pot over the fire, the motion the water made reminding me of a snake.

"Dewalt, you first." The man in question nodded and jogged outside to grab his pack before he went back into the study, closing the double doors behind him. Nana was waiting in the kitchen, a large basket under her arm.

"Don't you think he'll want this?" I saw she carried an assortment of different soaps—bars and liquid—and fluffy towels. I nearly groaned in anticipation as I spotted the lilac soap I'd always used, eager for my turn in the bath. Every once in a while, Nana would send us her homemade soaps, but I'd run out a long time ago. Rainier took the basket from her with a smile and carried it into the study.

"One of these arrived at Ravemont, and one was waiting when I got here." Nana pulled two envelopes out from under her arm, passing them over to me. My breath caught as I recognized Faxon's handwriting on the front of them, both addressed to me. Rainier returned from the study, and I felt him tense beside me as he saw Faxon's crest on the wax seal as I flipped over one of the letters. Not in the habit of receiving letters from Faxon, seeing the imprint of his crest in the wax made me nauseous, and the bottoms of my feet gave a phantom pang. Not bothering with a knife, I ripped the seal and pulled the letter out.

The prince swore a verit oath. She will not be harmed while under his protection. Do not follow.

I shoved the letter into Rainier's chest as I grabbed the other envelope. The same message appeared, also in Faxon's hand. I threw the second copy on the table and spun around, hand to my head. This letter served as confirmation that Faxon had done exactly what Lavenia claimed. I hadn't doubted her, but some small part of me had a glimmer of hope it was all a ruse. Not only did he sell her to Folterra, but he sold her to one of the Folterran princes.

"Cyran. The younger prince." Rainier's voice was steady. "This is *good*, Emmeline."

"How?" I whirled as I shouted at him. "How is it good?" Even though a verit oath was binding by death, it wouldn't stop another Folterran from harming her eventually. I vaguely noticed Nana leaving the room, slipping around the corner to the stairwell.

"Cyran is the lesser of two evils, by far." His facial expression was grim, but his tone was somehow hopeful—as if he truly believed we were better off with this turn of events.

"And how do you know which prince has her?" The letter had not been specific.

"The verit oath. Declan would never swear one. If Cyran has her, she might not even be in Darkhold."

"Making it harder for us to find her!" I was struggling to understand how this could be a good thing.

"Yes, but Cyran is more likely to work with us, and she'd be safer outside of the capital. We've intercepted his spies at the Cascade before; he's curious about my intentions. He is untested, young. Declan is over 200 years old, but Cyran, hell, he might not even be in his full divinity yet. I promise this is good, Em." He pulled my shaking hands into his and looked down at me.

"Alright." His eyebrows shot up, nearly to his hairline, and I would've laughed if I wasn't so scared. "I believe you. You know more than I do. I'm already a gods damn mess, I can't keep imagining the worst, it's killing me. I *need* you to be right. I—I need what you said to be true." My voice broke on the last word.

The door to the study opened, and Dewalt came walking out, combing his long, wet hair. Rainier dropped my hands, and I wiped at my eyes, brushing away the tears yet to fall.

"Cyran has her." He was blunt, and Dewalt only nodded, a grim smile on his face, before he headed outside.

Rainier went into the study, and I heard him open a window. I stood at the hearth, warming my hands, as I heard the sounds of water, presumably Rainier emptying Dewalt's bath and refilling the tub from the fire. I glanced out the front window, and sure enough, I saw water rising from the pot, slowly moving toward the house. How amazing was it that we'd all get fresh, hot water? Lavenia came walking in as I stared at the billowing water going into the pot, replacing what he'd just taken. It was mesmerizing.

"—go next?"

I shook my head; I didn't realize Lavenia had been talking to me. Apparently, my head shake was enough of an answer, and she went into the study, brushing past her brother as he came out and sat in one of the armchairs. It was surreal, seeing him there, his large frame filling out the old, worn seat. Nana had come back, presumably while I was staring out the window, and was tending to the food. I smelled roast chicken, and my mouth watered.

"Nana, where have you been sleeping?" It didn't matter; I was just curious and suddenly wondered how I'd set everyone up for the night.

"I've been sleeping in the Crandall's guest room. Lydia didn't want me here by myself, and I enjoy their company. Theo reminds me of your father when he was young. The young man and I came earlier, but he went right back to help his mother after tending to the horses. They'll be expecting me, and you seem like you have a full house." When we first came inside, Nana explained that when Bree was sent back here, she'd requested to come along, convincing Lord Kennon I needed her more than he did. I wondered how much she'd told my neighbors about Elora, and I surprisingly hoped she'd told them everything so I wouldn't have to. I still didn't know what happened to the bodies of the men who attacked me, and I'd need to visit with Theo to thank him, but also to find out exactly what happened after I left.

"I'll accompany you tonight when you go back. I do need to speak with him before we leave the day after next."

"Good, I'll be coming with you when you go." The woman put her hands on her hips, the same gesture which had once sent my legs quaking as a child.

"Nana, you can't be serious. Stay here. I'll be back. We can both go back to Ravemont together—with Elora." I couldn't help but wonder what Rainier thought about my statement, but he didn't turn his head from where he stared out the window.

"Darling, it's been years. Let an old lady die happy. Besides, I expect you'll be in Astana longer than you think." Her tone was unreadable. Even she worried about how long it would take to get Elora back, it seemed. I couldn't think about it.

"I'll talk to Rainier about it later." She crossed her arms and glared at me, and I shot her a look. "The *prince*. I'll talk to the prince about it." I heaved a sigh in Rainier's direction as I noticed his body shaking silently from the armchair.

"Come help me set up the bedrooms," I ordered him, my voice a bit harsher than I intended. As he stood, I couldn't help but notice how imposing he was in my tiny home. He was so much taller than me, my head only reaching the top of his shoulders, and it was all the more noticeable here, the ceilings low enough that I wouldn't be surprised if he had to duck through doorways. I turned to the stairwell and waited to hear his footsteps before I continued up, the candlelight from the landing flickering on the walls. I was suddenly embarrassed by the paintings hanging in our stairwell, evidence of a hobby I wasn't very good at. Elora and I had taken to painting in recent years and had filled the hallway with our work. But where I failed, she succeeded, creating beautiful landscapes from memory. I heard him stop for a moment as he studied one, my failed attempt at painting the meadow. Turning at the landing, I gently traced my fingertips over the bookcase there. Most of the books on it belonged to Elora, so she'd laid claim to it as her own, going as far as painting the wood. There were swirls of black and blue, looking like the night sky. Though the books blocked out the details on the shelves, I knew behind the ones on the bottom there was a town, alive at night. I knew about all the hidden stars that were also present across the top of the bookcase. My fingers grazed over the texture of the paint, finding every imperfection. She'd been so proud of it, and for good reason; it was beautiful.

At the top of the stairs, we turned to the left and went down the length of the hallway to my bedroom. The last time I'd been in it, I had stripped out of clothing and threw it haphazardly, but when I went inside, nothing was out of place. Nana had collected my laundry and put it in the basket it belonged before lighting the lamp on my nightstand.

"There are clean sheets in that closet next to you," I said to Rainier, who still lingered in the hallway. "I figured I'd put Dewalt and Lavenia in here."

Rainier stood there for a moment longer, his gaze flickering between me and the bed, a muscle working in his jaw, before he turned to the closet and opened it without a word. Not sure what that was about, I turned around and pulled the quilt off the top of the bed, setting it on the rocking chair in the corner. I didn't have time to launder it, but at least they'd have clean sheets to sleep on, a small comfort after a few hard days. I pulled everything off the bed, and Rainier walked over to the other side to help. Faxon's side. A pulse of anger went through me at the thought of him. I watched the man across from me fumble with the sheet, and I couldn't help but smile.

"Do you even know how to make a bed?" I grinned at him, wanting to fill the silence. It worked as one side of his lips twitched. He glanced down at the bed before looking up at me through lowered lashes, his sideways grin kicking up, making me question my sanity.

"I'm afraid I only know how to mess them up." Something hot tinged low in my belly, and I felt his eyes on me as I willed my skin not to flush. There was another feeling melding with that heat. I'd known he wouldn't be celibate, and I didn't have any claim on him whatsoever, so why did I care? Why did my chest grow tight and my heart thunder at the thought? I'd tried to ignore Lydia whenever she filled me in on the gossip of court—tales of the handsome prince who would bed women and fight battles, then turn around and charm dignitaries, smoothing over King Soren's indiscretions. I'd always brushed it off as nothing but idle chatter, but it seemed it was true. I schooled my features into something impassive, but I realized it was too late; my facial expression had already shown my hand.

"How many?" I kept my voice calm and curious even though my heart was beating a staccato in my chest, and hot jealousy pulsed through my veins.

"How many what?" His voice was low, almost a warning, as he stared at me, the muscles on his arms moving as he flattened the sheet to the bed. I wasn't sure if he just wanted to make me say it or not.

"How many beds?" I kept my gaze on the top sheet as he passed it to me, fingers lightly brushing mine.

"That's hardly an appropriate conversation to have. Especially after taunting me with the one you yourself have sullied." He sounded measured and calm, tone not indicative of the words he'd just said to me. It didn't matter I'd never actually done anything willingly with Faxon in this bed. It didn't matter that we'd have slept in separate rooms if we had the space. Rainier saw it as the bed I'd shared with my husband, and I didn't know what to say. Telling him my marriage bed was a cold one didn't seem a solution or a conversation I wanted to have. I didn't want to tell him I hadn't known passion since him. A part of me was resentful because of it. I'd been stuck in a loveless marriage, devoid of all touch and fire, while he'd evidently been sullying beds across the Three Kingdoms. I was frustrated that I hadn't experienced the kind of passion he seemed to. The hot flash of jealousy simmered in my stomach, and I turned to the quilt and unfolded it before he helped me spread it over the bed.

"Lost count, have you?" I turned away from him, not wanting to see his reaction. He didn't say a word before I grabbed one of my pillows off the rocking chair and turned back to him. "There is a trundle bed under the sofa in the study. You'll need this." I threw the pillow at him a bit aggressively, avoiding eye contact as I approached the closet in the hall. I planned to get fresh sheets for me to put on Elora's bed before I paused, realizing I didn't want to change her sheets at all. Forgetting about what had angered me only moments before, I crossed to the front of the house to Elora's room and leaned my head against the door, my hand on the doorknob.

Rainier abandoned and forgotten, I walked into her room, closing the door behind me. Her curtains were parted, so a thin shaft of moonlight fell across the bed. She had left it fairly tidy. The long-abandoned dollhouse against the far wall had books stacked in its rooms, the furniture and dolls pushed to the back, while the small dresser on the wall still held an assortment of knick-knacks. A small jewelry box sat open, and my hand hovered over her necklace I wore before I decided to leave it on. Her nightstand drawer was open, and I spotted the cover of her journal as I slid it closed. I sank down on her bed, inhaling her scent. Citrus and sun and a touch of sweat. It smelled like life, like summer. I laid down, drawing my knees up and staying there for a long time.

I noticed one of her long, white hairs embedded in her sheet, and as I pulled it out, it was as if the thread was attached to my heart, and pulling it released something in me I'd been trying to hold back. I'd been distracted by creatures trying to kill me or kill the soldiers, by Faxon's betrayal, by searching in Mira. By that frustrating man I'd left in the hallway. I'd been keeping myself busy specifically to avoid this, but something as simple as a strand of her hair in her quiet room sent me careening over the edge of grief. I closed my eyes and let myself sink into it, turning my head into her pillow and crying. I cried for the things I never told her; I cried for the life she could've had if we stayed at Ravemont, for the life she could have had if she weren't like Lucia. I cried for what she was going through. She'd been scared enough to bite someone's ear off, and everything I had done the past few days didn't feel like enough.

I didn't know how long I'd been laying there crying when the creak of the door drew my attention, and Rainier peeked his head in. I rolled over to face the wall, not wanting him to see me that way.

"How long have you been out there?" I wiped away the tears and tucked my hands under my chin.

"Since you shut the door in my face." I heard his slow footsteps, soft for his size, as he crossed the room. I sniffled, curling my body into itself.

"I'm not crying about you."

Rainier exhaled, a hint of a laugh behind it. "I'm not so vain as to think you've shed a single tear over me, Emmeline." I nearly laughed at how wrong he was. Pausing as the mattress shifted slightly, he lowered his body onto the foot of the bed. When he placed a hand on my leg, a solid weight resting on me, I didn't push him off. "I promise we'll get her back."

"Can you make that promise?" I snapped, not sure why I was angry nor why I took it out on him.

"To tell the full truth, no. But I'm going to make it anyway." Though his honesty was better than platitudes, it didn't help. I needed him to tell me he would fix everything.

"The one time I want you to lie to me, you won't." His hand stilled where it had been gently rubbing, and it was the only indication he gave that my words might have stung. A moment later, he continued his movements but didn't speak. The moonlight painted the walls, and I stared at it as I lay there, remembering nights sitting in the rocking chair in this room holding a fussy baby to my breast. I'd moved Elora in here before she was a year old because we kept each other awake otherwise. She was a light sleeper, every cough or rustle of blankets would wake her, and I was the same; every single thing she did woke me. I ran on little to no sleep for the first half-year of her life, catching myself holding my hand under her nose to feel her breathe if by some miracle she didn't wake at the smallest sound. The same chair I'd rocked her in sat in my bedroom, waiting to belong to Elora one day for her own children. The thought made my breath catch, and my tears renewed. She wouldn't have any children to rock if we weren't successful.

I had been trying to be so cold and removed from the situation with Elora to stay sane. I couldn't let myself think about it because this was what I turned into. A useless mess. But the scent of her, the hair embedded in the blanket, the nearness I felt to my daughter in this room was enough to turn my quiet crying into gut-wrenching weeping. It wasn't like my outburst at the inn; those were angry tears. This was fear. This was the realization that my own life depended on hers, and if we weren't quick enough to save her, I wasn't sure I'd be able to live it without her. When Rainier pulled his hand away from me, the lack of contact, of grounding to another person who seemed to care, nearly made me give up, the deep, shuddering sobs taking over my form.

But then he was there a moment later.

Rainier picked me up and pulled me into his lap, pressing me against his chest. He held me tightly, almost too tightly, and I clung to him, the warmth a comfort I should have seen coming. He didn't speak, didn't do anything other than hold me. And that simple tenderness broke me.

"I'm so scared, Rain. I am so gods damn scared."

"I know." His voice was soft, barely a whisper.

"She knows I'm coming for her, right? She—she has to know I'm coming. I wouldn't—I'm not like Faxon. Do you think she knows that? Do you think she knows I'm—"

"She knows, dear heart." He pulled me closer and kissed my temple. "She knows."

"She's probably so scared."

"Mm, yes. She probably is." Another harsh truth. "But she's also handling it well. I'm sure of it."

"How do you know?"

"She's yours." He said it simply, as if it was the most obvious thing in the world. I didn't reply, but put my hand on his chest, feeling the steady thump of his heart. He gave me a moment, my tears slowing by the minute. "The worst things that could happen to someone have happened to you. You lost your sister; you lost everyone, really. You've had people break promises to you—people you trusted. You made sacrifices you shouldn't have had to make. And your daughter was taken from you. But you're still you. You're still brave, still strong, still caring. You're resilient. Even if she's only the slightest bit like her mother, she's doing alright, Em."

I started crying again, and he held me tightly, letting me get it all out. I felt weak. Vulnerable. But I vowed I wouldn't sink into this again, and this was the last chance I'd give myself to be scared. I wouldn't shed any more tears. I would bring hellfire down on the people responsible for this, and I'd bring her back home safely. Or I'd die in my attempts. I wouldn't cry again.

I didn't know how long we sat like that, with his arms wrapped around me while I wept. Once my breathing had slowed, and I pulled my hand up to wipe my face free of tears and snot, Rain loosened his hold, but still kept me settled in his embrace. I wondered if he knew by instinct that I needed the touch.

I crawled off his lap, sitting next to him on the bed as I caught my reflection in her mirror. I appeared tired, but at the same time, there was something about the look in my eyes and the way my hair stood out from my head that gave me pause. I had a fire. A drive. Something I'd been missing for so many years. Something I was ashamed to only now have at the expense of my missing daughter. I ran my fingers through my hair and stood.

"Thank you," I turned toward him as I continued, "for everything."

Rainier still sat on the foot of the bed, gazing up at me. He took my hand into his and drew it to his lips, gently brushing my knuckles.

"I promise we'll get her back." I felt his mouth move gently against my skin as he said the words. I ordered myself to believe them.

I groaned when I took a bite of the roast chicken Nana made. I tasted rosemary and thyme, likely both things she found in my herb garden. She'd also boiled potatoes to go with it. Based on the reaction of everyone else as we sat around the table in the kitchen, it was one of the best meals they'd had in a while. I stole a look at Nana, and her satisfied smile told me she was proud of herself. She must have brought wine with her from Ravemont as well, as I found my favorite Nythyrian, a light and fruity chardonnay, sitting on the counter. I poured a glass for everyone to go with dinner, and the only sounds that followed were chewing and silverware on plates; we were too hungry and exhausted to discuss much else. It was Lavenia who raised us from our stupor a little while later as she began clearing plates from the table. I smiled when she ordered her brother to bathe, and I was pleasantly surprised when Rainier obeyed, forgoing the sibling bickering I expected.

"I need to take Nana to the Crandall's."

"Emmeline, I've been walking there every day by myself. I don't need you to escort me."

"Have you been going at night?"

"No, but it's not far."

Our standoff abruptly ended as a swift knock on the door drew our attention. I got up, but Dewalt beat me there, and when he opened it, Theo stood on the other side of it.

"I—I saw the soldiers." He glanced between me and Nana, and something like fear flickered in his eyes. "Is she back?" My heart cracked in half. I'd been so busy thinking about the mess I'd left him, I hadn't even thought about how he'd wonder about Elora. I walked over and put a hand on his shoulder.

"No, Theo. We are on our way to petition King Soren for aid." I made an assumption that Nana had explained everything. When I didn't sense any confusion, I figured I must have been right. He only nodded before clearing his throat.

"Alright. I came to check on Mistress Imogene. She said she'd be back by sundown." I whirled to Nana.

"*Mistress Imogene?*" I was incredulous. She'd never let us speak her name before; even the royalty who were currently staying in my house hadn't been privy to the information. Lavenia stopped washing up to turn around and stare at the old woman as well. I heard Rainier's booming laughter coming from the study where I forgot he'd been bathing.

"*You* still call me Nana, girl." She held herself in a way which tendered no argument, and I felt myself smile. She walked over to Theo and took his arm. "The boy can escort me." Theo's cheeks flamed, and the tips of his ears reddened to match.

"Thank you, Theo, for everything. Where did you bury them?" I lowered my voice, not sure if Nana knew about the less pleasant details.

"Mairin dealt with it. She burned them and sold the bones to a witch." I felt my jaw drop. It didn't surprise me she would take charge, but to burn them and sell the bones? That was something I wouldn't have imagined in my wildest dreams. Theo shrugged. "I suppose she'll bring you the money tomorrow. The whole town knows the prince is here." Anxiety twisted in my gut at the thought, the remnants of a life spent in hiding.

"I'll be back in the morning, Emmeline." Nana's hand touched mine on her way out the door, her veins and liver spots more prominent than I remembered.

CHAPTER 21

I SHOWED LAVENIA AND Dewalt upstairs to my room, and they were beyond pleased to sleep in a bed. I took a moment to grab a few things I would need before bidding my friends good night and shutting the door behind me. Lavenia was already in bed, eyes closed, and Dewalt seemed as if he wasn't far behind her. She was probably still exhausted, as I was, even if Dewalt had helped take some of her pain earlier that morning.

I trudged back downstairs with my robe and nightgown, torn between taking a bath and sleeping, but ultimately the dried blood and drool I found in my hair was enough to encourage me to bathe. The door to the study was open, and as I walked in, I saw Rainier refilling it for me, the rippling water hovering and sparkling in the low lamplight. He hadn't put on a shirt, and I watched light and shadow caress his skin, the muscles in his back taut as he bent over the tub, putting something in it from Nana's basket. The scent of lilacs and violets hit me, and I sighed, closing my eyes. He shot me a small smile over his shoulder before he stood, brushing past me on his way out, with one of Elora's books in his hand.

He closed one of the doors behind him, leaving the other slightly ajar. I felt bad, knowing he couldn't sleep until I was done, but since he had been filling the tub for me before I came in, I knew he'd insist. I eyed the trundle bed underneath the window with my pillow on it. I knew it wasn't comfortable; I should have given him better accommodations, but I wanted Elora's bed, even if it was selfish.

I undressed, carefully laying Rainier's shirt on a chair by his pack, careful to avoid walking in front of the door. I heard him fiddling with the wood in the hearth before he walked back across the room, evidently aiming to settle down in an armchair and read. I wondered which book he had picked. I laid my nightgown and robe on the table by the door and turned back, distracted by whatever Rainier had poured in the bath. It had turned the water milky-white, and dried purple petals floated on top. I lowered myself in, groaning in bliss. The water was hot, so much hotter than my normal baths. Usually, by the time I'd finished filling the beast and was finally able to relax within it, it was barely warm. Especially if Elora bathed first. I tilted my head back, submerging my hair. It was the first time since I left my parent's house that I'd had an enjoyable bath. I pulled myself to the other side of the tub and hung over the edge to examine everything Nana had supplied. I heard footsteps and Rainier clearing his throat from the door. Glancing over my shoulder, knowing I was covered by the milky water and my hair down my back, I smiled when I saw the back of Rainier's head. Although he had seen quite a bit of me when I was too exhausted and hurt and disgusting to care, he still positioned himself to give me privacy. As he faced the main room while leaning against the door frame, I was able to fully appreciate the long line of his body, the tapered muscles of his back, and the firm backside I could see through his pants. I drew myself out of the trance and cleared my throat before responding to him.

"Yes?" His back flexed as he crossed his arms, and I watched him greedily, thankful for the opportunity to look at him without fear of being caught.

"You sounded like you were in pain. Is your headache back?"

"It never left, but the noise was actually a good one. This bath is lovely, thank you."

"All I did was bring in the water." He turned then, still leaning against the door frame, keeping his eyes averted. I grabbed one of the glass bottles I recognized as being for my hair, a bar of lilac soap, and a washcloth. A cool breeze came through the open window as I moved to lay back, a hiss escaping my lips as I sank down into the water. Rainier must have felt it too, because he was in the room shutting the window in an instant. I sank even lower, chin almost in the water, as he turned around.

"It's still hot, though." I almost felt pathetic admitting I hadn't had a hot bath in a long time. Thankfully, he seemed to know what I meant by the way his eyes softened as his gaze met mine. The moment was fleeting, over the moment he quickly looked away, taking a step into the main room.

"Which book did you choose?" He stopped, settling back to where he leaned before, this time not bothering to avert his eyes. I busied myself and poured some of the contents of the bottle into my hand, lathering it in my hair, making sure only my arms lifted above the water. The scent of lavender permeated the air. The soft florals mixing together wasn't overbearing as I might've thought, but instead relaxed me.

"I picked the one with dragons on the cover. I didn't get to start it before I was worried about *someone* being hurt." His eyes twinkled with mischief, and I tried to shake the feeling that he was tracking every movement I made. I tilted my head back, rinsing the suds from my hair, and I felt his gaze on the long column of my neck.

"Oh, that's a good one. The girl falls in love with a prince, but he's cursed. He's the dragon who scours their lands. I'll let you get back to it." He quirked a brow as I smiled at him. Suddenly feeling shy, I spun in the tub, turning my back, effectively dismissing him. I needed to wash, and I wasn't feeling that daring.

When I heard him settle down in the armchair, I lathered my washcloth with the lilac soap, inhaling deeply. I'd always preferred this soap, while Elora liked the citrus bar. Lucia had liked one made with cucumber water, and I decided to ask Nana to make it for me, just so I could smell it again. Tracing the cloth over my injured arm, I noticed even the scabs were gone: four faint red lines were the only evidence remaining to show I'd been hurt, not even a day after the attack. I washed my face and the rest of my body, paying special attention to any tenderness where I'd been wounded the past few days. Once again, I sifted through my memories, attempting to think about injuries I'd had in my past. I had a few scars on my hands from cutting them while cooking, a slight burn on my forearm from losing the grip on a stew pot I was attempting to move, and of course, there were the scars on the bottoms of my feet. I would have thought if I could heal myself, those especially would have been a target of my divinity. I was almost certain at this point that unless I sent my healing toward a specific location, it only did the work itself if I was on the verge of death. I believed it had saved me twice now, in childbirth and after the onaán. I took a moment and stared at the old burn on my forearm, willing my divinity to heal it. I wasn't too hopeful, but I couldn't help my disappointment when the scar remained. With a sigh, I began pulling a comb through my hair, taking considerable effort. I always preferred to comb my hair wet, making defined waves rather than frizz. Considering how long it took me to comb out, I was pleasantly surprised the water was still warm by the time I finished. My headache had dulled a bit, just barely there behind my temples. I suspected the relaxation was helping and decided to lay my head back and close my eyes for a bit, enjoying the warmth.

"Emmeline." I heard Rainier's voice, and my eyes snapped open. "Did you fall asleep?" He was leaning against the door frame again, arms crossed, with a glint of amusement in his eyes and a hint of his crooked smile. I sat up with a start. Judging by the water temperature, I must have done exactly that. It wasn't cold, but it was nowhere near as warm as it had been when I got in. Glancing down, I realized whatever had been making the water milky was starting to fade or settle to the bottom, and if not for my hair, my breasts would be perfectly visible if Rainier came any closer.

"I did." I grimaced as I realized my robe was across the room. I didn't want to track water throughout the study, especially since Rainier would be sleeping in here. "Sorry. Would you—can you hand me my robe?" He started for the garment I'd left on the table by the door. "Close your eyes!" I added.

In a hilarious pantomime, Rainier held one hand over his eyes and brought the robe to me. I snatched it out of his hand and pushed him toward the door as he chuckled. Once I was out and felt sufficiently dry, I took my robe off and put my nightgown on. Walking past the window, I realized he'd want to empty the tub, so I opened it. He must have been listening for it because the second he heard it, he sent the water out, the stream barreling straight for me. I jumped aside with a curse and heard him laughing on the other side of the door. When he was done, I shut the window and went out to the main room with a glare plastered on my face. He peered up from his book, a picture of innocence, as I walked to the other side of the dinner table, headed for the pitcher of water I'd filled earlier, half tempted to dump it on him.

"Thirsty?" He shook his head no. I glanced at the book in his hand, noticing how little he'd read. "You didn't get far. Did you not like it?"

He turned his chair toward me, away from the lamp sitting between the two armchairs. I was suddenly self-conscious in my nightgown, realizing I'd left my robe in the study. The fabric was thin and had holes in some places, so I drew my arms protectively over myself.

"I've been distracted." He rubbed a hand over his face then, oddly agitated. It surprised me because he'd seemed rather pleasant when he woke me and handed me my robe.

"By what?" Something clenched in my stomach, fear or anticipation I wasn't sure which.

"I've been thinking about what you said the other day." I felt my heart lurch, knowing exactly what he was referring to. I was afraid if we kept rehashing everything, he'd change his mind about helping me with Elora.

"And?"

"I think it's time to explain myself." He wore a serious expression on his face as he watched me.

"Why bother? It's all in the past."

"Because I can't stand the idea of you hating me." I swallowed, uncertain about his statement. Though I'd said it—*to* him, no less—I wasn't sure it was true anymore. There was no way I'd tell him that, though.

"Who said I even cared enough about what happened between us to hate you?"

He sighed, glaring at me, knowing I was being difficult on purpose. "You cared." He paused long enough for my stomach to clench and tighten. "I think it's time I explain what was going on in my head. I was barely twenty years old, heir to a throne that belongs to a monster, and I'd been raised to believe certain things and act a certain way. And I think it's important you know how that might have reflected in my decision-making back then."

"Poor, tormented, little prince." When a glimpse of hurt flashed in his eyes, I sighed. "Go on."

"I had no say in anything back then. I never agreed to the betrothal. I hated Crown Cottage. I hated you and your sister that first year. Gods, you both were awful. You were what, thirteen or fourteen?"

I laughed, knowing full well just how awful we were back then. The two of us fought with each other and everyone else every chance we got. I remembered harassing Dewalt especially, less afraid of him than we were of Rainier. We couldn't stand the snotty prince who Lucia was promised to, and the idea she would have to marry him made her so angry. I'd always thought she was being a bit overdramatic. Even back then, I thought he was nice to look at.

"It's fine. We hated you too." He huffed a laugh, and I was momentarily distracted by the smile that accompanied it.

"You know I've always been raised with the knowledge that my duty lies with Vesta—one day I will be king. I spent my whole life being taught what was best for the kingdom, and I was told that was Lucia. That she and I would fix not only Vesta, but the entirety of the Three Kingdoms. Do you know how daunting that was for a teenager? From our betrothal until her death, I was burdened with the expectation we would fix everything. That we were both bound by duty to be the answer."

I nodded for him to continue when he looked at me expectantly. I'd never thought of Rainier's part in the prophecy—by marrying and bonding with the Beloved, he would also be destined for greatness. That if she were able to unite the Three Kingdoms, he would have a large part in it. I knew how overwhelming the burden was for her, and I'd never comprehended it was also his to bear in a way.

"And I decided long before that night that I didn't want to do my duty anymore if it didn't involve you."

My breath caught in my throat, and I was grateful I didn't choke. It didn't make any sense for him to say any of this—especially not now. I wasn't sure if I could even believe it. He'd left me, adrift and lost, with not a single person who would stand up for me.

I recovered quickly, ensuring he couldn't see a single emotion on my face. I didn't want him to see what I felt before I had the chance to process.

"Such pretty words. And yet..." I kept my voice steady and cool. Despite what he just said, it didn't change the past. I saw something like guilt flash through his eyes before his expression tightened.

"You have no idea how much I was struggling—to maintain my identity, my duty, everything I'd been raised to believe and to be. And that night in the cavern, I said what I did because when I was with you, I realized I didn't give a single damn about the rest of it. The Three Kingdoms could burn, and I wouldn't care." He took a deep breath, and I noticed his hands shook. "So, I *had* to stop it. It was my duty—to be what Vesta needed, to bond with Lucia, to do everything right. And you—you were a threat to that.

"I kept trying to find ways around it, ways to have everything. Ways to be a diligent prince, an honest man, and still have you. And I never found it until she died." I was unintentionally holding my breath as he spoke, the intensity of his words taking up all the air in the room. "And a small, sick, disgusting part of me felt relief when she died because of what it could mean for us. And even though I immediately banished the thought, I don't know if I've ever forgiven myself for it. What kind of person finds a fragment of relief in their friend's death? Not just my friend, but your sister. I felt so fucking guilty for that fleeting thought, for dropping the wards, for almost gods damn killing you, for everything.

"Part of me was angry about how I felt about you, really. I didn't want to want you. Shit, Em, I *still* don't want to want you. I hate the loss of control, and it's all I ever feel with you." I nodded slowly, waiting for him to continue while I felt my heart thundering in my chest. The implication of his words made my heart heavy and light at the same time. He waited a moment longer, those bright green eyes locked onto mine, before continuing.

"I hated that loving you came with those feelings of guilt, of not feeling good enough for Vesta, of not feeling good enough for you, for any of it. And I was a damned coward. You were right the other night; I do think I made a mistake." His eyes locked onto mine, and I saw regret in them, along with something more. Something that seemed a lot like hope.

I took a deep breath, willing my spine to become steel. He didn't want to want me because I wasn't what he dreamed of for himself. He still didn't want that for himself. So, none of this mattered.

"I'm not sure how that changes anything." It sounded like regret, just wrapped in a nicer package. I knew he expected me to feel disgusted with him because of his relief over Lucia's death, but that would make me a hypocrite. I missed her every single day and thought about her often, but if I said I didn't find any sense of relief afterward, I'd have been lying. Part of me was glad to be done with the Myriad, the Crown, and the expectations. He might have felt relief about his standing with me, but I felt relief about all of it. Maybe we were both disgusting and depraved, but I wouldn't judge him for it. Would either of us have traded any of it for her life, though? Absolutely not. I'd have endured it all with a smile just to have her back. But this helped me understand his actions better; he was young, and it was difficult to have that stress. Knowing that what he felt for me caused him to spiral so low sent a pang through my chest. But understanding and acceptance were two different things. I understood, but I couldn't accept that he'd let me beg—when I was so broken and unmoored—and he'd left me stranded on my own. The fact he thought it was a mistake meant little in the grand scheme of things.

"Finally being able to tell you changes everything for me."

I tried to remain calm, counting my breaths to center me, if only because I couldn't let myself unravel over the past. I had never thought about his perspective that day other than the fact he didn't want me. I'd lost my sister, and then the man I loved didn't—*wouldn't*—choose me. I'd lost everything. I'd been begging him for a reason to stay, and he'd been so wracked with guilt for his kingdom, for his dead friend, that he felt he had to let me go. But where did that leave me?

"Why didn't you tell me before? At the burial, or hell, before that? Why didn't you tell me how you were feeling?" At the very least, I'd have known he didn't want to break my heart. He gave a soft laugh before answering.

"Do you think you would've understood? *I* barely understood. I knew I wanted you and shouldn't and that was it. By the time I—I didn't truly understand until it was too late. I never thought you would have gone through with the marriage. You'd do what you always do, and you'd talk or fight your way out of it—you wouldn't accept it. But I was wrong."

He was exactly right. Knowing the conflict Lucia felt being the Beloved and even the comparatively small conflict I felt being forced to marry Faxon, I would have tried to understand. But it wouldn't have mattered. Between that and my feelings at the time, without her, without my other half, I hadn't had the fight in me to stop things. Duty won, as it always did.

"I couldn't do that to them, to my parents. Not without a good reason." I stopped myself from saying I wanted him to be the reason. He knew.

"We both wanted to call it off, you know. We'd been talking about finding a way out of it."

"You and Lucia?"

He nodded, leaning back in the chair, lightly resting his hands on his bare stomach. I tried not to look, finding a dark spot on the table to stare at. She'd offered to call it off, if I wanted. But she had never told me *she* wanted to. She would eventually be queen, bonded to one of the most powerful conduits in Vesta. Sharing his power, his throne. I couldn't have asked her to let go of that for me. She had always seemed hopeful about being a princess, being a queen. But if I'd known she wanted to—for her, not for me—then my answer might have been different.

"She was in love with someone, Em. She didn't want to marry me. She didn't want to do the ritual with me."

"You're lying." If Lucia had been in love, she would have told me.

"I'm not." He shook his head. "A week before I took you to the cavern, I talked to her. She knew about us."

"She knew?" I had told her it was only flirting, nothing more. How could I confess to her my feelings for the man she would be bonded to for centuries? The man she could come to love one day. The man she would share her life with after I was long dead and buried, having never performed the ritual, never been granted access to the font.

"Yes, Em, she knew everything. Hell, she knew before we did."

I took a deep gulp of my water, holding the glass tightly in my hand. I'd spent almost half my life thinking my sister died hating me, thinking I'd betrayed her. I knew she didn't love Rainier, not in that way at least, but she'd always seemed eager to be a princess, to share his power. Maybe she had only been showing me what she showed everyone else. Maybe she'd been making the best of a situation she didn't want. Finding out she was in love with someone—that she wanted to call it all off? My sister, who told me everything, hadn't told me, but she'd told Rainier? Though, I supposed I'd been keeping secrets of my own.

"But she seemed so angry when she saw us that night."

"Well, I don't think she expected what she saw." The smile he gave me was sheepish, and I swore I saw his cheeks darken. "But I imagine, based on my conversation with her, she was a bit angry you hadn't told her yet, and she'd heard it from me instead."

Honestly, it made sense. Of course, she'd be mad it wasn't me who told her. And I never had a chance to speak with her about it, to set things straight.

"You should have told me she knew."

"Yes, I should have. There are a lot of things I should have done differently, Em." He stared at me hard, and I averted my eyes.

"Who?"

"Who, what?"

"Who was she in love with?" There were countless soldiers there every summer and servants galore. Maybe she hadn't told me out of shame. I wished she would have known I wouldn't have cared who she was in love with. She could have told me. We could have commiserated over falling for people we couldn't have. I didn't know why, but my confusion and grasping had turned into something different. I was angry. Angry at my sister for keeping secrets. Angry at her for being dead, so I couldn't yell at her. Angry I'd been so hard on myself for so long. Just...angry.

"I—Em, that's not my place to say."

"She's dead, Rain. She's not going to be mad at you." My dead sister wouldn't be mad if he answered, but I would be if he didn't.

"We can talk about this tomorrow, the four of us."

"Four of us?"

"Lavenia and Dewalt. They knew."

"Am I the only one who didn't know?" I half-shouted, remembering them sleeping upstairs. I had thought for so long that Lucia had been angry at me, that she felt betrayed over Rainier. The look she gave me that night had haunted me for years. Yet she had told our three friends about her secret before she ever told me? It was odd to feel anything other than grief and sadness over my sister, the hot frustration having no outlet, no one for me to yell and take it out on.

"This is not the direction this conversation was supposed to go." Rainier stood, approaching me from the other side of the table. Someone had lit a candle, and the flicker of light across his skin was mesmerizing. Taut muscles flexed under glowing skin, and I noticed a dusting of dark hair below his navel, both serving as a distraction to my anger. I lifted my chin, dragging my eyes up his body to his face, not bothering to hide the path of my gaze.

"And how was it supposed to go, Rainier?"

"Well, I didn't want to talk about your dead sister. It's rather unromantic." His mouth twitched like he was about to laugh but wouldn't dare until I joined in. I felt the corner of my lips rise, and I pushed them back down by sheer force of will. That hot frustration with Lucia searched for an escape, but laughing at a joke at her expense was too much. Amusement glinted in his eyes. "I was supposed to tell you I was a fool. That no matter the cost, my duty should have been to myself first and then the kingdom. I was supposed to tell you I didn't regret anything between us. The only regret I have was not figuring out the mess in my head sooner and breaking down the door at Ravemont." I had to look away from his emerald scrutiny. It was almost too much, too intense, and I deflected.

"It doesn't matter now, does it?"

He walked over to my side of the table and took my glass out of my hand before refilling it. He drank from it slowly, flicking his tongue out to catch an errant drop of water from his mouth when he finished. I felt my own lips part as I couldn't help but stare.

"Doesn't it, Em?"

"I don't want to talk about this." What was there to talk about? My daughter was missing, my husband a traitor. Rainier and the past were the least of my concerns.

"Then what do you want, Emmeline?" His voice was a low challenge, and I tried to ignore the way it made my body tense.

"My daughter. I want my daughter back."

"Of *course*, and we'll get her. I promise you. Especially after what we've learned today, I'm more confident than ever about that." He took a step toward me, and I felt my breaths quicken. "But then what?"

"I don't know. I—I guess we'll go to Ravemont. It won't make sense to hide anymore." I glanced down, doing everything I could to not ogle his half-naked body, so close to mine. I narrowed my attention to the pitcher on the counter in front of me. My gaze traced the rim, focusing solely there, ignoring the large hand that gripped the counter next to it.

"Is that what you want? To go to Ravemont?" He asked like I had ever made any choices for myself. As if I hadn't spent almost half my life making decisions to keep my daughter safe and the other half being ordered to do whatever would benefit my sister.

"I don't know, Rain." I sighed, grabbing my glass back out of his hand. "It's a lot to think about right now."

"Let's start simple then. What do you want right now?" I could feel the heat of his skin, radiating warmth around him. I could feel his eyes on me. I wouldn't look at him—couldn't. I didn't want to think about any of this. I didn't want to think about the creatures that tore into me, in the form of a beast or the form of a man. I didn't want to think about the past, anything about that night, anything about Lucia. I didn't want to think about my missing daughter and the lengths we'd have to go to get her back. What I'd do to Faxon the minute I saw him again. I didn't want to think about what would happen after. What all of this meant to me and my life was all too much to think about. I didn't want to think about any of it. I didn't want to think *at all*.

I took a chance and peered up at him. He watched me, but my gaze was drawn downwards, toward his chest then to his waist, then moved to where the deep V-shape of his muscles disappeared beneath his waistband.

"A distraction." My eyes flew up to his mouth, studying the perfect fullness and softness. His lips gently parted at my words, and I saw his eyes rove over me, pausing on my breasts and again on my hips. I realized my wet hair was probably making my nightgown sheer in the places it rested.

"Just a distraction?" His voice was low, predatory.

"Yes, just a—a moment to refresh our memory," I stammered, feeling my face reddening.

I stopped breathing as he moved, taking the glass out of my hand and putting it on the table. He leaned in slowly, lowering his mouth to my neck, and he spoke so softly his words tickled my skin, sending goosebumps racing across my flesh.

"You think I could ever forget?"

My breath hitched, and it took me a moment to recover.

"That's all it can be. If it's not enough, then you need to stop." My voice was husky, almost unrecognizable. I was surprised I didn't stutter as I tried to convince myself all I wanted was a single moment. My stomach tightened as he chuckled against me and the light nip of his teeth against my neck sent a shock through my body.

"I've spent too much time imagining you like this. I'll take what you give me, Em."

His mouth pressed against where he'd nipped me, and I let out a small gasp. I couldn't move as his lips roamed, and he pressed the faintest hint of a kiss on the corner of my mouth before pulling away. I was frozen, leaning against the table, my hands gripping the edge. It began to hit me then. I'd never thought I'd see him again, absolve him for his part in it. His lips on my skin had haunted me as much as everything else. The smartest thing to do would be to step away, to stop our inevitable parting from destroying me. But I didn't want to. When he gripped my hips with his warm, steady hands, I thought maybe I could forgive him. Forgive us for the mistakes we made when our hearts were sore and young. He was here in front of me, offering the urgent passion I'd always wanted, and I didn't think I was strong enough to say no.

Maybe it was madness underneath my skin, or maybe it was fire, but warmth spread through my body. I reached my arms up, raking my hands through his short hair, pulling him away from my neck, and he stepped back a bit, straightening. In the candlelight, his eyes were dark as they searched mine, hesitance crossing his features. I stood there and let my eyes roam while I inhaled the smells of earth and rain which had always belonged to him. I vaguely wondered if he brought his own soap. I perused the muscles of his chest, marked with a smattering of soft curls leading down to his stomach, muscles tense—waiting. Without thinking, I reached my hand out to touch him, fingertips dragging across his abdomen, his skin pebbling as he exhaled a shuddering breath. He was as nervous as I was. Searching for the spot I'd marked him, my fingers grazed the sensitive flesh on his ribs, and he softly hissed as I touched him. I dragged my eyes back up to his, questioning.

"Here." His voice was gruff as he pulled my hand farther to his side, knowing what I was searching for. He placed my fingers on the distinct slice of skin I'd left behind, and in that moment, I simultaneously regretted hurting him while being grateful I'd left my mark. Pleased there had been a spot on his body that belonged to me, had been mine, all these years.

"I'm sorry," I whispered, my fingers still tracing the smooth skin, a slash of lighter pink against the darker brown. One of his hands went to my hip and pulled me toward him, possessive and rough compared to his other, which he used to hold my chin, lifting it to meet his eyes.

"Don't."

I wasn't sure who moved first, but in an instant, our lips met, and everything changed. His kiss was softer than I'd imagined, gentle yet insistent, and his lips were smooth and warm as they caressed my own. I was brought back to our first kiss in the meadow. He'd left me breathless, and I'd had an ache in my heart after that I didn't quite understand. The ache of a kiss containing promises made and the highest of hopes. An ache which echoed deep inside my chest even now, only having grown and matured with time. Every one of my nerve endings trembled and burned, heat spreading from where his lips met mine.

Gods, how had I ever thought that creature in the woods was him? Rainier was life and need and so enmeshed in who I was there was no mistaking him. Leaving one hand tracing his ribs, I gently lifted the other to his cheek, his stubble rough under my touch, following the outline of his jaw and down to grip his neck. He pulled me closer to him, both hands digging into me, spreading over the round curve of my backside. I opened for him, his tongue sweeping in over mine, tasting of the faintest hint of wine from dinner, and I pressed my body against his, my round curves meeting each sharp edge. I felt his length, already hard against my stomach, and I let out a soft moan of approval. The sound must have snapped something in Rainier because, in one swift motion, he pulled a chair out from under the table and sat, a hand tugging on my nightgown, pulling me toward him.

"Come here." His voice was a gruff demand, a need. An order I gladly obeyed.

I barely took a step before he reached out, grabbing me at the waist and settling me in his lap, a leg on either side of him and his hands on my hips. I was more than aware of my nightgown bunching up; the only thing separating our bodies was the thin fabric of his pants. His hands slid down, digging into me, gripping my ass tightly. Putting one hand on his chest, I used the other to grip his hair, pulling his head back to present his mouth to me. His lips lifted in a smile as he gazed up at me with hooded eyes, a heady desire glimmering within.

"Do you still hate me, Emmeline?" His voice was breathless as his hands slid up to my waist, waiting for my answer with a hungry look in his eyes.

I didn't know how to reply. The road we were going down was a path to tragedy from every direction. Part of me hated him for doing this to me again. For making me want to give him a part of me, with no plans for a future. He had even said he didn't want to want me, and yet here I was, wanting him back. I couldn't say I felt differently than him either. This was a sure and steady path to madness. A swan dive off a cliff, which only promised a watery death below. But it was thoughtless, a sweet obscurity over the worries and fears that consumed me. His lips and his hands released their hold, and I wouldn't trade the weightlessness for anything. But I still wasn't sure about any of it.

"I don't know."

"Kiss me, then. Don't stop until you decide."

I moved, lips crashing into his, a mess of tongues and teeth. Our mouths were open, his tongue caressing mine, his taste a promise of sweet destruction. He put one hand on my lower back, pulling me closer. With his other, he lifted my nightgown and slid his calloused hand up my skin, still slightly damp from my bath. He was slow and methodical, tracing each rib. I let out a small breath as he reached the swell under my breast, and his hand moved higher, lightly drawing slow, indolent circles across my pebbled flesh as he teased me.

My breasts felt tight, body flushed and tender as his fingers stroked my skin. He took his time. He'd never touched me like this before, our brief moment in the cavern the only time we'd done more than kiss, but something told me it wouldn't have been like this. This was sin and insanity and freedom wrapped into one. Every touch, every caress, was an erasure of the past which corrupted and destroyed. Finally, he stopped teasing, his thumb gently rubbing my peaked nipple.

I let out a small gasp, and I could feel his smile on my lips. I pushed into his palm, rolling my hips and feeling the thick length of him underneath me. The seam on his pants was sweet torture, and I wanted more. Feeling him, remembering him, a part of me was worried about pain. It had been so long, surely it would hurt. He'd been careful and patient back then, taking his time to check on me, watching me so carefully and sweetly it made me emotional, even now.

Those thoughts left my mind the second he rolled the tight bud of my nipple between his thumb and forefinger, and I let out a groan into his mouth as the pleasure from it bordered on pain. I felt slick between my legs and shamelessly rolled my hips on him again, torturing myself, not caring if I made a mess in his lap, realizing how badly I wanted that sweet pain. Suddenly, he released me, hand sliding back down to my hip as he ignored my cry of protest.

"Was that distracting enough, Em?" His eyes searched mine, looking perhaps for hesitation or something else.

"Very." I didn't know if he wanted me to say no, that it wasn't enough, that I needed more, but I considered it. Feeling how hard he was beneath me, I wanted nothing more than to continue. But if he thought we should stop, I wouldn't push. I'd spent our entire time apart under the impression he hadn't felt as strongly as I did. I'd only just found out he hadn't regretted us, and I didn't want him to start now.

His eyes flickered before he leaned forward, pressing his mouth against the sensitive skin where my neck met my shoulder, and I let out a quiet sigh. His lips were so soft and having them on me was a dream—a memory and prediction in one. He traced his teeth over where he'd kissed me, and I shuddered. Sliding one of the straps of my nightgown off, he slowly traced a path across my neck and chest, leaving open-mouthed kisses, before baring my other shoulder. I let out a breath and tilted my head back slightly, eyes closed.

"Do you want me to stop?" His voice was a low growl as he continued grazing his lips across my shoulder and neck. He'd learned a thing or two in my absence. The man before me was confident and demanding, so unlike the one who'd touched me with trembling hands. My nightgown felt spectacularly thin as those same hands roamed their way up past my hips, fingertips gently dancing up my sides. And I knew I wouldn't be satisfied with only this.

"Never," I whispered, leaning forward, my breath on his lips.

He let out a sound low in his throat, and any restraint he held onto cracked. Grabbing my waist and pulling my legs around him, he stood up, knocking over the chair he sat on with a clatter. I threw my arms around his neck, stifling a cry of surprise.

"I'll hold you to that, Em." He spoke into my neck before he continued kissing me there, carrying me across the room.

Feeling him against me, right where I wanted him, made me ache. His mouth moved to my lips, and he kissed me with a frenzied need as he brought me into the study and gently lowered us down onto the trundle bed. Bending down over me, he finished what he'd started and exposed my breasts, sitting back on his heels between my legs. My nightgown was rucked up around my hips, and he watched me as his hands roamed, feeling my soft skin beneath his calloused hands.

"Fuck, you're perfect." He exhaled before dipping his head to kiss my shoulder. Each large hand cupped a breast, a thumb swirling over each peaked nipple. He traced a path across my collarbones, his tongue and mouth grazing my skin. He was warm, heat radiating from his body—his beautiful body I'd always admired in every form. As I slid my hands across his shoulders, I decided this was my favorite version. Feeling him move, I delicately traced across his back and shoulders as he continued to kiss a path across my chest. I raked my nails through his hair, and he let out a low groan before he took my nipple into his mouth and rubbed the other between his thumb and forefinger.

"Rain..." I was breathless, the warmth of his mouth and body melding with my own, sending waves of dizzying heat across my skin and through my core. When he heard his name on my lips, he made a sound in his throat and gently teased me with the hint of teeth. I couldn't help it as I arched off the bed, pushing into his mouth and tilting my head back, a low moan escaping my lips. I put one hand in his hair and fisted the sheets underneath me with the other. He stopped kissing me for a moment, and our eyes met. The look he gave me took my breath away, and I was sure every feeling I had was written across my face. Every feeling I wasn't supposed to have, considering this was only a distraction. He watched me as he licked from between my breasts up to the space between my collar bones and then kissed his way back down. I gave a delightful shiver, never wanting it to end.

"Rainier?"

We both froze as Dewalt's voice drifted down to us, and we heard the creak of the stairs. Rainier sat back on his knees, and I bolted upright, pulling my sleeves back up and running my fingers through my hair.

"Get up!" I hissed at him. I stood, reaching for my robe as Rainier stepped behind me, tugging my nightgown down from where it had bunched at my hips. I felt his breath on my neck as he pushed up close behind me, continuing to kiss across my shoulder. I pulled away and threw on my robe before scampering back into the main room to cuddle under a blanket in one of the armchairs. Rainier walked to the table with no urgency whatsoever, the hard outline beneath his pants apparent. He was casually leaning against the table and drinking from my glass of water when Dewalt rounded the bottom of the stairs, rubbing sleep from his eyes.

He looked at Rainier standing there, and I held my breath, hoping he wouldn't notice what I couldn't take my eyes off.

"Heard something down here, everything alright?" His eyes scanned the room, finally resting on me. Surprise etched his features, but he didn't say anything else before he glanced to the other side of the table, spotting the overturned chair.

"Emmeline couldn't sleep, and neither could I. We've been keeping each other company. She's still the clumsiest woman in the world." Rainier gestured to the chair, and I hoped our friend believed the lie. It was an effort to keep myself from groaning as Dewalt raised a single brow. He wasn't stupid—he knew. I was frustrated; I wanted time to wrap my head around it all without having to think about the others finding out.

Dewalt glared at Rainier as he took a few steps around the table and slowly stood the chair upright. I watched Rainier swallow as he stared back at his friend. Dewalt slowly turned his gaze on me, and I felt his judgment weigh heavily as he scanned my face. His eyes lingered on my hair a few seconds too long, and I fought the urge to brush my fingers through it once more. I wondered if the source of his disdain was the obvious lying or if it was something else.

"Well, you two better try again. It's late."

"I'm feeling pretty worn out now." Rainier took another swig of his water before setting it down on the counter. Dewalt disappeared up the stairs after shooting us both a look I could only interpret as disappointment before Rainier walked back toward the study. At the last moment, he turned to me, a surprisingly soft smile on his face.

"Goodnight, Em."

"Goodnight, Rain." He blew out the lamp in the study, and I heard him lay down in the trundle bed while I sat there for a few moments, blissfully free of thought. Eventually, I stood, but I didn't move toward the stairs.

"Rain?" I whispered it, ready to leave him alone if he wasn't awake.

"Mm?" His voice was tired and quiet, and I felt a tinge of regret realizing he must have been on the verge of sleep.

"I don't. I don't hate you anymore." The room was silent, and I waited a few moments before I turned to go upstairs. He must have fallen asleep because I couldn't imagine he wouldn't reply to that. As I rounded the table, halfway to the hallway, I heard a low chuckle coming from the study.

"If I knew it was that simple, I would have kissed you sooner."

I rolled my eyes and headed up the stairs, but I'd have been lying if I said I didn't think about joining him in the study.

CHAPTER 22

I woke up disoriented, forgetting I was in Elora's room. I'd slept deeper in her bed than I had in days, and other than the confusion about where I was and the pang that went through me when I realized she wasn't here, I felt almost normal. I heard a voice cut through the quiet coming from below the window, and I wondered if it was what woke me. Stretching, I realized I'd slept far past dawn, the mid-morning light filtering in through thin curtains that needed replacing. I felt lethargic, not wanting to move. When I'd gone to sleep, everything felt heavy and relaxed. *Too* relaxed.

"He's going to get her killed." Dewalt's tone alarmed me. Was he talking about Elora? I sat up straight, confused because I was sure someone would have woken me if there was an immediate urgency. I heard another voice, quieter, but I couldn't make out what they said.

"She would. She won't see it differently." He sounded frustrated. I reached for my robe, putting it on as I eased over to the window, trying to stay out of sight. Something twisted in my stomach, telling me this was a conversation I wasn't supposed to hear. Part of me felt guilty for eavesdropping, but something told me this was important. I looked down and saw the source of the other voice. Lavenia stood facing Dewalt, arms crossed and looking grim. They were off to the side of the house, likely not realizing Elora's window was right above them. Lavenia was hard to hear, so I focused on her lips, hoping that between watching her and my limited hearing, I'd be able to understand her.

"And Emma will have our protection, Dewalt. I don't know why you're so upset about this; it's his decision to make." I felt my lungs tighten, and my heart drop. They were talking about me. I was the one getting killed in this scenario. It was preferable to Elora being the subject of this conversation, but not by much.

"You two don't know Keeva like I do. If she's still at court—" I saw Dewalt's head shake, his long, dark hair shimmering as it slid over itself. "We can't take Emma there." His foot tapped on the ground, full of nervous energy.

Who the hell is Keeva?

"Unless she wants a war, she won't do anything. You can try to talk to him if you want, Dewalt, but he's already decided. He's going to talk to her when we arrive."

"I've fucking tried. He's going to end up with his own Shika tattoo if he isn't more gods damn careful," he muttered, and I wasn't certain I'd heard him right. I hadn't seen any evidence of a constellation inked on him, though I supposed it could be under his shirt. "If there isn't an alliance, she has an army. She might not care about a war, Ven. Between Keeva and the others sulking about the court, Emma is as good as dead." He shook his head. I took a deep breath. Why was he worried about someone with an army killing me? And others? I had a sneaking suspicion in my stomach, and it made me want to vomit. I focused again, straining to hear what else was being said.

"Does she know?" He jerked his head backwards, toward the house, toward me. I jumped back from the window, so I wouldn't be seen if Lavenia happened to look up. I missed her response, but Dewalt's voice rose in volume.

"He can be so fucking—I think I interrupted something last night."

Shit.

"What do you mean?" I couldn't see Lavenia's face, she'd turned away, but her voice raised enough I could hear her.

"I heard a bang, woke me up. When I came downstairs, there was a chair knocked over, and her hair was a mess."

"That doesn't mean anything, D." She reached out to him then, a hand on his arm. "But I suppose if he's made up his mind about talking to Keeva, you may be right."

"Her face gave it away. You know how she is."

I cursed myself for my inability to hide my thoughts.

"You're angry." Her voice was quieter, her demeanor softening.

"No. I'm not—"

"She isn't Lucia." He froze.

"Divine *hell*, Ven. I know she's not Lucia. I know that better than anyone." He wrenched his arm back from her and turned, facing the house, and I saw his face.

It was him.

Dewalt had been in love with my sister, and she'd loved him back.

And I'd had no idea at all, until now.

He whipped around. "Seeing her everyday hurts because it's a reminder of exactly who she isn't." He gestured back to the house. "But we can't lose her too, Ven."

I felt intrusive watching him from the window as his shoulders sagged, and Lavenia put a hand on his neck, pulling his forehead down to hers. I walked away and sat down on Elora's bed.

This headache didn't come from my divinity.

Memories slipped past as I sat there, knees pulled up to my chest. Dewalt begging her to let him train her. Lucia sitting under the tree in the meadow while we trained, Dewalt's shirtless body glowing in the late afternoon sun while she watched with rapt attention. The time Lucia disappeared with Lavenia and Dewalt. Had Lavenia made herself scarce when they slipped away? Why hadn't they told me? Why had everyone kept it a secret from me? I didn't know why Lucia hadn't tried to end the betrothal sooner. Maybe she thought she had more time. We all thought there was more time.

I wondered what would have happened if she hadn't been attacked. Would she and Rainier have gone together to break off the agreement our parents had made? I was so unbearably sad, thinking about what could have been. What we'd lost. We thought we had time and youth on our side. The ache in my chest felt real, the emotional pain manifesting into a physical one.

A light knock rapped on the other side of my door, and I pulled my robe tighter.

"Come in."

Lavenia opened the door and hesitated, watching me where I sat, legs still tucked up into my chest as I stared at the floor.

"I saw you." I looked up at her and wondered if she could tell how tired I was. Fully rested and still exhausted. I raised my eyebrows, inviting her to speak if she needed to, but rather hoping she didn't.

"We won't let anything happen to you." She walked in, carefully closing the door behind her. I felt my brows crinkle before I remembered what she was even talking about, too caught up thinking about Dewalt and Lucia. Mourning my sister in a different way, mourning for Dewalt, so distracted I'd forgotten the rest of the conversation. I didn't move, keeping my legs tucked up while I watched her.

"Who is Keeva?" Lavenia stared at the ground, not able to look me in the eyes. That would have been answer enough, but she found her voice.

"She is one of the Nine." The Nine daughters of Nythyr, the assassin heirs and protectors to Queen Nereza. None were born to the queen, though she had her own harem, but all were chosen for their divinity and their beauty.

"And why would one of the Nine want to kill me, Lavenia?" The feeling I'd suppressed earlier was threatening to overpower me, nausea bubbling up my throat. Now accompanying an underlying current of fear.

"She doesn't. She won't." My friend shook her head, eyes dark.

"Dewalt seems to think differently." I knew I sounded annoyed. I wished she'd just get it over with. She sighed, rubbing her temples and looking just as tired as I felt.

"He worries she will not take kindly to your relationship with Rainier." She was stalling, and we both knew it. If she wanted to do this the long way, so be it.

"And why would my relationship—"

"They are betrothed, Emma." At that moment, I was glad I'd heard their conversation outside. It gave my subconscious time to understand, so I was ready when my suspicions were confirmed. I almost laughed, but I stopped myself, knowing how cold and bitter it would sound. What was it about being betrothed to someone else that made Rainier want to kiss me? Though I'd asked for it, I would have thought he'd have the common sense not to do it if he was engaged to be married and bonded. To an assassin, no less. Gods. "But he's going to talk to—" I cut her off.

"I don't see how that has anything to do with me. Dewalt said something about others at court who might also be interested in killing me?" I stood, pulling my robe around myself and crossing over to the pile of clothes I'd brought in. Lavenia paused just long enough to confirm, yet again, my suspicions weren't far off. "You know, I don't want to know. As much as I tried to ignore the royal gossip, it would seem he's earned his reputation. The others have nothing to worry about. As I've already said, *I do not want him.*" I had told myself it was only a distraction; it couldn't ever be anything more. I had said the same to him, so why did I feel betrayed? I turned my back to her, crossing over to the window.

"That's—" She sighed, frustrated. "What did you expect? That he'd stay celibate all these years? Did you?" More or less, yes, I had. But I didn't tell her that. It wasn't out of any loyalty to him. "You don't understand."

"Enlighten me."

"You should be talking about this with Rainier. None of this matters. You're his, and you'll be protected." I was angry that hearing his name brought me images of his hands on my skin, his tongue tracing a path of constellations across my chest, and I nearly boiled over.

"Did he sleep with her?" My voice came out embarrassingly weak. I hadn't expected celibacy. Hell, I *knew* he hadn't been. I expected honesty. I expected the man from last night not to be promised to someone. The nameless people at court were one thing, but the idea that he was betrothed and I was somehow party to hurting another woman didn't sit right with me.

"I don't make it a habit of knowing what my brother does in his bedroom, Emmeline. Like I imagine you didn't with your sister." She leveled a harsh stare in my direction, proving she knew the extent of what I heard. I curled my hand into a fist, my nails cutting tiny crescents of pain into my palm. "But as far as I know, they've never been alone together. Even if they had, it doesn't matter. He's claimed you."

"He cannot claim what does not belong to him. He should have told me before." Before he made promises in sighs and caresses, before he convinced me with his lips to soften my heart, before he held me with hands specifically created to burn every part of me. All while he was betrothed. Again. He could have told me that night in the tent when he discussed why he hadn't seen his mother. He had spoken so poorly of political alliances it made it clear to me this betrothal was more than a move for power. After everything he'd said, why would he agree to it if it was only for an alliance?

Gods dammit. I am so stupid.

"Before what, Emma?"

"I need to get dressed." I nodded toward the door, so Lavenia would leave. She got up, pausing at the threshold.

"He should have told you. You're right. But give him a chance to explain."

As I got dressed, I began to think about all the people in my life who kept secrets from me, made choices for me, did things and acted in ways that destroyed me. Doing and saying whatever they wanted to do as if I was no more than a possession to be had. Was I just someone along for the ride with men who chose not to include me in any decision-making? If I'd known about Keeva, last night wouldn't have happened. If Rainier thought I was going to go from belonging to my father, to Faxon, and now to him, he was sorely mistaken. I would belong to no one but myself.

When I stormed through the front door, stomping my way across the porch and down the steps, I wore my thickest breeches that still allowed movement. My hair was braided, and I wrapped it up around itself, a bun sitting on the back of my head. My plain, white shirt had the sleeves rolled up, and I'd dug out an old, leather bodice from years ago. It laced up the sides and the front, so I was still able to wear it, just not as tight as I used to. Lavenia and Dewalt were at the fire talking, the weather just crisp enough to necessitate it, storm clouds rolling in. It was after midday now, and I felt disgraced for how late I'd slept. Rainier was coming up the path atop Clyde with Thyra on another horse beside him, coming back from town, I guessed. I reminded myself I didn't care, averting my eyes toward my destination as I saw his head turn toward me. I knew he watched as I stalked across the clearing to the stable, and I hurried my pace in case he chose to bring Clyde inside. I went to the empty stall that wasn't remotely empty, full of random odds and ends I had to climb over. I found what I was looking for in the same place I'd left it.

I pulled my sword out of its sheath and inspected it, pleased that I'd sharpened the blade before putting it away the last time I'd used it. Even though it was old, it was still a decent weapon, the hilt simple with a tan, leather grip, faded in some places from my hand. Feeling the weight of it, I appreciated its balance. I climbed back out of the stall and stood there for just a moment, contemplating what I was about to do. I didn't want anything to do with the frustratingly beautiful man outside, but I needed him. As much as I wanted to give him a piece of my mind and cut him off all over again, I couldn't. Elora needed him, so I'd have to be careful about how I confronted him. Carrying the scabbard in my left hand and the sword in my right, I went back out to the clearing. Rainier was on the ground now, standing next to Clyde, while Lavenia spoke to him. His body language was tense, and I couldn't help but notice his hand move into a fist, the muscles in his arm flexing. Dewalt was gone, and I didn't see anyone else other than Thyra, who caught my attention and nodded, a twinkle in her eye. I wondered if she was listening to what Lavenia said, undoubtedly telling Rainier what I knew.

What I knew was he'd left me in the dark. Though it had felt like what we shared was restorative, his lips having a disarming effect on my senses, it was tainted by the knowledge she existed. What I knew was that I would not put myself in the position for him to choose duty over me once more. Some stupid and naive part of me had let him awaken that young girl within, and I didn't think I'd survive his rejection again. He might have been content with kissing me while he was betrothed, but I would not be a mistress. The fact I'd let him touch me while I was still married was blight on my soul enough, no matter how little those vows meant to me now. No matter that Faxon broke them first with his betrayal. The thing I was most certain about was that I would not be spending two years in a court where Rainier was married and bonded to someone, specifically a woman who would want to kill me. I needed to get this over with. I threw my scabbard to the ground, the noise drawing Rainier's attention. The expression on his face was full of regret and something like fear.

Good.

"Em—" He started toward me, and my name on his lips felt like a curse, so different from the night before. I shook my head and cut him off.

"You offered a deal, and I'm naming the time and place. Here and now."

He stopped after closing the distance between us by half. I saw something in his face break, and I hated that it took no small amount of strength to keep me from flinching. His face was a mirror to the look he gave me all those years ago when I'd demanded first blood. Anger started to replace the feeling of guilt in my stomach. How did he have any right to be upset?

"Em, let me explain."

"Get your sword out now, or I won't heal you when I'm done with you." I vaguely noted Thyra's raised brows behind him. He still stood there with his hands at his sides, his face soft. I lifted my left arm, bent at the elbow, resting my sword on it as I faced him.

"Don't hold back this time, Rain." I stood there waiting, watching as his face tensed, his mouth tightening. One of his hands flexed at his side before he raised the other to his sword. I observed as his eyes changed from soft—full of what looked an awful lot like pity—to hardened flint. He squared his jaw before he spoke, voice unforgiving.

"You are so gods damn stubborn. But if you think I'm going to let you make this mistake a second time, you're wrong."

He pulled out his sword as he said the words, and I moved, cutting the distance between us before I struck. Lunging, I aimed for his throat, and he bent backward, evading me as I expected he would. He dodged again as I used my off hand to help pull the sword back toward him. How a man so large could move so quickly, I'd never know.

At my third swipe, he finally lifted his sword, blocking me, and I spun in the direction he'd pushed me, turning into the momentum. I swung my weapon around with me, and he parried the blow. I continued to spin and aimed low for his knees, but he thrust his sword downward and stopped me, anticipating the movement.

He wasn't attempting to beat me, only checking me instead.

"Why does it always come to this, Highclere? Are you that scared of what I might have to say?" I ignored him.

He turned then, bringing his sword down from above as I stood back up and deflected him, twisting my shoulder a bit with the weight of the impact. I almost started to heal myself before I remembered our deal—no abilities. At the time we made our agreement, I hadn't been aware I could heal myself. How unfortunate. We might have come to different terms if I'd known. I felt myself smirk, picturing putting Rainier to sleep as I'd done to the tírrúil. It didn't last long as I felt a stab of pain in my shoulder. I could have gotten away with healing without him noticing, but I'd win this fairly or, I wouldn't win at all.

Even though it hurt, I pushed my sword against him, attempting to make a hit while he followed through, but he was too fast, bringing his weapon up to block me once again. The momentum spun me back, and I had to throw my sword behind me to stop his next move, an attempt at swiping my legs out from under me. He stumbled a step back, and I took advantage, throwing my weight behind me to finish spinning, bringing my sword right back around from the direction he stumbled.

I was disappointed when he ducked, and shocked when he came back up and shoved me backward, his empty hand splayed on my chest. As I tripped, he grabbed my sword hand and pushed me up against the corner of the stable behind me. I hadn't realized we'd moved so close to it.

"Good to see you're not holding back this time," I gritted out. Pinned against the building, I met his gaze, letting him see my fire and fury.

"You're mine for the next two years, ocean eyes." He grinned, and I saw red.

I grabbed the dagger strapped to my thigh and stabbed him in the gut, just to the side and below his navel. I'd have won right there if this were first blood, but it wasn't, and I knew, despite the roar of pain coming from him, I would still easily be overpowered. He grabbed my wrist, and I pushed him backward with my sword hand, pulling my dagger out of him as he went. He grunted and then immediately went to strike, and I fended him off with the dagger as I spun.

It felt like a pulse from Dewalt, the pain that shivered up my elbow when he made contact with the dagger. I vaguely heard screaming from Lavenia and what sounded like laughter from Thyra. I felt my braid fall down my back, loose and a liability. I was in a weakened position, having to parry behind my back, turning halfway to face him with both my weapons.

Left. Dagger. Hit. Turn. Right. Sword. Hit.

I fixed the grip of the smaller blade and attempted to reach back and hit him in the neck with it, but he threw my wrist down with one hand as he brought his sword down from above with his other. I barely spun backward out of the way as I heard other voices join Lavenia and Thyra. I groaned internally; I specifically didn't want an audience for this.

When he thrust forward again, I'd turned enough to block him properly. He was faster than me, though, and he swung again from the other direction. I had to check him with my dagger once again. I remembered how dangerous this was with him. He'd always been good at wearing down his opponent, and he knew I couldn't keep taking blows to my weaker side. I turned a bit to throw him off and brought my sword down behind him. Somehow, he managed to get his own between mine and his back and blocked me that way.

I let out a shriek of fury as a roll of thunder crashed. He was too gods damn fast.

He stood there for a moment and looked over his shoulder at me where our swords crossed. The heavens split, and rain started falling, heavy drops hitting my brow.

"I made an agreement for the kingdom." He barely looked phased while I was panting.

"Is that what you call it with all of the others? Is there a contract? Why didn't I get one?" I regretted my words immediately. It showed my hand. It showed I was bothered. It showed I gods damn cared. I knew he'd been with other women but finding out this secret made me wonder what else he wasn't telling me. What other secrets was he keeping? If he would have told me about Keeva before last night, before he made my body burn to an ember, then our conversation never would have turned into what it did. But he chose to keep that information from me.

Anger flashed in his eyes, and instead of replying to me, he threw my sword off with his elbow and brought his own around above him. I barely had time to throw up my blades, crossing them to stop him before he pushed down, making contact with my shoulder, forcing me to my knees. I bared my teeth as my arms weakened, and I felt the cool steel press against me. I pushed up into it, defiant, ignoring the pain as the blade sliced my flesh.

He looked down at me, and I watched his eyes soften and then widen when he saw the blood drip into the divot of my collarbone. He eased off me, pulling the sword from my skin but not dropping his guard. I felt the trickle of blood and water mix and slowly slide down my chest.

I should have surrendered then. Rainier already won, but I wasn't finished.

I shoved his sword off with my own while I spun on my knees, slashing my dagger around to his legs, cutting both his thighs in one swoop. He stumbled back and looked down, allowing me to stand up, my pants wet and sticking to my knees. I held my elbow up like before, dagger in hand, resting the blade of my sword on my forearm. My shoulder was already starting to hurt from the fight itself, and now it felt even worse.

He stood still, staring at me, the rain pouring down on us both.

"I should have told you. I was *going* to tell you."

For some reason, that angered me more than anything. Rainier knew all along he should have told me, and yet he chose not to. I was sick of people not telling me things. Maybe he thought I'd be scared away if I knew there was a betrothal, let alone to one of the most powerful women in the Three Kingdoms. I was angry that I thought it might have been a chance to get things right, and he'd already messed it up. I was frustrated with myself for wanting more even though I'd tried to convince us both it meant nothing, that it was all we'd ever be. I was angry that no one had been honest with me. I was just *angry*.

I lunged forward, and he blocked me and dodged when I swung back the direction I came from. When my sword followed through, I switched weapons behind my back, putting my dagger in my strong hand. I spun away then and threw up my sword in my left hand as his came down. It hurt as the vibration raced down my arm, but it distracted him long enough for me to get my dagger closer to him. But before I could make contact, he grabbed my wrist and squeezed hard. I yelled as I dropped the dagger, rage simmering in my veins.

I wrenched my wrist free, staggering backward as he came flying toward me. I still had the sword in my left hand, and though I was successful in parrying him, I knew I'd never be able to strike against him. I met every blow as he sent me stumbling toward the stable again. I tried to lunge and catch him off guard, and he palmed my sword, easily able to wrench it out of my grasp, throwing it behind him.

I fell back against the wall, hair falling out of my braid and sticking to my face. He brought his sword up and pushed the point in between my breasts, a pinprick of pain underneath my shirt, the fabric already plastered to my body with rain and blood.

We stood there for a moment while we caught our breath, thunder barely drowning out the sound of blood rushing in my ears. My chest heaved, a mirror of his own. The shirt he wore clung to every tense muscle of his body. His brows were lowered over his eyes, triumph and frustration warring on his face as he stared me down.

He slowly lowered his sword as he took a few steps toward me, and I glared as he came closer. He threw his weapon down, and he put his hand against the stable to the side of my head and leaned in. I gasped as his other hand gripped my braid and pulled, tilting my head back and up. I felt eyes on us as he aligned his face with mine, eye to eye and mouths close, his breath on my lips warm. Within those mossy green depths, there was a mixture of anger and sadness, and I forced myself to look into them, to let him see my feelings on the subject mirrored and surpassed his.

"It has been, is, and will always be you. And fuck, if that hasn't complicated my life enough already."

"Then let me simplify it for you. I don't want you, Rain!" I shouted at him, grateful no one would hear me over the storm. Grateful that if the angry, hot tears spilled from my eyes, they'd be lost in the rain on my face. He leaned closer and spoke quietly into my ear.

"Kingdoms and years and utter devastation."

"What does that even mean?" I pushed him back to look at his face.

"It means I'll wait."

He pushed off the wall behind me and turned on a heel, heading to where Lavenia still stood next to Thyra. The two women looked at me with vastly different expressions, Lavenia wore a look of pity while the warrior next to her exuded what I could only describe as pride. Rainier paused for a moment and looked over his shoulder, a smirk on his face, before he called out to me.

"It's going to be a fun two years, Emmeline."

I let out a growl, and he chuckled before continuing on his path. I slid down the wall to sit on the ground before I put my hand up to my shoulder, letting my divinity heal the cut. When I finished, I rested my elbows on my knees and hung my head, letting the rain wash over me and eventually slow while I sat licking my wounds.

He was betrothed to a Nythyrian princess. When Lavenia said he planned to talk to Keeva, did that mean he was calling it off? He'd said it was an agreement for the kingdom, but he'd spoken so poorly of being used as a political pawn that there had to be more to their relationship. Didn't there?

It didn't matter. I'd asked for a distraction, but this? This was too much. Maybe I didn't have a right to be angry because I'd made my position on the subject clear, but if Dewalt was right, there was a potential for me to be in harm's way. And whatever Rainier chose to say to Keeva could potentially upset an alliance while we were in the middle of trying to get Elora back.

No, I definitely had a right to be angry.

I looked up across the clearing to find him and have it out with him. It took me a moment because of just how many soldiers had gathered in the clearing, and I cringed, wondering how many people saw my defeat. When my eyes finally found him, I inhaled a breath as I saw the short woman with hair the color of a flame talking to him, no, yelling at him. The look on Thyra's face as she regarded the woman, nearly half her height, made me jump up and run across the clearing before Mairin got herself into trouble.

CHAPTER 23

I skidded to a halt in front of them, sliding through the mud, right as Mairin glared at me, eyes wild and furious.

"What in the Mother's name is going on?" She yelled at me, and I felt vague surprise at her reference to the old goddess before I was overwhelmed by her anger. "You left me bodies to deal with! Bodies, Emma! And Theo's face? Then I saw you yesterday with him!" She gestured wildly behind her to where Rainier stood, watching my fiery friend in wonder. "I tried to come last night, but of course, Old Man McLean decided to die, so I was busy. Then I finally get out here, and I see the Crown Prince of Vesta about to skewer you to the stable!" I registered Rainier's open-mouthed smile as he glanced between the two of us. I'd have rolled my eyes if I wasn't dealing with the spitfire standing in front of me. "What the hell, Emma!"

I took a deep breath, glad I'd redirected her rage to me. Grabbing her arm in mine, I walked toward the stream. I glanced over my shoulder, where Thyra and Lavenia still stood with Rainier, both women staring at Mairin with rather different facial expressions. Thyra seemed pissed, and Lavenia seemed in awe, a pretty standard split when it came to Mairin. Rainier started chuckling, and I heard him let out a low groan of pain. I let myself glance at him and saw the bloom of blood on his stomach, underneath where his hand rested. As much as I wanted to ignore him and walk away, I felt my divinity humming and knew I wouldn't be able to focus until I fixed him. I swore under my breath and stopped.

"You better come, too." I nodded pointedly at his stomach. Rainier clasped Lavenia by the shoulder and said something into her ear before he followed us.

"Do not think to finish the job, little viper," Thyra called out to me, a smile on her lips. I rolled my eyes and turned around, continuing toward the stream. When we sat down on the bank, I reached in and cupped water in my hands, splashing it on my face. It was cold as ice, and it helped me focus.

"I guess I should start from the beginning." I began telling the long and tangled story to Mairin—omitting any of the romantic entanglements which made it more complicated—while I healed Rainier. He laid down on the ground with his legs outstretched and crossed at the ankle, hands behind his head like a pillow. I healed his thighs first, taking only a few moments on each one because I'd barely managed more damage than a surface scratch. By the time I'd gotten to the part where Lucia had died, I thought he was asleep. Mairin had already known most of the story, like the rest of the kingdom, but didn't know Lucia was my sister.

I tried to skim over the part where I'd married Faxon within a week of her death, but Rainier chose that moment to prove his consciousness.

"Then she made the terrible mistake of running away and marrying that halfwit." I shot him a look and leaned over to untuck the bottom of his shirt, undoing the lowest buttons before I forcefully put my hand on his wound. I couldn't help but feel some satisfaction when he hissed in pain.

"I did run away. *From* him."

The crease between Rainier's eyebrows deepened as his eyes met mine, and his hand grabbed my wrist, demanding an explanation I didn't plan on giving him. Not now, maybe not ever. Mairin just watched our interaction with raised brows, waiting for me to continue. I shrugged before removing Rainier's hand from my wrist.

"Clearly, I was unsuccessful."

I continued the story, finally stopping with our arrival in Brambleton and the note from Faxon. Rainier grabbed my wrist again as he sat up, pulling my hand away from his stomach. I wasn't finished, so I stared at him in confusion. The wound had been deep, and there was still a decent slice on his abdomen—his well-defined and rock-hard abdomen. I had worked hard not to think about it while telling my story.

"Leave it." I stared at him as he buttoned his shirt and stood. He leaned down and whispered in my ear, lips lightly brushing against me. "I like having your marks on me." I pulled myself up straighter as he chuckled and sauntered away.

Mairin watched him as he walked and waited until he was well outside earshot before she spoke. "And how does that play into things?" I followed her eyes and saw Rainier talking to a few soldiers who had gathered in the clearing after a trip into town, unloading supplies from their horses.

"Well, he's going to help me get her back."

"Yes, you said that. What are you not saying, though?"

"It's of no consequence." I wasn't lying. I'd get Elora back, and we'd go back to Ravemont, the deal I made be damned.

"Do you want to explain the duel I witnessed, then? I've never seen you use a sword, but I know you well enough to know you weren't just sparring; you were trying to do damage." I grinned up at her. I hadn't made it known I could use a sword—and use it well. I'd only worked with Theo and the pell standing in my yard, so when would she have had a chance to see what I could do?

"When did you show up?"

"Right before you stabbed the prince like an insane person. Let me see your shoulder, by the way." She leaned over, reaching for my shirt, sliding it down. "Wow, you weren't lying. Not even a mark on you." I shrugged, oddly embarrassed. "The princess said it was about a bargain for you to kill King Dryul, but since you lost..."

"I have to spend two years at court once we get Elora back." I closed my eyes and inhaled.

"That doesn't sound too bad." I watched her observe Rainier before she turned to me, a look on her face as if she was debating saying something.

"It's complicated, Mairin." I wanted nothing to do with Rainier right now, and I had to do what was right by my daughter. Being at court would be a very different experience for her, and she'd be recovering from this whole ordeal. I hoped Rainier was right about Prince Cyran, and she was being treated well. It also felt counterproductive to be making plans for the future when I didn't have Elora.

"It doesn't seem complicated." She lifted a brow as she observed Rainier once more.

"What do you mean?"

"I can see it. Your auras are entwined." I just stared at her. "I guess since we are revealing our secret pasts, I have some things I need to tell you."

I waited, an eyebrow raised and hands clasped in my lap.

"I'm a merrow." I blinked at her slowly. Merrows weren't real. Merrows were make-believe horror stories created by our parents to get us to behave. Merrows were beautiful beasts who would trick and lure you to your death by drowning. My vibrant friend healed people, and she wasn't *that* scary.

"Yes, we are real. We rarely come to land anymore, too dangerous. The man you knew as my husband stole me from the water and destroyed my pendant, so I can never go back." I couldn't say anything. "He brought me here to get me as far away from the sea as he could, even though it didn't matter once he destroyed my only method of going home. I killed him and then decided to stay. Where else could I go?"

I was in shock.

Her husband had died from a wasting illness. Over the course of a few months, he went from a loud, boisterous drunk to a skinny, sickly man. To think Mairin killed him? I shook my head in disbelief. Merrows were evil. They preyed on people near the water, luring them with songs and seduction. They used a pendant, imbibed with magic from the earth and sea to go from land to water. The stories said men often died, trying to snatch them from the necks of merrow women to keep them on land. But those were myths. How could Mairin be one?

"I can prove it." She gave me a pointed look, and I was finally able to find my voice.

"How?"

"I'll show you, come on." She stood up, pulling me to my feet and walking across the clearing, straight to Rainier.

"You're not going to hurt anyone, are you?" She shot a glare over her shoulder at me, simultaneously annoyed and offended, and chose not to answer. She walked up to Rainier, boldly interrupting his conversation with Lavenia, and pulled him away. I followed behind, arms crossed over my chest, taking in the sight of my two worlds colliding while I grappled with issues from both of them. Mairin crashed into the stable, startling one of the horses in its stall.

"Why do I feel like I'm in trouble again?" Rainier looked from me to Mairin as he rested his hands on his hips. The light from the door did little to brighten the area, only illuminating their silhouettes and little else. I walked past Rainier to the dirty window behind him and tried to open it, grunting in frustration. The table sitting in front of it, full of odds and ends, made the angle awkward, and I couldn't get it. I heard Rainier behind me, felt him press against me as he reached around me and lifted the window. I was still angry at him, and I cursed myself for the way I arched at his touch, my back pressing against his chest. I heard him inhale a deep breath and his hand grazed my waist as he pulled away.

I heard Mairin mumble something behind me about consequence, and I felt my skin flush.

Rainier and I turned around, both of us waiting for her to continue. His hand brushed against mine, and I pulled it away fast enough to startle even myself. To my surprise and amusement, Mairin started to sing, eyes locked on Rainier's. It was a haunting lullaby, and her voice sounded ethereal and otherworldly. I glanced over at him and was stunned to see his eyes transfixed on Mairin, almost glazed over. Her song continued, and I saw how strange her eyes looked. They were almost covered as if a film had slid down over them. Eventually, the lullaby got louder and more frenzied. Then she spoke, her voice sounding both young and old together, yet still melodic.

"Get on your knees."

Eyes still glazed over, he did as he was told.

"Stand up."

He obeyed.

"Forget this happened." Mairin hummed a bit of the lullaby and stopped abruptly. I turned toward Rainier and watched his eyes as they cleared, and he stared at me in confusion.

"What do you want? I have things I need to do." He fidgeted and stared back and forth between us, his features changing to a look of unease.

"Emma." I turned toward Mairin when she spoke to me, squinting because it appeared as if that film over her eyes was back. When my vision finally cleared, the gaze I was staring into belonged to Rainier. I blinked a few times as I saw his mouth form a small smile. Pulling my arms down from around his neck where they'd somehow ended up, I whirled around to face Mairin, stepping forward to escape the hands lightly resting on my hips.

"What—"

"I am a merrow, Your Highness. What you just saw me do to her, I did to you and compelled you to forget it." I watched him, worried about his reaction once he learned he'd been compelled by a merrow with no recollection of it. I watched in surprise as his small smile turned into a wide grin.

"Amazing." He cocked his head to the side, and I realized he was curious about my friend, not at all frightened like I had been when she first told me moments ago. "You're quite far from the ocean, merrow."

"That's a long and sad story. Since we were airing our secrets, I decided it was time to tell Emma, and I needed to prove it to her. I didn't want her to feel like she had to keep any secrets on my behalf, thus my purpose for bringing you into the demonstration." She nodded to me, and I felt guilty for needing proof.

"What else can you do?"

"A little of this, a little of that." She gave him a sly smile, gesturing her hand dismissively.

"Are we bringing her with us?" he asked, crooked grin firmly in place as he addressed me.

"No, she has her patients." I glanced at her, shocked to see she seemed to be considering it. "Unless...you want to?"

"I think I may be able to help." She reached out and grabbed my hand, squeezing softly. "If you'd like me there, I will come." I couldn't control my smile, feeling a bit emotional that she wanted to help, and I nodded firmly as tears threatened my lash line.

"We leave in the morning, little merrow." Rainier nodded and walked out of the stable without giving me a second glance. Something coursed through me when he called her that, and I didn't like the way it made me feel.

"See, that's what I'm talking about." She dipped her chin as she walked to the window, hopping up on the table to shut it.

"What?"

"You flickered when he spoke to me." I studied her as she walked back to me, not sure what she meant. "You didn't like it—him calling me that." She tugged my arm into hers as we walked out of the stable, patting me like I was a feeble, old woman.

"You don't have to worry, Emma. You both burn for each other."

Seated tightly around the dinner table sometime later, shoved uncomfortably between Mairin and Nana, I wondered how I became the subject of discussion. I'd never had so many people in my house, let alone around my dining table, and a small part of me felt some joy from all the noise. Until it became about me. I'd invited Dickey to dine with us, worried about him after the death of his friend, and Dewalt, who had stayed away all day, went to fetch him. When the boy walked up the bank from the camp, my heart ached. His head and shoulders drooped, and he didn't look well.

"My lady." He had held out something I couldn't quite see since it had grown dark. "I found this after everything and thought you might want it."

He handed to me what was left of my bow, snapped clean in half, and the grip was missing. I had studied it in my hands for just a moment. It was one of the only gifts Faxon had ever given me, going out of his way to get it made for me. It was carved from yew heartwood, and the grip was made of a thin layer of leather, molded with time to fit my hand almost perfectly. I had treasured it.

"Thank you, Dickey. It served me well." I had paused, swallowing before I continued. I wasn't eager to talk about it but knew I had to. "I'm sorry about Sam. I tried, I did."

"I know you did, Lady Emmeline. Thank you. If it weren't for you, I'd be dead too."

I had waited until Dickey went inside before I walked over to the fire in the clearing and tossed the bow in, staring into the flame until Dewalt came to the door, calling me inside.

Now, Dickey was sitting across from me, describing exactly how I'd used that bow. Somehow, Mairin was running the conversation, and she'd wanted to hear about how I killed the tírrúil. I'd put a hand on her arm, a warning on my face when she asked Dickey to tell the story. I didn't want him to have to relive how his friend had died. But he didn't notice it and telling it seemed to make him feel better. I sank low in my seat, wishing I could disappear. I had done the bare minimum, and a boy still died.

"I heard my name, and I looked through the fire and saw Lady Emmeline through the flames." He shook his head as if in disbelief. "I thought she was some kind of war goddess—standing on her horse like that. Then I saw her bow, and I knew. I turned around, and there it was, already on my friend Sam." His head bowed when he mentioned him. "Then fire rained down on it, and it fell." I focused on the food in front of me; the meat pies Nana had cooked were tough, providing me a much-needed reason to be busy. "I've yet to thank you properly, Lady Emmeline. I owe you my life and my sword."

"You owe me no such thing, Dickey. You don't have to call me lady, either." I barely raised my head from the table.

"Yes, he does." Rainier's voice was quiet from the end of the table. He had finished his food, so he was relaxed and comfortable, an elbow on the arm of his chair while his hand traced his jaw.

"I'm sorry, Dickey. I was unaware our prince's opinion on how I am to be addressed outweighs my own." I aggressively stabbed a piece of meat from the pie in front of me before shoving it into my mouth, not bothering with the prince in question. Bold of him to demand respect for me while secretly betrothed and whispering promises with his lips against my skin.

"I heard I missed quite a show today." Dewalt served me a malicious grin. He was seated just far enough away that I couldn't kick him under the table, though it didn't stop me from trying. When I couldn't reach him, I fisted my knife in my hand and stabbed another piece of my food while I made pointed eye contact with him. My message was evidently not clear enough because he continued.

"Honestly, I thought you would've won, Emma. The old man down there doesn't like to slum with us soldiers and our swords. He prefers playing in the dirt." I heard a chuckle and ignored it.

"Emma has always liked to use her hands." Nana, of all people, chimed in. "Ever since she was little. Lucia fought with words, and Emma fought with fists. They were quite the pair." Everyone at the table laughed, and I looked at the little woman next to me, smiling lovingly, making it hard to glare at her.

"Emmeline excels at drawing first blood, but she doesn't have the endurance or patience to follow through with it." Rainier was talking about me as if I wasn't there, but I could feel the heat of his gaze on my face. "We'll have to work on it." I refused to engage with him.

"Yes, how is your stomach, brother?" Lavenia laughed from the other side of Nana, seated opposite her brother, before leaning forward in her seat to look at me. "To be fair, you did play dirty with the dagger."

"It was strapped to my leg; I didn't hide it. It's not my fault if he forgot about it." I shrugged and took a long drink of my wine.

"I didn't forget it. I just wasn't expecting you to use it on me. Just like I wasn't expecting you to challenge me today." I wondered when he would figure out that I didn't intend to speak to him. The apology he gave me while we fought wasn't even a real apology. It didn't tell me anything about his plans going forward. Until he gave me more details, I had no intention of speaking to him at all.

"You know we heard most of what you two said to each other, right? At least before the thunder started." Mairin eyed me when she said it, and I believed she meant to say it quietly, just for me. But the multiple glasses of wine she'd shared with Lavenia before dinner had other ideas in mind, her voice much louder than she intended. Everyone grew quiet. The only one who reacted at all was Dewalt as his head turned back and forth between me and the infuriating man at the end of the table. I noted Dickey and Lavenia taking a decided interest in their food. Eyes wide, I turned toward Marin and glared. Divine hell, this woman was going to be the death of me.

"Just a lover's quarrel, no more." Rainier was still leaning back in his chair, looking positively composed and unruffled. He wore that gods damned crooked smile as my eyes met his, and I wanted to smack it right off his face. Even before the mention of his betrothal, before he ruined everything, I'd intended to keep my *distraction* private. Until we found Elora. Until I had normalcy. Then I'd allow myself to think about it being anything other than what I'd said it was. I was beginning to realize my life was never going to be normal again.

I pushed my chair back abruptly.

"I'm going to bed." No one attempted to stop me as I marched up the steps and slammed the door to Elora's room.

I opened my eyes to a bright, blinding-white sun and spun around, blinking. Everything was too bright, the colors too vivid. I stood on a beach, the waves crashing in front of me. The water was too blue, almost the same color as the sky. I looked down and saw a seashell, a vivid red, the color of Mairin's hair.

Where am I?

Spinning around, I saw lime green grass as far as the horizon. The color was bright, almost sickly. I was wearing the nightgown I fell asleep in, but I was not cold. The sun beat down on me too, but I was not hot either. Everything felt strange. I'd never had a dream or nightmare quite like this before. I turned, looking in every direction, wondering where it was taking me. I began to walk, my bare feet not registering the difference between sand and grass. I continued for a few moments before I saw a silhouette on the horizon, and my heart rose quickly up into my throat.

Elora.

I began to run. Despite the otherworldly aspects of the dream, something told me this was truly her. If I could just catch up to her, I'd be able to speak to her. I ran and ran, but I didn't feel like I was getting any closer. I started screaming her name, hoping she'd hear me and could run to me, meet me halfway. My feet slid through the grass, and I continued running. I wasn't growing tired in this dream, my body unphased. I realized this was a new form of torture. I was about to stop when darkness fell on the horizon. It dripped down, more like a slow waterfall than a transition to night, and the darkness rushed out, barreling straight for me. I stopped, searching for her silhouette while I waited for the impact. When it crested over me like a wave, I closed my eyes.

I waited for the strike, and when nothing happened, I opened my eyes. I was in the same exact location, but it was night. The colors around me were muted, and the grass below my feet actually felt like grass, the cool blades moving around my feet, swaying in the breeze. I was shivering. It was cold here, and I studied the stars above me, twinkling, pinpointing the Damia constellation, misplaced in the night sky. When I looked back at the horizon, I saw a figure walking toward me, fast. Not Elora, but a man.

He was tall, though not quite as tall as Rainier, and slim. His sleeves were rolled up, and I could see faint muscles flex as he shoved one hand into a pocket. His pants were black, just as the shirt he wore and the jacket tossed over his shoulder. I found myself surprised that he was covered in jewelry. He had one long silver earring and thin chains of varying length around his neck, hanging down his chest. When he got closer, I was able to get a better glimpse of his face. Young. Much younger than I'd thought at first. Maybe the same age as Theo. But where Theo was gangly and awkward, the young man in front of me was graceful and collected, as if he'd never known discomfort. He had tousled brown hair, a few shades darker than my own, and skin so pale it looked almost pure white, especially in the moonlight. The tilt of his chin and the gait in his walk told me this boy was royalty. I knew exactly who he was.

"Hello, Lady Emmeline."

"Hello, Prince Cyran."

"She glares like you." He smiled at me before he tilted his head down, adjusting the buttons of the jacket he put on. He had a faint accent, crisp like cut-glass. "Elora says she loves you, by the way."

His tone was not unkind, but since he had my daughter, it came out as a taunt.

"I'd like to say it back to her in person."

"I've actually come here to see if that is something we can arrange." My heart stopped for a moment. Something told me this boy wouldn't respond well if I were too eager. I needed to temper my replies.

"Where is 'here' exactly?"

"An illusion. This is a product of my divinity." He gestured around us. "Mostly useless, I might add. Until now." I waited in silence, hoping he'd want to fill it. Hoping he'd give me more information if I was patient. "I'm sure you're worried about your daughter. I assure you, I have treated her with kindness. And as you should know by now, I swore a verit oath that as long as Elora is under my protection, she will be safe. She is much more comfortable with me than she would have been with Declan." His brother. I didn't know if I could trust this boy, if what he said was true. I hoped it was, for Elora's sake.

"She would be more comfortable with me."

"I wouldn't be so sure at the moment. She loves you, but, boy, is she mad at you." He laughed as he crossed his arms, rocking on his heels in emphasis. His hair fell down in his eyes, hazel and sparkling with amusement. "And her dear father."

"Is Faxon there too?"

"Yes, although he is far less comfortable than Elora. It's quite cold outside, and I imagine the chain around his neck chafes."

I couldn't help but smile at the image.

"Feel free to keep him. You mentioned arranging something?" I was too impatient to let him continue in this meandering way.

"Yes, I did." He nodded and cleared his throat. Despite his confidence, the gesture told me just how nervous he was. "My brother grows impatient. He sent me to procure Elora for him, and he is preparing to take her from me soon." I sucked in a breath.

"So, was it him who sent men to rape me? Or do I have you to thank for that?"

He blanched and cleared his throat again.

"I wouldn't know anything about that. The men who didn't accompany us on the ship were mercenaries. They'd been tasked with returning the injured boy back home at your husband's insistence, nothing else. I am...distraught to hear that happened to you."

"It didn't. I killed them both before they could. If such things truly cause you distress, let this be a lesson to you on whom you employ, princeling."

He gave a crisp nod, but I didn't miss the agitation on his face.

"I have managed to stall my brother for a time. But he has plans in motion now that I am not capable of changing on my own." I waited. "He plans to destroy the Cascade, and I am supposed to deliver Elora to him on the battlefield. For him to claim her as his bride upon victory." Though he spoke bluntly, this boy was not as much of a master of his emotions as he thought he was.

"And you don't want him to do that."

He inclined his head. "Nor do you, Lady Emmeline."

"What does *your* dear father want?" He laughed when I said it.

"My father is a barely functioning lunatic. He thinks your sister put a curse on him."

"Maybe she did." In fact, I hoped she had.

"Regardless, my father will die soon, likely by Declan's hand, and he is set to inherit the throne. He wants to destroy Vesta, and he wants a powerful conduit at his side when he does it. And who better than the Beloved?"

"Is the sibling rivalry that strong that you intend to connive against him?" He barked a short laugh as he paced past me.

"My *humanity* is that strong that I connive against him. Declan is more evil than my father by far. He plans to renew the slave trade, and there is talk of worse things he's done and will continue to do."

"Then what do you propose?"

"I am supposed to deliver Elora to the Cascade during the new moon. I know you are with the Bloody Prince." I wondered how he knew; had our movements been obvious? "Get him to fortify the Cascade and be ready for Declan. If you agree to my proposition, my most trusted guards will know the truth and assist to the best of their ability to get her to you."

"I agree."

"You haven't heard the rest of it. I want you to take me as a prisoner."

CHAPTER 24

THE MINUTE THE ILLUSION broke, I woke up and jumped to my feet. The moon was high in the sky, and I wasn't sure what time it was, just that it was late. When I went into the hallway, I saw my bedroom door was closed. I assumed everyone was long asleep, but it didn't stop me from thundering down the stairs.

The door to the study was open, and I saw the flicker of a candle in the room. When I turned into it, I was surprised to see Rainier asleep with the book he'd picked the night before, spread open on his chest. He'd made quite a bit of progress on it since last night, and I couldn't help but smile. The blanket had been pushed down around his hips, and I wondered how he was still asleep, the air cold and fire low. Even by the light of the half-melted candle, I could see an angry red line on his stomach, and I felt guilty for a moment before I remembered he was the one to blame for its continued presence. I flushed, feeling the phantom of his lips on my ear as he'd whispered why he wanted to keep it.

I pulled my robe tighter and rapped my knuckles lightly on the door. Rainier turned his head toward me and slowly opened his eyes, a sleepy smile lighting up his face. I felt a tightness in my chest as I watched him, and the hard pocket where I'd tried to hide my heart softened just a bit. He sat up on his forearms, and Elora's book slid down his chest.

"Hey, Em." His voice was deeper than normal, and a memory of me in his lap last night flashed before my eyes. I tried to dismiss it before it had more of an effect on me than I desired.

"I just met Prince Cyran."

His head cocked at an angle, and he took the book off his chest, setting it down next to him. "What do you mean you met Prince Cyran?"

I walked to Faxon's desk against the wall, pulling his chair out and spinning it to face Rainier before I sat down. "His divinity is the power of illusion. He visited me while I slept."

"How do you know it wasn't a dream?"

"I could tell." He nodded slowly before I continued. "He came with a proposition."

"Really." Rainier sat up and put his back against the sofa next to the trundle bed. "I can't imagine it's in our favor."

"Declan plans to attack the Cascade and claim Elora as his bride after he takes the fort. Cyran was sent to fetch her as some sort of prize."

"Did Cyran know you were with me when he told you this? That's quite a bit of information to give the enemy."

"He knows I'm with you."

"Then, it could be a trap. To lure our armies to the Cascade so they can attack elsewhere."

I'd wondered that myself. "I think he cares for her." Rainier gave me a quizzical look. "Elora. I think he's afraid of his brother, and he wants to protect her." I knew I might be wrong, but there was something tender in his eyes when he talked about her. Rainier pondered what I'd said before giving me a tentative smile.

"I told you this was good news. So, what is he proposing?"

"He plans to give us Elora in exchange for taking him prisoner." Rainier quirked a brow. "He wants us to take down Declan. If he believes Cyran has been taken, he'll make moves to get him back. I don't get the sense of true brotherly love from them, just that it would be an insult to the royal family. Cyran will be with us, giving us all the information he can."

Rainier ran his hand over his face. He looked tired. "Do you believe him?"

"I think I do. I want to talk to Elora first before we trust him."

I went on to explain that Cyran would appear in an illusion in one week, and he'd bring Elora with him. *As long as she behaves*, he'd said. I'd be able to see how well she'd been treated, and I could decide then if I wanted to trust him. The thought of seeing her in a week had sent hope flooding through my veins. Rainier sat in silence for a few moments, and I almost went back upstairs to bed to give him time to think on it.

"This doesn't change much. I'll still need to petition for troops to send to the Cascade. I'll need to do it in waves, so that Declan doesn't grow suspicious. I—*we*—will go there, before the new moon, and take Elora and Prince Cyran back to the palace. Then, I guess, make moves from there."

I nodded and stood, grateful there was a plan. The negotiations were complete, and I'd get to see Elora in a week, even if it was only an illusion. "Oh, and he has Faxon chained up outside like a dog." Rainier laughed in surprise before sobering.

"Was he part of the negotiations?" The way he asked it seemed like he was trying to gauge my reaction. I wasn't sure why.

"Cyran didn't seem too sweet on him. I told him to keep him, but I may change my mind yet." The need for vengeance still coursed through me. I walked through the study, about to head back up to bed, before turning to the candle and blowing it out. Rainier gently grabbed my hand as I passed. I turned to face him, the moonlight from the window shining in on his face.

"Stay, Em." His voice was quiet and rough, dark with desire or something like it. I couldn't miss the pleading tone. Did he not remember why I was angry in the first place? That nothing we'd said or discussed since had done anything to change how I felt?

"No."

He looked down and dropped my hand. "Why?"

I sighed and stared at him, showing as much ire as possible. "You have a wife who will want to kill me. I don't want to give her a reason."

"She is *not* my wife. She will not *be* my wife."

"Does she know that?" I crossed my arms and nodded when he didn't reply. By the time he finally spoke, I'd already left the room and was halfway to the stairs.

"You're awfully upset for someone who only wanted a distraction, Em." I paused, blood boiling. I was too tired to think of something to snipe back at him, so I slowly made my way upstairs in silence.

The next morning, we readied to head out for Astana. The soldiers who had been severely injured in the tírrúil attack were going to stay behind with the wagon to rest for a few days and escort Nana to the capital, leaving a week after us. It would give the soldiers a chance to get their strength back. I checked on them again, sparing some of my divinity for the more seriously wounded, and they seemed to be healing as best as could be expected. I was most worried about the man whose stomach I'd had to put back in, hoping there was no infection beneath the skin, but if his guffaw at my concern was any indication, he seemed to be doing fine.

Rainier and I told Dewalt, Lavenia, and Mairin about my interaction with Prince Cyran the night before. All three were skeptical about the verity of the interaction, but we both pointed out that we had nothing else to go on. I hoped to get more information the next time, such as where they were holding her. After our discussion, we all dispersed, heading to our separate last-minute tasks, and I carefully skirted Rainier's hand, which he'd attempted to rest on my lower back. I needed to be very careful. As much as I craved him—his comfort, his smile, his strength—I couldn't let myself fall into this with him again. He was a means to an end, and I didn't trust him. His purpose was to find Elora. I'd let myself depend on him to keep me going without breaking, and it had been a mistake. It was clear to me that path wasn't something that would ever work for us. This was something I needed to accept, should have accepted after all this time, and letting him steal moments with me was dangerous.

I walked over to Bree, who was already saddled and ready—my packs fit to burst on her. I'd grabbed a couple of outfits for Elora and packed them—that's how hopeful I was. My old sword belt was on my hips, worn and frayed. Between my cloak and the belt, I knew I'd be needing to replace parts of my wardrobe. I realized early this morning that my cloak was not compatible with this trip. It was already tearing and threadbare in spots before I even knew Elora was gone. In the days since, the cloak had been damaged beyond repair. I took the opportunity to seek Mairin out and asked her if she happened to have an extra cloak lying around since we'd be going back past her house on our way west. She thought for a moment before she shook her head. I'd headed inside and was fruitlessly searching through the storage closet in the study when Dewalt came in.

"Need help?" He was quiet and seemed like maybe he was the one who needed help. Seeing him brought an idea to my mind.

"Actually, yes. And you're exactly who I need to help me. Go get the ladder out of the stable and bring it upstairs." He eyed me suspiciously but followed my directions as I left the study. When he came up a few minutes later I pointed to the attic access. He leveled a glare at me and reached up, sliding the panel across before shoving the ladder into it and climbing up.

"What am I getting?" He called down before letting out a tremendous sneeze as he walked to the back of the attic.

"Lucia's trunk." I heard his footsteps pause for a second before they resumed. A few moments later, I heard scraping, and the trunk was hovering over my head. I grabbed the handle and helped him bring it down to the ground. "Let's take this in here." I grabbed the handle again, and we took it into my bedroom and set it on top of my bed.

I hadn't opened the trunk in a long time, since Elora was little and she'd wanted to see some of the fabulous dresses I'd described to her. I knew Lucia had a few cloaks in there for me to choose from, and I thought perhaps Dewalt would want to peek inside. Before I opened it, I turned to him. As soon as we brought the trunk in and set it down, he'd retreated, standing in the doorway of my room, looking uncertain.

"You don't have to if you don't—"

"I want to." He took a few steps closer to the trunk and took a breath.

I opened it and was struck by just how much I had managed to shove in there as the different fabrics sprang to life, as if they'd been waiting for me. I started pulling out different dresses, mostly in warm tones; Lucia loved pinks, reds, and oranges. She also had a fair amount of white because of Myriad events. I knew what I sought was at the bottom, so I kept gingerly pulling out dresses one at a time, carefully watching Dewalt as discreetly as I could.

I pulled out one of her favorite dresses. It had two layers—a light pink layer underneath and a sheer white fabric on top of it, muting the pink. It was long and soft, one of her more casual gowns. The bodice had tiny white flowers embroidered through the sheer fabric into the pink underneath. The sleeves were made from the sheer fabric only, offering a see-through look to it. I heard Dewalt make a noise, and I could see his eyes glimmering.

"This is what she was wearing when I told her I loved her."

I gently laid the dress down and slid my arm around his waist, leaning my head on his arm. Although we hadn't talked about it, he had to know I'd overheard them. I hadn't felt the need to speak to him about it and instead wanted him to only reach out to me if he wanted.

"It was her favorite dress." I smiled as I offered the words. I wasn't sure now if it was the dress itself or what was said to her while she wore it that made her love it. I waited a few moments before I turned back to the trunk, ready to bring more items out. "Do you—If you want the dress, you can have it." It would mean more to him than it did to me. But he shook his head.

"I don't think it would fit, but thanks anyway, Emma." I froze for a second and then burst out laughing. He smiled at me, his eyes still glistening from the memory.

"Well, if there's anything in here you want, feel free to take it. You loved her too." I squeezed his hand before pulling away, and I started digging, a bit less reverently than I had been, finally reaching the winter clothing. There was a small bundle of scarves and three cloaks. The first scarf was a deep crimson red, made out of the softest wool I'd ever felt. I'd envied it back then. I decided to take it; the weather in the mountains was bound to be torturous. Dewalt reached into the pile of scarves and found a plain black one, a bit lumpy and imperfect but otherwise nondescript.

"Can I have this one? Lavenia showed me how to knit so I could make this for her that last winter solstice."

"Of course, take it." I thought for a minute. "You weren't at the last solstice." Dewalt only came to Crown Cottage during the summers. I didn't remember him ever coming for a winter solstice celebration.

"I sent it with Lavenia. Lucia and I wrote letters back and forth after I left in the summer. It started as friendship and eventually grew into something else."

I nodded but stayed quiet. I didn't know they wrote to each other and was surprised I'd never seen any of the letters. For some reason, I thought what they had was brief and quick, a shooting star in the grand scheme of things, not unlike Rainier and myself. Little did I know they'd been cultivating a romance for much longer. An ache pierced my stomach, growing suddenly resentful of her. Had the two of them kissed? Made love? And she never told me? I supposed I didn't tell her when Rainier and I had first kissed, but I was going to tell her everything if only I would have had the time. Maybe she would have done the same.

"Thank you, Emma. Truly." I nodded as he turned to leave the room, the scarf already wrapped around his neck. "It almost smells like her." He gave me a small smile as he left.

I looked at the cloaks spread on the bed before me: a crimson one to match the scarf I wore, one of deep sapphire blue with beautiful silver vines embroidered on it, and a thick black one with fur sewn into the lining. I put the crimson one back and the blue one on. It wasn't Lucia's normal taste, so I was surprised she even had it. I carried the scarf and black cloak with me. I'd appreciate it in the mountains.

Once I added the thick winter cloak to my pack, carefully so it wouldn't burst, I inspected Bree. She seemed healthy and ready to go, having recovered from her infection. As I walked around her, a breeze blew through the clearing, and I pulled my cloak tight around me. I'd left my hair mostly down, a small pin keeping the front strands out of my face, and the wind made me realize I'd made a mistake. I climbed atop my horse, half-blind because of my hair flying everywhere and feeling awkward with my sword smacking into my thigh. I wasn't used to it.

Rainier circled around to me, riding one of the horses I'd acquired from the mercenaries. He'd given Clyde to Mairin, who wasn't used to riding horseback and figured the gentle steed would have been good for her. As he approached, Bree huffed at him. I wasn't sure if it was her standard snippy attitude or if she was able to read my own emotions, but I patted her gently with a grin on my face before I turned to Rainier. He faced me, and his eyes went to my thigh and hips, where the rapidly deteriorating sword belt sat.

"You need to replace that."

"Yes." I matched him in rudeness.

"Your cloak looks brand new. Did you sneak off to town yesterday after you stabbed me?" He raised a brow.

"You know, we are working on an average of me stabbing you twice in a seven-day span. If you keep bringing it up, I might make it thrice." He grinned, appreciating the challenge.

"I would hardly count what occurred back then, Emmeline."

"Well, it was the last time I saw you before a few days ago. If we include consecutive days of me being in your presence, it counts." He offered an exaggerated eye roll, and I forced myself to retain the scowl on my face.

"Fine. But you didn't answer my question." He started down the path, and I pushed Bree to follow.

"It was in Lucia's trunk."

"I always wondered if she ever ended up giving it to you."

"What?"

"Remember when I tackled you and ripped your cloak? That last spring, right when we got back from Astana." It was when I had disarmed him. I forgot he ripped the cloak I was wearing. It made sense that I forgot, it was closing in on summer, and I hardly wore a cloak after that day. "We went to a seamstress in Ardian, and I ordered it for you." I looked down at the cloak, scouring my brain for any memory of Lucia wearing it. It wasn't her typical color, so I would have remembered if she did. I just figured it was something that sat in her closet, unworn. "She must not have had a chance to give it to you." The entire time he spoke, he never glanced back at me. I didn't know how to feel about it. Truthfully, I was a bit mad at myself for letting all of her clothes just sit in a trunk in my attic. I'd taken them with me when I went to Brambleton, Faxon intending to sell them to supplement the money from Ravemont. I hadn't allowed him to, so instead, they sat.

"Evidently not. Thank you." He nodded but didn't reply further.

That was the last we spoke until making camp that night, and even then, it was limited. I shared a tent with Mairin and Lavenia, who stayed up entirely too late and were content with letting me keep to myself. I was still thrilled to have a plan and be on the way to the capital and one step closer to Elora, but I felt guilty about Rainier helping me.

After realizing the cloak I wore was one he'd given me years ago, I couldn't stop thinking about the past. Whenever my thoughts strayed toward the anxiety of the unknown with Elora, I redirected them. Somehow, they always ended up back on Rainier. If I wasn't busy worrying about Elora and the man who held her captive, I was thinking about the one person I didn't want to think about. I started puzzling over ways to avoid spending any time at court now that I'd lost our duel. I already knew he'd never agree to a rematch, but it wouldn't stop my attempt to get out of it. I was afraid if I stayed, I'd break. I couldn't watch him and hope things were different *again*. I knew now more about his reasons for breaking my heart all those years ago, but he'd conveniently kept important information from me. How was I supposed to believe he wouldn't break my heart all over again? How could I trust him when he was off to such a poor start?

I wondered what he would say if he knew just how much our distraction had actually meant to me. If I had been honest and opened up to him, would he have told me about Keeva? It was possible he was protecting himself just as much as I was. Maybe since he thought it meant nothing to me, he didn't have to tell me anything. I stopped myself from thinking that way. There I was again, justifying what he'd done. I shut it down. This was why I could not stay at court once we retrieved Elora. He could not be trusted, but neither could I. Sighing, I shut my eyes and vowed to end this dangerous line of thinking. Rolling over, I tried to remember the ending of Elora's book until sleep finally claimed me.

CHAPTER 25

It was nightfall on the third day when we reached the mountains. I'd seen them from afar for most of my life but being in the foothills of the Alsors put into perspective just how huge they were, the silver-edged cliffs cutting a stark line across the sky. There was a large outcropping which jutted out over a small lake, and we camped next to it, some of the soldiers deciding to climb up the jutting rock and take turns jumping into the water below. It was mostly the younger soldiers who braved the height and the water, and all of them were male. I shuddered at the thought of the sharp, stinging slap of the cold water. They climbed up the cliff side mostly or completely naked and jumped, arms and legs thrashing as they fell. It was a bit warmer outside than it was this morning, the sun having heated the ground all day. I'd even taken my cloak off halfway through, but I knew that water would be frigid. The sun was about to set when I heard whooping from behind me, where the daring were being reckless. Mairin, Lavenia, and I sat in a small circle around a fire sharing snacks from our packs while Dewalt and Rainier watched over their soldiers, arms crossed and laughing. I heard a particularly loud whistle, and I turned around to see what was happening.

I saw a rather tall woman climbing the rocks, completely naked. The blonde hair and braids were enough to tell me who it was. I stood up and walked over to Dewalt and Rainier, who were both watching the woman and smiling. When Thyra got to the top of the cliff, she sketched a bow for the onlookers and jumped, throwing both of her knees up into her chest and wrapping an arm around her legs, screaming the entire way down. I couldn't help but laugh. I turned to Dewalt who stood next to me.

"You next?" I grinned. He laughed and shook his head.

I watched Thyra make her way to the shore and walk out of the shallows, taken aback for a moment by how beautiful she was. Her body was feminine, but she had the defined muscles of a warrior. It was no wonder many of the soldiers eyed her as she wrapped a cloak around her body. She saw me watching her, and I smiled. With a wolfish grin, she approached us, bypassing the fire. She walked straight up to Rainier and opened her cloak, pushing her wet body against him in a hug to which he yelped and jumped backward. I felt my stomach drop, and the tinge of jealousy came back in force. She was tall and gorgeous and had the kind of body that hadn't known the changes of motherhood. Part of me wanted to strip and press myself against him there, to erase her naked touch. She stood back and wrapped herself up quickly, and I swore she looked at me a bit sheepishly before the mischievous glint returned to her eyes.

"You two jump, boost morale." She peered at Dewalt and Rainier. "Besides, you're already wet." I felt a grin spread over my face. She had soaked his shirt. Rainier threw back his head and laughed, the sight making my stomach twist. The fact I yearned for him when he'd completely blown my trust frustrated me to no end. I'd mostly ridden between him and Dewalt since we left my home, and the three of us had eventually fallen into an easy chatter. But I continued to hold my reservations. I hadn't planned on talking to Rainier at all, only focusing on the conversation with Dewalt, but he made it impossible, always drawing Rainier into our talks. I was sure now it was on purpose. The meddlesome prat. Though, it *was* easier to talk that way with him, stowing my anger away. I still didn't know what his intentions were going forward. He'd said it was only me, would only ever be me, but I couldn't give him the Nythyrian alliance. After our conversation about politics, I never thought it would have been an issue. He had already accepted a betrothal when we'd had that conversation, so his actions and words had scrambled my thoughts. I wasn't sure how to feel about anything.

"I'll do it if Ven does." Dewalt smirked. Lavenia and Mairin had both walked up when Thyra approached.

"No, sir. I'm not climbing naked up the mountain."

"I'll make a rift for you, Ven." Rainier piped up from the other side of Dewalt, a devastating smile on his face as he glanced past me to his sister.

"I'll do it." Mairin surprised me, and I whirled to face her. "I don't want to climb naked up the mountain either, though. Do I get a rift?"

She stripped before she got an answer. My gaze moved to Rainier despite myself, and I gave him a bewildered smile. He raised a brow and smiled back.

"Are you serious?" Lavenia was gaping at Mairin, who seemed to be blissfully unbothered by the fact she stood naked in front of people she had just met. Her long, curly hair hung in front of her, covering her body a fair amount, but I couldn't help but smile over her bare skin, even paler than my own, where no sun-touched freckles were present.

"Yes, do it with me. Or are you scared?" Her smile was a challenge.

"Oh, don't do that to me." Lavenia groaned. Dewalt gave her a look that said, *well, are you*? "Fine. Dewalt strip, you said you'd do it if I did."

The next thing I knew, all of my friends were naked in front of me, except Rainier, who, while not naked, had taken off his wet shirt. His body was a lodestone, and I struggled to pull my iron gaze away from him. He turned his back to his naked friends and rubbed his hands together to form a rift. It was surreal, being able to see down into the lake from where we stood next to it. I glanced up at the top of the cliff and saw a faint shimmer in the air, the only indication there was a rift there.

The three of them stepped through, perilously balanced on the edge of the outcropping. I snorted at the clear delineation on Dewalt's lower back, where the sun-bronzed skin met the much lighter skin of his backside. Rainier glanced over at me when I made the sound and raised a brow as he saw where my gaze landed. I grinned at him before I turned to the cliffs to watch our friends jump. Mairin dove in, graceful. I would have expected nothing less from a merrow. She came up out of the water and shouted.

"It's not even that cold!" I shook my head; I was not going to be tricked.

"The prince needs to jump, too." Thyra bumped her hip into his.

"I'll jump if Highclere jumps with me." He turned, an easy smile on his face.

"Definite no." I was not remotely interested in jumping, nor was I interested in letting him think I wasn't still mad at him. With the buffer of Dewalt gone, I was uncertain how to speak to him. Part of me was embarrassed because of the other night as well. I'd gone into it thinking I could handle it as only a distraction when clearly it meant more to me than I thought it would. When his lips burned into mine, it felt like more. Knowing he was betrothed made me feel stupid and small, and I wasn't ready to forgive him for it, nor did I know if he deserved forgiveness.

We both looked back as Dewalt and Lavenia jumped in together. They both yelled the whole way down. All three were laughing as they swam back to the edge of the lake.

"Your turn, Rainier!" Lavenia called from the water.

He shook his head at her, stepping a bit closer to the rift. I didn't know what came over me, but I felt spectacularly roguish for a moment. I caught Thyra's eye and gestured at Rainier, and she nodded enthusiastically.

He didn't see it coming when I shoved him through the rift straight off the cliff. It closed behind him as I watched Rainier fall into the water, arms pinwheeling as he let out a yell. Honestly, I felt a bit of my anger lift from me. He had embarrassed me, and this was a start at making him feel how I felt. There was still plenty of hurt radiating from me, but this felt like a step in the right direction. And, there was the added reward of hilarity in watching him.

Thyra howled with laughter, and many of the soldiers watching did too. Lavenia was standing in waist-deep water, and she threw her head back and laughed, the sun glinting off the golden beads in her hair. The biggest smile split my face watching his disgraceful descent. I watched as Rainier resurfaced, flipping his head up, sending water flying from his hair. His eyes locked onto me as he gave me a predatory grin, taut muscles pulling him through the water with a graceful ease. I felt my eyes bug as Thyra stared at me, a warning and a smile on her face.

"Oh, shit." I turned around and sprinted off, listening to the renewed peals of laughter from Thyra.

As I ran, boulders of dirt erupted out of the ground in front of me, almost every step I took. I easily ran past them at first until I took a chance and glanced over my shoulder. He was out of the water now, stampeding toward me like some sort of beast. One hand was outstretched as he ran, flicking his wrist to help direct his divinity. I looked back in front of me, and I screeched, running past a boulder much closer than the others had been. A moment later, I slammed into another with my hip as I tried to turn past it, the dirt breaking apart and falling as I hit it, not nearly as painful as it could have been. I should have expected he wouldn't fight fair, as I hadn't. I finally slammed into one and started to fall backward when he wrapped both arms around my waist, pressing his cold, wet body against my back. I shrieked, kicking my legs, as he picked me off my feet, dragging me back toward the lake. I was surprised he was able to pick me up with the same ease he used to, as if I weighed nothing, like I hadn't grown thicker at my hips and thighs. I didn't make it easy for him either, kicking and flailing to get out of his grip.

"You didn't think you'd actually get away with that, did you?" He laughed into my ear. I wasn't sure if it was the cold from the water or the heat from his breath that made me shudder, but he pulled me tighter as it rippled through me. We passed Thyra, who was still laughing.

"Help me, Thyra!" I cried out, a broad smile across my face.

"I hope the viper knows how to swim!" She called out while she watched.

"At least let me take my pants off! I need to wear them again!" He knew it was a ploy to get free. That's why, when we passed Lavenia wrapped in her cloak, he kept me locked in his arms.

"Help her with her pants, sis." Lavenia cackled and yanked them off along with my boots and socks. I worried for a moment she'd see my scars, but Rainier continued toward the lake. I kept kicking as he dragged me to the edge of the water and threw me in. It was relatively shallow, so I didn't fully go under. And

Mairin was right, it wasn't nearly as cold as I expected it to be. I was still soaking wet though. I shot up, ready to get out, when Rainier started marching into the water toward me, a man possessed. The grin he gave me promised he wasn't close to being done. I shrieked and tried to get past him, but he was taller and faster. He grabbed me by the waist and threw me over his shoulder as he walked deeper into the water, sending a yelp past my lips. I smacked at his back, but he didn't react, arm tightly wrapped around the backs of my thighs. Finally, when I thought he wouldn't be able to touch the bottom for much longer, he grabbed me by the waist and pulled me in front of him. He didn't throw me though, just lowered me a bit. My hands were on his shoulders as he hugged my thighs to his chest. I pushed off him with my arms, trying to wiggle free. He made a tsk sound as he let me slide down through his arms, lowering me into the water with him so we were face to face, his arms wrapped tightly around me again.

"Always fighting the inevitable, aren't you?"

"So it seems." I smiled. The water was a bit cold, but Rainier was warm. He pulled me near enough that my thighs were pressed against his. I was glad he held me so close, my shirt likely transparent in the water. He held me there for a while, and we gazed upon each other in silence, drinking each other in. The stubble on his face was thicker, the promise of a beard coming through. The facial hair made him seem more his age. The only signs of age I'd noticed before were the laugh lines and creases next to his eyes, but his strength and vibrancy were the same as I'd remembered. His eyes reflected some of the blue from the lake, looking like a deep pine green. Sunset was in full swing, but I could still see sunlight reflecting in them. I tried not to look at his lips, remembering what they felt like on my skin. Instead, I let my eyes roam to the scar on his brow. I reached up and traced it gently, and he closed his eyes.

"Where did you get this?" My voice was barely above a whisper.

"A pirate. He wanted my eye, and Dewalt had to stop him." I watched his mouth as he spoke and then his eyes as they slowly opened.

"Really?" This man had seen more and done more than I could have imagined.

"No." He huffed a laugh. "The truth is much more embarrassing."

I grinned. "The Bloody Prince has an embarrassing scar? I have to hear this."

"Don't call me that." His voice was a growl, and the look in his eyes haunted. I flinched back, the smile on my face gone in a second.

"I—I'm sor—" He cut me off with a deep inhale of breath as he braced one hand between my shoulder blades, pulling me against him once more.

"Don't apologize; you didn't know. I'm not exactly proud of the blood on my hands, Em." He exhaled slowly and forced a smile. "Let's forget about it. A truth for a truth?"

I cringed, wishing I could put my foot in my mouth. Of course, he wouldn't want to be reminded of the atrocities this war had made him commit. I latched on to his change of subject and threw myself in. "I promise my truths are boring but fine. How did you get the scar?"

"Gardening." I blinked at him and felt my lips part in surprise. His eyes darted to them for a second before his eyes met mine, and he chuckled. "I have a garden at my home in the capital. When I first moved in, it was a mess, and I helped the gardener from time to time. I had set a pair of shears up on a ledge and went to grab them, and I bumped them instead. Sent them flying right at my eye. I asked Dewalt to hit me, so it would look like I'd been in a fight. He refused, and I was too embarrassed to call a healer."

"That is *not* what I expected." I laughed, and he smiled, his expression soft as he watched me. I imagined Rainier surrounded by roses, clutching his hand to his eyebrow and a shocked gardener watching him bleed. It was a hilarious mental image, and it renewed my laughter, causing me to throw my head back and truly let go. He held me there for a moment as his gaze washed over me, an easy smile on his face. He ran a hand down my thigh and pulled it up, wrapping it around his waist before repeating the action on the other side. He brought his hands to rest on my lower back, still holding me close. My breathing tight, I focused on my hands resting on his shoulders. Drenched and standing in a lake as we may have been, I felt like I was playing with fire. I was a fuse, and he was a lit match.

"My turn." He studied me for a moment, to a point where I started to feel embarrassed, a flush creeping up my skin, and I looked away. I watched as our friends went into their tents to get dressed before I heard him take a deep breath. "Do you trust me?" I turned my head back to him. There was something vulnerable in his tone and his eyes as he stared into mine that gave me pause.

"In what way?" I could tell by the disappointment on his face he wanted an easy answer. But sadly, I had no way to answer the question simply. There was so much between us I wasn't sure if I'd ever fully be able to trust him.

"In any way."

I took a moment, debating how to put my feelings into words.

"I trust you with my life, my child's life." I swallowed. "But I do not trust you with my heart." I wasn't sure if that even mattered to him. Did he even care that he'd broken my heart back then and was in the process of breaking it again? I felt my cheeks flush in embarrassment despite the cool temperature of the water. He gave the slightest nod as he turned his head, gazing at the cliffs behind me while he worried his bottom lip with his teeth. He was betrothed to a princess; why would I think he'd even care about what I just said? When his eyes met mine, I saw a look of determination and a hint of fear which surprised me, almost as much as what he said next.

"Do you think that could change, given time?" It was so unlike him to talk to me like this. As if he were afraid of me, afraid to say what he felt. I didn't like it. I also wasn't sure I'd ever be able to trust him with my heart, but it gave me hope he seemed to want me to.

"I think it's my turn to ask a truth." I smiled at him, waiting for him to return it. Wanting him to smile. And he did.

"Go on then, Em."

"How often did you think of me?" I didn't know what answer I wanted from the question, but he didn't hesitate.

"Every day—when I wanted to, when I didn't want to. Even if I made it through a whole gods damn day not thinking about you, you visited me in my dreams."

"Me too." My answer came out full of emotion. I'd done everything to not think about him, not talk about him, and yet every day, he crossed my mind. Sometimes it was frustration and anger, sometimes longing. My emotions about him ran the gamut, but they were there every day.

"Will you ever give me a chance to earn your trust again?" He quieted, watching me expectantly.

"Rain, I—" I hesitated, eyes meeting his as I mulled over his question. "We've had enough secrets for a lifetime. You not telling me about Keeva? It was embarrassing to find out, and quite frankly, made me feel stupid and small. I still feel like there's more you haven't told me yet. And I shouldn't even be worrying about any of it at all right now."

"I'm sorry, Em. I was trying to find a way to tell you about her. I will tell you everything—every thought, every plan, all of it. What you don't know is minimal, at worst. It may take me some time, but I will tell you everything." I glared at him. "You will know *everything*. Every desire, every secret, every thought I've ever had will be yours to keep."

He leaned forward, pushing his forehead to mine, as he held me tight to him, and for once, I kept my mouth shut. The sincerity in his voice and body language was begging me to trust him. I knew there was no way I was going to be able to be around him without giving in to his pleading, allowing him to take tiny parts of me, tiny concessions, so I may as well lean into it. I started to think about all the different conversations we should have had if only I would have trusted him, kept him close to me and opened up to him. If I'd have stayed at Ravemont and leaned on the protection of the Crown, where would we be today? Imagining it almost felt like an insult to Lucia's memory, to think about my life not changing at all when she was dead.

"How do you not feel guilty about that night? I—It follows me. I can't escape it." I wished I could rid myself of the guilt I'd experienced every single day since Lucia died. We'd been responsible for the wards, and she died for it. He was the only other person who could understand the depth of it, the responsibility. Part of why I'd been so angry with him was because he'd been so unaffected by our hand in it. To me, it was all-consuming and inescapable. There was something about grief and love and regret that tangled. That made moving on despite fear almost impossible without unraveling. His eyes met mine, and I saw grief and pity as he watched me, sending a rush of anger through me. I banked it, knowing his emotions were from a place of love for my sister and concern for me.

"Em." He sounded sad as he tilted his head and reached up, gently tracing my jaw with his fingertip. "If it were you who died, would you want Lucia blaming herself for the rest of her life? Would you want that for any of us?" I looked down, staring at the line of water where it met his chest, watching its rise and fall with each breath. "It was a mistake, Em. Something all of us could have been responsible for, something *she* had done to sneak off with Dewalt the night before." I gaped at him, surprise blanketing my face and a small smile on my lips. He chuckled and grinned. "Honestly, you must have been so wrapped up in me you weren't paying any attention to her that summer; I'm flattered I was so distracting. They snuck out of the cottage almost every night, and I'm shocked you never realized."

"Not possible." I shook my head. I would have noticed what my sister was up to, wouldn't I?

"That's why I talked to her about us. I knew she wasn't invested in me, and telling her I was in love with her sister wouldn't be an issue."

In love with me. My eyes flicked back up to his at the statement. He didn't pause to let me react, just continuing to speak, and I wasn't sure if it was for my benefit or his own.

"She wouldn't have wanted you to suffer the guilt you've been carrying this long. She loved you so much, until the end. She pushed you away to protect you. You know that right?" My confusion was evident, so Rainier continued. "She saw where you both were being led, wouldn't take her eyes off him while you ran. She shoved you toward me, knowing I would protect you." I felt my eyes water as I listened to him. My sister had been protecting me? I thought I'd been helping her, staying with her since we got separated from the others, but it had been her helping me. She saw the King of Bones and chose to protect me, knowing the fate he likely had planned for her. She should have known I would have died with her. I would have stood with her until the very end. We were born together, and dying to protect each other would have been an honor. I felt the tears slip past my lashes and roll down my cheeks, hot against my water-cooled skin. I held onto his neck, my legs still wrapped around his body, as Rainier's hands lifted up and cupped my face on either side, brushing the tears away with his thumbs.

"She wouldn't want you to waste her gift on guilt." My eyes met his, and I knew he was right. I knew my sister would never want me to feel like I did a lifetime later because I'd never want that for her. I would have wanted her to be happy, marry Dewalt, have ten babies, and never think of me other than in fond memories. I'd maybe expect a namesake out of one of those ten babies, but nothing more. I wished it were me instead of her once again, but this time because I knew she wouldn't have wasted my gift as I'd wasted hers. I knew I'd done good—helping people in my small town who deserved it. I knew I'd raised a beautiful, kind, and smart daughter, but I'd spent so many years wrapped up in guilt and unable to pursue anything else that might have brought me any happiness.

I leaned in close to him, resting my chin on my arms, circling his neck as I looked up, watching the stars come out. I stayed there locked in his embrace for a while, watching the camp settle for the night and feeling the air grow still. I knew we'd need to get out soon—his body pressed up against me wouldn't be enough to keep me warm—but he seemed to know what I needed and held me tight against him, slowly rocking us to a song I couldn't hear. He always seemed to know when I needed that touch, that contact to ground me. Eventually, he pulled back, my arms extending to stay around his neck. It was strangely intimate, but I didn't shy away.

"My turn?" His eyes burned into mine, flooding with what seemed to be determination and vulnerability. I nodded, but I felt my insides twist around themselves, uncertain what he planned to ask.

"Can I kiss you?" It sounded so innocent and juvenile, I flat out laughed. He smiled his crooked grin while he waited for an answer, not the least bit perturbed I just laughed in his face. I quieted, averting my eyes and tracing a finger across a raised scar on his chest while I thought about it. He hadn't done much to regain my trust, but the fact he wanted to meant a lot to me. I still needed to find out if he was planning on calling things off with Keeva because all of this meant nothing if he didn't. Still, this felt different than the other night. The other night had been because I needed it. I had needed a distraction, something to focus on that wasn't every mistake I'd ever made or every fear I'd ever had. But this wouldn't be a kiss born out of need; this would be wanted. His eyes were full of hope when he'd asked just now, and I decided to let myself have it, let myself have a moment which might turn messy and complicated, but a moment that meant I was living. A moment I could own as a first step toward living a life Lucia had died for. A moment in a life of someone who chased happiness instead of hiding within guilt and shame and fear. I lifted my head and saw his smile had faded, his face guarded. I nodded, giving him permission, and I saw surprise flutter across his face before it quickly passed. I gave him a small smile which he returned.

He tucked a wet strand of hair behind my ear then cupped my cheek, tilting my face up to him. He pressed his lips to mine carefully, so painfully soft. His touch was tender and slow, so different from the frenzied kisses we'd shared before. Our mouths parted, and we kissed like that for some time, our lips gently caressing. His hand on my cheek slid back to cup my neck, fingers entwined in my hair, while his other arm wrapped tight around me. He slid his tongue into my mouth and lightly traced it over my own. I made a faint sound of content in the back of my throat, a whimper almost. He squeezed me tighter, a low rumble of appreciation coming from him that licked up my spine. This kiss was slow and calm—reverent. Intimate. I could feel the faint thrum of my divinity, which normally I only felt if I reached for, and I wondered if it was my soul's way of telling me this kiss was right. Our tongues explored as our lips caressed, and it felt like the most comfortable and natural thing in the world. I could have stayed in his arms all night, kissing him gently under the stars.

He pulled away, tracing my lower lip with his thumb, when he jolted his arm back like he'd been burned. I only had a moment to look at him in confusion when I felt it too. A tingle spread from my shoulder, ending in a slam to my elbow. I yelped, my arm still vibrating from the pain. I spotted a scowl on Rain's face as he turned us. Dewalt was standing on the shore, arms crossed, appearing for all the world like a disappointed parent.

"I suppose that means it's time to eat." He smiled softly before he leaned in to kiss me again. A short one before he jolted backward, another impulse sent down his arm. His eyes flashed to Dewalt in frustration as I grinned. He gave me a mischievous look before he leaned in, speaking quietly.

"Head back to the shore. I'm going to make him regret that." I grinned as he put me down, and I started to swim until I could touch before I eventually waded back to shore, arms folded across my body. I had a great view when a rift opened above Dewalt, and so much cold water dumped on him it made him fall to the ground. Rainier came falling out of the rift too, drawn down by the water, but he landed gracefully. He laughed so hard he doubled over, watching his best friend laid out on the ground. I finally made it out of the water and headed toward the fire while Rainier pulled Dewalt to his feet. I paused when I heard Rainier's tone as he addressed his second-in-command.

"There was no need to send an impulse to her. Do not punish her because I have dismissed your concerns."

Dewalt's eyes slid to me, standing behind Rainier. I shook my head slightly, eyes wide, hoping he knew I wasn't upset with him. It did hurt, and my arm was still tingling, but I wasn't mad. He dipped his head toward Rainier, eyes on the ground before he was dismissed.

Rainier took a few steps toward the fire and grabbed his cloak before he brought it back to me. I hadn't moved, uncertain how to feel about the way he'd just spoken to Dewalt. On one hand, I didn't want anyone treating me any differently, but on the other, something warm filled my chest, thinking he'd care enough to spare me from even mild discomfort.

"You didn't have to do that." He wrapped me in his cloak and walked me to the fire, his arm around my shoulders.

"You can't possibly be annoyed with me for helping you avoid impulses. You've always hated them." I laughed because he wasn't wrong. I saw his smile as he bent down, picking up my pants from the ground and handing them to me. I grabbed them and then hesitated, not wanting to put dry pants on over wet undergarments.

"Right, hold on." He closed his eyes for a second, and I felt my clothes dry around me as water slid down my legs before he whisked it away with a flick of a wrist. That was a fun, new trick. He grabbed the pants from me and knelt, shaking them open for me to step into. He pulled them up as he stood, fiddling with the buttons, safely out of view under the cloak.

"I liked your shirt better when it was wet." I felt myself flush, and I took over, fumbling with the buttons of my pants, swatting his hand away. Rainier laughed and grabbed his shirt off the ground and put it back on. It struck me then that he didn't have to shuck it off when Thyra got it wet; he chose to. The preening bastard.

He walked over to the fire with Lavenia and Dewalt as Mairin walked up to me, dry and in fresh clothes. She looked at me like she was about to say something that would ruin the evening for me, and I shook my head slightly, smiling after the man who was still stealing my heart all these years later, whether I trusted him with it or not.

CHAPTER 26

The night of the lake was spent much like the other nights during our journey. Mairin and Lavenia shared a bottle of wine, and I wondered where they kept getting it and how long they could keep it up. I sat with them for a short time, making idle conversation, while Lavenia asked Mairin about her patients and skills as a healer. Rainier and I had kept the revelation of Mairin being a merrow to ourselves as far as I knew, and I didn't think my friend planned to share the information. I eventually grew tired, the smoke from the brazier in the tent making it hard to keep my eyes open, so I bundled into my cloak and climbed into my pallet. I didn't know how long I'd been lying there on the edge of consciousness when I heard someone put a cover on the brazier, darkening the room. I was about to fall back asleep when I heard the two of them whispering, and my name came up.

"After hearing her story and meeting you three, I'm even more sad for Emma than I was before. She's lost out on so much these years."

"I know. We've missed out too, especially my brother."

"I don't think she's ever been truly happy while I've known her." There was a tightness in my chest when Mairin spoke. Elora had a good life, safe and protected, and I had been content because of it. I was a good mother, and I used my divinity to help people when I could. Maybe to Mairin, happiness meant something more, but I'd been happy enough. I knew things could have been better, but wasn't that the case for everyone? I almost rolled over to interject before I heard Lavenia.

"She's held him hostage. My brother had no closure. He's been looking for it for years. I think he needed it as permission to move on, to find a future in someone else. Mind you, he's been with other women, but nothing substantive. The last one I even knew the name of was Thyra when she first came to the guard almost a decade ago. None of the others were ever worth me learning their name."

He'd been with Thyra? I couldn't blame him; she was absolutely beautiful, a specimen of perfection who even drew my attraction. And it was almost a decade ago? That was quite a long time. I recalled how she pressed her naked body against him today, and I despaired, the beast in the pit of my stomach stirring. He was not mine. I had no claim on him. Not now, and definitely not then. His interactions with her now seemed platonic. I believed whatever they had was long over, but it didn't stop it from stinging.

"I wouldn't call what's happening now closure."

"No, I wouldn't either. I was hoping she'd have changed her mind, honestly, but she seemed pretty adamant the other night. Whatever happens with them is going to have to come from her. He'll never stop unless she makes him." Lavenia sounded almost bitter, and it was the first time I thought about the fact she might have feelings about the whole situation herself. They both quieted, and I heard them settle into their pallets for the night. I laid there for a while, fully awake and feeling guilty. It took me a long time to fall back asleep.

The next morning, I noticed the soldiers treating me differently. While all had been polite before, only a few had warmed to me. The ones I'd treated were the only ones who had spoken with me in the past, but with those injured men staying behind with Nana, there were only a few soldiers I interacted with on the journey since leaving Brambleton. The morning after the lake was noticeably different. Where there had mostly been indifference, it seemed opinions about me had changed. Some for the worse, but mostly for the better. As I waited for some sort of oat mash breakfast, everyone who left the line before me gave me a nod. Some even smiled. When one of the men winked at me, I couldn't help but stare at him as he passed. I shook my head, a bit mind-boggled. A moment later, Thyra was behind me.

"Good morning, Lady Emma." I turned to her, looking up. She was easily a head taller than me.

"Just Emma will suffice." I gave a brief smile, my stomach clenching because of my recent enlightenment.

"Good morning, Just Emma." She grinned. "Please don't tell the prince." She leaned down to me conspiratorially, and my stomach relaxed. I smiled at her before turning back around to the front of the line, something about her making it hard to feel uncomfortable. Another group of soldiers smiled at me, one of them offering a quick 'good morning' to me, and I nodded, not sure how to react to this sudden attention from people who had barely acknowledged me before. I exhaled a long breath through my lips.

"They like you." I glanced over my shoulder and saw her nodding to the soldiers as they passed. "Word of your swordsmanship spread, and they saw your push yesterday." I cringed. I should have known the few soldiers who witnessed our duel wouldn't have kept tight-lipped about it. I hadn't been thinking when I pushed Rainier. Of course, some of the soldiers could have thought it was disrespectful, and no doubt it was why one of the much older men sneered at me. But the younger ones all seemed to have found an endearment for me, which I found odd. I killed a tírrúil and incapacitated another, healed countless soldiers. One would think those would be the traits that would endear me to them, but it was the sword-fighting and playfulness with their prince that had earned it.

"Why make the face?" The soft lilt of her accent and the furrow in her brow made me forget my awkwardness with her. This giant of a woman was kind and friendly and seemed to like me. There was no reason to stunt a friendship with her over a man who wasn't ever mine.

"I probably shouldn't have pushed him in front of his soldiers. I got carried away." I gave her a tight smile, embarrassed about the whole situation.

"Prince Rainier has earned the respect of his soldiers many times. They—we—view him as brother. You would be happy for your brother to smile, no? It is the same."

A shamefully large part of me was happy when she said she viewed him as a brother.

"Even if I embarrass him in front of his soldiers?"

"Especially if you embarrass him in front of his soldiers. He's smiled more in the past week than he has in years." I found something interesting on the ground in front of me to stare at while I contemplated what she said. She ducked away a moment later, spotting a soldier to my right she wanted to speak to. I couldn't help but smile to myself. It had been a game for me when we were young to make him smile as often as I could. He had always been so stressed, and I kicked myself for never having truly understood the extent of it.

We were nearing the front of the line, and an older soldier got his mash before walking past me on the left. He spotted me and stopped in his tracks before ogling me and spitting on the ground, speaking a word I didn't recognize. "Fahyše!" I jumped back to avoid the spittle and stared back at him, jaw slack. I wasn't sure what the man said, but I knew it wasn't good. I felt something brush against my back a moment later, and the next thing I knew, Thyra had the man on his back, her knee on his chest.

"Thyra!" I don't know if I shouted her name in surprise or because I didn't want her to hurt someone on my behalf, but I stepped out of the meal line like I would be able to stop her. I knew whatever the man said wasn't good, but it wasn't as if I had any right to be mad. These men were helping me, and they barely knew me. And I had disrespected his prince, no matter what Thyra said, and I should have expected there might have been trouble to follow.

Thyra leaned over the man and said something in a thick, lyrical tongue I didn't understand. The man coughed, turning his head toward me.

"I'm sorry!" His accent was different from Thyra's, and I nodded, wanting the spectacle to be over. Thyra pushed down on his body with her knee, and the man was coughing again. "Lady Emmeline! I'm sorry, Lady Emmeline!"

"Thyra, let him stand." I stilled as I heard the deep voice at my back. The man on the ground stared behind me, eyes wide in terror. Out of the frying pan and into the fire. Thyra took her knee off of him but did not offer her hand for assistance. The soldier took a moment to sit up, breathing hard before he stood. Rainier moved beside me, appearing rested and fresh, with a frightening gleam in his eye.

"Rainier, don't. It's fine." He held up his hand for silence, not even sparing me a glance, looking more royal than I'd ever seen him, and I stopped talking. Disrespecting him in front of his soldiers was what got me here in the first place. Rainier looked expectantly at Thyra, waiting for her explanation.

"He insulted Lady Emmeline." I rolled my eyes at her, but she missed it. As if it wasn't already evident he'd insulted me. Rainier took a few steps toward Thyra and gripped her elbow, clearly wanting further explanation. She spoke quietly, and no matter how hard I strained, I couldn't hear what she said. Instead, I heard a thundering heartbeat coming from the man who insulted me.

A small crowd had gathered, and I felt the heat of a few people staring right at me. The person serving the mash had stopped, and the line was growing, everyone watching the four of us standing off to the side. I wrapped my cloak around me tighter. I saw Rainier tense as Thyra spoke to him, and she stepped away, coming to stand next to me. I eyed her pleadingly, but she only shook her head. Rainier turned his attention to the soldier in front of him, and I held my breath. The man was old, and the longer I stared at him, I realized he wasn't from Skos at all like I'd originally thought, and instead from Nythyr; I'd heard another language and assumed. My heart dropped in my stomach. Of course, he would hate me, especially if he saw what happened after Rainier dragged me into the water. I hadn't even known there were any Nythyrians in Rainier's guard. The fact Thyra spoke at least three languages fluttered across my consciousness before I was distracted by the men in front of me. Rainier's arms were crossed as he circled the soldier, like a beast about to attack its prey. I stared at Rainier, trying to draw his attention to me, but he never lost his focus.

I was about to say his name when he struck the soldier, punching him in the face. He immediately fell to the ground, eyes closed. I stepped forward in a panic, listening for the man's heartbeat, certain Rainier had killed him. Thyra grabbed my arm and pulled me backward as I listened, hearing an unsteady heart as the man's eyes fluttered open, and he raised up on his knees. Rainier punched him again, and I heard his heart skip and start pounding as Rainier reared back to hit him a third time.

"Rain, stop." I ran forward, pulling out of Thyra's grasp. "You're going to kill him!"

I dropped to my knees and ripped the man's shirt open, putting my hands on his chest, willing his heart to slow and steady. I put one hand on his face, already swollen and red. Rainier dropped his fist, watching me with dead eyes as he got his breathing under control. When the heart rate finally returned to normal, I lifted my chin defiantly to glare at Rainier, my brows drawn tight. I moved my other hand off the soldier's chest to join the one on his face when Rainier finally spoke.

"That's enough." The injured man coughed and opened one eye, the other still swollen shut. I didn't pull my hand away.

"I can't believe you." I was quiet when I spoke, aware of the spectacle we'd made. Aware that the rest of his men who weren't here to watch would still hear about what happened. His eyes met mine, and I saw anger flash there. I was relieved, even if it was directed at me, to see something other than the dead eyes he'd just used to look at me a moment ago.

"Lady Emmeline, that's *enough*." His volume rose, and it was Prince Rainier who stood in front of me now, and I knew I needed to listen or else it would be seen as disrespect and defiance in front of his soldiers. He was strategic, making sure those around us heard it, knowing I wouldn't want to make things worse. I pulled my hand away and sat back on my heels, glaring between Rainier and the man on the ground. Rainier crouched and spoke quietly to his injured soldier.

"You are banished from my guard. If you're lucky enough to make it through the mountains, you are banished from Vesta. You should know this *whore* is the only reason you live." I felt my mouth go dry, and I swallowed. I knew what the man said couldn't have been complimentary, but hearing it out loud made it worse.

Rainier stood, holding out his hand to me. I debated standing up without his assistance for a moment and then decided against it. He'd nearly killed a man over what he said to me. I didn't want to sow discord within his ranks any further, so

I primly took his hand as he stepped over the former member of his guard on the ground. I let go the moment I was standing.

"Come, I wanted to show you something before we leave." He offered me his arm, and I studied him for a moment, noticing his bruised and swollen knuckles. I heard movement behind me, the line for food having started again, everyone ignoring the broken soldier on the ground. My gaze hesitated over the man. He could have used a bit more healing on his face, but maybe he deserved the dreadful headache he'd have for the next few days. Knowing every interaction with Rainier from this point forward would be noticed, I put my arm in his, and we started walking.

"Are you going to beat every soldier who has a problem with me?" I kept my voice low, but my tone was light in case anyone chose to listen.

"If I need to. Are you going to heal every person who deserves a beating?" He countered, voice tight but pleasant to match mine.

"If I need to." He scowled at me, leading me to the cliff everyone had been jumping off the day before. "I'm serious, Rain. You can't do that, not over me."

"Come on." He tugged me along, but I pulled my arm free from him and stomped. He raised an eyebrow as he looked down at my foot, a slow smile spreading across his lips.

"That was adorable. Do you feel better now? If you need to do it again, go ahead. It was precious." I wanted to smack the smile off his face.

"Promise me you won't do that ever again."

"Promise you what? That I won't punish my soldiers when they disrespect you? That's a promise I refuse to make, Em." His smile faded, and the look he gave me told me I would find no give from him. I threw my arms out in frustration.

"You almost killed him. Promise me you won't kill one of your soldiers over me."

"Fine. Unless they put you in danger."

"*Intentional* danger. I don't want you killing anyone over an accident either." I knew how his mind worked, and I knew he'd keep his word to the letter. He pursed his lips as he studied me, and his eyebrows knitted for a second. He could tell this was important to me.

"Fine." He exhaled, like he was giving into the most absurd request.

"Fine, what?"

"Fine, I promise I won't kill one of my soldiers unless they put you in harm's way intentionally." I smiled and walked past him, continuing toward the cliff.

"You can be a real nuisance, you know," he grumbled from behind me.

"I know." I threw a grin over my shoulder, hoping it would ease his frustration. I stopped walking when we got to the base of the cliff.

"I'm not jumping in the lake if that's what you want." He chuckled and stood close behind me, one hand on my hip and the other reaching over me to point. I resisted the urge to heal his stupid knuckles.

"See that dark spot?"

"Not really." I squinted, and he laughed.

"Some of the soldiers were exploring last night and found something interesting, and I'd like to show you."

"What is it?" I was wary. A black spot on the side of a cliff was foreboding.

"It's a cavern, but there's an opening from above." He rushed out the second half of the sentence. My body must have stiffened in reaction. I shook my head before Rainier gently turned me to face him. "Em, it's beautiful. I thought—I can leave the rift open. It might be a good way to—"

"Rain, I don't think it's a good idea." The thought of going into a cave sent goosebumps racing across my body. I started shaking inside my cloak, and he noticed, rubbing his hands down my arms.

"It's alright, I understand." He pulled me close to him, hugging me to his body, a hand cupped around my head until the momentary panic had passed. A stark opposition to the man who nearly just bashed someone's head in. When he felt me still, he leaned back, a hand on each of my arms.

"What if I make a rift, and we just sit here and look? Would that be something you could handle?" I smiled up at him, struck by the thoughtfulness, and I felt a tightening in my chest. How was this the same man?

"Yes, I think I could handle that." His answering smile was the sun and all of the stars.

He took a few steps away from me, positioning the rift so we could sit on the rocks. He opened it, and I saw sunlight and a thin stream of water pouring down. I felt pulled to walk closer. I stood behind Rainier, leaning around him to peek into the rift.

The cavern was huge, at least a hundred meters tall, the only light filtering down from above. It narrowed at the far end, where it was much darker, and I could just make out a tunnel leading farther into the black. I attempted to inspect the opening of the cave, where the sunlight streamed in, but the angle of the rift prevented me from seeing it. It filtered down, illuminating dust in the air, shining upon a small pond of water, filled by what fell from above alongside the light. The water was a pale blue, almost the color of silver. A small stream led somewhere, behind where the rift was placed, so I couldn't quite tell where.

"It's beautiful." I breathed. I still stood behind him, leaning past to peer into the space. It reminded me of the place we'd discovered all those years ago, where we'd both explored and gotten lost in so many ways, and I was sure he shared the same memories. The cavern from my thoughts had access to the sea, the wind and waves crashing nearby, sending echoes throughout. This one was decidedly quieter, serene, but just as awe-inspiring. I felt my power within me pool and begin to thrum lightly, in a way I could only describe as excitement. Something that felt almost like a string of yarn spooled between this place and my divinity, pulling me closer if only I'd let it.

Rainier reached back, grasping my hand.

"The pond has moonfish." I could tell he was smiling when he said it.

"Liar!" Moonfish were incredibly rare, and I'd never seen one. Their presence was rumored to mean the area was god-touched, but I wasn't sure if I believed it.

"I'm not; there are hundreds. Do you want me to bring you one for proof?" He let go of my hand and took a step forward.

"No!" I grabbed his hand, pulling him back. I didn't want to hurt one to prove it to me. The only way I'd see one was if I walked inside, and I wasn't sure I could, even though I wanted to. It was strange to feel pulled like that, toward a place so like another, yet so different, the main feature in some of my worst memories. I stood there for a while, watching the water fall, the trickle echoing like the familiar sounds of my nightmares. It didn't bother me as much in the daylight, but I still didn't like it.

"How long can you keep the rift open?" I squeezed his hand in mine, and he brushed his thumb over the crook between my own thumb and pointer finger.

"As long as you want. I do suspect the guard will be ready to leave soon, though." I nodded, taking a step out from behind him to stand next to him instead. I started thinking of the cellar. I'd been able to go down there, and I came out again. I didn't get stuck. I was standing outside, perfectly free.

"Where is the entrance your soldiers found?" If Rainier's rift failed, there had to be another way out.

"Follow the stream. It leads to the lake. We'd have to swim eventually, but it's a way out. I checked." The unspoken words hung in the air between us. For you. I checked for you.

I nodded again, swallowing. A part of me felt a little insane for attempting to go into this cavern. But I was stepping outside of my comfort in so many different ways. What if there was a situation where I'd need to face these fears when rescuing Elora? I'd prefer to do it now than when it mattered.

"Alright." I set my features, determined.

"Alright?" Rainier looked down at me, a small smile forming while his brows lifted.

"If you get me stuck, I swear to Hanwen I will castrate you."

"I think you'd eventually come to regret that." He grinned, and I smacked his arm. "I'll leave the rift open, and I'll be right here with you. We won't get stuck, I promise." He squeezed my hand in affirmation.

I took a few deep breaths, focusing on breathing in through my nose and out through my mouth as I slowly moved forward. When I took my first step through the rift, I felt my pulse quicken, and I stopped, closing my eyes.

"Listen to my heart, Em." Rainier's voice was low and comforting, pulling me back to reality. I reached out, listening to the steady boom. I took a deep breath and started walking farther into the cavern. The trickle of water sounded musical once we were inside, the echoes bouncing off the walls. When we got to the edge of the water, I turned back to look past the rift. Rainier was right about the path to get out, the stream leading toward a dimly lit tunnel. I let out a deep breath before turning back to the pond, and I looked down.

"The descriptions don't do them justice, do they?" Rainier crouched down, still holding my hand, and I joined him. He was right. There were hundreds of tiny fish swimming in the pond, no longer than my index finger. They were the lightest silver, and they glimmered. In the light of the moon, they were said to glow. Their eyes were large and milky-white, and I was amazed these blind creatures could move around so gracefully. Watching them was mesmerizing, their movements nearly matching the beat of Rainier's heart. I held my free hand under the trickle of water, rolling my wrist beneath it.

"Do you believe what they say? That this place is god-touched?"

"Why not?"

"Well, I'd say the presence of rare fish is an odd way to show favor." I chuckled as I said it, and Rainier gave me a strange smile.

"The gods don't often do what we expect, do they?" His comment struck me as odd because Rainier had never been particularly religious. He'd always been of the same opinion as me. Whatever gods did exist had long since abandoned us.

"You believe in them now?"

"I do. I'll tell you why someday." I was curious about what made him come to that conclusion, his heart hammering in his chest. I realized then, I hadn't been focusing on my own breathing, and I was doing alright, still calm. I stood up, peering above us to the hole in the top of the cavern, the blue sky bright above us, and Rainier joined me. We stood there for a moment, and my arm began to tingle.

"Oh, no." I gaped at Rainier right as I saw all the muscles in his arm flex, the surge of the impulse going through him with ease. The pain slammed through my arm, much worse than it had been the day before. It brought me back to my senses, realizing where I was, and I felt a pulse of panic thread through me. I struggled to catch my breath for a minute, feeling like something was stuck in my throat. The next thing I knew, Rainier was folding me into his arms, squeezing me close.

"It's alright. You're safe. He must not have realized we were together." I scrambled with my divinity to listen to his heart, the steady beat anchoring me. When he sensed I'd caught my breath, he slowly unfolded his arms and pulled my hand back into his before leading us out of the cavern, back into the open air near the outcropping.

"Thank you, Rain." I was grateful he shared that with me and was patient while I tried to work through my fear, not pushing me but supporting me by just being there.

"No, thank *you*, Em. For trusting me." He lifted his hand to brush a hair off my face as he leaned toward me. When I realized he was about to kiss me, I froze. Over his shoulder I saw the soldiers—on their mounts and ready to leave. They were waiting on us, some even looking in our direction.

I imagined the man's face, full of righteous anger and disgust, right before he spat at me.

Whore.

I remembered Lavenia's voice from the night before.

She's held him hostage.

Rainier pulled back when he noticed my hesitance, his jaw tight, and a flicker of frustration moved across his features. A cool wind whipped around us, blowing the hair off my face. The air gave me chills, and it felt like a slap of reality. I couldn't do this with him. My heart had fooled me into thinking it knew what was best for me, and I was going to have to set it straight.

"I—Rain, what are we doing? What is this?" Lavenia said he'd been needing permission to move on. I was causing disquiet within his ranks and hurting his chances at an alliance with Nythyr. I should have been giving him the closure he needed all along rather than sharing stolen moments, sharing breaths after soul-shattering kisses. Allowing myself to distract my aching chest and fool it into thinking this was a mending instead of a painful impossibility. He deserved the closure I didn't know he was missing. That I didn't realize I needed as well. What we had these past days wasn't sustainable. I had nothing to offer him except myself and my daughter, and we were a burden. I could only imagine what they'd say about him at court. His judgment could be called into question. He'd said it himself—he had a duty. And I knew I couldn't stand between that. He made a choice all those years ago, and he chose Vesta. I couldn't let it all be for nothing. That was if he even wanted more from me, which I wasn't sure how he could. Who was I compared to him, compared to Keeva?

"What do you want it to be, Emmeline?" His voice was quiet but edged as he watched me, his eyes dark. I knew he was hanging on to every word I said.

"I don't think it can be what I want it to be." I paused while I searched his face, waiting for some sort of reaction to tell if he truly needed to move on like his sister had said. I could give him that, and after his actions earlier I thought I needed to, to keep his soldiers from growing to distrust him. Imagining what would happen if his mother got wind of him beating a soldier over a *whore* pushed me to continue. "I think I need to give you closure. You should perform the ritual with Keeva. I've already managed to—you can't just kill your soldiers over me, Rain." His face tightened, and I watched the muscle in his jaw twitch.

"Is that what you want?"

"No, of course it's not what I want. But what I want doesn't matter. You're going to be king, and you have to know how this looks." I paused and gestured between us. "You've wasted so much time." Waiting for me, searching for me.

"I don't care what this looks like. What about what I want? What if I don't want Keeva?"

"I don't know, Rain. You will always have my friendship; I won't disappear again." And I wouldn't. I couldn't go back to not knowing them, especially once they helped me get Elora back. There would be no going back to before, and while it was terrifying to think about, I was relieved I wouldn't lose him in that way again.

"Friendship?" He laughed, dark and bitter. "Your skin tastes like spring, and your sighs are a gods damn song. I'm not your fucking friend."

His voice bit into me, piercing the armor I'd created to shield myself from this, this danger and this hunger. I was drawn back to the study, his lips on mine and his hands all over me. The flame in my stomach flickered before it spread. I didn't want friendship either, but we couldn't have what I wanted. I didn't know why he was acting like this, as if my growing attachment was fine when ultimately nothing could come out of it. I squared my shoulders and faced him. My whole person focused on making my words stay calm and measured.

"We got caught up in a moment, that's all. We both agreed it was only a distraction. I needed something to take my mind off of things, and you didn't seem reluctant to help." It was a lie, and I tried not to flinch when I told it. He barked out a laugh, but it was cold, not a trace of a smile on his face.

"If Dewalt hadn't interrupted, would you have gotten *caught up in a moment* and begged me to fill that pretty, little cunt? Is that what friends do?" I clenched my teeth, not wanting to answer his question, and was taken back by his language. It didn't help my argument that the answer was yes. I undoubtedly would have done just what he said and regretted it after. I was a moth, and he was the flame to which I was drawn. I would've flown right in and singed my wings, happy to watch them burn.

"Do you often get caught up in moments, Emmeline? You weren't surprised Faxon fulfilled his needs elsewhere. Is that what you did? Though, I doubt you had to pay for it." He wore a mask of anger, and if it weren't for the heat of my rapidly darkening cheeks, I'd have thought my face a mirror of his.

"I make no apologies for anything I've done since you refused to choose me. You don't get to be mad or make ridiculous accusations about *anything*." I huffed out a breath, growing angrier every second. He had no right. And what if I had done what he was insinuating? He wasn't there, I wasn't his. "Truly, that's rich coming from you. You stand side by side with Thyra every day. How many others have you been with, Rainier?"

I saw his arm jerk as another impulse from Dewalt hit him. He threw his hand out, and I felt the ground rumble. I watched a trail of dirt flip over in a path toward the camp, clearly sending Dewalt a message. His eyes rose to meet mine, brimming with rage and something I might have mistaken for shame.

"What are you talking about?" He watched me, quieter for a moment, and it told me enough that I didn't want to know the answer.

"None of this matters. When Elora is back, she and I will go to Ravemont and be out of your hair."

"If I seem to recall, you have two years' commitment to court, Emmeline." He rubbed his hand against his chin as his eyes stayed on me. I couldn't believe he was actually going to hold me to that, but I shouldn't have been shocked.

"Just what I want, to be surrounded by women who want to kill me and bed you. Are you going to pardon Faxon and bring him to court too? To make my torture complete?"

"Women? Keeva is the only woman I'm betrothed to."

"Don't try to act like you haven't slept through half of your court. Your reputation precedes you." He barked a laugh.

"I generally don't fuck the women at court, but it's good to know you're worried about that." He leveled a gaze at me as if challenging me to continue the line of questioning.

"Generally, but not never?" Two years at court would be torture. Torture ending in death if the Nythyrian princess saw fit to punish him. I averted my eyes from him, watching the soldiers head west into the pass, the message from Rainier received. I saw his eyes flash to the soldiers as well before he answered my question.

"I suppose there are a few." The look he gave me was stony as if I was being unreasonable.

"And you're going to force me to be around Keeva, all the other suitors your mother will bring in if you don't choose Keeva, and however many women you've been inside? You're going to punish me with that for two years instead of letting us both move on?"

"Yes." He didn't elaborate. I threw out my arms, exasperated.

"I'm trying to give you a gift, Rain. Something you should have had all this time." He stared at me for a while. He had his arms crossed over his chest, the black shirt he wore clinging to every harsh curve and plane. His jaw was set, and he was so perfect that a large part of me wanted to take back every word I'd said. Every part of him was wound tight, and I'd have been afraid of him if he were anyone else.

"Don't you get tired of it?" The edge to his voice was so clear I could practically see the sharp glint on his lips.

"Tired of what?" The whisper held the weight of the question. I was exhausted.

"Running." His lip curled up in disgust. I could hear the rumble in his voice echo in the earth below us, threatening to swallow me whole. "The second you have a single, fucking doubt about anything, Emmeline, you run. You never give me a gods damn chance. You don't even try." My arms were limp at my sides, and I had no retort. Nothing to bite back at him, so I just stared. I saw his jaw clench and couldn't help reaching out. His heart was thundering. His eyes met mine and narrowed as he realized what I was doing. "Keeva was a means to an end. A choice I made for Vesta. You have no right to be upset about it because *you weren't there*. Kingdoms and years, Em. I've searched kingdoms, and I've waited for years. I had given up. But the minute I heard your voice at Ravemont, I wanted to go straight to the capital and call it off with her. And it's the first thing I intend to do when we get there. She will be gone, and she will not matter.

"And as for the others," He paused, even as he took a step toward me, tilting his head like he was debating what to say next, his tongue pushing hard behind his bottom lip. "Did you think of me when you let Faxon or whoever else fuck you?" I took a step back, stricken. I felt like I'd been physically slapped. The wind stepped up, and I felt my hair whipping around my face, mirroring the chaos I felt in my chest. He stepped forward as I moved back, pressing myself against a tree.

"Did you imagine my hands on you instead? My cock in—"

Before I knew what I was doing, I'd lifted my hand and smacked him hard across the face. His skin flushed darker where I hit him, but his eyes glimmered with something icy. He grabbed my wrist and pulled my arm to the side, pinning it against the tree. He leaned down so we were face to face while I pushed on his chest with my other hand.

"I don't care who you've been with, Em. Do you know why I've slept with enough women I have a reputation for it?" When I didn't reply, he surged forward, and his mouth caught mine, kissing me roughly. His free hand snaked up and wrapped around my neck, my pulse hammering against his thumb. He pushed his hips into me, and I opened my mouth, letting his tongue crash over mine. I felt the bark of the tree behind me digging painfully into my back and my head, but I didn't care. Every thought eddied out of my mind while he pushed his body into mine. Every bit of resolve I'd had was gone. There was only his lips and his tongue running over my own, over the roof of my mouth. His teeth tugged on my lips as he ground into me, and I arched my back, pressing my hips into him. He pulled his mouth from mine, panting.

"It was to get rid of the taste of you. You've crawled into my veins, and nothing I have done has gotten rid of you." He kissed me again as he ground into me, his teeth tugging hard on my lips. I swore I tasted copper when he pulled away from me, his face a breath from mine. "Every time I was with someone else, it was your face I saw."

I swallowed, and his eyes followed my throat. "You can cut their hearts out, banish them—I don't care. But you are coming to court with me, and you're not calling me your friend ever again." He let go of my wrist and pushed away from me, walking a few paces away and opening a rift. I saw our horses tied, waiting for us, the rest of the soldiers out of sight but not too far ahead in the distance. He stepped through and glanced over his shoulder.

"There is no moving on from this, Em. No closure, not for me. Believe me, if there was a way, I'd have found it."

CHAPTER 27

THE REST OF THE day passed slowly. The path through the mountains was arduous, requiring focus. Bree did extremely well, picking the sturdiest paths and avoiding areas other horses slipped in. It was a comfort to have her. When Rainier and I caught back up with the guard, he went straight to the front without a word. That was for the best, as I didn't think we had anything else left to say to one another. My mouth felt raw and swollen, the kiss reluctant to let me forget it. I was picking tree bark out of my hair for the next hour, angry and embarrassed.

No matter his feelings, no matter how he kissed me, the only way forward for us was to move on. He chose duty all those years ago, and I wouldn't let him waste that choice. I wouldn't let him waste the sacrifice we both made. He needed to do what Vesta deserved from a king. Vesta needed alliances. Vesta needed a king who wasn't distracted by an unknown woman—a woman who had already been branded a whore. He'd never be able to be with me in any official capacity, and I would not torture myself any longer pretending to believe in the possibility. Nor was I certain I even wanted that. Though the idea was next to impossible, if somehow it happened, being with him would mean I would be a princess and someday a queen. And where would that leave Elora? No, the idea was even more absurd the longer I thought about it. I had let myself feel something the night of the lake, the possibility of a future, of him being everything I'd ever dreamed of. And then my heart went off the rails, demanding more, demanding everything. It was his to break, and I wanted nothing more than to call his heart my own in turn. But all those years ago, he'd been right. He had known then what I was only beginning to understand. All I could give him was me, and I didn't think it was enough. He needed to make the best choice for Vesta after all this time. Lavenia was right; I'd held him hostage.

I began to spiral. It had been over three days since Prince Cyran's illusion, and the thought of seeing Elora soon was the only thing keeping me moving, eager to carry on and not circle down into hopelessness. I steered clear of my friends in the middle of the caravan. Mairin had melded right in with Dewalt and Lavenia, which didn't surprise me. She was kind and funny, and being around them seemed to draw out her personality even more. I could see her flaming hair from time to time when she tilted her head back in a laugh. The sight brought me a smile every time.

Surprisingly, Dickey stayed with me for most of that day. I believed with his friend gone, he was lonely. A part of me wondered if perhaps Rainier had sent him back to me because an hour or so after we arrived with the guard, I found Dickey waiting off to the side for me, a goofy smile on his face. "Lady Emma!" He waved, and I smiled at him, genuinely happy to see my young friend.

"Maybe one day I'll break you of calling me lady."

"The prince would break me first before that happened," he laughed.

"The prince can go—" I stopped, choosing different words than all the ones venomously flowing through my mind. "The prince can be rather pig-headed." The words that came out were still not kind but nicer than what I'd been thinking.

Dickey sputtered with laughter and quickly assumed a neutral expression which softened after a moment. "I heard about Makas. He got what he deserved." I was confused for a moment before realizing who he spoke of. My hands tightened on Bree's reins, not certain if I wanted to discuss the topic further. "No one else agrees with what he said, you know." I appreciated the sentiment, but I cringed internally. Of course, word had spread of what he'd said, even if he didn't say it in the common tongue. And despite what Dickey said, I was sure there were some who agreed with the man. I tried to smile at the boy, but I was sure it seemed more like a grimace than anything.

"I'm serious. Not a single person I've talked to is upset he was banished." I nodded. At least there was that. "There is a split about you healing him, though." He gave me a sheepish smile.

"What do you mean?"

"Well, some people thought healing him was foolish because he didn't deserve it. Others thought it was a valiant show of mercy."

"And what do you think, Dickey? Was I foolish or merciful?" It didn't matter, but I was curious what he thought.

"Merciful. The ones who see it as foolish didn't see you wield a sword against Prince Rainier." He grinned. "I know you're capable of being merciless when pressed." I felt myself grinning back as my face heated. "I was surprised you lasted as long as you did. I knew you had some training from when you asked for the swords, but not *that*."

We passed some time then with me filling the silence with details of my life at Ravemont and the time spent at Crown Cottage where I'd trained with Dewalt and Rainier. He asked a lot of questions about what Rainier, Lavenia, and Dewalt had been like when they were younger—his age, I realized. The rest of the time not spent talking about my formative years was spent in quiet or hearing about Dickey's life.

He had grown up knowing Rainier for most of his life. When Dickey's mother died, his father didn't know what to do with the child, still too young to be unattended. Rainier had given the soldier a year of pay while he mourned the loss of his wife and handled his affairs to ensure Dickey's care. And when his father died a few years ago, Rainier sought him out, offering him a job as a stable hand. Eventually, Dickey convinced Rainier to let him join the guard, and he'd been training ever since.

Dickey introduced me to the soldiers around me, who all seemed deeply respectful and refused to call me anything but Lady Emmeline, much to my chagrin. When the party finally stopped for the evening, I was grateful and freezing. I'd pulled out Lucia's black cloak and wore it on top of the blue one, my hair tucked into the crimson scarf of hers I'd wrapped around my neck. It was soft and smelled faintly of cucumber, allowing me to pretend she was just not around at the moment, waiting to yell at me for stealing her scarf. I spent a fair amount of time in front of the fire warming myself, all while keeping a watchful eye out for Rainier. I didn't know if I wanted to see him or not. But when I finally decided to go to the tent, and I hadn't caught sight of him, I felt the small curl of disappointment in my stomach. Should I have sought him out? What would I say to him? When I opened the flap to the tent, Lavenia was in there already taking off her boots.

"Emma." Her nod was curt, and I wondered why. Evidently, I'd angered more than just Rainier with our fight that morning. I nodded back before I undressed and climbed into my pallet. I laid there for a while, replaying the earlier argument. I couldn't believe all of the events of the day. Rainier almost killed someone, he helped me face my fears and go into the cavern, and then we'd fought. And kissed. There was a lot to think about, yet I didn't want to think about any of it. I decided I wasn't going to try to discuss things with him again until after Elora was back; my head wasn't in the right place. If he called off his engagement with Keeva in the meantime, then it might provide me with more clarity. Or she'd kill me, and it wouldn't matter.

Despite the stupidity of it, I let my mind wander and allowed myself to visualize a scenario where things could be different. I couldn't offer anything to Rainier but burden. It wasn't the first time I damned my divinity. If I were more powerful, more rare, a capable conduit...I stopped myself. There was no sense going down that road.

I traced my finger over my lips and ran a tongue over a sore spot where he'd bit me. Even though he came at me all feral and demanding, I hadn't been afraid of him. I thought about him grinding his hips into mine and remembered his words. I wasn't sure if what he said was supposed to comfort me or not. That every woman he'd been with had been some sort of stand-in for me.

What he'd said about Faxon had been a slap to the face. When I let Faxon into my bed it wasn't as if I was an eager participant. Surely, he had to know that. I had been nearly catatonic, lost in grief, and barely present. I hadn't told him no, knowing what would come with marriage, what was expected of us, but I hadn't told him yes, either. I hadn't imagined anything, let alone Rainier, because I wasn't truly there. In the years since, there were occasions where Faxon forced other things on me. Things I didn't want to do but weren't going to cause a child. It was rare, and it only happened when he'd been drinking. When he'd force me to use my hand, never bothering with my mouth since I'd threatened to bite. When he would grab my wrist so hard, I was afraid he'd break it. When he would take my hand and put it on him, refusing to let me go until he was done working himself with it. I wasn't sure if it made him feel powerful or what. I knew his own hand would have felt better. The first time he did it, my thoughts had gone to Rainier, only because of the one time I'd gripped *him* before he had slid into me. But any time after, I specifically didn't think of Rainier. I didn't want to taint the memory. So, I tucked him away, wiping my mind blank.

It was only after those moments, the days and weeks after Faxon stole parts of me, when I let myself think of Rainier. When I'd touch myself to reclaim my hands, knowing they were for my pleasure, not Faxon's. My hands were mine to control, belonging only to me. Moments when I let myself think of my hand around Rainier and the sting of him. When I let myself think about his expression. When he gazed into my eyes as he moved inside me, desire and adoration on his face. It wasn't Faxon's hands I imagined were Rainier's. It was my own. And I hadn't done it to try to forget him like he'd been doing when he imagined me. I did it to remember him. To remember what it felt like in the moment to be cherished and cared for. To not feel alone or weak or pitiful. Even though he didn't choose me in the end, every moment we were together, I had always felt precious.

In the quiet of the tent, I remembered all of those things, and I found myself wondering if Rainier was also struggling to sleep. Had he told Dewalt what we'd said? I felt well and truly alone, and I found myself crying quietly. The straw in my pallet poked into me, and I was reminded exactly why I was here and what we were doing.

I missed Elora. I missed checking on her at night even after she was old enough to not need me to do it. I missed lowering the wick in her lamp when she stayed up too late reading. I missed her laugh and easy smile. I mourned our life we had because I knew it would never be the same. Even after we got her back, if she wasn't completely traumatized, the simple life we had led was over. I knew nothing would ever be the same, and I felt my heart tear in two. I did my best to keep my sobbing quiet, and thankfully Lavenia left me to it. I fell asleep before Mairin ever even joined the tent.

I didn't see Rainier at all the next morning, and it started to bother me. Mairin was nowhere to be found when I woke up, although the rumple in her bedroll told me she'd at least slept in the tent. Lavenia was still cold with me, and I debated saying something to her, but what was there to say? When Dewalt came up in line behind me while I waited for breakfast, I gave him a tight smile over my shoulder, wondering if he'd speak to me, not sure I wanted him to.

"I've been sent to check on you." His tone was pleasant but not particularly open. I tried to keep the relief out of my face. I didn't want anyone to know how desperately lonely I'd felt the last day. I didn't understand it; I'd been alone for so long—why did that one day feel worse than all those years combined? Perhaps because I'd had a taste of what it could be like, and I didn't want to let go of it.

"Rainier?" He bowed his head in affirmation but said no more. "I'm fine." I turned away.

"Spoken like someone who isn't fine," Dewalt grumbled behind me.

"Why did he send *you*?"

"You certainly woke up in a good mood." I turned and saw his eyebrows raised high, a look of unimpressed boredom on his face. "I was the only one who volunteered." Had they called a meeting to discuss who drew the short straw? Had it been such a chore that Dewalt was the only one who wanted to speak to me? Not even Mairin? It felt like a betrayal. And like any other time when my feelings were hurt, I lashed out.

"I thank you for your sacrifice, Dewalt. I apologize for the hardship you've faced in having to talk to me. Tell him I'm fine."

"Don't be an ass. We're all here because of you—for you." I whipped around to face him, feeling my braid slap against my back.

"I know that, Dewalt! And you know how gods damn grateful I am for it. You should know, better than anyone else here, how I might be feeling. My daughter has been taken by monsters. Taken for a man who is supposedly worse than his father—the man who *killed my sister*. Declan is somehow *worse* than the man who killed Lucia. I've been betrayed by the only other person in the world who was supposed to love her as I do. Do you know how that feels? And it's my own damn fault! I didn't notice, couldn't even fathom a situation where he would do that. Now, on top of all of that, I have to deal with Rainier beating his soldiers and talking about forfeiting alliances because of me. It's as if he forgot the whole reason he didn't choose me in the first place. I'm sorry for being an ass, but listening to the only man I've ever loved say a lot of confusing things doesn't help matters."

I realized my voice was loud by the end of my tirade because of the way the food line had quieted. I glanced around and felt a flush rising, my breathing rapid. If Dewalt couldn't understand now, I wasn't sure he ever would.

"Nothing to see here." He barked out the order, and everyone around us moved back into action as Dewalt took a step toward me, bracing both his hands on my shoulders. His expression was unreadable as he peered down at me from beneath his lowered brow.

"You love him?"

"Of course I love him. I never stopped." I couldn't have prevented my answer from rolling off my tongue if I tried.

"Then let him love you back. Let it be enough."

I felt my face soften as I looked at him, realizing how awful I must have seemed. He averted his eyes, and I felt a sharp pang of guilt. He'd give anything to be arguing with Lucia. I tried to find the words to say, but he cut me off by clearing his throat.

"Do you want to start training again?"

"Yes." My reply was instant. He'd given me a break the last few days. My muscles had been screaming since I'd fought Rainier, and I hadn't even thought about touching my sword to train. But the thought of spending this energy, distracting my thoughts—I knew instantly I would not deny myself of it.

"Good. Tonight, before dinner."

He said no more as we retrieved our food, but he sat next to me as we ate. It was silent, but I didn't feel so alone.

Thyra joined us to train after we made camp that evening. Dewalt and I had spent some time going over basic stances and holds when she marched up, carrying a sword instead of her ax I'd grown accustomed to seeing.

"Hello, little viper." Her grin was mischievous, and I couldn't help but laugh.

"Thyra wanted to join us to sharpen her skills with the sword." Dewalt offered the information without meeting my eye. My friend's face was almost as readable as my own sometimes, and I knew someone had told him I knew about Thyra and Rainier.

"I prefer the ax, so I need practice with the sword at times." I suspected she was just as good with a sword as she was with her ax, and I wondered if there was some sort of ulterior motive to her joining us to spar. I took a breath and sat, drinking water out of a canteen while Dewalt warmed up with Thyra. She was left-handed, which I found interesting. Eventually, Dewalt stopped and gestured for me to come over.

"Thyra, you strike. Emma, block." Thyra nodded, and we both took stances apart from each other before she advanced. Her fighting style was similar to Rainier's, and it bothered me more than it should have. Though she used her height over me to attempt quite a few overhanded swings, I met every one with ease, used to this approach. Everyone had always used my height to their advantage, something I had to compensate for from the start. She may have had the height Rainier did, but not nearly as much of the power. I knew if she were to have her ax, it would likely be a different story. It was slower and heavier, but if she could move it, it would give her the strength the sword lacked. After a while of back and forth, Dewalt called for us to stop.

"You do well for being so short." Thyra's breathing was a bit heavier than it had been before sparring, but overall, she seemed unaffected.

"You do well for being so tall." Her booming laugh echoed as she walked over to her canteen, and I smiled. I liked her. I wondered why Rainier stopped sleeping with her. She was beautiful and intriguing, kind and funny. What could have made him lose interest? More importantly, why did I care?

A few moments later, Dewalt instructed us to switch roles. Before we started, I noticed Lavenia and Mairin walking toward us in easy conversation. I felt a pang of jealousy over the fact my friend had barely seen me the past two days and had already fallen in so quickly with the people I'd known for so long. They sat down next to our canteens and watched while I lunged toward Thyra, over and over.

It went much the same as when she attacked me. She was good at anticipating my movements and parried with ease. I circled her, searching for an opening, but never found one, and I grew frustrated, throwing fast and frenzied attacks. She easily anticipated and blocked each one.

"Easy, Em. Don't get sloppy." I felt my heart slam in my chest at the sound of his voice, and I was grateful I was the only one who could hear it. I forced myself to keep going, not averting my eyes to look where I knew Rainier was standing. Slowing down, I decided to take a more methodical approach with Thyra. She wasn't as fast as me, so I needed to find a way to send her blocking in one direction while I hit her from another. I struck a few more blows at her, which she predicted, before I lunged to her weak side. When she went to block me there, I spun and brought my sword down low, about to slam into her thigh before I stopped the swing. Thyra let out a breath of frustration before she smiled at me, grabbing me with her free hand and pulling me in for a one-armed embrace. It surprised me, but I accepted the gesture either way. Dewalt slapped me on the shoulder, a grin on his face, and I broke from the hug, turning around to see Rainier leaning against a tree behind me with his arms crossed.

"Good girl." The look he gave me was dangerous. It returned the feeling of the tree on my back—the bark scratching into my skin and his hand on my throat. I pushed it deep down, eager to bury the memory. His shirt was a deep burgundy color, and the top few buttons were open, revealing the swells of muscle in his chest. A small smile danced on his lips while I watched him, and I felt the need to knock him down. I let my gaze flicker over him in annoyance and rolled my eyes before turning back to Thyra.

"I hope you join us again. It was fun."

"Yes, maybe I will teach you ax and shield. You are too short and impatient to be shield-maiden but still fun to learn." Everything about this woman should have intimidated me, but I only found warmth and kindness from her.

"I would like that, Thyra. Thank you."

She nodded and left, heading toward camp, and I tentatively walked toward Mairin and Lavenia, not sure if I would be received. I wasn't ready for Lavenia to be cold to me again, but I didn't want to leave, to stand in a line for food alone. Nor did I want to go to the tent and cry myself to sleep again. Mairin looked up when I approached.

"Are you done moping now?" I felt heat flame my cheeks and knew from her expression the hurt I felt was evident. Her features softened as she continued. "You seemed like you needed some space."

"I'm not sure what you're talking about."

"You never caught up with us yesterday, and you avoided us today." She shrugged as if it was obvious. When I realized the reason for Lavenia's coolness might have been because she thought I was avoiding her, my veins flooded with cool relief. Maybe they hadn't volunteered to speak to me because they thought I needed space, even though I'd never felt lonelier.

"Oh. Well, maybe I did. I'm alright now, though." I gave a weak smile as they both studied me. Lavenia's eyes were searching, and I avoided making eye contact.

"Good. Sit." Mairin patted on the ground next to her, and I sat, nearly crying in relief when she pulled my head to her shoulder. Lavenia stood, striding over to where Dewalt and Rainier spoke in low tones. I wasn't sure if she was trying to give me one-on-one time with Mairin or if she wasn't ready to speak to me, but I tried to remain optimistic and assumed the former. I sat there leaning against Mairin, her wiry curls wafting into my face in the light breeze, enjoying the nearness and warmth of my friend. Her hair smelled a bit bittersweet, almost like nutmeg and cloves, the scent familiar and comforting.

"We're going to go get food for us; we'll be right back," Lavenia called over. I noticed it was Mairin she was talking to, not me.

"Bring us back some?" Mairin called back, a smile in her voice.

"That was the plan." The three of them started walking toward camp, and I couldn't help but notice Rainier's eyes sweep over me, the last of the three of them to turn away. Mairin waited until they were out of earshot before turning to me, her tone demanding.

"What was the fight about?" I sat up.

"How do you know we fought?" She glared at me as if I was too stupid for words. Which, to be fair, wasn't wrong. I inhaled. "The same thing we've always been fighting about."

"Which is?"

"Everything." I huffed a laugh, hesitating before continuing. "I heard you and Lavenia talking the other night; I was trying to give him closure."

"Why?" The question surprised me.

"Because he needs it." She just stared, waiting for me to continue. "Mairin, I can't go to court."

"Why can't you?"

"Let's see, where to start?" My voice was dripping with sarcasm, and I tried to remember I was talking to my friend, tempering my annoyance before I continued. "First, my daughter is my priority, and she might not want to stay. Second, he is betrothed to someone who will want to kill me. He needs the alliance it will bring, and I won't jeopardize it. Third, I will not be a mistress, even though I'm sure I'll be branded a whore either way."

"Only one of those makes sense." I stared at her. "Elora might not want to stay, and you have to do what's best for her, especially after everything that has happened. But the rest?" She made a dismissive gesture with her hand.

"I don't know about you, but I personally like being alive."

"From what I've heard, he's calling it off. Won't she return to Kieża?"

"Probably, but that wouldn't stop her from bestowing him a parting gift of my head. Besides—the alliance. He shouldn't be calling it off at all."

She shrugged. "I don't think she'd risk it. And I'd trust him more than you to know what alliances he needs and doesn't need."

"I won't be a mistress, Mairin."

"Who says you would be? He's not bonded."

"Yet." I sighed, tilting my head back to look through the canopy of trees. The faintest hint of stars were starting to appear, and I wondered, perhaps, if Lucia was among them. "King Soren is old, and Rainier will have to perform the ritual and wed soon. If Keeva leaves, I'm sure the queen has a whole host of other suitable conduits to replace her."

"Why are you so determined it not be you?" I paused a moment, blinking. Of course, it couldn't be me.

"Future kings don't bond for...love." It felt strange to say it, presumptuous even. But was it so far from the truth? He cared for me—that much was clear. The attraction was there. But was it love? "I doubt that's what he feels for me, anyway. Kings bond for power. They bond for mates who will give them strong offspring, to carry on their legacy. I can offer neither."

"You just learned you can heal yourself, Emma. Who knows how far your divinity goes? You cloistered yourself away when you came of age. You could be more powerful than Rainier, for all we know. And you're more stupid than you look if you think that man wants anything less than everything from you." I snorted; she was being obnoxious, now.

"Well, I can't give him any children. Elora nearly killed me."

"But she didn't. Because of your *powerful divinity*." I threw my arms up and stood, pacing in frustration.

"It doesn't matter if you think I'm powerful or if I even start to think it. It's not up to me—or even Rainier for that matter. It's up to the king and queen and the Myriad."

"I know this."

"Then why are you arguing with me about it?"

"Lavenia told me all of this. She also told me the Myriad hate her, and they grow worried she will inherit the throne."

"So? What does that have to do with me?"

"*So*, she thinks they'd agree to him bonding with anyone as long as it kept her off the throne."

"Why do they hate her?" Lavenia was kind and truly cared. Vesta would be just as lucky to have her as queen as it would having Rainier as king.

"Because she is not a he." Mairin spat out the words, and my nose crinkled in disgust. I still hated the Myriad, though I'd been so far removed I had no idea they would have any preference about that. The throne had always gone to the oldest child, but I supposed the bloodline hadn't had a female heir in over a millennium. "There's also the fact that she has made it clear to anyone who will listen that she does not want the role. They've taken offense." Mairin laughed.

"What about Dewalt? They could ascend to the throne, and Dewalt would be king."

"They claim Dewalt isn't of proper breeding, having been born with no title. They don't want him either. Besides, they've both been rather vocal in their support for Rainier and disdain for an ascension that involved them."

I exhaled a breath, pacing back and forth. Making sure no one could hear me, I eyed the path back to camp before I continued speaking.

"None of this matters if he doesn't even want to bond with me, Mairin. He seems to care for me, and there is definitely an attraction, but who is to say it isn't just unfinished business?" Even though I practically whispered it, saying it out loud was a weight off my shoulders. I'd been holding back from him because I knew we could never perform the ritual thanks to my underwhelming divinity, but the quiet, destructive voice inside was more afraid that if I let him have me, he'd no longer want me. I was the woman he left, bereft and afloat. Guilt and regret weren't reasons to be with someone.

"I am." She nodded confidently as she said it.

"You are what?"

"I am the one to say. Auras, remember?"

I crossed my arms and scowled at her. "The auras tell you when something is more than just attraction? Can you definitively tell me what we have is *more*?" I was skeptical. From what she'd said, it seemed like auras changed minute to minute based on feelings and interactions.

"Sometimes." She gave me a small smile with one side of her mouth quirked up more than the other. "Certain relationships gleam. They look a bit different."

"And ours looks different?" She nodded. "How so?"

"You're twin flames, Emma."
I froze.
"One soul, two bodies."

CHAPTER 28

THERE WAS A TICKLE in my chest, and I felt it slowly rising up my throat until I started laughing. It was nervous laughter, laced with disbelief. The timorous chittering turned into a deep belly laugh, and I brought a hand up, pushing to the stitch in my side. My friend just looked up at me from her seat on the ground, head tilted and a curious expression on her face.

"You're so full of shit, Mairin." My laughter trailed off as I watched her. She wasn't laughing. We stared at each other for a few moments, and I was about to speak when I heard Dewalt's low chuckle behind me. The three of them had returned with our food. Stew again, I realized distractedly. I was getting sick of it.

"Someone is in a better mood." Dewalt flashed me a grin, and I made a face at him accompanied by my middle finger, earning a laugh in return. I could see Rainier smiling at me out of the corner of my eye, but I didn't spare him a glance. They crossed the small clearing where we had trained, and Rainier pushed a bowl toward me, forcing me to make eye contact with him. He had that gods damn crooked smile on his face, and his eyes were bright. Hopeful, even. He spoke quietly so no one else could hear.

"If you wish to stay angry, please do so nearer to me. And not so quietly."

His hand slipped out from the bowl, lightly touching my fingertips. I felt a jolt, like lightning, when his skin touched mine. My eyes strayed to the bowl, and I looked at the contents; however unappealing they'd started to become in recent days, I found them especially fascinating in that moment.

He was wrong. It's not that I *wasn't* angry exactly. It was more that it wasn't him I was angry with. It was the situation; it was me. I'd started to realize part of me just always simmered with anger, and I'd kept it tamped down and locked tight inside me. Being around him again, the lid I'd shut down so forcefully was prying loose. I was angry about my sister's death, my unceremonious marriage to Faxon, my isolation, my missing daughter. His decisions and reactions from back then were still part of that list, but not enough to blame all of my rage and frustration on him. No, I wouldn't direct it toward him, but it had started to consume me. A whirlwind of feelings had come to the surface. A pot boiling over. But I was the one who wanted fire, who had asked for it. I exhaled a breath and held eye contact for a moment.

"You want me to scream at you?" His eyes flashed dangerously, and he leaned in, lips brushing against my ear.

"I want you to scream *for* me. But I'll take what I can get." He pulled back, a lazy, satisfied smirk on his face.

I felt my whole body flush, my skin raising, and I focused on maintaining slow, steady breaths so he wouldn't see what he did to me. After what Mairin had just said and Rainier's admission, I'd somehow forgotten how to inhale properly. It was pathetic being so worked up. I shot a look at Mairin, one which promised later discussions. What she'd said was a revelation if it were true. I knew she hadn't said anything to Rainier yet, based on how he'd acted with her before when she showed him her abilities. Maybe he knew more about merrows than I did because he didn't have a single doubt when she showed him what she was. And if she'd told him what she told me? I didn't think he'd be asking me to shout at him. I think he'd have stolen me away and made me his. The thought sent my heart rocketing once again.

This was what I'd wanted all those years ago. I'd wanted him to choose me. I'd wanted to be together and perform the bonding ritual. Why was I so hesitant about his attentions now? Especially knowing Faxon was not long for this world, what was there to stop him from giving me everything? Had I begun to understand the sacrifice he made back then? With King Soren's age and health a factor, Vesta needed security, and Rainier could give it to the people. The people in the small town of Brambleton, the slums of Mira, the immigrants and refugees—those people needed him and the security he could and would offer. My mere existence in his life was a threat to what he could give them. But other than those loyal to Keeva, would I be that poor of a choice? I had the benefit of seeing some of the work that needed to be done in Vesta's poorer cities. My divinity, while not anything monumental, was something that could be seen as a balance to Rainier. The hardened warrior could use someone whose divinity could save and heal. Maybe it wasn't such a far-off dream.

I averted my eyes and sat next to Dewalt, who nudged his arm against me, giving me a small smile. Rainier settled down on my other side, and I felt the heat from his leg against me, electricity traveling through my veins.

I had a hard time eating my food, all appetite having left me. I sat quietly, making sure to engage in the pleasant conversation occasionally, not sure what I'd agreed to or disagreed with. Everyone else finished, their dishes stacked in a pile on the ground in front of us, while I stared into my bowl. Suddenly, there was a loud screech above us, and I saw something falling from the sky. My head jolted up as some sort of rodent slammed to the ground, and it came running toward us. Mairin squealed and skittered backward, and I was about to jump up myself when Rainier put an arm across my legs to calm me.

"It's one of my shifters." He peered up into the sky then, arm still across me, and I followed his gaze to see a hawk circling us slowly before dropping to a low hanging branch. My attention was drawn back to the mouse as it began to grow. It was the size of a small cat by then, and I watched it in horror, one of the more gruesome things I'd ever seen. It was a giant mouse, the size of a dog when it stood up on its hind legs. Its spine straightened and lengthened, the fur slowly disappearing and the small claws stretching and filling out, turning into hands and feet. The spine kept lengthening as the snout shortened, pushing back into a face. The sounds coming from the transition were unsettling, the cracking and popping of bones loud in our quiet clearing. It was all over in a matter of ten minutes, but I watched the entire time, with equal parts amazement and revulsion, until I realized the shifter was completely naked. He was an average-sized man, shorter than both Rainier and Dewalt. His coloring matched what he'd looked like as a mouse; light brown hair and eyes made the man generally nondescript. His voice was quiet and higher-pitched than I'd have imagined, wringing his hands in front of him as he spoke.

"Our friends from Skos have moved. A thousand men. They're positioned west of the Aesiron."

"Did you say west?" Lavenia's face snapped to the man. "How did they get past the bridge?"

"Evidently, Nythyr has opened their pass." Rainier's tone was dark. The Aesiron Bridge was a divider spanning between Nythyr and Vesta. It was impassable by sea except for certain tunnels which could be opened, allowing ships through. Skos, located far east of Vesta, rarely traded farther west than Olistos, on Vesta's eastern shore. Other than sailing northwest around Nythyr and back south between the landmasses, the only other route for traders from Skos to move west of the Aesiron involved one of the tunnels, of which there were only two. I wasn't sure who the "friends" from Skos were, but since it was clear the term was used sarcastically, I gathered the Vestian pass remained closed. I'd heard of no issues with Skos from my corner of society, but that didn't mean there weren't any.

"No sightings of the girl. Declan claims the younger prince is taking care of a 'most precious gift.'" His voice didn't hold back his disgust, and I felt my lip curl.

"Yes, Cyran appeared to Emmeline in an illusion." Rainier nodded toward me and, as if he suddenly realized I hadn't met his shifter, introduced me. "Aedwyn, this is Lady Emmeline. Em, Aedwyn is one of my most trusted spies." The naked man in front of me bowed, and I nearly laughed. To be so formal yet so nude. There was a sharp screech from above, and I saw the hawk ruffle its feathers, almost angrily, from its perch on the tree. Rainier gave me a wry smile. "Other than his sister, Aerfen, of course. She's up there." As if on cue, the hawk fluttered down, landing gently on the man—her brother's—shoulder. My stomach clenched a bit, worried the talons would break his skin, but Aerfen was careful. I smiled, feeling exceptionally uncomfortable smiling at this predator.

"My sister does not like to shift right after a flight. She prefers to rest in her hawk form, less soreness that way." The hawk shrieked quietly and lightly ruffled its wings. "But be assured, she is happy to meet you as well." I gave a more confident smile to the two of them. Something about the pair was deeply unsettling but also deeply familiar. The language of twins. It made me glad Aerfen stayed in her shifter form.

"Cyran holds the Beloved in wait for Declan. We are not sure exactly where they are. Hopefully, Emmeline can extract the information during the next illusion. Perhaps Glenharbor? I know there is a royal estate there. We have reason to believe Cyran wants to plan a coup over his brother." Rainier explained the rest of the illusion to Aedwyn. And Aerfen, I realized. It was strange to think of a hawk understanding him. If either shifter was surprised by the information they'd just received, they didn't show it.

"When do you want us to leave, Your Highness?" Aedwyn still stood naked in front of us, seemingly comfortable in the cold. Rainier gave them their instructions, asking for an update four mornings from now after I'd met with Prince Cyran. My heart gave a small leap; I'd be seeing Elora in three nights' time. I tried to temper my hope in case Prince Cyran decided Elora hadn't behaved, but it was a struggle. The thought of seeing her for even a moment made me lighter.

"Aedwyn, send me Thyra," Rainier called after the shifter, who walked toward the camp, completely naked and unashamed with his sister perched on his shoulder. I watched his retreat in silent consideration of the fact I'd just met two of the rarest conduits in the world. Rainier cleared his throat, and I turned to my small group of friends sitting around me. He studied me for a moment as if considering saying something. I noticed his temple throb before he turned to Dewalt. "So, Declan is making moves to ally with Olag."

"It would seem." Dewalt's face was dark and tight, deep anger thrumming through him.

"Who is Olag?" I assumed it was the 'friend' from Skos, but I didn't know what any of that meant.

"A monster." My head whipped toward Mairin, surprised my friend knew of him. This also surprised Lavenia, who raised her brows as she studied the fiery redhead. "Not me, but I've heard stories." Lavenia nodded at Mairin's explanation, but Rainier noted the confusion that remained on my face.

"He's a slave trader from Skos. The fact Nythyr opened their pass, I—" Rainier rubbed his hand over his face. "He must have an extreme amount of coin or Queen Nereza an extreme amount of gall. Likely both."

"How? Where are slaves even still traded?" It had been outlawed centuries ago in Vesta, early in Soren's reign, one of the few good things he'd done. And more recently, in Nythyr and Folterra, but nearly 100 years separated the Three Kingdoms from the last slaves. Cyran had mentioned Declan's desire to bring the trade back, but how could a slave trader exist in the Three Kingdoms when it had been outlawed for so long?

"To the east. Olag specializes in warriors and women," Dewalt spat out.

"Sometimes both." Thyra came walking from the path to camp and sat, no, *threw* herself down next to Rainier as she reached into Dewalt's bag for an apple. I looked at her, surprised, and realized what she meant.

"Oh," I said, dumbly. "You?"

"Yes, little viper." She took a bite from her apple, her eyes on Rainier. "Do I finally get to kill the man who sired me?"

From what she explained, Thyra was raised as a warrior. The daughter of Olag and one of his victims, he'd taken her shortly after she was weaned and raised her to fight. And when she came of age, he sold her to the highest bidder.

"I am not so unlike you, little viper." She didn't elaborate, but her statement gave me pause. Though my father hadn't taught me to fight, he *had* sold me. Both men had sold something they didn't have any right to own. She continued her story, and my frustration only grew. Her training as a warrior was supposed to provide her protection from whoever purchased her; Olag led her to believe the man who bought her would only utilize her for her abilities with her ax.

Olag lied.

Thyra had paid for those lies in blood and fear. She didn't go into detail, but the shuttered look on her face told me there was deep trauma behind it. My heart ached for her. For someone with such a disastrous childhood and upbringing, how she managed to smile every day and befriend people as easily as she did drew deep respect from me.

"Then these two saved me." She put an arm around Rainier and nodded toward Dewalt. I liked her and trusted her, but I had to fight against my instincts to slap her arm off the man. "And I've been saving their asses ever since." They both glared at her, Dewalt giving her a middle finger as Rainier pushed her away, though both men smiled. It reminded me of the two young boys from so long ago, both impossibly handsome and devilish.

"It was shortly after—" Dewalt took a breath. "Lucia died, and we ran around doing King Soren's bidding for a while. We'd heard news of a slave ship trying to make port for supplies in Olistos, blown off course from a storm."

"It was good practice for me, with the water. I did my best to destroy the ship—"

"And nearly drowned half of us," Thyra added, and Dewalt snickered.

"And nearly drowned half of them in the meantime." Rainier grinned. "But we were ultimately successful. The only ones who drowned that day deserved it." Thyra gave a quiet nod, and I stayed silent for a few moments.

"I'm so sorry all of that happened to you."

"I have made peace with it, and my destiny is here. Swearing my life and sword to Prince Rainier has been one of the best decisions I've ever made." The man in question hung his head, peeking up at her out of the corner of his eye, and I tried hard not to overanalyze the fondness I saw there. "I will continue to serve him as king and swear fealty to his queen—as long as he lets me kill my wretched sire." She turned to him with a questioning look, and he gave a grim nod.

"If it comes to it, you will be the one to kill him." She grunted an assent before she stood, turning toward camp, and Lavenia was quick to join her, a silent signal that it was time for all of us to retire for the night.

"Em, hang back a moment." Rainier was behind me, not having followed the rest of us, merely pulling himself to his feet. I felt my stomach twist as I took him in. I wasn't sure what he wanted to talk about, but his somber expression made me feel like whatever it was wasn't good. Rainier watched me, studying the embroidery on the cloak he'd given me as I pulled it tighter around me.

"It is important to me that you are comfortable with Thyra."

"What?" I sputtered. That wasn't what I expected. "I am." It was Rainier's turn to be surprised. "I know you and her—never mind, it doesn't matter. I like her." My smile was sheepish, and his gaze narrowed.

"I was left with a distinct impression after our last conversation that it was a point of contention for you. I feel compelled to explain the nature—"

"I'd rather you not. It's fine." I thought I was being rather accommodating and understanding, but I wasn't sure if hearing about things between them was something I could handle. He took one of my hands in both of his and started tracing the lines of my palm. It was soothing, the only reason I didn't pull away, allowing him to continue.

"What she went through, that's not my place to talk about. But I can talk about what was happening with me." He swallowed, and his eyes followed his fingertips, gently moving across my skin. "I found out you were gone. You know, a part of me—perhaps a delusional part—thought you wouldn't have married him. I had faith you'd weasel out of it because I never knew you to do something you didn't want to do." He sighed, looking up with remorse in his emerald gaze. "But I'd just found out you were married and gone, and Thyra and I were drunk, and we both had things we were working through." He paused, and when he started speaking again, his voice had found the resolve it needed to finish saying what he needed to say. "It was my first time since you and her first time by choice."

He stared down at my hand, his perfect features clouded with emotion. I turned over what he'd said in my mind. Thyra was his first time since me, seeking comfort after finding out I was gone. But based on all the conversations I'd had recently, I gathered it took them some time to find out. How long had he stayed celibate after me? Even though he'd said as much during our argument, I was still surprised to know I had that much of an effect on him. I wasn't sure why he felt the need to tell me about Thyra specifically. Between the gossip and his own admissions, it was clear there were plenty of women. I didn't expect him to abstain when there was no hope of reconciliation between us. Why would I have expected him to remain faithful to something that didn't exist? My desire to avoid court wasn't so much about Thyra as it was about being reminded and perhaps adjudicated against the women with whom he'd shared parts of himself. It felt like torture, especially if we could never be more.

Unless Mairin was right.

I pushed the thought away. Even if I was his twin flame, not all twin flames ended up together in every lifetime. In fact, the histories of twin flames were often bloodied and tragic. Thyra didn't bother me much, for whatever reason. I thought of the monster residing in my stomach, dormant for half my life yet awakened in his presence, and knew it reacted toward Thyra just as it did toward Mairin. I cared for both women, respected them. Thyra treated me as an equal, as a friend. I wasn't certain about her choices of nicknames for me, but I liked her. Besides, it sounded like what they had done was more about comfort than it was anything else. I squeezed his hand.

"It's alright, Rain."

"She has become one of my most trusted soldiers and a good friend. It never happened again, and, quite frankly, she's a little disgusted it ever did." He forced out a dry laugh. "But I will release her from her vow if you wish it."

Ah.

He was afraid I'd want him to send his friend away. A friend who had comforted him in a time of weakness, one caused by me, however unintentional it was. His friend who had started to become my friend. Instead of worrying about why I'd have any sway in his decision and bringing it to his attention, I chose kindness and understanding instead.

"Of course not, Rain." I brought up my other hand, and I cupped his in my own. "Besides, she tackled the soldier who—well, I'd like her on my side when there's a real threat." Rainier bristled, but it didn't stop the light in his eyes as his gaze met mine. "Come on. I'm tired."

I dropped his hand and turned toward our tents awaiting us. I was exhausted, but I knew I needed to talk to Mairin. A few steps later, I hadn't heard Rainier start to walk after me, and I glanced over my shoulder to see him still standing there, watching me. I jerked my head up the path, giving him a look to get him to follow, and he finally moved, shoving his hands into his pockets.

"I don't think I'll ever figure you out, Emmeline Highclere."

"No," I agreed. "But if you do, let me know. We could compare notes."

By the time everyone settled in, snow had started to come down. Though it was still early into autumn, the mountains didn't seem to care about the seasons, the air cold and blistering. There was a cave carved out of the side of the mountains with perfect coverage from the wind and elements—a hospitable place to make camp. It was more than big enough to accommodate everyone, including a giant fire in the center, painting shadows on the walls around us. When we came to the mouth of the cave, I paused for a second, Rainier a step behind me.

"I can rift you directly into your tent if you want."

"You've been in it?" I grinned at him cheekily, and his cheeks darkened. Had I embarrassed him?

"Well, no. I suppose I'd rift you into my tent first, but it's a much shorter walk."

Dewalt had asked me if it would be alright when he'd scouted the location, and of course, I said yes. It was safe and warm, a boon for the soldiers. I supposed I could have insisted on my own tent being outside the cave, but it seemed a fussy thing to ask. When I'd answered, I'd remembered braving the cavern with Rainier, and perhaps I was a bit too confident. My breath hitched, and my hands felt sweaty as I stared past the fire where I knew my tent waited.

"No, it's fine." I took a few steps in and counted my breaths, the anxious habit forcing itself on me. But I was doing alright. I didn't like how many people were in the cave at once, but at least the opening was wide and visible. I kept walking, my eyes locked on my goal. I didn't even realize my hands were shaking until I felt Rainier's large, warm one sliding into mine, his fingers lacing with my own.

Embarrassed, I whispered to him, "My hand is sweaty."

"I know," he whispered back before squeezing tighter. I smiled as I focused on his thumb gently circling the back of my hand. When we finally reached the tent, Rainier held the tent flap open, and I started to walk through, dropping his hand. He held on a moment longer than I did, and I considered not letting go.

It made no sense that inside the tent, much smaller than the cave, I felt safe rather than crowded, but such was the nature of the beast. It especially made no sense that it wouldn't feel crowded, considering it was. Thyra, Dewalt, Lavenia, and Mairin were scattered about the tent, comfortably chattering with each other. Dewalt was lying on my pallet, so I slid his legs off as I sat down on the end of it. He sat up and shoved a bottle of wine into my hands. Rainier still stood in the opening, surveying his friends in front of him. Mairin and Lavenia were sharing their own bottle of wine, sitting on one of their pallets, while Thyra stretched out on another. I took a long swig from the bottle before holding it out, watching Rainier.

"A thousand men from Skos alone, Rainier. Declan wants war." Dewalt nodded to the bottle I held out. "Drink."

Rainier took a few steps across to me, taking the bottle out of my hand before tilting it back, taking a long draw of it before he spoke. "Why are we all here? Our tent is bigger."

"I go where she tells me." Dewalt nodded toward Lavenia, who seemed to be having an intense conversation with Mairin, both of their heads tilted toward the other. I knew I still needed to talk to her, but Mairin seemed occupied. I wondered if I was reading more into it than I should have been, but I had the distinct impression the rest of us were intruding.

"Scoot." Rainier walked over to the end of my pallet where I sat and bent over, putting a hand to the side of my thigh and pushing me closer to Dewalt. I slid, glad to break the contact sending shocks ricocheting through me, and he sat down next to me.

"Do you think it will come to war, or do you think Cyran's coup will be successful?" I sat back a bit so Dewalt and Rainier could see each other, and the three of us could talk with ease, passing the bottle back and forth.

"It is always war with men like my father," Thyra slurred. I noticed the bottle she held wasn't full of wine but something clear.

The four of us got lost in a long conversation about the events to come. The Cascade had strong defenses, but Rainier still worried about a full-scale assault, even with our advance notice from Cyran. The three of us finished our bottle of wine quickly while Thyra nursed her own bottle of what I assumed was something much stronger. Dewalt went to fetch another bottle of wine, and Thyra peered at Rainier with surprisingly steady eyes.

"Nythyr will not ally with us." Her eyes flickered over to me for a second, and I understood her meaning. If he called things off with Keeva, there would be consequences. I threw my head back and finished the remains of the bottle in my hand. This was why I'd said all the things I said before.

"Queen Nereza made her decision when she opened the pass to Olag. Nythyr has always remained neutral; I would not have expected that to change either way." His eyes flashed a warning to her, and I was grateful when Dewalt came back in, passing the new bottle to me first. I drank for too long and coughed a bit after, wiping my mouth with my sleeve. Rainier turned to me and grinned.

"Do you remember when D shot wine out of his nose?" Dewalt groaned, and I started laughing so hard I started coughing again. Rainier reached behind me, lightly rubbing my back to get me through it. I burned from his touch.

"Do you remember when you ripped your pants and exposed your ass cheeks at Ravemont?" Dewalt retorted, and Rainier's laugh boomed enough to interrupt Lavenia and Mairin's conversation, the former grinning with the memory while Mairin wore a dreamy expression.

"You should have seen Lady Highclere's face when he came inside. She was mortified. How about when Emma fell into the creek?" She offered.

"Hey! Lucia pushed me—how does that count?" We were all laughing by then, enjoying reminiscing. I learned some interesting stories from Thyra about Dewalt and Rainier's escapades before Dewalt bonded with Lavenia. Apparently, the two of them had no qualms about sharing rooms while they participated in activities with women. I groaned, feeling an ugly, stunted emotion in the pit of my stomach.

"We grew out of it," Dewalt offered, and Rainier averted his eyes. The fact he felt embarrassed kept the monster within me at bay.

Mairin and I told stories about different patients we'd treated, including a more harrowing tale about a child stuck underneath a wagon. Everyone listened with rapt attention, waiting with bated breath until we revealed we had saved the little boy. Thyra whooped in elation while the others sighed in relief. It felt like it had been hours of talking when Thyra finally rose, unsteady on her feet.

"Goodnight, my friends. Sleep well." When she got up to leave, it drew my attention to Lavenia and Mairin behind her. They were wrapped up in each other, legs tangled and seeming content. I glanced at Dewalt, unsure if he'd be jealous or what kind of limits he and Lavenia set with each other, but it seemed whatever boundary Lavenia and Mairin may have had was weakening. He watched from across the tent as the two of them exchanged a small kiss, and I saw him adjust the way he sat. I blushed when I realized why and looked away, trying not to see something I didn't want to. Instead, I found the striking face of the man beside me. I studied Rainier as he glanced past me, realizing what I had just figured out. His hand moved, and I realized with a start it had been resting on my thigh. I hadn't noticed, or, more likely, it felt so natural I hadn't cared. He leaned in—sparkling, green gaze catching mine—and I thought, for a moment, he was going to kiss me. Here, in front of everyone. I didn't know if I would have stopped him, either.

"I think it's our cue to leave." His breath was hot on my ear, his tone a dark promise. I swallowed, nodding. Judging by how intensely Dewalt and Lavenia were making eye contact while she kissed Mairin, I felt like it was long past time for us to leave. The three of us stood as one, and Rainier pulled me to the entrance of the tent. I heard Dewalt behind me make a beeline straight to Lavenia. I couldn't help but grin.

The temperature in the tent had been much higher than that of the surrounding cave, and I'd left my cloak on my pallet, so I was shivering when we stepped out. Rainier turned to me with a sideways smile, and I started laughing nervously. I hadn't exactly been around anyone who acted on desire so brazenly, and part of me felt scandalized. Rainier chuckled before he noticed my shiver and took his cloak off, wrapping it around me.

"They're probably going to be a while." His grin was boyish as he rubbed his hands up and down my arms over the cloak, warming me up. "Fire or tent?" He

nodded in turn toward each option. I could tell by the look in his eyes, the dark fire blazing underneath the green, which place he wanted me to choose. So, I did.
 "Tent."

CHAPTER 29

When we walked in, Rainier moved straight to his pallet and sat down, pulling his boots off. I noticed someone had laid a rug on the ground, and it was more cozy than the last time I slept in his tent. I paused, lingering in the entryway before walking over to the chair sitting at the small table in the back. "Why do you have this in here?" My finger traced over the table as I lowered myself down into the seat.

"Sometimes I have to write correspondence, and someone along the way thought it would be a good idea."

"Isn't it terribly bulky to worry about bringing on a horse?"

"Normally, we have the wagon, but since it got left behind with Nana, we made it work. It folds though, watch." He walked over and lifted the top of the table up, showing me how the legs folded together and the top folded down. When he put it back together, he took a step back, and I looked him over. He still wore the burgundy shirt from before, buttons still unfastened at the top. His black pants seemed a bit different than the ones he'd been wearing during our trip. These were smoother almost, the fabric not as rough as most breeches. I wondered if those were part of the capital fashions he spoke about. My gaze drifted down to his bare feet.

"Your feet are still huge." I peered back up to his face as his eyes lit up, and I watched his beautiful, full mouth spread in a smile.

"Feet don't tend to shrink, do they?" He knelt in front of me, pulling one of mine toward him and unlacing my boots. The light danced across his features, and I memorized his face. Gods, I'd missed him. The fire popped in the brazier, and my eyes were drawn to it before moving back to him.

My twin flame. I didn't know if I believed it. The soul I had found in past lives, in this one, and would find again in the next. I almost couldn't catch my breath thinking about it. Aonara and Ciarden were the first twin flames, lightness and darkness. Two halves of one whole. There were so few recorded instances of twin flames they'd become more legend than anything. The thought that Rainier and I were predestined by the gods was overwhelming, partially why I hadn't believed Mairin. But I was beginning to, the more I thought about it. We had found each other again, and I didn't plan to let him go. It seemed as if the Nythyrian alliance had already broken, and I wondered if, perhaps without it, I wouldn't be too much of a threat to his ascension. With no possibility of an alliance, did he have to bond and marry for Vesta? Or could he do it for himself? Make his own choices? I pushed the thought aside when I remembered my divinity. I might not be a threat, but I'd never be suitable. I wasn't sure when I planned to tell him what Mairin had told me. Part of me wasn't sure if I should tell him at all.

He pulled my boot off and eyed at my foot.

"No, they certainly don't shrink. Before you know it, we'll be sharing shoes." I kicked at him with my socked foot, and he chuckled, holding it tighter as he began to rub it. I let out a small groan, and he pushed on the same spot again harder, eyes darkening as he looked up at me. It felt delightful. He sat back, getting comfortable with his legs crossed, and pulled off my other boot.

"Do they do that often?" Another groan crossed my lips as he slid a thumb down the arch of my foot, working on spots I didn't even know were sore. He slid his hand up the back of my leg, working my tight muscles into putty.

"Who? Lavenia and Dewalt?" I nodded. "Do they have sex often? Or include—" I cut him off, feeling the flush going up my neck, matching the redness in my face from the wine.

"They were just so open about it." We knew what they were doing and had to leave to give them privacy. It was strange to me, foreign. I couldn't imagine anyone being so open about that.

"It's part of being bonded. It craves the connection—the mind, body, and soul. Dewalt and Lavenia are extremely in tune with their mind and soul. They've somehow become more annoying since they bonded. Sometimes they even finish each other's sentences." He smiled but didn't look up, full attention on my feet. I hoped they didn't smell too badly. "So, they don't feel the need of the body as often, but from what I understand, when they do, it's hard to resist."

"They've always been annoying together." We laughed because it was true. Dewalt was Rainier's best friend, but he spent almost as much time with Lavenia and Lucia all those years ago. I'd always been separate, and I wondered if it was part of why I didn't fight to stay in their lives. Rainier slid his hands down and pulled at my socks, his fingertips warm on my cold skin, and I relished his touch.

"When we travel, it gets harder to maintain their bond. If we stayed, they wouldn't have stopped." He cringed, exhaling on a shudder, clearly speaking from experience.

"Oh, no!" I laughed, "I'm sure you learned the signs quickly, then."

Rainier stilled, holding my foot in his hand, and his expression turned confused before he pulled back, lifting my leg. My mouth dropped in horror when I realized my mistake. I'd drank too much wine, and I wasn't thinking. I tried to pull out of his grasp, but he only tightened his grip.

"What the fuck is this, Emmeline?" His gaze was murderous, and I shut my eyes, exhaling slowly.

"I told you I ran away." My voice was a whisper. He lowered my leg and picked up the other to examine the twin scar on the bottom of my other foot. He traced his fingertip over the raised skin—a filigreed letter C encased in a circle.

C for Calvert.

"Faxon branded you." I kept my eyes closed, finding it hard to breathe while overwhelmed by his thunderous heart. I took a deep breath and opened my eyes, finding him watching me carefully.

"I tried to run the night before. I only made it a quarter of the way to Olistos before his brothers found me, and we were closer to the Calvert home. Faxon wasn't there—he'd gone south to search for me—but his father told me if I wanted to wander like livestock, then..." I gestured to my feet.

C for cattle.

Rainier's gaze smoldered, dangerous fire dancing within.

"And when Faxon found out?"

"What about it?"

"What did he do, Emmeline?" His temple was throbbing.

"Nothing." He nodded as if I'd affirmed his suspicions. "Well, that's not exactly true. He was glad of the inconspicuous placement." A low growl rumbled from his throat.

"Have you tried to heal them?" He resumed rubbing my feet, gentle but firm, the same way he had before taking my socks off, paying no attention to the scars marring them.

"I've tried a few times since the onaán, but I think it's been too long. I'm sorry." I was whispering again, afraid for some reason I couldn't quite understand.

"Divine hell, why are you sorry?"

"I don't know. I should have listened to you back then. If I had your help, things might have been different."

He didn't speak for a while, brow furrowed as he watched his hands work.

"Maybe. But I'm here now, quite literally at your feet." He gave me a soft smile before he pulled each of my feet up and delicately kissed my ankle bones, the softness making something in my chest hurt.

"At my feet making questionable decisions. Those things have been in socks and boots for days." I pulled them away laughing, glad for the excuse to provide some levity. I felt a bit lighter now that he knew I hadn't entirely given up back then. I hoped we could move on to lighter conversation, the heavy topics making me emotional. I was warm, flushed with embarrassment and emotion, and I moved to take his cloak off.

"Not cold anymore?" I shook my head, and he stood up, taking the cloak from me and hanging it up.

"Do you wish you were bonded?" I blurted it out and slapped my hand to my mouth the second after I asked it. So much for lighter conversation. The wine had loosened my tongue more than I wished.

"Doesn't every conduit?" He countered as he turned back to me, his eyes narrowed a bit and his face guarded.

"Then why haven't you? It's not like you haven't had the opportunity." I grimaced when I realized how pathetic I sounded.

"I think you know why I haven't, Em." He crossed his arms as he stared down at me, his jaw clenched.

"That's bullshit, Rain. You're trying to tell me you waited for sixteen years? Because of me? You can't just go around saying things like that to me. It's confusing."

"There's nothing to be confused about." He shrugged when I cast a glare in his direction. "To my credit, you're the one who keeps bringing it up. You brought it up at the lake, and you brought it up now. I've been content to just do and say what feels right with you. You're the one complicating things, not me."

I almost retorted with a biting remark, but something stopped me, and I stilled. I sat there for a moment and thought back. He did have a point. Past his initial explanation at my home the other night, he hadn't said any of the things that confused me or made me think about us or the future unless I pushed him. And if he was telling the truth, he hadn't performed the ritual because of me. I didn't know how to feel. I sat there for a few moments, thinking, while he quietly watched me.

"Is there any more wine?" I finally blurted out, embarrassed. I liked the warmth the wine gave me and the confidence. I decided I wanted to stop thinking, stop complicating things, and just be in the moment with the man who may or may not be the other half of me. The man who had dropped everything for me and my child. The man who had included me in every decision regarding her. The man I'd missed every day since Lucia died. He chuckled, a half-smile on his face.

"No, I don't have any wine in here. I could go find some if you want me to?"

"No, no, that's alright."

"I do have a bottle of spirits. I don't know how much more you should drink, though, if you don't want to feel like hell tomorrow."

"I've never tried. Does it taste like wine?"

Rainier snorted. "It tastes like fire. It's not like wine—you don't drink it slowly. Quick, small sips."

"It burns?" It seemed fitting.

"Mhm, a little." He went over to a pile of his belongings in the corner of the tent and pulled out a bottle of amber liquid.

"Is that what Dewalt poured on my arm the other night? That certainly burned." I cringed, remembering how badly it hurt.

"Oh, I hope not. That bottle was a clear liquor, not my favorite. This is the good stuff." His expression grew serious before he turned to me. "My rifting won't fail you again." I cocked my head, not sure what he was getting at.

"With the tírrúil. I forgot you're not exactly helpless." He gave me a sheepish smile. "I thought I was about to see you torn to shreds so I couldn't form the rift. You saw I was struggling; that's why you ran, right?"

"I didn't want you thinking it was your fault. If I was going to die in front of you, I wanted you to blame my actions, not yours." I laughed a bit, but his expression was somber.

"I'd have blamed myself either way. But you didn't die. You took down a tírrúil three times your size, ran off and healed my soldiers, all before healing yourself. You're a warrior, and somehow, I forgot. I won't forget again." He exhaled quickly and shook his head. I didn't exactly feel like a warrior, but it didn't seem like a point to argue. He squinted down at the bottle in his hands, turning it around before opening it and tilting his head back, taking a quick sip before turning it upright. Giving a little exhale, he wiped his mouth off with the back of his free hand. "Yep, still burns. Would you like to try?"

What the hell, why not?

"Maybe just a little." He gave me his crooked smile, but his eyes were dangerous as he crossed the distance between us. I made to take the bottle from him, but he put a hand on my shoulder.

"Tilt your head back." I did as I was told as Rainier walked around the chair behind me. My breathing stopped when his warm hand went to my throat, tilting my head back farther. The gentle but firm touch made heat flare through me before the alcohol even touched my lips, curling tightly low in my stomach. His gaze met mine before I closed my eyes and opened my mouth, wondering if I'd imagined the lust and fire in his eyes. The alcohol hit the back of my throat, a small amount, and I swallowed. He was right. It did taste like fire.

I exhaled quickly as the position of his hand on my neck changed, and then he was bent over me, his mouth on mine, the heat of what we'd drank burning my lips and my throat. The taste of that fire propelled me, and I pushed up out of the chair, turning my body as I did to keep his lips on mine. He threw the chair between us out of the way and closed the distance, pulling my body against his. His desperation to get to me, the aggression of his movement, the ease in which he tossed the chair—all of it caused heat to pool between my legs. I stood on tiptoe to kiss him as I started fumbling with the buttons on his shirt. I wasn't thinking, wasn't analyzing. I was doing what he'd said, doing what felt right. His hands were on either side of my neck and in my hair as he kissed me, my braid unraveling with each movement. His tongue twined with mine, and I let out a small groan. The buttons were taking too long. I needed to feel him, to taste him.

A sound remarkably close to a growl came out of my mouth as I gave up and pulled his shirt out from his pants, trying to yank it up his body. I would rip it if I had to. I felt him laugh on my lips before he pulled away, finishing the buttons and removing it. He didn't have a chance to set the shirt down before I was on him again, and I vaguely heard it fall to the ground. I stood on my tiptoes, kissing across the swells of his chest as I pushed him back toward the pallet. My hands slid over his warm skin, and I couldn't help but marvel at his body. He was gorgeous, built like a dream. He smelled good, and I realized he had to have his own soap, likely washing up like the girls and I did every night. I found myself wanting to know all of those little routines—what kind of soap he used, which shoe he put on first, how often he shaved. I'd lived for so long without him that now I'd gotten a taste? I wanted more than scraps.

I wanted everything.

"Em, slow down." Rainier put his hands on my shoulders as the backs of his legs hit the pallet behind him.

"No." Despite my words and pushing him back, forcing him to sit, I paused, looking down at him, his head level with my chest. "Unless you want me to stop?"

"If you keep kissing me like this, I don't know if I can control myself." His lips were parted, and I realized he was panting a bit, his chest swelling as he breathed. I reached out and heard his heart pounding. Did I want him to control himself? I didn't know if I wanted him to hold back. I decided I didn't care. I wanted to take, and I'd do what felt good.

"Good thing I'm in control, then."

I leaned down and kissed him, both of my hands on either side of his face. He met my movements, his tongue brushing against mine in languid strokes, kissing me thoroughly, stoking the flame of my desire. When he raised his hands to my waist, I pushed him backward and slowly eased to my knees between his legs. He watched me, eyes full of lust and surprise. Perhaps I was being reckless. It didn't matter what was guiding me, just that there was a fire building inside of me I wanted to ignite. I leaned forward, kissing down his stomach, finding the wound from our duel and licking it, pressing a kiss to it afterward on my slow descent downward.

"Come here." He grasped my hand and pulled. I resisted, wanting to take my time, pressing soft kisses up his stomach and chest, climbing atop him as I did it. When I moved, he put his hands on my ass, his fingertips digging into me. I kissed up his neck and leaned down to press my lips to his mouth, grinding my hips into him. He groaned as I felt him twitch underneath me. I couldn't help but smile.

"Do you feel what you do to me?" His voice was thick as he pulled me by the hips up the length of him, rubbing against me so I'd feel just how hard I'd made him. I kissed him and rolled my body again, teasing. His hands stayed on me, pulling me over him again and again, and I wished we had on decidedly less clothing. I was panting as my mouth pushed against his, wanting to consume him, taste his fire. My fire. My flame, my heart.

"I do feel," I stopped speaking and smiled down at him, feeling the mischievous grin spread on my face. "But now I want to taste." He exhaled a sharp breath as I pulled away from him, kissing down his body with a confidence I didn't know I was capable of.

"No, Em. Not until I make you come on my tongue." His words were filthy, and they sent a shock down my body, pulsing low between my legs. He grabbed me under my arms, trying to flip me, but I stopped him.

"Let me. Please. I want to choose this. I need to make this choice." I couldn't explain it, but I needed to touch him first, explore his body without my own being a part of it. I needed to show him how much I wanted to choose him, and I needed to show myself I was capable of being the person who made decisions for my own body. That I was an active participant in this decision, not forced, not someone swept up in the pleasure, caught in a moment. That it was me who wanted it, who wanted him, and I was taking what I wanted no matter the risk.

"Are you sure?" His hands bracketed my face, looking up at me intently, understanding of my request even if he didn't know the details.

"Yes, I'm sure. I want this. Can I have it?"

His eyes softened as a smile pulled up the corners of his mouth, and he laid back. "You've always had me, Em. But you already knew that."

I stared into his eyes for a moment too long, overcome by the emotions I saw there, before I began to kiss down his body once more. I'd never done what I was about to do, but it didn't matter. Everything with Rainier came so naturally if I just let it. If I stopped fighting, stopped running. If I stopped thinking about what everything meant, I could just focus on doing what felt right. I felt a tremor go through him as my fingers slid along his waist to his pants. I undid the top button and watched his skin pebble.

He was breathless, eyes closed, as my fingertips moved tenderly to finish unfastening his breeches.

I saw the muscles in his stomach tighten as I slid my fingers in his waistband. I kissed them, following the path of curling hair which led me lower, as I pulled down his pants and undergarments as one. He lifted his hips to help, and his length finally sprang free. "Gods," I whispered it, my eyes wide. I'd never truly laid eyes on him, our previous coupling having been rushed and fumbled, not to mention how long ago it was, and I was nothing short of intimidated. He was huge, both long and thick. When our eyes met, I swore I saw a glimmer of boyish pride on his face.

"If I didn't already know I could..." I trailed off, looking at his beautiful, masculine body in the light of the flickering brazier.

"Oh, you can. I'll refresh that memory of yours," he grinned, "and show you just how perfect we fit together."

I stared at him for a moment, meeting his intoxicating desire with my own, before glancing down, my tongue darting out over my lower lip, and I grasped him firmly at the base as he groaned. He let his eyes close for a moment before propping himself up on his forearms, and his expression turned serious.

"You don't have to if you—"

My tongue cut him off, and he pushed his head back into the pallet, a hiss of pleasure escaping him. A small bead of moisture had formed on his tip, and I leaned down and licked it off. Putting my hand around his length, my fingertips not quite touching, I leaned down, maintaining eye contact with him, wanting to watch his response. When I spoke, I knew he'd feel my breath on him. "It feels right."

We watched each other as I slowly slid the tip of him into my mouth, my tongue exploring, swirling around the thick head of him. He let out a deep sigh, and his head fell backward, slack. I took my free hand and shoved on his chest, pushing him down off his forearms. He moved to put his arms behind his head, relaxed and comfortable, just like I wanted him. I slid my hand down his length, my tongue following after, feeling the velvety softness of his skin. I wasn't sure how hard to grasp him; I didn't want to hurt him. Swirling my tongue over his sensitive tip as I took him into my mouth, I watched him as my lips slid down. He was warm, and his breath had turned slow like he was focusing on every inhale and exhale. He opened his eyes to watch me and reached down, gently swiping my hair out of my face. I took that moment to slide my hand down with my lips to take more of him, slowly matching the timing of my mouth to that of my hand.

"*Fuck*," he drew out the word. His eyes closed, and I continued, sliding my hand with my mouth. "Emma," he breathed my name like a prayer.

I mumbled a reply with him inside of my mouth, and I wondered if he felt it. As I continued, I noticed his hips twitching in response. Watching him as the expression on his face grew pained, I wondered if I was squeezing too hard. I lifted my mouth off him while continuing more gently with my hand. "Am I hurting you?"

"Quite the opposite." He exhaled hard, his nostrils flaring, and I saw the desire in his eyes.

"You were just making a face. I don't—If it's not good or I'm hurting you, please tell me." I felt silly and immature, not knowing what I was doing, and the pained look on his face made my newfound confidence dwindle.

"Em, dear heart, you're not hurting me. I'm trying not to hurt you." His eyes were soft, and he reached down a hand to trace my jaw. I felt something flutter in my chest.

"You won't hurt me." At least, I didn't think he would. "I want you undone."

"I already am, Em. Every day since you came back to me."

I felt myself flush as his gaze met mine, eyes full of desire and something else I wasn't willing to identify. I leaned back down, putting him in my mouth again as I watched him. This time when his hips twitched, he let himself thrust into my mouth, and I understood why he'd been pained. He'd been trying to stop himself. Looking up at him as he pushed into my mouth, moaning my encouragement around him, I showed him he wasn't hurting me. Eagerly meeting each thrust, I loved watching him let go for me.

"You're taking my cock so well. Gods, you're beautiful."

He reached down with both hands, twining his fingers in my hair as he pushed into my mouth. I picked up the pace, sliding my mouth and hand down his length as he bucked beneath me, a deep, guttural moan coming out of him. I threw off his rhythm when I pushed myself down farther, bringing him to the back of my throat, hollowing my cheeks. He grunted, and I felt his body shake beneath me as his fingers twisted tighter in my hair, and he lost control. He pulled back and slammed into my mouth, and I groaned, loving the base need flowing through him. He did it only once more before he stopped, putting his hand on my chin, pulling me off him.

"There's no way in hell I'm going to finish before you do. Come here." His voice was rough as he started pulling on me and bringing me up his body. I straddled him and began rubbing against him, unable to stop. I didn't want to stop pleasing him; I wanted to see him lose himself. He pulled me down to his mouth, kissing me thoroughly, deeply. His tongue speared into my mouth, just like his cock had, not caring that my lips were slick and swollen from taking him.

"You have no idea how badly I want you." He threw one arm around my waist and flipped us, so I was on my back beneath him. "You have too much clothing on for what I want to do to you." He started kissing down my jaw, down my neck, and his soft lips felt amazing on my skin. But there was a tingle in the back of my head, something making me hesitate. I was nervous, and some damned part of me flashed into the memory where I'd made my vows to Faxon, and I balked. I didn't care about the vows, considering Faxon had betrayed me so thoroughly, but something about Rainier and his honor made me hesitate. My presence in his camp was scandal enough. There was so much that was imperfect to me—it didn't feel right to continue much further with him. If Dewalt hadn't interrupted, I knew I would have done exactly what Rainier said I would, but I wouldn't have been ready then like I wasn't now. I didn't want to have a single regret. I was so angry I even thought any of this with Rainier on top of me, his beautiful naked body hot and smooth against me, that I couldn't help it when I groaned aloud in frustration.

"What is it?" He pulled himself from my neck.

"Nothing. This just—I haven't—Oh, *divine hell*." There were too many things to say at once, and I was struggling. Rainier stayed where he was, hovering over me, waiting patiently. I took a deep breath. "As much as I want you, and believe me, I do—badly," His eyes flashed as I spoke, "I just don't think I'm completely ready. I haven't—" I inhaled, struggling to handle this like an adult. "What I just did, I've never even done before. I haven't done anything like this at all since before Elora was born." His eyes widened, but he didn't say anything. "And even then, it wasn't—this is different. *You* are different." I swallowed, steeling myself for the next part. "And I'm just not ready to go much further. It doesn't feel right, not yet, anyway." He put his weight on one arm next to me and rolled a bit, his hip on the pallet, but he left a leg draped over me. He didn't say anything, just studied me, and I began to feel nervous.

"I'm sorry, Rain. I just—we messed this all up once already, and I don't want to do that again."

"Don't you dare apologize, Em. When you are ready, I'm going to make up for so much lost time." His smile and the look in his eyes were a promise that brought heat low in my stomach. "We should stop."

"But you didn't finish. I don't want to stop; I just don't want to go too far." He chuckled then as he pulled my hand to his mouth and kissed it.

"You know, I wasn't planning on fucking you tonight. Not in secret. Never like that again. I won't keep you a secret to keep you." I watched as his kiss traced up my wrist. "I had no intention of it happening in a tent surrounded by my guard. I want you spread out for me in a bed, sober. Ready to hear everything I have to tell you and feel everything I have to give you when we finally make love, Em." My heart skipped and began racing through my chest.

"Then what *were* you planning on?" I barely recognized my voice, a husky whisper. He leaned forward, and I felt his length press against my leg, hard as ever, as he pressed his lips to my neck just behind my ear.

"I wanted to taste you, too." His words were a whisper, and chills chased down my body at the heat and promise behind them. He traced a finger across my collar bone before moving down my chest.

"Starting here . . ." He lightly circled my peaked nipple, already hard under my shirt, before he dragged his hand downward, circling my navel. "And here." I froze, not breathing, as he touched the part of me I was most insecure about, and I willed him to continue for a few reasons. "And finally, here." His hand slid down farther, rubbing at the seam of my breeches, and I exhaled, a light throaty sound coming out with my breath.

"Now, do you think we can remove some of these clothes?" I swallowed and nodded, barely able to function because of the low throb between my legs. Rainier's hand rested in that spot, unmoving. I decided then I needed him to move. I sat up and pulled my shirt over my head, my hair finally falling free from my braid as I moved. I laid back again, lightly tossing the shirt across my stomach. He already saw me the night of the tírrúil attack, but I was still nervous for him to see how my body had changed. It wasn't that I was ashamed of it, but I knew his memories of me were different. The body he'd wanted then was quite unlike the one I wore now. He chuckled as he rolled on top of me, my thighs opening on instinct to cradle his hips between my legs.

"That's much better." He leaned in and kissed me, his soft lips against mine a delightful contrast from his hardness pressing between my legs. He didn't linger, pushing his lips to my pulse point on my neck, tracing down, until his lips fastened onto my tight nipple. I couldn't help it when I arched off the pallet, the delightful warmth and wetness of his mouth overwhelming.

"So sensitive," he murmured as his tongue trailed to my other breast, and I nearly lost my mind when he grazed his teeth over my nipple and lightly tugged. I cried out, arching off the pallet even farther as he swirled his tongue over the small hurt. He swiped my shirt off of my stomach and continued kissing down my body.

"I hope you weren't covering up for a reason." He looked up at me, his head tilted with the question, and I felt my cheeks burn.

"You got harder, and I got softer." I gave a nervous laugh as I deflected, squeezing his biceps to illustrate my point. He studied me for a moment before he started kissing my stomach, dragging his tongue over me between kisses.

"I love your soft." Another kiss. "You don't have any idea how much I've fucking needed your soft." I felt my throat constrict. I didn't know what I expected him to say, but it wasn't that. I could tell that our time apart had hardened him to a degree, in more ways than one, and I knew he referred to more than my body. I wanted to give that to him—my gentle, my tender. And the fact that he needed it? I was only more inclined to give everything to him. I slid my hands over his muscled shoulders, the smooth warmth of his back under my fingertips. He reached for the button on my pants as he peered up to me, waiting. I gave a nod as I felt my hands start to shake.

"I want to hear you say it." Though his eyes were dark in the firelight, I could see them simmer with lust and mischief.

"Please." My whisper was half-choked.

"Please, *what*?" He bent down to lick around my navel, and I inhaled sharply.

"Please touch me." I nearly moaned the words.

"That's a good girl." His answering grin was feral as he unbuttoned my pants, sliding his fingertips into my waistband and hooking his fingers in with my undergarments, pulling both down my body. He sat back as I lifted my hips, and he pulled them off over my feet. I delicately laid my legs on either side of him as his eyes traced a path down my body, roaming from my collarbones past my breasts, my soft belly, and down to that spot between my legs, spread bare before him. I watched as he knelt over me, the shadows of the firelight flickering over his body, his arousal apparent. He was everything I'd ever dreamed and more. I watched as his hand wrapped around the base of his cock, and he slid it up his length once and again a second time. I exhaled a shaky breath as he leaned over me, his hands pinned on either side of my body before he lowered himself, so he was pressed against me, naked skin on naked skin.

"You are the hardest lesson in self-control." I felt him reach down and rub himself against me, my wetness making him glide easily over me, every muscle in my body tightening as he did it. I considered changing my mind, considered grabbing him and sliding him inside me, and when he started kissing down my body again, I felt almost disappointed. He eased backward until he was on his knees on the ground, and he put a strong hand under each one of my thighs as he pulled me closer, almost to the edge of the pallet. I felt so exposed, open to him, and my heart rocketed through my chest. I let out a small sound of surprise, and he chuckled, the smile on his face so handsome. It didn't seem fair that I was destined for him, that the man in front of me was meant to be mine, forever. And all he got in return was me. I would count my blessings for the rest of my days if Mairin was right.

He wordlessly hooked one of my legs over his shoulder and pushed down on my other knee, spreading me wide open. His eyes met mine as if giving me another chance to stop him.

"Please." I pleaded again, a low whine rising from inside me. He grinned then as he wasted no more time. He used one hand to spread me open as his tongue moved down my slick center, hard and claiming. There was nothing gentle about the way his tongue moved over me, and I let out a whimper of pleasure.

"Gods, I've been dying for the taste of you. You're so wet for me." His tone was almost reverent. I felt his breath on the most intimate part of me and nearly trembled. He turned, kissing my inner thigh, tracing his lips up to where my leg met more sensitive areas. Nibbling and sucking the sensitive skin, he moved his way back to where I needed him, gently sliding his tongue between the delicate flesh. He was taking his time. Dragging his tongue back down, he circled my entrance for only a second before he pushed in deeply. A strangled moan burst from my lips as he feasted on me.

"Am I the first to taste you?" He paused only for a second before his tongue continued its torture, pushing deep into me, deeper than I thought he'd be able to, and I groaned.

"Yes." My voice was ragged, breathless. No one had touched me like this, made me feel like this. What he was doing felt almost decadent; too much for me to handle but too good to let him stop.

"Mmm, a shame. Not that I mind." His tongue skimmed up the length of me again. "You taste exquisite. You taste like mine. If I'd gotten a taste of you back then, I would have died without you." His words were a growl against my sensitive skin, and I shuddered against him.

He lowered his mouth to my clit and gently sucked. I let out a loud cry as I dug my hands into his hair. He traced his tongue from base to top again before focusing solely on that sensitive spot, sucking and nibbling ever so gently at the bundle of nerves until my eyes were rolling back in my head. I couldn't stop the moans that kept coming from me, and I was almost embarrassed. Nothing had ever felt like this before. Rain's encouraging noises vibrated against me, and it made it harder to stay quiet.

He stopped for a moment while he adjusted our bodies, bringing my other leg over his shoulder as well, pulling me even closer to him. I whimpered at his absence, and he looked up, grinning like a man possessed, his lips glistening in the light, before he returned his tongue to my clit. I pushed my head back and closed my eyes, luxuriating in the sensation. He used one hand to keep me spread open as he traced tiny circles on that spot, my legs twitching to the rhythm he wrote on my body.

"Give me those eyes, Em."

I opened them, finding him watching me. He held my gaze, tongue still working me, as he slid one finger inside me. I cried out again and lifted my hips in answer. I couldn't control myself as I began undulating, grinding on his hand. I couldn't help it; I needed more. Wanted more. I felt him huff a laugh against me, and another moan broke past my lips. Release began to build low in my stomach and spine as warmth spread through my body. I bucked against his hand and face as he slid his finger into me, curling upwards into a spot that made me see stars. My voice came out a yell when I said his name, consumed. The fire was building throughout my veins, and I knew I couldn't take much more.

"I want to hear you say my name again, just like that. Come for me, Em." I felt him adjust again; it looked as if he grabbed himself, but I couldn't see to be sure, let alone focus on much more than his tongue on me. His mouth was still there, nibbling out a beat on my clit he matched with his fingers as he slid one more inside me. I rolled my hips, moving on his hand with reckless abandon, pushing upwards against his mouth. I saw the muscles in his shoulder flex and realized he was matching the beat on his own body. There was nothing more arousing than watching him pleasure himself while he pleasured me. I felt white-hot all over, and I grabbed my breasts, squeezing tight, melding pain and rapture, as I ebbed over the edge.

"Divine fucking hell, Rain!" My voice was a shout, and I couldn't stop myself as I nearly screamed, the orgasm crashing over me. Trying to keep my eyes open as I watched him, I felt them roll back as I arched off the pallet. He kept licking me and slamming his fingers into me as I moaned through the shockwaves, feeling myself pulse around his fingers. He exhaled hard on my center and let out a guttural sound as he finished, collapsing onto me.

The world stopped spinning, and everything went in slow motion as I laid there in the throes of ecstasy, too exhausted and sated to move. His head rested on my thigh for a moment or an hour, I couldn't be sure, before he started kissing up my leg, and I shuddered. He stood then, and I watched his ass flex as he walked to his pack, where he grabbed a cloth and poured water on it from his canteen. Walking back, he pressed it to me, gently cleaning where he'd licked and where I'd become slick for him. I was still so sensitive I jerked a bit, and his touch became even more gentle, a small smile on his mouth, almost smug. Instead of my usual desire to humble him, I smiled back, exhaling as I watched him, in awe of the man he'd become. Part of me hurt, knowing I could have had those smiles all these years, this intimacy, this fire. I scooted farther up onto the pallet and pulled a blanket over me, suddenly aware of my nakedness. He cleaned himself up and knelt down where he'd been a few moments ago, cleaning the rug as well. I felt myself flush, thinking about the mess he made. I clamped my legs together tightly, remembering how it felt when he rubbed his cock on me. I needed to control myself. He finally put a damper on the brazier before he returned, crawling onto the pallet next to me and sliding underneath the blanket, his warm skin against mine.

He pulled me toward him and tucked me into his chest, kissing me on my forehead as he ran his fingers through my hair. I pushed a leg in between his, entwining with his warm body, wrapping my arm around him as I delicately traced my fingers across his back.

"I don't want to add to what you're going through; I don't want to complicate things for you. But I can't—*won't*—go the rest of my life without doing that again. I hope you know that." He gave me another smile, but I could tell it was a question he'd love for me to answer in time. But I wasn't ready yet.

I didn't have words, so instead, I tilted my head up and kissed him, soft and sweet. He had one arm tucked under me, his fingertips gently twirling my hair, while the other arm traced designs on my lower back, just like what I was doing to him. He kissed me back gently, and we both fell asleep like that with our lips on each other.

CHAPTER 30

The next morning, I woke up pressed to Rainier's chest, his heartbeat and breathing slow and steady. It was still dark since our tents were in the cave, but I could hear the soft sounds of the camp waking up. I had the slightest ache behind my eyes, but nothing worth mentioning. The blanket had slid down around our hips, but considering how warm we were, there was no reason to pull it back up. In fact, it was almost too warm. I gently rolled over, keeping his arm around my waist as I turned. He gave a low rumble and pulled me back against him.

"I'm sorry. I didn't mean to wake you," I whispered as I wiggled playfully against him.

"I wouldn't do that unless you want my tongue inside you again." His voice was a low growl as he began nuzzling my neck and ear, and I clenched my thighs together tightly, feeling my body flush. His hand on my waist slid up and cupped my breast, and what he'd said started to sound less and less like a threat. I felt him harden against my backside, and I inhaled a sharp breath.

"Who says I don't want that?" I felt brazen, the confidence of the night before still there, but it felt almost dirty talking like that. He groaned quietly and adjusted his body, the arm underneath me coming up to cup my other breast, gently pinching and rolling my nipple, and I let out a soft moan.

A throat cleared, and it wasn't Rainier's.

I shrieked as I opened my eyes and saw Dewalt standing at the entrance of the tent, staring down at us. I dimly realized he was standing only in his undergarments as the blanket was thrown higher, covering me. I rolled over quickly, pressing my chest against Rainier, who shook with silent laughter. I smacked his chest in frustration. I was thankful the light was low, the brazier barely embers, and the sunlight hadn't reached too far back into the cave.

"Why aren't you wearing pants?" Rainier called out to his friend, talking to him as if he weren't just touching me that way in front of the man.

"Things got a little intense last night. My pants did not survive." Dewalt replied as I heard him rustling around on his side of the tent. "Sorry, I didn't hear anything, so I thought you were both still asleep. Evidently, I was wrong." I could hear the smirk in his voice, and I cringed, feeling my face flush. It was bad enough he had witnessed anything, and now he was apologizing for it. I wished he'd just stop talking altogether and leave.

"She was much louder last night." Rainier chuckled deviously, and I smacked him on the chest before I pinched his nipple. "Ow!" He laughed as he grabbed my hand in his, pulling it to his lips.

"I know." Dewalt's voice told me exactly what he meant.

"Divine hell, get *out*!" I shouted as Rainier started laughing again.

"Alright, alright. Let me pull my pants up, woman." A moment later, I heard the tent flap open and shut. I bolted upright, still naked, and looked around for my shirt, irritation flooding through me and into my voice.

"Did you know he was standing there?"

"No, I was focused elsewhere."

"Well, I know you both used to—to do things in the same room as each other, so I feel I should make it clear I am not interested in that."

"Nor am I. Did you not feel me throw the blanket over you?" I found my shirt and tugged it over my head, shooting a glare at him over my shoulder when he sat up.

"Hey, come here." His voice was soft as he put a hand on my jaw, turning me toward him, a smile playing across his lips. "I'm just happy we don't have to hide with them. I don't want you to be a secret. I know we have to be discreet for now, but after I talk to Keeva, no more secrets." I felt my face soften as something in my chest tightened. I needed to talk to Mairin, so I could tell him what she'd told me. I didn't like keeping secrets either. He leaned forward and kissed me gently, moving his hand to splay across my back, and I felt my breath catch again. It was all too good to be true. I pulled away, knowing a smile lit my face.

I searched the room and spotted the rest of my clothing. Rainier got up and walked to his pack, and I froze, watching every muscle, every divot and harsh curve of his body. I didn't move as he stepped into undershorts, a form-fitting garment that only went part-way down his thigh. I didn't stop staring as he stepped into his pants or as he shrugged on a shirt. When he turned around and started doing his buttons, I was still staring. He glanced down at me, and his eyebrows raised, watching me sitting there, still half-naked, enraptured.

"I need my pack." I blurted out dumbly. He chuckled and finished buttoning his shirt as he walked over, leaning down to kiss my forehead.

"I'll get it."

A few moments later, he came back, setting down what I needed in front of me, with my cloak laying across it. "As much as I want to stay here and watch you get dressed, I have to make my rounds. Ride next to me today?" I nodded, an easy smile on my face despite the tightening in my chest. I wondered when the ache would stop or if I'd always feel this way. Would I always ache for the missing time? Would his smile and affection for me always make my heart sore?

He tidied up the corner where he stored various items, and I couldn't miss the shudder when he picked up the bottle of liquor from last night. I felt the same, though the heat and taste of it helped push me to take what I wanted. I didn't regret it.

He left a moment later, sending a small smile my way. I put on fresh undergarments and the breeches from yesterday before I started pulling a brush through my hair. I was braiding it, trying to imitate the ones Thyra wore, when I heard my name from outside the tent.

"Come in." Mairin and Lavenia entered, both wearing grins that irritated me more than they should have.

"Have fun last night?" Lavenia winked, and the smirk on her face was more than enough to annoy me.

"I don't know, did *you*?" Two could play that game.

"Don't tease her, Ven." It was strange to hear Mairin use her nickname, but shouldn't have been surprising. "We heard how much fun she had—no need to ask her." I leveled a glare at the two of them as they grinned back.

"Did you two need something?" Lavenia threw her head back and laughed while Mairin gave me an apologetic smile. I narrowed my eyes on her. "Actually, I need to talk to you." Mairin nodded, and when I turned and gave a look to Lavenia, she took the hint.

"I'll go grab some food for us." And she was gone.

"Tell me everything." I stood up, crossing my arms over my chest as I started to pace.

"Um, well, I like her a lot." Confusion flooded me before I realized what she was saying, and I snapped at her.

"Gods damn, not about that." I saw her face though, and I softened, feeling like an ass. "I'm sorry, that was shit of me. I do want to hear about it; please tell me. Gods, I'm sorry." Mairin gave me a small smile, so out of place on her normal obnoxiously grinning face.

"There's not much to tell. I enjoy her company a lot. And Dewalt's too, to my surprise. They're...easy. Uncomplicated." I nodded, knowing she spoke true.

Dewalt and Lavenia seemed to have an uncanny way of finding out what worked for them and doing it, not worrying about anything else. They'd always been that way. It didn't matter how it worked, just that it worked for them, and they were happy. "You should try being uncomplicated. It's nice." She smiled, and I laughed.

"About that. What exactly do you know about twin flames? I—I'm not sure what it means. Are you certain about us?" She tilted her head to the side, watching me with eyes a lighter shade of green than Rainier's, and the thought of him sent a small ache through me.

"I should have told you that first day, but I didn't know if you wanted to hear it. I was trying to gauge how you'd react, if you'd even be open to the idea. It's hard to explain, but I can try." She studied me, and I nodded. "Everyone has their own unique aura which exists on a spectrum of color and light, no two exactly alike. When you were dueling with him, your auras were mingling and expanding, and all I could see was blazing gold behind you. I've never seen two souls exist on the same exact spectrum until that day with the two of you. And when I say never, I mean never. Ever since I met him, whenever I see one of you two, there's this ... tug, in my mind. If I see him, I picture you, and the opposite holds true. That's never happened before." I took a deep breath as she continued. "I'm sure you've heard the legends, and not a single one is exactly right. Aonara and Ciarden were twin flames, drawn to each other. They were mirrors—their flaws and strengths perfect counterparts."

"Then why did they kill each other?"

Mairin snorted. "Many believe that's part of the story the legends get wrong. They didn't kill each other; they chose to *contain* each other, for lack of a better word. Or one was killed, and the other could not live without them. Some say twin flames are reincarnations of the gods, but I don't buy it. Especially after seeing how clumsy you are." She grinned, and I smiled back in agreement. Believing we were reincarnations of the gods was not going to happen. "Either way, your souls *are* connected, *have been* connected, and *will be* connected. What you choose to do with that?" She shrugged. "It's certainly something of consequence."

"Lady Emmeline, you need to come outside the cave." It took me a moment to place the voice. The boy must have been right on the other side of the tent. I wondered if he heard our conversation.

"Just a moment, Dickey!" I called back, wanting to finish my conversation with Mairin.

"Prince Rainier bade me bring you immediately, my lady." I frowned at Mairin as I grabbed my cloak off of my pack and put it on. A moment later, I was outside the tent as Dickey led me to the front of the cave.

"Is someone hurt, Dickey? What happened?" I was worried, wondering what the cause for Dickey's stress could be. He sounded anxious.

"Yes, someone is hurt, but—" He broke off as we neared the edge of the cave, and I saw a small group standing just outside. Faces I recognized turned toward me, and I found Rainier's immediately. He seemed angry and pained, and I stopped short as I noticed something on the ground at his feet. Something moaning in pain. I took a few more steps, confused why no one was helping the person on the ground.

"Is he alright? What happened?" I looked down at the man on the ground, his face swollen beyond comprehension. I knelt beside him, about to heal his face, when I pulled my hands back like I'd been burned.

It was Faxon.

When I realized who the man was, I lost control of my body and ran. I found myself in Rainier's tent, searching for water, something to keep my stomach at bay. I hadn't yet eaten, and I could feel the urge to vomit. As I ran, I heard Mairin yell out to me, but Rainier advised her to give me a moment. I silently thanked him as I put his canteen to my lips.

"My lady?" I was surprised to hear Thyra's voice, and I opened the flap more out of confusion than anything.

"The prince decided I should tell you the facts because I do not know either you or your husband and will not influence you in any way." She gestured to the pallet for me to join her, and we sat.

I was a bit confused, wishing he was here with me. From what she'd said, it seemed like this was Rainier offering me a choice. He was allowing me to decide and take Faxon's fate into my own hands. I resented him at that moment, wishing he would make the decision for me.

"He was found wandering this morning near the outskirts of our watch perimeter. We did not find any other tracks or impressions of anyone else. It is as if he simply appeared." She pressed a small envelope into my hand, sealed with a crest I didn't recognize. "This was in his pocket."

He is your problem now.

Cyran sent him back to me? Why? He had to know how I felt. Was this some kind of sick gift? Had he tired of the man as well? Knowing Cyran cared about Elora, I wondered if she knew what Faxon had done. Had the princeling sent him away to protect her?

"The moment he was discovered, we brought him to Prince Rainier as he made his rounds. He did not speak to anyone. The prince felt compelled to interrogate him with his fists until he fell to the ground. Once he fell, he moaned your name." I sucked in a deep breath. Rain did say he would kill my husband; it would seem the promise was due for collection.

"Was he asking for me?" My stomach roiled.

"No asking, just moaning. I believe he was beaten before he was brought to us. His face was a mess, and his shirt was covered in dried blood. I don't know if the prince made much of a difference when he hit him, to be honest. Princess Lavenia attempted to compel him, and nothing happened. Dewalt feels they may have used a mindbreaker. He has not responded to any questions since he arrived, other than to cry when asked about you." I made a face, disgusted. Did he even know I was here? Had Cyran told him he was delivering him to me? If the man knew what was good for him, he wouldn't be asking for me. I was the last person he should want to see. As far as the mindbreaker aspect of Thyra's news, I wasn't sure I agreed with Dewalt. What were the odds Cyran even had a mindbreaker? I found it unlikely, considering most were hunted down and executed after the Great War.

"The prince bid me explain your options. Execution or imprisonment, he has left it up to you. If you choose execution, he will personally ensure the task is completed in a manner you deem appropriate."

I studied the letter in my hands. My problem now, my problem *always*. That was all Faxon had ever been—my problem. I wasn't sure what punishment I wanted, but I knew I wanted answers. Thyra left the tent, and I had a few moments to myself. I wanted to know more before I decided, the situation different than I anticipated. Taking a deep breath, I stood up, stretching to my full height before making my way back outside. Seeking out Rainier's eyes, I was disappointed when he refused to look at me. There was a moan coming from the lump on the ground, and I couldn't bring myself to care, almost wishing Rainier would have finished him off with his fists. Honestly, after he learned about the brands last night, I was surprised he didn't. Dewalt and Lavenia shared a grim look as Mairin approached me.

"What do you want to do?" Her hand was comforting on my shoulder. I put my own over my mouth as I stared down at the thin and bloodied body of the man I'd once called my husband. He moaned and writhed on the ground as he rolled over, allowing me to see the mottled bruises on his face. I glanced over at Rainier again, and he averted his eyes. He wasn't his normal, overbearing self, and I found it unsettling.

When I imagined seeing Faxon again, I expected him to be himself, healthy and capable. I expected to scream at him, yell at him, and then slice his throat. What I didn't expect was this blubbering mess on the ground in front of me. The hatred for him still simmered deep in my body, but underneath, there was something surprisingly like pity. I was caught in a difficult spot, between serving the justice he deserved, satisfying the burning anger and wrath inside me, and hiding behind the pitiful familiarity and memories of the man with whom I'd shared my life. The man who must have loved us in a way because he couldn't have faked so much with us, could he? The man who helped me tend my herb garden and could be rather funny when in a good mood or dreadfully pedantic when in a foul one, spouting off information from one of the books we bought about herb use as if I had never read it. The man who took Elora fishing, who taught her to ride a horse. When considering killing him before, I could think of nothing but the terrible things. But now, with his life in my hands and his body broken, I couldn't help but think about the parts of him that could be good. The man who might never recover from a mindbreaker if Dewalt was correct. The man who sold his own blood. Would it be a mercy to execute him before he was driven to madness? Did he deserve mercy?

"Do you think I can undo the damage from the mindbreaker? I'd like to question him if we can." I directed my question to Dewalt who turned to Rainier.

"You could certainly try." Rainier finally deigned to look at me then, and I couldn't read his facial expression. I paused for a moment, then knelt back down in front of Faxon and pressed a hand to his face. I watched the swelling go down, and his moaning quieted. I could tell most of the bruising was old, hidden under the new swelling Rainier had bestowed upon him. When I finished with his face, I pulled my hand back, rubbing my temple. The slight ache behind my eyes had turned into something more.

"Faxon? Can you hear me?" There was an edge to my voice, a quiet ruthlessness. Part of me wanted him to answer, to recover, so he could end his pathetic life with the knowledge I was the one who decided it. Another part of me wanted him to go quietly, never realizing the full extent of how he'd broken me. He was lying on the ground in the fetal position with his eyes closed. He didn't answer, and I glanced up at Rainier to see what he thought, but he turned away from me, his hands on his hips as he started to pace.

Mairin knelt next to me and whispered, "His aura is different. I can barely see it; I don't think he's truly there."

"Can you tell me if it changes? I'm going to try." She nodded as I placed my hand back on his head, ignoring the heat from Rainier's stare.

I didn't know what to focus on as I tried to heal him. I thought of our home and Elora. Our horses and the creek next to our house. I thought of Ravemont, the bow he gifted me, everything I could think of that might mean anything to him. I could tell the difference between normal wounds and what the mindbreaker had done, confirming to me that Cyran did, in fact, have one in his employ. My divinity struggled, and it felt almost like wading through mud. The toll was much higher than other times I'd healed people, the mindbreaker's work making mine more difficult. My head started to pound, so I pulled away, attempting to muffle a slight grunt of pain. Rainier's eyes met mine, and he seemed angrier than I could have imagined. Based on how he reacted when I spread myself too thin with his soldiers, I couldn't imagine he would approve of me doing it for Faxon.

"It's a bit better, but barely. I don't know if you'll get much out of him." Mairin had knelt beside me the entire time, keeping an eye on us both.

"Thank you, Mairin." I rubbed my temples and grimaced, readying myself to stand before I decided to try one more time. "Faxon, can you hear me?" After a few moments, I stood, searching for Rainier, who still paced angrily nearby.

Then Faxon reached out and grabbed my ankle, causing me to yelp.

"Emma?" His voice was a croak, weaker and raspier than the last time I'd heard him speak.

"Do not *touch* me." I pulled my leg away from him as I glared, a thick feeling of repulsion sliding through me, the sulfurous taste solidifying on my tongue. I felt Rainier at my side, his hand on my lower back, steadying me.

"You have white eyes." Faxon's voice didn't sound quite right, and I gaped at him, confused.

"Do you know where you are?" He peered at the people surrounding us, taking in all the faces looking down on him before he hung his head, staring at the ground.

"On the precipice of war." He didn't move.

"Oh, gods." I turned to Rainier, frustrated, before I lowered my voice. "Mairin saw his aura. I don't think he's going to be of any use."

"Meeting expectations as usual, Faxon." He gave me a small grin as he rubbed my back. I saw Faxon's eyes track the movement.

"I suppose she's yours?" He was crying, emotional as he considered the two of us, and I felt nauseated. He struggled to sit up, and I watched as Rainier only stared down at him. "I always suspected she spread her legs for you." His eyes moved back to me. "I loved you, but you wouldn't let me. You made me do all of this. You never let me in." He started to sob, slumping over.

I heard some quiet grumbling around me, and I was glad the group was a small one. The words didn't sting as much as he had intended. I'd always belonged to Rainier, as he had always belonged to me. I knew that now. Knowing Rainier's love only proved that what Faxon had felt wasn't love; it was a sorry imitation on its best days.

"You don't break the people you love, Faxon. I was just a pretty prize that came along with an estate, and it has always chapped your ass you never got to run it. You can go straight to hell with any talk of love between us. You never loved me. Do you even know what love is?" My voice was quiet and lethal. Rainier watched me, affection and sadness in his features, and he squeezed my hand before kneeling in front of Faxon. I froze, but he surprised me.

"Why waste what valuable time Emmeline has allotted you? Help us undo what you've done. Where are they holding Elora?"

"Time is catching up to us." More nonsense.

"Do you know where your daughter is?"

He merely cocked his head, confused. "She is not the prophecy."

"Answer the question!" My head was pounding.

"She will die before the Beloved will rise." His voice grew louder as he struggled to his feet. "You will be covered in her blood, and it will stink of your curse. Your curse. Your curse. Your curse. Your cur-"

Rainier walked slowly around Faxon, pulling both of his arms behind his back. He didn't struggle, falling backward slack without another word.

"What do you want to do, Em?" Rain was quiet, and he watched me with sad eyes. My chest was heaving after what Faxon said. I didn't know what a mindbreaker could do or what could have caused him to say those things. I couldn't help it as I let out a sob.

"Why? Faxon, why did you do this to her? To our family?"

"It had to be done. She is safe—I made sure of it. From you. She's safe from you."

I didn't think. Sick and horrified by what his mad mind insinuated, I stepped forward and put my hand on my husband's neck, feeling his heartbeat and forcing it to slow. I watched as his knees buckled as he fell. Then everything turned black, and I fell too.

CHAPTER 31

I woke up in a familiar position, with a familiar scent wrapped around me and an ache in my head. "I passed out again, didn't I?" Rainier's arm around my waist pulled me tighter. I glanced down and realized it was Bree we were riding on, and I felt a small comfort at the fact.

"You should have warned me you weren't feeling well. I would have taken care of it." The admonishment was clear in his tone.

"You wouldn't even look at me." I distracted myself, playing with the embroidery on my cloak.

"I couldn't be part of your decision, Em. You know that. But I said I'd be the one to do it. I know Thyra told you." He sounded frustrated.

"Why couldn't you be part of it?" I wished he would have decided for me. I was torn from my decision. Had it been a mercy for me to kill Faxon? Was it mercy for him or a mercy for me?

"I couldn't influence you; you had to decide for yourself. If it were up to me, you wouldn't have healed him at all. If it were up to me, he'd have been dead before I brought you out of the cave. I would have handled it and told you he was dead. I almost did it too. After what he's done to you both? But it wasn't up to me."

"I had to heal him—to see if he knew anything." I began to think about what he'd said. That Elora would die, her blood on my hands. That he was keeping her safe—from me. I shook my head, refusing to think about it. He was a broken man with a broken mind. It wasn't logical. None of it made sense. I would never do anything to harm her, and he knew that. Thinking about it would only push me to insanity.

"I know." He let out a long exhale.

I tilted my head back into him and rested my eyes. My head was a dull throb, and I willed my divinity to do my bidding, hoping not to make it worse.

"Did you bury him?" I didn't know why I felt sad; Faxon deserved his death. Nonetheless, I had killed my daughter's father. The man who helped me raise her to be kind and brave. The man who built her a dollhouse. The man who picked out books for her, knowing she'd devour them almost immediately, and yet he'd still smile when she'd beg him for more. The man who had claimed to love us both. But that man was the same man who sold her to the enemy.

"Under a bush at the mouth of the cave. There's a stone to mark it." He paused, stiffening. "We can take a break before we go too much farther, and I can rift you there."

"No, I only asked for Elora. I don't want to go back. Honestly, I'd love to never think about him again." I threaded my fingers through his hand around my waist and settled myself more comfortably against him, somehow managing to fall asleep quickly, my head tucked under his chin.

I slept off and on the entire day, grateful to not be in my thoughts. Rainier woke me periodically, offering me food and drink like a small child. Eventually, I told him to knock it off, and I'd let him know if I was hungry or thirsty. I suspected I might have hurt his feelings a bit, but I didn't spend too long feeling bad before I fell back asleep.

I woke up to my ear popping and my headache mostly gone. I hadn't realized how close we were to leaving the pass. The western side of the Alsors was treacherous—a steep, downward slope I tried to not think about. Bree was a good horse, sturdy and smart, and I trusted her to keep us safe. This side of the mountains was a ruddy, brown color, quite different from their eastern ridge, which almost glowed a dull silver. I gazed at the horizon below us and saw nothing but grasslands. It was the flattest land I'd ever seen, stretching as far as the eye could see.

"Where are all the trees?" Rainier chuckled and gave me a quick kiss behind the ear. I glowed at his touch.

"These are the great plains. Not many trees, but home to most of our crops. I forget you haven't been this far west before."

"Are there trees in Astana? I don't know if I can handle life without shade."

"Life, huh? So, you've decided to be a woman of honor and respect our bargain?" He teased.

I tried to look over my shoulder at him to glare. "As long as Elora agrees." As long as he spoke to Keeva. As long as Mairin ended up being correct, and he could finally choose me after all this time. Quite a lot had to occur to get us to stay, and since I didn't want to get into any of it, I stayed quiet.

"That's fair. It's going to be a hard transition, no matter what. Hopefully, I can convince her with all of the royal luxuries I can throw at her." I could tell he was smiling, and I knew if I allowed it, he'd try to bribe her in any manner possible. Imagining him funding an expensive wardrobe for her and a private library just to convince us to stay put a smile on my face. I cringed a bit, thinking about the conversations I'd have to have with my daughter about my history with Rainier. Thinking about Elora and Rainier interacting with each other was both strange and comforting, and the thought brought a smile to my face before the cruel reality sank in.

"I don't think court will be the problem. I think it will be me."

"What do you mean?"

"I've failed her in so many ways, Rain. And I just killed her father." I exhaled, worried. I'd have to tell her the moment I saw her. If I kept it from her longer than I had to, she'd never forgive me.

"If it's easier, you can tell her I killed him. I imagined it a thousand different ways at least."

"No. Thank you, though. I think it's best I stop lying to her." I felt him nod. "I wonder if she knows Prince Cyran kept him tied outside. Did you see the marks on his neck?"

"I did. It earned the boy some respect from me."

"Rain, it was cruel."

"Was it? You and Elora deserved so much better. Deserve so much better."

"And let me guess, you plan to give it to us?" I teased as I squeezed the hand still entwined with mine.

"Until the day I die." I nestled back into his chest, the warmth from his words moving through me like a caress.

"Fair warning, she has a smart mouth and can get into some terrible moods." I couldn't wait for them to meet. She'd give him a run for his money.

"I've had all the practice I need with her mother."

I let out an embarrassingly loud laugh and pushed my elbow back into him.

I stayed awake after that, and we spent our time in easy silence or light conversation. Rainier told me about how Bree fought him off at first, but he'd tamed her with an apple and soft words, and he made a joke about how he wished it would have been that easy with me. My headache stayed away, and although

I felt a little tired, my divinity undetectable, I was none the worse for wear. Attempting to manipulate the work of the mindbreaker had worn me down.

"Why do you think they sent him to us?" Did Faxon go too far, or had the prince just found him to be useless?

"You'll have to ask him tomorrow night, but if I had to guess, he wore out his welcome. He was locked up a week ago, and you said Cyran seemed to care for Elora. Do you think maybe Faxon said or did something to her?"

"A fortnight ago, I would have said no, but now, I'm not sure."

"Maybe Prince Cyran just grew tired of him."

"But why break his mind before they sent him back?"

"Now that, I do not know. Maybe to prevent us from doing exactly what we tried to do."

I nodded, and we grew into a quiet comfort once more, my body pressed against his. No one approached us, and it was serene and comfortable. I needed time to process everything; so much had happened in the past day. I hadn't expected Faxon to show up like that. I thought he'd give me excuses, beg for forgiveness, or at least prove how evil he was. I thought he'd show he had no remorse or regrets about what he did.

It almost felt like what I did was unfair. He was a man with a broken mind, and I did what I had intended to do from the start, despite the fact the circumstances had changed. What if Elora couldn't forgive me? What if everything I'd done would break my relationship irreparably with my daughter? Not to mention, I'd killed someone. I'd killed people before, but they'd been attacking me or mine. I didn't feel any remorse for those people. They had died by my hand, and they deserved it. But had Faxon? Was it justifiable for me to kill him? Elora was being taken care of, and we were making moves to get her back safely. Was it fair for me to kill the man? To use my hands and divinity to speed his heart up enough it burst? Was that what Aonara intended I use her gift for? A large part of me felt remorse for what I did, and it was the last thing I would have expected. I wanted relief, and his death hadn't given me that. A thought occurred to me in a rush, and I pushed away from Rainier, sitting upright.

"I murdered Faxon." The words rushed out of me, and I felt Rainier still behind me.

"I wouldn't say that."

"He's dead, and I'm the one who did it, am I not?"

"Yes, but—"

"So, I murdered him. He didn't have a trial." I was not judge, jury, and executioner, but I'd played the roles well, hadn't I?

"The traitor in the cellar didn't have a trial either. His execution was not a murder."

"You're the one who did that, not me. I'm not royalty." Rainier could do what he wanted with no problem, no hesitation. At least to an extent. Of course, the person had to deserve it when they were executed, or there would be consequences with the people.

"You could be."

I only let myself react for a half-second, frozen in place, before I chose to ignore it, not about to get into a completely different conversation that was just as heavy.

"But I'm not, and I killed Faxon." He leaned forward, pushing his warm chest against me, breaths steady as he tightened his arm around my waist.

"He deserved death. I would have executed him myself if not for you. I had to let you have the choice—to be able to choose mercy if you wanted. And, honestly? I'm glad you didn't want to offer it to him. But you are not a murderer, Emmeline. I *am* royalty, and I gave you a choice of punishments. Your choice doesn't make you a murderer." A small, whispering part of me wondered if I somehow still showed mercy today but pushed the thought away.

"Just because you say it, that doesn't mean I won't be condemned in death or by Elora." I didn't know why my thinking had turned so dark.

"Then I'll be right there with you because I've done much worse. And Elora will forgive you. At the absolute least, she'll be distracted by all the things court has to offer. All the books we'll buy her. Hell, we'll just give her a line of credit at the bookstore." I could tell he was trying to cheer me up, and he succeeded a bit, especially with his use of the word 'we.'

"How is her book?"

"I finished it. A little predictable, but I can see why a young girl would like it."

"Oh? Why, old and wise one, would a young girl like it?"

"The prince changed for her. She helped him see the error of his ways and all the mistakes he made."

"And what's wrong with that?"

"A good man will know when he's made a mistake and do everything he can to make it right. He won't need a beautiful woman to tell him." He pulled me closer, kissing the top of my head. "But I'll let you tell me, anyway."

I smiled as I tilted my head back. I didn't know where things would go from here, but I knew the two of us would weather it together.

Dewalt came up next to us, and the two men began to discuss where to make camp. They had to be careful because of where different fields were in the process of planting. Between the two of them, they decided to stop a short while later, and for the life of me, I couldn't figure out how they knew to stop. It all looked the same to me.

While everything was being set up, I sparred with Rainier, Dewalt calling out instructions and criticism throughout. After a while, though *I* was freezing, Rainier took his shirt off, and I nearly got stabbed, distracted by him. He came rushing at me, all bared muscle and naked flesh, and I forgot where I was. I snapped out of it at the last second, barely twisting out of his way and deflecting the blow he'd intended to give. Dewalt had launched into a fit of laughter, and Rainier chuckled, giving me a chance to catch my breath. I glared but couldn't help my smile. Eventually, Lavenia and Mairin came to watch, bundled up in a cloak together, the winds piercing on the plains. I worked on my patience while we trained, waiting for a better opening instead of settling for the fastest one. By the end of it, we both had a sheen of sweat coating us, and I threw myself down onto the ground near our friends.

"I prefer you both when you're not fighting." Lavenia grinned as she said it, and I threw a clump of grass at her. Rainier groaned as he sat down next to me, shirt back on, relaxed with his elbows resting on his knees. The five of us sat there for a long while, just lounging and chatting. Mairin had revealed to Dewalt and Lavenia that she was a merrow, and I was glad to not have to keep a secret from them. She spent some time talking to us about her years since coming to land but refused to speak of where she came from. My heart ached to know she had family and a life in the water she could never return to.

Eventually, Rainier laid down next to me, pulling my hand into his and rubbing it. It felt incredible, considering how sore I was because of my sword. The more I used the thing, the more I realized I needed a new one or to attempt to fix it. The balance wasn't quite right, and the grip was loosening.

A while later, as we sat around the fire and ate, I suddenly realized I didn't know which tent to go to. I was sure I'd be welcome in either, but it felt presumptuous to assume one over the other. I decided I'd wait and see which one Dewalt went into, and then choose the other. It seemed like a better plan than asking. What I didn't plan on was his strategy being the same as mine. We both stood outside the two tents with the packs we'd retrieved from our horses and waited in silence together, everyone else having already retreated inside.

"You know, I'm fine with either, Emma." His arms were crossed, and he peered down at me.

"Come talk with me." I grasped him by the hand, not giving him a choice but to follow me. When I sat back down by the fire, he plopped down beside me with long legs bent at the knee and his legs spread wide as he began to draw on the ground with a stick. "Do you ever feel guilty?"

"Plenty, but I assume you mean something specific?" He chuckled, but the smile didn't reach his eyes. I think he knew this was a serious conversation, and it meant a great deal to me to choose to confide in him.

"About...moving on without her? Without Lucia?"

"No, because I haven't." He shrugged. "I have felt guilty for *not* moving on, though."

I studied his features, harsh in the light of the fire. His sharp nose and angled cheekbones cast dark shadows across his face, making him look less approachable than the typical smiling Dewalt.

"What do you mean?" He dropped his stick, staring down at the swirls he'd been drawing in the dirt.

"She would've wanted me to find a love like ours, and I never did. It's impossible, but she would have wanted me to try, and I never have. I feel some guilt over that, but not enough to make an effort." He let out a sigh. "You know, I'd forgotten the details of her face, the exact shade of blue." He looked at me, staring into my eyes, memorizing the exact color she and I had shared. "Thank you for helping remind me." I nodded, not trusting myself to speak and stay composed. He let out a long breath before he leaned over, bumping his shoulder into my arm. "Sounds like you're feeling guilty, mouse."

A flood of affection for my friend spread through me at the nickname. I'd earned it by creeping up on him and Rainier one night when they were trying to sneak out of the Cottage. It was our first summer there without our parents, and it was the turning point when we'd stopped being a nuisance to the older boys and instead became friends. I quietly sidled up next to them, scaring them half to death, and insisted on joining their late-night mischief, daringly stealing a bottle of wine from the kitchens to impress them. I smiled, then took a breath to explain.

"I've been allowing myself to be distracted by all of this because it keeps me from thinking about Elora. I feel guilty I'm not weeping over her every waking second. But I can't, I can't let myself fall into that, or I won't be of any use. And, I guess, part of me just has a feeling everything is going to be fine, or at least close to it. I'm hopeful it will all work out because of Rain's optimism. He is keeping me sane in one way and driving me mad in another.

"I feel guilty Lucia died protecting me, and I'm here barely living. How can you feel guilty for two opposite things? I feel wrong for not living the life she'd have wanted for me, and I feel wrong when I try to live that life and accept all of this with him. You know, she's almost been dead longer than I ever had her, and it doesn't feel like it's any easier. Will it ever get easier?"

Dewalt chuckled then and put his arm around my shoulders. "No, I don't think it will. We just learn to take one day at a time and hope it doesn't kill us. You want my opinion, though?"

"Of course, always."

"You've spent enough time doing it one way. I think it's time to stop punishing yourself and try the opposite."

I sat there for a few minutes with him, leaning into my friend and thinking. Eventually, I looked up from the fire and saw Rainier standing in the entrance to his tent, hands in his pockets as he watched us. I stood then, grabbing my pack, and leaned down, kissing Dewalt on the cheek.

"Thank you, friend," I called over my shoulder as I crossed the distance to my tent, Rainier's eyes fixed on me the entire time, a guarded expression on his face. He maintained the expression until the last second, when I stood on tiptoe and pushed my lips to his, one hand snaking up his neck. After a moment, I broke away and edged past him, straight into the life my sister wanted for me.

CHAPTER 32

THE NEXT MORNING, I woke up on the ground between the two pallets Rainier had pushed together the night before. In our sleep, we must have somehow slid them apart and fell between. His insistence on taking care of me, long after my headache had dissipated, was a source of contention the night before. But this morning, I was grateful for it, likely the only reason we were fully clothed and protected from the cold ground below us. When we first laid down, Rainier held me close, all soft caresses and kisses. Neither of us spoke, enjoying the easy silence after I chose us by going to his tent. His guarded expression told me he might have been anticipating another outburst from me, but I was done with that. I was leaning into this. This love was a light, a love that came back to me and brought me back to the land of the living. It was a love that made me want more—from him, from us, from life. I knew I needed to tell him about the twin flame nonsense but wasn't sure how he'd react, and since I wasn't ready for anything to change more than it already had, I kept it to myself.

When I opened my eyes, I studied Rainier's face, slack with sleep. The scar through his eyebrow was the biggest one on his face, but I noticed another small one across the bridge of his nose and one at the top of his chin, a slight marring of the demarcation between his mouth and the skin below it. I reached up, lightly tracing his full lower lip, and as he began to stir, I leaned forward and gave him a closed kiss. He made a soft groaning sound and pulled me in closer to him, and kissed me back, trying to part my lips with his tongue. I'd yet to replace my toothbrush after accidentally stepping on it, shattering the bone handle. I hoped the shops in Astana had a more diverse selection. I pulled back from him, murmuring about morning breath, to which he kissed me more enthusiastically. I laughed and leaned into the kiss, returning the ardor. When he finally pulled away and opened his eyes to look at me, I got lost in them, the flecks of gold vivid in the low light.

"It seems we've broken our bed." There was a sparkle of amusement in his eyes as he spoke.

"It would seem so."

"I could have thought of better ways to break it." I rolled my eyes as he leaned in and kissed me again before he flipped onto his back. "We will only ride for a few hours today, and then I'll rift us to my home in the city."

"When was the last time you were there?"

"Maybe a year ago? I don't imagine the servants have changed the place too much, so rifting shouldn't be a problem."

"Do Dewalt and Lavenia live there too?"

"They have a room there, but they also have their own home. It's farther from the city, though, so they'll likely stay with us. If that's alright with you?"

"Of course, that's alright with me. It's your home."

He studied me before he sat up, stretching. "Are you ready for tonight with Elora?" He asked because I'd spent a good portion of time last night agonizing over Elora's potential reaction to Faxon's death. I sat up next to him.

"The more I think about it, the more I want to vomit. What if she isn't even there? What if she hates me for what I did to him?"

"You're strong, Em. And if you need to be weak, I'll be strong for you. We'll get through it." He pulled me into him, kissing the top of my head. "I wish I could be in the illusion with you."

"I wish you could be, too. Maybe Cyran will bring you along this time." We both stood then, separating to get dressed and handle our needs. I did notice Rainier watching me as I took my shirt off, and I shamelessly turned to give him a decent view, eliciting a groan from him.

"You dirty, little wretch." He smirked at me as he stripped his shirt off.

"Dirty is right. I need a bath."

"I have a better idea. I'll show you tonight."

"What is this idea?"

"It's a surprise. I promise you'll like it, though."

I started to braid my hair and then remembered Rainier had liked it better down, choosing instead to pin it at my hairline, just to keep it out of my face.

True to his word, we only rode a few hours before we slipped away, leaving our horses in Dickey's care, and Rainier created a rift. Peeking through it, I saw dark floors and not much else. It was dim within the room, and I realized him being gone for a year was the reason for it. Dewalt walked through and sneezed, confirming my suspicion, and Mairin and Lavenia followed.

"I built this house with you in mind."

"What?"

"I did. You'll see. Maybe it's part of why I've hated coming here for so long." He grabbed my hand and pulled me toward the rift with him. "I've never been happier to go home than I am today, though." He shot me a dazzling smile, and the rift closed behind us as we stepped through.

Dewalt opened the curtains and a window, and I looked around. The ceiling was high with wooden beams crossing the top, and the floors matched, dark oak if I had to guess, not unlike the floors at Ravemont. The cream curtains blew in the slight breeze from the open window, mildly contrasting with the light blue walls. A large fireplace took up one wall of the room, the grey stone stretching across the entire face with a long oak mantle. There was greenery and candles nestled across it, books, and other items I wanted to inspect decorating the shelf as well. The furniture within this room, what I assumed to be a living room, was large and comfortable looking, with an ottoman to prop your feet upon next to the most inviting sofa I had ever seen. All cream, with throws and pillows of various shades of blue tossed all over it. The room was decorated simply and beautifully, with comfort in mind—much different than what I would have expected for the Crown Prince. The others went through a hallway in search of their rooms, I supposed. I spotted a glimpse of something through the window Dewalt had opened and walked across to peer outside. Finding the garden Rainier had discussed earlier, I was surprised to see different shades of purples, blues, and pinks throughout, with a beautiful pergola covered in vines.

I heard a creak to my right and turned to see Rainier opening up glass-paneled doors leading out to the garden. He nodded his head, indicating for me to follow, and I joined him. The walkway through the garden meandered, the dark grey stones creating a path I followed, marveling at all the different flowers he'd managed to accrue. Some were tall and climbed trellises that hung over the path while others were left to flourish in their wildness, spreading across the grass with no sense of direction. There was a peaceful solitude in the garden, and I wondered at its beauty.

"You did this?" He laughed from ahead, waiting for me to catch up.

"No, I helped in the beginning. I had the vision, but my gardeners have kept it up for me since then. It's best in the summer, but there is still plenty blooming this late in the season."

I took his hand and wandered through the garden with him, noticing the various bushes I suspected would be full in the summer, their blooms resting this late in the autumn. He took me to a particularly large bush that had dark purple blooms all over it. "This is the only one that blooms this late, but most of the plants are lilacs. There are violets, and I'm sure you saw the hydrangeas from the window. And quite a few others I don't remember the names of." His crooked smile was going to be the death of me.

My favorite flowers and my favorite scents. I didn't have words. He meant what he said earlier—my influence was evident in this house. From the flowers to the colors and decor inside, even the dark wood floors. It was perfect. He took me further into the garden, showing me a swinging bench nestled into a secluded area surrounded by tall hedges.

"Why?" I was just a memory by the time he built the estate.

"I decided if I was going to torture myself thinking of you, your scent would make it more palatable."

My breath hitched, and I swallowed. He never stopped when it came to me. Knowing he built this house with me at the forefront of his mind was almost too much to think about.

"It's beautiful, Rain, it's perfect." I turned away, not sure why I was tearing up. His home was faultless, every detail like something I'd dreamt up myself. He came up behind me, wrapping his arms around my waist and resting his chin on the top of my head.

"Then why are you crying?" I wiped my eyes quickly and turned in his arms.

"I don't know, truly." I smiled up at him, and he returned it, leaning down to kiss me. Putting one hand on the back of my neck and the other at my waist, he kissed me deeper and more passionately than I'd ever been kissed. I felt something shift as if the world had aligned for this moment. For me to find Rainier again, fall for him again, love him again. For me to be wrapped in his arms in the beautiful garden he'd made for me. When he broke from the kiss, he pressed his forehead against mine, and the intimacy made my chest tighten.

I heard a gentle clearing of someone's throat and pulled away from Rainier, turning to the doors we'd come out.

"Your Highness." A slightly older man with salt and pepper hair bowed at the waist before righting himself.

"Sterling!" Rainier beamed at the man, who returned the smile.

"I did not realize you would be back today. You have my apologies for the state of the house. It has only been me, at your insistence, but I have called the others back, and we will have everything ready by nightfall for you."

"A little dust never hurt anyone, Sterling. It's no rush. As you said, you didn't know because I am an irresponsible madman who forgot to send word." Sterling's answering smile told me he was used to Rainier's boyish charm. Rainier turned his stunning smile toward me, and I watched his eyes soften before he turned back to the man waiting at the door.

"Sterling, I'd like you to meet Lady Emmeline Highclere. Emmeline, this is my butler, Sterling Tiller." I was taken aback when Sterling bowed to me, realizing I'd turned into some sort of heathen, forgetting the niceties of court. I'd need practice before tomorrow. I found myself falling into a curtsy while Sterling gaped at me in horror. Rainier gently cupped my elbow and pulled me out of the curtsy, chuckling as he did it.

"The servants don't particularly like being bowed and curtsied to, Em." He turned to Sterling then. "Not that you don't deserve the same respect and reverence I do, Sterling. I just know you hate it. If he had it his way, I'd be calling him Mr. Tiller." I felt my skin turn what I knew was a bright shade of red as Sterling nodded his agreement with Rainier.

"I'm so sorry. I've been away for a long time. I forget myself." My vision dropped to the ground.

"It is nothing. A pleasure to meet you, my lady." Sterling directed his attention back to Rainier. "If you and your guests would like to make yourself scarce for a few hours, sir, I would suggest it. I'll open all the windows, but I can't imagine the dust won't affect you all, especially His Grace." Rainier chuckled before he replied.

"Noted, Sterling. We will plan accordingly. I have business in the city I must attend to; I'll bring Dewalt with me." I started, realizing the person they'd been referring to was Dewalt. The butler gave a shallow bow before walking back into the house.

"I am so embarrassed." I buried my face into Rainier's chest, and his arms wrapped around me.

"Don't be. As you said, you're out of practice. You can practice your curtsy with Lavenia while you're in the city."

"I'm going into the city?" I turned my head so he could hear me but stayed pressed up against his broad chest. He was warm and solid, and I didn't want to move.

"To Lavenia's seamstress, remember?"

"Oh, Rain. You don't have to do that. I'm sure the dress I brought will suffice."

"Nonsense, I want to."

An hour later, I was at a small shop in the city center with Mairin and Lavenia. The store boasted so many different fabrics and colors along its walls I could barely concentrate on what the woman in front of me was saying. The ceilings were tall, and there was fabric shoved into every shelf, every color in the rainbow and a multitude of patterned fabric represented. Eventually, Mairin gripped me by the arm and took me back to the dressing room the woman had been telling me about while I ogled the walls.

"Strip," Mairin ordered, no small amount of annoyance in her tone.

"Naked?" I knew things were different in Astana, in the city, but when the seamstress visited Ravemont, I always wore a slip or some sort of petticoat, and I hadn't thought to pack one.

"Down to whatever you plan to wear beneath your dresses." Lavenia walked into the room then, and I turned my back to Mairin, giving her access to the buttons I needed help with. I'd changed into my cotton dress before we left—the time for traveling clothes had passed. If I were to be referred to as a lady and bowed to, I decided to act the part. When I stepped out of the dress, Lavenia took one look at my undergarments and shook her head.

"Gods, you've been away too long. You need to lose the stays and shift once we get back." She tossed me a short satin robe from the back of the door, and I slipped it on before heading back out to the back of the shop. The seamstress squinted up at me when I stood on the dais. I was not tall by any means but still managed to tower over this woman. Her hunched back and jagged teeth recalled a story to me Elora had once read about a crone, one that gave her nightmares. The woman mumbled to herself as she took my measurements, pulling a pencil out from between her teeth to jot down the numbers. When she removed my robe and got to my bust, she shook her head and climbed down, disappearing into a storage room in the back.

I crossed my arms over my chest, standing awkwardly above my friends, completely naked save for my underwear. Though I'd been daring and allowed myself to be naked with Rainier, I wasn't remotely comfortable standing there with so much of my body on display. About to step down and put my robe back on, I stopped when the woman came fussing back into the room, holding two different garments out to me.

"This is a brassiere. I assume you've never seen one?" I shook my head; I had never seen such a thing. "Try these—they should be the right size. They're more comfortable than stays." One garment was a dark cream color and plain, while the other was a deeper navy color, covered in lace. I took the cream one from her and went to make my way back to the dressing room, unconvinced I'd be able to figure out how to put it on. The seamstress clucked at me, a scowl on her features.

"Everyone in here has them. Just put it on." She seemed impatient, but the woman was doing a huge favor by getting at least one dress ready for me by tomorrow, so I obeyed. I made eye contact with Mairin, allowing her to see my discomfort at exposing my breasts. She made a face toward the seamstress, who was bent over digging through a basket of materials, then pulled Lavenia away to inspect some of the fabric lining the walls. I studied the garment in my hand, discerning where certain parts ought to go but had no idea how to fasten it behind my back. I struggled only a moment before the seamstress helped me. The fabric was soft, and I understood the appeal immediately. I caught a glimpse in the mirror and couldn't help but stare at myself for a moment. The fabric clung to my breasts and helped appealingly support them, and it wasn't digging into my skin or squeezing me half to death. A definite improvement over stays.

"There you go. You can have both. I have bottoms to match that you can have as well." The woman went to measure my bust then, making tiny sounds of approval as she did.

"You don't have to do that!"

"Rainier is footing the bill, Emma. Calm down." Lavenia laughed at me as she approached, grabbing my old stays from the dressing room and unceremoniously dropping the garment in a bag in the back of the shop. It seemed to be full of discarded remnants intent for repurposing.

"He offered to pay for a few gowns so I'd look appropriate for court, not a whole new wardrobe."

"Funny, then why did he tell me to help you pick out a whole new wardrobe?" Lavenia didn't spare me a glance, her eyes on her nails while she picked at them instead. I glared but got no response.

After the measurements had been taken and noted, I went back into the dressing room with Mairin so she could help me button up my dress, where she revealed the seamstress was likely a witch based on her aura. It made sense, and I figured that was how she planned to deliver a gown so quickly. When we left the dressing room, Lavenia was going over a list with the woman, detailing all of the different items Rainier had sent her for. Mairin grabbed my arm and dragged me out of the shop after we waved our quick goodbyes.

"Come, I want to show you something." She pulled me out into the sun, and I shielded my eyes, giving them a moment to adjust to the bright light. Though the wind was biting, and we were well into autumn, it was a warm day, likely the last of them before spring returned.

We stuck close to the side of the buildings as the streets were crowded, full of horses and carriages, and countless people walking. The smell of the city was not one I was prepared for. Even the quarter we were in, supposedly the nicest in the city proper, smelled worse than the most wretched slums of Mira. I wasn't sure if it was because of the sheer number of people and the bodies that pressed against you, no matter which way you turned, or lack of a sufficient waste system, but it was not a pleasant scent. I knew King Soren didn't much care for the problems of his poorest people—who all seemed to congregate in the cities, the cost of land too high with no guarantee of their ability to work it. I made a note to ask Rainier about it, sure he would want to do something about the smell and the overcrowding if he spent any meaningful time in the city. I felt my nose scrunch as I tried to keep the worst of it at bay.

Mairin led us up the street a bit before we attempted to cross it, weaving through people who all seemed to be hurrying to their next destination. I was bumped into no less than six times during the brief walk. The building she took me to had no windows and just one nondescript door. The walls themselves were made of dark marble, and there were bronze inlays throughout. It was a luxurious building, but from the outside, I couldn't tell what it was. She pushed us through the doors, and I immediately understood the lack of windows.

Books. There were books in every spot of the giant octagonal room going from the floor to the open ceiling several stories above where we stood. Ladders on tracks allowed access to shelf after shelf, stocked full. There were small walkways you could access from the ladders, leading to even more shelving, each one covered in countless tomes. The small skylight in the center of the ceiling was the only light source in the room, other than the low lamplight, likely to preserve the pages themselves.

"Great Divine. I've never seen so many books in one place."

"This is one of the first places I went to on land. I heard of it from my sisters," she whispered as we walked, not breaking the spell of silence in the room. My heart ached a bit when she mentioned her family. I couldn't imagine a world where my sister was alive but I couldn't see her whenever I wanted. Mairin could go anywhere in the world, anywhere at all, except for her home. And the way she spoke of it, I knew she thought of it often.

"Elora is going to be in heaven here." I browsed for a while before noticing a corridor in the back, leading to even more books. I found a beautiful, gilded copy of one of my favorite books, a story about an iniquitous king with a golden touch and the woman who put a stop to his black-hearted ways. I pulled it off the shelf, gently turning the pages to look at the illustrations at the beginning of each chapter, when I heard a cough and turned to my left, making eye contact with a man only a bit taller than me. He had onyx hair and eyes that tilted up a bit at the corners, with a pair of spectacles almost too small to be useful resting on his nose.

"Are you Lady Highclere?" The man squeaked out the words, barely audible even with all the quiet around us.

"Yes, I am. And you are?" I gently slid the book back onto the shelf, curious.

"I am Reminy. I work here. The Crown Prince came in an hour ago and told me to watch for you." I smiled, realizing Rainier must have stopped here after rifting us before he went to handle the business he needed to attend to. The business he wouldn't speak to me about, for some reason. "I have been told to put whatever books you'd like on his account. Did you want this one? A beautiful edition, is it not?" Reminy took the book back off the shelf and walked over to a counter I'd failed to notice, right near the corridor that led into the other room.

"Oh, I shouldn't. I already have this book; I just thought this edition was beautiful." I followed him to the counter as he wrote down the title in his ledger before handing it back.

"I was told to insist." He gave me a shy smile, and I decided to acquiesce in this, knowing Rainier likely harassed him about it.

"Thank you, Reminy. I appreciate it." I took the book from him and smiled. "I expect you'll see more of me here and likely my daughter as well."

"I look forward to it." His smile was warm, and I couldn't help but appreciate the way his cheeks pinked.

Mairin walked up then, her arms full of books that she put down on the counter in front of Reminy. "She'll take these, too." She huffed and grinned at me. Reminy was already writing everything down. I decided not to stop him, but I gave her an annoyed look.

"What? I've gifted you with incredibly valuable information; the least I should get is some books out of it." She shrugged, and I couldn't help but chuckle.

When Reminy was all done and her books loaded into a canvas tote, Mairin dragged me out of the bookshop, as if *I* was the one who made us late. We ran back down the street to the fountain Rainier had rifted us to when we first arrived in the city. I saw Lavenia standing, leaning over Dewalt, who sat on the fountain's edge. As we made our way, I realized she had a cloth pressed against his lip. I rushed over and pulled the fabric away to see his mouth swollen and bleeding, a tooth resting in his outstretched hand.

"Put that back in and hold it where it goes. What happened?" I turned to Lavenia for an explanation, and she shook her head. Dewalt put the tooth back in, and I held my hand over his mouth, healing the split lip and willing his gums to grasp back onto the tooth. I hoped it happened recently enough that the tooth would grip.

I felt Rainier's presence at my back, and I glanced over my shoulder. He was holding a piece of raw meat on his eye, and I did a double-take.

"What happened?" I was exasperated as I finished healing Dewalt and turned back to Rainier, gently peeling the meat away to see his eye rapidly swelling shut. I pushed him down next to Dewalt and repeated my question for the third time.

"Keeva happened." Dewalt leaned over to speak, and Rainier grinned up at me.

Apparently, Keeva punching Rainier and throwing a vase at Dewalt was a better reaction than they were anticipating. Properly healed and rifted back to Rainier's home, we found ourselves sitting on the massive sofa, waiting for the two of them to explain.

"Did you know that was what they were doing?" I posed my question to Lavenia, who quickly shook her head, taking on the same exasperated expression I wore.

"I told you I was going to end things with Keeva the minute I was back in Astana, Em. I got sidetracked for a moment by a beautiful woman in my garden, but it was still my top priority. I wanted to speak to her before the guard arrived." I could have punched myself when I felt my stomach twist after he called me beautiful. It was pathetic, and I felt like a schoolgirl pining after a boy. He had to do it on purpose to distract me.

"And you thought you should bring Dewalt to help end a betrothal to the woman?" Lavenia glared at her brother, arms crossed.

"He wanted a witness." Dewalt shrugged. "I don't blame him; the woman is insane."

"The same woman who supposedly will want to kill me? Wonderful. Why did you want to tell her before the guard arrived?"

Rainier looked at me with a bored expression on his face, willing me to understand something painfully obvious.

"I trust my guard. What I do not trust is them to control their tongues. Word will spread about you, and I wanted to tell Keeva before she heard anything untoward."

"She took it well, it seems." Mairin's face lit up in a mischievous grin, clearly amused by the whole situation.

"For Keeva? Undoubtedly." Rainier nodded, missing Mairin's sarcasm. "She was a bit put out because she'd already done her task from the Myriad."

"She'd already done her task? What was it?" That bitter beast that resided low in my stomach stirred, and I felt it in my tone. He snorted, likely reading my voice.

"She stitched me a cloak by her own hand. The Myriad must be desperate for me to marry. They're getting rather boring. How hard is it to make a cloak?" He huffed a laugh.

"Hard for her, it seems, since she was so mad she wasted her time on it." I shrugged, and he grinned.

"Oh, dear heart. I have no doubt you could make a much better cloak for me." I kicked him, pulling my foot out of his lap where it had been resting, and he grunted, covering himself in protection. "Watch it!"

"So, that's it? Did you tell our parents?" Lavenia's face was stern as she waited for her brother's answer.

"I sent them a message, don't worry about it." Rainier's tone told me I, in fact, should worry about it.

"You didn't go see them? That's going to go over well." She rolled her eyes, exasperated.

Sterling rescued Rainier from his sister when he came in to announce dinner. We walked into another room of the enormous house to find a long dining table. The dark oak floors continued throughout. The room had floor-to-ceiling windows, which allowed the moonlight to fill it. The chandelier had over a hundred tiny candles in it, and I wondered if someone had to light them all by hand. On the wall opposite the windows was a massive painting in a silver frame. I took my seat to Rainier's right and studied it. It looked familiar, and I jolted in shock when I realized what it was. Rainier noticed my surprise and slid his hand onto my thigh when I turned to him.

"Did you paint that?"

"No, I commissioned a seer in the artist quarters. She painted it from my memory."

"It's—wow. It's a flawless re-creation." I had to avert my eyes for a moment because it was so realistic. The view was from inside the cavern, looking out to the water. It was a misty, grey day, and the sea in the painting was wild and rough with great waves cresting over the rocks. I could almost hear the sound of the water hitting them, the echo reverberating throughout the vast space, taste the salty mist in the air, feel the spray on my skin.

"Is it bothering you? We can cover it." Rainier's hand squeezed my thigh gently as he asked, and I felt another surge of warmth and affection for the man beside me.

"No, it's alright. It's beautiful. The artist did an amazing job." I stared at it for a few more minutes as the meal was brought out to us, served in multiple dishes that we plated ourselves.

Everything in front of us smelled delicious, and I wasn't sure I'd have room on my plate for everything I wanted. I grabbed some asparagus, a baked potato, and a chicken breast, as well as a bowl of salad. It was the best food I'd ever had, and Rainier watched me with delight as I let out a slight moan after biting into the chicken.

"I keep a small staff: Sterling, my butler, Mellise, my maid, and Deandra, my cook. I have a few stablehands and the gardener, but those three are the only ones who help care for the household. If you eat Deandra's food like that in front of her, she's going to fatten you up in no time." The crooked smile he gave me was full of tenderness that matched what I felt for him.

"I don't need any help with that." I grinned and shoved a bite of potato in my mouth. He leaned closer to me and spoke so only I could hear.

"I've grown quite acquainted with your ass in front of me in the saddle. It may be rounder than it used to be, but all the more delicious for it." I felt myself flush as his hand gripped my thigh possessively. Mairin eyed me from across the table, a single eyebrow raised, before I reached for my glass of wine and drank deep.

We all finished our dinner, and the servants whisked away the dishes before we even left the table. The other three went out of sight down a dark corridor before I heard them climb the stairs. I made to follow when Rainier grabbed my wrist, pulling me against his chest.

"Do you want to sleep in your own room?"

"I should, shouldn't I? The servants?" He shrugged.

"The only one who lives on site is Sterling, and he won't bother us. Melisse and Deandra go home after dinner." I was surprised he didn't keep more of his staff here full time, and I appreciated his simplicity.

"You did say you had a surprise for me. Unless you meant the bookstore?"

"I wondered if you'd wander there today. Do you think Elora will like it?" He tilted his head with the question, and I stood on my tiptoes to kiss him. His consideration of Elora surprised and affected me every time. I wondered if I'd ever grow accustomed to it, the easy acceptance of a girl he'd never met, all because she was mine.

"I think she'll love it, thank you."

"I already put her on the account, as well. Speaking of Elora, we need to get you to bed." I nodded, and a thin exhale escaped my lips.

"I'm not sure I'll be able to fall asleep."

"I can help with that." He gave me a coy smile, and I snorted but let him lead me to a small hallway off the back of the living room I hadn't noticed before. His rooms were on the lower level and were likely enormous based on the size and height of the living room beside it.

The door at the end of the hallway swung inwards to reveal a large, open room. The ceilings mirrored the living room, the oak beams against white walls raised to a peak in the middle. The floor was the same dark color as the rest of the house, but there was a giant rug stretched across a large portion of the room, grey and fluffy. The wall opposite the door was a deep navy blue, almost black, with a giant bed centered against it. Nightstands on either side of the bed held small lamps which flickered with low light, giving the room a cozy feel, despite the size. There were windows on either side of the room with a set of paned glass double doors that likely let out to the garden. The windows were open, a cool breeze coming through, pushing the dark blue curtains to billow. Despite the draft, I was warm due to the fire crackling behind me. The fireplace took up a large portion of the wall the door was on, with a small sitting area in front of it and bookshelves built into the wall on either side. It was the door on the other side of one of the shelves that Rainier pulled me toward, and I found a bathroom bigger than my entire bedroom back home. There was a giant closet off the entrance, where I could see a variety of button-down shirts and jackets hanging before Rainier pulled me past the door. The room itself was different shades of white, from variegated marble patterns on the floor to the white porcelain bathtub before me. It was enormous and built into the corner, with an L-shaped waist-high wall creating two of the four sides. It was more of a small pool than anything else. He turned on the spigot, and after a moment, pulled my hand under the water, already hot. He nodded to the wall where the water came out, explaining the water reservoir system above the fireplace that kept the water hot. It was more efficient than the boiler that heated the water for the rest of the estate. Walking behind me, he gently pushed my hair in front of my shoulder as his fingertips trailed down my back.

"Something about unbuttoning your dress makes me want time to slow down." Deft fingers went to work on the fastenings, and I closed my eyes, reveling in his touch. I couldn't believe I was here, in Rainier's house, being undressed by him. The man who had haunted my dreams and nightmares for the past sixteen years—longer even. The man had been a part of my dreams the moment I met him twenty years ago, since sharing a bottle of wine with him and his best friend in a dark garden. This man was a picture of patience and devotion, and I took a moment to bask in the knowledge he was mine. Regardless of what was to come—our rescue of Elora, his father's illness, the pressure for him to wed—none of it could go wrong with us at each other's sides. He kissed my bare shoulder as he slid my dress off it, continuing to unbutton all the way down. He turned me before pulling the dress off my other shoulder, and it slid down to the ground, puddling around my ankles.

His pupils dilated when he saw my new brassiere—bra as Lavenia called it—and the matching underwear I obtained from the seamstress, and I felt a warm flush spread over my chest as I squeezed my thighs tight. I reached for his shirt and started to unbutton it, but he pulled away.

"I want you to relax, and if I get undressed, I certainly don't think either of us will be relaxing tonight, at least not for a while. And you have an appointment to get to." He turned back to the bathtub and pulled a glass bottle off the edge, dumping a portion into the swiftly filling tub, the scent of lavender blooming. He kissed me, his hand on my neck and his thumb caressing my jaw, before he carefully pulled away.

"Call for me when you're done." His eyes slid over me again before he stiffly walked out of the bathroom. A bit disappointed, I slipped out of my undergarments—wishing I'd asked him to help me with the bra because it was not as simple as I thought it would be—and slid into the water. It was delightful and warm, and I almost had to swim by the time the tub was full. I found a bar of soap and sniffed, the smell of rain and earth enveloping me. I grinned and used it to wash, knowing I'd smell like him. After washing my hair, I pulled the small lever in the bottom of the tub to drain it and called for Rainier.

He came walking in, this time stripped of all clothing except those tight undershorts that showed me exactly what he spent his time thinking about. I was standing in the tub, my nakedness on display, and watched a tremor go through him. He turned the spigot back on, and with a flick of his wrist, the water stopped going straight down into the tub, controlled by his divinity. Instead, the hot drops fell from above, like a rainstorm, and I laughed in delight. He climbed into the tub with me, still wearing those shorts, and turned me around roughly, kissing the back of my neck and shoulders while his hands roamed over me, gliding across my wet skin. He put one hand on my waist as he cupped my breast with the other, pulling me backward. He sat on the edge of the tub, and I stumbled, my bare ass landing in his lap. I felt how hard he was and reached back, pulling onto the fabric between us, trying to tear them off. He swatted my hand away, so I grabbed at his muscular thigh instead. Grabbing one of my legs, he pulled it up to rest on the outside wall of the tub, spreading me open. He reached down, sliding his fingertips down past my stomach and the light patch of hair between my legs, straight to the waiting heat. I groaned as I pushed my head back against him.

He leaned down and nipped my ear as he teased, rimming my entrance with the pad of his fingertips. He dipped two fingers into me quickly, and I moaned.

"You're going to make me come just from touching you. You're assaulting my senses. Smelling my soap on your body," he whispered against my neck, inhaling deeply before pushing a soft kiss against my nape and sending delightful warmth through my body. "Tasting you on my lips, feeling your soft skin against mine." He trailed his free hand across my breast and stomach, fingertips lightly dancing on my pebbled flesh, while his other hand moved to my clit, where he started rubbing forcefully enough to drag a deep, low moan from between my lips. "Hearing you cry out, seeing you spread wide for me . . ." He pulled me against him, arm tight around my waist, as the leg I stood on started to shake. I felt his hard length against my back as he kept touching me, rubbing me, working me, and I already felt like I was about to come. I was completely relaxed in his arms, trusting his every move. He nipped at my neck, and I bit back a moan when he did once more, hard, before pressing a kiss to the wound. My chest was heaving, and my breathing came out rough and wild.

"I want to touch you. Let me touch you." I slid my hands down his sides, pulling at the clothes he still had on, jerking roughly as his fingers continued, pulling me closer to release.

"Take what I give you, Em." He let go of my waist and reached up, grabbing one peaked nipple roughly between his fingertips and squeezing. It was enough to send me over the edge, and my body jerked against him erratically as I screamed his name. He grabbed me by the waist again, keeping me upright, as his other hand continued rubbing me until I fell slack against him, twitching under his touch. He helped me turn to face him, and I drew a kiss from his lips like I needed it to survive.

I felt his smile as he pulled away, sliding his hands down my arms.

"I'll never get tired of watching you fall apart for me. Now let me put you back together."

CHAPTER 33

A SHORT WHILE LATER, I was in one of Rainier's shirts, wrapped soundly in his blankets. He brushed my hair out in the shower, and it felt like one of the more intimate things he'd ever done for me. He was gentle, massaging my scalp while he did it. I was mildly put out when he wouldn't let me touch him because I wanted him to feel the way I did. He argued that I needed to relax, and though I knew he was right, it didn't make me less grumpy about it. Rain spoiled me when he pulled out citrus lotion and slathered it over my body before wrapping a fluffy towel around me. Bringing me into his closet, he picked out a shirt for me before ushering me into the bedroom, promising to hold me after he bathed. I lay in his bed for a while, thinking about everything. I did some quick math and realized we would be getting Elora back in just over two weeks. The fact Rainier was so confident, and her captor seemed eager to work with us made me so optimistic the last week, I'd barely allowed myself to fear anything regarding her. My thoughts were more concerned with her well-being afterward. Had Prince Cyran been good to her the entire time she was there? Or did it take time for him to warm to her? What kind of things happened in the meantime before he took on the role as her protector? Did she see what happened to Faxon? I wondered how she'd react to me. Was my omission about the prophecy unforgivable, or would she understand? Would she forgive me for what I did to Faxon? After what the boy prince had said about her anger, I was worried she might not show up tonight.

I didn't even realize I had fallen asleep until I woke up standing in a doorway. My teeth were chattering, and I looked down, realizing I was only in Rainier's shirt. The thought hadn't even occurred to me that I would need to dress for it.

Shit.

The last time I had worn a nightgown that came down past my knees, and I'd still been cold. I tucked my arms around me as I glanced around, realizing I was in some sort of meeting room. I sat under a low ceiling made of wood with a table below it, a map outstretched on top. It almost seemed like we were on a ship, wooden slats making up the walls and floor beneath my feet. There were no windows, lending to my suspicions, but everything was perfectly steady, too still. There was no light fixture in the room, but everything was still bathed in light, a trick of the illusion. I thanked the gods I was alone as I padded over barefoot to the table, taking a seat on the other side of it to face the door. I waited only a moment before I heard the sounds of footsteps. Two sets, based on the heartbeats. I was surprised my abilities worked within the illusion, but there was no sense in questioning it. Prince Cyran rounded the corner, followed by a woman roughly the same age as him, the resemblance between the two clearly marking them as related despite her jet-black hair compared to his brown. They were both dressed in royal finery all the way down to the exquisite jewelry. Had they slept like that? Prince Cyran was dressed in black with the same chain necklaces and single earring as before, tall boots laced to his knees.

The woman, his sister perhaps, wore a crimson dress cut to the navel, revealing the swell of her breasts before thin wispy fabric billowed downward, fading to black at the bottom. I searched my memory for her name but fell short.

"Lady Emmeline." Prince Cyran was curt in his nod. "This is my sister, Princess Ismene." I stayed seated a moment too long before realizing I was expected to curtsy for them. I stood up quickly, knowing how absurd I looked wearing only Rain's shirt, and gave the weakest curtsy imaginable, ensuring I stayed covered. It was clear I was wearing a man's shirt, and I balked at the thought of Elora seeing me in it. I watched Ismene's lip curl as she took in my attire, and a grin flickered over Cyran's face.

"Did I get the date wrong?" His grin turned into a sneer as he regarded my appearance.

"No. Honestly, I forgot I needed to be dressed. I don't tend to sleep in such stunning attire. In truth, I don't even own such finery." I gave a small smile, hopeful my groveling would ease any offense. I needed these two to work with me, and offending them wasn't doing anything in my favor. Ismene's sneer stayed plastered on her lips, but Cyran's turned into a smirk.

"Here." He held out his hand, and a cloak appeared in it from thin air before he passed it to me. I was grateful, standing up to pull it around my body.

"Thank you. Is Elora coming?"

"As of now, she is undecided. Ismene is here to help her decide." I looked at the girl next to him, her sneer turning into a mixture of boredom and contempt. She seemed so close in age to Cyran, and I couldn't tell if she was an older or younger sister. I studied the two of them before slowly sitting back in my seat.

"Different mothers, born within a month of each other." Cyran read my curiosity and supplied the answer I never asked, and he grinned at my expression. "I'm older."

"What is keeping Elora?" I didn't particularly care about their ages. I wanted to see my daughter.

"Did you know Faxon planned to sell her?" Ismene's voice was deeper than I anticipated, quiet and sensual by nature, with the tightly clipped accent her brother shared.

"Of course not." I felt the look of disgust on my face in an instant. "Does she think—are you kidding?" Cyran held up his hand, and I slammed my mouth shut, glaring at him.

"I didn't think so, but one can never be sure." Cyran nodded to Ismene, prompting her to continue.

"And did you know she was the Beloved?"

"I've never presented her to the Myriad."

"But you suspected." A statement, not a question.

"Yes."

"And you never told her." Another statement.

"Correct."

"Why not?" Ismene's careful tilt of her head made me feel like prey. I knew Ismene and Cyran probably weren't in full power of their divinity, yet Ismene's calm and watchful stare reminded me of a cat waiting out a mouse.

"Her father and I couldn't agree on telling her. I'd always thought we were protecting her, but I planned to tell her after she returned from her trip in Mira, regardless of his wishes." Cyran and Ismene shared a glance to which Ismene nodded. Realization raced over me, a cool shock to my system.

"You're like me, aren't you?" She gave me a curt nod before folding her hands in her lap.

"She's the best harrower in Folterra." Cyran gave his sister a smile that had her rolling her eyes.

"Harrower?" The term was unfamiliar to me.

"Is that not what you call it in Vesta? Someone who can communicate with the heart?" Cyran cocked his head at the same angle as his sister, and I almost laughed. Different mothers, perhaps, but raised the same.

"I've never called it anything. I've never met another. Until now, I suppose."

"Why did you send Faxon to me? What did you do to him?" It was my turn to ask some questions, and I made sure I listened to them just as Ismene listened to me.

"That's a question for your daughter." Cyran's brows furrowed as he spoke. "And I let my seer help mindbreak him. He deserved it."

"What do you mean?"

"I *mean*, I have a mindbreaker, and I let a seer join in on the fun as a special treat."

"I can't help but be curious as to what exactly he did, although I'm sure it was warranted."

"On that, we can agree. How is he? I'm sure as much of a delight in madness as he was in sanity?"

"He's dead." Cyran and Ismene's brows both shot up as their eyes met.

"By whose hand?" Ismene stared at me, mouth agape.

"My own. It was mercy after what you did to him, but I'd have done it either way."

"The effects might have worn off eventually."

"Doubtful. And the result would have been the same. Faxon was dead the minute he sold his daughter." I spat out the words, forgetting about minding my tongue.

"You killed him?" Her voice was quiet, laced with a certain hardness I wouldn't have expected. I glanced up at the door I'd appeared in and saw Elora standing there. I took her in, the long, white dress she wore flowed off her, and she was barefoot. Angry, red marks marred her wrists, likely from some sort of restraint—obsidian perhaps—but her pallor was healthy. She seemed cared for, well-rested. I watched as a single tear rolled down her cheek, and she brushed it away with the back of her hand. Angry. Her hair was unrestrained, the tight curls flowing down to her waist. She was beautiful, and it made me heartsick that it wasn't truly her standing in front of me. Cyran jumped to his feet, looking between the two of us as I rose as well.

"I told you to stay—" Cyran started to whisper to her, but I cut him off.

"This isn't how I wanted to tell you. Your father betrayed us, Elora. I'm sorry."

"He was no father of mine." Elora's jaw jutted out, tears forming at her lashes, and I could tell she was fighting to keep them at bay. Cyran took a few steps toward her, reaching out his hand before she turned away from him, back to me. I stood, making my way around the table, wanting nothing more than to fold my daughter into my arms, to let her cry into my chest and pet her, playing with her hair as I did it.

"Stop, Mama. Don't." I froze, terrified by the confirmation of my fears coming true. She couldn't understand. "Papa—Faxon—told me everything was going to be fine, that he was keeping me safe. But then, a few days ago, he told me I meant nothing to him because I am an extension of you. What did you do to him, Mama?"

My jaw dropped. He hated me that much? He was that embittered by my lack of love for him that he'd do this to her? The fact she used his name hit a sore spot. I didn't blame her, not one bit, but I knew it was a wound within her that probably festered.

"Nothing. I didn't do anything to him. I—I didn't love him, but I didn't do anything."

"We've heard rumors." Prince Cyran turned to face me, arms crossed.

"Prince Rainier called off his betrothal." Ismene supplied, body language matching her brother.

"Yes." I nodded, pulling the cloak around myself closer, fully aware of every touch of the fabric underneath it, the shirt belonging to the man in question. I didn't like where this conversation seemed to be headed.

"Did you have anything to do with that, Mama? Is that what Papa—what he meant?" Elora's voice was full of accusation.

"I—I suppose I may have had something to do with it, but I don't know what your father was talking about. He did this to us before I ever—" Her face fell as she watched me, every emotion on her face telling me what she thought of me, what she assumed I'd done. "I had not seen or spoken to Prince Rainier since long before you were born. I only sought him out after you were taken, I swear it." I looked at Ismene, my brows lifting, begging her to confirm what I said.

"She's telling the truth."

"He was the only person I knew who could even help me, Elora. But I hadn't seen him since we buried Lucia." Elora's face turned into something more contemplative, but the furrow between her brows told me she wasn't sold on my confession.

"And yet, you had something to do with him calling off the betrothal to the Nythyrian princess." Cyran waited for an explanation I wasn't willing to give. So I just stood, watching Elora as she pleaded with her eyes for me to explain. I wanted to tell her everything, but I was afraid of sharing in front of Cyran. I offered her as much truth as I could without revealing too much.

"The prince and I, Rain . . ." Her eyes widened at the familiar name. "Rain and I were in love before your Aunt Lucia died, and we parted ways at her burial. I was given to your father, and I never saw or spoke to Rainier again until what, two weeks ago?" I felt the sting in my nose and knew I was on the verge of crying. I didn't want to tell her any of this in this forced way. Ismene nodded, confirming the truth.

"Wasn't he betrothed to Aunt Lucia, Mama?" Her eyes flared with judgment and more insinuation.

"Yes, but Lucia was in love with someone else." She rolled her eyes as if the whole situation was beneath her.

"Why didn't you tell me?"

"About Rainier?"

"About any of it! The fact you didn't love Pa—Faxon, that you'd been in love with the Crown Prince!" She was incredulous, and I only realized then how absurd this must be for her. I felt a tear roll down my cheek. "Let alone the fact I'm the gods damn Beloved, Mama!" I'd never heard her curse before that moment.

"Supposedly." Ismene cut in, earning her a glare from both Cyran and Elora.

"I'm sorry. I'm so sorry, Elora. I was trying to protect you, and I guess I was trying to protect myself. Thinking about all of it hurt. Thinking about Rain hurt." I looked at her pleadingly, hoping she'd understand. "Please forgive me."

"You've kept so much from me." She shook her head and started for the door, and I let out a sob. The entire room shook, and I fell backward, landing roughly in my chair. Cyran was at Elora's side, holding onto her, and I watched the soft way she gazed up at him. I was right about one thing at least.

"Where are you?" Prince Cyran cocked his head. I slowly eyed the room we were in, and he gave an exasperated sigh. "Where are you sleeping? Are you safe? The illusion is fighting me."

"I—" I hesitated, afraid of revealing too much, worried about Elora's reaction. But the time for lies and half-truths and omissions was over. "I'm safe. Rainier has a home in Astana. I'm asleep there."

"It would seem he's trying to wake you." Cyran raised a brow. "Let's try to calm down a bit. My illusions work a lot like dreams, so I wouldn't be surprised if you were crying in his bed right now." I took a deep breath, avoiding Elora's eyes. I didn't deny I was in Rainier's bed, nor did I plan to. I changed the subject.

"Is the plan the same?"

"Yes. Is the prince sending troops to the Cascade?"

"We are petitioning King Soren tomorrow, but Rainier has the pull without his father if he needs it."

"Good. Ismene will remain with our brother, helping work against him."

"Your brother has allied with Olag, has he not?"

"Yes. And based on the fact I already know about the broken engagement; I wouldn't be surprised if the Nythyrians were to join the fray if they haven't already." I closed my eyes, rubbing in between them, realizing my presence might have made this all the more difficult.

"Why don't you tell me where you are, and we can come get her before the attack on the Cascade ever happens?"

Cyran scoffed. "Declan has spies everywhere. Doing that would get both myself and Ismene killed for acting against him."

"But he wouldn't know you told us. Rainier has spies too."

"It doesn't matter; I can't tell you anyway. He had his mindbreaker place a gag on us. If I even try to speak of our location, I'll stop breathing."

Ismene nodded in confirmation, and I sighed, dropping my head into my hands.

"May I speak to my daughter, alone?" Cyran glanced at Elora, who hesitated, rubbing her arms before agreeing. The royals walked out of the room, and I wondered how large the illusion was. Would Ismene and Cyran just wander an endless hallway until they were called back in? I waited a few moments before I pulled her into my arms. She fought me at first but then let out a small cry as I wrapped myself around her.

"I'm so sorry, honey. I'm sorry I hid things from you. I'm sorry your father did what he did. I'm trying. I'm doing the best I can." She sniffled and pulled away from me.

"I know, Mama. Was Papa—Did Faxon say anything about me?" I felt bad that she was struggling with calling him something else as if she felt she had to. Though, it had only been yesterday when Faxon said all those horrifying things. How was that only a day ago? I couldn't share what he had said, regardless of my newfound insistence on honesty.

"Oh honey, you can still call him Papa. You don't have to—"

"No, no, I cannot. He doesn't deserve it. What did he say about me?" She snapped, and I recognized the rage in her eyes, the promise of violence. Hanwen would be proud.

"He wasn't... right. I tried to heal him because I wanted to find out more about where you were, but he never told us anything useful. When I realized his mind was gone and he couldn't help me, I killed him. But you should know I would have killed him either way for what he did."

She looked down at her feet, not as upset by the statement as I thought she'd be.

"He slapped me. That's how it happened. Cy already hated him, but when he saw the marks on my face, he just snapped. My guard told me he beat him and sent him to the mindbreaker."

I nodded slowly, watching her, tracing her cheek for any signs of injury before finding none. "I don't blame him, honey. I'd have done worse. Do you like the prince?" Her eyes grew wide, and her cheeks flushed.

"Cy? He—He's not that bad. Everyone has been kind to me."

"I heard you bit someone's ear off." She grinned at me before she pushed the smile back down.

"They attacked me in the woods; I don't know what they expected. Cy was less than thrilled about it." Her eyes widened in panic for a moment before she blurted out her next words. "Is Theo alright?"

"Yes, he's alright. I found him and healed him. He's worried about you, of course."

"It was so scary, Mama. Until we got to Cyran, the soldiers weren't nice to me. And Papa, well, he told me everything would be alright, but he wouldn't look at me if he could help it."

"They didn't hurt you, did they?" She shook her head, and I sighed in relief. After my interaction with the mercenaries, I was so frightened they might have hurt her like that. After what Faxon did, I wouldn't have trusted him to stop them. "Do you think we should trust Cyran? Rain seems to think we should."

Elora nodded slowly. "I think so. I'm still mad at you, but this is awful. Cyran is *scared*, Mama. I don't want his brother to get to me. I've heard stories . . . "

"He won't." My voice portrayed a confidence that wasn't altogether real. "Rain and I are going to be at the Cascade. We'll get you back, I promise."

"And then what? Where do we go? Everyone will know I'm the Beloved." I could hear the panic rising in her voice. I shushed her, pulling her tighter against me.

"Don't worry about that yet. Prince Rainier has offered us his protection. We can go wherever you want to go."

"What about Cyran?"

"Well, he'll probably stay in Astana until everything is over with Declan."

"Do you want to stay in Astana?"

"I want to stay wherever you want to stay, Elora. Rainier has offered multiple options to us, and we can always go back to Ravemont if that's what you'd want."

She made a face about Ravemont, surprising me. I always thought she was curious about her ancestral home, but her expression told me otherwise.

"Are you going to marry him?"

I gaped at her. Not only was I surprised by her question, but I also hadn't meant to make it seem as if that were a possibility. Not only that, but just a few moments ago, she'd been staring at me like the soldier who called me a whore. I paused for a moment, stumbling over my own thoughts on the situation.

"He's a conduit, Elora. I don't think either of us has thought about that at all." So much for honesty. I'd thought about it. I'd thought about every aspect of it. Would he even want that? Was it even possible? I had agonized over the idea of the ritual, and I thought about the responsibility. It was too much, so I tried to push it all away every time it entered my mind.

"Why does it matter that he's a conduit?"

"Because I am not a strong one like you, so I have little to offer him. I don't know if it would even be allowed, and I don't know if he would even want that with me, baby. We're talking centuries here, Elora. Centuries of being stuck with me, and you know firsthand how bad that could be."

"Mama." She smiled at me, a knowing look on her face that surpassed her years. "Do you still love him?" I only hesitated for a moment, wondering what to tell her.

"I might." She tilted her head in consideration as Cyran rounded the corner.

"Have you ladies made up yet?" Based on the laughter that spilled from his mouth and the joy lighting his face, the glare Elora shot him was meant to kill. The way his expression lit up at the sight of her made him appear rather handsome, and I understood why Elora blushed when I asked about him. His build was narrow but strong, and he had kind eyes, full of laughter and misbehavior. "I can't hold the illusion much longer, so you'll have to bear with me."

Cyran went on to explain what to look for at the Cascade, utilizing the map on the table. Declan didn't anticipate us knowing about the attack and had made little to no arrangements for hiding Elora. She'd be in a carriage far back from the battle, only to be brought out upon victory. His suggested plan was to rift to her location and pull her through it quickly. Cyran would allow himself to be taken in battle, and we were to plan accordingly. Elora tensed when he revealed that aspect of the plan and argued with him over it until I assured her Rainier's men wouldn't hurt him. When he was finished speaking about logistics, he left the room again, and I pulled Elora into a long embrace, both of us crying as the room began to shake.

"To the moon, Elora. I love you to the moon."

I woke up with a gasp, disoriented. I couldn't see, and the room was stiflingly hot. My arms sprang free from either side of me, reaching for Elora, trying to clutch her to my chest. When I realized I wasn't in the illusion anymore, I let out a sob and tucked my arms close to me.

"Come here, love." Rain's voice renewed my tears as he pulled me tight against his chest, brushing his fingers through my hair. The tenderness was doing nothing to stop my crying, only fueling it further. The illusion had been too short. I cried into his chest, not caring if I covered his freshly cleaned skin in snot and salt. He held me and petted me until my tears finally lessened.

"She's alright, isn't she, Em?" He sounded timid, afraid for the answer, and I realized this entire time he thought something might have happened to her.

"Oh gods, yes. She's alright. It was just too short. She's scared, but she's alright."

Rainier let out the breath he'd been holding, and I nearly started crying again.

"But you were able to see her?"

"Yes." I paused, wiping my nose and eyes on my sleeve, Rain's sleeve. "She is quite mad at me, though."

"Like you expected?"

"Worse. Faxon fed her lies, and she believed them. He made her think he sold her because I betrayed him. I think he insinuated I was unfaithful."

"Well . . ."

"No, stop. You came after."

"I sure did." I could hear his smile in the dark, and I smacked his chest. "*Were* you unfaithful to him?"

"No, Rain. I'm offended you even asked. It's absurd! Utter foolishness. Not only did he think it, he was convincing enough to make Elora consider the idea. Gods, when would I have had the time? I haven't done anything . . . like what we did the other night. Not since before she was born."

"Even with him?"

"Especially with Faxon." I paused, wondering if I should reveal everything to him, and finally decided honesty seemed to be the best idea for everyone important to me. "Faxon drank. Sometimes when he drank, he'd . . . use my hand. But that was it, and I didn't ever want to do it."

I felt him tense beside me before he pulled me closer, kissing my forehead.

"I wish I could bring him back just so I could be the one to kill him." He stilled before he nuzzled into my neck, inhaling me. "I'm sorry."

"Why are you sorry?"

"Because gods dammit Emmeline, I made so many mistakes. I let you challenge me to that gods forsaken duel, and then I respected the outcome. I should've taken you and ran, the Crown be damned, and saved you from so much."

"You know I wouldn't have let you do that. And to be fair, you didn't respect the outcome since you did return to Ravemont." I laughed softly, somehow able to look back at it without anger.

"I could have tied you up and made you understand." He huffed a small laugh.

"I'd have hated you, Rain, and you know it."

"I know. Still, what he did, all the things he's done—and I wasn't there to save you." Surprise crossed his features, and he kissed me gently before pulling back to take me in. "The fact you still did what you did the other night with me means more now than it did before. Thank you, Em."

"Don't thank me; I wanted to do that. I—you still helped me through it in a way. Afterward, I'd remind myself what it was like when you used to love me. I knew your kind of safety and security existed out there, and I'd experienced it, however fleeting. Don't say sorry or thank me because you've helped me more than you know."

His gaze met mine, and the look on his face almost broke my heart in two. Every feeling I couldn't voice and every moment shared between us all showed on his face, and I buried mine in his neck, not able to handle the intensity of it.

He placed his hand on the back of my head, holding me, before whispering, "I never stopped, you know."

"Me neither."

It was the closest we had ever been to saying it. We never said it back then, and both of us had only admitted to it in passing now. It felt like a line drawn in the sand, and I wasn't sure I was ready for the freefall once we crossed it. He held me tight, and I slid my leg between his. We laid there for a while, his hands rubbing down my back while I settled into his embrace.

"They knew about the betrothal and suspected I had something to do with it." I felt his body go stiff, and he cocked his head to look at me, despite the darkness of the room.

"How?"

"I assume he has spies, too. He suspected Nythyr may have already joined with Declan because of it."

"I was afraid of that."

"You were afraid of that? You knew they might ally with Folterra? Then why would you call off the engagement, Rain?" It was one thing to cost him an alliance, but this? To gain another enemy? My voice rose, and I sat up. Climbing out of bed, I walked to the fire and put another log on, allowing the room to brighten so I could see him. It wouldn't help with how hot it was, but, nevertheless.

"Did you just ask me why I called off the betrothal?" His voice was quiet, laced with frustration. He sat up in the bed, shirtless and disheveled, while I stood at the foot of it, arms crossed and staring at him.

"Yes! If you knew scorning her would lead to another ally for Folterra, why would you do something so stupid, especially with what's about to happen at the Cascade? I thought you'd lose an alliance, and that was bad enough. But for them to ally against you? To sway Nythyr over to Declan?

"Keeva is not a woman scorned, Emmeline." He sounded dismissive, as if I had no idea what I was talking about. "She had no illusions of love between us; we were a means to an end. I was her mother's opportunity to sink her claws into Vesta, and she was my guarantee of the Crown and the ruse of an alliance. Nythyr opened their pass while my engagement was still intact. Queen Nereza made her intentions clear; the union never mattered. The only thing that has changed is they will be more open with their duplicity."

"I still don't understand why you'd do it now and not after Elora was safely back. Surely, Nythyr wouldn't join an active cause against you if you were still betrothed. Why do it now?" I raised my voice, frustrated he'd take risks that endangered our mission to get Elora back.

"Highclere, what the hell do you think I was doing in Ardian?" I watched as his hands gripped his thighs where he sat cross-legged on the bed. I took a moment to think, drawing back to what my father had said to me about the reason for his visit.

"Something to do with the Myriad, I don't know!"

"My gods damn task for Keeva." I felt my heart start to pound in my chest, the animal in my stomach iced over in a cold panic. He'd been so close to performing the ritual. He gave me a small smile, one without any warmth. "Yes, Emmeline. I was in Ardian to get my task and was supposed to return to the capital to perform the ritual immediately afterward. *And I never even went to the temple.*"

"Why didn't you?" My voice shook because I already knew the answer.

"YOU." His voice rang out, with a rumble in the ground to underlie his anger. "Because you fell back into my life like a gods damn forest fire. I made a choice, and it sent a clear message the day I left Ardian without my task, and I've been sending clear messages every day since with you by my side. I knew my engagement was over the moment I left with you. Keeva knew the moment I left Ardian. What I did today was merely a formality."

"Why would you do that for me? You're risking a war, Rain! Folterra *and* Nythyr?"

"There will always be *another fucking war*. You already know why I did it. If you thought for a second I'd have told you no, you wouldn't have come to ask me for help."

I stood there, crestfallen. He made a decision to help me, which sacrificed the stability of Vesta, risked his ascension as king, risked a war, and completely changed the trajectory his life had been on. I still had no idea what would happen between us, if he planned to let Lavenia take the Crown to be with me, or what his intentions were, but I knew now just what he'd risked and turned away from by choosing to help me. His mouth was set in a tight line, and he narrowed his eyes at me.

"Oh, don't give me that look. Do you think I only did it for you? I knew what would happen when I made my choice. I chose myself by choosing you. And I'm going to keep doing it. I'm going to keep choosing you." He shook his head before he lifted his hands, palms out in offering. "I love you, Emmeline. I have loved you from the start, and I will love you until we are both just a whisper on the wind. It's your eyes I see when I close mine, your heart I want to hold, and I'd set this whole damn world on fire if you wanted to watch it burn."

I stopped moving, stopped breathing. This was it—the freefall. The line in the sand. Loving Rainier was the most terrifying and exhilarating thing I'd ever done. Loving Rain was like breathing, like dying. Inevitable and compulsive. It was something once admitted, I'd never come back from.

"How? We—the Crown." I didn't know what I was asking, but the words tumbled out of my mouth. And yet, he understood.

"My father is dying, and I have to marry. Come on, Em, catch up." His serious expression changed to a rueful smile. My heart was racing, and my stomach was churning. He couldn't possibly mean what I thought he did. It was insane.

"You can't be serious. The Myriad won't allow it. Your mother won't allow it." He pulled himself out of bed, wearing only the undershorts from earlier, and opened his nightstand. I knew we were destined to be together, but I never thought like this. I never imagined, never wanted this. I only wanted him; I didn't want a crown. I didn't want to stop Vesta from making alliances it needed, however frail. He turned, a small box in his hands, as he walked over to me.

"Rain, I can't. I don't want that."

My jaw dropped, and my heart stopped as he slammed down on both of his knees in front of me, taking one of my hands in his.

"Marry me, you beautiful, venomous fool."

CHAPTER 34

"Stand up!"

"No."

"Rain, stand up. Are you insane? Faxon's body isn't even cold. I only came back a fortnight ago. I know you have to hurry and marry; I understand. As much as it pains me, I'll let you go so you can be the king you're meant to be. But we both know it can't be me." He was born for it, raised and educated to be a better king than his father before him, and I couldn't stand in the way. We'd find each other in the next life. We'd always find each other. Rainier didn't move, just stayed on the ground in front of me, those piercing, emerald-green eyes on mine.

"You haven't even had a chance to think this through, Rain." I watched a beautiful smile spread across his lips, nearly destroying me in the process.

"I've had almost twenty years to think this through, Emma."

"Stop. You have not."

"Did you ever stop loving me?" He squeezed my hand in his, and I felt nauseated.

"I just told you I didn't." He stood up, and I crossed my arms and turned away from him, gazing down into the fire.

"And I said the same to you. I haven't stopped loving you since you bullied your way into my life when you were fifteen years old. I haven't stopped wanting you. I've tried to put my duty first, and I've made some mistakes along the way, but my love for you has been constant. I've loved you from the start."

"There's more to this than love!" I turned around, throwing my arms out in frustration. If there was some way I could say yes, and not be the voice of reason, I would have done it in a heartbeat. I could not be queen. I almost started laughing, thinking how badly Lavenia didn't want this because she wasn't prepared. If only she knew what her brother was asking of me. If he would have let the Crown go to his sister, I'd have said yes in a heartbeat. Even if it hurt my friend or went against her wishes, I would have said yes. There would have been no hesitation or questions. I'd have fallen to my knees and screamed the word. But he was asking me for so much more than just to marry him.

"Yes, of course, there is more to it. There's the protection you and your daughter would be offered if you were my queen, there's—"

"You won't protect us unless I say yes?" I shoved him backward, shouting at him.

"That's not what I said!" He took a step forward, fists clenched, and I felt my jaw shoot out in defiance. "I'm saying no one would dare try to take her again if her mother was the gods damn Queen of Vesta. They'd die trying."

"You realize how selfish that would make me? Becoming queen for no other reason than to better protect my daughter?"

"The fact you think it's selfish only proves—it doesn't matter. I'd hope there are other reasons you'd want to be queen, present company included." The corner of his mouth quirked upward.

"You think loving you is enough reason to rule a kingdom, Rainier?" I knew what I said hit its mark when his face tightened, all traces of his smile gone.

"As if loving you has ever been any sort of blessing, Emma." I saw red.

"Then why bother with this?" I gestured to the box in his hand, shouting and willing the tears forming in my eyes to go away.

"Sometimes, I wonder if maybe my life would've been easier if I never met you, Em. But the fact is, I did. I met you, and my heart has beat for only you ever since. My heart is yours to break, borrow, and bruise. The only way this ends is death. There is no one else for either of us. You know it, I know it, our friends know it. Mairin just met me, and even she's said as much!"

"Yeah, Mairin seems to think she knows a lot." I bit the words out, immediately regretting them.

"What do you mean?" His eyes narrowed as he stared down at me, instantly recognizing the facial expression I wore.

"Nothing." I reined my features in, averting my eyes.

"*What do you mean?*" He bent down, eye level with me, an unforgiving look on his face.

"It's nothing!" I shouted at him, pushing him again before I turned to walk away, but he grabbed my wrists and held me tight.

"You little liar." He was angry beyond words, but the longer I looked at him, he began to appear hurt. The earth below us was shaking slightly, and I realized he wasn't doing it on purpose, his emotions strong enough that controlling his divinity was a task he couldn't manage at the moment. His eyes searched mine, pleading with me for honesty. I didn't want to tell him. Telling him meant I'd been hiding it from him. Telling him meant I was still fighting him, even though I knew we were predestined. But I couldn't lie to him anymore. My body made my decision for me when I felt my shoulders drop, my defensive position lost, all open and vulnerable in the way I held myself.

"She says we're twin flames." I looked down as I said it, not wanting to see the hurt from the secret I'd kept. His hands tightened on my wrists.

"We're what?" His voice was breathless, and I lifted my eyes back up to his, shining in the low light.

"We are twin flames, Rain." My voice was louder, breaking on his name. He let go of my wrists and took a step back, the space between us a slash to my heart. The ground was shaking hard enough I grabbed onto the chair behind me for support, letting out a small gasp. He glanced at me for a second, and the movement stopped abruptly. I watched him turn away from me, pulling his hand up to his mouth, rubbing his jaw roughly. He paced for a moment, and I watched the muscles in his arm flex as he kept tracing his hand along his jaw. He walked over to the garden doors and threw them open, a cool breeze ripping through the room. I found it interesting he didn't question me or question Mairin. He took it as fact, and I wasn't sure if it was because he knew more about merrows than I did, or if it was because he was so certain in me, *in us*, it didn't seem like a stretch to him.

"How long have you known?" His back was to me, the fire dancing a pattern across his broad shoulders.

"A few days."

"Specifically." His voice was a knife in my stomach, cold and unyielding.

"She told me after I sparred with Thyra the other night while you and the others were getting us food."

"So, you've spent the night in my arms twice since then without telling me?"

"Yes." I hesitated. "I was going to tell you." I let my voice trail off, knowing it wasn't enough.

"When? When were you planning on telling me?" He turned and took a few steps toward me, and I dipped my head the second I caught his eyes. His gaze was piercing, and I swore I saw a faint shimmer, emotions welling at the surface, and I knew I'd start to cry the minute I gave into it.

"I don't know, Rain. I needed to talk to Mairin again, and then Faxon happened, and I just needed a moment to wrap my head around all of it and what it means." He stopped, standing a few feet in front of me, and I kept my eyes on the ground.

"And you didn't think I might need to wrap my head around it, too?" I finally raised my eyes to him, and to my surprise, I found myself not filled with tears, but righteous anger instead.

"No! I didn't think you needed to wrap your gods damn head around it, and given the fact you just *proposed* to me, I clearly wasn't wrong, was I? You have proven to me over and over again how you feel. I have fought you every single time when you've made it clear, and in this, I knew you were certain. I stopped questioning it. I knew where you stood, and I thought you'd understand when I eventually told you. That you'd understand why I might have needed a gods damn minute!" I was shouting again, and I hoped to the gods wherever the others were staying in the house was far, far away from Rainier's suite.

"What I understand is you're *mine*, and by not telling me, you made me think there was a chance you weren't." He dropped his crossed arms to his sides and took a step toward me.

"I'm not *yours*. I'm not a—a thing to be kept." I knew that wasn't how he meant it, but I didn't care. As he approached, I pulled my arms protectively around me, and his eyes raked over my body.

"You might not be my property, but you are mine as I am yours." He was close enough to smack, to touch, to hit, to kiss.

"Says Mairin." Meeting his eyes, I knew my defiance was wearing thin.

"Says the *gods*. Are you trying to tell me it doesn't explain everything?" He was incredulous—the idea that we were anything but twin flames, predestined by the gods, was absurd to him now that the possibility was here in front of him.

"No, I just needed a minute, alright?" I pushed him away but he grabbed my wrist, pulling me closer to him.

"Well, time's up." Holding my wrist with one hand, he opened the tiny box with his other. I gazed up at him, my breath shaking and throat working, as I felt cool metal slide onto my ring finger. I refused to look at it, to look anywhere but into deep green eyes reflecting the flames behind me and the flames in my heart.

"I didn't say yes."

"I know."

And then his hand was grabbing my hair, holding it in his fist, as he pulled my head back, roughly kissing the length of my neck, nipping me with his teeth. He used his other hand to rip his shirt from my body, the buttons falling to the ground. I reached to help, to free the buttons instead of ripping them, and he forcefully threw my hand aside, almost angry, a low growl vibrating against my throat. With one last hard tug, he finished ruining his shirt, and it fell to the floor. He pulled back from my neck, his eyes raking down my naked body as his fingers drew delicate circles across my breasts. I was molten gold under his hands, shining and heated.

"You belong to me, Emmeline." I glared up at him as he flicked one sensitive nipple and then the other when I didn't reply. He slid his hand down, tracing the swell of my breast, my stomach, down, down, down to my warm center. His fingers brushed through my wetness, and I closed my eyes, willing myself not to react, not to cry out for him, not to show him just how much I needed him. My body was a traitor to my will as I arched into his fingertips, both of my hands braced on the chair behind me. He withdrew his touch, and I opened my eyes as he lifted his fingers to his lips, slowly sucking on them as he looked at me.

"You taste like you belong to me." I felt an ache deep inside me, and I glared up at him as I pressed the flat of my palm against his hardness, the thin fabric doing nothing to hide what was waiting for me. He used both hands to grab me by the ass, pulling me against him, trapping my hand between us, as his lips found mine. Lips and tongue and teeth crashed together. I tasted myself on his lips, and I found it so indecent I let out a soft groan, thinking of his tongue inside me. I rubbed down the length of him with my palm, rough and unforgiving. He let out a soft grunt as he moved his hands to my thighs, pulling me up so that my legs wrapped around his waist. I threw my arms around his neck as I rolled my hips, rubbing myself against him just like I liked it, the sweetest torture.

He bit my lip as he moved, slamming us into the bookshelves on one side of the fireplace. He was a force, a wild flame, and he was going to take and destroy and burn me alive. He used one hand to brace against the books while the other slid down my body, skimming over my breast, then my ribs, finally settling at my hip, while he pushed his body against mine. We kissed like we didn't need air to breathe, like we wouldn't have the time. He tugged my bottom lip into his mouth, causing me to moan and push against him. I cut off his answering groan by biting his lip, hard enough to hurt. Letting him see I wanted it to hurt. I wanted everything between us to feel the same: frenzy and passion and pain. I loved this man, that much I knew to be true. I loved him in a way I'd never been able to love anyone else. The type of love which burns bright and quick but no less devastating. But we'd never stopped burning.

His tongue slid between my lips, forceful and thorough. It was a preview of what was to come when we made love. Because that was certainly happening. As sure as I drew breath, I knew it was the right time. I would pour him into my body as I'd already poured him into my soul. The rest would come later.

He slid one hand to my neck, pulling my hair into his fist, as he moved my head just where he needed it. His lips drifted down to my neck before he clamped down, biting hard enough that I cried out and ripped my fingernails down his back. He hissed and ground his hard length against my soft center before he took my mouth again. A fierce need drove through me. The need to make him mine. To show him, finally, that I was on the same page. I wanted him just as desperately now as I ever had. I needed him.

He moaned into my mouth before he spun us around, carrying me to the giant bed we'd been lying on not long ago. He slammed me down as I let go of his neck, and I fell, my hair fanning out around me, my body fully bared. Heart and soul, body and mind, I belonged to him. I was his, and it was clear he intended to claim, to prove it as fact. He climbed on top of me, his tongue forcing past my lips, and I held back, biting his lip hard. When he pulled away, his eyes were full of delight and mischief. A promise that I'd pay for the small hurt. He slid down lower, kissing down my neck, my breast, swirling his tongue over one nipple then the other as he kissed between them, inhaling the smell of his soap on my skin before he looked up, grinning.

"You smell like mine." He continued kissing down my body until he roughly positioned my legs, bent at the knees, and lowered himself, tracing his tongue clear up the center of me. He watched me as I moaned, and my back arched; the feeling of his tongue for only a moment was torture. I wanted his tongue inside me, his fingers, his cock. I wanted him to fill me, and I ached at the lack of him. He gave me another long lick, ending with a flick to my clit. I grunted at the need, at the feel of such a tease, and glared down at him. He gave me a devious grin before he pulled my clit into his mouth, sucking me, allowing the slightest caress of teeth on the sensitive spot, and I threw my head back, moaning loudly.

"This is definitely mine."

I hissed in frustration, angry he was stopping to talk. He stared up at me, gaze narrowed and brows lowered.

"Who does this belong to?"

I glared down at him, annoyed at the interruption, frustrated by his need to possess, but he just watched me expectantly, his lips glistening in the low light. He leaned back down and nipped my clit, and I cried out before he stopped again, watching me. I let out a whine and pushed myself up, trying to close the distance between his mouth and that spot.

"I asked you a question, ocean eyes."

I groaned and slid my hand down. If he wouldn't do what I needed, I was perfectly capable of doing it myself. He grabbed my wrist before I even got close and held my hand down at my side.

"No, Em. You don't come until I say so. I'll ask you again, who does this sweet, little cunt belong to?"

He flattened his tongue as he licked me from base to clit, his tongue dipping just inside my entrance before he stopped. He hovered just over that bundle of nerves, his breath hot on me, waiting for me to answer. The need for him to fill me, to fuck me, to make me come, finally outweighed my desire to defy him.

"You! It belongs to you." I shouted at him, eager for him to continue.

"You're gods damn right it belongs to me."

He dipped his head and picked up where he left off, nipping that sensitive spot before he slid his tongue down the length of me. I arched into him, pushing up into his face, grinding myself onto his tongue. His hands spanned the backs of my thighs as he pushed them back, knees approaching my chest, opening me up farther to the assault of his tongue. Moving one hand down to slide through his hair while the other gripped the sheet, I scratched his scalp, dragging my fingernails across his skin as he continued nibbling and sucking on my clit. He made a soft, contented sound I felt through my body, and I was almost overcome by the intimacy. Gods, to know I could make him make that noise while he made me feel like this? I felt powerful.

His tongue circled my entrance before he slid his mouth back up to my clit, and he shoved two of his fingers inside me. I was ready for him, slick, but the use of two at once was a surprise. The sensation pulled a deep moan from low within me. I already felt so tight, but it wasn't enough. I heard him groan as I felt myself squeeze around his fingers tightly, desperate to be filled. Desperate to have him inside me. Desperate for more. He moved, fingers going in and curling upwards as he placed his other hand palm-down, lightly applying pressure right above my pubic bone. I started panting and writhing, feeling a whole new layer of bliss and pleasure I'd never felt before. He beat a rhythm with his fingertips inside me, and I arched off the bed, an endless moan coming from the back of my throat. He had sat up so I could see his outline in the light of the fire behind him. In the low light, I could barely make out his face, but his eyes glinted with lust as he took me in. I didn't hide my expression, allowing him to see how crazed he made me. I had one hand in my hair, tugging, the sting pulling me back to reality. I whimpered as I dragged my other hand up to my breast, kneading and rubbing, while he continued destroying me, bringing me to the brink of something savage and wild. He kept at it until I was screaming his name, coming on his fingers. Every muscle in my body tightened and released as I came down from it. I laid there, a wanton pile of limbs, shaking as he withdrew his fingers. My body clenched, not wanting to lose the feeling of being filled. He kissed up my legs while I caught my breath, giving me a lazy smirk when I met his eyes.

"Divine *hell*, Rain."

"If this is hell, dear heart, I must be truly wicked because I'm never leaving."

I smiled as he kissed back up my stomach before he stood, and I whined as the heat of him left me. I wasn't done with him yet. He looked down at me and gave me a devastating grin when he pulled his undershorts off. His hard length was the dirtiest silhouette in the light of the fire. My breath shuddered, and I caught his eyes as his gaze traced over me.

"Tonic?" I asked him, breathless, hoping he was taking it because I knew I'd let him do this either way. Knew I wanted him inside me. Knew I wanted to feel everything he had to give me and more. He climbed atop me, and I cradled him between my thighs, his hard cock resting against my naked, wet skin.

"For the last fortnight."

I should have been surprised, maybe even annoyed at his presumption, that he'd been taking it since the moment I re-entered his life, but I wasn't. I was grateful for it now, just for the fact he'd handled one of my worries, and I didn't have to think about it at all. I just had to live in this moment. He knew at the beginning where this would end, and deep down I knew too, no matter how hard I fought it.

I locked eyes with him as I reached down between us, positioning his broad tip at my entrance. He used one hand to guide himself, rubbing through my wetness, making him slick for me, so it would feel good. So I wouldn't hurt. He moved back and notched himself at my opening and froze. His gaze met mine, full of love and lust and fire and life, and I knew what he was waiting for.

"I'm yours, Rain. Every part of me."

He closed his eyes as he exhaled, leaning down to kiss me deeply, as he pushed his hips into me the slightest bit. I inhaled sharply against his lips, and he stilled, not moving. He was so thick, and I felt myself stretch around him, the sweet pain I'd been somehow craving and afraid of. Eyes closed, I focused on my breathing, hoping the faint smile on my lips told him everything he needed to know. He stayed hovering over me as he slid in a little bit more, filling and stretching me, little by little, so he wouldn't hurt me. He took his time, allowing me to adjust, making sure I could take him. I was glad that I'd told him my history, so he knew to be gentle with me. He was my history. He was my present and future. He was every moment, every breath. I opened my eyes and peered up at him, the love and concern on his face so intense I couldn't help it when I let out a choked sob. He froze.

"Have I hurt you?"

"No, no. I just—I feel like I'm finally . . . home." I lifted my hand to cup his cheek as his face softened, flooding me with more emotion as I felt a tear slip down my cheek. He turned his face into my hand and kissed my palm before he whispered into it.

"I can't believe you came back to me." He eased in a bit more before pulling back out, only to repeat the process, going deeper each time, letting me rest and adjust between each thrust. I truly felt like I'd finally found my place. Ravemont hadn't been home to me in years, and Brambleton never was. Everything just felt like a resting point until this moment. Everything that brought me here was temporary, but this, where we were, was forever. My home had never been a place. My home had always been Rain.

Finally, he pushed all the way in, his body flush against mine, and stayed there while I rubbed my hands down his back, letting myself feel the fullness, the tightness—the sensation on just this side of pain. Then he pulled almost all the way out, and I groaned before he slid back in firmly, the gentle thrusts from before giving way to this. Something more visceral, something primal. Something possessive and complete. And then he started truly fucking me, keeping a pace that set me panting as I pulled him closer, my fingernails slicing into his skin, marking him. I raked my nails down his back, a claiming of my own design as he slammed into me over and over, murmuring my name into my neck.

"Emma, Em—*fuck*, you feel—you're perfect."

I reached down, grabbing his ass as he pushed into me, guiding his movements as I pulled him deeper inside me, and I matched him, lifting to meet every thrust. He pulled out almost all the way, one more time, before slamming back into me, hard. I threw my head back, moaning his name, wanting more. Wanting everything. We were fire and cinder and ash, a flame once lit that could light the world. A glimmer of ember on a breeze, a spark of passion ignited.

"The sounds you make, divine hell. Those sounds are mine." He groaned as he slammed back into me again, and I nearly screamed. The smack of his body against mine, the pressure, the push as we slowly moved up the bed with each thrust. Gods, I wanted to stay here forever, with him buried inside me and his tongue on mine. I pushed up, grabbing his lip between my teeth, and pulled him down to me, kissing him like I was never going to get the chance to again.

He broke from my kiss and reached down, grabbing one of my legs, pushing it up and back, hooking it over his shoulder. I cried out as he kept pushing into me, hitting me deeper and harder than before, and I felt my release start to build, a tingle at the base of my spine spreading warmth throughout me. He leaned his body down, pushing my leg back with him, as he kissed me fiercely, and opened me up even further to his cock. The angle provided friction that sent me wild, grabbing onto my breasts and panting.

"Look at how pretty you are with me inside you." He had pulled back from me so his eyes could move to where we were joined, attention rapt on where he slid in and out of me. He slowed his pace, rolling his hips as he thrust into me. Using one hand to grab the back of my neck, he pulled me up so I could watch where he moved, where our bodies met. So I could watch where his thick length disappeared inside me and slid back out, glistening in the light. It was hypnotic, feeling every movement as I watched.

"You feel so good, Rain." I struggled to even speak, panting in between each word, drawing out his name.

He slammed into me hard as he reached down with one hand, rubbing tight circles on my clit, and I felt myself on the edge, ready to fall, and I gave in for a moment to his touch, the slick feeling of him sliding through me before I smacked his hand away and put a hand to his chest. He slowed, panting, and I felt him twitch inside me as he lowered my leg back down, unsure if I'd stopped him because it hurt. It hadn't, but there was a reason I stopped him.

"I am yours, but I want to know if you are mine." I undulated beneath him. Pushing up into him, rolling my hips as I moved on him, and he groaned, his eyes flickering closed before a small lazy smile spread across his face.

"Of course I am. In every way."

"Then let *me* ride *you*."

I'd barely spoken the words when he flipped over, pulling out of me as he laid back on the bed, pulling me over him so I straddled his hips.

I reached between us and pulled his cock upward, and I rubbed him back and forth, the thick head of him sliding up and down the wet length of me. He watched and let out a soft groan while I teased him. I braced one hand on his stomach as my other guided him into me, and I slowly sank down on the length of him, our groans meshing together, a delicious song of fulfillment between us. I looked down on him under me, the broad expanse of golden-brown skin, scarred from a battle-hardened life, taut muscles that flexed as he tensed, the light smattering of hair on his chest, and the face of the man I'd dreamed about for so many years, soft with emotion as he gazed at me, though his eyes were filled with fire. I would never get sick of him. Somehow, with me on top like this, he felt even thicker than he did before. I sat there for a moment on top of him, gently circling my hips, until Rainier reached up, lifting me and slamming me down on top of him, thrusting up into me as he did it. Something between a moan and a scream escaped my lips as he set me free. I put my hands on his chest and rolled my hips forward and began to ride him, my breasts bouncing with the movement. He kept his hands on my waist as he met each thrust, and I felt his eyes on me as I tilted my head backward, moaning. His hands slid up to cup my breasts, teasing my nipples as he did it. Finally, I leaned down over him, kissing him fiercely, biting his lip, and exploring his mouth with my tongue. His hands were on my ass then, and I slid up his length until he was barely still inside me before I pivoted, slamming myself back down on him. I did it again, and he groaned as he thrust up into me, meeting my movement.

"You're mine, Rain." I smiled on his mouth as he panted.

"I am. Until my last breath, I am yours."

"And even then, we'll find each other. I'll always find you." I breathed it against his lips before I unleashed myself, riding him with reckless abandon, a frenzy of motion, of lips on lips and skin against skin. I clenched around him, pulling him to the edge with me as I felt the warmth licking up my spine. I sat back up, using my hands to balance on his taut stomach as I moved, feeling filled and stretched. He moved one hand to my clit and started rubbing me with his thumb. My movements were a call to motion, a call for Rainier to meet every one, and he responded in kind. It felt so natural and right. There was nothing left between us. There was no protection for my heart, no stepping back across the line. There was no line, not anymore. There was only this, only him. There was only us. I groaned with each thrust, louder and louder, as I barreled toward oblivion.

"There it is, that's it. Come on my cock, Em." His voice was rough and desperate. He sat up, pulling my legs around him, as he pushed his forehead to mine.

Our lips met, and I kissed him deeply, spearing my tongue into his mouth like he was speared into me. I opened my eyes and his met mine. We didn't say a word, just shared breath, shared the moment, shared our fire and our passion, our love and our strength, before I threw my head back and cried his name. He held me roughly, one hand around me and the other in my hair, while I crested the wave. The orgasm flowed through me, and I felt my body squeeze him, pulsing him to release. He called out my name and bucked wildly into me for a few strokes before I felt his hot warmth inside me. I heard the glass lamp next to the bed shudder, the ground below us rumbling along with Rain.

Panting, I collapsed into him, my head against his shoulder, as I felt him continue to spend inside me. He held me tightly in his arms as he pressed a kiss to the top of my head.

"I love you doesn't feel like enough." He murmured against my hair, squeezing me tightly.

"It doesn't," I agreed. "But I love you too. Until we are just whispers on the wind."

CHAPTER 35

I HAD ONCE BELIEVED that to know love was to lose it. Maybe I still did. Perhaps it *was* love to know there was a price and to find it worth paying all the same. Perhaps it was love to have an unshakable madness burrow under your skin, asking you to choose that which terrified and exhilarated you, over and over, knowing one day it wouldn't be a choice. Knowing that one day—when you are truly dependent on it—it will leave. By accident, choice, or time, it will be gone. Perhaps love was risk. Perhaps love was taking a leap and hoping you could withstand what happened after. I didn't know much about it, not this kind, not in the way many seemed to know about love. But what I did know was it had found me and never left. This love had been there all along, waiting for me to choose it. This love felt like daylight, golden and warm. The first rays of sun after a long, hard night. This love felt like courage. Like the first timid steps on an uncertain path. But I was changed and made anew, still soaking in the afterglow of the light we had become. And I knew there was no going back.

I felt the sun shining on my body and squinted, opening my eyes. The curtains were drawn back, and the sun splashed over Rainier's chest, along with my hand resting on top of it. The ring on my finger caught the light and was sending a beam straight into my eyes. Nestled in the crook of Rainier's arm, the sounds of his breathing were soft and slow enough to tempt me back toward sleep's embrace. I adjusted my hand so I could study the ring I'd refused to look at the night before. The stone in the center was a blue-green color, teardrop-shaped, and tiny delicate vines made up the band, a sprinkle of clear stones embedded along it to resemble flower buds. I delicately turned my hand, careful not to disturb Rainier, as I watched the light dance over the facets of the gems. It was truly stunning, something that fit my hand and tastes perfectly. I'd never worn a ring with Faxon, the simple band used in the ceremony immediately discarded and left to sit in a small bowl on my dresser at home. It felt foreign on my finger, but I couldn't take my eyes off it.

"It changes color with the lighting." Gravelly with sleep, his voice was quiet. I hadn't noticed a difference in his breathing, but he must have felt me move.

"I'm sorry if I woke you." He pulled my hand up to his mouth, bending my fingers at the knuckles before pushing his lips to them.

"You didn't. The stone changes color depending on the type of light. Sunlight makes it look like this. But candlelight or firelight makes it turn a sort of violet-red color." I pulled my hand back down to inspect the ring closer, trying to determine how it could possibly change color.

"I still haven't said yes, Rain." I tilted my head up and watched a small smile spread on his full and tempting lips.

"I know." He placed a sweet kiss on my forehead before he disentangled himself from our entwined limbs, sliding to the edge of the bed. I studied his naked body—the swells of muscle across his shoulders, the long scar that went diagonally across his back, and the strong curve of his backside. I sat up, scooting to where he sat, and traced my fingers down the long scar, my cold touch causing his skin to pebble before he shivered.

"What's this from?"

"When we first took back Varmeer. It had to have been, what, ten years ago now? I made some mistakes, got overwhelmed. Dewalt and Thyra had to drag me out of the fray. Thank the gods we had a healer then, or I'd have certainly died."

The idea had my stomach clenching, and I banished the thought as I pressed my lips to where the scar began.

"I suppose I have a lot to thank the gods for." He wore an earnest expression as he turned to me. "Do you remember where we stopped on our way to Mira? The divine statuary?" He was talking about the tunnel of orange leaves where I'd prayed to Aonara. Where he had pressed a coin into my palm, and I'd pleaded, sobbing, for Elora's return.

"I remember."

He smiled, and it was breathtaking.

"The coin I gave you to pray with had been all I had left in my pocket. I prayed there the day before." Confused as to why he'd been there in the first place, my head tilted in question. His smile softened as he watched me, his eyes dancing across my face, memorizing me. I knew the look because I'd done it to him so many times. "The offerings you saw there, they were all mine. I stopped there and prayed to them, Emmeline. You know how I used to feel about the gods. But I prayed anyway."

"Why? What were you praying about?"

"I was on my way to request the task and saw the divine statuary, and I stopped. And I begged. To forget you. To rid me of this—this poison that has been in my blood all these years. It didn't feel right to request a task for her, with you still firmly planted in my heart." His smile faded, and he studied me, waiting for my reaction. Part of me wanted to avert my eyes or resent him for calling me a poison. Again. But I wouldn't. I would never turn my back on him again.

"I'm glad they met expectations as usual and didn't listen." I let my smile spread, and he threw his head back, laughing.

"I think they *were* listening if only to do the exact opposite. I decided not to request my task that day and went back to Ravemont instead, where you were waiting for me." He put his hand on my neck and pulled me into him, so our foreheads rested against each other, and we sat there for a long while, reveling in the glow of what we'd become.

Standing in the closet, Rainier's ripped shirt pulled tightly around my body, I stared at three of the most beautiful dresses I'd ever seen, hanging on the rack in front of me.

"You shouldn't have done this!" Mouth agape, I stared between him and the gowns, shocked by how much he must have spent on me. He shrugged on a shirt, all black, buttoning it in such a casual manner, I almost thought he couldn't hear me.

"You'll look beautiful in them, but I already know I prefer them pooled on the floor." His gaze didn't stray from his buttons, but his lips kicked up in a grin. Once finished, he ambled over to a drawer and opened it, gesturing to countless wrapped parcels within. I chose one, unwrapping it carefully, and out fell a set of delicate undergarments. Rainier picked them up and handed them back to me, not uttering a word, but I watched his smile grow. By the time I opened them all, carefully arranging them in the drawer, Rainier was fully dressed, head to toe in black, looking sleek and impossibly handsome. He raised a brow as he took in my expression—utterly lost—before plucking a set of matching undergarments out from the drawer and sliding one of the dresses in front of me.

"These. We slept through breakfast, so I asked Sterling to prepare an early lunch. Join me once you've finished?" He leaned forward, fingertips delicately touching my own, as his lips softly pressed against mine. I sighed at the tenderness and nodded as he left.

The set of underwear he picked was an exceptionally light blue. So light in color they were almost white—made of satin and impossibly soft against my skin. They were simple, not nearly as frilly as some of the other sets. When I put the bra on, I noticed tiny, delicate flowers embroidered on the cups, a shade of blue only slightly darker than the rest of it that it was almost imperceptible.

The dress itself was a darker blue. It had multiple layers, the bottom-most layer being the darkest, and it swept back into a short train. I began to wonder if I would even be able to put it on myself without managing to rip it when I heard a light knock on the bedroom door and Mairin calling my name. I replied, and she came bounding around the door, wearing a green dress I'd never seen before. It was relatively plain but still looked new and shiny, and I wondered if Rainier had outfitted the whole house or if she'd bought it herself.

"The prince thought you might need some help." She gave me an easy smile, and I noticed how well-rested she appeared. Her freckles stood out starkly across her pale skin, but her curly orange hair was vivid and shining. She reached up, pulling the dress from its hanger. "You told him? Truly, I thought it would take you longer."

"It was an accident; I didn't mean to tell him." I stepped into the dress, and she hauled it up as I slid my arms into the sleeves. "Did he say something to you?" I glanced over my shoulder at my friend as she fastened each button down my back. The dress fit perfectly.

"No, but I can tell. Your colors are different." Maybe one day I'd understand what auras looked like to her or what it meant, but I didn't think it would be any time soon. I almost asked her about it but decided against it, knowing the explanation I got before was likely the best I was going to receive. I walked over to the mirror and tugged at the garment a bit, helping it settle better on my hips. It was truly stunning. The darkest blue layer was a perfect length in the front with a short train at the back, manageable enough it didn't need a bustle. The lighter shade of blue fabric on top became sheer at the bottom, allowing the dark blue to show through. It was the color of the summer sky and had beautiful flowers dispersed across it. I saw what seemed to be blue delphinium flowers and light purple freesia in the pattern, and I felt like I'd fit right in outside in the garden Rainier had planted for me. A light-blue sash, the same material as my undergarments, cinched the dress in at the waist. The same fabric lined the sweetheart neckline, only showing the top swell of my breasts, making me feel feminine but still covered. The sleeves were the same light blue patterned fabric, form-fitting to my arms, and only came down a bit past my elbows. The back of the dress dipped a bit lower, an upside-down triangle of skin showing

"Do you want me to put your hair up for you?" Mairin was watching me as I turned in the mirror. I was shocked that such a beautiful dress looked so good on me. The seamstress was most definitely a witch, I laughed to myself. I debated, knowing Rainier liked my hair down, but relented, suspecting he'd appreciate my exposed back just as much.

Minutes later, I wore a beautiful braid that wrapped around the back of my head, joining the rest of my hair in a low, loose bun. I lightly fingered the plait and began to give my thanks to Mairin when she suddenly grabbed my hand.

"What's this?" The ring. I hadn't taken it off. Her brows were in her hair, and my heart was in my throat. I pulled my hand back.

"It's nothing." I crossed my arms, tucking the evidence away.

"Emmeline, it looks like something. Something *of consequence*." I felt my lips tug upwards in a smile.

"I haven't told him yes." I was still thinking about everything, about how it would work going forward, if I could accept being a queen one day, how Elora would feel. I hadn't even spared a second thought about all of the issues that would come from the Myriad and his mother.

"You also haven't told him no." She studied me for a moment. I debated taking the ring off and leaving it on my nightstand, only temporarily, to avoid questions until I made up my mind, but I decided against it. It was rather beautiful, and after last night, it wasn't in me to part with such a beautiful gift from him, no matter how fleeting it might come to be.

"I haven't. Let's go eat."

It turned out everyone in the house had slept past breakfast, all of us recovering from the road, so Sterling organized a full lunch. Dewalt and Rainier already sat at the table and had started in on their plates, loaded full of meats and pastries—the fruit on the table neglected. I let out a snort at the sight, and they both glanced up at me as I walked into the dining room, Mairin at my side. Dewalt's jaw dropped, and the grip on his fork went slack. Rainier jumped to his feet, actually stumbling as he pulled out my chair for me. Startled by the impression I made, I hesitated before stepping forward.

"I know I've looked rough the last few days, but—" Rainier interrupted my nervous jest, placing a kiss on my temple, his hand on my waist.

"Every day, you shine, but especially so right now."

When he grabbed my hand and pulled it toward his mouth, kissing my knuckles, his eyes met mine, and I felt myself smile. I didn't know what to do with all of my feelings. Once I sat, Rainier hovered over me, grabbing a plate and filling it, pointing to each item spread before us to see if I wanted it.

"I can do that, you know." Ignoring me, he continued to load my plate with a little bit of everything.

Mairin stood on my other side, selecting her food as well. At one point, both of them stood over me, and I stared across the table at Dewalt in bored annoyance, and he grinned.

"You are radiant, Emma." I raised a brow as Dewalt bit into a puff pastry, no small amount of delight on my face when he got cream on his nose. "I'm serious! No offense, but you've looked like shit on the road. You clean up nice." Rainier chuckled as I barked out an obnoxious laugh, my hand raising to my mouth to cover it, when Dewalt's eyes widened. His facial expression changed so many times in less than a minute, ranging from sad to shocked to happy, and it took me too long to realize why. I was sure it was hard for him to see me, twin to his lost love, happily wearing an engagement ring. A reminder of what he'd never have. When his expression landed on happy, he lifted his eyes, about to ask a question. I gave the slightest of head shakes, and he closed his mouth, brows furrowed. I wanted to speak to him privately before I decided; the barefooted country boy who became a duke might have valuable insight for me. I mouthed the words *talk later* to him, and he gave me the slightest nod before digging back into his food. Rainier finally lowered my plate in front of me, food stacked on it so high I'd be lucky if it didn't tumble off the plate onto the table.

"Where's Lavenia?" I gave a happy wiggle as I bit into a delicious pastry with some sort of raspberry cream filling in it.

"Getting ready for court. She always takes a long time to pick out her wardrobe," Dewalt explained between bites of cured ham.

"Our mother always has some sort of critique for us, and despite the fact she's thirty-two years old, Lavenia hasn't learned to ignore her." Rainier offered me a glass of orange juice, which I declined, content with the coffee in front of me.

"And what she says to Lavenia is about what she wears?"

"Well, Lavenia makes sure that is what she talks about." Dewalt snorted across the table from me as Rainier continued explaining. "Our mother is always going to have something to say; Lavenia just makes sure it's about her clothing and nothing else."

"The critique used to be about me until this new strategy." Dewalt gave me a devilish grin from across the table.

"Does she not like you?" Dewalt was generally carefree and friendly to most everyone he met, only showing his prickly attitude to people he was comfortable around. I couldn't imagine someone not liking him, even if it was the Queen of Vesta. Chills moved down my back when I realized if Rainier had his way, that would eventually be my title.

"Not in the slightest. And you should prepare yourself for the same treatment." He chuckled as Rainier shot him a glare.

"No, you should *not*. My mother is abrasive on her best days when you get to know her. But she had to be, being married to my father. She dislikes Dewalt, no offense brother, because he isn't serious." Dewalt shrugged and nodded before stabbing a piece of sausage. "She believes he acts rashly, and it could hurt Ven." Before his friend could interject, the hurt and frustration on his face apparent, Rainier held up a hand to quiet him. "A belief not shared by me. With you, Em, I believe that once everything is explained to her, she will see in you what I do. In the meantime, I suggest giving back what you receive in kind."

"What is it you see in me, exactly?" I teased, not expecting an answer.

"I see a deliberate and intentional woman. A fierce protector and determined warrior. I see someone completely unaware of just how important and worthy they are." His hand slid on top of mine as Mairin made a choking sound next to me. Dewalt put his fork down forcefully and stood up.

"I'm going to vomit." He picked his plate up, walking it into what I assumed was the kitchen.

"Oh, don't leave me here!" Mairin called after him, laughing.

"If your mother sees all those things in me, you might just have some competition." I gave him a silly smile as he threw back his head and laughed.

After we finished eating, I requested a tour of Rainier's home. Popping our heads into the kitchen, I met Deandra and Mellise, who were running around cleaning up before they shooed us out quickly, not ones to have their space invaded. Hand on the small of my back, he guided me through the living room to another hallway that led to a more formal living area, complete with a grand staircase. It appeared to be the front entryway, and I laughed to myself when I realized we had yet to use the front door. Upstairs, there were four different suites with yet another living space that opened up to a balcony over the back garden. He took me into one of the empty suites, and I was surprised, not having realized just how massive the rooms were. The one we were in was almost as big as Rainier's room downstairs, a bookcase on one wall and a wardrobe on the other with a large four-poster bed in between. The bathroom, shared with the suite next to it, had a giant claw-footed tub, deep enough to fully sink into. The view of the two suites looked out over the back garden, a trellis underneath the window that I knew would be covered in purple blooms come summer.

"This could be Elora's room." He was leaning forward, his hands on the windowsill as he gazed down at the flowers. I walked over to the bookcase, my fingers tracing along the spines, as I lost myself in thought.

"What if I say yes, and Elora hates it here? What if she hates my decision, hates all of it? Then what do I do?" Eyeing him over my shoulder, I watched as his brows furrowed, his focus on the garden below.

"I don't think it's possible she would hate it, but on the off-chance she does, I suppose you both could go to Crown Cottage until she came of age or changed her mind." The thought filled me with such intense agony I knew it wouldn't be an option for me, and I wouldn't ship her away from me. No, Crown Cottage wasn't acceptable. It was either Ravemont or Astana.

"Would she have a tutor?" He crossed the room to stand near me, observing as I slid one of the books out.

"She could. If that's what you wanted."

"Where would we go after your father . . . ? Would we have to go to the palace?" He put his hands on my hips and nuzzled against my neck from behind, his warm body pressing against mine.

"Considering we would be king and queen, we would do whatever we wanted. But I'd think we would have residences at both, for convenience's sake." His lips trailed down the column of my neck.

"Do I have a garden full of my favorite flowers at the palace?" He kissed the base of my neck as his arm wrapped around my waist, drawing me into him.

"We will convert every single one. I'll have the gardeners start tonight—just give me the word."

The word. Telling him yes. Accepting that to be with Rainier, I would eventually become a queen to thousands.

"What if the people hate me? What if they decided my head would be better off in a basket?" He stilled for a moment before continuing his ministrations across my exposed upper back.

"They won't," he replied simply, not offering anything else. I turned in his arms to face him, lacing my fingers behind his neck.

"How do you know?"

"If they love you only a drop as much as I do, they'll think of you as the greatest queen Vesta has ever seen." I snorted.

"Most of the people have only seen your mother as queen. There are only a few conduits even able to draw a comparison." No mortal alive had ever seen a change in rulers.

"Then you see how low the bar is, Emmeline." His smile and his words drew a cackle from me, and I flushed before immediately feeling guilty.

"Your mother is fair; she is not a bad queen. You shouldn't say such things."

"No, you're right. My mother is not a bad queen. But she is not good enough to make up for what my father lacks."

"And you think I'd be able to make up for what you lack?"

"I don't think, I *know*. We are two halves of one soul, Em. Who could be more suited to the task?" His head dipped, and he pressed his forehead against mine. "You know how this ends; I don't know why you're questioning it."

"You just said it yourself. Someone has to balance you out." I kissed him, allowing my tongue to explain the rest.

CHAPTER 36

A FEW HOURS LATER, after a thorough tour of the house and grounds, we met Dewalt and Lavenia in the entryway of the estate. Lavenia looked equal parts breathtaking and scandalous. She did not wear a dress but instead wore black high-waisted pants which stopped just above her ankles. Ankles I was sure she would break considering the height of the black heels she wore. She paired the rest of her outfit with a closely tailored black jacket on top with a thin slip of a chemise underneath. Half of her braids had been pulled up into a round bun while the rest hung down. She took one look at her brother, and I watched her features screw up in annoyance.

"We match." A small giggle escaped my lips as I realized Rainier was also dressed head to toe in black.

"If you'd have joined us earlier, you would have known that and had time to do something about it." His sister rolled her eyes.

"Let's just get this over with." Dewalt stared at me with such a glazed-over expression of irritation it dawned on me just how often he would have to mediate between the two of them, and I felt a bit of pity for him.

Rainier opened a rift in front of us into a rather cavernous bedchamber, gesturing for his sister to lead the way. Lavenia stepped through, followed by Dewalt, and Rainier grabbed my hand as we crossed into the rift, closing it once all four of us were firmly in the room. His fingers brushed against the ring on my hand, and he twirled it for a moment. I tensed, worried that my lack of answer was upsetting him. I wanted to say yes, truly, but the thought was so daunting that I needed more time. Leaning down, he spoke quietly in my ear, clear in his intention that whatever he had to say would stay between us.

"Unless you intend to give me an answer now, give me the ring; it will not go unnoticed here."

"Will they not think it's from Faxon?" I didn't want to give up the ring even though I hadn't given him an answer. It was mine, no matter how I decided.

After our moment earlier, I assured him that I'd give him an answer by tomorrow, depending on how things went this evening.

"No, she will not think it is from Faxon." He scowled as if the very idea was offensive. Which, I guessed it was. "I had it made a long time ago when I was much more forthcoming with my mother. She will recognize it."

"A long time ago?" I twisted the ring off my finger, and I watched his lips move into an almost undetectable frown.

"A story for another time." He held out his hand and pocketed the ring. I felt I needed to say something to ease the hurt.

"I will be quite upset if you lose that." He gifted me a crooked smile before he promised he would guard it preciously.

Lavenia and Dewalt had left the room already, and I took in my surroundings. The bedchamber was enormous and yet confining with no windows and little light. Everything but the furniture and door was made of cool, grey stone, and there was a draft that made me shudder. It was much more primitive than I expected, especially in comparison to Rainier's estate. Tapestries hung on two of the walls, older than I could imagine. The furniture seemed newer, at least—a four-poster bed with drawn curtains sat against one of the walls while a small, delicately upholstered bench rested at its foot. I supposed the curtains were to keep the draft at bay, and I knew I'd be more appreciative eventually, but for now, I found them confining.

"I think I'd prefer your estate." I took the arm he offered, and he chuckled.

"This is the oldest wing of the palace. I am rarely here, so why waste the finer rooms on me?"

The throne room was not what I expected. It was round, for one thing. The only light filtered down from the giant glass dome above us, letting in the rapidly diminishing glow of the setting sun. Behind the thrones was a morose assemblage of headless statues, each a likeness of someone the Vestana bloodline was proud to have slain. Long fabric hung in strips from the tall ceiling, shrouding the figures in a dark cloud of shadow and silk brocade. Growing up, Nana had told us stories of King Soren and his father, King Alric, who had passed his aggressive vindictiveness down to his son. I assumed most of the likenesses belonged to Folterran royalty, and I was momentarily distracted by the singular female figure standing to the left of Soren.

She was slight—much thinner and shorter than the surrounding effigies. Less detailed than those around her, it appeared she'd been sculpted hastily, and I wondered why. Though plain, wearing only an unadorned dress with no added texture, she appeared new compared to the others. An addition from Soren and not his father, I presumed.

Larke. His first wife.

I wondered what she looked like, the headless statue offering little to my imagination.

Pulled out of my reverie by a cough from Dewalt, I continued my visual exploration, indulging in the first sight of a room not widely accessible. To either side of the dais were two rows each of chairs belonging to members of the council and higher-ranking members of the court, empty because Rainier requested an informal meeting. They faced inwards, ensuring the councilors' place in their monarch's line of sight.

What surprised me most was the location of the thrones. The dais was not elevated as I'd imagined but instead sat recessed into the ground in the center of the room. We entered on a wide staircase that led downward, and I shuddered when I remembered Nana's stories explaining the peculiar arrangement.

Alric's divinity was similar to Rainier's—organic manipulation—though he used it in more brutal ways than one could imagine. It was said that the king used the recessed area as punishment for those who spoke against him, drowning would-be apostates in boiling water, heated by flames he'd conjure from above, all while he sat in an air pocket on his throne and watched. Though I knew he'd never do such a thing, I was grateful Rainier didn't inherit the gift of flame.

The four of us stood on the steps, waiting to be called upon. I watched Dewalt next to me out of the corner of my eye, following his lead the best I could, knowing my expectations would be more similar to his than that of Lavenia and Rainier. I swept into a curtsy when the time came and kept my head down, hands tightly clasped in front of me to keep them from shaking. At one point, I felt Rainier shift on my other side, and I hoped he was about to reach out and comfort me, but I saw his fist clench instead as if he was holding himself back. I only looked up when King Soren began to speak, his voice much frailer than I remembered yet equally cold. His skin was pale, almost translucent, and sallow. His presence was as equally haggard as his voice. His hair was white as snow and ragged, and the crown which sat atop his head seemed heavy enough to break his neck. Those beautiful, emerald eyes I loved appeared dark and cruel set in his scrunched face.

"It is a rare day when our son chooses to grace us with his presence, is it not, Shivani?" He wheezed, and it seemed as if it took a significant amount of effort to speak.

"It is. And with another Highclere girl, no less. Likely intent on ruining all chances of his performing the ritual, I bet." I blinked, and my jaw dropped. That was not what I had anticipated in the slightest. The queen was beautiful—her hair pulled back tightly to the crown of her head where it burst into soft, springy curls resting on her shoulders. She didn't wear a crown but a diadem instead, the thin band crossing over her forehead. Considering she only performed the ritual with King Soren in the last two hundred years, she didn't look much older than her son. Her umber skin was still smooth with only a small amount of crow's feet at her eyes. Her dark hair was going grey at her temples, but it only accentuated her regal demeanor. Lavenia took after her mother, but where my friend's face had kindness and humor, Shivani's held a shrewd cunning designed to intimidate. I felt both men on either side of me tense, and I swallowed as Rainier plastered on a charming, confident smile that managed to put me at ease.

"I'm sure Lady Emmeline will forgive your harsh words, Mother, as it must be a shock to see us on short notice. Father, did you receive my message?" The king grunted in assent. "So, you know our presence is of great importance, not to be confused with such a trivial matter as my performing the ritual."

Queen Shivani was the one who replied, disdain evident on her face. "And yet, we've been told Princess Keeva is leaving the capital, counter to our insistence that she stay. Her chambers are being cleared out as we speak." The queen gestured past us with a flick of her wrist. I wondered if she was who we needed to convince more than King Soren; she was the more imposing of the two of them by far. "Lavenia, I would hope you are prepared for your brother to fail, but somehow I do not think you are." She tilted her head and narrowed her eyes at her daughter, scanning her from head to toe before turning her attention to me, a more thoughtful look on her face as she gave me the same treatment. Her eyes didn't leave me as she addressed her son.

"I understand you're here to request assistance to retrieve the Beloved, Rainier. Is there a reason you saw fit to bring your plaything?" A low warning growl sounded from Dewalt as Rainier moved, taking the steps two at a time as he approached his mother. I remembered Rainier's words from before—to give back what I received in kind—and I cleared my throat.

"Your Majesty, may I?" Queen Shivani raised an elegant brow and afforded me a brief nod as Rainier froze, turning to glare at me over his shoulder, a warning written across his face. My hands were loose at my sides, and I resisted the urge to clench them.

"Respectfully, if you know why we are here, you also know the Beloved is my daughter. To feign the belief that I am present as no more than a plaything does both your children and your role as their mother a disservice. I assure you, I have no interest in impeding Prince Rainier's ritual, and in fact, protested his intended dismissal of Princess Keeva. You know why I am here, just as you would be if our roles were reversed. I hope we can come to a mutual respect, as you are the only person in this room who can understand precisely what I am going through."

She pondered me for a moment, moving her tongue behind her lip in a gesture reminding me so much of her son, it was unsettling. I let out a slow, unsteady breath and refused to make eye contact with Rainier. I could feel him watching me, but my show of bravado would be for nothing if I burst into tears at the sight of him. I watched Queen Shivani's mouth tighten, but I swore I saw her eyes soften before she spoke.

"There is the manner in which you effectively disappeared once your sister died and are now claiming your child is the Beloved with no evidence." The tone of her voice was softer but still had an edge to it. It hadn't even crossed my mind that there was a possibility for doubt.

"Her powers are identical to that of Lucia's, stronger even."

"So you say." I was surprised to hear King Soren's voice interject.

"Why would Folterra have any interest in her if I were lying?" I saw the queen's eyes flicker to Rainier, and I wondered for a moment just how forthcoming he used to be with his mother. Did she think Folterra would be interested in Elora as a means to get to me, specifically to hurt Rainier? It was improbable, considering how discreet our short-lived romance had been. Surely, if Folterra wanted to get to Rainier, Faxon would have arranged for me to be taken instead of our daughter. And even then, it would make little sense.

"It could be a falsehood designed to lure us into an attack." King Soren grumbled and trailed off. I couldn't help it as my head tilted to the side. The old man was paranoid. Did he think I'd lie about my daughter and willingly give her up to start a war with Folterra? For what purpose? I knew my father blamed King Soren, and I was devastated when Lucia died, but what an insane leap in logic to think I'd help start a war over it.

"My spies have confirmed Prince Cyran has her. There would be no reason for them to take such care of a frightened child unless she was of great significance." Rainier's voice was loud, and since he was getting visibly frustrated, I chose to ignore the insinuation that my daughter's significance came only from her divinity. I knew his heart, but I made a mental note to speak about it to him later. Her importance had nothing to do with her status as the Beloved.

"My son will remember I have spies as well. The girl is no child; she is nearly of age, and I can think of one reason a young prince might want her." As the king spoke, Queen Shivani snapped her head in his direction, a look of warning on her face not dissimilar to the one her son gave me moments ago. I took a steadying breath, willing ice to flow through my veins to staunch the fire smoldering underneath my skin. I watched Rainier's fists clench and felt Dewalt's arm brush against mine as he took a step toward me. Protective of me or what I might do, I wasn't sure, but I focused on where my arm touched his. A pinpoint of concentration anchoring me in place.

"Father—" Lavenia's anger was clear, and I didn't want the aggressive energy in the room to continue, so I attempted to cut it off.

"Then your spies will have seen that she is chained in obsidian when she is let out of her chambers." It was a bluff, and the only reaction I received from my lie was Rainier's shift in posture. A vision of Elora's wrists in the illusion had flashed before my eyes, the faintest red marks apparent. Rainier's spies hadn't yet found Prince Cyran, and I was surprised King Soren had succeeded where they had not. Our information was collected from my illusions and the very first visit the shifters made to Darkhold. I had no idea if they still kept her chained in obsidian, but I didn't think sharing Prince Cyran's cooperation was a better plan. Nor did Rainier, or he'd have mentioned it already. It was clear his father was slipping into a deeper paranoia than I thought possible.

"Yes, she was. Until recently. Until she began to exercise her divinity with the dark prince." My heart sank, knowing it was a confirmation to him that Elora played a role in a plot against him. We would have to explain Prince Cyran's involvement and hope to the gods the king understood. "I do believe she could have been the Beloved. But by practicing with the dark prince, I think, instead, she is more likely cursed. She has already become a threat, and I issued an order less than an hour ago to handle the problem."

Everything stopped.

The second the words left King Soren's mouth, I knew I wouldn't walk out of the throne room alive. I saw Queen Shivani's arm immediately extend toward the king, pulling Soren's hand into hers, with an expression on her face which told me she had no idea about the order. The queen started whispering desperately to the king, the desperation of a mother. Everything moved at half-speed, and I watched as Rainier reached for the sword on his hip. I had no idea what he intended to do with it, but I didn't wait to find out. I acted on instinct.

Running down the stairs, I quickly closed the distance between us. Even standing two steps below me, Rainier was still slightly taller than me. By the time I reached him, his hand was on the hilt of his short sword. In a swift motion I didn't know I was capable of, I swatted his hand away and unsheathed his sword myself.

"I'm sorry," I whispered to him as I launched backward, ignoring the tear I heard from my gown and nearly tripping over my train as I drew his body toward me. My free arm was around his neck, pulling him down to the ground hard, and he groaned. I was a step above him, standing over him with his back resting against my legs. With my free hand, I pulled his head up and back, baring his neck to the long blade—his blade—I held in my other hand. Against my better judgment, I chanced a glance down at him, those deep, green eyes gazing straight up into mine. Within them swirled fire and rage. I shook my head and trained my eyes on the king.

"You will not harm my daughter," I gritted out, my voice dangerous. Queen Shivani's eyes hardened as she took in the image of me with a blade to her son's throat. I could tell she had been arguing with King Soren on my behalf, but her jaw slammed shut as she watched me, familiar anger dancing behind her eyes.

"This is your only chance, Lady Highclere. If you step away from the prince right now, you can still leave this room with your life." King Soren's low grumble echoed through the room. No one believed the lie, and he knew it. The two guards on either side of the dais watched the king, awaiting orders. They were useless; King Soren was more powerful than both, although I wasn't sure how his feeble body and mind might have affected his divinity. I watched his attention shift down to Rainier on the ground, then back up to me, and I hoped I imagined the flutter of realization behind his eyes. Hoped he didn't realize I'd only been able to disarm Rainier and pull him down because he trusted me. That he was mine, and I was not a plaything.

At that moment, I had no plan. I obviously couldn't kill Rainier. Grabbing him was an impulse. Panic started to rise in my chest, tightening my lungs and making it hard to breathe. Soren's words had made me desperate, willing to do anything to stop him. I could feel my chest burning and knew I'd start gasping for air any second, the familiar, suffocating panic I'd felt so many times before. Rainier leaned against me, the warmth of his back pressing into my leg. I glanced down, and the moment my eyes met his, he closed them. I reached out and felt his heartbeat. Slow. He was calm. He trusted me. I saw movement in the corner of my eye; Dewalt and Lavenia moved down a few steps but made no moves to come near me.

"If you kill my daughter, what life will I have?" My voice sounded stronger than I felt. "If my daughter dies, so does the dream of peace, so does your son, so do you. The only curse she suffers is that from the gods." I narrowed my eyes at the king. Even if he canceled his order to kill Elora, he'd die for giving it in the first place if I had anything to do with it. Rainier's steady heartbeat focused me. "Elora is a child who did not ask to be the Beloved, who did not ask to be taken by the Folterrans. Do not touch her," I growled out. I realized in horror how hard I was pressing the blade to Rainier's throat. With a sharp intake of breath, I watched a bead of blood trickle down, absorbed by his shirt. Before I could pull away, Queen Shivani stood.

"Soren, rescind the order." The king gaped at her, shock and outrage mixing on his face. "No one will be killing *anyone's* child today." The stare she directed at me could melt steel. She was the only one in the room who knew what a mother would do to protect their child. Whether she suspected I was bluffing or not, she wasn't willing to take the risk.

She turned to her husband and knelt, taking his hands in hers. I let up on my grip on Rainier's hair, trying to press my divinity toward his neck as my fingers grazed his scalp. I heard a quiet rumble from him, and I realized he was purring at my touch. I would have laughed if the situation weren't so dire. Hair was sticking to my forehead and the back of my neck, and I felt a cool breeze across my face, lifting the sticky strands away. Where was the air coming from? I looked down at Rainier and saw his fingertips gently gesturing at his side, and I blinked. *His* breeze. I started as I realized he was the cause of it. He had learned to summon the wind. I felt my lip tug upwards before I wiped my face of any expression. I pushed my leg into him, trying to support the way he was sitting; I knew he couldn't be comfortable. Finally, the queen turned back around to face us.

"We will put a hold on the order, for now, but will not take it off the table. It will need to be discussed further." She trailed off, extending her hands outward in supplication. I released my grip on Rainier and dropped his sword. My knees buckled, and I all but threw myself to the ground. Leaning forward, I buried my face into his back, a sob bursting past my lips. What the queen had promised wasn't enough.

"Is her cunt that sweet?" I lifted my head to see the king addressing Rainier before his eyes locked on me. "Pray to the gods the dark prince thinks the same about your daughter, or I will not have to lift a finger."

The move wasn't calculated but animalistic. In one movement, I came up onto a knee and reached for my blade under my dress. Pushing Rainier down, I let the dagger fly over him. My aim was true, but so was his. A wild gust of wind blew across the room, knocking the blade off course.

The room erupted.

The guards on either side of the dais launched into the air, the stone underneath them forcing them upwards. I registered the king stumbling to his feet, the queen at his side, her hands grappling up his sleeve. I'd never seen a siphon before, but as she tore at his clothes to touch his skin, I recognized it as her trying to stop him from using his abilities. On me.

I was still on my knees when Rainier slammed into me, throwing me backward onto the stone steps. In one graceful movement, he slipped his hand behind my head as we slammed down, the small of my back and upper shoulders taking the brunt of the impact. I groaned as the edges of each step dug into my back.

"Stay here," he growled into my ear, close.

He climbed off me and stood, turning around to face King Soren, his hands raised as if he were about to call upon his divinity.

I rolled over, wincing. When Rainier landed on top of me, he slammed my ribs into the steps we'd been seated on. Once my vision focused, it hit me that he actually shifted the ground below us, making the steps bow into a divot where I lay.

"Stand down!" The king's voice bellowed throughout the room.

"I will not." Loud and arresting, Rainier's voice was calm, not showing a single sign of agitation.

"She tried to kill us both. She will not live."

Without risking raising my head, I adjusted to watch as the king pushed Queen Shivani away, and in his hand, he held a ball of glowing crimson and violet fire. His dark green robes, made of silk, reflected the flicker of the flame. He glowered at his son.

"She tried to kill you after *you* tried to kill her daughter. Neither of you succeeded. You will both forget it and move on." If my life hadn't been on the line, I'd have argued with him. I had another name to add to my list of people I would kill before this was all over.

"And what of her threats to you?" Queen Shivani was seated on her throne, and her chin jerked to Rainier as she spoke. Her hands were clasped in her lap, appearing as if she were about to pose for a portrait.

"Mother, you wound me," he said, almost teasing. "Did you truly think she could kill me?"

Yes. No.

The king released the fireball in his hand, although he still looked enraged.

"She will be executed, Rainier, by my hand or yours. I'll give you three days to decide."

I didn't see the guards poised at the top of the steps waiting for their orders, and with a flick of Soren's hand, they rushed down the stairs. Rainier's eyes met mine as one of the larger guards picked me up and threw me over his shoulder. I kept my head lifted, maintaining eye contact for as long as I could. When I mouthed the one word he'd been waiting for, I saw his face twist in pain.

"Yes."

CHAPTER 37

When I was tossed into my cell, it was with no small amount of force. After we left the throne room, I'd moved my hands to the neck of the giant carrying me and slowed his heart enough for him to collapse. I didn't want to kill him, he was merely doing his job, but I couldn't help but take some small satisfaction when I heard the sound his knees made as he fell to the ground. I didn't know what I was thinking—it wasn't as if he was the only guard. Granted, there was only one other soldier escorting me because I didn't seem threatening at first glance. It surprised me they still managed to underestimate me when I'd just thrown a dagger at their king's face—one which would have hit its mark if not for Rain. I wondered if Dewalt appreciated the form considering it was his training responsible for it. Before I could get three steps in my dress, the other guard was tackling me, pulling my arms behind my back. He was careful, avoiding my bare touch. I didn't make his life easy, struggling against him the entire way, so when he threw me into the cell and slammed the door behind him, I wasn't surprised.

"Don't pull that shit again, or I'll put you in the chains. I'm eager to see how well the obsidian works."

I growled at him, still pissed off about everything, and he slammed the tiny peephole closed, plunging me into darkness before I heard his receding footsteps.

I knew there was a flickering torch in the hallway, but only the slightest sliver of light was visible under the crack of the door. I pushed and pulled on it even though I knew he'd locked it, hoping luck would be with me. I heaved a sigh and started fumbling around the room, navigating by feel. Based on the smell and the sounds I could hear, I was afraid I would find company in my cell among rats. I kicked against what felt like a cot on the ground and reached, feeling a thin cushion of sorts. I collapsed onto it and closed my eyes and took calming breaths, finding it especially difficult considering every inhale reeked of rot and shit. Stuck in a small room devoid of light was too much for me to handle, and I was about to go somewhere much darker mentally. I had to calm down. I focused on my heartbeat, trying to maintain it.

The low rumble I could feel in my bones was helping to soothe me. Rain was fighting for me, fighting for us. I knew he'd have fought either way, but I wondered if my answer to his question had motivated him further. I didn't like that he was upset enough to have trouble maintaining his divinity, but I took reassurance in the fact that I could still feel him in some way.

I sat for a while, replaying the events of the last hour in my head. Perhaps I shouldn't have thrown that dagger. I should have waited, bided my time until I was able to kill him without witnesses. I wouldn't let myself think I'd jeopardized Elora by throwing the knife. It was reckless, and I'd acted on instinct, unleashing a feral rage Soren breathed life into. I could have hurt her in the process. I tried to calm down, knowing Rain wouldn't let that happen. He'd force his father to completely rescind the order, and if he didn't, the queen would. She would see it from the perspective of a mother; knowing what the king said forced my instincts to act. I hoped. Either way, I wished I ignored his words and kept my temper. Now, Rain was having to work miracles to get me out. Though I didn't doubt his abilities to remove me from the dungeons, the entire palace was warded against rifting, Rain not being the only conduit with the ability. But I knew he would find a way to get me out. I knew he'd come for me, without a single doubt. He was confident he'd have control of the Vestian armies if he needed them, so I had confidence his power would hold in other ways.

My head rested against the wall, better to feel the ground rumbling, and my eyes were closed when I felt a familiar tingle in my arm, ending in a shock of pain.

"Ow, shit," I mumbled to myself as I rubbed my elbow. I got to my feet and walked to the door, pressing my ear up against it. I wondered if the impulse was just a reassurance they were working on a plan. But then I felt the tingle again, and this time my elbow jerked backward hard enough that I cursed loudly.

"Hello?" I called out, unsure if the thick wood would allow my voice to carry. Another tingle—this one much longer than the last—drew out so long I thought maybe it was just leftover pain from the previous impulse. And then it hit me so hard I thought my arm was shattering, and I screamed.

"What the hell!" I threw my body against the door, listening for any sign of footsteps, hearing a scuffle at the same time I felt another tingle.

"Stop, stop! I'm here! Stop!" The needling feeling stopped, but the pulse still went through me, and my already sore arm began to twitch. "Holy Hanwen, stop it!"

I finally heard something in the lock of my cell, and the door swung inward a second later, revealing Lavenia standing in the torchlight. "What the hell were you thinking?" She shouted at me, pushing me backward.

"I messed up!" I stumbled, blinking while my eyes adjusted.

"No shit! Gods damn it, Emma! You're lucky you aren't already dead." She crossed her arms, shivering. "Divine hell, it's cold down here. Aren't you freezing? And the smell, gods."

I shrugged. It certainly wasn't warm, but I wasn't that uncomfortable either. The smell, though—*that* was putrid.

"He sent me down here to see if you were hurt."

"Are you sure he didn't send you down here to hurt me? Four impulses, Ven!"

"I couldn't find you, so I had to make you scream. I won't pretend I didn't enjoy it. Anyway, are you hurt? I have to get these keys back to the guard I compelled them off of."

"I'm not hurt. Well, not bad enough that I can't handle it. My divinity, remember?" I paused. "Wait, you're not taking me with you?"

I couldn't see her face in the dark, but I saw her head dip lower. "I can't. There are too many people I'd have to get you past. You can tell Rainier is dealing with it." We could hear the pebbles on the ground rattle a little louder as she said it. "He is doing the best he can. My father may be evil, but you're a gods damn fool."

"I know."

"I don't know if the fact you know you're an idiot makes it any better." Though she sounded angry, I could hear the echo of a smile. "Oh, and he wanted me to bring you this." She grabbed my hand, pushing something small and metallic into my palm. "Which, excuse me, but what the *fuck*?"

"Dewalt didn't tell you?" I slipped the ring on my finger and sighed. I didn't plan to take it off ever again.

"You told him before you told me?" Incredulous, offended even, her voice rose in pitch.

"No, he saw it on my finger this morning. I hadn't decided yet when he saw, so we didn't talk about it."

"But you're decided now?"

"As of the moment I was getting carried out of the throne room, yes." That reminded me. "Is that soldier alright, by the way?"

"Which soldier?"

"The big one who carried me out?"

"I have no idea what you're talking about. What did you do?" Her tone of accusation would have been amusing if the situation were different.

"I, uh... made him pass out. He must be fine, or else you'd have seen him when you came down here." She started laughing before pulling me into a hug.

"You're so gods damn stupid. It may take some time, but we'll figure it all out. Gods, Dewalt and I are going to have our hands full dealing with the two of you." Her voice softened. "Try to rest." She looked past me and wrinkled her nose, no doubt at the sight of the pallet on the ground. She spun around and walked back into the hall, fiddling with the lock to another cell. I wasn't sure if she knew it was empty or if it was a lucky guess, but she came back a moment later, dragging another pallet behind her. Her terrifyingly high heel got stuck in a gap in the stone floor, and she stumbled before gracefully righting herself and throwing the other pallet at my feet. Looking at it, I wasn't sure if it was much better, but I could stack them and make it marginally more comfortable.

"I'll try to get you a blanket or a pillow. Hopefully, this will be your only night in here."

"Thank you, Ven."

"Don't thank me; it was his idea. I'm so mad at you I didn't want to come."

I smiled as she shut the cell, locking it behind her. When I laid down on the pallets, I tried to block out the stench as I felt the faint rumble in the ground. I fell asleep quickly, crashing from the emotions and rush of energy I'd had before.

I thought it was morning when I woke up, but I couldn't be sure. The room was still pitch black, and I could hear nothing. I laid there for hours, reliving everything that had happened and how different last night was to the one before it. Two nights ago, I had been wrapped up with Rain, pouring ourselves into one another, and last night I was alone in a cold cell, cuddled next to rats for all I knew. I wondered if things would have been different if I walked into the throne room with his ring proudly on my finger. Honestly, it might have gone worse. They'd have been mad on top of it all because I brought nothing in the way of alliances and little in the way of divinity. Queen Shivani might not have spoken out on my behalf. I spent most of the day laying there thinking, deciding if Rain got me out, I'd never question anything with him again. With my head resting against the wall behind me, I realized with a start that I didn't feel that low, reassuring rumble in the ground. I put my hand flat on the floor, ignoring the feel of various debris underneath it, and cursed when I couldn't feel the slightest hint of his divinity. It worried me, and I wondered what he was doing.

It felt like days had passed. I was ravenously hungry, my stomach rumbling, and I figured it had been more than a day since my last meal. Not long after, I heard a key turning in the lock, and a half-loaf of stale bread soared into the cell, landing at my feet before the door snicked shut. I debated turning my nose up at it; I'd be out in a few days, or I'd be dead—I could wait for decent food that didn't land in filth. Ultimately, my grumbling stomach won out, and I ate it. After I was done and realized I had no water to wash the dryness down, I thought it might have been a mistake.

More hours passed, and I snoozed on the pallet or paced the room. I noticed a small hole in the corner, the smell telling me its purpose, and I hoped I'd be out of the cell before the need to use it overtook me. Eventually, I heard the sound of another key in the lock and was surprised to see Dewalt's towering figure in the doorway. I jumped up and hugged him, hoping he was there to get me out.

"Gods, you're rancid." It didn't stop him from hugging me back, patting me gently.

I laughed and stepped back. "Sorry, I haven't had my bath yet. No one will give me a straight answer about it either." He chuckled as he came into the cell, closing the door behind him, and I felt my face fall. "I take it we aren't leaving."

"No, they're doing patrols. I compelled the guard to forget his next round, but I figure we should shut it just in case."

I sat down on the pallet, defeated. I had hoped that Rain would have worked his persuasive skills enough that I'd be out by now. For the first time, I worried.

"If he can't get me out, will you still go after Elora? At the Cascade?"

"Don't even start that shit. He's getting you out. Don't be stupid."

"Alright, but what if he doesn't? You'll still get her, right? Promise me."

He sighed, exasperated. "Of course, Emma. I promise."

"Thank you." I sighed in relief, knowing that no matter what, they would save her. "Why are you here, Dewalt?"

"Thought you might want some company. I can't stay long, though." He sat down on the pallet next to me, making a sound of displeasure as the scent wafted up at us.

"That's kind of you. Thank you for not yelling at me. Or impulsing me to death."

He chuckled and leaned back, resting his head against the wall behind him. "I heard about that. Can't say you didn't deserve it." I grunted at him. My elbow was still sore. "I do have to say, though, I'm rather proud of myself for only imagining throwing a dagger at his face over the years. You actually did it within the first hour."

"You heard what he said, Dewalt." He grunted in assent. "He's vile. An evil bastard. How do they belong to him? How can Rain and Lavenia be the way they are with parents like that?"

"Servants, nursemaids, and tutors. Shivani was around more than Soren, but both were hands-off. Rainier helped with Lavenia a fair amount since she's younger. But you're right; it's pretty amazing they didn't turn out worse."

"I didn't realize you were officially royalty until the other night. You're a duke, though, not a prince. Why not?" Sterling hadn't addressed him as he would a prince.

"I had to assume a title when I performed the ritual with Lavenia, and I refused the one of prince. I didn't want any titles, but I had to have something, so yes, I am a duke in title only. I do not have a duchy—all our land belongs to Lavenia."

"I take it you don't like being a duke?"

"It doesn't affect me. When people say 'your grace,' I cringe, but other than that, it doesn't mean much. It's a title."

"You don't have any responsibilities?"

"Oh, I do. Lavenia and I live a bit closer to the plains than Rainier does. We own quite a bit of the land the farmers care for, and our duty is to protect and help provide for them. Though, it doesn't often feel like a responsibility because we enjoy doing it. We've been chasing her brother all over creation, but I'm eager to finally go home and relax. I'll make a farmer out of Ven yet." I laughed, imagining Lavenia in her outfit from the night before, digging potatoes out of the ground. "Something tells me you're not asking out of pure curiosity. Does this have to do with the ring I saw?"

I could hear his smile as he spoke, and I chuckled, leaning against him. "You're smarter than you look."

"You're not." We both started laughing, and it took me a moment to stop.

"I hadn't said yes when you saw it at lunch. I wasn't sure what I was getting myself into—if I could be a good queen, or if it was something I'd even want to do. I don't think I could get away with refusing a title, considering he will be king."

"But you've said yes since then?"

"I have."

"What changed?"

"Seeing firsthand how much better Rain and I would be."

"Oh yes, queens who throw blades and ask questions later are a prime example of confident leadership." He elbowed me, and I snorted. I knew he was joking but still felt like I needed to defend myself.

"It *was* a lapse in judgment—I'll give you that. Rain is so much better than his father, though. I only have to do just as well as his mother, and Vesta still improves." He grunted in agreement, and we sat in silence for a while.

"Lucia felt a lot like you do. She was afraid she wouldn't be a good queen. I think the fear of disappointing your people or being good enough is part of what makes people good leaders. Soren is old and doesn't give a damn. He sure as hell doesn't care if he's a good leader. But a healthy fear makes us better, makes us work harder. Lucia would have made a good queen, and so will you."

"Thank you, Dewalt, truly."

We sat in silence for a while before Dewalt locked me back in my cage and left. I could hear the rumble again in the ground, vibrating in my chest. I knew it was because Rain was distressed and having a hard time keeping his divinity in check, but the feeling brought me comfort enough to sleep.

Minutes or hours later, I couldn't be sure, I heard the telltale sound of someone about to enter my cell, and I sat up. Dewalt had brought me a blanket, and I threw it off me, ready to see whoever was coming to visit me, hoping it was Rain.

It was not Rain.

In the dim lighting, I couldn't see her face. She was slim with long, flowing hair, and she stood a bit shorter than I did.

"Hello?"

"I've heard you're headed to the gallows." I didn't recognize her voice, a strange lilt to it I couldn't quite place. "So, this trip might be a waste, but it's important to send this message."

"What are you talking about? Who are you?"

She strode toward me, her movements oddly graceful.

"I am Keeva. Youngest of the Nine—and the most deadly, or so has been said."

I stepped farther back into my cell. I knew she couldn't have been thrilled with the broken betrothal, but I couldn't control Rain's actions. How had she gotten the key to my cell?

"You're fatter than I thought you'd be." I snorted. What was this woman playing at? A jilted ex-lover? Rain had told me there was no love between them. "I would have thought the woman to win the elusive prince's heart would have been extraordinary. To oust one of the Nine, surely you would have to be a woman of exceptional beauty or power, yet you seem to be neither."

I laughed dryly, not sure what she wanted from me. "You're right—my divinity is not impressive. Though, the prince does tell me I am beautiful. I wonder if that says more about you than it does about me."

A low growl, unsuited for her slight frame, came from her as she advanced toward me. "I do not understand it. We would have been greatness, and instead, he chose to make me an enemy." Her approach toward me was slow and unsettling.

"He harbors no ill will toward you. Why would you be enemies?" I knew Nythyr had opened their pass, already forgoing the alliance, but still. Was the broken engagement that insulting?

"Why wouldn't we be?" She tilted her head, and a second later, blinding pain tore through my right leg at the shin. I collapsed to the ground, a scream and a curse on my lips. Reaching down, I felt my leg and nearly vomited. My bone was poking through my skin, and she hadn't even touched me. "He will learn."

I shrieked as the pain mirrored itself on my other leg, high on the thigh this time, and I knew if I reached down, I'd find bone once more. I was screaming and sobbing, unable to form words. No one was going to hear me, and this woman was going to murder me. Dewalt had been right; I was going to die at her hands. She stepped closer again, and she kicked my leg out of her way to approach. The piercing throb flowing through me tore a garbled wail out of my throat, and my vision was white with agony.

She stood over me and spat, her hair hanging down and brushing against my face. I did the only thing I could think of and grabbed onto it, hauling her downward with my remaining strength. She fought me, rearing back, but I held on, grip tight in her silky hair. She was surprised, unprepared for me to fight back, likely the only reason she didn't snap more of my bones in that instant. I could tell I was about to pass out from the pain and, based on how wet I felt, blood loss. Perhaps she'd nicked an artery with a shred of my bone. I was going to die, but I wouldn't die alone. I shoved my hand around her throat and squeezed, focusing on her already fast heartbeat and speeding it up. She put her weight on one of my broken legs, and I screamed, the pain about to push me over the edge of consciousness. She was panting as her heart rocketed, and she collapsed. I kept my hands on her until I heard it, the overbearing silence that came after a heart beat fast enough to stop it for good. This wasn't like the tírrúil—I didn't just knock her out. I killed her as I had Faxon.

I didn't have the strength to roll her off me, but I used my remaining moments of consciousness to send whatever divinity I could muster to that artery. If I could just stop the bleeding, I would deal with the rest later. I was glad for the dark to claim me, hoping the pain wouldn't follow me there.

CHAPTER 38

THE GROUND BELOW ME shook, and I woke up with a scream on my lips. The pain was immense, and I bellowed when something moved on top of me. A weight was being pulled from on top of me. A body. The movement jarred me, and my legs felt like they were on fire. I didn't think I'd opened my eyes, yet I could see white dots of light in my vision, the pinpricks of agony which kept me from falling back into unconsciousness.

"Oh gods, Em—"

"Focus. She's alive, come on."

I blinked. Everything was blurry and dark, save the light from a torch. For a moment, I was terrified, thinking someone was coming to finish me off. The two blurry figures, both enormous, were familiar, but my mind couldn't focus. The touch was gentle, and I didn't think they'd hurt me. I was short of breath, unable to inhale deeply, and when I turned my head, I felt dizzy. The room was spinning. Not caring about the rotten air, I took deep gulps, trying to force my lungs to expand. I was so tired. Tired, confused, and not to mention wet. Where was I? Why was I wet?

"Make the rift. I've got her."

An arm tucked under my knees, and I started screaming again; the torque of gravity on my shin was unbearable. The overwhelming scent of fetid air in my nostrils was replaced by peppery sandalwood and a hint of sage as I was held against someone's chest. Dewalt, I belatedly understood. They had come for me. The ground shook harder.

"*Make the gods damn rift.*"

My head was tilted back, my hair falling in a curtain over his arm, and I tried to lift my neck. I couldn't, too weak to do much of anything except moan. Eventually, he shifted me, propping my head against him. I felt Dewalt's heart beating fast without using my divinity at all. He was scared. Was I that bad off? I heard the sound of a rift, and then it stopped. Again, it repeated. Open and close.

Silence. He was struggling. Rain couldn't focus. My Rain. He was here—my heart, my love, my life.

"Rain," I whispered, needing him to know I was alright and that I loved him, that I chose him. He needed to see so he could take me home. His hand was on my forehead a second later, pushing my sweaty hair off my face. Why was I sweaty?

"Em, I'm here." He lowered a kiss to my forehead, and I nearly choked on the sob that tore through me.

"I said yes." He coughed a bit and let out a soft groan, thick with emotion. "Now, take me home." He brushed his lips against mine and turned around. I was unconscious before he succeeded.

I was sure Dewalt tried to be delicate when he laid me down, but the jostle of my limbs on the bed was enough to rouse me. Shrieking, my voice hoarse, I knew where I was this time, slightly more lucid than before. I could smell the sweet alyssum and lilac from the garden, their scents wafting in on a breeze. We were home. But my coherence meant the pain was worse, too. Why was I still in so much pain? Dewalt moved away, and I heard low voices coming from the foot of my bed. I opened my eyes and immediately closed them again, the room too bright. I tried again, squinting and panting, struggling to draw breath.

I shouldn't still be in this much pain.

I didn't know how long I slept, but it was daytime, and I thought Keeva came at night. I shouldn't have been struggling to breathe. Why was I still so weak? Why hadn't my divinity healed me more?

I pushed up onto my elbows and looked down. My dress—drenched in blood, the pattern of flowers unrecognizable—covered my legs, but I could still tell everything was at the wrong angle. I guessed my divinity wasn't good at setting bones, the reason for my abundant agony. Maybe I was right in assuming Keeva had nicked an artery, and the only thing my abilities could do was keep me alive, explaining my exhaustion and shortness of breath. And the blood. Gods, there was so much blood. I could feel it, sticky on my body. Rain was at my side a second later, trying to get me to lay back down.

"Healer. Do you have a healer? Where's Mairin?" Did they have another me? My friend could help set the bones.

"I only have a mortal healer close enough to help, Em. But Mairin is probably—"

"I'm here, I'm here. Divine *hell*." My friend was a welcome sight when she burst into the room, harried and wild as she took in my appearance.

I finally collapsed, accidentally stirring my legs, and I had to take a moment to roar through the pain.

"Worse than childbirth," I gritted out through my teeth. Grabbing Rain's hand, I squeezed, and he knelt next to the bed a moment later. "Talk to me."

"The bones need to be set so her divinity can work. Get her ready. I'm going to wash up." Mairin was pure healer as she charged into the bathroom.

Rain swallowed and moved away to do what Mairin said, and I growled.

"Dewalt, you do that. Rain, I need you."

Rain was back at my side within a breath as Dewalt moved to the foot of the bed, gently pulling up my dress. I hissed, the slight movement still too much. "Cut. It."

"What do you need from me, dear heart?" Rain held one of my hands tightly in his grip while his other hand gently cupped my face.

I screwed my eyes shut as Dewalt began to slice into the beautiful, ruined dress. "A distraction."

"The last time you asked for a distraction, I ended up lying in your study with aching balls." The sly devil dared to grin, and I snorted as Dewalt finished cutting away my dress.

"Hanwen's ass, Rain. Why would you say that in front—"

"In front of me?" Dewalt scoffed, and I avoided looking down at where his hand pulled my dress taut as the blade ripped through the fabric, glad for the distraction Rain's comment offered. "As if I didn't already know. I might not prove it often, but I'm not stupid. Nor am I blind. Either that was the best damn water he'd ever drank in his life, or something else got him riled. By the state of your hair, I guessed it was you."

I laughed before it turned into a moan, body disturbed by the movement. Dewalt looked down at my legs and whistled. The two men both peered grimly at my lower half, their expressions a mixture of horror and fear. I didn't look at my legs; I didn't want to start vomiting.

Dewalt approached the side of the bed where Rain stood next to me, hand holding mine, letting me squeeze it through the pain. "Emma, they seem healed. I—It's like it healed wrong."

"Help me sit up so I can see." Rain slid an arm behind my back to prop me up, and I inhaled a breath, trying to calm my revolting stomach. Shards of bone were halfway melded together, protruding from my skin. What new hell had my divinity wrought? It certainly tried, didn't it? "Gods above, is my shin like that too?" Dewalt examined me and shook his head. At least that was one victory. I pushed back against Rain's supportive arm, and he helped lower me slowly to the bed, worry etching every part of his face. My first instinct was to reassure him that I would be alright, but I wasn't so sure myself. What if we couldn't fix it? What if I never walked again?

Mairin returned, eyeing what we had just discovered. "Dewalt, go find something for us to use as splints, so she doesn't move them in her sleep. I'm going to set this first one, but one of you is going to have to re-break the other so I can set it too."

The two men exchanged a weighted glance, and I squeezed Rain's hand while looking up at him. "You're going to have to hold me down, love." He nodded, appearing sick to his stomach, before walking around to the other side of the bed and gently climbing up. Both of his hands pressed down on my thigh, firm yet gentle, holding me in place as Mairin moved into a better position. I felt her cool hands on my skin, and I inhaled, focusing my divinity as she swiftly set the bone. I cried out but managed to stay awake, panting and sobbing, picturing my bone healing, the white shards knitting back together. I could feel tears rolling down my cheeks, and the pain from both hurts—my shin and my other leg—started to overwhelm me. Though Rain was next to me, gently petting my forehead and hair, I could feel that pull back to the dark.

"I think I'm going to sleep for a moment, my heart." He carefully leaned over me, lips pressing gently on my forehead.

"I'm sorry, Emma. I'm so sorry."

"Why are you sorry?" I never heard the answer before the dark claimed me once more.

I woke up to a damp cloth being rubbed across my brow, cool and soothing. Breathing deeply, I indulged myself in sorting the different smells assailing my nostrils. The faint scent of the garden mixed with the intoxicant that was petrichor, earth, and something inherently male, and I knew it was Rain who tended me. It was dark in the room except for the light of the fire as I opened my eyes. There was a fleeting pain, fading in and out, in one leg, and no pain in the other, and I nearly choked on my relief. I was calm, my heartbeat and breathing measured, no longer erratic and grasping. Cautiously, I adjusted my leg, the one that didn't need breaking a second time, and was relieved I felt no discomfort.

"Are you awake?" Rain's voice whispered close to me, and I turned my head toward him, smiling at him in the dim light.

"I am. Have you not slept?" He had dark circles under his eyes, and I was worried. We were past the worst of it, and I knew he needed to rest.

"I've been dozing off and on. You were sweating." I did feel flushed, and I wondered about a fever. Needing to check my wounds for heat or redness, I rallied my body to obey, but I still felt weak. Nothing compared to before, but I still didn't feel quite right. The dull ache behind my eyes told me my divinity had been hard at work while I was sleeping; the tightly thrumming hum I usually felt was reedy and shaky. Most times, I never noticed my divinity. But when it was taxed, I found it harder to ignore. Rain's hands were chilly as they slid up my back to help me as I sat up, and he stood, lighting the lamp, before sitting on the edge of the bed beside me.

"How long have I been asleep?"

"Almost three days."

My eyes widened; I was shocked it had been that long, but it explained why my pain had lessened so drastically. I wasn't hungry yet, my body still in shock, but I was thirsty, and it made sense considering how long I'd been asleep. My shin was nearly completely healed, with no signs of infection, yet there was still a faint line where the bone had broken the skin. My thigh was a different story, warm to the touch and red. I couldn't see bone, thankfully, but the wound had barely knitted closed. It needed to be disinfected. Would the torture ever stop? I sucked in a breath, knowing it should be the last of it. One more burst of pain, and then I'd spend the rest of the divinity I could and go back to sleep, waking up significantly better. "Can you help me to the bath?"

"You can't mean to bathe with that?" His eyes lingered on my leg for a moment before gaping at me.

"No, I'm not bathing yet. I'll need some alcohol. Not the good stuff." He frowned when he realized what I meant to do. "It's almost over. See how it's red and hot? I need to clean it. And then I'll finish healing it, curl up next to you, and sleep until I'm better. I may need to drink quite a bit of water first though, my mouth feels full of sand." I gave him an encouraging smile, and he nodded before pulling me to the edge of the bed, a hand behind my knee and at my back.

"Wait, I need to check something." Grabbing onto him, I turned, swinging both legs over the side of the bed before putting a small amount of weight on the better one, and I was glad it held. I stood, balancing only on that same leg, but didn't tempt fate by staying on it too long. I knew I'd tire easily.

"I think it'll be better in another day or so. Until then, you're stuck carrying me." He gave me a look that touched on annoyance, and his lips curled down into a frown as he gently scooped me into his arms.

"If you can carry my heart, I can carry your body." He pressed his lips to mine, firmer than all the delicate brushes he'd given me since finding me in the dungeon, and my heart sang. Carrying me into the bathroom, he gently situated me on the bench at the back of the tub before leaving the room to get the alcohol I requested, and I leaned back. I knew I'd told him I didn't intend to bathe, but I wanted to—the stench of my captivity and all that came after was almost vomit-inducing. My clothes were filthy, and I gazed at the arms of my sleeves longingly, distraught over the destroyed fabric, the beautiful pattern of flowers that once made up my dress ruined. I ran my hand up one sleeve, and the beautiful ring Rain gave me caught my eye. I was still staring at it when he finally walked back in, carrying two different bottles and a glass of water I drank in one long gulp.

"I brought one to hurt and one to numb." He had a grin on his face that didn't quite reach his eyes.

"Numbing first." He handed me one of the bottles, and I tilted my head back, taking a deep draw. I immediately regretted it, sputtering and coughing as a few droplets landed on my leg, making me hiss in pain. "Get it over with, please."

He looked at me warily, and I could tell he hated this almost as much as I did. He reluctantly walked to the side of the tub and pulled the remains of my dress out of the way, tilting the bottle over the wound, making quick work of it. I grunted out a string of curses but managed not to scream. It wasn't as bad as having your bones broken and set. I held out my hands over the center of the tub, and he helped me disinfect them before I slid them on top of my thigh and closed my eyes, leaning my head back against the cool tile behind me. I just needed to get the wound shut so I could bathe. It was all I wanted at that moment, to feel clean and whole and folded into Rain's arms. I focused my attention on my wound and ignored the sharp pain behind my eyes, but I knew I was grimacing. Rain climbed into the tub, sitting on the bench behind me and readjusting me to lean against him. He soothed me, playing with my hair, gently caressing my arms, and pressing-open mouthed kisses over the curve of my neck and shoulder.

"I smell wretched." I could feel the wound knitting together slowly, the taste of metal in my mouth once again.

"I know. I've been lying next to you for three days." He didn't pause in his attentions, and I laughed.

"I want to feel clean, normal. I want to take a bath and then sleep for another day." He kissed the top of my head in response. I wanted to keep talking to him and distract myself from the growing pain behind my eyes. A thought occurred to me, and I felt guilt I'd never thought possible before.

"Is Elora safe? Your father rescinded the order?" Divine hell, how had I forgotten to ask about her?

"She's as safe as she was before. The order was rescinded, and the assassins never left the palace."

"Thank the gods." I sighed, tilting my head back. I didn't move for quite a while, just relaxing and soaking in his heat and strength. It wasn't long before the ache in my head increased. "Tell me how you convinced your father to release me."

"I didn't. It was Ven." His tone was off—something about the way he said it not quite right.

"He would listen to her, but not you?"

"Mmm, my mother helped as well."

I knew there was something he wasn't telling me. "Out with it, love."

He sighed. "Lavenia is compelling him while my mother siphons his power."

"They're what?" I shouted, twisting toward him, my leg forgotten.

"He is the one who sent word to Keeva; he let her know you were in the dungeons. The bastard knew what she was capable of, and when he taunted me with the information, he blocked me from leaving. Dewalt and I killed four of his guards before Lavenia stepped in. He wasn't expecting her to use her divinity on him; she'd always been so gentle with him in the past. She compelled him to order his men to stand down, and Dewalt and I ran. She must have made him lower the wards too so I could rift you out. She's been compelling him ever since. He fought it at first, but when Dewalt went to check on Ven, he found my mother at her side, helping her."

I exhaled a shaky breath, moving my hands back to my leg. "What will he do when she stops? I—should I run?"

"She will not be stopping. With his divinity siphoned away, she can hold the compulsion for longer."

"What do you mean? Can't his guards tell? Won't people ask questions?"

"They think he is sick. He *is* sick. It is no surprise he is secluded in his chambers."

"And then what? They can't just stay with him forever."

"No, but they can stay with him until we perform the ritual."

I'd already said yes. I knew what it entailed, but to hear him say it was almost astounding, and I inhaled a quick breath. The idea I would be performing the ritual at all was a shock. I'd gone from anticipating an almost mortal lifespan, but now I had centuries. With him. My head gave a dull throb, and I peeked at my leg. I'd been distracted, so I was pleasantly surprised to see the wound had healed; only an angry, red line remained. I'd have to continue to send my divinity to it when I could, hoping to fight off any infection which might occur. Bending my leg at the knee and uttering a pleasant sound at what I found, I spun myself on the bench. Rain was there in an instant, arms out, easily anticipating what I needed and waiting for me to grab onto him.

"And after the ritual?" Putting my weight on the newly healed leg and finding I was satisfied with the results, I plopped back down on the bench, already feeling tired from the mild exertion.

"After the ritual, he will die."

I stopped for a minute, my mind snagging on the words he said. "He'll die?"

Rain appeared satisfied with my wounds since he turned the knob on the faucet and spun me, quickly unbuttoning the dress. I felt myself frown. I'd envisioned him undressing me a thousand different ways since the other night, but never had I imagined this. Malodorous and wounded, I was entirely dependent upon him. The soft glow from the candle on the counter helped it feel more like what I'd imagined, but it wasn't the same.

"Yes. The four of us have decided."

"What do you mean you've *decided*?" He slid the shoulders of my dress off of me, and an anxious knot formed in my stomach.

"My father is not long for this world, Em. The way he's been since before I was born is undermining every good thing he has ever done. It's time."

"Who decided this?" I held my hand to my chest, keeping the dress from falling off me.

"My mother, Lavenia, Dewalt, and I. My family."

"I suppose I missed quite a bit while I was asleep. Who could have guessed the conversations would be about regicide. Or is it patricide? Which takes precedence?" His hands rested on my shoulders, tenderly working my taut muscles, and I tried to resist the touch. "I suppose my opinion on the matter doesn't count?"

"It depends on what your opinion is." He moved in front of me, tugging my arms free from my sleeves and pulling the dress down off my chest. I stood, focusing my weight on the better leg, and he helped me slide the ruinous fabric past my hips so I could step out of it, and we worked together to finish undressing me. The water was nearly up to my knees, so I sank to the ground and leaned back against the bench, my body entirely submerged. Rain turned the water off, undressed, and slid down next to me.

"My *opinion* is that I don't want to be the reason for it. Your mother made it clear what she thought of me, and she's known your father to be like this for some time and hasn't done anything. I don't know how that could change because that bitch broke my legs." He turned and pulled me, sliding me across the bottom of the tub to situate me between his legs, and began to wash my hair. I groaned and leaned into his touch. "I don't want anyone blaming me in the future. You all decided without me, but it feels like I was a factor." Rain took a deep breath as he massaged my hair and scalp, the scent of lavender filling the air. I thought this might have been my favorite part about saying yes to him. I'd never wash my own hair ever again if it was an option.

"Shivani is complicated. There's no way for me to explain her behavior because I don't understand it myself most of the time. But you weren't the deciding factor for her. Elora was. I think the idea he could do something like that to a child and tell you, her mother, with not an ounce of remorse? This decision isn't about you. He has become a monster, and we must put him down."

"How?"

"That hasn't been decided yet."

"When? Can it wait until after we get Elora?" It was not lost on me how strange it was to schedule someone's death. Someone's *murder*. Rain finished rinsing my hair and pulled me back against him, head resting against his chest.

"Yes, it could wait, but I want you to have my divinity before the Cascade. I want to teach you to rift." I tensed, remembering how hard it had been for him to learn. I hadn't thought of the implication of having his divinity, and it intimidated me. He took a washcloth from the side of the tub and lathered it in soap, the smell of lilacs and violets filling the air. We sat in silence for a moment as he washed me, trailing over my shoulders before clearing his throat.

"I know you said yes in the heat of the moment, but I'm not letting you take it back." His touch somehow felt more possessive as he pushed me forward to scrub at my back.

"Who said anything about taking it back?"

"You seemed nervous a moment ago—about my divinity. I thought maybe you changed your mind."

"No, never." I was in this for good. "I *am* nervous, though. You were so bad at rifting at first, Rain. How could it be useful for me at the Cascade? I'll end up rifting over a cliff." I started laughing, and he chuckled.

"You never know when it could help. Besides, you're a grown woman, not a young boy with a beautiful girl on his mind. You'll likely be better at it than I was back then."

"Well, it would be hard to be worse." I stuck my tongue out at him over my shoulder, and he reached around, pinching one of my nipples. I shrieked, turning to face him as he pressed those soft, full lips to mine, and I melted. I was relaxed, feeling clean and safe, sinking into the warm embrace of the man I'd always loved, surrounded by the soft floral scents I'd always loved. I broke from the kiss when a realization came over me.

"Is Nana here?" Either Rain ordered soap especially for me, or Nana had arrived in Astana.

"She's here, yes. She is staying with Deandra. I think it will be good for them to have each other." I nodded in agreement. Deandra was a little older, not quite as old as Nana, and I thought their personalities would mesh well. "You'll be surprised to know Theo came with her."

"What, why?"

"He requested to join the guard."

"And you told him no and sent him back home to Lydia, correct?" Theo was only seventeen years old. I loved him almost as much as I loved my daughter. To have him join the guard? Terrifying.

"Of course, I didn't do that. He's a good kid. I guess his mother is moving to Mira, and he said he didn't have anything left in Brambleton. Quite frankly, he seemed a little lost. Besides, won't it be good for Elora to have a friend here?"

"Alright, you have a point. I'm surprised Lydia finally left. Since John died, she'd brought up going to live with her sister a few times, but always stayed. I never thought she'd leave Brambleton. Still, you keep that boy safe. I don't like it."

"Only because you said so."

Rain grinned at me, and I glared before leaning in for another kiss. I was getting greedy with them. I wondered how long this would last. Would I be craving him forever? Though I was tired and injured, my head aching, I pulled myself into his lap, wanting to be closer to him. He adjusted me, so he almost cradled me before grabbing one of my feet in his hand, pulling it out of the water.

"These giant things need washing." He grinned down at me as I swatted him on the chest before I snuggled into him. He held me there for a while before he picked me up and put me on the bench, kneeling in front of me and gently washing my lower half. He was careful on my legs, and I was pleased I felt no pain at his touch. He moved upwards, and I inhaled a breath. It was still so new to me for Rain to see me naked, and I couldn't help my nervousness, sliding my arms around my stomach. He tracked the movement, and I watched his brow furrow, but he said nothing before handing me the washcloth.

"I'll let you get the rest. You feel uncomfortable, and I need to wash as well." Rain pushed up and kissed me once more, and I was torn between explaining myself and just letting him go about his business. He pulled away and grabbed another washcloth, quickly cleaning himself while I used my own, awkwardly sitting naked on the bench at the back of the bathtub, before lowering myself back under the water.

"I'm not used to being naked around anyone." I felt like I should explain that it wasn't him making me uncomfortable. He eyed me cautiously as he washed his chest, waiting for me to continue. "I never undressed in front of him."

"Never?"

"No. Even before Elora was born, I avoided it."

"What was your reason? Is he why you cover up in front of me?" He frowned as he finished washing then sat down next to me.

"Well, I told you I haven't done anything sexual since before she was born. I never trusted him to take the tonic. After Elora, I was afraid of having another like her, not to mention I almost died giving birth to her. There were a lot of reasons. Not wanting to do those things with him was the main one. As for why I cover myself? I don't know. Maybe it's because you originally fell for a different version of me." His gaze narrowed, and I gave him an apologetic smile. "A version that didn't jiggle or have stretch marks." He finished washing and slid down in the water next to me.

"The parts of you that jiggle are some of my favorite parts, though." He slid a hand down my side and under my ass, cupping me as he pulled me back into his lap. "You've seen my body, all of my scars, and I don't believe you love me any less because of them. Do you?"

"No, of course not."

"Your stretch marks are scars, proof you grew a life and nourished it. I wish I was there to see it. To see you swell with a baby and coo over an infant." His smile was gentle, almost dreamy. "Preferably my own babe, not Faxon's. But it would have been beautiful to see, all the same." He chuckled, but I felt an ache at his words. I imagined his hands sliding over my stomach, round with pregnancy. I felt a sleepy smile grow on my face to match his before my eyes snapped open.

"An heir." I nearly shouted the words.

"What?" He was just as startled as I was.

"I . . . You can't marry me."

"Not this again." He shook his head and pulled me tight against him.

"No, I'm serious. Elora almost killed me. I can't give you an heir."

"Then I won't have an heir." He shrugged. "Maybe Lavenia will have a child one day, and it can be my heir. It's not worth worrying about."

"Not just an heir, Rain. A child. Don't you want children?"

"Yes, and I will treat Elora as if she is my own." A surge of affection raced through me, but my panic countered it.

"I appreciate that more than you can understand, but you know it's not the same thing."

"It doesn't matter."

"But it does!"

"You've said yourself that I keep proving to you how I feel, over and over again. Must I prove it to you again? *It does not matter.* I would be overjoyed if you blessed me with a child, do not mistake my words. But I will not give you up for anything, even that." He glanced over at the candle on the counter, noticing how long we'd been in the bath. "I hope I don't have to spend the rest of our lives convincing you, but I will if I have to. I will tell you every single day how I feel. I do not need a child from you to love you. All I need is you. I will kiss every stretch mark, every freckle, every single part of your body. I will suffer through watching your exquisite ass jiggle because of how much I love you. It is a price I am willing to pay." He grinned, mischief in his eyes as he stood, easily sitting me on the edge of the tub before wrapping a towel around me. "But now, it's time to sleep. I suspect you'll sleep most of the day to regain your strength, and I need to go to the Myriad." He toweled off, heading toward the closet, and I watched his firm ass as he went.

"For a task?" He walked back out, carrying my hairbrush and a nightgown I'd never seen, and he was no longer naked.

"Yes. I anticipate it being simple, but I'm quite pressed to get it done quickly. I have a beautiful, stubborn, and passionate woman waiting for me." He pulled the gown over my head before turning his attention to my hair.

"I can brush my hair—my arms aren't broken."

"No, but they were probably next, and I like taking care of you."

While he worked out my tangles, bad from days in the cell and lying in bed, I told him what happened with Keeva, and it brought him some joy to know the hair she was apparently vain about was part of her downfall. He told me how he had Mairin compel him so he could break my leg. Dewalt had taken a look at the bone sticking out, already joined together at an odd angle, and promptly vomited, thankfully hitting the floor and not me. Rain was afraid he wouldn't be able to do it, so he asked her to force him and compel him to forget doing it—he didn't want to think about it later. I felt guilty for what I put everyone through.

"I'm sorry for getting thrown in the dungeon. I shouldn't have done what I did."

"No, you shouldn't have, but I don't blame you. I honestly can't believe him. His cruelty has only increased since I saw him last. When he told me Keeva was on her way to visit you, I thought I was going to kill him right there, but I didn't have the time." Rain helped me to bed and lay facing me while he told me more. "The rest of your clothes showed up while you were in the dungeons, and yesterday I nearly lost my gods damn mind thinking about how close you came to never wearing them. Fuck."

He wrapped me in his arms, nestling his head in the crook of my neck. He needed my comfort, needed to know I was alright, and I did everything I could to make him feel my love, stroking his upper back and neck until he fell asleep.

CHAPTER 39

I SLEPT THROUGH THE entire next day, only waking up when the sun was setting. The smell of something delicious cooking roused me; I was ravenously hungry. When I opened my eyes, I scanned the room for Rain and was disappointed he wasn't back yet. My thigh still looked angry, but it wasn't warm, only hurting when I touched it. My shin was much better, but both injuries were rather itchy. I laid there for a short while, focusing on my bones mending stronger and my wounds healing. I was scared to put weight on them without Rain there to support me, but my hunger won out, and I slid off the bed, carefully trying one leg and then the other. I felt much sturdier than the night before, but I didn't want to overdo it.

After a few moments in the closet, mouth agape as I stared at my new wardrobe, I selected the softest things I could find—a fleece sweater dyed a faint lavender and sleep pants similar to the ones Rain wore in Brambleton. I was especially grateful for the way the smooth fabric caressed my tender skin, not constricting or agitating my wounds in any way. Since the hairbrush from last night was nowhere to be found, I ran my fingers through my waves before heading out to quiet my angry stomach, not bothering with shoes.

Mairin and Dewalt were seated at the dining table, and they looked up in surprise when I walked in. Giving each of them a kiss to the temple, I thanked them for their efforts, ignoring how strange it was to see two distinct people from two very different parts of my life keep company with each other so comfortably.

"I tried to warn everyone." Dewalt read a book as he ate, slurping up noodles as he flipped each page. I smiled softly and nodded.

"You did. Thank you for trying to protect me, D." He waved a dismissive hand while he continued to read, never looking up from his book. "Dewalt, I mean it. Thank you. You were right."

"Don't thank me. We should have placed a guard at your cell. Hell, I should have stayed with you while Rainier bartered for your release. I should've known better."

"Stop. You did more than I could ever ask for. Thank you." He lifted his head, seemingly accepting my sincerity with a grim nod before returning to his book.

"Do you know when Rain will be back?"

"No. But he did ask me to inform you that Shivani and the Myriad have set the ceremony for three days from now. Two days later, we leave for the Cascade." I was surprised. Between the illusion of Soren's renewed illness and whatever the king broke in Shivani, Rain's status apparently became an object of worry for the Myriad. I would have expected a much bigger fight from them—some claim against our divinity's compatibility, perhaps, since I was so weak, and he was so strong—but to cooperate with apparent ease? Dewalt set down his book, leaning back in his chair to study me. Sometimes when he stared at me like that, I felt deeply unsettled, like it wasn't me he was looking at. I knew it was difficult for him to have me here. I knew he was happy for his friend, but I was sure seeing what we'd turned into was hard for him. Lucia and I shared the same face, same eyes. Though our hair and personalities were different, I could imagine it wouldn't be easy for him. Mairin dismissed herself to go to the palace and check on Lavenia, and I found myself feeling awkward, focusing on the food in front of me while still keenly aware of Dewalt's presence.

"It's been a whirlwind, hasn't it?" His voice was quiet as he picked his fork back up, wrapping the noodles in it.

"It almost doesn't feel real," I agreed. It was hard to believe I'd ridden into Ravemont less than three weeks ago.

"You're still sure, though, right? After Keeva? It's not going to get less dangerous, Emma."

"I know. I *did* just kill one of the Nine." I cringed, suppressing a shudder. "Is that common knowledge yet?" I swore the look he gave me was one of pride before he answered.

"We've managed to stifle it for now, but when she doesn't show up back in Kieża in a few weeks, there will be questions."

"Great. Just what Vesta needs." I sighed and shook my head. "Already making a mess of it, aren't I?" He laughed and stood, carrying his empty plate with him. Before he left the room, he turned, studying me with a serious expression out of place on his normally jovial face.

"He'd never forgive you, but if you change your mind—if this is all too much—you have to tell him. He wouldn't want you to do something you're scared of doing."

"It's not that simple. I don't know if he told you, but—" I hesitated, debating on telling him more. I was uncertain if my friend with the quick smile and sad eyes could handle what I had to say. I pushed ahead, knowing I shouldn't avoid it. "Rain is my twin flame. Mairin read our auras."

His jaw dropping was the only indication he was surprised, but he recovered and smiled, albeit sadly. "There's no getting around that, is there?" He stiffly turned toward the kitchen to drop off his dishes.

"No, I suppose not." The way he spoke filled me with sorrow, and I wasn't sure what either of us may have been sad about specifically; there was too much to choose from.

After Dewalt left and I finished my food, I retreated to the bedroom, lonely without Rain there with me. I reminded myself that I hadn't been around him for a long time before these last few weeks, and I survived just fine. Perusing the books on either side of the fireplace, I picked one, settling in, warm in front of the blazing fire. My legs were mildly sore, but I propped them on the arm of the sofa as I read. I'd only been up for a few hours, but I knew I'd only be able to read a few chapters before I crawled back into bed, seeking peaceful sleep. I wanted to wait for Rain, but it seemed he wasn't coming home that night.

When I woke, the sun streamed across my face from one corner of the bed to the other, where my head rested. I didn't remember crawling under the blankets, and I was confused about how I got there; the other side of the bed was crisp and untouched, with Rain nowhere in sight. Had Dewalt moved me to the bed? Had he come in to check on me? I glanced at the nightstand to see my book lying there with a small slip of paper resting on top.

Unfolding it, I saw tight, crisp handwriting I hadn't seen in a very long time. Rain had come back last night, and I felt a tinge of disappointment I hadn't woken up. He'd even slept next to me, tidying his side of the bed without my awareness at all. Dewalt was taking me to the Myriad today, and Rain hoped for an easy task for me. I was curious about what his own had been and was eager to find out. My thoughts turned to worry when I began to wonder what the Myriad would ask of me. They'd asked Keeva for a cloak, which was laughable. Would I get the same treatment? I doubted it. Perhaps that was why they weren't kicking up a fuss; they planned to give me something impossible for my task. If I couldn't complete what was asked of me, they wouldn't approve of the bond and we'd be denied access to the font. It was quite unfair. Of course, my mind raced toward the woman who had almost killed me and the consequences we might face because of her death. I was not sorry, but I didn't want to think about her at all.

Hours later, properly outfitted in a simple traveling dress—cotton and emerald green to match Rain's eyes—I was cursing the fact I'd have to ride to the temple side-saddle. I wished I'd chosen breeches, but something told me they expected something different from a future princess and queen. I was dreading this visit. I hated the Myriad. I hated what they did to Lucia. I hated that they seemed to think women incapable of leadership. Dewalt watched me as I successfully, but clumsily, mounted Bree side-saddle. The horse was not a fan of it and huffed in frustration before I soothed her, grateful for my fussy mare's presence.

After a ride that was too long for side-saddle and too short for my nerves to calm, we arrived at the temple on the outskirts of Astana. It was more ornate than the temples in Mira and Brambleton. The building itself was plain, comprised of porous white stone, and the four giant windows across the front were bright and attention-grasping, two on either side of the large oak doors. Each window contained stained-glass depictions of life-sized versions of the gods. Rhia was positioned furthest to the left, a babe in one arm for fertility and an apple in her free hand, the symbol of wisdom. She wore a long white dress, drawing one's eyes to the bottom where tiny shards of glass depicted her toes. For a stained-glass portrayal, she seemed relatively lifelike, almost familiar. Aonara stood tall in the next window, and I took a moment to look at her open palms, white glass representing the light she held in her hands. I was disappointed when my perusal was cut off a moment later, the door opening and a novice escorting us into the temple. I was surprised they allowed Dewalt in with me, but I didn't dare say anything.

The temple interior was tall, with high ceilings and columns made from white marble. I would have thought it beautiful if I hadn't been distracted by a distinct feeling of being watched. Above us, a beautiful mural of the gods and goddesses decorated the arched ceiling, and, although we weren't given time to appreciate it, I could tell it was ornate, immense in its elaborate perfection. After leading us behind the altar, the novice stopped just inside a small room, gesturing to a long wooden bench against the wall. We sat, and the novice turned and left without a word.

"This is unsettling." I leaned over to Dewalt, keeping my voice low.

"You're telling me. I hate it here."

We didn't wait long before a door in the back of the small room opened, and a short, bald man with a ruddy complexion walked in, hands clasped in front of him. His white robes dragged behind him on the ground, and I was impressed he didn't trip over them.

"I understand you are Emmeline Highclere?" His voice was much higher-pitched than I would have expected. I nodded, and his mouth stretched into something like a smile. I thought it felt like a threat.

"Your Grace." He nodded his head in deference to my friend, and I suppressed a smile when I remembered Dewalt's comment about the phrase. His expression was sour as he nodded back at the master. "I am Master Filenti. Lady Highclere, you will follow me while His Grace waits here." I shot Dewalt a nervous glance, but he only nodded.

I followed Filenti into a narrow passage that ended in a tall, open room. There was no marble, but instead, the walls were hewn out of rough, grey stone, not a single window in sight. A rudimentary chandelier hung from a chain high on the ceiling, made of two crossed pieces of wood, and it barely emitted enough light to see the corners of the room. Other than a few chairs off to the side, it wasn't furnished, and the only color came from old tapestries hanging on the walls, covered in depictions of the Great War. It reminded me of Rain's bedroom at the palace. Three other masters were sitting in the chairs, waiting. The two men already seated watched me as I took my place where Filenti gestured, as he took his seat among the others. Only one of them didn't stare at me with some sort of disappointment, and it was a woman. I'd never seen a female master—or a mistress as it was.

Filenti cleared his throat before he spoke. "Lady Highclere, your task is a simple one. Show us your divinity and what makes it worthy of the Crown Prince of Vesta."

I blinked. I had no idea how to show my abilities. "Uh . . . do any of you have any ailments or injuries?" Looking at one another, disdain clear on their faces, they shook their heads. All but the woman; she remained still. "Alright, do any of you have a knife or something sharp?" I hadn't brought my dagger, thinking it might have been frowned upon, but now I wondered if I seemed horribly unsuited to take care of myself. Though I guessed since I was marrying into royalty, would they expect me to carry weapons?

One of the masters stood, pulling a letter opener out of a pocket of his robe, and handed it to me. A letter opener, of all things. I made sure they were all watching as I turned my hand over and sliced it open. The letter opener was not sharp, so

I had to apply a fair amount of pressure to cut through my skin. None of them reacted to it.

"Though healers are the most common conduits, and their value speaks for itself, I am more rare. I've never met a healer who could also heal themselves." I clasped my other hand to my wound and willed my divinity to move toward it, showing my unmarked palm to them a moment later. I passed the letter opener back to the master who presented it, and he promptly cleaned my blood off with a handkerchief before proffering the cloth to me.

"Thank you." I cleaned away the blood and glanced up, a grimace on my face, not sure what to do with the handkerchief. Its owner did not smile as he took it back from me.

"What else?" Filenti didn't seem impressed by my healing, and I was mildly offended.

"Well, the healing is honestly amazing. I had two broken bones three days ago, and now I don't." I felt my stomach clench, realizing I probably shouldn't have told them about that.

"How did you break them?"

Shit.

"A tumble down some stairs. Unfortunately, my divinity doesn't help me keep my balance."

Unruffled and seemingly annoyed, Filenti sighed as he chose not to comment on my lack of grace. "I understand you have a type of ability to do with the heart?"

"I do, but I'm not sure how to demonstrate without hurting anyone. I'm a harrower, I believe is the term?"

"I'm aware of it, yes." The master inclined his head, but his brows furrowed.

"I can hear heartbeats, and with a touch, I can slow or hasten them. Even stop them."

"We'd like a demonstration."

"I—I'm not sure how to go about doing that. If I slow it enough, the person will pass out. They'll be fine, but..." I trailed off, staring at the four of them. The woman was the only one not looking at me, staring straight ahead instead.

"We want you to show us how you stop a heart. Then we want you to start it again."

"What?" I felt my eyes grow wide.

"Mistress Miriam has come today to allow you to demonstrate." The woman still stared, unmoving.

"I've never stopped a heart and restarted it. I could kill her."

"That is a risk she has agreed to." Filenti's grew impatient.

"How will you know if I am successful? I could just slow it enough and then hasten it again and say it stopped."

Why did I say that out loud?

"I will know because I am also a harrower, Lady Highclere, though my gift is only auditory. I cannot affect anyone else." My jaw dropped; finding out once again about another person with my abilities was unexpected. I recovered and crossed my arms, feeling the glare on my face as I spoke.

"I still don't want—what if I can't restart it?" I watched Miriam, waiting for her to meet my stare. To agree with this was preposterous.

"Do you want to perform the ritual with Prince Rainier or not?"

Divine hell.

"Am I done after this? If I do it, will that be enough?" My heart raced, and I was struck with the sudden knowledge Filenti could hear it. Good, I hoped he could hear just how terrified I was that I might not be able to bring her back. And what if I couldn't? What then?

Filenti nodded slowly.

"And if I fail? If she dies?"

"Mistress Miriam knows the risks, and she has agreed to it. No harm shall become of you if that's what you mean. I have a contract here if you'd like to look over it, releasing you from any responsibility." Filenti held a paper out toward me, and I briskly cut the distance between us, snatching it out of his hand. "I had a copy delivered to the palace this morning, but you may keep this one."

I glanced over it, skimming to see that what he'd said was indeed true. But still, responsibility in front of the Crown and Myriad was different from the accountability I would feel in my soul and upon death. That I'd knowingly contributed to killing a woman? Even if it was an accident? But what choice did I have? I wondered if Filenti was getting some jealous, vindictive kick out of this. Since he couldn't do what I did, he wanted to make me do something like this with my own gift? My thoughts strayed to Keeva, oddly enough. The Myriad must have mixed up our tasks. I was infinitely more suited to make a cloak, and it was apparent where her proclivities had lain. I paced for a moment, still watching Miriam stare straight ahead. I reached out, spearing my divinity at only her, ignoring the men around her. Her heart was racing. She didn't want to do this. What did these men have to gain by making me do this?

"May I talk to Mistress Miriam in private before I do this?"

"Absolutely not." The man with the handkerchief spoke. He had a long thin nose, and his eyes were rather close together. I didn't hide my scowl. I didn't know what to do. Something told me it wasn't just the ritual on the line if I didn't do this. I walked toward the woman and studied her. Why her? She was a bit older, likely in her fifties. She had dark brown hair, threaded with silver, and it was pulled back in a bun that made her features look more severe. Her eyes were gray, and she had a slight overbite. I knelt in front of her and gently touched her neck, still unsure about what I planned to do. I stifled a gasp as a voice broke into my mind, drowning out my internal thoughts.

"Do not react—listen to me carefully. They suspect you are not what you appear. Do not prove it by bringing me back. If you try to save me, they will kill you, and thousands more will die because of it. You have to stop my heart. The seer has foretold it. It is the only way. I am ready."

Feeling my heart rocketing and my eyes enlarging, I pulled myself together. I couldn't lose my control, especially not when Filenti could hear my heart. I pulled my hand away, taking slow measured breaths.

"I'm sorry, I need a moment. I've never successfully done this, and I'm nervous."

"Take your time." Filenti nodded, and the man with the long nose turned to glare at him.

I started pacing. Miriam had been in my head, and she sounded agonizingly desperate. This was a punishment—that much was clear. What had she done for them to volunteer her in this? They thought I wasn't what I appeared to be? What did that even mean? Thousands would die? I reached out again, listening for her heartbeat, and it had slowed considerably since speaking to me. Had she calmed because she knew I heard what she had to tell me?

"Why is she the volunteer and not one of you three? Surely, one woman cannot be braver than the three strong men before me." I hoped perhaps one of them would stand up for the fearless woman.

"You would do best not to hurl insults at us. You are only here because King Soren is on his deathbed. You are barely worth our time, let alone the time of a crown prince." The master with the handkerchief spoke, his voice thick with disdain.

"If she dies, will I still be sufficient?" I felt disgusting asking it, knowing she would die if I did what she asked. But I had to know.

"Yes, I thought we established this." Filenti stared at me, annoyance growing in his features.

I began to pace again, thinking about how Dewalt could help if I could only get him in here. She said a seer had foretold this, and it was the only way. Why would she lie? Believing her would kill her and not believing her would allow her to live. What could she have gained by lying to me? It made no sense. I wanted to know who this seer was. Who could possibly have predicted an outcome where I had to kill someone? I watched the woman, continuing to listen in, her heart a sure and steady thump, and her eyes flashed to me for just a moment, just brief enough I could have imagined it. And in that glance was trust, acceptance, and perhaps determination. I squared my shoulders and walked back to her. I wanted to trust myself on this, but trusting myself meant trusting her. Trusting her meant killing her. I took a deep breath and put my hand back on her neck, knowing the decision I made was hard-won. A glimmer of a tear was the only sign of emotion she wore, and she blinked it away.

"Tell her I'm sorry I wasn't better."

My nod was imperceptible. Though I couldn't ask aloud who she meant, I'd do my best to get her message across.

"May the gods fight for you and goddesses protect you."

I bit down on my lip, hard. She looked at me with a storm in those grey eyes, urging me forward, pushing me down the path which led to her demise. Courage, that's what the storm was. Bravery in the face of fear. She closed her eyes, and I focused, slowing her heart, each beat a nail driven into her coffin. Eventually, it fell quiet, and she slumped forward. I nearly let out a sob, but I stayed there, frozen, making sure to appear as if I was focusing hard. Thankfully, the screwed-up expression I was surely making could be interpreted as concentration rather than loss. I kept one hand on her neck, and the other grasped hers. I didn't move, didn't use my divinity. I trusted this woman. I trusted the voice that hadn't faltered.

"May your divine slumber be peaceful, and your heart be full." My words were a whisper, a final comfort to a woman who had sacrificed for reasons I could not know. I felt the tears slip down my face before turning to Filenti and unstopping my emotions.

"I told you I've never done this!" I cupped my face in my hands, feeling the rage and grief race through me. "Her blood is on your hands, and now I have to live with it. I have to live with the knowledge that a woman is dead because you were curious." Filenti didn't seem bothered as he glanced at the woman, but his lips had turned down into a frown.

"I had high hopes you'd be successful."

"You weren't the only one. Am I done here? Did I pass your test?" I struggled to maintain my composure and keep the earlier bite in my words.

"Yes, yes. You may go."

I rushed out, found Dewalt, and nearly sprinted out of the building. By the time I got to Bree, I was shocked my legs weren't in more pain than they were, the stress of running and walking throughout the temple getting to them. Dewalt watched me in silence, helping me climb onto my horse and trying to help me arrange my skirts, looking at me in trepidation. I wasn't ready to explain it to him, not yet anyway. Hell, I wasn't ready to try to figure it out in my own mind, let alone tell him what happened. Bree shook and huffed, already disagreeing with the way I'd mounted her, and I nearly screamed in frustration.

"To hell with side-saddle." I slid my leg over to sit astride her and wore the mare out in a gallop the entire way home, Dewalt keeping pace behind me. I took us up the long lane of the estate, realizing this was the first chance I'd had to take it in. It was beautiful. The outside was all grey stone and dark brown oak. The large windows made it appear welcoming, the covered front porch with a small sitting area a comforting and relaxing sight, made even better when I saw who sat there. I couldn't have been more relieved to see Rain before me, his absence over the last few days palpable, and I needed him for this. He saw me storming up the drive and jumped to his feet, coming down the steps. He was radiant in a crisp white shirt, unbuttoned to the middle of his chest and his sleeves rolled up. He pulled a hand across his jaw, freshly shaved, and he seemed to shake out the stiffness in his body, shoving his hands into his pockets by the time I thundered to a stop.

"What is it now?" He sounded tired, so very tired, as he helped me down from Bree.

"We need to talk." I dragged him from the house as Dewalt tended to the horses. Rain's estate had land, and there was a small pond he'd shown me on our tour the other day. I didn't want anyone to overhear us because I was truly terrified, not speaking as I tugged him along the path. When we finally got there, I couldn't hold it in any longer.

"I just killed a woman because she asked me to." He blinked, shock etching his features, and I burst into tears.

CHAPTER 40

I BARELY BREATHED AS I raced myself to recount what happened as fast as I could. What was asked of me, what Miriam said to me, what I had done. By the time I finished, I was no longer crying but angry and breathless instead. Rain held me the entire time I spoke, and it brought me some small comfort. I pulled away and started pacing while he stood in silence, thinking. I felt an ache in my thigh and ignored it, pushing my divinity toward it instead. I knew I should have been resting, but I couldn't. I needed to move.

"They are clearly interested in your divinity." His temple throbbed.

"Yes, but why? I'm just a healer, and apparently not the only harrower either."

"Just a healer." He shook his head. "I've never seen another healer heal themselves, Highclere."

"Yes, but again, why is that important? I can only help myself with that. Why would it be useful to the Myriad?" He surveyed the pond, a muscle working in his jaw as he considered.

"And you said Filenti is a harrower but can't do what you do? He can only hear the heart, then?"

"I guess. He was disappointed when she—when I didn't bring her back." When she died.

I continued pacing while Rain crouched down, poking at something in the water with a stick, still deep in thought. The woman's grey eyes swam in my mind. She had seemed at peace at the end when she offered a prayer for me. How could she have looked at me like that, with courage I couldn't even begin to understand, knowing she was facing her death, and pray for *me*? I took a moment to offer one up for her and another one, begging the gods to understand and forgive me if I'd chosen incorrectly. Part of me thought about cursing them too for putting me in this position in the first place, but I decided against it.

"She had a message for someone." Rain glanced over his shoulder in question. "She wanted me to tell someone, a female, that she was sorry she wasn't better.

Maybe her child? I'm not sure, though I suppose I'll have to add that to the mystery of Mistress Miriam."

"Why did you do it? Why did you stop her heart?"

"I don't know, I told you. I just trusted her. And she brought up the seer."

"What made you trust her, though?"

"She was . . . off. She didn't interact with me as the others did. And her voice was so calm and strong. I don't know. Maybe I was wrong. Maybe I should have refused to do it and left."

"Well, if she was telling the truth and you refused, it sounds like they would have done worse to both of you. If she was lying?" His face tightened, lips flattening. "Why would she lie only to bring about her death?" He stood up, observing the water, and I was grateful his mind had worked in the same way mine did. It made me hopeful I'd made the right choice if it was the same one Rain would have made. "I've never liked Filenti. I've worked with him in the past, and he's always made me uncomfortable."

"Is he who gave you your task?"

"No, I went to Lamera for mine. That's why I was gone so long."

"Why did you go all the way to the Seat? Wait, how did you get back last night?"

"A day and night full of rifting. I'm sorry for not waking you; I was exhausted and had an early morning today."

"Why didn't you just go to the temple in Astana?"

"As the future king, it is expected of me to go to Lamera. They would've given one at the temple in the city, but if I didn't meet with the Supreme, it might have looked like a snub. I was only going to go to the temple in Ardian for Keeva because I didn't care if it fell through, and I'd been staying at Crown Cottage, so it was convenient. I only went to the Supreme because I wanted everything to go as smoothly as possible for us, dear heart."

My heart warmed a bit before the ice in my veins held it in its grip once again. "I take it your visit went smoother than mine?" I was still marching a path in the dirt, full of nervous energy.

"He chastised me a bit for Keeva." I gaped at him in horror. How could they already know? "For not *choosing* Keeva," he corrected, and I let out a sigh of relief. "But he seemed relieved I was finally there, finally ready."

"Did he seem interested in my divinity?"

"Nothing more than curiosity. He knew you're Lucia's sister. He even said he was surprised we hadn't performed the ritual sooner since I'd known you so long."

"Did he ask where I've been this whole time?" I watched his mouth pitch up into a slow, crooked smile.

"I told him we lost touch, and you married another man but finally came to your senses."

I glared at him. "That does not make me sound particularly loyal." Rain shrugged, his grin fading.

"I couldn't exactly tell them the truth, could I? I'm especially glad I didn't, after what happened here. He will eventually learn Elora is the Beloved, though. And he'll know you were hiding her. But we'll handle that when we have to."

I nodded in agreement. "What are we going to do?"

"Nothing, yet. Not until Elora is safe. One problem at a time, Em." He strode toward me, determined, and hugged me tight against his body. I was surprised he was so calm. I wanted to act. I wanted to throw Filenti in a cellar and help Rain torture him until he explained everything. I imagined doing to him what I did to Miriam but succeeding in what he'd asked of me, restarting his heart instead. Doing it over and over until he begged for mercy. He had made me kill that woman. But Rain was right, of course. Elora was our priority. She had always been the most important thing, and we were getting so close. I grew anxious thinking about the days ahead. I'd be performing the ritual, learning Rain's divinity, and then rescuing my daughter in a handful of days. I couldn't let myself ponder what would happen after.

"Does Dewalt know why you raced him back here like a screaming demon from the pits of hell?"

I snorted. "No, but he didn't question me." For which I was grateful.

"Of course, he didn't. Let us go explain, or he will worry."

Rain started back through the trees toward his home, and I tried to keep up but my leg was starting to ache. The better of the two seemed to be holding up fine, but my left leg was giving me trouble. No longer running on anger and adrenaline, the trek back seemed endless. Glancing over his shoulder when he realized I'd fallen behind, Rain stopped to glower at me as I caught up.

"You're limping. Why didn't you tell me you were hurting?"

"I'm fine. I'll rest when we get there." He shook his head and scooped me up like a sack of potatoes, tossing me over his shoulder.

"Rainier!" I slapped his back, not pleased at all. He responded by smacking my bottom hard enough to make me yelp, and I beat at his back even harder.

"Stop it, or I'll do it again." I let out a sigh of frustration but stopped wiggling and fighting against him. He laughed, low and seductive, before rubbing where he smacked, easing the sting of it. "I'll kiss it better later." I snorted and then pushed up a bit, so my head was upright, growing dizzy watching the ground below us.

"Are we dragging her back to the temple for her task?" Dewalt's voice called out, amused. So much for worrying.

"No, her task is complete. Did you truly not tell him anything?" Rain chuckled and carried me up the porch steps, refusing to put me down.

"All I know is she came running out of there and pulled me out with her. She had some colorful words about riding side-saddle, though."

After talking to Dewalt during dinner—a decadent meal of roasted duck with red currant jelly served with roasted potatoes and glazed carrots—Rain left once again, quieting me with ravenous kisses as he explained why. With King Soren comatose, Rain was having to take over some responsibilities, and he wanted to check in on his sister. It took everything in me not to whine about it considering I was the reason anyone was there having to do those things in the first place. I treated myself to a bath and a book by the fire, but I struggled to focus, worrying about my daughter. Though the threat of the assassin from Soren was no more, she was not safe by any means. The new moon was quickly approaching, and I was growing ever eager, anxious to speak to Elora, to hold her in my arms, to bring her home. Thinking about bringing her here to this beautiful home full of wonderful people with whom I had reconnected was overwhelming, and it brought me such intense joy I was overcome with grief when I realized she might not want to stay. She might hate it, might resent me. What if she didn't like Rain? I thought about how she'd asked me if I was going to marry him and fought a smile when I remembered my response. Only hours later, he immediately proved me wrong by throwing himself on his knees before me. I didn't recall a negative tone in her voice when she asked, in fact, I recalled a sly smile gracing her lips when she asked me if I loved him. She'd seemed more curious than anything else. With a start, I realized it had been one week exactly and that Cyran might see fit to invade my dreams. We hadn't made a plan for this, but all the same, I supposed I should at least try to rest just in case. Climbing into bed, I set my book down and willed sleep to claim me.

But sleep would not come. My legs were aching, even with flooding my divinity downward, not bothering to ration it, and I couldn't help but think about Miriam. I wondered if I could have brought her back like they'd wanted me to. As I had wanted to. Could I have started her heart again? Could I have started Sam's after the tírrúil attack? I had tried, willing it to begin beating under Rain's pumping hands, but I'd been using my healing gifts rather than my harrowing. The moments leading up to his death echoed in my mind. He had been dead by the time I got there, his heart no longer beating, but I'd tried anyway. Maybe if I had gone there a moment sooner, chased them the minute I knew they were hurt, maybe then he would've lived. Maybe I would've been able to heal him enough and keep his heart going or start it again if it stopped.

They think you are more than you appear.

Why did she speak in riddles? Why couldn't she have been more clear? Maybe it had something to do with being Rain's twin flame? Perhaps the Myriad suspected there was more to us than a normal pair of conduits who wanted to perform the ritual? But then why had Rain's experience with the Supreme gone smoothly? I focused my divinity on my own heart, trying to calm its beating. One problem at a time—Rain was right. It would definitely be a problem, though, the minute the Myriad caught wind of Elora being the Beloved. I was surprised they didn't know already, given what happened in the throne room the other day. They would try to do to her what they did to Lucia. But now, after what I'd been a part of today? I would never allow it. I supposed her protection from them might be one more perk of being queen. The Myriad had been so firmly enmeshed in royal affairs for so long, though, I wondered how hard it would be to extricate from it.

The moment my eyes grew heavy, there was a knock at my door. I sat up, confused. Rain wouldn't knock. I pulled a match out of my nightstand and lit my lamp, calling out for whoever it was to enter.

"Hey there." Lavenia's voice was low and quiet, tired.

"Ven!" I jumped out of bed, glad to see my friend. The woman who helped save my life by stopping her father. From keeping him at bay. But how was she here?

"I just wanted to check on you. I heard things were pretty rough for a while."

I smiled and wondered if her first stop upon returning was to see me rather than to go rest. "I'll be good as new by tomorrow. You sound exhausted. Are *you* alright?"

Lavenia sat down heavily on the end of the bed. "He's far gone now. I don't know if it was my compulsion or not, but I was there all day today and didn't need to use it once. Mama is staying with him and will siphon him if she needs to until I can get back. But neither of us think he'll wake again."

It was strange to hear her refer to Shivani the way she did, but I imagined the two of them had spent a fair amount of time together the last few days, and maybe some closeness between them had been restored. "He's dying?"

She gave me a look and snorted. "He's *been* dying. I think we just hastened it along." She hung her head, and I didn't know how to react. Rain had said they all agreed to it, but I was sure the decision weighed heavily over all of them. Save for Dewalt; I couldn't believe Dewalt would feel any remorse for the king.

"I'm sorry. Thank you—for everything." I grasped her hand, and she squeezed mine.

"I'm sorry too—for impulsing you so much. And you're welcome." Her expression was somber, but the sigh and slight smile she afforded me seemed more like relief than anything. "I'll have to check with Rainier, but I think we're doing the cleansing tomorrow."

I cocked my head. "I have no idea what you're talking about."

She rolled her eyes and sighed. "Of course, he didn't mention it. I forget the real reason for it; it's such an old tradition for royalty. It doesn't even mean anything anymore. Something to do with the cleansing of our pasts and coming together as a family or something. It's turned into an excuse for a day of pampering. It will just be you, me, and Mama. If Elora were here, she'd participate too." We exchanged a sad smile but knew with Soren's ailing health, we didn't have time to spare.

"Ordinarily, your father should be there to participate with Rainier, but there is no time. It'll just be him and Dewalt."

"Divine hell, I suppose I should send a message to him. 'Hello Papa, do I have a surprise for you.'" Lavenia gave a mild chuckle, yawning before she headed to the door.

"I'll see you tomorrow."

"Thank you, Lavenia." She waved my words away and left.

I didn't fall into an illusion but had restless dreams instead. Though I didn't remember a single one, I had an uneasy feeling in my stomach when I woke. I was lying in the center of the bed on my side, and Rain was behind me, a heavy arm around my waist. Sighing, I wiggled happily against him, having missed him while he attended to all the responsibilities I inadvertently thrust upon him. His absence the past two nights was bothering me, and I felt pathetic for it. I interlaced my fingers with the hand wrapped around my waist, and he tugged me backward toward him in his sleep. He gave a soft snore, making me smile. I loved waking up in his arms or on his chest or just near him. I'd never felt that sort of intimacy. When I shared a bed with Faxon, I tended to sleep on the edge of it, curled away from him. In all our years living in hiding, I only remembered waking up to his touch once, and it was an accident, my cold feet seeking body heat in the night. Even in Rain's sleep, he held me like he was going to lose me. I adjusted in his arms before falling back into unconsciousness, comfortable and relaxed, my uneasiness gone.

I didn't think it was too much later when he woke me, nuzzling my neck.

"I don't know if I'll ever get used to this."

"Mmm?" I kept my eyes closed and snuggled against him.

"Every morning I wake next to you, it takes me a moment to realize I'm not still dreaming." I made a happy noise in my throat and felt the smile spreading across my face.

"I've missed you."

"I know." I snorted, and he kissed that spot, right behind my ear, making my skin pebble and my heart soar. "I met with my shifters; They suspect Cyran and Elora are in Evenmoor but haven't had time to follow up. Aedwyn and Aerfen will be checking to see if Declan suspects anything. I've also had to tend to concerns within the council. Some of them aren't thrilled we are bypassing their approval for the ritual. But surprisingly, Mother has helped me deal with it, since my father ... well, did Lavenia speak to you last night?"

"She did. He still hasn't woken up?"

"No, and I hope he doesn't. It makes things easier. With him unwell, my mother gave me free rein. Until he dies and we are crowned as king and queen, everything will have to go through her first, but she's given me almost absolute permission to run things as necessary."

"I was told I'm to spend the day with her and Lavenia while you and Dewalt do the same? The cleansing or something, she called it?" I felt him nod.

"Dewalt and I are leaving in the afternoon for a short hunt and a night of smoking draíbea and drinking. I don't think you'll have as much fun with Ven and my mother."

"Ass." He chuckled and kissed me lower, moving down my neck.

"You, my venomous little demon, will be pampered, plucked, and prepped for me to defile you tomorrow night." I chuckled, squirming away, but he hauled me back against him, rewarding me with a twitch from him against my backside.

"Pampered, sure, but plucked? Am I too hairy for you?" He slid his hand under my nightgown and rested it on my stomach, gently caressing around my navel, and I didn't flinch or pull away. This man loved me and everything that came with me, rounded belly included.

"I was teasing, dear heart. I'd have thought you'd be more focused on the defiling part." His hand slid lower, cupping my heat.

"Something tells me you won't be waiting until tomorrow to defile me."

"Your intuition is spot on, Em." His finger slid down my center, and I exhaled, relishing the sensation. His movements were lazy and comfortable, much like the two of us. After the passionate night we'd shared, it was a pleasant surprise to have this easy, warm tenderness. I basked in it.

"I've missed your hands." I folded my leg to give him better access and rolled into his touch.

"Is it just my hands you've missed?" His lips tickled the skin on my neck as he spoke.

"Of course, I've missed this, too." I gave a soft laugh as I reached behind me, grabbing his hard length through the undershorts he wore. "I haven't missed these clothes, though." I began pulling at them, and he took his hand off me for a second to finish what I started. I felt him spring out and hit my ass, and I giggled before reaching behind me and pumping him, rubbing my thumb across the already slick head. He bucked gently into my hand, letting out an exhale on my neck. He froze for a moment before I felt him tilt his head up, looking down over my body toward my legs.

"You're not in any pain, are you? If you're still healing—"

"The only pain I have is the ache of wanting you." He gave a low, rumbling laugh before he hitched my leg up, grabbing the back of my thigh and spreading my legs apart. I reached between and grasped him, guiding him to my entrance.

"I've ached for this ever since I spilled inside you." His filthy words were rough and made my heart race. Groaning, I slid him through my wetness before positioning him just so, ready to thrust into me. He took me slow, still careful. I wasn't sore anymore after the night we shared, but I still wasn't used to him. He was so thick that I could feel my body stretching to make room for him. He let out a low, measured breath as his hips punched forward, keeping a leisurely pace as he kissed along my neck. I moved my hand down, tracing where we were joined, feeling his slick cock moving in me, and I sighed. Gods, he felt so good. When his hand found my clit and pinched it, I cried out in surprise.

"You're perfect, Em, you know that?" His whisper tickled my skin as he rubbed me in tight circles with increasing pressure, all while he firmly thrust into me, and I could feel myself clenching around him.

"Perfect for you, maybe." I was breathless as I tweaked my nipple, moaning the words.

"Only for me," he growled. "You're mine, and I'll never let you go again."

Someone rapped on the door.

He groaned and buried his head into my neck, still moving inside me. "What is it?" He barked out, clearly frustrated. I would have laughed if I wasn't trying to keep from whimpering. I heard Sterling's muffled voice behind the door.

"I'm sorry, Your Highness, but the queen's carriage is here for Princess Lavenia and Lady Emmeline." I deflated, not wanting this moment to end and certainly not wanting to spend the day with Queen Shivani.

"It is not midday, is it?" He called back, still teasing my clit with his fingertips, pushing me closer despite the distraction.

"It is, sir. My apologies." Rain groaned and moved into me with renewed purpose, slamming my body while he brought me to the edge. I stifled a moan, pulling my pillow over my face while I reached behind me, grabbing his ass as he pounded viciously against me.

"Gods damn it." His voice was quiet, meant for only me to hear, and I smiled before he raised his voice. "She'll be out soon, Sterling. The queen will have to wait."

He bit my ear, and I stifled the moan with the pillow when I came, pulsing around his body, my hips jerking as his fingertips continued their ministrations. He crashed into me hard and bit my shoulder as he finished with me.

"I quite like the idea that you're going to feel how good I fucked you for the rest of the day." He pressed an open-mouthed kiss against my neck, curling his body around mine.

"It would seem my day can only get worse from here."

CHAPTER 41

THE QUIET WAS THE most uncomfortable silence I'd ever experienced in my entire life. I was shoved into a seat next to Lavenia as we sat across from Queen Shivani. When Sterling had said the carriage arrived for us, I assumed he meant to take the two of us somewhere to meet her. I was especially ashamed I'd been the reason for our tardiness, having been busy being ravaged by her son, when I realized she'd been waiting in the carriage the entire time. At Rain's recommendation, I wore my own simple, cotton blue dress and a braid in my hair. Lavenia wore a long tunic with skin-tight leggings underneath, so I felt confident in my attire. Until I saw the queen.

Shivani's clothing was likely less formal than her standard garb, but she still looked every bit the regal ruler I recognized from the throne room. She wore a long, loose dress in jewel red. It wasn't fitted to her body, slack and flowing instead, and it had long, sweeping sleeves. The embroidery on it was magnificent. Gold and silver patterns traced across the fabric, matching the gold and silver jewelry she wore.

We were headed to a hot spring in the mountains to the northeast. We would cut a diagonal path across the plains, so the trip was shorter, but it would still be a few hours in the carriage. I had not anticipated hours of silence with Rain's mother, but I found myself not able to find any words. I'd been sitting there for the better part of an hour while the two of them made inconstant and awkward conversation when Shivani finally turned her attention to me.

"I remember you, you know." She wore a soft smile, but her eyes held no kindness. I sat for a moment, waiting for her to continue. I wasn't surprised she remembered me; I was the twin sister of the Beloved to whom her son had been betrothed. When she stayed silent and continued to watch me with those calculating eyes, dark as night, I wanted to wriggle out of my skin but decided to reply, just to see what she would say.

"I remember you, too." As if I could forget the Queen of Vesta. Her smile grew, and she gave a light chuckle.

"You were much wilder than your sister." It surprised me she thought that. I had generally been quieter than Lucia. My sister had a quick temper, though mine wasn't much better, and she was the first person to lash out at anyone she felt had wronged her. Or me, for that matter. She was always a protector of sorts, much better with words, ready to launch a full-scale debate on the person she was angry with, whereas I would falter and stutter, unable to convey my message. I'd grown more confident in adulthood, but as a girl, I was timid unless I was around people I felt comfortable with. Only my friends and family were familiar with that side of me. I had certainly never been comfortable with Queen Shivani. I gave her a small uncertain smile, unsure of what to say.

"Wild *in spirit*. Your sister always seemed content to do as she was told." I opened my mouth to object, but she gave me a knowing look and continued. "Oh, I know she could pitch a fit. But she always gave in to what was asked of her in the end. I assume it was because of your ordinary divinity and perhaps some pity, but you, *you* got your way a lot. When the two of you started to train with the boys, I knew it was at your insistence and not my daughter's." I wasn't sure if I should have been offended or not, but when she gave a warm smile to Lavenia, I was pleased to see it returned. Perhaps it wasn't that Shivani was unkind, but instead, she didn't make an effort to mince words.

"I think you may be right. Being the unimportant sister was limited on advantages, but disinterest afforded me some freedoms." I gave a light chuckle and watched as Shivani's eyes narrowed on me.

"And look at you now. More advantage than you know what to do with." Her lips pursed, and I schooled my features as Rain's words rang through my head.

Give back what you receive in kind.

"It's amazing how much things can change. I imagine it might be similar to suddenly realizing your husband is a monster—something we have in common. Though, I didn't have decades of evidence to prove it."

Lavenia stiffened beside me, but I made sure to give a simpering smile to the queen.

"It would seem most stories are more complicated than they appear." Her nod was terse, but her eyes weren't filled with the anger I was expecting, just assessment. I nodded back, feeling slightly ashamed.

"How are your legs?" I supposed it made sense the queen knew what happened, but I was still surprised by her inquiry.

"I'll have a scar or two, but back to normal. I imagine they'll ache in the cool weather, though." I grimaced.

"It is lucky you have not drank from the font yet, then. Perhaps it will help heal you further." Her gaze moved down my covered legs.

"Is that part of it?" I was inordinately underprepared when it came to anything involving the ritual. I was never supposed to participate.

"Did you never discuss any of this with your sister when she was being prepared for it?" I shook my head; I did everything I could to avoid thinking about my sister performing the ritual with the man who had stolen my heart. Shivani's eyes softened, and her tone gentled. "And your parents did not perform the ritual. I suppose you would not know, then." I shook my head again, feeling like a child.

"The font is life-giving. Some say Aonara created the first healer out of its waters." A warm smile, though small, lit up her face. "If a man were to take a drink from the font with his dying breath, it would sustain him for a long while. That is why it is so heavily guarded. It is our greatest gift from the gods. I imagine it will fully heal your more recent ailments."

It made sense for it to be guarded, but I wondered if anyone had considered giving the waters from the font to the sick and injured who might need it. Why did only those with divinity have access to the life-giving blessing? It had always been monitored and distributed by the Myriad in such a way, but had no one thought to question it?

"Do you have anything else you'd like to ask about the ritual?" Sensing Lavenia's worry in her question, I wondered if she thought I was going to panic at the last moment and run.

"Honestly, I have no idea what I'm doing." I shrugged, and Shivani laughed. I was confused by her kindness nestled between coarse words. "I don't even know what time I'm to be ready tomorrow."

Lavenia and Shivani exchanged a knowing look.

"My brother is too excited to think about the logistics, it would seem, and since you have no idea what you're doing, we've been in charge of arranging it all. He was supposed to give you all of this information, but it must have slipped his mind." She rolled her eyes.

"He has been busy the last few days. Between his task, Elora, and the other duties he's had to take over since . . ." I trailed off, not knowing what to say about Soren.

"Yes, yes. I should have known not to use him as a go-between and just tell you directly."

"Yes, I think you're right. You should have known better." Shivani supplied, earning her a glare from her daughter.

Lavenia took a few moments to explain the following days' itinerary, and I was beginning to feel overwhelmed.

"Are you excited for Rainier's divinity? Dewalt was able to start compelling almost the moment we finished the Mind ceremony, but I didn't get access to his divinity until after the Body. You don't need me to tell you about that part of the ritual, do you?" Lavenia waggled her eyebrows.

I felt my whole body turn a brilliant shade of red. I couldn't believe she said that in front of her mother, the queen. I still couldn't tell if Shivani hated me or was actively trying not to hate me. Either way, I was appalled Lavenia said it in front of her. Thankfully, she didn't react, and I chose to deflect to something I was truly worried about.

"Honestly, I'm afraid of his divinity. It's rather staggering, isn't it? He has so much power. I mean, I'm still finding out things about my own power, and now I'll have his to contend with."

"He is rather powerful, but it seems there's more to you than we originally thought all those years ago. I can't say I'm not thrilled he will be able to heal himself, though. What a lovely gift to share with the bonehead." I laughed in surprise, shocked to hear Queen Shivani say that about her son. Lavenia grinned and grasped my hand tight as she assured me.

"You'll do fine with his powers, Emma. I've seen you learn so much about your abilities the past few weeks; I know you'll be fine." I hoped Lavenia was right.

"How did your task go, Emmeline?" The queen's question was innocent enough, but I wondered if someone had reported what happened at the temple to Shivani. Had she seen the contract?

"It was fine. They had me demonstrate my divinity." I hoped my tone made it clear I didn't want to speak about it.

"Was it Master Filenti?" Her face seemed tight with displeasure. When I nodded, she sighed but didn't press further, instead, turning to her daughter. "Did Rainier finish his task yet?" Lavenia smirked, watching me with a smug look in her eyes.

"He finished!"

"What was it?" I asked sweetly, trying to conceal my eagerness for the answer.

"You'll see!" Her voice was chipper, and I shot her a glare.

The rest of the ride was spent mostly in silence, but it felt less tense than it had before. When we finally reached our destination, it was late afternoon, the sun heading steadily for the horizon. It felt a little silly to ride all the way out to the mountains to take a dip in a hot spring, only to turn around a few hours later, but I wouldn't pretend I wasn't excited about the experience. When the carriage finally stopped and we stepped out, I was amazed for a moment. There was a large cabin built straight into the side of the mountain, and my jaw dropped at the sight of the waterfall beside it. It was gorgeous—bright aqua blue water falling into a small pool. We hadn't gone that far north, but I supposed fall was in full swing, the weather here significantly colder than the city. I pulled my cloak closer to me, the blue one which had been a gift from Rain all those years ago, and we made our way up the many steps. It was a long walk, and by the end of it, my legs were aching. I wasn't sure how much of it was exertion and how much of it was from being weak due to my injuries, but I sent some of my divinity downward, just in case.

"Remind me again why Rainier didn't just rift us here?" Lavenia wasn't thrilled about the walk either. Shivani didn't bother with a response as she led us into the cabin. It was built of beautiful golden oak, and I was nearly knocked back by just how hot it was as we crossed the threshold. I almost wanted to step back outside into the chilly fall breeze, the air inside wet and heavy. The cabin was sparsely decorated with simple furniture, not quite outfitted to live in. Instead of a dinner table and chairs, wooden benches lined the walls of the large open room, accompanied by thin runner rugs that ran the length of each one. A servant bustled out from a back room, a younger woman with skin paler than mine and dark brown hair swept back into an intricate design of braids and curls. She reminded me of Thyra. She swept into a deep curtsy.

"Your Majesty, it is a delight as always." Shivani inclined her head as the servant bustled through, welcoming us, and led us into the room she came from. I was amazed. It was less of a room than it was a back patio, opening up to the snow-covered mountainside behind the cabin. Steps led downward directly into the hot spring, the water a brilliant blue-green, and the pool curved and arched into a stream leading back into a cave on the side of the mountain. Lavenia and Shivani were already peeling their layers off, and I was surprised; I had figured there would be more to it than the three of us stripping naked and climbing into the water. By the time I'd finished taking off my cloak, Lavenia was at my back, assisting me with unbuttoning my dress.

"You need to lose this dress when we get back home." She was laughing, and I felt a surge of warmth in my chest at the thought of home. Since Ravemont, my view of home had become something different. Even in my little house in Brambleton, I hadn't known that permanent security, of a place where I could find comfort and safety. A slice of the world to call my own. I'd always longed for

Ravemont, wanting to return and know the security and memories it offered. But looking back, though I'd only been there for one short day, it wasn't home to me anymore. Everything that had made it a home was gone—Lucia and Mama were gone, and even Father wasn't the same anymore. Home had turned into an idea more than a place. It was the people and the safety I felt, and I hadn't experienced that anywhere until Rain brought me to his estate. Until he made me certain I was his, and he was mine. It was a gift that his estate had been made specifically for me. I couldn't wait to further perfect that belonging by bringing Elora to live there—if she'd have it.

By the time I stepped out of my dress, Shivani was already in the hot spring, her hair pulled up in a bundle with a protective red jewel-toned scarf covering it. It matched what she wore, the same gold and silver embroidery weaving a pattern across it. The servant scurried about, picking up our discarded clothing and creating neat piles on a bench off to the side. It felt a bit awkward being near her in only my undergarments, but I brought my dress to where she worked and folded it, placing it neatly beside the other piles she'd made.

"Oh, my lady, you don't have to do that!"

"I know." I smiled. I didn't want to be treated with such deference. "I'm used to cleaning up after myself." Her eyes widened a bit as she bustled away, moving over to a basket full of towels. I finished undressing, carefully placing my undergarments neatly on top of my dress, and I was glad for Rain's small staff. After Ravemont, I had a short period of adjustment where I had to learn how to run a household. I had never done laundry or cooked a meal in my life, but through much trial and error, I figured it out. It wasn't hard exactly, but it was often thankless, and I knew I'd never take a servant for granted ever again.

Crossing over to the stairs, I tentatively lowered one foot into the water and hissed. It was warmer than I anticipated, and I stood still for a moment, acclimating to the heat, arms crossed over my naked body. I wasn't comfortable being on display in that way. It wasn't as if I ogled her, but though Shivani was a mother twice over, her body didn't seem to be as ravaged by the changes of motherhood as mine was. Lavenia had always been thin as a twig, and her mother wasn't much different. Slowly lowering myself into the water, step by step, I unbound my hair, letting it hang free over my breasts. I tried to shake off the insecurities—it wasn't until after giving birth to Elora that I felt insecure about the way my body looked, but I wouldn't change that for all the confidence in the world. Besides, my body had served me well. It was strong, nourished, capable. Mine.

Lavenia noticed my slow hesitance and gestured me over to the benches carved into the stone, where she and her mother sat. Lavenia's arms spread out behind her on the lip of the pool as if presenting her nudity, and I was jealous of her unabashed boldness. She didn't bother with a scarf as her mother had, opting instead to pile her hair high on her head, currently tilted back in utter relaxation. Shivani peered at me from a half-open eye, equally comfortable as her daughter in posture.

"You have good hips." I gaped at her. "I watched you get in. Your hips are good for children."

I laughed nervously before averting my eyes. I didn't think it was prudent to discuss the unlikelihood of providing grandchildren for her. Part of me wondered if she'd fight us performing the ritual if she knew I would give Rain no heir. And because of that, I wanted to keep it quiet, at least until it was too late to do anything about it. Ideally, I wouldn't tell her at all and let her assume we had issues with conceiving. Although, as I sat there, I wondered if telling her about my previous experience wasn't the worst idea. That way, when years passed without an heir, she wouldn't be as surprised.

"My hips weren't the problem with Elora. I nearly bled to death." Shivani pulled her head up, watching me contemplatively.

"What happened?"

"The midwife never told me much—something to do with the way Elora was attached to me wasn't quite right. Knowing what I do now, I believe it had something to do with the placenta. I'd bled intermittently throughout the pregnancy, but when I went into labor... Mairin said I was lucky Elora was even born. That most pregnancies like mine don't make it to term, and if they do, the babes don't make it."

"Your healer was right. Most don't survive it." Looking up, startled, I caught a glimmer in Shivani's eye, and my heart sank. It seemed she understood too well.

"Mama?" Lavenia sat up to stare at her mother.

"Almost a century before Rainier was born, I birthed an infant that never took its first breaths. My healer caught the issue early on, spent almost every waking hour by my side, pouring her divinity into me to prevent it, but we—I still lost the babe. It was early enough that the blood loss wasn't life-threatening, but I still took quite some time to recover. Physically and otherwise." Her voice had grown quiet, and she took a quick breath, almost to shake off the sadness. "I imagine you and your daughter—Elora, is it?" I nodded. "Your divinity likely carried you both."

When I realized my divinity stopped me from bleeding out, I began to wonder. Shivani might have been right. The silence was heavy as Lavenia moved over toward her mother, resting her head on her shoulder.

"I'm curious about Elora." She cut the tension of her admission with a subject I wasn't sure I wanted to broach. Not only had I never thought of Elora interacting with Queen Shivani, I was surprised, and part of me was instantly suspicious. Shivani had close ties with the Myriad for the entirety of her reign as queen. Was she only interested because of her status as the Beloved? "Obviously, any heir would have to be of Rainier's blood, of course, but I suppose he could grant her the title of princess if he wanted. I'd like to know more about the girl who brought out such ferocity in you."

"She's my daughter. Of course, I'm fierce when it comes to her."

Annoyed, I didn't reply further. Did she say all of that out of an assumption that I would expect Rain to somehow name Elora as his heir? Or that giving her a title was important? It was absurd, even if it was something Elora would want. I was mildly offended by the implication but kept silent, tilting my head back in an attempt to relax. I sensed the queen's fixation on an heir might be an issue. Rain hadn't cared, had assured me that it didn't matter if I couldn't give him that, but what Shivani said rolled around in my head, not allowing me to focus on anything else. Rain's own words about wanting the blessing of children joined hers.

Something like cautious curiosity lit in my gut, and I tugged my lower lip into my mouth, nibbling on it as I thought. Shivani might have been right about my divinity carrying us. If Shivani had two healthy children after she lost the first, who was to say that might not be the case for me? Perhaps it was a one-off, something that wouldn't happen again. And if it did, if I knew earlier on what might be the cause, could I spear my divinity into the right direction? Could I fix it before it even became a problem?

It was a lot to think about in consideration of the future, and it was too much pressure to put on my mind with everything else happening. Between Elora and the battle with Folterra, the unfolding situation with Keeva and the Nine, the ordeal with the Myriad, and my impending bonding ritual, I couldn't spare a thought for a far-off possibility.

But in that far-off future, would I even want that? I was sure Rain would, but I nearly had a full-grown child. Did I want a baby? I allowed myself some cautious daydreaming as I relaxed, mulling over the different futures that may come to pass. Eventually, I opened my eyes and found Shivani watching me. I glanced at Lavenia, resting as I had been, head tilted back on the ledge behind her. Her mouth was slack, and I wondered if she was even awake.

"I must say, I don't know what it is about you that he's so taken with." Shivani's eyes narrowed as she addressed me. "You bring nothing in the way of politics. I doubt you even know the names of anyone on the council." She continued without waiting for a response. "Your divinity is interesting but not nearly as powerful as his. You are of average beauty. Does he choose you because of your daughter? Is she that powerful? I do not think that is it because he never seemed anything other than burdened when he was set to marry your sister. Not to mention, from your outburst at the palace, I do not suppose you'd ever allow him to use her as a weapon. A good thing, as a mother—to not want your children to be used. I do respect that. You are motivated when it comes to your child but clearly hot-headed in your defense." She stopped for a moment and studied me, tapping a finger against her chin. I didn't say anything, merely meeting her gaze with my own. "Maybe it is a sort of nostalgia, for when his life was simpler." She paused as she rubbed her chin with the same fingers. "He will make a great king, but I'm not convinced you will make a great queen."

While I'd been wondering the same thing myself, her blatant questioning of me rubbed me the wrong way, and I snapped out at her. "It is lucky then that it is not you I need to convince, but the people." I attempted to keep the scowl off my face, but the way her brows furrowed and lips pursed when she looked at me, I hadn't adequately hidden my emotions.

"I suppose that is true. Once Soren is dead, I will continue with my duties long after the coronation until Rainier deems it appropriate for you to take over." I didn't reply, wondering if she'd discussed this with him already. It didn't seem like him to determine something like that for me, but it was possible. I didn't mind that she'd continue on, but I hoped I would be permitted to learn what was expected of me in the meantime. The way she said it made me wonder if she meant for the arrangement to be long-lasting. I supposed with Soren dead, their bond would break, so unless she found another person to perform the ritual with, the arrangement wouldn't last forever.

As much as I luxuriated in the warmth of the spring, I didn't want to be there any longer. I would rather have been in Rain's bathtub, awaiting his return. I supposed he would be busy with Dewalt for the night, but since the night he proposed, we had had little time together, and tomorrow I was going to commit my mind, body, and soul to him. It was a large leap for me to make mentally, and I just wanted a few more moments in his arms to help come to terms with it. Not to mention, I needed to find the words I was expected to say to him tomorrow in front of everyone. No, I wanted to leave, even if it meant enduring more silence with a woman who didn't understand my presence.

CHAPTER 42

I woke up to an empty bed once more. The other side was disturbed, and I vaguely remembered Rain kissing my forehead before he left at dawn. Still, I was annoyed, though I took some solace in the fact Rain couldn't escape me tonight. Lying across the very end of the bed, I found a white robe made of thin white silk with a tiny pattern of purple embroidered flowers traveling up the side. The hot spring had been sulfuric and slightly oily, and I hadn't bathed the night before, so I took the robe with me into the bathing chamber to tend to all of my needs. Once finished, I took some extra time drying and combing my hair, using some scented oils I recognized as Nana's work.

Absentmindedly adjusting the robe as I came out of the bathroom, I glanced up and couldn't help my shriek. Both Rain and Dewalt sat at the end of the bed, waiting, one of them with averted eyes and the other wearing a hungry expression.

"You scared the hell out of me!" Pulling my robe even tighter, my eyes widened. "What if I was naked?"

"It's a good thing you're not then, my bride." Within a moment, he was on me, picking me up at the waist. I heard the door snick shut, thankful Dewalt had more sense than the man holding me in a death grip.

"What is going on with you?" I was exasperated. A small part of me had been worried he'd changed his mind or somehow finally realized I came to our pairing with very little, and he had doubts over it, explaining how little I'd seen him the past few days. An even larger part of me was terrified about getting married again in the first place, especially considering the outcome of the last. With him dead. The logical part of me knew I was overthinking, letting anxious thoughts get the better of me. He had been patient all these years, with no hope of ever seeing it through. We were twin flames, something he had fewer doubts about than I did. I was being ridiculous; I needed coffee, or perhaps something stronger.

"Oh, it is but a small thing." He put me down, and I saw the corners of his mouth curl up. I couldn't help mirroring the smile. "Today, I make you mine." He leaned down and gave me a slow, perfect kiss, thoroughly casting aside my fears from only a moment before, and I put my hands on his chest, tugging him closer by his lapels before he pulled away. "But right now, you need to put some warmer clothing on. I have something to show you."

"Oh?" I raised my brows as I walked into the closet, pulling out some thicker leggings and wiggling them up over my hips, feeling his eyes on me as I dressed.

"Your hair is different." I turned toward him, noticing an impossibly soft-looking sweater on his side of the closet that I grabbed and pulled over my head.

"Just a small trim. The servant at the cabin, Ashra? She did it while I waited for your mother and sister. I didn't let her cut too much; I know how much you like it." He grinned and grabbed me, pulling me into another deep, thorough kiss. He was in one of the best damned moods I'd ever seen him in, and it made my heart soar to know it was because of me. Once I was ready, he grabbed me by my hand, half-walking half-running out the door to the garden. Instead of meandering down the path we'd walked before, he turned sharply, following a smaller path through the plants running parallel to the house. It seemed as if we were heading for the stables, and I slowed down, forcing him to match my pace. I knew it was likely I'd be on my feet for most of the day, and I didn't want to tire myself out prematurely.

"Are your legs hurting you?" I shook my head, ready to explain, but he cut me off by hoisting me into his arms.

"Rain! You need to calm down!" He chuckled but didn't obey. I flung my head and arms back in dramatic fashion, not particularly enjoying being hoisted unceremoniously and carried around like a baby. Seeing his handsome smile though, I couldn't be too aggrieved. "What is this even about?"

"It's a surprise." My eyes lit up.

"Put me down. I just need to go a bit slower. Is it your task?" His eyes gleamed, but he didn't reply, just set me down gently before he took my hand in his. What could possibly be in the stables? I wondered exactly what his task was, not for the hundredth time. It clearly involved something physical, and I wondered if I was about to receive a cloak. After what Filenti made me do, I simultaneously hoped Rain's task was that simple while also being jealous he hadn't had to make the kind of choice I did. I cringed at the memory, and I refocused my attention on the stable. Did he get a horse? He couldn't possibly be this excited about a horse. I couldn't think of anything I'd be this excited about, save for Elora's return.

For a brief, painful second, I thought maybe, somehow, he'd gotten her back already, and that's where he had been. I tried to let the thought disappear, knowing it was entirely unlikely. He wouldn't hide her out in the stable; he would have brought her directly to me. But still, my mind knew no logic. At that moment, I had been briefly hopeful I'd find her waiting for me. I wanted to let go of the hurt blazing through me, but I couldn't. She wasn't waiting in the stable. She wouldn't be here for today, arguably the most important day of my life after her birth. And when she did return, she would be different, affected by trauma untold and walking into a disparate life. I turned my head away, not wanting to ruin the day or Rain's mood with my tears. I took deep breaths, albeit shaky, and managed to calm down before he pulled me to a stop. He turned me, cupping my face in gentle hands while eyes of moss-green searched mine.

"What is it? I can't fix it if you won't tell me." I could hear a small tremor of fear in his words, a vulnerability I'd rarely seen in him before. I reached out, listening to his heart race, and I realized he could have been worried about more than just why I was crying at this moment. Was he as anxious as I had been earlier?

"You can't fix it. Not yet anyway." I wiped my eyes, determined not to ruin his spectacularly happy mood with my somberness. He watched me for a moment longer before folding me into his arms, recognition on his face.

"Elora."

"I—For a second, just a moment—" I backed away and inhaled a shaky breath before continuing. "I thought maybe she was here, and that was why you were so excited." He made a low sound in his throat, and the sorrow in his eyes was palpable. He pulled me tight against him, and I sank into his warmth.

"I'm so sorry, dear heart. I wish that were the truth. I wish she were here to witness the promises I make you and hear the ones I have for her. I wish she could hear me promise to love you both to the best of my ability. But I gave you my word that we'd get her back, and I plan to keep it." He was grave as he continued, pulling me tighter as his voice lowered. "I wanted you to have my divinity before we went to the Cascade. To better protect you. But if you think we should wait for her to perform the ritual—I don't know how much longer my father has, but we could try to wait."

I pulled back from him and stared. We didn't have time, his father could die any minute now, but he offered to wait to make things easier for us, for *her*. I knew he loved me and wanted to protect my daughter, but the fact he'd so willingly accepted and said he would love her surprised me. I thought back for a moment, searching my memories. Everything he'd ever said about her was from the perspective of a man who wanted to love her as his own, and my heart broke right in half. This man would never have done anything to hurt her as Faxon had. Rain would never betray us as Faxon did. He wouldn't have betrayed *anyone* like that, let alone his own child or mine. She had seen me broken and cold with her father her entire life. She'd never seen me truly happy, never seen me love the man. I just had to hope she'd understand that performing the ritual with Rain, marrying him, was almost just as much for her as it was for me. I reached up and traced his lips with my fingertips, watching the corners of his mouth curl upwards. He lightly kissed them in return.

"I don't want to wait, Rain. I think we've waited long enough, don't you?" His answering smile was everything. I didn't think I'd ever tire of it.

"We're almost there. Come on." He grabbed my hand, leading us around the corner of the house to the stables. One of the doors was open, and it took a minute for my eyes to adjust, but I saw three figures standing inside. Rain opened the other door, allowing light to flood into the room. They were dressing figures and on them was the most beautiful armor and weaponry I'd ever seen.

"I was asked to prove I could protect you—truly a throwaway task." He chuckled. "I did a quick demonstration of what the Supreme wanted, but I didn't think the gods would approve of leaving it at that." I looked at him questioningly, wondering what he meant. "You don't need me to protect you. The gods know it. I know it. And I thought this was one way to make sure our enemies know it." I took a step forward to examine the figure in the middle. I'd never seen female armor like this before. Most of the soldiers I'd seen wore leather cuirasses at most, but this was something a knight would wear. Or a king leading his soldiers into battle.

Or a queen.

My eyes nearly glazed over as I took in the assorted pieces. Leg armor, arm guards, pauldrons, hip shields, a breastplate—all of it hammered and polished to perfection. The armor was made from beautiful, darkened steel, almost fading to black in some places. The piece which drew my attention the most was the breastplate. It had an intricate raised design of flowers across it, with detailed petals etched across its entirety. The other pieces had such accents as well, but nothing as complex as the breastplate. Vines, leaves, and petals tangled in a sinuous pattern across the face. I traced my fingertips over the designs, enamored.

"Rain, these are beautiful." I smiled up at him, allowing it to spread across my face. Truly, he'd done so well. He picked out items for a queen. For his queen. He beamed, crooked smile spreading, before drawing my attention to the weaponry.

Between the other two figures, I found a new bow, a short sword, and two daggers, each attached to a thigh and ankle belt. Every weapon was more lovely and perfect than the last. The hilt on the sword was ornate but not so much as to impede my grip. A stone that matched my ring was inlaid on the pommel, while the guard had a beautiful design of flowers and vines on it. I unsheathed it and weighed it in my hands. The balance was perfect, the blade precise. I smiled when I saw the sword belt that came with it, remembering Rain scolding me about mine. I was thrilled about the ankle belt as well. With all the dresses I'd been wearing, I'd taken to using my thigh strap and wrapping it around double.

Rain had taken a few steps back to lean against the wall of the stable and watch me, and when I turned toward him, I was reminded again how lucky I was. He seemed enraptured, happy to watch my joy. As long as he loved me, I'd forever feel this way. I matched his smile as I approached him slowly. Looking over the long leg jutting out a bit in front of him, the trim waist, the crossed arms corded with muscle, my patience already wore thin. I wouldn't be able to wait for the night to end. Gods, he was too much.

"You'll need a squire for when we go into battle. And a second."

"I—alright." I paused for just a moment, barely long enough to think, before I already knew my answer. "Dickey and Thyra." Rain's eyebrows raised. "That was actually pretty easy." I gave him a quick grin.

"Dickey is no surprise, but Thyra?"

"Who else?" He stood for a moment before nodding.

"You're right. I'll ask her for you." He leaned in, about to kiss me, when I felt my nose wrinkle.

"Shouldn't that be something I ask her?" A look of surprise crossed his features, only for a moment, before a sly grin replaced it.

"I told you you'd make a good queen." He pressed his mouth to mine, his tongue teasing at the seam of my lips, and I opened to him, lightly caressing his tongue as he pushed into my mouth. He groaned a bit before pulling away, all too soon. "I'm sorry, I have to get you back to Lavenia and Mairin before they have my head."

"So, is this the last moment I get alone with you before tonight?" I tucked my fingers into his belt loops and pulled him toward me, using more force than necessary as I pulled his hard body against mine.

"Yes, so make it count."

It felt like Mairin and Lavenia spent hours getting me ready, and I didn't even have the dress on yet. Thanks to my careful attention to it that morning, my hair was all soft waves and easy to manage. Mairin left most of it down, but she pulled strands from around my face back into loose braids, weaving in tiny purple and white flowers. Lavenia made sure Mairin left adequate space for the diadem I would gain at the ceremony, another detail Rain hadn't mentioned. She explained there were so many crowns and diadems the Crown possessed, dating back millennia, that she was able to pick what she wanted from the trove. She had three she wore on rotation. Rain would eventually help me pick out others, but the one I was to wear today had been picked out to match the dress still awaiting me at the palace. My eyes lingered on the circlet Lavenia wore, a thin band of gold, inverted into a peak which rested on the top of her forehead, pointing down. At the tip of that point, there was a delicate ruby matching the color of her dress. Her dress was rather typical for what I imagined she'd wear to a royal ball, and I supposed her relationship was good enough with Shivani at the moment that she hadn't wanted to cause a stir with something specifically chosen to annoy the queen. Mairin's dress was the mirror of Lavenia's but in green. Both of their skirts were full and deeply pleated, elegant yet understated. They both chose to wear their hair down, and I'd never seen them more beautiful.

After Mairin finished with my hair, Lavenia moved in, adding kohl to my lashes and lining my eyes with it. When I caught a glimpse in the mirror, I saw the dramatic effect and wanted to wash it off. "This is too much, Ven."

"Nonsense." She pushed me down when I began to rise and pulled out a champagne-gold colored powder that she brushed on my eyelids, softening the black. She brushed more of the gold over my cheekbones and lips, and I raised a brow at her. Certainly, my face was completely covered in that rosy gold shimmer.

"The gold is tradition; Rainier will have it on too." I glanced at myself in the mirror and smiled, imagining Rain covered in the same gold I was. It wasn't as bad as I imagined, the powder softer and less bold than how it appeared in the palette in Lavenia's hand. She held out a pair of earrings to me, tiny and delicate, just a stud made from the same stone as my ring. In this lighting, they looked like the violet-red Rain had described.

"A gift from me." Her eyes were warm as she smiled down at me. "I'll spare you all the weeping and just tell you that it's about time, sister."

She may have spared herself the weeping, but she didn't spare me. That one word hit me, hard and square in the chest, and I squeezed her hands tightly in mine. I missed Lucia so much, and I wished she was here. The truth, that if she were here this wouldn't be happening at all, was a hard one to contend with. To have Lavenia call me her sister was an opening of a wound and a healing all in one. An end and a beginning I wasn't expecting. The initial rip took me by surprise, but the warmth which flooded through after caused me to stand and throw my arms around her. It had been so long since I'd had a sister, and to find one in a friend who also loved the sister I lost was a blessing. I held her tightly, trying hard to limit myself and keep the hard work she'd done intact. Eventually, she placed her hands on my shoulders and pushed me back, a glimmer of a tear in her eye.

"You saved him."

Later, safely tucked away in a carriage, I felt unprepared. Though Lavenia had set aside dainty slippers for me to wear, I opted for the boots I'd owned for years. Something about them steadied me and helped bring balance to the fact all I wore under my cloak was the silk robe I'd had on for most of the day. Over the robe, I wore Lucia's thick, black cloak, and I tried not to think about her absence. She should be with me. She'd have the assuring words I'd need to hear, debating me about the situation until I acquiesced, naming her the victor. My sister would find a way to convince me of my worthiness, the surety of my decision, and find a way to make me laugh in the process. I didn't often think of her in this manner, the what-ifs too painful, but for the first time, I found myself lighter after, as if she were really there to say the words I needed.

I hadn't expected the crowd. It was stupid of me; the last royal bonding ritual had been almost ten years prior, and it would give the people something to celebrate. I smiled, remembering when I'd heard vague details about Lavenia and her duke, not realizing the duke was Dewalt. I'd paid no heed then, trying to push my former friends to the back of my mind. I heard a shout from outside, and I swore I heard the words *peasant princess*.

"Pay it no mind." Lavenia reached over, mistaking my expression for concern. But I found the moniker interesting. Was it because I was the daughter of a minor lord, or was it because I'd lived in Brambleton? Had gossip of my isolation spread? Was it a good thing? Perhaps it would work in my favor. While I hadn't starved thanks to my father's stipend, I knew all too well the effects of poverty on those less fortunate than me. And now I'd be in a position to help—to do more than use my divinity at no cost. I pulled back the curtain just a sliver, taking in the sea of faces that crowded the road. Some eyed the carriage warily, while I saw others wearing expressions full of hope and excitement. I spotted a small girl, no older than six years, clinging to her father's ears from where she sat atop his shoulders. She was missing her two front teeth, and her raven hair tumbled down around her face in loose curls. I saw eyes of the brightest green light up when she saw me, and a grin spread across her face, the gap-toothed smile and dimples reminding me so much of Elora at that age. I smiled and gave a small wave, aimed only at the little girl, before sitting back and allowing the curtain to drop. I hadn't once been confident in my abilities to take on the role of princess and eventually queen, but for the first time, I was optimistic, hoping Rain and I would have the ability to change things for the better.

Before I knew it, we were in Lavenia's chambers. Her rooms were in a newer wing of the palace and significantly nicer than Rain's. I remembered with a shudder where we'd be sleeping, and I wasn't looking forward to the stark and dreary room we'd been in before. The thought promptly left my mind when Lavenia pulled out the dress. My dress.

The fitted bodice boasted a deep, sweetheart neckline, tapering down to a skirt covered in flower petals. Starting at the waist, all shades of purple and blue flowers covered the fabric, trailing down delicately, almost as if the petals had fallen from above. Thin layers of silk made up the creamy layers of the dress, light and flowing, ending in a long yet manageable train. The off-the-shoulder sleeves were made from the exquisite, thinnest silk, cuffed at the wrist, loose and billowing on the arms.

"I'm speechless." I walked over to the bed where she'd laid the garment and tenderly traced my fingers across the flowers. The petals were soft and felt real, and I questioned it at first before remembering the seamstress was a witch.

"That's a first." Mairin quipped playfully from behind me. I shot her a look, but the smile I had on my face took the sting out of it.

"You have lady's maids to help you get ready if you want them." I shook my head; I'd rather get ready alone than have lady's maids fuss over me. Lavenia smiled, nodding. "Mama hates when I don't use mine, but I don't care."

"Alright then, let's get down to it." Mairin took charge, lifting the dress and holding it open for me. I kicked off everything I was wearing except my lacy bottoms and hustled over, stepping into the gown. When she finished fastening the gown and pulled the corset lacing taut, I noticed it only went halfway up my back. I shuddered a bit, thankful Mairin had left my hair down. After slipping on the dainty slippers set to complete the outfit, I finally turned, allowing myself a moment to ogle my reflection.

I had never felt particularly beautiful in my life. I'd been the child who could disappear behind her sister. The girl who worked things out with her fists and not her words. I'd prided myself on my ability to go unnoticed, always managing to slip through the cracks. But seeing myself in this beautiful gown, Elora's necklace resting on a neck that seemed elegant, long hair flowing over graceful shoulders, and the gold dust across my face, I felt like something out of one of Elora's stories. The dress was flattering, tucking in at the waist and flaring enough at the hips, creating a figure I didn't realize I had.

"Witchcraft." I looked at Lavenia in the mirror, and she started laughing, one of her head-thrown-back cackles, and pulled out the gold dust again, touching up the imperfections and adding some to my collarbones.

There was a quick rap at the door, and Mairin cracked it enough for me to see Dewalt on the other side.

"It's time." His eyes met mine, and he froze.

"Pick up your jaw, fool." Mairin kicked him in the foot, and Dewalt was drawn back into the moment. We both knew it wasn't me he was seeing, and I felt my heart tear a little. He was as handsome as ever, dressed in tailored black breeches and a structured velvet jacket, a black and dark-grey brocaded vest peeking through underneath. He had a sword belted on his hip, polished to perfection. I wished more than anything that Lucia was here to see him. He took my hand and pulled it to his mouth, kissing my knuckles.

"Emmeline, painfully beautiful as always." I squeezed his hand, and he let go, both of us hurting over the ghost of my sister but not having the words or courage to speak of it. "Here, you'll need this." Dewalt handed me a ring, a large vine made of gold, clearly meant for Rain, and I slipped it onto my thumb. We made our way through the palace with me at the back, ensuring the others didn't step on my train by accident. Finally, we approached a small door off to the side of one of the hallways, and they slipped through it, directing me to continue walking. I followed their direction, unsure of where I was going until I found the small alcove leading into the gathering space.

I stopped, watching him.

Rain had his hands locked behind his back, the right one twitching in the nervous way I hadn't seen since he was a boy. From behind, the outfit he wore seemed to be the same as Dewalt's. The sword on his hip wasn't one I recognized, the hilt encrusted in more jewels—rubies, emeralds, and sapphires—than could ever be necessary. My eyes trailed up, only barely distracted by his broad back, the jacket tight over the stretch of muscles, and saw the crown which sat atop his head. It was the same one he wore the first time I met him. He had been a snotty prince, too good to pay any attention to the twin girls who were more nuisance than friends at that age. I remembered him continuously adjusting it throughout the day, and I'd found silent satisfaction in it causing him trouble. It was a simple gold, unadorned with jewels, more a circlet than a true crown. It suited him. I saw him peek his head into the room a bit, likely seeing the others taking their seats, before he turned around slowly, knowing I'd be waiting behind him. Where Dewalt's vest had been a dark-grey pattern, Rain's was gold. Shimmering threads sewn into the fabric that caught the light just so. He also wore gold on his face, dusted carefully down the bridge of his nose, across his cheekbones, and on his lips which slowly arched as his eyes rested on me. He looked like a god. His eyes were smoldering, a need and a hunger shining through. I watched him swallow as his gaze slid from my toes upward, the heat of his attention making me feel the ghost of his touch as he lingered over my hips, then my waist, before moving up to my breasts and collarbones until finally resting on my face. I didn't need to reach out with my divinity to know his heart was racing, matching my own.

"The sun itself could not shine as brightly as you." He crossed the distance in one stride before cupping the back of my neck and softly brushing his lips against mine. He pulled away much too quickly and offered his arm. "Come, you must make me whole."

Slipping into his hold, I smiled up at him. I felt a sense of calm and peace I hadn't felt in a very long time, even before Elora had been taken from me. It felt like the world was in balance, and the stars had aligned, with the sole purpose of bringing me to his side. I wondered if the gods looked down, the twin flame bond between us shining brightly for their attention, and I knew, whatever unknown future lay beyond for the two of us, I'd never been surer of it than with him by my side.

CHAPTER 43

I kept my head down, staring at my hand resting on the inside of his forearm, and tried to calm myself, resisting the urge to firmly grasp his bicep. I felt my fingers dig a bit harder than I meant to, and I heard a chuckle before Rain's other hand found my own, fingers intertwining with mine. The balcony we stepped onto was enormous; over fifty people sat outside to watch the ceremony, with plenty of room to spare. I only recognized a few, glad to see Nana sitting next to Mairin. Queen Shivani waited for us, the mountains visible behind her while she stood in the last ray of light before the palace blocked the setting sun. Normally, a Myriad master would perform the ceremony, but the Supreme had given Shivani permission to perform it for her son, an honor he didn't bestow on many. She was resplendent in a gown of deep emerald, her hair loose and unbound, and I was taken back by how youthful she looked.

Myriad novices lined the aisle we walked, and I felt my stomach twist, severely unnerved by their presence after what happened with my task. They all held branches of greenery above the aisle, sprigs of baby's breath interspersed among the branches, and the novices shook them as we passed beneath. I was surprised when both Rain and I got wet, and I gasped a little, stuttering a step and grabbing his arm tighter. His fingers squeezed mine, holding me upright and sturdy, rubbing a reassuring thumb across the back of my hand as I glanced up at him.

"From the font," he murmured, assuaging my confusion. The water didn't burn or feel strange, but I knew the life-giving powers of the font were real. I'd seen the effects of drinking it, but I wondered the meaning behind sprinkling it over us. Was this a waste, or did it have any real meaning? Maybe my skin would benefit from it. The idea almost made me laugh, pushing the novices out of my head for the moment. When we finally reached Shivani, there was a small bench for us to kneel on, and Rain held my hand tightly while I lowered myself, helping to situate my gown before joining me. He kept my hand tightly in his grasp as we both looked up to his mother, and I attempted to remain serene. It was beyond my comprehension that this could be real. This man who had remained steadfast in his search and love for me over the years was publicly claiming me as his own, his equal, and it wasn't a dream. He was mine as I was his, and this proved it to the world. He was the other half of me, and never had I held such hope in my heart as I did kneeling next to him.

Queen Shivani started speaking, but I did not hear a single word she said. I felt the heat of Rain's leg next to mine and his calloused hand holding my own. I saw the shadows on the mountains we faced, growing longer in the fading sun. I heard the crisp cool breeze and felt the heat of fifty pairs of eyes. And then there was the heat of one specific set of eyes. They met mine, and I saw every single fleck of gold, the brilliant green full of promise and passion. I gripped his hand tighter, and he slowly closed his eyes, his unspoken signal for me to join him in the calm surety between us. I reached out, listening to his heart and his alone. It was sure, and it was steady, counting on the future we would have and the kingdom we could build.

Eventually, Shivani watched Rain expectantly, and I realized he was just as distracted as I was. Looking up at her for a moment, uncertainty on his face, until she glanced down pointedly at my hand, and he realized what came next in the ceremony. I couldn't help but grin up at her, the motherly gesture not lost on me. I was surprised to see her eyes crinkle at the corners when she smiled back. He took my hand in his, sliding my ring off and replacing it with a tiny band shaped to fit around the engagement ring he slid back in place a moment later. Glancing up for approval, I took the ring that waited on my thumb and pushed it onto his ring finger, letting my fingertips gently touch his palm as his eyes met mine. It seemed like such a small thing before, but it felt like so much more now. To have him wear this ring signifying he was mine and mine alone. He met my smile, and I saw nothing but affection reflected back at me from the mossy depths.

When Queen Shivani pulled out a dagger—small, black, and plain—I was struck by how uneasy I felt. There was power radiating off it, the pull of it similar to that of my divinity, a soft thrum that held me in its grasp. Rain let go of my hand, offering his own to his mother. She flipped it over, using the blade to slice his palm, murmuring a prayer to the gods under her breath. I swore I saw some sort of white light in the air, a faint shimmer hovering between the blade and his hand. She reached for mine next, and, though nervous, I offered my palm to her. When the sharp edge broke through my skin, she murmured the same words as before, and I winced, the sting a bit harsher than I expected. There was a slight burning sensation to it, and I knew, this time, that I was right, my eyes widening as I watched the faint shimmer in the air above the wound. The sting of pain lessened when Rain grasped my hand in his and held it out, catching my eye and nodding down at the blood dripping from our hands, proud he'd saved my dress from staining. Warmth rose in me, and I felt it wrap itself around my heart. We both looked up at his mother, ready for what was next. The handfasting. The definitive end to the Mind ceremony. The intermixing of our blood with the words and promises that swore us to one another. Using the ceremonial red ribbon, Shivani bound our hands together before leading us through the divine vows, both of us repeating each line in unison.

> While we both wish it, I will give to you freely, sharing myself and my divinity.
> I will share my hopes and fears, sorrows and joys.
> I will be your home and your hearth, your steadfast and stalwart.
> I will shoulder your burdens and swallow your secrets.
> I will be your shield and your sword, your contrition and courage.
> Yours will be the name on my lips and the hands on my heart.

I inhaled after we finished and felt tears prickling my eyes. Rain's gaze met mine, and I saw every ounce of surety and love I felt for him, reflected in his own. I would be everything to him, as he had and would be everything to me. He had already upheld all of the vows we'd just said, and I felt an intense heat flooding through me, the warmth of calm and confidence that came with the acknowledgment of all we shared and would come to share. My divinity was thrumming at a pace I'd never felt, the vibrations of my soul resounding on the edges of my physical self.

After we finished saying the words, Shivani took the diadem from a small pillow I hadn't noticed and lowered it onto my head. It was gold to match Rain's, but where his was smooth and simple, mine was delicate and intricate. Designed to look like vines, the gold weaved in and out of itself with a sprinkle of diamonds and pearls nestled down in the twists and turns. I glanced at Rain, a small smile on my face as I took in his expression. His eyes flickered with delight and triumph as if this moment was what signified his victory. This moment of crowning me as the woman he would put first the rest of his life, as the woman he would love and cherish and share his divinity with—this moment made all the rest worth it.

I didn't need to be reminded of what came next, the words having echoed throughout my mind the last day. We shifted on the bench to face one another, the quiet sounds of the guests around us falling to the wayside. Those in the first rows might have heard us if they strained, but no one else mattered. Rain lowered his forehead, gently resting it against mine. His voice was a whisper, meant for only me.

"You have held my heart in your hands since the moment I met you, Emmeline. Every beat and every skip you have possessed. Every thought and every dream, every secret and every fear has belonged to you. You ignited a flame in me which has burned and sputtered and raged. Ours is a fire that will never go out. Ours is a fire that will swallow us whole, and I'd rather burn with you than live in the dark."

Eyes closed, I swallowed a sob. The earnest emotion rang true in his voice, each word a line in a song. Though he spoke of his heart belonging to me, I felt a clear fist around my own, knowing it was his hold on me. Knowing that if I reached out, our hearts would beat as one. I felt a single tether spread between us, a string of gold neither of us could see, but we could feel, and we could sense. The string that led us to this day together—the string that weaved a story of us. I felt it as surely as I felt the chaotic thrum of my divinity, and I knew he did too. I took a deep breath before speaking, voice low and quiet to match his.

"Before I knew you, I searched for you, and I've never stopped. I found your eyes in the leaves. I found your smile in my child's laughter. I found your patience in my heart and your courage in my own. Just a spark, a tiny flame all those years ago, which I protected and fed. A tiny spark I could never snuff, and now you've stoked it into a roaring fire. A warmth that protects and endures and sustains. A spark of hope and an ember on the wind of promises made and kept."

I felt a tear slide down my cheek as the golden string snapped into place, the connection I could see on the edge of consciousness if I only looked harder. The thread, that if plucked, would make the most beautiful sound I'd ever heard. I closed my eyes and reached out, feeling his heart beat in time with mine. Rain squeezed my hands in his before tilting his head a small distance, breaking the space between us with the brush of his lips. If Shivani said anything, which based on a distinct whoop from Lavenia, she did, none of it registered. The only thing I knew was the tug between us and his lips on mine. I had to remind myself again—this was real. That so many years later, I'd chosen the life Lucia sacrificed hers for. I'd chosen the life I'd never let myself dream of for long. The life that terrified and elated me, and the love that had almost consumed me. The love that spanned lifetimes, and the love that chose me every time. I'd chosen the man in front of me, whose soft lips caressed mine, and I was never more certain of any choice I'd ever made. His hand cupped my face, and he pulled back from me to gaze into my eyes.

"My bride, my wife, my Emmeline." And then his lips were on mine again, and everything else drifted away.

"Do you see the door right there?" Rain pointed across the chamber, and I spotted it, hidden behind a few council members who lingered on that side of the room. It was recessed into a small alcove, likely a servant door leading to some other area of the palace.

"Yes?" I wasn't sure why he was giving me a tour considering the size of the room. There wasn't much to it, the small chamber stuffy and crowded. A large, round table sat in the center, taking up quite a bit of space, with a dozen or so chairs surrounding it. Three tall windows opened up to the Alsors, with thick, red, velvet curtains that hung heavy on their fixtures, blocking the view. The air in the room smelled old and stale, and I wondered how often the council even met. This, in turn, sent me into a spiral about how little I knew about any of this. I didn't even know how often council meetings were held. I didn't know which decisions required council approval, which ones could bypass a majority ruling, nor the limit of Rain's power as Crown Prince. Soren had ultimate command, of course, but even he had to answer to the council on some decisions. And I knew nothing about any of it. Lucia had additional tutoring sessions when we were younger; a royal aid instructed both her and Rain on everything they could ever need to know about their future responsibilities. I felt woefully underprepared. This chamber would become an ever-present staple in our lives, and it all began with this meeting. Ten council members gathered within the room, and they all stood to deliberate if I should be declared as Crown Princess. I worried, not for the first time, that they would find me sorely lacking and not want to cooperate. I couldn't bring anything in terms of knowledge or leadership. All I had was a heart willing to serve Vesta and an understanding of the people who needed our help. But a council that had served Soren, especially in the last few decades, wasn't one I sought to impress if I truly thought hard about it. Rain bent, lips hinting against the curve of my ear.

"It's an alcove for private meetings, dear heart." His tone held sexual implication.

"Surely, you cannot be serious?" I'd only met two members of the council before Rain bustled me away with the excuse of explaining how the council members would decide if I was fit for my title. I had glared at him when he said it, frustrated by the fact it was information I needed to know. It was another reminder for the council members that I shouldn't be here. That I didn't know what I was doing. I had insisted upon a true explanation even though he'd tugged me possessively to his side, desperate to be touching me as much as he could.

"I need to taste you on my lips right now." His words sent a shiver down my spine, and a blooming heat settled low in my stomach. I pulled his hand into mine, gently pressing our wounds together. My divinity itched to heal us both, the sliced flesh making that low thrumming almost unbearable, but there was no sense in healing it. The Body ceremony required the same connection as the Mind did when performed, an intermingling of our blood caused by the divine blade Shivani used. I pulled his hand up to my mouth and kissed the back of it.

"You've waited this long, my love." I raised my brow, giving him a coy smile, and he groaned. A laugh bubbled up my throat, but it was quickly stifled when my attention was drawn behind him, where two of the council members watched me with shuttered eyes. They spoke quietly, not looking at each other and only watching me. It was the first time I felt truly uneasy. With Lavenia and Dewalt, the council voted before the ritual was performed, allowing them a chance to argue and debate over his lack of title and if they found him worthy for one. With me, they hadn't had the chance, the meeting bypassed because of Soren's illness. Though I had little doubt Rain would have married me regardless of their stance on my title, it seemed the assembly was designed to persuade against the marriage to someone the council deemed inappropriate. I sipped on my glass of champagne, meeting the scrutinous gaze of one of the men. He was tall, almost as tall as Rain, but much slimmer. He watched me as if I was a stain on an otherwise new shirt. It made me uncomfortable, but I wasn't about to let anyone on the council think I was a meek, quivering fool who'd been swept up in a great romance with a prince. Although at moments, I felt exactly that. Like when Rain put his hand on the small of my back to press me against him and whisper about just what parts of me he wanted to taste and which places he'd give special attention to. I felt myself flush, and my nipples hardened before I lightly pushed him back.

"Stop it. I'm in a glaring match with one of your council members." He huffed a laugh as he pulled away.

"One of *our* council members," he corrected with a raised brow. "Which one?" He saw where I stared and gave a brief glance over his shoulder before turning back to me, annoyed. "Scias. He will be replaced the minute I am formally king. He is originally from Kieża and an original pain in the ass." He chuckled under his breath. "He's almost as old as my father."

I widened my eyes at him in panic. I'd heard no news of Keeva's death. Not even a whisper. I supposed it served me well that the assassin princess visited me in secret. But certainly, whoever was meant to accompany her back to Nythyr had to know she was missing.

"Rain, does he—"

"No one knows. Be calm." Rain pulled me into his embrace, pressing my head against his chest as he wrapped his arms around me.

"Her servants? Guards? Someone has to—"

"They've been taken care of. No one knows, Emmeline."

That made me start with fright, pulling away from him with force, my hair snagging on the stubble gracing his chin.

"You didn't." Chin jutting out to keep my demeanor strong, I demanded answers.

"I didn't, no."

"But?" My voice broke, "Rain…"

"Those who could be Coerced were spared. Between Dewalt and Ven, they believed Keeva left for Nythyr without them. But the men who planned to report back, bringing down the Nine upon you and Vesta with a vengeance? Those men no longer draw breath, and I will not apologize for it."

"But you said you didn't." How many people had died because of me? Because of Keeva?

"I said that I did not execute them. It was Thyra, if you must know."

My jaw dropped. "Thyra?"

"She was quite distraught about your injuries. We are lucky it wasn't more. She wanted to kill them all."

Blinking, I crossed my arms as I stared up at him, warring emotions consuming me.

"You chose your Second well, wife." A grin played upon his lips, but I didn't share the sentiment. I'd killed someone, even if she'd tried to kill me first. And how many others died because of it? I wasn't sure how to bear it, just that I had to.

"If anyone finds out…" I trailed off, eyes darting over to the men staring daggers at me.

"Oh, they will eventually. There's no getting around it. But not today. Besides, you're a princess now. You have immunity." I could hear a tone of pride in his voice. I was *his* princess. Even if I still needed to get through the next hour to be formally recognized as such.

"Oh, but I had my sights set on *queen*." I pulled back, crossing my arms like a pouting child to match the whine in my voice. He gave me his lopsided grin and a deep laugh which tugged on the golden thread, pulling from my heart. He took a breath, his smile dropping a bit.

"Alright, let's get this over with." Rain took my arm in his and turned, heading toward the two council members who had been attempting to burn holes through my head for the last quarter-hour.

"Lord Ellington. Sir Scias." He tilted his head in respect to the men who gave quick bows, replying in unison. Lord Ellington begrudgingly took my hand, placing a kiss on my knuckles, and I had to force myself not to pull it back from him.

"Lady Emmeline, it is a pleasure." His face told a different story, and I was sure mine mirrored it. He couldn't let go of my hand fast enough. I felt Rain tense beside me at his choice of title, however, I had no intention of splitting hairs. Though I didn't hold the title of princess quite yet, it didn't stop the other council members I'd met from deferring with the formal 'Your Highness.' Which, I had to admit, wasn't something I'd get used to anytime soon. I didn't care about my title, but the respect which came with it was not something Rain was willing to negotiate, and I supposed I shouldn't either.

"Lady Emmeline." The man who had held my glare from across the room was much taller now I saw him up close. Taller than Rain by a hair, he glared down his nose at me, the distaste still plain on his face. When he took my hand, he spoke, but only to me.

You will not last, fahyše.

He was in my mind, just like the Myriad woman had been. And the last word he said, I recognized it. It was the same word that doomed a man to death at Rain's hand before I stopped it. The word uttered that brought Thyra down on him, his spit hitting the ground just before he did. I remembered it just like I remembered his face after Rain was through with him.

Whore.

It was so quiet and faint I would have thought I imagined it if it weren't for the racing heartbeat coming from the man. The heartbeat of adrenaline and rage. The sound a drum of deep disrespect and pungent anger. In a surge of frustration, I grasped his elbow with both hands before he stepped away and looked him in the eyes. I wanted him to know I was not weak, nor was I to be disrespected like that or taken advantage of. It was clear he assumed so little of me that he would brazenly say such things to me, even if only in my mind, the wife of his crown prince. As if my word would be no match for his own.

"Do you feel that?" His eyes grew wide as his heart stampeded, racing faster than the adrenaline rush he'd gotten when he called me a whore. "Does it feel like your heart might burst in your chest?" He tried to pull away from me, but my grip was strong. "I will not think twice next time."

He stared down at me, lips parted in shock or fear. When I finally released him, he stumbled backward, disgust and horror on his face. Rain stared between the two of us, stiffening. The look I shot him was a warning to not interfere, and he acquiesced. This was the first time I'd been challenged, and of course, it was only minutes after our vows. But he knew just as well as I did that to do this, to live this life by his side as not only his wife but also his queen, I would need to set my standard and draw the line without him.

Rain pulled us away under the guise of introducing me to more council members, his grip firm on my arm. Between each introduction, he studied me, waiting for an explanation I refused to give. I knew if I told him, there would likely be bloodshed on this day, one of the most important days of my life, and I didn't want that. If Scias said anything aloud, I'd let Rain handle it, or I'd keep my promise to the vile fool. But I wanted to give the man a chance to learn his lesson. A few of the other council members were less than receptive of me, but at least half seemed to be genuinely content with the events that had passed. Introductions complete, the ten council members, Dewalt, Lavenia, Rain, and I sat down at the table. Queen Shivani stood at the chair I assumed to be reserved for Soren, her presence serving as a replacement for her indisposed husband. Clearing her throat and folding her hands together, she let her sight settle on her son, a soft fondness on her features I'd never seen before, while everyone in the chamber quieted down.

"We will make this brief so the festivities may begin, and our bellies will be full of food and wine. Crown Prince Rainier Vestana has taken a bride today and formed a bond with a conduit. Council of King Soren Vestana, will you recognize Emmeline Vestana, formerly Highclere, as your crown princess?" I inhaled the tiniest breath at the new stylization of my name, and Rain squeezed the hand he held under the table. I wasn't sure if he thought it was nerves or doubts, but I offered him a smile, reassuring him that it was merely a surprise.

As "ayes" resounded, the final two men, seated to Dewalt's right, remained silent.

"Lord Ellington?" Queen Shivani turned toward the man expectantly as if he were slow and not paying attention. She put a hand on Rain's shoulder next to her, and I was curious if it was to make it easier to siphon his abilities if necessary. How many times had she assumed that role with Soren? How often was she dousing his flames? Did she think Rain capable of that same rage?

"I have some concerns, Your Majesty." Ellington's voice was higher, nervous. His heart nearly beat out of his chest.

"Do you care to share them, Ellington?" Shivani's voice was tight and clipped as she spoke.

"Did Crown Prince Rainier not have an arrangement with Keeva of Nythyr?" Without giving Shivani a chance to respond, he continued, the rapid flow of words he spilled buoying him. "And right before the arrangement was to take place and the alliance strengthened, a woman, one who has not been seen or heard from in recent years, took her place at our prince's side? Does that not sit well with anyone else?"

I heard one or two murmurs of assent, and my blood chilled.

"Emmeline had been in hiding until the Folterran forces kidnapped her child. It was a mere coincidence Prince Rainier's assistance coincided with his engagement to Keeva." I was surprised Shivani was the first to come to my defense.

"Why was she in hiding? This child is supposedly the Beloved. Why was she not formally identified by the Myriad?" Scias blurted out, earning himself a strict glare from the queen and a scoff from the man beside me.

"*Princess* Emmeline's daughter was not formally identified by the Myriad in an effort to protect her after what happened to her sister. You may recall Martyr Lucia?" Rain's voice heated, dripping with derision. "Emmeline chose to protect her daughter and keep her hidden until she came into her divinity." Quiet and precise, the anger in Rain's tone threatened to rise. I knew the secret I'd kept so carefully hidden for so long would come to pass as common knowledge, but I still wasn't prepared for how naked it made me feel. Rain's hand moved to my thigh and squeezed, the grip harsher than he likely intended, but I withstood it, needing the discomfort to anchor me. Shivani's icy gaze on her son moved to me, and I looked at her with apology, knowing Rain spoke out of turn. She pursed her lips before addressing Ellington and Scias.

"Once she has been retrieved, she will be formally identified by the Myriad, but I believe what she speaks is true."

I stared at Rain in horror, the reality of what Shivani had said hitting him in the same moment. A slight head shake that did nothing to quell my fear was his only response. It was clear we couldn't discuss it now, but did it mean it would never happen? King Soren couldn't die fast enough. If it was between Queen Shivani forcing Elora to be tested and identified by the Myriad and me placing my hands on the king myself, ensuring his heart stopped and Rain became king, I'd kill the man in an instant. It wasn't as if I didn't want to do it anyway.

"And we are going over a child who we don't even know for certain is the Beloved?" Scias was yelling, his face flushed with anger, and his hands were fisted where they rested on the table.

"Yes." Shivani's answer was simple, her voice terse.

"You will go to war with my kingdom over—" Shivani cut him off quickly.

"Vesta is your kingdom, Scias, is it not?" The councilor snapped his mouth shut and turned to Rain, who I knew sat furious beside me. It was my turn to squeeze *his* thigh.

"And you are willing to risk good men and an alliance with Nythyr for this," he paused to sneer at me, "*witch* of a woman?" He shouted, and the chamber grew still and silent. I took a deep breath, inhaling through my nose and out through my mouth. Lavenia, who sat on my other side, pulled my hand into hers. I watched as Rain's head turned slowly toward Scias, giving the man a few moments to take back what he said, but the councilor remained taciturn. When Rain finally spoke, his words were lethal.

"What did you call my wife?" I sat perfectly still, and so did most everyone else in the room. The other council members didn't appear to be surprised that Scias had earned their prince's ire, but I paid special attention to those who seemed to sympathize. One woman with a pronounced widow's peak looked particularly angry, giving Rain a bold and withering glare. The oldest member of the council, I couldn't remember his name, glanced back and forth between the two men, and seemed to be warring with himself about speaking out on Scias's behalf.

"This fahyše is going to lose you men! Nythyr, trade—" Scias' accent had come out, his voice thickening as he yelled and shook in anger. It cut off, though, as we all felt the small rumble, the only hint Rain gave of his disintegrating calm. He let go of my thigh, and I knew then the path our day had taken. Killing a council member on our wedding day was not something I wanted from him, no matter how much he might want to, and I tried to express that by the look I gave him. But when Rain stood and Queen Shivani hadn't said anything, I knew it was up to me to diffuse the situation. I didn't care as much about Scias as I cared about it being a blight on our day. It was likely I'd have to get used to being called a whore—in his language and the common tongue. I had to make an effort and prove myself as capable. I willed my divinity to steady my heart rate, and I felt a cool sense of peace come over me. I sat forward, grasping my champagne flute like a lifeline before I cleared my throat. Every head in the room snapped to me as I spoke.

"That is twice in the last hour you have called me a whore, Sir Scias." I forced a small laugh, attempting charm. "I am starting to believe you are not fond of me." Taking a sip of my drink, counting each fizzy bubble that popped against my tongue, I feigned nonchalance. "Do you not remember my promise?" He stared at me, a mixture of shock and defiance on his face. With Shivani as their queen, I would have thought the councilors wouldn't be surprised to have a vocal woman in their midst, but I gathered that perhaps they'd expected something different from me. A daughter of a minor lord who had hidden within the poorest of the kingdom, they must have thought I would be meek and mild, grateful and compliant because of the opportunity. I watched Scias' jaw move, clearly debating retorting. Rain slowly lowered in his seat next to me, and I felt his burning gaze on the side of my head, clearly agitated I hadn't divulged the details of my earlier interaction with Scias. I ignored him, steeling myself to maintain my icy countenance, and addressed Scias with the calm indifference I hoped would serve as a deterrent for him to continue down this path.

"In case I was unclear, I will reiterate. I told you if you ever called me a whore again, I would stop your heart. Though, I did say it more with my divinity than with my words. I did not think it would be so soon. As I am reluctant to sully my wedding day with your death, I do hope you can find it in you to control yourself?" I was doing everything I could think of to keep my voice steady and measured, the tension in the room overwhelming. Scias' throat worked as he struggled with what to say next. Part of me hoped he would say something stupid. He was clearly sympathetic to Nythyr and likely Keeva, the woman who had tried to kill me only days ago. The kingdom would not be worse off for the lack of him. Scias leaned back in his chair, drumming his fingers on the table in front of him, before he bent forward once more, exploding with anger as he addressed Rain.

"I will not allow it! I will not approve of this. She is a whore, and you've been bewitched." Spittle flew from his mouth, and I watched the mistake register on his face as he paled. "Your Highness," he tacked on, his voice meek. He underestimated Rain. He underestimated my husband. The man who chose to be my defender and protector. I had known in the back of my head that we wouldn't get through this day without bloodshed. I knew the minute Scias called me a whore, breaking into my mind, that he did not have much time, but I had hoped to get through the day at least.

"That makes three, Scias." Rain's voice was cold and unrecognizable. Dewalt rose from his chair at a nod from Rain, and I held my breath. Shivani watched her son quietly but did not say a word as he walked carefully toward the man who had insulted me. Scias knew what he had gotten himself into, and he sat straighter, his nostrils flared. Dewalt grabbed Scias by his forehead with one hand and his jaw with the other, pulling his mouth open. That's when he began to struggle, and I saw Dewalt's muscles flex as he held him still. I didn't want to watch, but I forced myself, knowing this was because of me. This was the first drop of blood spilled on my behalf because of our marriage, and I was only mildly disturbed that I had no desire to stop it. The consequences were upon Scias, and I would not intervene.

Rain pulled out his dagger and swiftly grabbed Scias by the tongue, slicing it off in one fell swoop. Dewalt let go, and he fell unceremoniously to the ground in a strangled scream, blood rushing out of his mouth.

"If anyone else feels they cannot hold their tongue, I will be happy to do it for them."

Rain's voice boomed in the chamber as he threw the tongue down on its owner. No one said a word to refute him, nor did anyone make a sound, the only sound the gurgled screaming of the man who laid on the ground, now without a tongue. The councilor with the widow's peak was a bit green around the gills, but no others seemed moved by the spectacle. "Duke Holata will take his seat on the council." Rain looked to his mother across the room, the only one of the two of them with the ability to appoint Dewalt since Rain was not yet crowned king, and she nodded before turning to our friend.

"Duke Dewalt Holata, do you accept the position of servitude on King Soren Vestana's council?" Dewalt murmured his assent. "And do you recognize Emmeline Vestana as Crown Princess?" The queen seemed nonplussed by the councilor moaning on the floor, choking on his blood. It disturbed me that I hadn't felt compelled to help him, my divinity a quiet hum that betrayed no demand to heal and fix, almost as if it knew. Rain bent over Scias and wiped off his dagger on the man's shirt before sheathing it and returning to my side.

"Aye, Your Majesty." Dewalt dipped his head, and his eyes twinkled as they met mine. He gave me a grim smile, a look that told me he suspected this might happen, and I realized I hadn't taken a proper breath in a few moments, inhaling deeply.

"Lord Ellington?" The man who started the original line of debate had promptly shut his mouth and sat back, allowing Scias to take the brunt of the altercation. It seemed Scias was the only one with a spine between the two of them.

"Aye, Your Majesty."

"Delightful, I am *starving*." I blanched, listening to Scias' garbled blood and moaning had done the worst thing to my appetite, but evidently, Queen Shivani's stomach was made of something stronger. "Crown Prince Rainier and Crown Princess Emmeline, will you lead the way to our festivities?"

Rain stood and pulled my chair back before offering me his arm, leading me around the table so as not to pass Scias on the ground, Lavenia and Dewalt filing behind us. Rain leaned toward me as we walked, speaking softly against my ear.

"I'm sorry to do that today of all days." I could tell he was sincere, but I wasn't sure if he needed to apologize.

"He deserved it. Do try to behave the rest of the night, though?"

"I don't know, Em, if my tongue isn't inside you soon, I'm liable to—"

Despite the shivers racing down my spine at his words, I cut him off with an elbow, and I heard Lavenia snicker behind us.

"You know, princesses aren't supposed to elbow people." Dewalt groaned a moment after he said it, and I grinned, knowing Lavenia had helped me prove his statement wrong.

CHAPTER 44

The ballroom was vast. I had never seen a single room so large. It had opulent, white marble walls with veins of gold throughout, onyx floors, and crystal chandeliers hanging from the vaulted ceilings. During the day, I was sure the stained glass would create beautiful, colorful paintings on the walls. Each window encased a depiction of the kings and queens of Vesta, including the present rulers. I studied the glass which held Soren's likeness, a dated image of him created centuries ago, likely before he ever bonded with Shivani. His hair was blond—I could tell that the glass used was butter yellow—and the green eyes, the same ones I couldn't get enough of on the face of Rain, were almost black, with the moonlight doing little to illuminate the glass. I thought it was more fitting that way, truth be told. My eyes moved over Shivani's image, her decadent, red dress taking up much of the piece, the various shades reminding me of blood. I tried not to think that one day, Rain and I would take up a place in the glass of the ballroom, a truly bizarre thought reminding me just how little I knew of our future.

When we finally made it inside, the councilors took their seats, followed by the rest of the royal family, until Rain and I were formally announced. Once we walked in, he surprised me by pulling me against him and giving me a fierce kiss that I melted into, ignoring the loud reception it garnered. He had one arm wrapped tightly around my waist, bending me back enough that one of my feet popped up, while the other snaked into my hair, holding my head still as he kissed me thoroughly. It was as if he wanted to write his name on my tongue and breathe his essence into my body. It was all surreal to experience the intensity of his love and the depth of his passion—especially in front of the nobility of his kingdom—as his *wife*. When he finished kissing me, completely rendering me both thoughtless and speechless, he pulled me up, holding me tightly as he gazed into my eyes. Those green pools glimmering with untold promise held everything he wanted to say but didn't have the words for.

"Mine." His lips spread into a wide smile.

"Yours." I agreed before giving him a quick, soft kiss.

We were whisked away to the center of a wide table that held more food than I would have thought possible. There was a surprisingly large platter full of cut and cubed cheeses, and I wondered if it was an intentional detail Lavenia had included, just for me. We made ourselves a simple plate, but I barely picked at it. Nervous energy had tided me over since breakfast, and I wasn't sure my stomach could handle much of the food, regardless of how delicious it tasted. I searched the room for people I knew. Mairin was seated at a table with a blonde woman that I took too long to recognize as Thyra. Her hair was only half up, and she wore a plain wine-colored dress that didn't look quite right on her despite her beauty. I noticed a sword belt hanging from the back of her chair, and I smiled, confident in the Thyra I knew. I sighed, remorseful over her fears and need to kill the men who might threaten me, but thankful for the woman all the same.

Drunk on my emotions and nerves, and perhaps too much champagne, I set my plate down and walked straight over to the warrior, dragging Rain along with me. She saw us coming and hastily set her mug down, splashing what I assumed to be ale out on the table. She went down into a clumsy curtsy, and I nearly laughed, catching myself so as not to make her feel bad about her attempt. It was worse than mine.

"Be my Second."

Her eyes widened as she rose out of the curtsy.

"I'm sorry, my la—Your Highness, what?" I was startled by the change in title but ignored it, pressing on, glancing at Rain who nodded encouragingly.

"Rainier would like me to pick a second in battle, command, whatever it's called, and I would like it to be you."

Thyra's jaw dropped, and it felt like an achievement of sorts to catch her off guard.

"You want me to be your Second, Princess Emmeline?"

"Oh gods, don't make me take it back. But yes, of course, I want you to be my Second. Who else?"

"I am most honored. Yes, of course." She dropped down to one knee before I could stop her and stared up at me expectantly. I stared in confusion before Rain leaned down and spoke quietly in my ear.

"She needs to pledge an oath now." He pulled his sword out of its sheath and handed it to me. I gaped at him, and he shrugged, almost as if to say I'd gotten myself into this mess. I studied her for a moment; her eyes were blue like ice, and deep laugh lines made up most of her face. Rain leaned into me, offering more advice I needed.

"One shoulder, then the other."

I raised the heavy sword to Thyra's shoulder and gently lowered the weight onto it.

"I charge you, Thyra of Skos, to defend and protect the weak and oppressed and to show no mercy to those who do not deserve it."

I lifted the sword to her other shoulder as she watched me diligently.

"I ask of you, Thyra of Skos, to follow me, and abide in my company, advise me in my best interest, and—" I hesitated, not sure how to finish. I'd heard oaths like this before, but I was on the spot, doing my best to make it sound respectable. "I ask you to have patience with me while I learn and strive to be better." She smiled at me as I pulled the sword back, waiting for her to do something.

"Thyra of Skos, do you accept the oath as Princess Emmeline Vestana—gods, I love that—as Princess Emmeline Vestana has presented it?" Rain grinned and took his sword back.

"I accept." Thyra stood and grabbed me at the wrist before I pulled her in for an embrace. "Thank you, Princess."

"I should have put something in the oath about you calling me that. Please, Thyra, call me Emma. My friends call me Emma."

She nodded and backed away before sitting back down, abruptly as if her legs failed her. If I didn't know any better, I would have sworn the warrior woman who called me stupid the moment she met me shed a tear as she looked away.

After an unnecessarily extravagant dinner, a small troupe of performers set up began playing music. I watched as Dewalt dragged Lavenia and Mairin out to the clearing in the middle of the floor, and they all began skipping, jumping, and dancing to the fiddle. I felt melancholy, wishing I could participate in the joyous fun without any trouble brewing in my heart. While this day was one I'd never imagined could happen and left me absolutely incandescent with love and relief, my heart was not quite in it without my daughter.

"Care to dance with me, my wife?" Rain's lips brushed against my cheek, and I turned to him, smiling over how the gold dust had spread across his face. I lifted my hand, tracing my fingertips over his cheekbone and jawline.

"Soon? I'm feeling a bit sad at the moment. Elora would have loved this."

He started to slide into the chair next to me, but I stopped him, placing my hand over his. "But you should dance, my love." I nodded at his sister and our friends, and his lips tipped up before he pushed a kiss to the top of my head.

"I will keep you company until you're ready to join me."

"Rain, please. Go have fun. I just need a few moments alone."

He nodded slowly, understanding my desire to sink into my thoughts. I felt the threads of our bond light up faintly, the connection almost purring at our synchronicity.

"We will have countless more celebrations she will enjoy, I promise. Join me when you're ready." He gently traced his fingertips over my exposed shoulders as he walked past me to join our friends, and I watched them dance together with a smile on my face, feeling luckier than I'd ever felt before. Rain twirled his sister around him while Mairin led Dewalt through a complicated dance to the beat of the music, Lavenia laughing at them with her head tilted back, a beautiful swirl of red dress and black hair blurring as she spun. I imagined myself and Elora out there next to them, light with joy. We'd be getting her back so soon, and I was starting to count the hours. I knew afterward there would be a time of transition and healing and honesty, but I was eager for the time after. The normalcy we would grow into, although nothing about this new life was normal. I dreamt of the three of us sitting in the garden at Rain's estate. Our estate. That home was as much mine as it was his from the moment he built it; I just didn't know it. I imagined falling asleep with both of them in the hammock, Rain murmuring tales of his adventures to her as we drifted off. I could hear Rain and I telling her the story of the two of us. Of the love we felt which drew us over the years, the love we could finally claim. The love we'd hope for her to experience one day. Part of me was devastated, sorry for the fact she lost her father, but she'd lost him long before his death. I wondered if she ever truly had him. But I knew Rain would be everything to her he could be, everything she could ever hope for, and the thought was a beacon of light in this long dark.

"How does it feel to be a princess?" I startled out of my dreamy state when Queen Shivani spoke. I gave her a small smile, uncertain of her tone, as she lowered herself into the seat next to me.

"Well, I suppose I don't feel any different at the moment." Other than the title and the diadem I wore, nothing had changed.

"Oh, but you will. There is much for you to learn and much for me to teach you." Though I did my best to portray the opposite on my face, I internally cringed. I knew as the reigning queen, Shivani was inarguably the best person to learn about my duties from, but the thought of working with her and learning from her provided me with such unease I thought I'd much rather figure things out myself. She began explaining and listing some of the many meetings I'd start to attend with her, and I felt my senses glaze over again as I stared out at the people dancing. I saw a shock of white hair at the back of the room for a brief second. Leaning in my chair, I searched, attempting to find the person again. I'd only seen two people in my life with hair that color, and it wasn't possible either were here. I stood, ignoring Shivani, gazing past the people on the crowded dance floor. That was when I saw her.

The woman who stood at the back of the room was tall, Thyra's height. Her hair fell past her lower back, and it swayed in a slight breeze despite the still air in the room. I felt myself walking toward her, all sound in the room having become a dull buzz in my ears. She wore an all-white dress and a half-smile—almost sad as she looked at me. I skirted the tables to avoid those dancing, and she eventually turned away from me in a manner that could only be described as a glide. A memory itched at the recesses of my mind. I'd seen her before. I'd been hallucinating, blood loss and childbirth having nearly killed me, but I remembered seeing her. She'd been with another woman who was the opposite in coloring and clothing, and they'd whispered to one another, quiet as they watched me dying, before turning and walking away from me in the same manner. If this woman in the ballroom was the moonlight, the woman with her in my memory was night itself. Perfect compliments and equals. I'd seen them both while I was barely conscious, and because of my midwife's insistence that I'd been seeing things, I'd pressed the memory away, locking it down with the trauma of Elora's birth, never to be relived. But the woman I saw just now made me wonder what it was I saw back then. As she glided away, I felt myself pick up my pace, swiftly walking across the ballroom as she whipped around into a hallway. Picking up my skirts, I began running to catch up to her, but when I turned quickly into the hallway, she was gone. I stood there for a moment, watching the end of the long hallway and knowing there was no way for her to have disappeared.

"What did she say?" The hand that grabbed my arm belonged to Dewalt, though it took me a moment to understand what he was saying.

"Who?" I blinked up at him, realizing I felt a bit dazed.

"The queen. Did she upset you?" He narrowed his eyes as he examined me, scanning my features.

"No. She didn't upset me. I thought I saw someone." My gaze flickered back down the hallway. I didn't know how to explain it to Dewalt. My heart told me deep down, I knew both women, the one from the ballroom and the other from my memory, but my mind was not willing to admit the possibility. I shook my head as Dewalt stared down at me. He worried his lip before taking my arm in his.

"Come on. You owe me a dance, mouse."

Leading me back out into the ballroom, his steady grasp on my arm helped support me as I couldn't focus, too engrossed on the women from my memory. He led me onto the dance floor just as the performers switched their songs to a slower pace, a young woman singing in the place of the grizzled old man, her song low and melancholy. Placing one hand on the small of my back and taking my hand in his other, Dewalt twirled me around in a slow dance I vaguely remembered learning years ago. I heard a low rumble of thunder followed by the beginning of rain. I was glad the storm had missed us during the Mind ceremony.

"You sure jumped headfirst into it, didn't you? The life she would've wanted for you?" He smiled as he looked down at me, but the tone of his voice was bitter. I had anticipated some of those emotions from him and readied myself for the possibility, but I was worried. I would take the brunt of his frustration, the closest thing to the real woman he was missing.

"I guess I did."

"Funny, how it's the life she would have lived, isn't it? This was supposed to be her." His expression was sour. "It's a shame it took you so long to take her place. The wait was torture for Rainier."

"I'm not taking her place, Dewalt. This is *my* place. I love him; I was always supposed to be here. Just like Lucia was supposed to be with you."

He sighed and averted his eyes, watching our friends dance with each other, his expression softening as Lavenia twirled Mairin in a wide circle before he turned back to me.

"I'm sorry. I'm being unfair."

"You are, but I understand."

"If she didn't die, she still never would have been mine."

"You don't know that."

"I've been thinking. Ever since you told me you two are twin flames. Part of me wonders if that's what Lucia and I were, and that's why I just feel . . . lost. But then I feel stupid for thinking I could ever have possibly deserved her."

"You *did* deserve her Dewalt. You did. The longer I've had to wrap my head around the fact that it was you, the more I realize just how blind I was. I wouldn't be surprised if you were twin flames. You should ask Mairin."

"I have. She said there's no way to know."

"She's wrong. Here." I placed my hand over his heart. "You know. Just like Rain and I knew. He never left my heart all those years."

"May I cut in?" Rain surprised me by appearing next to me the moment I said his name, almost as if I summoned him. He smiled at his friend, who hesitantly returned it after looking at me.

"Of course. Thank you, Emmeline." He gave a curt nod and backed away, striking a purposeful path through the room, heading toward the hallway he'd found me in. Rain took his place, pulling me against his body. He was warm and unyielding, in not only body but other ways too. He was home, and being wrapped in his arms was a balm.

"That seemed intense." He watched me warily. I sighed, giving him a tired smile.

"Yes, but not unexpected." I tucked my head into his chest and abandoned the structured dance both men had been leading me on. Rain held me tight, and I let myself breathe in the comfort of his arms. Dewalt was right, I had jumped into this headfirst. But I had also been right. This was my place. Here in Rain's arms was where I was always meant to be.

"I'm sure it's hard for him. The two of us bonded over our shared loss of the Highclere twins. Granted, I never lost you quite like he lost Lucia, but we bonded over it anyway. But now I've got you back." He pulled me closer and kissed the top of my head.

"It can't be easy."

"Did you know he sent me three impulses when you showed up at Ravemont?"

"Three?" I was incredulous. "That's like what Ven did to me in the dungeons. It ruined my whole night."

"Yes, I was already in the stable when he sent them. I had just returned from praying, and I ran inside the house in a panic. I didn't know what could have possibly warranted three impulses. Servants were crowding the door, and I almost pushed through them until I heard you. I thought I was hallucinating. I froze, and my heart just plummeted. I immediately convinced myself I was wrong, and it almost felt like losing you again. But then you kept talking."

He took a deep breath, and I could hear the emotion thick in his throat, making my heart ache.

"Emmeline, I had just asked the gods to let me forget you. And there you were. It took everything in me to gently push past those servants. You were there in the same room as me. You were in trouble, and you needed me. Gods, Emmeline. *You needed me.* I didn't even care that you were married. And when I saw your face, when I made you stand up? I wanted to throw myself at your feet."

I felt a tear break free as I looked into those gold-dappled green eyes I had come to know so intimately. I stopped swaying with him, pulling away to gaze upon him as I spoke, a surety coming over me that I needed to show him just how deeply I felt for him. I'd said it in my vows and told him I'd loved him, but since I'd come back, he had been the one who made it overwhelmingly clear, and I thought it was past time I made my feelings as clear as he always had.

"I love you, Rain. I loved you back then, and I've loved you every day since. Loving you is the most terrifying thing I've ever known, but I need you to know, I'd suffer all these years again as long as it led me back to you. I know I try your patience, and I'm not the easiest person to love or the most vulnerable with my feelings. Hell, even this is difficult for me. But I will never give you any reason to doubt my love again. Good gods, I've never been happier than when I'm in your arms."

A smile spread across his face as I spoke, and he cupped the back of my neck, pulling me in for an agonizing kiss. The music picked up, and more people flooded into the open space to dance, but Rain and I were frozen. He grasped me by my hips and pressed my body against his, propriety be damned. Tilting my head back, he deepened the kiss before sliding his tongue against the seam of my lips. I let his tongue in with a slight moan, and then his hands left me.

I heard the sound of a rift.

The next thing I knew, we were in the pouring rain. I pulled away with a gasp, and Rain pushed me against a wall where the drizzle couldn't reach us anymore.

"What are you doing?"

"Making love to my wife." His lips found purchase on my neck, his hands back on my hips as he pulled me against him.

"Where are we?"

"Our garden." He murmured against my skin, soft lips marking my collarbone.

I looked past him, and, though only lit by torches on the walls behind me, it appeared as if the garden from his home had been duplicated here at the palace. I started when I realized we weren't on the ground level but a balcony. And yet there was dirt for the plants to grow.

"You did this?" Rain must have used his divinity to make this possible.

"So many questions tonight. If you don't want to be interrupted, you need to stop talking." He put one hand over my mouth as he kissed lower, pulling my dress below my breast and popping my nipple into his mouth, sucking hard. I let my head tilt back against the wall of the palace, and I moaned, still loud, if muffled.

He pressed his hand harder against my mouth.

"Quiet, dear heart. You don't want us to get caught by a servant, do you?" His voice was low as he pulled my leg up around his waist, hiking my dress up my thigh. He unbuttoned his pants before pulling his hand away from my mouth and kissing me, resuming the frenzied clash of tongues that brought us to the balcony from the middle of the ballroom. Gliding his hand between us, he slid my panties aside and roughly pushed two fingers inside me, hard and deep, eliciting a groan from me that I tried to keep at bay.

"I'm going to have to fill this mouth with something since you can't keep quiet." He slid those fingers out of me and then brought them to my lips. "Suck."

I blinked at him for just a moment before slowly opening my mouth. Pushing them past my lips and teeth, he repeated his order, and I closed my lips around his fingers, sucking my own desire from his skin.

"Now you know just how good you taste, *princess*."

The look on his face was pure mischief as he pulled his fingers out of my mouth slowly, and I sucked on them, nipping him lightly. He hooked one of my legs up into his elbow as he pushed me back against the wall. With his other hand, he pulled my panties aside once more, roughly, as if he couldn't do it fast enough, and then shoved into me. The only thing that kept me from crying out was the sudden boom of thunder and the flash of lightning which lit up the entire balcony, startling me into silence.

He slammed into me as he kissed me, his free hand coming to rest on the side of my neck. I could feel my back scratching against the stone behind me, and I didn't care. I'd heal myself later, or Rain could, I supposed. It almost felt good, mixing the pain on my back with the pleasure rolling through me. His kiss was demanding and harsh, taking what he wanted from my mouth as he took what he wanted from my body.

"You were made for me, Em. You fit me so perfectly."

I started panting as he slid into me over and over again, and it was all I could do to not moan out loud. I bit my lip as a low groan crept up my throat, and I threw my arms around him. He picked up my other leg and pushed me harder against the wall, holding me up completely, and began to piston into me hard. I had no control over any of it, a complete wreck in his arms, lost to what he wanted. And what he wanted was to possess me fully. I wouldn't stop him if I could, wanting to give him every part of me. I could feel my divinity thrumming, and those tiny threads connecting us were glowing brighter, sounding in our unconscious. In a quick, violent movement, he dropped one of my legs as he slammed my hand up into the wall behind me, pressing his own against it, our wounds from the divine blade pressing together, melding our blood as we made our promise, skin against skin. He poured his body into mine as the heavens opened further around us. The sound of the rain hitting the ground overpowered the sounds of our skin slapping and the heavy breaths coming from us both.

His free hand supported my lower back, helping me to wrap my legs around his waist, and he pressed us harder against the wall, using it as leverage to thrust into me, so deep that I couldn't tell where I ended and he began. He fucked me hard, bouncing me on his cock, and I tilted my head back against the wall, my hair pulling against the rough stone. Adjusting, he pushed into me from a different angle, hitting a spot that made me cry out, and he took my lips between his teeth and bit. Hard.

"What did I tell you, naughty thing? Do I need to fill your mouth? Do I need to punish you?" His eyes flashed as he kept the same pace, sliding out a bit farther each time and then slamming back into me even harder. It felt so good that I never wanted him to stop. I knew I would be sore, but I didn't quite care. I wanted every part of him, the gentle and loving Rain and the vicious and angry. I wanted all parts in all ways, and this was one way he gave it to me.

"I think I need punishing." Each word was punctuated with a thrust from his hips. And then I let loose, screaming out his name, knowing what was in store for me, before he abruptly set me down, a sinful grin taking over his face. If he wanted to put something in my mouth, I had an idea I knew he'd like, and the thought of sucking my desire off of him in another way made my body tense and flush, and I clenched around nothing, wishing he was still inside me. I hungrily watched as he took a step back and assessed me, my dress falling back down to my feet. I nearly dropped to my knees to take him into my mouth before he spoke.

"Over to the railing." He pointed out to the garden where the rain was still coming down with a vengeance. I gawked at him. It was thundering and storming, and I was still fully dressed.

"I don't want to ruin it." I gestured to the beautiful gown I wore.

"Take it off."

"Right h—"

"I said, take it off." He stepped forward and spun me so I faced the wall, growling when he struggled with the corset bindings, and did his best to undress me quickly, pulling the dress down for me to step out. Gently laying it across a bench against the wall, his gaze was full of lustful intent. His eyes did a lazy perusal of my body, clad only in the dainty slippers, champagne panties, and the diadem I wore on my head. He was fully clothed, including his crown, the only evidence of what we'd been doing was his length jutting straight out of his pants. I bent down to pull one shoe off before he stopped me.

"Leave the shoes and the diadem. Then I want you bent over the balcony. Now." Pausing to stare at him for only a second, I slid out of the panties. "Touch yourself while you wait."

Thankfully, the weather had been temperate today, so the rain itself wasn't bad, but the wind sent a cool chill down my spine as I walked naked into the downpour. I turned around, watching him as he pulled his pants off, the thick muscle of his thighs tensed and flexed from the exertion of taking me against the wall. I stole another moment as he took off his jacket but then decided to obey him, leaning into the railing, tracing my hand down and finding my clit. I brushed down farther, dragging my fingertips through my wetness, before I moved back up, rubbing tiny circles on that sensitive spot. Fluttering my fingers there, I glanced over my shoulder to see him finally approaching behind me, naked and ready. A flash of lightning lit up the surrounding area, hitting every indentation and curve of his taut muscles. He was so gods damn perfect it took my breath away. A vision come to life. The sky was still open, rain pouring heavily, and my body was slick with it, the wind cooling me, spreading goosebumps across my skin. When he reached me, he stood back, watching me touch myself for just a moment before sliding his warm hand up my backside, rubbing slowly across my soft, wet skin. His hand grazed up my back, his caress firm, and a low moan from deep in my throat crossed my lips.

The next thing I knew, he was kneeling behind me, licking the most sensitive part of my body. I sighed deeply, his warm tongue a stark contrast with the cold air blowing over my pebbled skin. He spread me open with his fingertips, tongue circling my entrance, sensitive from him taking me against the wall. I moaned, not able to help myself before I felt a tight slap on my ass, and I squealed before he rubbed the sting away, his tongue continuing its ministrations at my opening.

The thunder rumbled through me, and the rain picked up, lightning flashing over the mountains in the distance. The storm was wild and dangerous and beautiful, mirroring the way it felt to love Rain. He slid his fingers against my clit, knocking away my own, working me in small circles as he tongued me. His other hand slid up my ass, grabbing and massaging me.

"Gods, Rain, that feels so good. I love you." He sped up his pace, and I was breathless, repeating myself over and over, barely able to speak. My hair was soaked, and water ran down my back and arms, dripping off my chest and rolling down my legs. He pulled away abruptly, and then his hands were on my hips, pulling me back onto his cock, my cry lost in the storm.

"It's more than love, my wife. I crave you, I need you, I cannot live without you; I *burn* for you."

I let out a sob as he slid back into me, overwhelmed by my feelings and the sensation. When I was bent over like this, it felt like he could tear me in half, his thickness stretching and filling me. I felt like I was falling, body weak and limbs heavy. His hands grasped my hips, holding me up, while his fingertips dug into my skin and left bruises. I was weightless and too heavy all at once, getting sucked under the wave of desire.

"Hold on to the railing, dear heart."

I grabbed onto the balustrade like my life depended on it as he pounded into me. His hips struck a tempo that made me feel like I was on the edge of a cliff, about to fall. I was lost in the sensations, feeling full, and I could feel my breasts swing at each thrust. The sound of his skin slapping against mine was amplified by the rainwater pouring down over our bodies. My divinity thrummed, and I could almost hear an echo along with it. The golden string was taut between us, and I felt another one grow as I had during the Mind ceremony. I could have sworn I saw the glow but knew it was just out of sight, all in the space where my soul resided. Bending over me, he placed soft kisses down my spine as he thrust even deeper, pushing himself into me so I would never—could never—be rid of him.

"I hear your heart." Rain panted as he pulled me up, my back against his chest. One hand stayed on my hip, while the other reached around to my breast, rolling my nipple in his fingertips. "I feel your divinity. It's in harmony with mine."

His words were a caress against my ear. At this angle, he felt even bigger than before as he moved gently inside me. He had slowed his pace when he pulled me up, just moving against me tenderly, lovingly, and I slid my hand up behind me, cupping the back of his neck. When he kissed me in that sweet spot just behind my ear, I melted. And when I listened for the thrum of our divinities, I realized Rain was right, and the song our shared power made was beautiful. I was nearly brought to tears as I listened to it, the sound a comfort for the soul. For a soul who had been so lost and alone, to finally feel this with him was too much. A cold breeze blew past, and I shivered just a second before it abruptly stopped. I was close when Rain reached a hand around me and sent one of his fingers to work on my clit, pushing me ever closer to the edge. There was another rumble of thunder close enough it made the palace shake underneath us, almost making me lose my balance. Rain grasped my hip tightly to steady me before turning my head to the side, holding me just so, and kissed me as he thrust, his fingers pushing me closer and closer to the edge while his tongue swept into my mouth, his lips a caress on mine. He tasted like everything I could ever want. When he broke from my lips, I looked into his eyes, willing him to see every bit of love and emotion I felt for him, and he let out a small gasp.

"Gods, Em. Your eyes."

I didn't have a chance to ask what he meant when I finally ebbed over the edge, a free fall into every emotion and feeling I'd been terrified of but now knew as the warm embrace of Rain. Of life. I felt him pulse inside me as he crashed over the edge with me. Lightning struck close by, illuminating the grounds below us, and the thunder that followed nearly threw us to the ground. Rain wrapped his arm around my waist, pulling me close and away from the railing, and I closed my eyes, sagging against him—spent. My divinity was throbbing, and I felt the power rolling down the string, the space which I now knew housed both mine and Rain's divinity, a rolling vibration between our souls, a sharing he'd told me about before, but we couldn't understand until now.

He picked me up, carrying me like a child, and brought me back to the wall we'd been pressed against. Navigating his way to a door, he walked us through it, fully naked. It led into a bedroom, large and comfortable, similar to the one I'd been in earlier with Lavenia. A vast improvement upon what I'd expected. I wondered if Rain was offended when I said I preferred his estate and arranged this suite for us because of it. I didn't care where we slept, as long as it was together. But I glanced around to take it all in. The room was rather dark, the low light of the fire barely able to light our path in from the garden, but I could make out a large carpet, perhaps a deep wine red in the light, and a tremendous bed, thick velvet curtains drawn open to reveal what appeared to be comfortable bedding. He kissed my forehead as he sat me down on the bed and then backed up a bit, watching me with something I could only describe as concern on his face. I felt myself frown, confused over his reaction after what we just shared.

"What is it? Are you alright?" I sat up as he swept the water away from my body, shooting it flying into what I assumed was a bathroom. Sitting down next to me, he pulled a blanket over us before taking my hand and looking at me in earnest.

"Did you mean to do that?"

"Do what?" I didn't know what he meant.

"Pull from my divinity like that?"

"What do you mean?" I still didn't understand. I had felt the string, the divinity, the thrum, but I hadn't pulled on it. Not that I knew of, at least.

"You couldn't tell? You tugged from my divinity when you . . . when you lit up."

"What are you saying? Do you mean the lightning?"

"That wasn't lightning, Em. That was you."

I shook my head. "Rain, you aren't making any sense."

"Your eyes were white when you kissed me at the end. And then, when you finished, you lit up. You *glowed*."

I stared down at my hands. They seemed normal, the same pale ivory I knew. But they weren't glowing. I felt bewildered, and I was sure Rain saw it on my face when his eyes met mine. He leaned in, caging his body around me, searching my face before he kissed me softly, trying to calm me with his lips.

"Your eyes looked like Lucia's, but I never saw her skin glow like that. Did you ever see her whole body glow? You—Em, you're strong, stronger than me, I could feel it. You made the ground shake and the wind stop too."

"That's not true. Rain, that was thunder. And I—" I remembered the wind stopping abruptly, but it couldn't be. "The wind stopped on its own. I couldn't have done all of that, let alone at once."

He shook his head quickly, adamance ruling his features as he looked at me, eyes bright. "You shouldn't have been able to, but you did, Em, I swear it. Do you have a headache?"

"I think I'm getting one, but it's because you're saying ridiculous things, not because of my divinity. Or the champagne. Maybe both." There was no way I could have done those things, especially when I hadn't been trying.

"It's not ridiculous if it's true."

"Lucia could only shoot those bolts of light out, Rain. And then the—the last time, before she—when she knocked down all those soldiers, it used up all of her divinity. All of it! That's why she couldn't fight—But I feel fine. You're saying I lit up the grounds? From *glowing*? That's impossible." He just watched me, his face bleak. I couldn't comprehend what he was trying to tell me. It made no sense.

"Has Elora ever done anything like that?"

"No. She's never done that either." I held my breath, wary over what he was getting at.

"So, you're stronger than both of them." I gaped at him, waiting for more outrageous things to spill past those perfect lips. He gave me a meaningful look, willing me to understand. But I couldn't believe that. If it were true, it changed everything. When his lips parted to speak, I stopped him.

"Don't say it," I whispered, unwilling to deal with the idea at full volume. Pulling me against his chest, we laid back on the bed, and Rain held me tight against him, his warmth attempting to permeate the chill that had settled over my body. We didn't speak as he held me, and I lay there in shock. When he noticed I was shivering, he threw one leg over me, holding onto me as if I might fly away. His fingers tangled in my hair while he gently caressed my back, rubbing soft circles down my spine, comforting me.

"Faxon said my eyes were white." The realization hit me sharply, and I jumped. I tried to remember everything else he'd said that I'd blown off as useless chatter from the mind of someone who wasn't quite there. A seer had helped mindbreak him. Could the seer have known I'd have eyes like Lucia and Elora one day? Rain pulled me tighter, gently caressing me in an attempt to soothe.

"He said she wasn't the prophecy either, Em." I inhaled a breath, everything inside me tightening. It was unfathomable. If she wasn't the prophecy, then—what did this mean? For me? And at the same time, relief. Unending, blissful, all-encompassing relief. I would give anything to take the burden from her.

"And the Myriad wondered about my divinity, too. They suspected . . . fuck, Rain. What about Elora? What if the councilors find out she isn't the Beloved? Will they still allow—"

"Fuck the councilors," he scoffed. "And if she isn't, and you are, it protects her. If she isn't the Beloved, it protects your daughter. It protects our daughter, dear heart."

My heart warmed for a second before my world flipped on its axis for the second time. I remembered something else Faxon had said, something Faxon had said to Rain.

"Oh, gods!"

I suppose she's yours?

He hadn't been talking about me.

CHAPTER 45

I JUMPED UP FROM the bed, wild-eyed and frantic. Naked, I looked around in a panic, trying to find something to wear while I made sense of the mess in my head. I needed to move, to walk, to think.

"Did I say something wrong?"

Ignoring him, I made my way over to the door where Rain sent water before, opting to settle for a towel if there was no alternative. It was pitch black, only faint shapes discernible in the light, and I shoved out my arms to grab onto something and found soft cloth after only a moment. I pulled down a hand towel, using it to clean up the mess between my thighs before continuing my search, patting along the wall in desperation. My divinity hummed, and I felt a surge of annoyance before a sudden thought struck me. Holding out my palm, I focused, attempting to put Rain's theory to the test, and I gasped when my fingertip began to glow. Staring at the white light emanating from my skin, I allowed myself only a moment to come to terms with it. There were bigger things to worry about. Using the light, I was able to see a robe hanging up and grabbed it with my other hand, extinguishing my divinity before I pulled on the garment. Once back in the bedroom, I realized it was Rain's, the bottom of the emerald satin fabric dragging across the crimson rug. He watched me warily as I set to pacing in front of the fire, expectant but quiet. There was nothing I could say to him, though, not until I was absolutely certain. Shivers of fear from before gave way to unparalleled shaking—a combination of panic and chill, and perhaps a bit of hunger since I'd barely eaten.

"Em?"

I waved a hand to silence him as I walked back and forth. I hoped he'd think my behavior was because of my divinity and what that could mean, but the reality was much worse. I allowed myself that moment in the dark to contemplate it, and I wouldn't bother with it again. If I was the Beloved, the overwhelming emotion I felt was relief. If I was the Beloved, Elora was not. But none of that mattered, not when all I could think about was what Faxon had said to Rain before he died.

I suppose she's yours? I always knew she spread her legs for you.

I had only ever been with two men. Rain was only the once, and we had been interrupted only moments into it. Though I was no expert, I did know that what we had done could have resulted in a child in rare circumstances, but the likelihood seemed slim considering how briefly we were joined. When I considered that Faxon had consummated our marriage just one week later, continuing to lay with me regularly until he was satisfied I'd provided him an heir, I thought the odds of Elora belonging to Faxon were immense. It hadn't even crossed my mind that Rain could . . . I stopped myself. I was overthinking it. Faxon had only meant it the way I'd originally interpreted. I was the person he spoke of, not our daughter. It was impossible; there was no use letting myself think it.

She is not the prophecy.

Faxon had said many things that day, and I'd considered them all delusory ramblings of a man half out of his mind. But it seemed as if he was right about Elora. How could he have known? Shaking my head, I muttered to myself as I paced. What other things had he said? He hadn't said that my eyes would turn white but instead said they *were* white in that moment. Had a vision been implanted into his mind? Just because he might have been right about Elora not being the Beloved didn't mean he was right about anything else. Not once had I doubted she was the one the prophecy spoke of—because she was just like Lucia. The Myriad had determined Lucia was the Beloved, and though they were wrong because of her death, it stood to reason, they'd at least be searching for someone with the same abilities, like Elora. But they'd been wrong before. It could have been a fluke for Faxon to be right about that.

Elora not being his daughter would help explain why he sold her. But if I never even knew, how could he know? There was no way to know, was there? Elora looked like me. I had a feeling I was right; the only reason Faxon would have given up his child, the girl he seemed to care for and love, would be if he found out she wasn't his and acted in anger. Perhaps he found out somehow and decided to sell her and run away. But Faxon still paid those debts to protect me. If he had thought I had a child with someone else, would he have bothered? Especially if he thought I kept it secret on purpose? I'd never told him I'd been with Rain; it was none of his business. And besides, how could I have known Rain sired her when it was so preposterous?

I felt hands on my waist, and I jumped, flinching away from Rain's touch. He wore a blanket wrapped around his shoulders and concern etched across his face.

"Em, I told you I would love her as my own. Is this not what you imagined? If you think I've overstepped, I will not apologize. I meant what I said." He sounded frustrated, and I struggled to listen to him, my instincts wanting to explain, but I couldn't do it. Paying attention to him was out of the question until I'd figured everything out.

"What?" I pulled away from him, continuing to pace.

"Is that what upset you? You jumped up right after I said she was our daughter. You have plenty to be upset about right now, I suppose, but I assumed you'd be pleased."

"It's not that. I—I can't even explain—" A thought occurred to me. One question which could help solve my inner turmoil. One question I could ask him. But after posing it, he would start to wonder, and I'd need to make sense of things fast.

"Rain, were you taking the tonic back then?"

"Back when?"

"When we—Before." I froze, waiting for him to understand. His brows bunched before he answered, clearly confused.

"No, I wasn't on the tonic back then. You were the fir—Why are you asking me that, Em?" His eyes narrowed on me, and I averted my own. I couldn't look at him until I knew for sure. This could break us, could ruin us. I was terrified of being right. I was terrified of him thinking I'd hidden from him. Terrified of him being angry at me for the lost time.

Unbidden, another image appeared in my mind. The two women who whispered to one another as I bled out were at the forefront of my thoughts. They were present at her birth. If they were who I thought they were, why were they there? Could their presence have had something to do with the improbable situation that started to seem more and more possible the longer I thought?

I set to pacing again, shuffling through all the evidence in my mind which pointed to Rain being Elora's father. He stood near me, arms limp, and as much as it pained me, I froze him out, not able to handle explaining yet. I had only moments before he understood, and I needed to gather my thoughts.

I imagined her face in my mind, searching it for any traits belonging to him. It had never occurred to me to look for his features because we'd been called back in the middle of our tryst, and it was nearly impossible. But she'd always had darker skin than mine, but so had Faxon—though not by much. Her eyes were blue like mine, and her hair was white like my sister's. But where mine was wavy, Elora's had always been rather curly. I'd always thought it came from Faxon's side, two of his brothers having mild curls, though hers were far tighter. Her expressions, though, they'd always belonged to someone other than me. I had always assumed Faxon, but now? Hell, I had even said it in my vows to him. Her smile had always reminded me of Rain. Every time her face lit up in a grin, and especially when she laughed, I saw him. But I always thought it was because I'd seen parts of him everywhere. I had been looking for him, and I had found him in different ways. Her smile was childlike wonder and joy, just as Rain's had been, but that wasn't it at all. I saw his smile in hers because he was a part of her.

He grabbed my arm.

"*Emmeline.*" Rain's face was grave, features stern and eyes wary, his voice a command. Where I'd averted my eyes before, I finally let them meet his. Let him read me this way, the intimate way he had always been able to do. Let him see the emotions, the confusion. The doubt and relief. The regrets. All of it.

The moment I saw understanding cross his face, I fell to my knees. His expression cracked, his brows meeting in the center and his mouth going slack. His emotions mirrored mine, but the moment I saw the heartbreak in his eyes, I wasn't sure I'd be able to continue. He dropped to his knees with me, the blanket curling around him, while he held onto my hands. I forced myself to meet his gaze, to live in his sorrow as he took me in, tears gathering on his lashes.

"She's mine?" His voice broke, hoarse and pained.

I tried to speak, but the words wouldn't come. I let out a sob and mouthed my confirmation. Rain took a gasping breath as the tears threatening to fall down his face burst forth. He nodded as if what I said made perfect sense, and he pulled my hands to his chest. I watched our hands clasped tightly and listened to his heart stampeding through his chest. We both knelt together, accepting this new truth into our lives. With my hands on his heart and my own heart in my throat, we stayed there for countless moments.

He heaved a deep breath and wiped his eyes, letting my hands drop from his chest, and I almost couldn't breathe as I awaited his anger and frustration. I braced myself for accusations and harsh words, terrified of his reaction. I'd wanted all of him, the sweet and loving and the angry and vicious, and I thought I was about to get the latter. I couldn't control myself as I let panic bubble over into my words. "Forgive me, please. I didn't know, I swear it. Rain, I didn't know." He shushed me and pulled me closer, tucking me into the blanket with him. We sat on the floor, huddled together, as we untangled our new reality.

"When was she born?" Quiet and shaky, he sounded nothing like the demanding or harsh Rain, nor the delicate and loving Rain. This was new territory, and I was so sad to do this to him, to tell him something he should have known for a long time. What he *would* have known if I would have deigned to see him. It was a special kind of pain to know that if I had only allowed him to be a part of my life that one of us would have figured it out. The knife was sharp in my gut. When she was a babe cradled in my arms, and I had searched her face for pieces of me as I fed her, I'd found little comfort. Oddly enough, my mother, who had been avoiding me, not even present for Elora's birth, had come to me one morning when I was feeling particularly overwhelmed by the tiny, wailing creature in my arms. I suspected Nana had sent her after walking in on me crying for the infant to just be quiet. Mother came to distract me and gaze upon the little love, caressing her fat cheek. She'd commented on the audacity that children had, to spend nine months on the inside only to come out looking like their father. I'd laughed, but looking at her, I hadn't seen Faxon either. Now I knew why. It wasn't until she was a toddler that she began to look like me. If I had seen them together before then, there was no doubt in my mind that I would have known.

"Spring Equinox." Rain did the math as I had done already, and by the expression on his face, came to the same conclusion I had.

"I wasn't on the tonic, but we stopped before I . . . I didn't—I know it isn't impossible, but—" He didn't seem doubtful, just confused. He was right, it didn't seem possible, but I had already thought of the probable explanation. I took a breath, cutting him off, readying myself to verbalize what I'd been thinking.

"At dinner, I think I saw a vision of Aonara."

"What? Dinner tonight?" His confusion only worsened, eyebrows up to his hairline, and he seemed exhausted.

"Yes. She had the hair—white—and she was so pale. I followed her before I danced with Dewalt, but she disappeared after she turned the corner." He nodded slowly, waiting for more.

"Now, if that was all it was, I might have just shaken it off. But she felt different, familiar almost. The way she moved and just the way she looked at me, I don't know. But Rain . . ." I shook my head, barely believing myself. "Rain, I've seen her before." His face was ashen, and all he did was blink at me. "When I was in labor with Elora, I hallucinated two women. But now, I don't think they were hallucinations. I think—I saw Aonara and Rhia. The midwife told me I hadn't seen anyone, and I was half-dead, so I believed it. I mean, it would explain it, right? Even if you didn't—if Rhia was involved—I don't know."

He stared down at his hands, not truly seeing anything. "But why was Aonara there too?"

"I suppose to bless her. Her eyes were white from the very beginning."

Rain lifted his head and watched me, his expression pained, and I wanted to hold onto him. My heart broke knowing I was responsible for what he was feeling. I was almost certain the women I saw all those years ago were the two goddesses. Their presence hadn't been a comfort or discomfort at the time, just a confusing thing to think about after the fact. I'd explained Aonara's reason for being there, but the only reason for Rhia's presence had to have explained how Elora could be his. Perhaps she'd accompanied her sister to ensure her blessing had come to fruition. The longer I thought, the more sure I felt. It would explain everything.

"Does she look like me?"

I couldn't help it as a sob broke past my lips, his quiet hope more than enough to destroy me. He grabbed my hands, pulling them into his lap, and the simple motion of him comforting me undid me. He was the one being told about what he'd missed, and yet he was consoling me. The tears streamed down my face, the guilt and sadness mingling so thoroughly when I thought about my daughter. *Our* daughter.

"She looks like Lucia, like me, I never sus—Her hair is curly." I gave him a tentative smile, hoping I could offer him something. "I thought it came from Faxon's side, but I suppose I was wrong."

Rain didn't speak, his eyes empty. I wished I could crawl inside his chest, be his heart for a moment. Just long enough to ensure it was me who broke, to save him the pain.

"What made you—How did you realize?" He swallowed, a loud gulp breaking the silence.

"I was thinking about all the things Faxon said. When he said it, I thought he was referring to me being with you. But now I think that when he said 'I suppose she's yours,' he was talking about Elora. Thinking about what he'd said, and then hearing you call her *our* daughter, well, it just clicked into place."

He nodded slowly, eyes searching mine. I wasn't sure what for; if he expected some sign that I was alright and not fragmented into tiny pieces, he wouldn't find it. I was fractured and raw, and my wretched, selfish heart felt traitorous for still beating. When he stayed silent, watching me with a broken expression, I wanted to tell him anything I could to make him feel close to Elora. To his daughter. If Rain couldn't forgive me, at least he would still have her.

"Her smile. I always saw you in her smile, and I always thought it was just because I was busy looking for you."

He made a sound in his throat, almost like choking, and then there were more tears rolling down his cheeks. I couldn't handle seeing him in so much pain, and

I reached up, brushing them away before I cupped his face in my hands. It was all my fault.

"I'm so sorry, Rain. I wish—Oh, gods. I kept her from you, and I didn't mean to! Rain, please—" I broke off, words failing me as shuddering tears moved through my body. He pulled me against his chest, placing me in his lap, and we cried together in each other's arms, my heaving gasps in total opposition to his quiet, silent tears that landed in my hair. As my tears slowed, I kept whispering my apologies, begging him to forgive me.

He stroked my hair and held me tighter while I wrapped my arms around him. "I know. I know, dear heart. Shh, please don't cry."

We sat there until the storm outside stopped, and we were in complete silence. Rain had murmured to me, shushing me as I cried in his lap. Truly, I'd never been more selfish in my sorrow; I should have been the one comforting him. He gazed down at me with a calmness I wasn't sure I could possibly be capable of before he spoke.

"Well, maybe it was *my* blood that made her bite the mercenary's ear off." He offered me a small smile, and I stared at him a moment before I let out a loud snort. I started crying again, laughter dulling the pain. Tears of joy mingled with regret and heartbreak.

"Maybe it was. You did cut off a tongue tonight." I inhaled, wiping my face free from tears yet again as I sat up, twining my arms around Rain's neck before meeting his eyes, face solemn. "Please forgive me, Rainier. I would never have kept her from you if I knew."

"There is nothing to forgive." He brushed his lips over mine before pulling away, pressing our foreheads together instead. "She was mine the moment you said yes. All this means is that she's been mine all along. Thank you for taking care of her for me, all this time."

My sharp inhale caught me off guard. "Don't thank me. I—don't thank me. You missed so much of her life, and it's all my fault."

"No, it's *our* fault. We both could have done so many things differently. And it doesn't matter. You're the one who has raised her, so I know Elora is good and kind and brave. You took good care of her, Em. I already felt like I knew her because I know you. And now, I know part of me is within her. I could have missed so much more, but now I have a chance to be her father. I suppose I should be thanking Faxon for letting this happen."

I laid my head against his chest, listening to the steady heartbeat. I knew it was a jest, that he wouldn't truly want her in the hands of the Folterrans, but there was truth to it. If she hadn't been taken, we never would have known. He never would have had a chance. She wouldn't have known this beautiful, generous, kind man as her father, better than anything Faxon could have ever dreamt of being. He and I would never have had this chance: to try again, to love again, to begin again.

Eventually, we moved to the bed, comforting each other with our lips and bodies, making sure we knew how the other felt without words. We had a long road of realization ahead of us, and we'd weather it together. I wouldn't let myself think about what would change if I was the Beloved. As for what would change with Elora, I found myself not sure much would change at all. Rain would have treated her as his own no matter what. He would have been adamant about getting to know her and having a friendship with her, and he would have loved her. That didn't change because we realized the truth. I wondered if she knew, if Faxon had told her, or if it had been made clear to the Folterrans. Based on my conversations with her in the illusion, I wondered if she suspected. All of her questions about Rain had been more than curiosity on behalf of Faxon's pride. I finally tired, my body pressed against Rain, against my husband. As I fell asleep, I felt myself smiling softly, realizing I'd had a piece of him all these years and never knew it.

We woke before dawn, preparing to finish our ritual by partaking in the Soul ceremony. We barely spoke on anything important, just cautiously existing in the other's orbit. After the emotional undressing we'd done the night before, both of us were raw, and we carried it in our countenance, both of us afraid to hurt the other or bring up things we couldn't quite handle in the moment. Dressed for travel and ready to rift to Lamera, we planned to get breakfast from the kitchens before we left. Upon opening the door to leave, we were surprised by a Myriad novice, waiting in the alcove across the hall, clearly having slept there the entire night. They were waiting for us to prove our divinity had been shared.

The novice sat up, and Rain slammed the door shut, bringing us both back into his rooms before turning to me, panic in his voice.

"Shit, we didn't even—"

"We both did last night. It's alright."

"Well, I can't prove the harrowing, and you didn't exactly do any of yours on purpose. You need to do it on command; we can't exactly repeat last night in front of the novice." I shot him a glare to counter his crooked smile. "I mean, we could if you'd like, but I thought you weren't alright with people watching. Or is it only if Dewalt is the one watching? Because if it is, I un—"

I cut him off, knowing he wouldn't stop unless I made him, though I couldn't help the small smile on my face. "You first. Cut your hand."

Rain glowered at me before reaching for his dagger, slicing his arm open.

"I said hand!"

"I'm right-handed. It was either here or my palm, and I don't want to ruin whatever the divine blade did." He was talking about the mark from our handfasting. I didn't argue with him, realizing he had a point. My own cut was still open, though no blood flowed. How had that only been a day ago? So much had happened since then.

"Putting your hand over it may help you, but all you have to do is will your divinity toward the wound. Imagine the skin mending from the inside—" I started to walk him through the process, but Rain cut me off.

"There."

I gaped down at his arm in surprise. His skin was unmarked and fully healed. "Well, that was fast." I gave a nervous laugh, worried I wouldn't be able to master his divinity as easily. It had taken me years to learn how to heal a simple cut like he just did in only a moment. He shrugged.

"It's easier to learn now that we're familiar with our divinity. You should try to rift."

"Fat chance. I'm not falling off a cliff this morning."

He snorted before rolling his eyes. "Just open a rift by the fire. And don't walk through it if it seems dangerous." The second half of his instruction had a tone attached to it which earned him a glare.

I turned my back, spreading my hands apart as I'd seen him do, and closed my eyes, picturing the fireplace in front of me. When I heard the telltale sound, my eyes popped open. There in front of me was a rift, the grate with the roaring fire behind it in plain sight. I glanced over my shoulder to Rain, watching a grin spread across his face, and I caught the glimmer of the rift out of the corner of my eye from across the room.

"Looks safe to me, Em. Go on through."

I gave a soft smile and took a tentative step toward the folding in reality before stepping through it. I realized a moment too late it wasn't quite perfect—the two floors didn't mesh together, causing me to have to step up as I went through. An ideal rift was seamless, but this was pretty close, especially for my first one. I let it close behind me, and I turned to face Rain from across the room. His grin turned into a beaming smile as he crossed the distance and picked me up, arms wrapped tightly around my waist. It made me a bit giddy when he hoisted me up like that as if I were still the young girl from our past.

"I told you. We'll practice a bit on our way to the Seat." Placing me back on my feet, he stole a quick kiss.

"Are we going to tell them about me? That I may be the Beloved? I don't want Elora to be a target anymore."

"I think until we have her back, we shouldn't say anything. She is more valuable to Folterra as the Beloved. If our plan goes awry, Declan won't kill her. He'll still want to use her. If he finds out *you* are the Beloved, not her, it would only endanger you both. Not to mention, we aren't prepared to protect you from whatever Filenti is up to." He rubbed a hand over his tired face, exhaling slowly. "Let's just make it out of this next week alive and see what happens."

I agreed with him, knowing as long as Declan thought she was the Beloved, she was safer. A part of me worried, though, that perhaps Cyran knew Elora wasn't what we thought. What Faxon had said to me had come from the prince's seer, and surely they would have told him what they'd seen. I hoped if the boy did know, he'd have the sense to keep it to himself. I hoped his feelings for Elora were true, and he'd try to keep her safe. He had chosen to work with us, a risk in itself, to keep her away from Declan.

Could Elora know? The only one who seemed to doubt her status as the Beloved was Ismene. Had Cyran been acting to keep Elora from knowing the truth? Perhaps I was giving him too much credit for deciphering the information from the seer. I didn't understand what Faxon had meant until my divinity proved to be much stronger than we thought. Maybe Cyran hadn't figured it out yet, either. I supposed it didn't matter, though. Once we got her back, we'd have a lot to discuss, and I thought, perhaps, she'd care a bit less about that than she would about the identity of her true father.

After we proved our divinity had passed through our bond, the novice who waited in the hallway scampered away, and we finally made our way to the kitchens. Saving his abilities for the trip, Rain led us through corridor after corridor and down countless stairs to get there. At one point, he even attempted to take us on a shortcut behind a tapestry before he realized it hadn't been used in ages and was full of cobwebs neither of us felt like dealing with. When we finally reached our destination, Rain rapped a knuckle on the door, and a frazzled woman answered it, frustration across her features. From the sounds emanating from within, they were well into breakfast preparations for the rest of the palace, and we were an interruption. But when her eyes met Rain's face, the cook gave him a tired smile before grabbing a basket from inside and shoving it into his arms. He thanked her with his crooked grin before turning and opening a rift. Through it, I saw an open field with one, single apple tree in sight. We walked through, and Rain pushed the basket into my arms before promptly climbing into the branches. The air was chilly, and I was thankful he'd reminded me to bring my cloak as I wrapped it tight around me. I could see the Alsors far off in the distance, and I determined we were a few hours west of Astana.

"What are you doing?"

"The animals have gotten the ones down low." He grunted and heaved his body further up into the tree, his feet disappearing in its branches. The tree itself was about fifteen meters tall, and its branches spread almost as wide. It was a giant of an apple tree and all on its lonesome in this vast green openness. I watched two apples fall and bounce off the gnarled trunk before coming to rest at my feet.

"You just knocked some down, Rain. We can eat these." I walked to the golden-green apples on the ground and gathered them, putting them in the picnic basket before looking directly above me, watching him carefully pick his way across a thick branch.

"I want the sweeter ones, the ones that ripen in the sun." He caught me watching him and smiled before plucking a few apples and tossing them down. I caught them easily as he swung down from the branch like he'd done it a thousand times before. He grabbed one of the apples out of my hands and took a bite, a grin on his face as he offered it to me. I couldn't help but smile before I opened my mouth, waiting for him to bring it to my lips. After the last day, something as simple as eating an apple was a comfort I didn't know I needed. The fruit was sweeter than I anticipated and tender—the juice dripping from my lips. Reaching up to swipe the mess off my face, Rain slid his thumb into my mouth, and I sucked the nectar from it. When he tilted my chin up and kissed me, the sweet taste of apple on our tongues, I wondered if I had finally started to understand the meaning of contentment.

We ate our breakfast the cook had packed away, goat cheese and pumpkin bread with a drizzle topping which tasted like coffee—a perfect compliment to the apples—and Rain explained where we were. There were several points he had set up over the years that made rifting to the Cascade easier. The points he spoke of were areas he could rift to, tasking someone in the vicinity to keep the locations relatively unchanged and cared for. This apple tree was the biggest in all of Vesta, and there was a lone farmer who cared for the area, ensuring Rain's mental image always aligned with what was actually there. There were several more points along the path that had the same treatment; an abandoned watchtower, the personal well of a tanner who used to be part of Rain's guard, a small footbridge, and a few more he didn't bother describing. Nara's Cove, named for the birthplace of Aonara, was the last rifting point on Vestian soil before we would have to cut southwest across the Mahowin Strait to get to the Cascade. Luckily for us, Nara's Cove was just a few hours east of Lamera. In the coming days, we'd be traveling this same path on our way to the fortress. But today, we'd stop at Nara's Cove, staying on the continent, and head northwest instead, toward the Seat of the Myriad.

After we finished breakfast and Rain felt properly rested, we rifted to the next point. During the breaks between each location, I practiced, bringing myself to different areas around where we stood. He bade me pay close attention so I'd be able to visualize each one on our way to the Cascade, hoping I'd be able to make bigger jumps with more practice. I did my best, trying to memorize as much of each location as possible, down to how many boards there were on the footbridge. Rain made it sound like that was a bit excessive, but I thought it would be better to be too detailed. It had taken him a long time to learn how to travel this far, but my handle on my divinity was much more advanced than his was when he began learning. Not to mention since the Body ritual, my divinity felt different. The light thrum was no more, and instead, I almost felt my entire being vibrating. It was unnerving almost, getting used to this much louder feeling, not quite on the edge of consciousness. But with that change came confidence I'd never imagined. I knew what I felt was unfettered divinity. Rain was extremely powerful, so was it his divinity merging with mine that made me feel this way? Was this what all bonded conduits felt? Or did it have something to do with our suspicion? With seeing Aonara the night before? Had her presence been her blessing me?

When I briefly mentioned the feeling, Rain didn't seem to know what I was talking about, and I concluded it must have been because of what we had begun to suspect. The longer I sat with it, the power, the more certain I was that we were right. I was the Beloved. I had been goddess blessed. Not just by Aonara, but Rhia as well. I wanted to hear the original prophecy from the Supreme if he'd give it. As I had heard it, the Beloved was blessed with gifts from Aonara, but I didn't feel like I was particularly burdened with something from the Goddess of Light. I believed the glowing, as Rain had described it, would have been from her. But what I felt didn't exactly feel like light, but instead felt like straight, tingling power—overwhelming and barely controlled.

When we finally landed on the docks at Nara's Cove, I felt nervous. I didn't have the appetite for lunch, though it was past afternoon, but I accompanied Rain through the fish market as he led us to his favorite vendor. The graying and weather-hardened old man was familiar with Rain, not bothering to bow to his prince, but still offered me a small one—a barely perceptible bend at the waist. The man, aptly nicknamed Grizz, fried a fresh cut of salmon, adding thyme and dill, chives and lemon juice until it was seared to perfection. Rain practically inhaled it, offering me his last bite as an afterthought, and I declined with a smile before he finished it. Grizz didn't have much to say, but I could tell he was proud he'd caught the favor of the prince.

Because he had just traveled to Lamera a few days ago and his memory was fresh, we were able to rift there, only having to make one stop along the coast in between. My feet were sinking in the sand at our last stop when he opened the final rift, and peering through, all I could see was stars, easily a hundred of them. I heaved a breath, grasping Rain's hand before we stepped through, trying to remain calm, not allowing myself to panic. We were here to drink from the font, and that was it. With my task out of the way, there should be no reason for the Supreme to look further into my divinity. Besides, what Filenti was up to in the capital might have no relation to the Supreme. He could be an ally for all we knew. I doubted it, but the thought helped put my mind at ease.

That is, until I saw the giant cathedral in front of us. I had forgotten. Facts learned about the Seat of the Myriad during childhood tutoring had long since trickled out of my memory. Made entirely of lava-stone, the building was impenetrable by divinity. Even the intricately designed stained-glass windows were made from the thinnest obsidian glass. The twin spires reached into the heavens, black and threatening, casting an almost evil shadow on the ground behind us though it was barely past midday. Even if I knew the purpose of the basalt stones was to add a layer of protection to the font within the cathedral, there was something almost sinister about the building. The effect of the mineral's dampening force repelled my divinity, the harsh thrum inside of me turning into a staccato, itching to break away from me and the building I stood in front of. I was reminded of the dagger during the Mind ceremony and the opposite effect it had on me, almost begging for me to touch it. I'd never held obsidian before, but something told me this visceral reaction I was having had more to do with *my* divinity than divinity in general. Rain's expression wasn't one of nausea like mine surely was.

"Do you feel that?" I whispered up at him, staring up at the giant red cedar doors, appearing eerily blood-drenched in the midday sun at the top of the stairs.

"Feel what?" He squeezed my hand, and I felt him watching me.

"Dread. Revulsion. Like if we step inside that building, we won't step out."

He watched me as my gaze was drawn upwards, my eyes on the statue of Aonara sitting on the smaller peak of the building between the two spires. The shape of the cathedral was an 'X' with a statue of each of the gods at the end of the branches. I remembered some of my lessons as I tried to place where each of the gods stood. Aonara faced east while Ciarden faced west; Rhia sat to the north and Hanwen to the south. All four were carved out of the same basalt stone, and none struck me as a particularly welcoming likeness compared to the drawings in the pamphlets the Myriad passed out. I studied Aonara, trying to draw a comparison between the statue made out of this dark rock and the ethereal vision made of moonlight I'd seen before.

"We'll be alright, Emma. I was just here the other day. We'll drink from the font, go home, and prepare for the Cascade. One step at a time." He took my arm and planted one foot on the bottom-most stair, and I froze, my divinity's wild fragmented beating sending shivers up my spine. I was terrified.

"I can't." I was whispering again as I pulled away from Rain. Taking a step back, I looked at him, meeting his confused gaze with my frantic one.

"Em, we have to. We'll lose each other's divinity if we don't drink."

"We can just keep doing the Body ceremony."

"Emma, you know that's not how it works. Unless we complete the whole ceremony, it'll just wear off. You *know* this." Rain's voice was patient if firm. As if he was talking to a particularly stubborn child.

"You really don't feel that, do you?" Though it was dry, with not a cloud in the sky, something cool and wet dripped down the back of my neck, following the path of my spine. When I lifted my hand to wipe the water away, I found I was completely dry. What the hell was happening? What was this place? Rain's expression softened as he watched me before softly shaking his head. "Rain, I'm scared."

"I know. But you're one of the most courageous people I've ever met. If anyone can do this, it's you." He held out his arm again and waited. I knew he was right. My thoughts were drawn back to Miriam. The Myriad Mistress who looked me in the face, looked *her death* in the face, and prayed for me. She had made a choice in the face of fear, to do the right thing, whatever it was. The least I could do was honor her memory and show courage in the face of fear, of the Myriad, to do what I needed to do. We didn't have a choice if we wanted to share our abilities. And to protect Elora, I'd utilize every advantage we could get our hands on. And then after, after it was done, we would utilize our advantage to figure out what Filenti was doing, to avenge the woman who looked death in the eye and comforted her.

While inside, I wouldn't be able to hear heartbeats or heal anyone, and the thought made me feel naked and vulnerable. That was likely the reason for the debilitating energy my divinity was giving off, nothing more. Or at least that was what I needed to convince myself. I took Rain's arm and a deep breath.

"Let's hurry." I steeled myself, attempting to create the courageous person he claimed I was before we quickly climbed the stairs.

CHAPTER 46

I COUNTED THE STEPS as we walked. There were ninety-seven leading to the twin set of wooden doors, each of which were easily twice Rain's height. When we reached the top, I tilted my head back to look at the pointed arch above the doors. Within it, recessed into the wall, was a detailed relief sculpted into the stone. Larger than the rest of the figures within the scene, Aonara and Ciarden were in the middle, performing a handfasting ceremony. Rhia and Hanwen were on either side, encased in ornamental circles. Rhia held two babes, one in each arm, while Hanwen held a shield and spear. To the side of each door, there was a bust of a drake, jutting from the wall. Both beasts had their maws open in a silent scream, each tooth nearly as long as my forearm. Drakes were creatures of myth and nightmares, monstrosities created by the gods and for the gods, only walking the earth during the time of their creators. If the sculptures were any indication of their size, drakes would easily have been as tall as the giant doors which stood in front of us. The stories told us they were creatures of muscle and aggression—determined destruction in the form of sinew and scale. The monster to my left had spikes rising from the center of its skull, moving toward its spine. The other creature had twin horns jutting out from either side of its massive head. Hanwen was often depicted riding one into battle, he and his mount standing tall over the men who sat on horseback on either side. I shuddered at the thought.

 A low creak came from one of the doors, drawing my attention. I'd been trying to ignore the dread stemming from my chaotic divinity, but seeing the cloaked and covered novice standing in the door, beckoning us forward, I latched onto Rain like a lifeline. My fingers dug into his arm much deeper than was likely comfortable, but he pulled me along patiently. We stepped over the threshold, and the door shut behind us, taking all of the air in the room with it. I truly struggled to breathe for a moment as my eyes adjusted to the deep dark within the cathedral. The high chandeliers set in the ceiling did little to lighten the space, their flame barely able to puncture the quiet dark below it. It was stifling. I reached for the well of my divinity and found nothing—the thrum gone, the connection snapped. I felt for those tiny golden threads between Rain and I and nearly fainted at their absence. I clutched him tighter, knowing our only way through this was forward. He placed his other hand atop mine and brushed his thumb in gentle circles over the back of my hand. I felt his gaze on me but knew if I met his eyes, I'd lose control of my frenzied emotions. I was barely holding it together, the intense discomfort something that made me nauseated and terrified to my core.

As my eyes adjusted, I was able to take in the impressive display of architectural perfection before us. I could see clear across the length of the cathedral, an open space from the entryway all the way to the opposite end filled with countless chairs for worshippers. The space was bracketed on either side by an arcade, the tall, pointed arches reaching easily fifteen meters from the ground. The ceiling itself was made of intersecting pointed arches, ribs dark against the light-colored plaster. The novice led us toward the right arcade, our footsteps muffled by the long carpet stretching the length of path, passing through to the northernmost section of the cathedral. Moving beneath another pointed arch, we made our way through to a giant library filled with ancient texts, the scent of old parchment wafting through the room. The ceiling wasn't as high in this room as it was in the main part of the cathedral, but books covered every bit of available wall space.

"They're taking us straight to the Supreme," Rain whispered, his voice barely a breath as he held my hand tightly on his arm, attempting to lace his fingers through my white-knuckled digits.

Leading us down a darkened hallway, the torchlight on the walls doing little to illuminate the dark stones, the novice brought us before a closed door and rapped their knuckles lightly before turning and walking away.

"Is that our royal visitor?" The voice I heard was weaker than I anticipated. I'd heard stories of the Supreme, and though most tales spoke of a kind and wizened man, there were quite a few portraying him as cunning and headstrong. Rain dropped the arm I held onto and grasped my hand firmly. He caught my gaze, his emerald eyes nearly black in the dim lighting but glittering with life all the same. His expression told me to have faith in him, his eyes promising safety and resolution I wasn't sure he could give. Nonetheless, I would trust him.

Rain opened the door and pulled us into the room, nodding to the Supreme. Following his lead, I did the same, not sure what proprieties we were supposed to offer each other. The room was lit better than the cathedral itself, one chandelier hanging down to light the space. Rich earth tones filled the room; sage curtains hung from the narrow window, a rust-colored rug, plush, laid beneath our feet, and the furniture was made of deep walnut. It was cozy and warm, a fire crackling behind the grate.

"Your Holiness." Rain spoke the words, and I quietly murmured the same.

"Your Highnesses, congratulations are in order." The smile the Supreme gave was warm, matching the deep brown eyes watching with curiosity and a joviality which surprised me. The man who stood before us was only a bit taller than I was, dressed in the white robes I was accustomed to from members of the Myriad. I knew the Supreme was a conduit, gifted in divinity not dissimilar to my own. My original divinity. He was a healer and a renowned one at that. I wondered how he could possibly stand to be in this place all hours of the day, to live in it, unable to use his divinity unless he ventured outside. I pushed the thought away, realizing again that I seemed to be much more affected than the other conduits who stood with me. The Supreme chuckled, pulling both of our empty hands toward him, and I was struck by how cold and smooth his hand was. As the Supreme, he had drunk from the font without performing the bonding ritual, supposedly granted divine permission from the gods. Though his face told of age perhaps a decade older than Rain, I knew he was far older. His dark brown hair was cropped short, allowing me to see a gnarled scar going from ear to ear over the crown of his head. His smile was kind, and his voice reminded me of my father—from when I was a small child, the voice that soothed when I'd gotten a scrape, the voice that stayed calm when he mediated mine and Lucia's arguments. It helped, this calming presence when my divinity felt strangled.

He held each of our hands in one of his and closed his eyes, head tilted toward the heavens, and began to chant. It was a language I didn't know, but the cadence told me it was an old language, one ours may have been fully rooted into. I watched him curiously, this performance a distraction from the absence of the thrumming that had been part of me for as long as I could remember. Finally, his eyes opened, and he smiled.

"A blessing for you both," he explained as he let go of our hands. "Now, do either of you have any questions for me before I escort you to the font?"

Rain startled, the jolt of his arm imperceptible to anyone but me.

"*You'll* be escorting us? I assumed it would be one of the masters taking us."

"It will be me." He smiled again, and I calmed a bit. There was something about him that soothed, making me second guess my trepidation. Being inside the building was still uncomfortable, but the Supreme himself was comforting. "I go when I deem it important. I anticipate the two of you will be King and Queen of Vesta soon enough and integral to—well, to quite a variety of plots."

Rain nodded, and though I could feel his uncertainty, his grip on my hand loosened the tiniest amount.

"No questions?" He looked between the two of us, and we stayed silent. "Well, off we trot." The Supreme clapped his hands together in a way that vividly reminded me of our old butler, Mr. Carson. The chipper tone accompanying the clap was jarring coming from the man who was in charge of the Myriad.

As he led us back down the darkened hallway, I practiced my nonchalance, wanting to bring up the prophecy in a manner that wouldn't be suspect. I didn't want to bring his attention to Elora too much or the fact I was curious. I felt like I could trust this man, but I knew from experience I couldn't trust anyone. Rain was the only person with who I felt that kind of trust, and even it was hard-won. We went back out through the library and crossed under one of the arches of the arcade before going toward the western side of the cathedral, away from the doors we came in. Off to the side of the massive empty space, near where the branches of the building crossed, there was a small door—barely noticeable. It was made out of a dark wood, perhaps black ebony, and it blended in with the stones around it.

Upon opening the door, the Supreme grabbed a lit torch off the wall and dipped it to the ground where the wall met the floor. There was a flash, and a trench of oil ignited, spiraling down a circular stairwell, the fire dancing across the top of the liquid, lighting our path. We walked for what felt like an hour, and I lost count of how many stairs there were. I was pleasantly surprised as the stifling of my divinity lessened the farther we descended. I could feel the thrum in me returning, and I couldn't help but smile, feeling better almost instantaneously.

Finally, the Supreme took a step down and then forward, no longer descending in a dizzying spiral. We were at the bottom of the steps, and I couldn't see a single thing. I stopped, closing my eyes, and I could barely see in my subconscious the thin threads of gold connecting me to Rain. I heard a snap of fingers accompanied by a whooshing sound and opened my eyes.

Candles. Hundreds of candles in an underground cave.

And a stream.

I sucked in a breath, and Rain stepped behind me, putting both of my hands in his and resting his chin on my shoulder. "The stairs are right there, and we have our divinity again. We can rift out, Em." His thumbs rubbed circles over the backs of my hands while his words soothed me, the heat of his breath warming my ear.

"It is a bit . . . *dank* down here. We have a piping system, of course, that brings it up into the cathedral, and we send barrels to the various temples. But I assumed since you both came all the way here, you wanted the purest form of their gift."

The Supreme sounded reverent, and it was clear the man had a great respect for the gift the gods had granted.

"Of course, Your Holiness. Thank you." My voice surprised me, not coming out as high and squeaky as I thought it would, but calm and measured.

He nodded, watching me almost curiously in the candlelight. "Your daughter may be the Beloved, is that right?"

I felt my body tense as Rain squeezed my hands tighter. "She may be. I've never brought her to a temple."

"Yes, after the tragedy with your sister, that does not surprise me. I hope you'll allow me to apologize, though it was no fault of the Myriad. It was most distressing to hear the tale." The sad smile he gave me seemed genuine, but the words he said had a ring of something other than pity. Something which almost bordered on amusement. I didn't like it.

"It was rather distressing to live it, Your Holiness." My voice was sharper than I'd intended. The man had been kind and comforting upstairs, and things had gone much better than I expected. It would do me no good to ruin it now. "Actually, I was wondering if you had any of the original translations of the prophecy I could share with my daughter? As I'm sure you know, she's been taken, but the second we get her back, I wanted to make up for lost time and help prepare her for the responsibility."

The Supreme eyed me warily, maybe uncertain of my intentions after I'd snapped at him. I hoped my tone was apologetic enough.

"I believe I can spare a text that contains the original translation for the Beloved. Though, I'd give it only with the understanding you'd bring her to me personally to determine if she is the true Beloved or not."

I felt a warm bead of sweat trickle down my spine at the thought.

"Yes, Your Holiness, of course." Rain answered for me, pressing his chest against my back, steadying me. He knew we would do no such thing, and he lied directly to the Supreme's face.

"Good!" The Supreme clapped, the smile back on his face. "Let us perform the ritual of the Soul, quench your thirst, and send you on your way."

He turned around, hopping over the thin rivulet of stream, and I nearly snorted in amusement. First clapping, now hopping. The stream was small, no wider than my arm, and it wound in and out of the lit path. We walked for a few moments before finally making our way to an open circle surrounded by candles. I expected a small sort of pond to be at the center, but when we reached it, I was shocked to discover it was barely more than a puddle.

The Supreme pulled a few items out of his robes, and my divinity sensed them before I could see them. Another dagger and a goblet. This dagger was different than the one Shivani used, but it felt the same. I wanted both items desperately. I wanted to touch them, to take them.

"Kneel." The Supreme gestured to the small puddle on the ground below us, the quiet bubble of water from the font pulsing. Rain and I knelt on either side of the font, facing each other.

"With this final declaration, the two who kneel before the font choose to complete the ritual, joining the Mind, Body, and Soul as one. They make an offering of their lifeblood to the gods and to one another, forging an unbreakable bond betwixt and between them." The Supreme spoke quietly, holding the dagger outstretched in one hand and the goblet in the other. The flickering of candlelight made it impossible to read his expression, but it twisted his features into a darker version of the man from before. He took Rain's hand and eyed his palm. "Oh. You could have healed that."

"We weren't sure if we were supposed to or not." My husband's voice was sheepish as if being reprimanded.

"Now, now, young man. Were you not paying attention when we last met?" The Supreme's tone was chiding, and I felt vaguely unsettled. He'd been a soothing spirit when we were in the cathedral, but now he was grating against my nerves. He hummed before pricking Rain's fingertip, drawing a single drop of blood. "One drop in the goblet, then rinse your hand in the font."

Rain did as he was told, and the motions were repeated for me. When I rinsed my fingertip in the water, it stung the tiniest bit, and I could see a slight shimmering on my finger as it healed instantly, my palm not far behind. The Supreme bent down then, dipping the goblet into the font, filling it.

"Drink, and be one." The Supreme smiled down at us as he passed the goblet to Rain. He took a long swallow before passing the goblet to me, the candlelight shining in his eyes showing the intense love and devotion he felt for me, and I knew he saw the same in my own. I raised the cup to my lips, watching him beam at me as I tipped it back. I nearly sputtered at the sulfurous taste mixed with something else, something sickly sweet. Dewalt had been right; it did taste like shit.

And then I felt it, the final thread. Gold and glowing and strong. I looked across the font at Rain, a soft smile forming on his face. He felt it too. I reached out with my divinity, letting it glide across the threads and felt his meet mine in the middle. Where mine felt warm and light, his felt cool and grounded. A perfect balance. A dance, a meeting, a merging. I could feel a surge of excitement coming from across the thread, and I startled, realizing I could feel Rain's emotion. He laughed then, his smile wide and open, likely feeling my surprise on the other end of the thread. Dewalt and Lavenia hadn't mentioned that. I wondered if Rain had known to expect it, thus his amusement. He stood, pulling me up into a chaste kiss, and I let myself relax the tiniest bit.

When we left Lamera, we both heaved a sigh of relief. Neither of us wanted to be there any longer, and I was more than disappointed—I'd failed to get any sort of book from the Supreme which could offer more insight into the prophecy.

After drinking from the font, the Supreme escorted us back to his library and office. He pulled out several books for us to sift through, all of them barely held together by their bindings. I knew they were at least a thousand years old, some even more. The Supreme opened each book to various sections and translated the more formal language into something we were better able to understand. It wasn't that the language was foreign, but it was from a time when it was slightly different. Some of it meant the same, and yet some of it was slightly changed, just enough to distort the meaning minutely. It was fascinating and overwhelming at the same time. Though I wanted to leave desperately, the awful leaching of my divinity almost more painful when we came back up from the font, a part of me wanted to stay and pore over the texts with the Supreme helping translate what I read. Eventually though, Rain and I decided it was time to leave. It was an unspoken agreement, eye contact made that we were both able to interpret perfectly.

But when I asked the Supreme which tome he'd lend us, I realized I misunderstood his offer.

"Why, my dear, I told you I would lend it out *only* if you brought her to me so I could determine if she indeed was the Beloved. I'm sorry if there has been some sort of misunderstanding?" He held out his hands in supplication and glanced back and forth apologetically between the two of us. "I simply cannot lend these out to just anyone." He paled then before clearing his throat. "Not that you two are just anyone, but I shouldn't lend these out at all. I planned on making an exception if she were the Beloved, but . . ." He trailed off, his meaning clear. He would not be letting us take any of the books with us. Rain was poised to argue, but I gave him a look. We could not appear too eager.

"I understand. Thank you for showing us what you have. I wish we could stay longer; I'd truly love to learn more from you. Perhaps when we return with Elora, we can accompany her for a lesson with you." While I did wish to learn more from him, bringing Elora back here was out of the question.

"It would be my pleasure." The Supreme stood, brushing his palms down his robes in a surprisingly common gesture. "Now, let me have a novice bring you something to eat on your travels."

When the Supreme left the room, Rain and I shared a glance before standing. It would do us no good to speak of it while still inside the cathedral, but I was sure Rain could feel my disappointment even without the bond, muted by the lava-stone once more. I took a few steps over to inspect the display of gears and statuettes which sat on a handsome sideboard at the back of the Supreme's office—bending down to take a closer look. I pressed the small button at the base, and it sprung into action. The miniature gods were on display in a moving clockwork of gears and platforms, and they spun, interacting with each other in turn before spinning back to their original location. I had watched three revolutions by the time the Supreme came back.

"Ah, I see you've found my kinetica. A rather neat, little toy."

Rain came up behind me to look as well. "Where did you get this? It's incredible." Rain's voice was true, and I smiled at his appreciation. When the man was in awe of something, it showed. He was easy to read in that regard, and I found joy in his delight.

"It was a gift. From your father's first bride, actually."

Rain's head shot up. King Soren's first wife was a subject no one dared to bring up in Vesta. For fear of death, or worse.

"Yes, I knew Larke, and I was rather fond of her. We studied together when we were children until her sister died. Your father was promised a bride as part of the treaty, and Larke had to abandon her studies with the Myriad to fulfill the Folterran's end of it." His gaze was far off when he spoke. "She was brilliant, one of a kind. She made this herself." His smile was sad as he traced a finger across the bottom platform. He sighed before turning to us.

"The novice in the entry will have your basket packed. I hope you have safe travels, and I will pray to the gods about your success at the Cascade." The Supreme took my hands and squeezed before sending us on our way.

It was hours later, after I'd successfully rifted us from the well to the apple tree, when I felt Rain's trepidation through the bond. He'd been quiet, almost lost in thought during our trip back, and I didn't push him. His feelings had changed frequently, and I worked on learning to block it out like I could with harrowing, not wanting to invade his privacy. But finally, I decided he had enough time to dwell on whatever it was that was responsible for his eddying thoughts. I turned to where he sat with his back against the tree and was about to speak, when he interrupted me.

"I got you something." His voice was quiet, but I could hear and even feel the mischief coming from him.

"Oh, really? Nicked something from the Seat, did you?" I chuckled as I approached him, guessing he meant something else with his words, and I'd be met with a kiss, knowing full well he hadn't had the time to get me anything at all.

"Actually, yes." He grinned as I sat down on the ground across from him. It was night, the new moon swiftly approaching, and it was difficult to make out his features. I stared at him in confusion as he opened up his jacket, digging through one of the inner pockets.

I gasped as he placed his gift in my hands. "You didn't! Rain, are you kidding?" I was in shock. I could feel the amusement mixing with a bit of hesitation coming from him as I looked down at the book in my lap. I traced my fingers over the title, remembering the lesson the Supreme had given only hours before. "*The Divine Instruction*? When?" The slim text had only a hundred or so pages in it, and the book itself was barely larger than my opened hands in which it sat.

"When he was worrying about our dinner, and you were distracted by the kinetica." He gave me a sheepish grin.

"Rain, he's going to notice! He probably already has!" I reprimanded him even though I was secretly elated he'd taken the book. I felt a tug of amusement down the bond and realized he'd felt my excitement, counteracting my rebuke. I studied the book, flipping through its pages. I needed to know what was in it. I needed to know exactly what was expected from me. I couldn't help it as I looked up from the book and smiled at him, though his expression wasn't the same grin from before.

"Yes, well, I've been thinking about that. First thing, what's he going to do? Start a war with Vesta over a book? With what army? We can deny it or take the blame and apologize, play it off as a hysterical mother worried about her daughter."

"You can't be serious." I glared at him, making sure to let all of my anger seethe through the bond. A hysterical mother? He'd been the one to take it, not me! Hysterical father, more like! And then I was mad all over again, at myself this time, for being unable to control my emotions. The swell of joy that flew through the bond at the thought of him being a hysterical father would only encourage him further.

Gods, how am I supposed to keep up with my spinning head?

"I'm teasing, dear heart." He gave me a wicked grin, surely having felt the dizzying emotions I was sending toward him. His expression sobered before he continued. "Second thing, I don't trust him."

I looked at him in confusion. The Supreme had seemed infinitely warmer than I thought he would have been. He'd only made me uncomfortable once, but it had been about Lucia. Any time anyone who didn't know her spoke of her, it made my blood run cooler. But the way he spoke to us before the font, and our time spent studying texts, even the way he spoke of Larke, all of it made me trust him more. But Rain had felt the opposite, and I wondered why.

"Em, I never told him about going to the Cascade. He surely has spies in the palace, and then the way he talked about—" He paused, clearing his throat before he spoke again, voice quieter. "Larke. It was odd. No one talks about her at all, let alone fondly. If my father ever found out he spoke of her, that he was keeping trinkets she'd made? My father has not been a good man late into his reign, but he used to be. Larke—she was never good." He shook his head. "Obviously, he never spoke of her to him, or all of Lamera would be nothing but rubble."

"Do you know anything about Larke? I've always been curious."

"Barely. Other than father killing her, of course, what the Supreme said was the most I've ever heard about her. Mother told me she committed atrocities Father wouldn't even speak of." I nodded, confirming the same. It itched at me, not knowing anything else about the Folterran princess who was supposed to end the centuries-long feud with Vesta but somehow only fueled it further and died for it. With Soren on his deathbed, I wondered if anyone would ever know.

"Besides all of that, I asked him to show *us* the prophecy, and he declined. I could understand if he didn't want us to take it to the palace and show Elora, but to not show us in his study? As he said, we are very soon to be the ruling monarchs. I don't like it. So, I took it, and we're going to read it now and leave it here."

"We can't just leave it here!" I couldn't believe he wanted to leave one of the oldest books to have ever existed out here in the middle of a field.

"I'll put it in the basket and encase it in stone, and we'll bury it under the tree."

I rose a brow, dubious. "And what, we're going to memorize it?"

"Yes. We aren't going to leave this tree until we have it memorized. It's getting cold, though, so come here." He took the book from me and set it down in the grass beside him, to my horror, and then pulled me into his lap. I promptly snatched the book from the dampening grass and held it open in my hands.

Thankfully, this tome had a bit more modern language in it. Showing Rain my neat trick with the glowing fingertip, I had him skip to the end, showing us the pages that the Supreme stayed away from.

When I finally found it, I read it three times, certain I wasn't reading the right thing. Rain, feeling my shock and confusion, leaned around me and pulled the book a bit closer to him so he could see and read it out loud.

The Beloved and the Accursed: two sides of one coin,
Blessed by the gods, lives forever adjoined.
Both touched by the light and the dark,
With wrath's caress and fecundity's mark;
Bloom, blood, and bone are the ties which bind
The betrayer, body, and bane to their future descried.
One will wrest peace from the grips of such blight,
While the other will do naught but turn from the light;
In each hand, they hold the death of another
And the fate of the kingdoms bound by lovers.

I felt his shock mirror my own, and my breaths quickened. I started to jump up, but Rain wrapped his arms tightly around me, holding me in his lap. The pressure of his arms on me might have made me feel trapped in any other situation, but the tight grasp he had on me grounded me. The Beloved wasn't only blessed by Aonara, but by all four of the gods. I knew Rhia had given me Elora, but I couldn't recall ever seeing Ciarden or Hanwen in a vision as I'd seen the goddesses. Maybe I wasn't the Beloved. Maybe the Beloved didn't even exist—yet. Something like relief coursed through my veins, but the mention of an Accursed made it fall flat. The prophecy spoke of two individuals. If I was interpreting it correctly, both the Beloved *and* the Accursed were blessed by all four of the gods. And as for the part about bones and blood, I had no idea what any of that meant.

Was the Supreme guarding the prophecy as a secret? What we'd just read was not what had been taught. Is that why he had been unwilling to show it to us? Did the Masters and Mistresses know too? If they did, why did they ever think Lucia was the Beloved? Lucia might have been blessed by Aonara, but none of the other gods, that was certain. The questions and confusion ran rampant and untethered through my mind. I could feel Rain's worry and confusion as well. He held me close, and I focused on his heartbeat, counting the beats as I'd done so many times before.

"I'm not the Beloved," I whispered, my voice flat.

"You still could be, Em. At the absolute least, you're blessed by the goddesses." Rain's tone surprised me. I couldn't quite place it, and the emotion I felt from the bond wasn't helping me. If I had to guess, he was optimistic.

"We don't want me to be the Beloved, right? Rain, I don't want anything to do with being a harbinger of war or involving myself in the Accursed turning from the light."

"Right. We don't want you involved in that if we can help it."

"What aren't you saying, Rain?"

"The last set of twin flames was recorded a millennium ago, before the Great War. I looked it up. What are the odds we are twin flames, *and* you've been blessed by the goddesses, and that's all there is to it?" I wanted to argue with him, but he held up his hand, cutting me off. "Even if you're not the Beloved, you are more important than many other conduits alive today. When it comes down to it, if there were a war, you'd be involved. Besides, it's possible you could become the Beloved one day. We always were taught it was from birth, but clearly, some of the things we learned were wrong."

I watched him quietly, unease coursing through me as he spoke.

"All I'm getting at is, don't get too comfortable with the idea you aren't the Beloved. I'm not certain. And if you are? If this prophecy is correct? You need to be prepared. We all do."

CHAPTER 47

We didn't rift back to the palace but instead went to Rain's home. Our home. It wasn't an easy thing, training my mind to view the place as mine as well. I supposed I'd need to retrieve my belongings from my home in Brambleton and bring them here after Elora decided if she wanted to stay or not. I couldn't imagine a situation where she'd prefer to go to Ravemont after how she reacted during our last meeting, but it was possible. Knowing she wasn't the Beloved made things better for her. I would relieve her of the belief as soon as possible and hoped it would help lessen the weight of my omissions. I was uncertain, though, of how to break the news to her that Rain was her father. And how would we tell Lavenia and Shivani? Would they even believe me? There wasn't *that* much resemblance between the two of them, and it was certainly possible Faxon was her father, or else I wouldn't have believed it all these years. It was going to be a shock. And, of course, the news would have to be shared with the citizens of Vesta eventually. Though I'd been called a whore often enough I was relatively nonplussed, being viewed as such by the public was a bit different. I would be their queen one day. As I collapsed on the sofa in the living room, I felt Rain's worry through the bond.

"You're thinking awfully loud, Em."

"Life has changed a lot in the last day, and I'm just trying to keep up." I gave him a soft smile when he lifted my legs and sat down under them. I'd slipped my shoes off before I sat, not some sort of heathen to put my filthy boots up on the fine cream sofa, and Rain took the opportunity to rub my feet. It had been a long day. I'd grown more and more confident in my rifting throughout our travels, and I was shocked I'd been able to pick it up so quickly. But now, my head had a slight ache, and the chandelier felt extra bright. When we arrived, Sterling had already retired to his rooms, and I didn't even know how late it was anymore. When Rain's strong thumbs pushed against the arches of my feet, I felt my eyes roll back as I nestled further into the comfortable pillows beneath me. I felt warmth down the bond and peeked one eye open to look at Rain.

"I'll never get used to this. Feeling your love for me this way. Why didn't you tell me?"

"How would I have known?"

"I figured Lavenia and Dewalt would have said something." He studied me for a moment, his hands stilling.

"This isn't... normal. I assumed it had something to do with being twin flames. Maybe the font helped expand the connection?"

"Oh. I thought—well, it doesn't matter what I thought. Huh." I was surprised, expecting this sort of connection to be present between all bonded conduits. It was rather convenient. I supposed it only made sense that we'd have something special about our bond. Still, it was a bit overwhelming to feel so unique. I laid there, letting his hands relax me, and I sank into his touch, my eyes growing heavy.

"Emmeline! Go to sleep!" The voice was far away, almost as if it were at the end of a long tunnel. I opened my eyes and looked around, wondering where it came from.

"Did you hear that?" I asked Rain, and he blinked at me before shrugging and shaking his head. "I swear someone just told me to go to sleep."

"Considering it's after midnight, it's not a bad—" He stopped, and I felt his panic a half-second before he spoke, turning to me with wild eyes and a paling face. "Cyran."

"Oh gods, do you think? It was a man." I slammed my eyes shut and tried to focus on the voice, willing him to talk to me again or pull me into slumber. I didn't hear him again, no matter how hard I tried. I wondered if I only heard him the first time because I was on the edge of sleep. But how could I possibly expect to fall asleep now? Terror and adrenaline rushed through me, and I knew it would be impossible.

"Emma, breathe with me. Calm down. We need to get you to sleep." His racing heart erupted through my thoughts, and I knew he was just as worried as I was. I waited for a few moments, trying desperately to calm down to be able to fall asleep, and I couldn't. "I can try to slow your heart if you want me to."

"No. I don't even trust myself doing it." But what he said gave me an idea.

"Take my breath. Rain. Take my air." He was going to have to make me sleep. I didn't particularly want to get punched into a comatose state, so the thought of cutting off my air supply was the next best thing. Just enough to make me pass out, just enough to connect me with the man who had my daughter. I couldn't think of another way.

"No, Em, what the hell?" His falsely calm demeanor shattered as he shouted at me. I inhaled a deep breath, trying to soothe us both.

"I'm clearly not going to be able to do it on my own, and we need to know if it was Cyran and find out what he wanted to tell us. Take my air until I pass out. You'll know I'm alright when I start breathing again, and you'll be able to hear my heart. Then wake me up in a few minutes?" I was sitting up, awkwardly pulling my feet out of his lap as he watched me, eyes dangerous.

"I don't like it." His brow was furrowed, and he squeezed my ankle.

"Well, me neither, Rain! But it has to be done." I laid back down, waiting for him to do it. "Don't warn me, j—"

Air whipped out of my mouth, and I felt my throat clamp down while I tried to inhale deeply, against my better sense. I didn't want to fight it; I wanted to sink deep into unconsciousness and quickly, but my body wasn't having it. I was only a little bit scared, though, knowing it would pass, and I'd be asleep soon. He wouldn't kill me, and we had to see what was happening. I tried to channel the calm my logical brain was experiencing while the animal inside me bucked at the pressure. I reached down, trying to grab Rain's hand. Finally, as he hovered over me, his voice a soothing caress of words I couldn't understand, the edges of my vision began to blacken, and I closed my eyes.

"Emmeline! Finally! Get to the Cascade!" It was black, and I couldn't see anything. Cyran's voice echoed in the space, and I didn't even feel my body. It felt distinctly like being on the verge of sleep, that quiet ease into unconsciousness before your body jerks, bringing you back from the brink of temporary death. But I didn't wake up.

"Where are you? Where's Elora?" The panic which had taken over my body moments before was now taking over my mind.

"I'm trying to stay asleep. We're on our way—early. He took Elora, and I'm trying to figure out where she is. Get there *now*!" Cyran was panicking, and I reached out, wondering if I could hear his heartbeat. I was unnerved, scared this could be a trap.

His heart was pounding so fast I could barely distinguish it into separate beats.

"Ships and on foot. A thousand men. Hurry!"

I plummeted, falling through the dark, awareness of my body slipping back into my mind. I sat up, gasping for breath, Rain coming into blurry focus. I felt my hands snake up to my throat against their will, clutching to get air. I took a deep breath through tears, and rasping, I managed to get out the words he needed to hear.

"Go. Now. Cascade."

Within an hour, we were assembled with Rain's guard at the barracks. There were hundreds of soldiers stationed at the Cascade thanks to his careful maneuvering since we'd been in Astana, but we were still outnumbered. I wasn't sure how Rain intended to do it, but our plan was to take the same path he and I traveled earlier that day, maintaining the rifts so the entire guard could get through. I wasn't sure we could do it and still arrive, divinity reasonably untapped, ready for whatever might happen when we got there. What I was sure of was I hadn't had a chance to let the panic and hysteria climb up any further. We didn't have the time. The minute I got words out to Rain, he'd disappeared through a rift to rouse Dewalt and the others before rifting straight to the barracks. It took me a few minutes to catch my breath without pain, and I had to drink an entire pitcher of water, the dryness in my throat causing me to cough incessantly. With Rain at the barracks preparing his men, Dewalt and Lavenia ran to ready the horses, and Mairin came running into my bedroom in a harried state, under the impression from Rain that he'd left me unconscious and barely breathing. By the time we rode in, not traveling by rift to save my divinity, the guard was nearly ready.

Thyra found me shortly after we arrived, carrying a heavy chest with Dickey. When it slammed down, Dickey was on his knees in a heartbeat, opening it. I felt a lump in my throat when I realized it was my armor. I knew I'd be wearing it at the Cascade, but the reality was staring me in my face. I looked up and found Rain's gaze on mine as he spoke to one of his men. He gave me a quick nod, and I felt something like pride push across the bond to me. Swearing, Thyra pulled out a padded garment from the trunk, having to tug a bit to pull it out, and she brought it to me, strapping it across my chest. It was almost like a tunic, and I knew it would protect me from the harsh angles and metal of the breastplate. Between the two of them, they had me fully armored within minutes. I was grateful for Dickey, knowing I'd chosen my squire well when he brought out all my weapons and let me choose which ones to arm myself with. Thyra, to my surprise, was braiding my hair back similar to hers but let most of it hang loose down my back.

"A warrior queen." She murmured it, more to herself than to me, as she faced me with a small pot of black paint, shoving her thumb into it and swiping it in a thick line across my eyes and bridge of my nose before she dragged a bit down my cheek from under each eye. Thyra repeated the process with her own eyes before quietly turning back to the now-empty chest on the ground, carrying it away to the barracks. I glanced around, noticing none of the other female soldiers wore the same paint, and I felt humbled, knowing she chose to share her traditions with me and found me worthy of them.

I glanced down and let out a shaky breath; I looked every bit the warrior queen she'd labeled me. My sapphire cloak from Rain billowed around me, and the dark armor seemed almost black. The hair Thyra hadn't braided blew in the wind as well but stayed out of my face. I caught the gaze of a few of his soldiers, who all peered at me with deference, but I could feel a quizzical, if not dubious, nature about their glance. I realized, to them, I was a princess. A future queen. The only useful version of me they'd seen was when I picked off a tírrúil with an arrow and then brought one down with my touch after it had thrown me to the ground. A few had witnessed my spar with Rain, but I hadn't yet proved anything to most of them. Compared to Lavenia, who they'd known and fought beside for years, and Queen Shivani, who was renowned for her unique abilities, I was untested, no more than a royal who barely deserved to be there. I was the reason for all of this—the upheaval of troops and traipse across the continent. I'd known some of his guard might have resented me, and I'd been upset about it before. I had asked these people to risk their lives. Granted, the Cascade was worth protecting in its own right, but I couldn't help feeling responsible. I tilted my chin up, pulling myself up to my full height, though it was not much, and purposefully made eye contact with each soldier who would meet my gaze. I tried to show my pride in them, my confidence. These people were looking to me now, either for encouragement or to question my tenacity. I would give them what they needed to the best of my abilities.

Rain finally blew out one of his coded whistles signaling our departure as he made his way to me. I felt his gaze track over me in assessment. His emotions pushing down the bond were too numerous and fluid to pinpoint exactly, but the one I felt most clearly was determination as he approached. He wore armor as well, and my chest tightened as I took him in. His breastplate matched mine, the darkened steel hammered to perfection. But where mine had the intricate floral etchings, feminine yet deadly, his was simple. There was no need for it, its purpose solely to protect his body. His appearance promised pain and retribution, and I basked in the knowledge that he would bring it to those who took our daughter from us.

"I'm going to do the last rift into the Cascade, and I want you as rested as you can be. So, that means you need to get us to our apple tree, dear heart."

I nodded, ignoring the fact that my divinity wasn't at its full capacity because of all the rifting we'd done before. I didn't have a choice. I knew both Rain and I would fight through a headache and more. I knew we would fight to the death for her, divinity used and gone, or not. But the fact we'd both be tapped when we got there was unsettling. I pushed aside the nervousness, knowing there was no point in it. We were doing this, getting to the Cascade and retrieving our daughter.

The guard was organized into two rows, and I walked to the front where Dewalt and Lavenia were at the head of each line, waiting for us. When I opened the rift, it wasn't quite as wide as it needed to be for the two lines to go through at once, so Dewalt led his line first until Rain came up behind me, putting his hands on my hips and his breath on my ear. His touch strengthened me; I felt the way our divinity pooled together, opening a deeper well inside of me. His whisper in my ear guided me through stretching the piercing of reality a bit wider, and Lavenia began leading her line of soldiers through as Dewalt's line finished up. When Rain and I followed through, I let the rift close behind me. The squeeze he gave my hip as we walked through told me he wouldn't be letting go until we got to the Cascade, likely realizing the benefit of the connection. Opening it with him wasn't nearly as taxing as opening one by myself.

By the time we reached the docks at Nara's Cove—hours later—my divinity wasn't nearly as tapped as I thought it would be. I had a mild headache, only slightly worse than what I'd had before Cyran's illusion. Since Rain and I had held onto each other during each rift, we were able to move and recover faster. It had taken the two of us nearly twice as long earlier in the day, but we didn't have that kind of time now. Dawn was breaking, and I stared out across the water, straining my eyes, knowing full well I wouldn't be able to see land, let alone the Cascade. The guard picked up some rations, certain that once we rifted inside the fortress, most would stay there and defend it, and rations in case of a siege would not go unused. I felt for my weapons, anxious to use them and terrified of needing to. I didn't bother with my bow, opting to carry as lightly as possible, knowing the moment I spotted Elora, I'd abandon the battle, and I'd need my sword to cut through the thick of it. As the sun fully breached the horizon, illuminating the sky more and more, I felt Rain's presence next to me. He spotted it when I did.

"Smoke." I felt him tense, and the sharp tang of fear made its way down our bond.

Just there, on the horizon, almost imperceptible, there was a cloud of black smoke. It seemed too close to shore to be from the Cascade, but I inhaled a sharp breath. We needed to go. It didn't matter what we'd be walking into. We needed to leave now. I started to pull Rain away, back toward the soldiers who were amassing supplies, before he stopped me.

"If they're not there already, they will be soon. I think the smoke is from the village." He shook his head, a shudder going through him. "I think they sacked Clearhill." The Folterrans had sacked their own town, full of women and children. The town that was supported by the money Rain's soldiers spent. That he'd worked hard to create peaceful relations with. It was left defenseless, its own men forced into the Folterran armies. Had there been men from Clearhill who destroyed their own village? Had the Folterrans protected their women, or were they considered traitors for fraternizing with the soldiers at the Cascade, doing what they could to survive? Rain drew a hand down his face before he looked at me.

"You stay safe in the fort until we get word on where Elora is, alright, Em?" I opened my mouth to argue, but he cut me off, putting his hands on either side of my face, bending down to meet my eyes. "Look, one of us has to be safe and protected so the minute, the *second*, we know where she is, we can get to her. I have to help lead my men, so you have to be the one who stays safe for our girl. In case I can't. Promise me."

I swallowed before nodding, his eyes burning into mine. The fear and love rolling between us almost tangible, I swore I could reach out and grab it. I took a deep breath before kissing him. Desperately. Like it could be the last time. As if, by making this promise with my lips, I was keeping a bigger one. Not a promise that I'd stay safe, but a promise we'd make it through this. We'd survive and find Elora. We'd be a family. We would have everything we should have always had. A life, friends, kindness, love.

"I promise."

CHAPTER 48

When Rain and I opened the rift into the Cascade, we were met with quiet chaos. The courtyard was full of soldiers, all working with purpose. With practiced efficiency, the guard who accompanied us went through the rift, lining up according to Dewalt's orders. Once the last soldier passed and we followed, Rain pulled me along, nodding to his soldiers already at the Cascade, as we made our way toward a man who was clearly in control—holding command over the organized madness to which we bore witness. He was a bit older, maybe mid-fifties, with a handsome face that looked accustomed to the expression he currently wore, the seriousness of the situation evident by his tight mouth and drawn brows. His sleek black hair was longer, flipping out around his ears, with grey peppering his temples. His cropped and tidy beard was more silver than black, and he met us with purpose, clasping Rain to him and slapping him on the back.

"You're here early, gerizëk." His accent was faint, Nythyrian if I had to guess, and his dark brown eyes held more warmth than the smile he gave Rain, tempered by the tick in his jaw and stress etched across his features. "My lady." The man took my hand and kissed it quickly before dropping it. "Raj Koli, it is a pleasure."

"*Your Highness* is Emmeline's appropriate address, Captain." Rain corrected gently, a small smile on his lips as he took in the surprised expression on his captain's face. "And if anything, you're the pain in my ass."

"Forgive me, Your Highness. I'd heard rumors from the men, but I thought I'd have been invited if they were true." Raj shot a glare toward Rain that I wasn't sure was as fake as his tone implied. "What do you think?" His eyes twinkled as they met mine. "Who is the true gerizëk?"

Rain laughed, and I smiled, quietly taking in their interactions. It almost seemed as if Raj were a mentor of sorts. "I'm sorry, brother. Things have been hectic, to say the least. What are we looking at here?" His tone turned serious, and the captain crossed his arms to match it.

"Twenty boats off the coast, maybe a thousand men. They burned Clearhill, and those on foot set up camp there with what supplies they didn't burn. Most of the people got out and came here. The elders and the children are in the central keep, and the women have been helping where they can. Two hundred men in Clearhill, all mercenaries from Skos. We'd just had a shipment, so we are prepared for a siege, but I'm worried about what they have on those ships. If they breach the walls, the supplies won't matter. I figured we'd just hold them off and bunker down in the keep if they made it through. I sent for you, but it appears you got my message before the bird even left."

As Rain nodded at his captain's report, our eyes were drawn upward as a screech filled the air, breaking the busy silence. A falcon circled above before it dived down, headed straight for us. Rain threw me behind him and pulled out his sword before the shifter could stand up. This man's change was almost instant, unlike Aedwyn's transition I'd witnessed. His dark umber skin was on display as he rearranged his body, so he was on his knees. I recognized him as one of Shivani's personal guards and breathed a sigh of relief.

"Soren is dead, Your Majesty. Long live the King!"

An intake of breath resounded around us, and Rain's eyes moved between the shifter and me with a look of surprise on his face. We'd known it was coming, but it wasn't something any of us expected to happen now.

A ripple of movement caught my eye as the soldiers around us fell down into a kneel, fists on their hearts. Shouts of "Long live the King" echoed within the courtyard, loud and tremendous. My breath caught in my throat as I saw a tear in Raj's eye as he began to kneel, and a wave of recognition crashed through me. Rain, my Rain, was the King of Vesta. A role he'd hold for centuries, a role he'd been born for. It was the first ascension to the throne in almost a millennium. I let go of his hand, and he stared at me, bewildered, as I sank down onto my knees, fist on my heart.

"No, no, no, no. What did I tell you about kneeling for me? You kneel for no one." He grabbed my wrists and pulled me back up fast enough I stumbled. He tugged me to his side, arm around my waist, before he shouted in triumph, hand fisted on his heart. "Long live the Queen!"

Everyone in the courtyard echoed him, and I felt nothing but pride coming down the bond. It was surreal. The role I'd never wanted, never prepared for, the role I'd hold by his side. I had no idea what I was doing, but based on the faces gathered around us, we gave them hope. Hope for something different, something better. I spotted Dewalt and Lavenia on the ground not far from us, with wide grins a slash across their faces. I spotted tears in Ven's eyes, and I wasn't sure if it was grief for her father or pride in her brother. Dewalt winked at me as Rain pulled me in tight against him, his fingertips anchoring my body to his.

"Now rise, and get back to work!" Rain's first order as king was followed with expediency. Everyone moved, including the shifter who made way over to us, his nudity no obstacle.

"King Soren died in his sleep early this morning. The queen just missed you and sent me in her stead." He paused and cleared his throat, looking at me before correcting himself. "I apologize for my error. The queen *mother* sent me."

I gave him a soft smile, assuring him I knew he meant no offense.

"She asked me to return quickly, but I can stay if you need me, Your Majesty." He stood up straighter, rolling his shoulders back, eager to help his new king.

"No, Warric. Go back. Actually, I have a message I'd like you to give her from me, and I do not want you to tell anyone else. If I catch wind anyone other than you or the queen mother knows this information, it is your tongue I will come after first. Understood?"

Rain squeezed my hand, and I looked at him in confusion. What message was he sending? Warric nodded but seemed uneasy.

"I want you to tell her Emmeline's daughter is my child. By blood."

I was surprised the shifter's face didn't change much with this revelation, though it grew heavy with trepidation. My face, on the other hand, was likely one of shock. I knew we'd eventually have to tell her. But now? Why was everything happening *now*?

"Yes, Your Majesty. Anything else?"

"I'm sure you can anticipate her reaction may not be pleasant. But please make sure to pass on my sincerity and know we will answer any questions she might have as soon as we return." Warric nodded and was in the air within a moment. Rain turned to me, amusement flickering in my direction.

"She needed to know; best to let her find out when we aren't there." He shrugged and let out a quiet chuckle. I didn't know if I agreed with him, but I wasn't going to argue. There was no time to argue. Rain needed to be talking to Dewalt and Raj, deciding our best methods of defense. We were vastly outnumbered. Rain had been sending small regiments to the Cascade for the past week, but it was difficult to send them discreetly, so there were still two Folterrans to every one Vestian. We had no idea where Elora was, just that she was likely to be nearby. Was she on one of the boats or being held at Clearhill?

Rain pulled my hands into his and looked at me, pain in his eyes. "She needed to know because Elora is my heir, Emmeline. Since you're not of the royal bloodline, the crown would pass to her in the event of my death."

I flinched at his words, the thought of his death something I had no intention of entertaining on this day or any other. Especially not now, as we stood on the brink of a battle where we were outnumbered, and the stakes were so high. He pulled me close and pressed his lips against my temple as he felt what I was feeling, words escaping me as the thoughts ran rampant through my head.

Our moment was interrupted by a bellow from Raj, who had made his way to the battlement directly above the gate. Rain opened a rift above us and pulled me through. It felt like a waste of divinity, but I knew even a moment could be the difference between success and failure. Staring out to the sand and grass below us, I spotted the messenger.

One heavily-armored man on a horse. I glanced out toward the horizon and saw a small contingent of soldiers, but it was too far to count how many. Rain tensed next to me, a grim expression on his face, as he brought us closer to where Raj stood. The messenger called up with a heavily accented voice, thick and with a burr, his voice much louder than he should have been capable.

"King Dryul will be taking control of this fortress, as it is on Folterran lands. If you choose to surrender at this moment, he has promised a quick death. If you do not? It will be anything but. Either way, you will surrender."

I felt a trickle of dread down my spine as the man spoke. There was so much on the line. The lives of all the soldiers here, the citizens of Clearhill who must be viewed as traitors by now, Elora. I trusted Rain knew what he was doing, the Bloody Prince was a name known across the Three Kingdoms for a reason, but still. The fear was settling low in my stomach, and I had to focus to take measured breaths.

Rain, however, was a picture of calm. He approached one of his archers who had his bow already aimed, stationed at a crenel, looking through the gap at the messenger below.

"May I?" The soldier passed the bow into Rain's outstretched hand and positioned himself so his quiver faced his king. When Rain stepped forward to the gap, bow in hand, his face was hard. A picture of determination and rage. Ice and fire.

"Tell your king his death belongs to Queen Emmeline Vestana, sister of Lucia Highclere. And she is not known for mercy." The minute Rain finished calling out, he loosened an arrow into the ground at the horse's feet. Its rider whipped his steed around, and Rain followed his retreat with six more arrows right behind them, landing deep into the sand. A show of accuracy and restraint.

Raj turned around with a raised brow and a hint of a smirk.

"That certainly sent a message." He chuckled as he walked down the length of the parapet, barking orders down into the courtyard, sending his soldiers to their various positions. I watched him while feeling a few different emotions coming from Rain, none of them good. My voice was quiet as I spoke, a ghost of a smile on my face.

"I'm not known for mercy?" I felt the amusement for a brief second before it lent back into the turmoil of conflict simmering within him.

"Well, they don't know much about you. But I think if you're allowed the opportunity to kill the King of Bones, you'd be anything but merciful. Consider it your wedding gift since you didn't earn it in our duel." He shot me a crooked grin, and I felt it to have the exact type of calming effect I needed. He pulled me to his side, hand on my hip, breathing me in.

"You'll actually let me kill him? I thought you wanted me to stay here until we figured out where Elora was?"

I felt his lips move against my skin when he spoke. "I do want you to stay here until we retrieve Elora, but I'm going to leave Raj with you—and of course, you'll have Thyra. Just in case something happens, and I can't help you get her. But once we have her back, as long as we are able, we'll go after the king. Together. I do owe you his head, after all."

An hour later, the boats on the coast had moved closer. The side of the fortress facing the sea was built right on the edge of a deep drop-off. The ships could come right up next to the fortress if they wanted, and it seemed like that was their goal. The mercenaries from Skos were marching, getting nearer every moment. Thyra, as my second, would not leave my side, and Raj made rounds checking on all of his soldiers as we stood on the parapet. I learned a bit about him from Thyra, eager to talk about something to keep my racing mind at bay. He was a widower with two children, a little boy and a teenage girl. They all lived here in the fortress. Both children were acting as assistants to Lavenia and Mairin, who had created a small healing area within the dining hall. I was worried, children had no business being here. Evil men didn't care. No small part of me was glad the children and my friends would be out of harm's way. I knew Lavenia was a capable soldier, and she'd die defending those in her care if she felt she had to, so keeping her away from the fight, yet still useful, felt like the best way to protect her.

When Rain said goodbye to me, heading down into the courtyard, I made sure to keep the tears at bay. I was terrified of how this would turn out. An overwhelming fear flooded through me, certain I wasn't going to walk out of this with both Rain and Elora. All I wanted was their safety; I didn't care what I had to do or who I had to kill to get it. And the thought was petrifying. I stood in the front corner of the battlement, offering a solid view of the approaching ships and men on foot and only a few steps to glance down into the courtyard. A few steps to see the side of his face, strong arms crossed over his hard body. I closed my eyes, visualizing the bond between us, the strings of gold, and plucked one. The sweet tone of our fire and love energized me, and when I opened my eyes, he was looking up at me, a soft smile on his face. Whatever I did, he'd felt it. He'd felt it, and he did it back, the song a melody in my veins. The overwhelming feeling of love and fear and pride simmered between us, making waves up and down the bond. We held each other's gaze until the first pound of the battering ram.

Rain's eyes tore from mine, and he started barking orders to his men. He'd already had them fortify the gate after raising it. I watched as he climbed the small mountain of dirt he'd cleared away, using his vantage point to yell for his men. To lead them, to encourage them, to be their king.

I scanned the horizon, searching for Prince Cyran, Declan, King Dryul. Anyone who I thought might know where Elora was. I looked for a carriage but knew if she were in one, she'd likely be out of sight. Raj ordered his men, helping those who fell to the mercenaries' return arrows, moving replacements into the crenels. I could see why he was in charge. He had a vicious efficiency, almost callous. But from the few interactions we had, I could tell he was kind, and Rain trusted him. A shout drew my attention, and I took a few steps toward the sea before I realized what caused the men to cry out.

Floating platforms. The boats had unloaded floating platforms with giant ladders balanced on them. Rungs as wide as Rain was tall and almost high enough to reach the top of the parapet. And they were closing in. Enemy soldiers placed wooden boards across the platforms, and the warriors nimbly jumped over to the ladders and began climbing. The archers did their best, but the soldiers were on the other side of the platform, protected by what they used to climb, making it hard to get a clean shot. I realized with horror what was happening when the soldiers reached the top of their ladders and cut loose rope, dropping smaller ladders up against the walls, which the invaders swiftly climbed.

I drew my sword, waiting to use it if necessary, hoping to save my divinity as long as I could. The sounds of the battering ram on the gate were a loud drumbeat as I watched the first Folterran soldier breach the wall. He was promptly felled and thrown back over, but then all hell broke loose. Thyra pulled me further away from the battlement facing the sea as dozens of men climbed over at the same time. The majority seemed to be mercenaries from Skos, and they attacked with the ferocity they were known for. They wore shields on their back and had axes in hand. A few of them wore the same face paint Thyra and I did. The shudder of the battering ram made me startle as I looked down, realizing we were directly above the gate. I made a scan of the area again, searching desperately for Cyran, and didn't see him anywhere. I was feeling particularly useless, trying to stay out of the battle like Rain had asked, to stay safe until we found her or saw her. I itched to partake, to help slay the men who fought for the one who stole my daughter, who stole my sister from me.

That itch turned into need as I saw Rain's men on the battlement becoming overwhelmed. They were tired, their morale low. We were outnumbered here, archers unprepared for hand-to-hand combat. They'd been roused in the middle of the night to prepare and had been up, fully armed and clothed in thick leather and steel in some cases. They were hot, worn-down, and exhausted. And it showed. The archers had mostly abandoned their posts, allowing more and more soldiers to make their way over the ledge. It struck me then, with a force that caused a stitch in my breathing. These weren't just Rain's men. They were *my* men. I'd already seen a few soldiers die, and I thought with a pang about having to inform their spouses, their loved ones.

A loud bang and splintering from below told me the gate had been breached. And I felt the victory through the bond before I heard Rain's cry. I whipped my head around, searching for him. Before the Folterrans breached the gate, Rain had been prepared, using his divinity to hold the dirt mound over the pit he'd dug out earlier. For all the Folterrans knew, it was packed dirt, ground they could walk on. But they fell down into his trap. The pit was full of spears that now impaled dozens of Folterran soldiers, the unlucky ones who ran through the gate first. It soon filled, and the Folterrans began to use the men's bodies as a bridge into the fortress, swiftly gaining back the advantage. I saw Rain swing back into action as more men climbed over the top of the parapet.

"My Queen, permit me to fight with Raj. The soldiers, we're . . . this is bad."

"Of course, Thyra. Go. I'll be fine here." I gripped my sword tighter, ready to prove my point, if necessary. Looking around me, I found a bleak resignation of death and loss weighing heavily on faces I knew and faces I'd just met. Soldiers were falling left and right. Our soldiers needed something, needed help, needed spirit. It was not time to break yet. I decided to do something about it and climbed into a crenel at the corner of the battlement and raised my voice, hoping I'd be heard. Hoping that my encouragement as their new queen, my readiness to fight apparent, would help them.

"The gods did not bring us here today to lose! The gods brought us to defend light and honor! Today you fight for peace! Hanwen will guide us, and Aonara has blessed us. Fight for justice! Fight for your king!"

I screamed it to my people, my soldiers, screamed at the top of my lungs. I knew they'd heard it when I felt warm pride through the bond, and an answering war cry rang out, echoing around me. Sheathing my sword, I held out my hands toward the dozens of soldiers still clambering over the parapet and reached for my divinity. I would put proof to the words the soldiers had just heard, prove Aonara had blessed us. I hadn't done more than play with the flame at the tips of my fingers, but I knew there was more. That power I'd felt swirling within me, stronger than I could comprehend. I coaxed it into my fingertips, the warm white energy inside me thrumming with an intensity I was afraid to possess, afraid to use, and I unleashed that divine light. The divine light which would identify me as goddess blessed. I harnessed it, and I let it wash over and through me. It flooded my veins, tingling. My fear dissipated immediately, washing away with every other dark thought I had. It felt so right, as if it had always been a part of me. I knew I could wield it as Lucia had, but with more control. I could spear it toward our enemies, throwing them into the frigid, deep water. I hadn't yet done much with it, but I felt more in tune with it than my original divinity. It would do as I asked, protecting me and mine. My divinity was an arrow, and I was the bow. We were strung tightly, taut with power, and I released my grip, allowing my divine light to strike true.

CHAPTER 49

I DIDN'T QUITE KNOW how my divinity would manifest using the abilities Aonara had blessed me with. I'd only used them to that degree once, during the Body ceremony, and it wasn't even intentional. When I reached for it, amassing the light inside me, inside my being, I let it guide me. It felt different than the glow I'd summoned to my fingertips, a bit more wild and frenetic. I let it move where it wanted to, trusting it to do what I wanted with it. It felt natural, intrinsic, more honed to me than the abilities I'd carried my entire life. I trusted it, letting the power course through me before I let it free.

And it worked.

The soldiers from the Folterran army toppled backward, the impact of my divinity falling over them like a wave of white, molten fire, and they were gone. The soldiers flew over the side of the wall, falling to the water below. The bright blinding light was tempered by the sunlight, which bore down on us well into the late afternoon. Not a single one of my soldiers was injured. The ones who were engaged, trying to push the enemies backward one moment and then looking at an empty parapet the next, whipped their heads around to find the source of the light, the saving force that drove death back. More men were coming, mercenaries scrambling up the platforms, either uncaring or unaware of what I had done. There were too many ladders pushed up against the wall, and I decided that would not do.

Running down the battlement, I scanned for Thyra and Raj. Thyra was fussing over a wound on Raj's shoulder, his back pressed against the wall, while the weathered captain stared up at me, an expression of frank assessment.

"Thought your daughter was the Beloved." I couldn't read his eyes, couldn't tell if it was judgment or curiosity or something else altogether. I didn't quite care either, other than the fact I needed this man's trust and guidance.

"Honestly? Recently, I'm finding out I don't know shit, Captain." I gave him a sheepish grin, and to my surprise, he returned it, so I carried on. "We need to get rid of some of these platforms, and I think I might be able to do it. Where do you want me to start?"

A moment later, Raj was on his feet, and Thyra and I followed as he led us to the other end of the battlement, where no one had dared continue climbing after I blasted soldiers off the parapet. Other men were still clambering up from other areas, but there was a backlog, most of the soldiers coming from one boat at the opposite end of where we stood.

I climbed up, both of my feet wedged in a crenel, while Thyra stubbornly held onto my knees. With the sun beating down, I had to admit the black paint she'd put on my face had its merits, so I placated her and let her hold me around the knees, even if I thought I looked foolish. I glanced down and to my left, where more boats were making way to the platforms, doing a quick scan for Cyran or Elora before I used my divinity to destroy not one but two of the platforms. I stood tall, my sapphire cloak billowing in the wind, my armor sleek and beautiful and on display, and I let out a shout that came from the deepest depths of me. Warrior queen, indeed.

This time, the light let me form it. I didn't know what I was doing, but when white flames burst forth, I didn't hesitate. The platforms below me were completely engulfed in white-hot fire. And then the fire was spreading, hopping to another platform, this time with soldiers climbing it. I watched as they fell, screaming. Growing dizzy, I tried to climb down and nearly fell backward into Thyra's arms, grateful I'd let her hold on to me.

"Your Majesty?"

"Thyra, if you don't start calling me Emma, I will use this fire on you. I'm fine."

It was a lie. I was dizzy and painfully thirsty, my head starting to ache. Maybe I'd done too much too fast. In an instant, I was worried, a dose of my panic going through the bond, scared I'd pulled too much power from Rain somehow as I'd unintentionally done the night before. We weren't touching, but I wasn't sure how it worked. Was our well of power always connected? I could feel it even now, simmering on the other end of that string, but I wasn't sure if I could take from it if I wanted, and now didn't seem like the best time to try. Could I have hurt him and left him without his divinity? The ability to heal himself?

I rushed toward the front corner of the battlement between the gate and the water, searching below me in the courtyard for Rain. Thyra surged in front of me, preparing to guard me from the skirmishes that had moved above the gate, the Folterrans trying to take out the archers who shot down at the mercenaries on foot. I felt Rain's fear in response to my panic, and I calmed immediately. His soothing relief echoed back down the tight string a second later. There was something so strange and yet familiar about sharing our emotions this way. I wasn't sure I'd ever get used to it. But the fact we had some inkling of feeling, of awareness, without having to see each other was a comfort. I turned to go toward the back corner, hoping to recover my divinity in quiet safety. I was halfway back when I stopped, looking through a gap in the parapet to see where we stood, and that was when I saw him.

Prince Declan.

I knew it was him the moment my eyes locked on him. A slightly broader version of his younger brother, tall but still lean. His skin was so pale I could see a hint of blue veins above his collarbones. His hair was lighter than Cyran's, a golden blond that fell to his shoulders. Though I knew he was over two hundred years old, he didn't appear much older than me. He was standing at the prow, waiting for a board to be lowered onto a platform so he could cross. The gleam in his eyes told me he'd seen what I'd done. He knew. He gave me a slow and decidedly evil grin as he murmured something to the man beside him.

Fuck. He knew. Where was Elora? Now that Declan had seen my divinity, he'd know what she wasn't. My heart moved up my throat, and I tried to calm its erratic beating. I should have known better.

He moved then, agile as he crossed the wooden plank, climbing across to the platform disappointingly untouched by my fire. The man he'd spoken to followed him, and that's when I finally paid attention. It was Cyran. Maybe he knew where she was. They were climbing the ladder when Raj stumbled behind me, loading a bolt into a crossbow, ready to fire and aiming at Prince Cyran.

"No! You can't!" I grabbed his arm, stopping him, and he looked at me again with an unreadable expression. "He's . . . Aim at the boy if you must, but make sure you miss. Declan, though, he can go if you can get the shot."

He nodded and aimed again. He didn't have to pretend to miss either. When his arrow came deadly close to Declan, a flick of the wrist sent a shadow at it, knocking the arrow completely off course. I didn't know what to do. I stared in a mix of horror and confusion, watching both princes reach the top of the platform, about to climb the next set of ladders.

I wasn't in any shape to use my divinity yet. I had black dots in my field of vision, resting my hand on Thyra's shoulder to keep me steady on my feet. The good news was the fire was spreading, nearly decimating half of the platforms and slowing the number of men climbing, a bottleneck forming at the two platforms near the front corner of the battlement. The minute I had control of my divinity again, I'd use it to destroy what was left. It would slow the men left in the boats, forcing them to make for land.

Raj ushered Thyra and I toward the back corner where I'd hoped to recover, moving me as far from Declan and Cyran as possible, but I felt eyes tracking me. He was coming for me. He knew I might be the Beloved, and he would try to take me. Use me as he had planned to do with Elora. I felt a pit of dread opening in my stomach. Looking over my shoulder as they breached the wall, I saw that my soldiers were no obstacle. Declan used his shadows to toss both his and my soldiers out of the way, moving with a vicious speed which told me I'd have to make a stand here on this parapet. Thyra made the realization at the same time as I did, charging to engage with Declan, Raj only a step behind her. I pulled out my sword as my Second ran, a flicker of anxiety running through me. I was scared, my divinity tapped and weak, my body just as delicate from using so much so quickly. It wasn't like when I healed too much, the headache that knew no end, but instead, a frailty that made it hard to even stand up. I watched Cyran fall a few steps back, half-engaged in combat with one of the soldiers Declan had tossed aside.

I watched as Declan's sword met with Thyra's ax, and I became mesmerized by the sharp glint of light reflecting off of it. It called out to me. The dagger and the goblet and now this sword. I wanted it; I needed it. The pull of it was stronger than the other items, and I felt my expression glaze over as I watched it move, the sun catching on the edge of steel. He pushed Thyra out of his way, and she fell, landing on her leg in a way that made her cry out. Then he was engaging with Raj, all while maintaining eye contact with me.

"Why hello, Your Majesty. Or am I to call you mother, considering the impending nuptials?" The words slithered out of his mouth as he gave me a feral smile that sang of cruelty. I gagged, disgust rolling through me, and he saw it. Raj feinted left and then came to his right in a surge I was sure Declan wouldn't be able to deflect, yet he managed to easily. Thyra was scrambling to get up from the ground, and he tossed his arm behind him, making shadows wrap around her wrists and ankles, holding her to the ground.

"Though, I suppose it's not too late to call off the wedding, considering I feel a bit misled."

I advanced, brandishing my sword with two hands. I was weak, my body shaky like I was on a ship out to sea. Even holding the sword felt difficult. I shouldn't let him get to me, knowing how weak I was, yet I did it anyway. I could engage in verbal sparring with him while Raj kept him occupied, fighting with a fervor Declan didn't match. The prince wore a bored expression on his face as his shadows whipped out from around him, biting at Raj, while Declan lazily brandished his sword.

I called out to him, finally replying, willing my voice to be stronger than I felt. Make him think I had every bit of divinity I could have at my disposal. "Misled? Surely you didn't think anyone would *want* to be your bride, did you? You had to force the bond, if I recall."

He chuckled, his dark laugh sending a shiver up my spine. "I was promised the Beloved by your lovely husband. Well, former husband, I suppose? I spent a hefty amount of coin for her, and yet I think he sold me the wrong woman."

And then Raj was down, Declan slamming the pommel of his sword up against his head and shoving him into a wall, blood pouring from the captain's ear. Declan grabbed Thyra by her braid and dragged her toward me. I backed away, still brandishing my sword. I felt helpless, too weak to do much more.

"I am not the Beloved." This man seemed to like to hear his own voice, so I decided my best line of action was to get him to keep talking. Maybe Rain would come. I didn't think I could do anything on my own, with my body feeling this way. My sword was shaking in my hands, and my head felt like it was cracking in half, and I was sure he could see the signs of how I felt.

"Mmm, so you say. But I don't like games of chance. I've read the prophecies, Emmeline. And that's why I'm afraid I have to kill you." He clicked his tongue and tilted his head, a look of mock concern on his face. "And Vesta's newest queen, too. How sad."

I froze and blinked, confused. He wanted to kill me? He'd had Elora all this time, and she was alive. Untouched, safe even. Had Cyran kept her alive this whole time from his own force of will? Declan threw his head back and laughed, an evil sound devoid of anything human. Thyra struggled against him, and he didn't move, completely unaffected by her fight.

"After my brother reported her abilities or lack thereof, I realized your daughter was not the Beloved. She had none of the other abilities, and her Light divinity was weaker than it should be. Believe it or not, I don't revel in killing children, so it came as a bit of a relief, as you can imagine. I'd originally planned to take control of the Beloved, ally with her. But then the prophecies made it clear I'd have to end whoever it was. I considered ransoming her to make back the money from my poor investment, but then I heard a delightful little rumor. About you, Your Majesty."

He pulled Thyra to her feet, and she tried desperately to stomp on his insole.

"A rumor you just proved to be true with that little stunt just now with the holy fire. Using your daughter as bait was Cyran's idea." He jerked his head backward at his brother, who only stood leaning against a parapet, pleading with his eyes. Did he betray me, betray us? Did he take advantage of my desperation? He seemed to think Elora was the Beloved when I saw him last. Was he that good at lying? I didn't know who to believe. "Do you fancy showing me how the others have blessed you? Go out with a frightful display, if you please?"

Declan rambled on, casually leaning against the wall of the battlement as he held Thyra by the braid, talking about what would happen once he killed me, how he would be the one to fulfill the prophecy. I didn't care about the gods forsaken prophecy, if he was the one it spoke of or not. Accursed or not, he'd want to kill me either way, so I needed to be smart. I stared between the two men at a loss. And then Declan's sword, the sword that called to me, that sang a song and filled a void, that same great and dreadful sword lifted to Thyra's neck, and he issued a command.

"Take your dagger out, and slit your own throat. *Now.*"

Thyra's eyes were wild and frenzied, horror crossing her features when she saw me reach for the blade. I couldn't let her die. I wouldn't look at my protector, my friend, my training companion, as the life ebbed from her eyes. I lifted the dagger to my throat and saw Cyran's eyes widen in a panic, begging me not to do it. And I decided to trust my instincts, trust *Elora's* instincts. To trust this prince, who I only hoped loved her as much as I thought he did.

Not sure if it would work, I grasped my dagger by the blade and tossed it, sending it flying end over end toward Cyran, toward the ground at his feet. At the same time, I sent the last of my divinity toward Declan, a white burst of light and heat making him and Thyra fall to the ground. I had hoped in the frenzy of the distraction, Cyran would use his sword against his brother, or somehow free Thyra from his grasp.

Cyran scrambled for the dagger, but Declan was already standing, brushing his pants off.

"Did she miss you, brother?" I didn't have a chance to hear Cyran's reaction before shadows were shooting at me, and I was defenseless. Cyran held my dagger, staring between me and his brother, and I realized I'd forgotten one simple thing.

Blood.

Whether Cyran wanted to see his brother fall or thought he was morally incapable of good, Cyran couldn't be the one to kill him. No matter how much love he might have for my daughter, how much pity he might have for me, Declan was his blood, his brother. It was too much to ask, and I'd miscalculated. It was when my arms and legs were moving of their own accord, the shadows latched around my ankles and wrists, around my neck, around my waist, that I finally realized what was happening. I was a puppet, a marionette on Declan's strings. I reached for my divinity, that empty well of power, and found nothing. If only

I could reach my white-hot light and bring it to the surface, surely the shadows would fall away. I frantically searched the bond, grasping at Rain's divinity, attempting to utilize it somehow, but it was just out of reach if it was there at all. I was climbing the parapet, facing the dark, deep water, unable to even look down below me, fully controlled by the shadows detaining me. Just before I stepped off the ledge, I heard the rift. Rain was too late. His shout tore through me as I jumped. I didn't feel fear at first, the sensation almost like flying. But when I plunged down, down, down to the flaming platform floating on the surface of the water the terror flooded my veins. If the wooden bottom didn't break the moment I hit it, sending me into the inky black drink below, I'd break bones and be unable to heal, my divinity completely tapped.

When I hit the platform, it was sturdy. It hadn't burned yet. And it was for that reason I was able to hear the startling crack as the back of my head slammed into the wood. Seeing stars and barely breathing, I lay there. I felt the pure pain and anger coming down the bond, and I heard Rain's roar. I couldn't feel my divinity, but I hoped maybe I had a small amount. Just maybe I'd be able to heal myself. I reached for that well again, finding it empty once more, not enough of Rain's to risk taking from him. I didn't sit up, worried my skull was fractured or my neck broken.

I was in and out of consciousness, unaware of how long I laid there before one of the rungs from the platform shifted and fell down into the hollow where I lay. I looked up, staring at the small square of blue above where the sky peeked through when the man bent over me.

The bronzed man, handsome and scarred, terrifying and strong, bent over me and studied me. Where had he come from?

"Whose side are you on?" I murmured, almost hoping for a mercenary, hoping he would end my misery sooner, rather than one of my soldiers risking themselves to rescue me. The idea of someone pulling me out and dragging me up the platform was not an appealing one. He chuckled, though, crow's feet wrinkling at his eyes.

"I haven't decided yet. You're definitely making it interesting, little one."

And then he pushed two fingers to my forehead, and I heard a voice in my mind. *Get up.*

I blinked, and he was gone. As was my pain. The thrum of my divinity was back, stronger than ever. I reached into the well of power, and I realized with a start that it was significantly deeper than it had been. I offered up a silent prayer, closing my eyes and breathing deep, understanding with an unsurprising surety who had just saved me and blessed me with an unfathomable gift. Hanwen had turned the tides, granting me unimaginable access to my divinity.

I slowly stood, and I delicately examined the back of my head, right where the braids ended and my hair hung down freely, feeling blood on my fingertips. There was no wound, but my hair was wet and sticky, matting together. Another rung broke free from the platform above me, the fire-covered beam coming dangerously close to my head. I was going to have to climb out of here, climb through the fire. I set my jaw and shimmied through a gap in the side, carefully tiptoeing the edge of the platform while keeping my hands out of the fire.

"My queen!" It was Thyra's voice, shrieking from the battlement. I called out, unsure if she'd even be able to hear me as I started climbing, carefully choosing the placement of my hands. With the well of my divinity full again, I considered trying to put the fire out with the water below us, but I was scared to use it, wanting to save it for fighting Declan if it was needed. I didn't know exactly how deep that well went, but I didn't want to find out if I could avoid it. Thyra called for me again, and I bellowed at the top of my lungs, hoping she'd know I was alright, that she'd tell Rain somehow. The desperation and rage coming from our bond told me that he might not know I was alright or even alive. I hadn't felt him the entire time I'd been at odds with Declan, and I wondered if we were distracted or overcome, we wouldn't be able to sense each other. I struggled to control my emotions, trying to let my love flow through me to him, but it was laced with so much fear, so much worry that he would fall to Declan, that I was afraid it could have been confused for the dying thoughts of a woman who loved him. A moment after I yelled, I nearly lost my footing at the cool sensation of relief flooding through me from Rain.

A loud thump above me shook the entire platform, threatening to splinter it into ashes. Looking up, I saw Raj, bleeding from his ear and the wound on his chest, but alive. Conscious. He laid down and held his hand out, reaching for me.

"Can you put out the fire?" He called down to me, and I noticed his arm being licked by the flames, and I grimaced, not wanting him to get hurt for me. I picked up my pace and focused, willing the air to leave the fire, to suffocate it. I thought it might keep it a bit safer for me to climb than just dousing it. The water on the charred wood would make it soggy and slick. I kept climbing and was disappointed the flames didn't snuff, but I did notice they were smaller, at least. Easier to avoid.

Finally, I reached the captain's hand, and he pulled me onto the platform before turning back to the ladders leaning up against the battlement. I saw Rain then, a flurry of movement, and the clang of his sword told me they weren't fighting with their divinity. Relief soared through me, knowing Declan's divinity was almost as strong, maybe stronger than mine. Though I knew his shadows came from Ciarden, I wondered if the god had perhaps bestowed a more formidable blessing upon him as well. If he was fighting Rain with his sword, maybe he'd drained himself of his divinity. I saw the golden-blond head turn toward me, and I ducked, pushing myself behind Raj, hoping Declan wouldn't see me, hoping he'd be distracted enough for Rain to get a maiming blow.

I saw Thyra then, struggling to stand against the wall, but with her arm wrapped brutally around Cyran's neck. She knew about his role in our plan, his supposed alliance, and his feelings for Elora. I was confident she wasn't actually hurting him, but I was glad for her to keep up the ruse for Declan. Even if Cyran had betrayed us, I needed to be sure before doing anything to him. I watched, frozen, unsure of what to do. To stay on the platform would be catastrophic if the flames continued, but to climb up might distract Rain.

Declan decided for us when he faltered, spotting me standing tall on the platform to his left. And that's when Rain acted. He threw open a rift behind Declan and tackled him into it, letting it close behind him. I screamed his name and started scrambling up the ladder, my body moving into action before my mind even comprehended what he'd done. I had no idea where he'd gone. I knew he did it for me. He wanted Declan as far from me as possible, and he might have just gone to his execution for it. If Declan was god-blessed by Ciarden as I suspected, who knew if Hanwen would help him too? He seemed to think he was the Accursed. Had he already been blessed by Hanwen? His divinity might come back stronger and faster than Rain's, and then he'd be dead.

That gods damn stubborn, stupid, stupid man.

I clambered over the wall and screamed, sending all my rage and terror through the bond. Let him feel. Let him know if Declan didn't kill him, I would.

Thyra released her hold on Cyran as I rounded on her. "Did you see where the rift opened?"

She shook her head, and the grief tore through me. My heart was pounding, and breathing was a struggle. I was going to lose them both today; I was certain of it. I might never even find Elora. Cyran slid down to the ground, his back to the wall with his head in one hand, the other braced on the floor next to him. In that moment, I didn't care if he was practically a child; a child with an evil brother, a child who might have seen untold violence and terror, a child who might have loved my daughter. Declan's words rang through my ears, telling me that using Elora as bait was his idea. If Declan had known Elora wasn't the Beloved, had

Cyran known? I didn't care if he was innocent. I didn't care about anything but the truth.

I took a few steps forward, crushing his hand under my boot, pushing down as hard as I could as I leaned forward. To his credit, he didn't cry out, just bit back the pain with a grimace. But I wanted him weak. I wanted him sniveling. I wanted him to have a reason to fear me because I was dangerous—wild and on edge. I gathered my hand into a fist and pulled the air from his lungs. The hand that wasn't under my foot went up to his throat, and his eyes were panicked when I spoke, low and deadly.

"Talk. Did you lure me here? Did you know she wasn't the Beloved?" I released the hold on his air, and he took a deep gasping breath, glaring at me with watery eyes.

"He told me Elora wasn't the Beloved the morning after the last illusion. He told Ismene before, but she couldn't tell me. He made her swear a fucking verit oath, so she couldn't outright say anything. I did give him the idea to lure you here because that was *our plan*. I didn't know you were—"

I cut off his air again, needing a moment to determine if I believed him or not. The situation was too high tense, his heartbeat rapid the entire time, impossible to trust it to distinguish truth from lies.

"I'm not." It was starting to feel like a lie. Only one more blessing and all four gods would have meddled in my life. The thought of Ciarden blessing me was something I didn't want to think about. Something told me the God of Dark had to have good reason to bestow a blessing. Something malicious. "Do you know where she is?"

Releasing him, he took another deep breath. He wasn't nearly as winded because I didn't cut him off for long. "She's with my father. That's all I know."

My heart stopped.

"King Dryul? I thought you said he was delusional. Declan trusted him with her?"

"Declan doesn't care about her, remember? She's useless to him now. But my father wanted to see you and insisted."

I fought a shudder. The King of Bones had my daughter, and he wanted to see *me*.

"And you have no idea where he is?" I eased my foot off his hand, realizing I'd been pushing down the entire time. He pulled it into his lap, rubbing it.

"If I had to guess, probably in Clearhill. He gets sick, so I can't imagine he'd be on a boat."

"Do you know anyone who would know? A captain or other soldiers who might know for sure?"

Cyran looked past me, gazing around the battlement, and stood, walking over to glance down in the courtyard. He grabbed the back of my arm and pulled me closer to the edge. Thyra was right at my side, huffing and puffing as she was on her injured leg.

"He'll know." I followed the point of his finger, and I felt Thyra stiffen beside me.

"Olag." His name was a whisper and a curse on her lips.

CHAPTER 50

THYRA SPRANG INTO ACTION, a hiss on her lips as she tried to run toward the staircase at the back corner of the battlement, stumbling on her injured leg as she went. I took steps to follow her, to block her from acting with the purpose and fire I knew was simmering under her skin. Before I could get close to her, Raj had his hand gripped tightly around her arm.

"I think the queen is going to want him alive. Let me get him."

Raj looked over his shoulder to me, and I nodded. I didn't particularly want the captain out in the fray, potentially injuring himself worse, and by the way Olag was laying out soldier after soldier, I wasn't sure if we'd be able to get to him without one of us getting hurt. I wracked my brain, trying to figure out a way to find Elora, to distract myself from my missing husband. It was up to me to get her back, considering I had no idea where Rain took Declan, and I had no idea if he was coming back. I tugged on the bond, feeling for rage or fear, or *something*, and yet all I felt was the faintest hint of annoyance, barely perceptible. Part of me wondered if it was my own mirrored back at me. I shook my head, forcing myself to draw my focus away from him. I thought for a moment as I healed Thyra, moving my hands down her leg, watching her expression until I found the soreness at her knee. It seemed like a minor injury, so I wasn't worried about the small drain on my divinity. I hadn't even noticed what I'd used when I took Cyran's breath. Finally, the beginnings of an idea began to form.

Once Thyra and Raj were healed, and I explained my plan, she grumbled at me as we waited. She wasn't happy about having to question her father, but my assurances that she could have him and do whatever she wanted after I was done was enough to assuage her. I watched with bated breath as Raj made his way down to the fray, pushing mercenaries aside with ease. He was strong, but I could tell it was his height that was his biggest weapon, his long limbs able to reach his attacker before they could make contact. Cyran kept his distance from me, standing in the shadows of the stairwell. I wanted to keep the ruse going in case this all worked out, and we could resort back to some semblance of our original plan. When Raj made contact with Olag, and the men began to fight, I noted the similarities the ogre shared with the woman he'd created. He was tall, not surprising ,considering Thyra rivaled Rain in height. He had the same blond hair, though peppered with silver, and the same ferocity I'd seen Thyra fight with. But that was where the resemblances stopped; where her face was kind and open, a bit fuller in the cheeks, his was all rage and pain. Thyra and I both tensed as Raj stumbled with a grace that told me he needed lessons in acting, and I held my hands out, ready to act. When he dropped down on one knee, we moved. I opened the rift, and Thyra was through it in an instant, her dagger at her sire's neck before he could close in on Raj.

"Hello, Da." Her voice was a growl as she pushed the blade against the side of his neck, her other arm locked around one of his while drawing blood where the edge of the dagger pushed into his skin. He gave a rough laugh, his whole body shaking.

I walked slowly around him to look him in the eye. My lip curled as I took in the monster who had trained his daughter to be an unrivaled warrior, capable of committing atrocities for the highest bidder, and then left her to be used in other unspeakable ways, knowing full well the coin he got for her was worth more to him than her protection and safety. He was mortal like his daughter, his weathered face putting him around sixty years old, but he was enormous and strong, built like a wall made of stone. His eyes narrowed as they lingered over the braids and paint which marked my face, courtesy of the daughter who held his life in her hands.

"Of course, my daughter favors the peasant princess." His accent was thick, and his voice gravelly as he spat out the words. I was afraid Thyra was going to act before I had a chance to extract the information I needed.

"It's queen, actually. But peasant queen just doesn't have the same ring to it, does it?" I cut off the air in his lungs while giving him my middle finger, and his eyes bulged in his head as his mouth worked like a fish caught on a line. Raj was already on his feet, helping Thyra drag the giant man to the keep. Suffocation made him pliant, and I had a smile on my face as I pulled out my sword, energy renewed as I knocked the mercenaries out of the way who stood in our path, utilizing small bursts of divine light to aid in the task. The courtyard was nearly empty, the fighting mostly taking place outside the fortress.

I led the way into the dining hall, accidentally slamming the door open farther than I meant to, the loud noise barely perceptible amid the loud echoes of injured men. I let go, allowing Olag to get a deep breath. The moment he started struggling against Thyra, I cut him off again.

"This pig's ass should know that breathing is a privilege, and I'm not feeling generous," I spoke to Thyra, but the words were meant for Olag. We led the swine into the kitchen while Raj went running through the dining hall to find Lavenia or Mairin. It was loud and stifling, soldiers groaning and vomiting and dying on the ground. My chest tightened as I took one last look over my shoulder, horrified at the destruction which had been wrought on our people, and the door swung shut behind me. My divinity trembled, begging me to heal them. To help. A moment later, Cyran had joined us, slipping in through a back door of the kitchen. I wasn't sure how he knew the layout of the Cascade, but I imagined he had a thorough understanding of it because of his spying Rain had said he'd been doing for years.

I hadn't been paying attention, hadn't been feeling for his emotions past my initial tug. I reached out again, trying to follow our golden bond, but there was nothing to feel other than a light simmer of anger. I wondered if he was too far away, but I could tell he was there, the strings between us pulled tight and thin.

Lavenia came running in, drenched with sweat and covered in blood I didn't think belonged to her, Raj on her heels. "I heard you flexed your divinity up there. The soldiers who can talk won't shut up about it." She gave me a quick grin as she grabbed a towel off the counter and wiped the sweat from her forehead. Rain had given her brief details of my newfound abilities on our trip to the Cascade. We had opted to keep the information about Elora to ourselves, not wanting anyone else to know before she did.

"Yeah." My response was noncommittal as I shrugged, releasing my hold on Olag. He went slack against the wall Thyra had pushed him against, his head lolling but eyes open. "I need to find out where Elora is, and supposedly, he knows."

Lavenia nodded her head and walked toward him, pulling herself up to her full height before inhaling deeply. I knew she hated compelling people, but this man deserved every ounce of discomfort and pain she could inflict. "Tell us where the girl is and who guards her."

"In a tent with King Dryul." He bit out the words, coughing as he spoke, angry that his lips and tongue had betrayed his mind.

"Where is the tent? Are there any other guards with the Bone King?"

"Outside Clearhill. No." He shuddered, trying to pull away from Thyra, and I snatched the air out of his lungs again.

"Where specifically outside Clearhill, you pungent ass." Lavenia was growing increasingly impatient, and I didn't blame her. I released him so he could speak.

"Near the shore." Lavenia sighed, about to continue her line of questioning.

"That's enough. Raj, if I rift us to the horizon toward Clearhill, will you be able to get me there?" He nodded slowly, an appraising look on his face. Olag made to move, and Thyra's dagger was on his neck in a heartbeat. I decided not to risk anything when it came to him, and I closed my hand in a fist, suffocating him until he went limp, his enormous body a pile on the ground, heartbeat slow. I turned to Thyra.

"He's all yours. Do what you think he deserves, but show him no mercy." She nodded, watching me with narrowed eyes, clearly suspicious of what I was about to say. "Raj and I are going to go get Elora. I don't want to do it without Rain, but since he left . . . well, I have no choice." The captain nodded, and I was surprised by his instant approval as he crossed the room to stand beside me.

"Your Majesty, I am your Second. I must go with you." Thyra appeared stricken, torn between hurt and hesitance, glancing between Olag's limp form and me.

"You're my Second, Thyra. That means you obey me." I shook my head stiffly, the motion shutting her argument off at the stem. I would not rob her of this revenge. "Come." I nodded to Cyran. "I'll lock you in a cell before we go, properly kidnapped." The boy balked, his face falling as he took a step toward me.

"I have to help Elora. Please, Emma. I can help with my father."

He looked as if he were about to cry, and I watched him for a moment, contemplating. King Dryul would have to leave this encounter dead. If he didn't, his father would know Cyran had helped us, and the boy would be viewed as a traitor. It was a risk for him to join me. And his expression when he asked me, the way his voice cracked when he said her name, all of that told me he was being honest. If he didn't love her yet, he was close. He was a child willing to risk his safety for her. A small part of me still felt I couldn't trust him. Folterran royalty had never been known for their trustworthiness. A vision of her clinging to him in the illusion made me push that aside. She'd trusted him, and I'd seen love light up her eyes. She was young, and he could break her heart, but I'd recognized the look. It was the same look I gave her father.

"Alright, princeling, let's go."

There was no sign of Rain. He wasn't in the field outside the fortress, wasn't anywhere I could see, and I could barely feel his emotions at all. I was angry and worried. What if Declan had gotten the upper hand, and that man who burned bright, who destroyed me and put me back together, was dead or dying? Kingdoms and years and utter devastation. Is this what he unknowingly meant? Was this utter devastation?

The three of us stood on the battlement above the gate. I picked a tree on the horizon, hoping and praying to the gods I'd be able to form the rift. I didn't want to push through the men who were still outside, fighting to the death in the field below us. It took me three tries before I was finally able to form something. Peering through, it appeared to be the right place, and Raj confirmed it, walking through first. Cyran and I followed. The sound of battle shifted to behind us rather than around us, and we started on a run toward the town and the shore.

"There, I see the crest." Cyran pointed out a spot of red in a sea of brown tents where the Folterrans had camped the night before, waiting to give the Cascade the chance to surrender. It was a vast green field marred by tents and supplies, but I could see hints of life, flowers growing in between them. "Rift there and wait. I can go in and distract him while you two rip open a slit in the back. Once you get away, I'll try to hold him off for as long as I can."

My eyes narrowed on him; this child was willing to risk his father's wrath for Elora? King Dryul was no stranger to filicide. It was death that waited for him if he tried to fight his father. "I think I'm distraction enough. You stay with Raj and get her out. I'm not leaving him alive, Cyran. Besides, you said he wanted to see me. Let's give him what he wants. I don't see any other soldiers, do you?" Though I didn't hear any heartbeats aside from the two in the tent, Raj did a cursory sweep, assessing with his captain's gaze before confirming what I'd said. I could tell Cyran wanted to argue with me, wanted to sacrifice himself or prove himself to Elora. It was a death wish, and I wouldn't allow it. I wouldn't allow the boy she might love to die in front of her. And I trusted the two of them to get her away safely before she could possibly witness what may happen to me.

But I wasn't afraid. I was blessed by three of the gods. I'd seen Dryul's strength, heard the rumors of his divinity, but I still had confidence mine was stronger, especially in his frail and deluded state. I had the absolute certainty my need for vengeance was stronger than anything he could do to me.

The rift spat us out on the side of the tent, and Cyran and Raj circled around to the back as I went straight to the entrance. I hesitated for a moment before I pushed through, almost blind.

"At least one of my sons still has respect enough for me to send you here. Was it Cyran? Declan didn't seem inclined to wait."

It took me a moment to realize I wasn't going to adjust to the dark. I'd thought it was due to the red material of the tent, but I soon came to the conclusion it was dark because of his shadows. I couldn't see a thing. I waited, not sure if my divinity could cut through and shed light upon us, but I listened for the voice, sounding eerily similar to King Soren's.

"I'm here, what do you want?" I didn't bother to pull out my sword, knowing his well of divinity was untouched. There would be no time or need for weapons. I heard a gasp toward the back of the tent and a muffled cry of *mama*, which made my heart soar and plummet at the same time.

"It seemed like an interesting bookend. I killed your sister, who we thought was the Beloved, so it only makes sense for me to kill you too."

We acted at the same time. His shadows were twining, tightening on my body as my light exploded, burning the tent around us in a white, blinding heat. I hadn't intended for that outcome, but knew it might make things easier for Raj and Cyran to get her out. Dryul laughed, a malevolent and vicious thing, as he sat down forcefully on a chair in the tent. I saw Elora, seated on a pillow with wrists fastened together, a chain made of obsidian wrapping them tightly. She had a rope holding her legs together and a cloth in her mouth. I felt the rage bubble up in me and wondered if Rain could feel it. Would it summon him?

I didn't notice the men crouched low behind Elora until Dryul's arm shot out, and shadows went flying, slamming Raj right in the chest. The captain fell to the ground, twitching, and I cried his name, hoping he was alright. Needing him to be alright. Listening for his heart, I knew it was still beating, and I hoped it would stay that way. I slowly approached the king, my hands raised and my divinity crackling between my outstretched palms, and I sent a burst of that fire toward him, though his shadows served almost as a prism, sending the white bursts of light in all directions, diluted. When Dryul looked at Cyran, his dry chuckle grew louder, even turning into a cough for a moment.

The tent was falling around us, pieces of cloth and leather falling down, and I used the wind, harnessing Rain's ability as if it were second nature, to push it all at Dryul. More shadows poured out of him, wisping the debris away.

"My, you devious thing. This is the only time I haven't doubted you're mine." The king watched his son with cold eyes as he laughed, echoes of a cough in the back of his throat. The son in question dove forward to Elora and began working on her bindings. She gazed at him like he'd arranged the stars into their constellations, especially for her. Hoping to catch Dryul off guard, I sent my light toward him, and it launched out of me like lightning. Gone was the holy fire, and in its place was a burning crackle that enveloped him.

Dryul projected shadows in response, and they dodged past my light. One wrapped around my throat and squeezed. I grabbed for it with my hand, stupidly, as I started gasping for air. Then my hand was glowing, lines of light erupting from my skin like scars. The white heat emanating from my fingertips touched the shadow, making it retreat, and I inhaled deeply before pointing my hand at Dryul, fingertips spread, and blew white-hot fire at him, like a dragon from a fairytale. His shadows encircled him, creating almost a black shell of protection covering his body. I groaned in frustration as I caught Cyran pulling the cloth out of Elora's mouth. I chanced a look at her, my baby, my life, before she called out to me.

"Mama, watch out!"

Dryul was wrapped in his shell made of shadows, so I was confused when an arm gripped me around my neck, pulling me up, so the tips of my toes barely scraped the ground. I put my hand on the arm, light coming from my fingertips, and it went straight through, the shadow of a man disintegrating around me. I tripped as I dropped to the ground, but my attention was drawn back to the king as he rose from his chair, stumbling toward me, his shadows propelling him and giving him the appearance of floating. I pulled into the well of my divinity, trying to turn the dirt below us into some sort of rock I could launch at him, but I wasn't there yet. I hadn't had a chance to manipulate the earth, and it didn't come to me as easily as the wind. The best I could do was make the ground rumble beneath us.

The moment I stopped, Dryul launched himself at me, his shadows propelling him forward. I was taken by surprise, not expecting him to move toward me so quickly, and I was barely able to grab my dagger from my thigh in time before I was pressed to the ground with the king's body on top of mine. I heard Elora screaming at Cyran to let her go so they could help me, but he hadn't gotten her wrists free yet. I was glad for it, I wanted her out of here. I didn't want her risking herself to help me. Dryul's sharpened fingernails dug into my throat, and I reached around, trying to bring my dagger down into his back. He was frail, skeletal, but I was aiming for his kidneys, trying to deal a killing blow. His shadows kept grabbing onto my wrist, keeping me from making contact. I felt my skin start to glow and heat emanated from me, pushing his shadows away. It was in my attempt to stab his back that I felt a sharp pain in my side, a deep searing ache telling me I'd been stabbed myself.

I vaguely heard Elora's sobbing and Cyran's comforting whispers as I reached up, trying to gouge the king's eyes out. Not quite hitting the mark I wanted,

I dragged my nails down his face, and the howl that came out of Dryul was animalistic and unearthly. The glow from my hands had faded, and I realized I couldn't feel my divinity anymore. The hum stoppered and empty. It felt like I was in the cathedral again, that menacing building that suffocated and pulled, that repelled and nauseated. I tasted bile in my throat, and the pain in my side stung.

"I'm sorry." Cyran's voice was no longer a whisper but instead a loud commanding tone with just a hint of a crack in it as he pulled Elora to her feet. Barely holding Dryul at bay, I couldn't focus. I saw her turn her head, gazing up at the boy in question, and I coughed, choking on the bile in my throat when the look on his face unnerved me.

"It's alright, go! Get her out!" I pushed at the king, using my nails to dig into his neck.

Dryul struggled on top of me; his shadows had bound my legs together, and they were slowly working their way up my body. I tried to push the light out of me but found nothing. No hum of energy, no thrumming of power. What had he stabbed me with? Did he have an obsidian blade?

I attempted to twist away, tried to dislodge what dug into my side. And that's when Cyran stepped into my field of vision, Elora in front of him with a confused expression while the prince positioned her with his hands on her upper arms. His eyes met mine, and everything stopped. The heartbreak in hazel depths, the terror, the pleading, the apology.

His hands moved up.

One hand was on her forehead, holding her head against his chest.

The other held a dagger.

King Dryul had his hands on my throat, his hot, rancid breath on my face.

I pushed Dryul hard as I saw Cyran's lips move, his mouth next to her ear.

And then he pulled the dagger across her throat from ear to ear.

Her blood spilled, watering the flattened wildflowers beneath us.

Utter devastation.

I was everything, and I was nothing.

An overwhelming inferno rose through me, and I burned white-hot.

The symphony of pain and rage crescendoed through me, a swell and a peak as I screamed. The earth-shattering scream no one should ever have to know burst out of my throat as strength I didn't know I possessed surged through me. I tossed the king off me without a second thought as I watched Cyran gently lower Elora to the ground, her white dress covered in blood. I ripped the obsidian dagger out of my side as I ran across the tent. Listening for her heart and already finding silence.

She wasn't Sam.
She wasn't Miriam.
She wasn't my sister.
She was Elora, and I was here.
I'd bring her back, I just had to get to her.

I didn't realize I'd still been screaming until something slithered its way into my mouth. I heard the king shuffling behind me as the shadow forced its way down my throat. Shadows at my ankles. The ground was shaking, a rumble of sound rolling outward, the earth underneath us threatening to crack open and swallow us whole.

That's when I saw him, standing behind Cyran and Elora . . . her body.

The black, wavy hair and skin the color of moonlight would have elicited lust and fear if I could have been able to feel anything other than agony. His head was tilted down, and he looked at me through jet-black lashes, an alluring smile in place showing elongated canines. Handsome and cruel, he licked his lips and raised a brow, and I felt it. Ciarden's blessing.

The shadows around me grew pliant, their touch seductive, sensual. Only a second had passed since I started moving to Elora. Cyran having his hands on her drew up the fire inside me while the shadows spun around me. I was a vortex, a conquering night.

When Dryul's hands grabbed my shoulders, trying to pull me back, the shadows, *my* shadows, moved of their own accord. Black billowed around me, the sunlight extinguished as the shadows expanded and spread. Racing from me, they were animal in form and demonic in sound. The creations made of despair beyond imagination. Dryul's hands dropped from my shoulders, and I didn't turn around to see what happened, only barely registering the stopping of his heart. The shadows returned to me, thin wisps encircling my body, the creatures I'd created gone.

I was screaming again, the white-hot fire inside me turning into something else. Something different, something that eviscerated, something that hunted and killed. Cyran backed away from her body, tears streaming down his face. The holy predator inside me cocked its head before I exploded, white light enveloping us, blasting the boy away.

Within a moment, I was on her, my hands on her neck, pouring everything inside me into her. My healing, my divinity, my soul. I'd die before I let her leave me.

Live.

Live live live.

CHAPTER 51

Rainier

It was easy to forget Declan was over two hundred years old. He wore his arrogance like armor, and he never stopped talking. After walking this earth for so long, one would think he'd understand the importance of quiet. The intimidation of a look alone was more powerful than it had any right to be if used correctly. But Declan chose words more often than he didn't. When I'd rifted us to the cliff side near Clearhill, quiet and abandoned, I hadn't thought of the repercussions on my morale of hearing him so clearly and constantly.

"I suspect my little brother may have deflowered your daughter, Rain. Oh, you know about her by now, I expect?"

I ignored him; if Declan was right, if Cyran had—it didn't matter. Though she was mine, and as her father the idea of it sat sour in stomach—it didn't matter. Emma had said Elora loved the boy. He was just trying to get under my skin. Though the rage did slide up my back when he spoke *her* name for me. Only Emma called me that. Only Emma was allowed to call me that. But she was safe, I'd heard her call out. I'd seen her a split second before Declan did, triumphant and beautiful atop the platform. Alive. That was why I brought him here—for her. Declan, ever the braggart, had cooed his victory over the Beloved. That he'd killed *my wife*, and I was next. Though it was faint at first, the bond I shared with her told me how he was wrong. Her power over me, that call down our bond, had brought me to the battlement. I could feel her fear, her helplessness, and I never wanted to feel that ever again. Not in this life or the next. When I saw Thyra's face relax into one of relief and I felt Emma's determination, I nearly sobbed.

I'd have taken him sooner, but I had to see her. I had to make sure she was alright, even if it was the last time. My gaze had landed on her, and I had seen her in one piece, and then I looked away. I couldn't look at her, couldn't meet her eyes. She knew as well as I did that Declan's divinity was stronger than mine. I'd felt the tug of her tapping into mine the moment before I reached her; she knew how little divinity I had left, and the rift I made took the last of it.

I couldn't look at her, knowing I'd already chosen to leave her.

I'd been able to pull from her divinity when I rifted out—I wasn't sure how she had any left, but I wasn't going to pull from her again, not without me there to protect her. My only hope was his divinity being truly depleted, since he was fighting me with his sword on the battlement. If not, and he had a well of power to tap into, it was too bad. Emma needed her divinity, so I resigned myself to being brutalized by his shadows. But the gods must have been looking out for me for once, Declan clearly having used the last dredges of his abilities when walking Em over the battlement. Gods, seeing her jump was a horror. She'd fallen slowly, her hair streaming above her and her arms out on either side of her. A vision from a nightmare.

"I heard she's quite polite. I hadn't met her until today, of course, but Cyran told me such *interesting* tales about her. I think he quite fancies her. Did you know she paints?" He shook his head as he lunged, and I parried, continuing our dance. We were evenly matched; where I made up in height and strength, he made up in speed. We clashed and dodged and parried and swung while he continued his drivel, and part of me wanted him to just kill me, so I didn't have to hear him any longer. "Of course, you didn't know. There's quite a bit no one knew about that little mystery. Even the dimwit of a man she thought was her father didn't know she wasn't his until recently. The sniveling sot couldn't shut up when he found out about your whore's treachery. Did you know a seer told him? It's quite a funny story, actually. A libertine told him she was pregnant with his baby, and he went to a seer to make sure. She informed him that not only was the libertine's babe not his, but he had no living children at all. The decent thing to do would have been to soldier on and continue raising the child. The little beauty can't help her poor parentage."

I growled, pushing him back toward the cliff. He was trying to rile me, and I'd be damned if I said it wasn't working. I'd had quite enough of people calling Emmeline a whore, and I didn't want to hear him speak of Elora. My daughter. Gods, it was strange to think about even now. I knew she was mine. I knew with every fiber of my being that the child belonged to me. The moment I realized it, she fell right into place, into an empty part of my heart, perfectly sized to fit the love I already had for her. I'd already promised to love her, but this . . . having a piece of me, a piece of Em? The best of us in one person was more than I could ever ask for. I paid attention to the bond then, expecting the faint confusion and worry I'd been feeling, the threads weakened by distance, but instead, I felt a much sharper tang of fear and worry and rage. Where was she?

"I think she'll be quite put out if your whore queen kills my little brother. I've been told by the servants she slept in his bed on more than one occasion. I'd be a bit disappointed as well; I did raise the boy, after all. But alas, he did get himself caught by that slave woman. Maybe your whore will work out a trade with me. My brother for her bed-warmer?"

I had him closer to the edge of the cliff, fully ready to shove him if given the chance. A wisp of a shadow, weak but still a threat, flew toward me, Declan's free hand open and extended. Acting on instinct alone, I threw my hand up to blow the shadows away with my wind, and instead, my hand glowed the faintest bit, and the shadows scurried back to their master.

He gaped at me and stumbled. I almost did too, not realizing I'd have access to her blessings from the gods. I'd only been able to use her base divinity, but considering I hadn't had much time to try, it wasn't altogether surprising. It was then that trepidation rose in me, an overwhelming panic and fear of something about to happen. But it wasn't coming from me.

"Emmeline."

I whispered it, her name a prayer on my lips. Oh gods, if something happened, and I wasn't there... Were Thyra and Raj alright? My sister?

Declan recovered and lunged toward me, a guttural sound escaping him in lieu of words for once. I blocked him and pushed, somehow managing to disarm him, his sword falling to a ledge down the cliff side, completely out of reach. His dagger was out a split second later, and the black color of it told me all I needed to know. Told me that if shoved into me, my divinity would be choked. Too bad for him; it was already severely diminished.

That was when I felt it.

The pure anguish coming through the bond. When the ground began to shake, I fell to my knees, facing the sea of tents behind us.

No.

Declan was on the ground a second later, thrown by the earth and rocks moving below him. What pulsated through me was soul-shattering, heart-stopping pain. My breath caught, and I cried out, needing to be with her. The urge of my body to find her, to grab her, to protect her was overwhelming.

She had to be close, had to be.

I wouldn't let myself think about what could cause that pain. I couldn't. There was no feasible explanation for the sorrow, for the agony. The grief. Not one I would accept.

I would never accept that. Ever.

Yet, I knew. The base, logical part of me knew.

Elora.
The child I'd never met, the girl I'd loved the minute I knew she existed.
Dead.
That was the only explanation, the only possible outcome. I could feel myself shattering. Every muscle in my body, torn. Every blood vessel distended. Every bone broken, every thought forgotten. Every dream had come true, every wish and desire was mine, only to be taken away from me like this. I pushed myself up, not sure where I was going, just following our bond. And then I saw them, the black death hurtling forth, and stopped in my tracks.

The shadows had taken form. The blackness, the swirl of inky black midnight, had taken the shape of something enormous, bigger than a horse. Dozens of them, all stampeding toward me. I didn't care, running headfirst toward the tents into the camp. King Dryul must have been there if he was sending shadows out. And she was there too.

Pull from me, dear heart. Kill him. Pull from me and save her.

My heart made a desperate cry, pleading that somehow she'd hear me. She could burn out my divinity. She could burn out every part of me just to bring her back. I would burn for them. Burn for this love, their love. Ignite myself and be thankful for the brief chance I had to love them. I'd find Emmeline again—it was foretold. But for Elora, I'd sacrifice myself, self-immolate to save her, to save them both.

And then came the light. I cried out with relief as I was thrown to the ground. Blinding, powerful, consuming, *hers*. I couldn't see, crawling in what I hoped was the right direction. Dragging myself blind and terrified, only knowing my destination by my soul's pull.

I blinked and pulled myself up, only barely able to see through the white dots in my vision, when I saw a jaw-dropping sight. Thorns had grown from where the light came. Branches with dangerously sharp thorns had burst from the ground, creating a large dome. That had to be Em, some sort of manifestation of my divinity. But when I reached for the bond, there was nothing.

No emotion, no well of divinity, no threads.

She couldn't be dead. She had to help Elora. They couldn't be dead.

They *couldn't* be dead.

They couldn't leave me. Not now, not ever.

It was those thoughts of desperation, pure need to get to them, overwhelming despair rippling through me, when the obsidian blade sank home into my back, just below my ribs, and I stumbled to a knee. Within a moment, a rope was around my neck, tiny shards of lava glass embedded in it cutting my throat as my head was pulled back. Declan's sneering face looked down at me before he raised my sword, the one I'd left abandoned at the cliff, and brought the hilt down on my head.

To be continued late 2022

Keep reading for a bonus scene from Rainier's point of view.

RAVEMONT

One of the stablehands was dealing with a fussy mare, a beautiful bay horse that I hadn't seen before I left, when I returned to Ravemont. I'd been gone all day long, much longer than I was supposed to be, and I was exhausted. The kid was trying to lead the horse to a stall, and she was having none of it. She had planted her feet and was huffing at the boy as he tried everything to get her to move. Though I was in no gods damn mood for it, I figured it was my duty to prevent this dimwit from getting a hand bitten off. She was probably just nervous and needed some reassurance, but this imbecile was cursing at her and yanking on her like he'd never touched a horse, let alone worked with them.

"Quit. Just go. I'll handle her." I barked it out harsher than I meant to, but I was in such a foul mood it was probably lucky that I wasn't worse. The kid let out a yelp that crossed with a whimper before he skittered out, and it told me maybe I was a bit shittier than I thought I was. Oh well, I'd been through it today and didn't care.

I had literally one thing to get done today. One. And I was doing it the laziest damn way possible. I wasn't going to the Seat; I was going to the temple in Ardian, for fuck's sake. It should have been simple. Get a task, do what they ask of me, then leave. That was it. Coming to Ravemont first was a mistake. Lavenia had said as much. But I couldn't go before I tried one last time. She had some choice words for me after I asked her to compel Kennon for information about her, but I didn't give a shit. She'd been in a mood ever since Brenna broke things off with her, so she would've found a reason to be angry one way or another. Dewalt had already refused me, which pissed me off to no end. He would have done it in a gods damn second if he could have. But they both said the same thing: if she wanted to be found, she would've been by now. Fuck them both. This was my last chance.

I led the gelding I'd borrowed back to his stall, only using a small bite of the carrot I'd gotten from a farm stand on the road back, saving the rest for the mare. I was going to need to look into investing in another horse. I still missed Nico, and the stallion had been dead for nearly a year. The mare that remained planted just outside her empty stall would have drawn his attention. He tended to be drawn to any mare but especially liked the stubborn ones. I chose to ignore the parallel between me and my fucking horse, because gods damn did I know about a stubborn woman.

It's been sixteen years, asshole.

I should have been long over it, long over her by now. I should have fallen in love with someone, performed the ritual, had a child by now. But, no. It wasn't the first time I'd thought she was a witch, or at the very least found one to curse me for my stupidity. I had thought of Emmeline Highclere every single day of my gods forsaken life since that last day. It wasn't for lack of trying; gods knew it wasn't. I was never going to be rid of her. No, truly, I wasn't. The seer I saw in desperation over the summer told me she would be with me for the rest of my life, no matter how much I tried to rid myself of her. This woman, this bane of my gods damn existence, would follow me forever, and I wouldn't have anything to show for it.

I'd tried to forget her that night with alcohol and nearly killed myself in the process. A small part of me still resented Dewalt for his intervention. But I'd have done the same for him. Hell, the worst part of me wished she was dead, just so I'd have a reason to be pining like this over a woman that didn't want anything to do with me, who probably didn't even think of me. Who probably had a whole family in Nythyr by now. And those children would look like her and Faxon. That was the worst part of my imagination. Her children weren't supposed to look like another man, and even my subconscious tortured me with it. Her eyes and his weak chin. Disgusting.

I sighed as I advanced toward the mare, holding that carrot casually in front of me. I'd have to let her approach me. While I waited, I tried to calm myself down. I'd been in such a bad spot on my way to the temple, just on the outskirts of Ardian, that I actually stopped and prayed. I was on the path, going that way instead of rifting because it had been so long that I couldn't do it, when I stumbled across a divine statuary. In a moment of sheer hopelessness, I stopped. I emptied my pockets and asked the gods for help. I still didn't know what I was thinking, but I was desperate. I just wanted her out of my head. I couldn't go request a task for another woman with this one so firmly embedded in my soul. I spent a long time there, much longer than I meant to, longer than the temple would even be accepting visitors, and by the time I left, I knew I wouldn't be getting back to Ravemont before dark. I'd try again tomorrow.

The mare finally took a few tentative steps towards me, and I stood still. She was well cared for, her mane sleek and glossy. She only took a quick nibble of the carrot, barely taking any into her mouth, while she assessed me. The boy had already brushed her and taken off her saddle, so as soon as I got her into the stall all I'd have to do was remove her harness. It was just a matter of convincing her it was time to go in there.

"If I told you I had a really bad day, would you be more willing to cooperate?"

She just stared at me for a second before taking another bite of the carrot in her mouth, and I yelped, drawing my arm back quickly. She'd fucking bit me.

"I thought we had an understanding, ma'am." I looked down to inspect the damage, and then that pain went shooting through me again, the tingle landing in my elbow when I realized. She didn't bite me; it was Dewalt sending impulses. Two back-to-back? What the hell? "I'm sorry, that was rude. But it's time to get in your stall because I think my day is somehow about to get worse." I backed into the stall and was pleasantly surprised when she followed. I gave her the carrot, fighting past another impulse while I removed her harness and then slipped out. I'd have to check on her after I figured out what was happening with Dewalt.

I opened a rift into the hallway outside the great room, where I figured they'd have retired after dinner. When I stepped through, I was surrounded by servants that stood just outside the door, clambering to look into the room.

What the fuck is going on?

I heard Lavenia telling someone to sit down. I started to push through the servants; gods there were so many just standing here. Didn't they have things they needed to be doing?

"My daughter. Elora. She—"

The voice cut off. *That* voice. My heart stopped and restarted. I froze, brought both hands to my face, and rubbed over it. It had clearly been a very long day. Shit, is this what the seer meant? Between dreaming about her and obsessing over her, was I going to start thinking every woman I heard was her? I felt my stomach plummet, a rock falling off a cliff when the cool realization struck that there was no way it was her. It was almost like losing her again. She continued speaking, whoever the woman was, and I took a few steps forward, moving another servant out of the way. It sounded just like her. If this was how the gods thought to repay my prayers, divine hell. I had done a lot of terrible things in my life, but to deserve this? I could see Lord Kennon and his nurse sitting on the sofa, the old man staring as if he'd seen a ghost. Finally, I pushed past the last servant and stood still as Lord Kennon answered.

"Emmeline, she can stay. Gemma knows everything."

My hands were slack at my sides as I was finally able to see the woman who sat on the ottoman across from my sister. *The* woman. The only woman. She was silent as she stared at Lord Kennon. I couldn't see her face, but I nearly slapped myself. It couldn't be her. I'd officially gone mad. I had gone mad, and this was just a fever dream or a hallucination. The imposter—because this couldn't possibly be Emmeline—gave a shake of her head, the messy golden-brown hair a gods damn perfect replication of hers was wet, darkening the back of her shirt.

"Elora is my daughter. She's like Lucia." That breathy, husky voice was exactly as I'd remembered it. The woman turned her head at an angle to look at Ven, and I caught just a glimpse. The pale, ivory skin was flushed, and I saw blood at her temple. Something twisted in my stomach at the sight before I understood what she said. A daughter. She had a daughter. Did she look like her? "They were attacked on the Mirastos Path, a few hours' ride north of Mira. Elora and my husband were taken. Two men came back to the house to... I don't know, kill me, I guess."

I nearly growled at the idea before I saw Dewalt out of the corner of my eye, the only bit of my vision I could spare. I pulled my eyes away from her, from Em, and I looked at him. I didn't know what I looked like to him, but I was sure the last vestiges of my sanity were fighting me, and he'd see it on my face. He gave a single nod, and the look in his eyes told me my worst nightmare and greatest gods damn dream had come true. It was her. It felt like my ribs cracked open, my sternum split, and that spot that I'd tucked her away, that soft spot tucked inside my rib cage, had ripped at the seams. I began to bleed.

"That was their last mistake, I presume?" Lavenia was still talking to her when I looked back at Emmeline. Gods, it was really her.

"I found our farmhand nearly beaten to death afterward. The men had brought him back, used him to find our house. He told me what happened and he thinks they are taking them to a ship. I came straight here. I knew that Rain . . . Prince Rainier was supposed to be here, and I thought, well I didn't know what to do and—"

Me. She needed me. Lavenia cut her off, but I didn't hear a word she said. Emmeline was here in front of me, and she needed me, and all I wanted to do was show her just how backward that was. I took a step forward, a moth drawn to her flame, and everyone in the room seemed to realize I was in it, servants practically throwing themselves to the ground. None of them captured my attention, though; I was only focused on her. She slid off the ottoman and turned toward me in one graceful motion, with her head down and eyes on the ground. It was so unlike the woman I knew that I felt a keen sense of disgust in myself. She thought this was what I'd need to help her? This compliance and submission? Gods, this was going to be hell.

"Lady Emmeline, stand up. You've never once knelt before me—why start now?"

If you liked that Rainier POV, I have another one, and boy, is it steamy! Sign up for my newsletter to receive your copy!

ABOUT THE AUTHOR

Jess Wisecup was born and raised in Ohio. Growing up, Jess loved to read and dove headfirst into any fantasy world she could get her hands on. She is a stay-at-home mother who has lived all over the country the past six years, and currently resides in coastal Virginia. Her husband, two kids, and two giant dogs keep her busy. If she isn't busy writing, she's busy reading and drinking iced coffee.

To learn more about Jess or her books, visit her at https://beacons.ai/jesswisecup for all social media and website links, or scan the QR code below with your mobile device.

Make sure to preorder BETWEEN DESPAIR AND HOPE, releasing LATE SUMMER, 2022!

ACKNOWLEDGEMENTS

I can't believe I am finally at the point of having to write this. This book was a project I started in May of 2021, intending to write the story I'd been looking to read myself. I've been an avid reader my entire life, with fantasy and romance taking the forefront of the books I have loved to read the most. Fantasy and romance together are my favorite by far, and this year my passion has been reignited thanks to authors like Raven Kennedy, Sarah J Maas, Holly Black, Caroline Peckham & Susanne Valenti, and so many others. As I have entered new phases in my life, such as motherhood and *gasp* my thirties, I've felt just a bit too old to relate to some of the younger female protagonists. I deeply love the characters in the fantasy romance books I've read, but I've always wanted to read about someone like me, and I no longer fit those roles. I searched and searched for a story like that, and I wasn't finding anything that particularly interested me. So, I decided to write it myself. I hope you enjoyed it because this story is very much a part of me.

Firstly, I have to thank my Nebula Allies: Abby Mann and Emily Dugan. Without the two of you sharing my passion for my story, your wisdom, opinions, and most importantly, your thirst for my characters, I don't think I would have finished it with the fervor I did. You are two of my biggest cheerleaders and have become two of my greatest friends, and I love you. Another invaluable person whose influence will be felt throughout the series is my friend Heather Nix. Through discovering strange midwestern dialects and making an off-handed comment that change the trajectory of my entire story, I don't think this book and series would be the same without you.

I would be remiss if I didn't thank Hollee Mands, author of Little Fire (go read it right now) and one of the kindest people I've spoken to in this journey. Messaging her to fangirl over her debut a few weeks before my ARCs dropped was such a wonderful decision. I was stressed, dealing heavily with imposter syndrome, and feeling a bit lost about how to continue with this journey. To hear from a tremendously talented, recently debuted indie author and gain her insight and support was something I never would have imagined, and I am so thankful for every bit of advice and guidance she offered me. It meant more to me than you know!

Though I hope they never read their mother's smutty book, I have to thank my children for giving me first-hand knowledge about how far a parent would be willing to go, the mountains they'd move, and the overwhelming all-consuming nature of motherhood. I love you both to the moon.

Most importantly, I must thank my husband, Nick. For tolerating long, lonely nights when I wouldn't leave the computer, for picking up the slack around the house when I was in too deep, and for supporting me in every way to make this dream come true. And of course, for helping to create our own fairytale. I love you.

Printed in Great Britain
by Amazon